Saurgan
Saudamos
Shadamehr's Keep
Dwarven Territories
Karkara
mpire
Vir
Forden
Saumel (The City of the Unhorsed)
Enesh 'Sar
SEA OF STIAGA
Goresh 'Sar
SEA OF SAGQUANNO
Gatu 'Sar
Rehn
the Orks
KAS

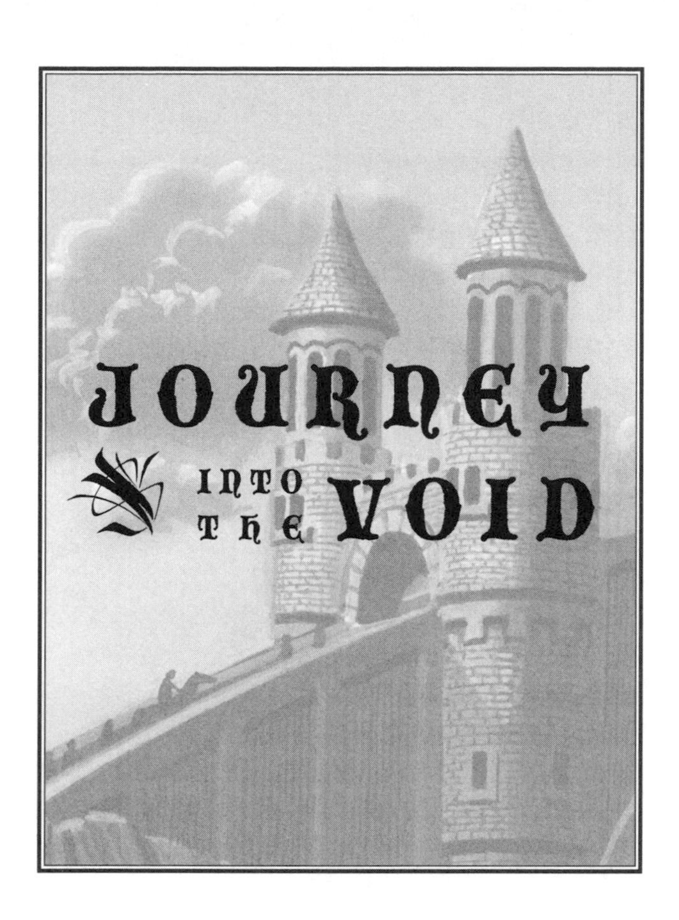
JOURNEY
INTO THE VOID

The Sovereign Stone Trilogy by
Margaret Weis and Tracy Hickman

Well of Darkness

Guardians of the Lost

Journey into the Void

An Imprint of HarperCollins*Publishers*

JOURNEY INTO THE VOID

Volume Three of the Sovereign Stone Trilogy

MARGARET WEIS

and

TRACY HICKMAN

A. DuPierrez

This is a work of fiction. Names, characters, places, and incidents either are the product of the author's imagination or are used fictitiously. Any resemblance to actual events, locales, organizations, or persons, living or dead, is entirely coincidental and beyond the intent of either the author or the publisher.

FIRST EDITION

Designed by Kellan Peck

Printed on acid-free paper

Library of Congress Cataloging-in-Publication Data
Weis, Margaret.
Journey into the void / Margaret Weis & Tracy Hickman.—1st ed.
p. cm.—(The Sovereign Stone trilogy ; v. 3)
ISBN 0-06-105178-0
I. Hickman, Tracy. II. Title.
PS3573.E3978J6 2003
vi813'.54—dc21 2002038894

03 04 05 06 07 JTC/QW 10 9 8 7 6 5 4 3 2 1

Dedicated to my daughter,
Elizabeth Baldwin,
with a mother's love and pride

ACKNOWLEDGMENTS

We want to thank Larry Elmore for a wonderful journey through his fantastic world. We are so grateful to him for permitting us to travel alongside.

—Margaret and Tracy

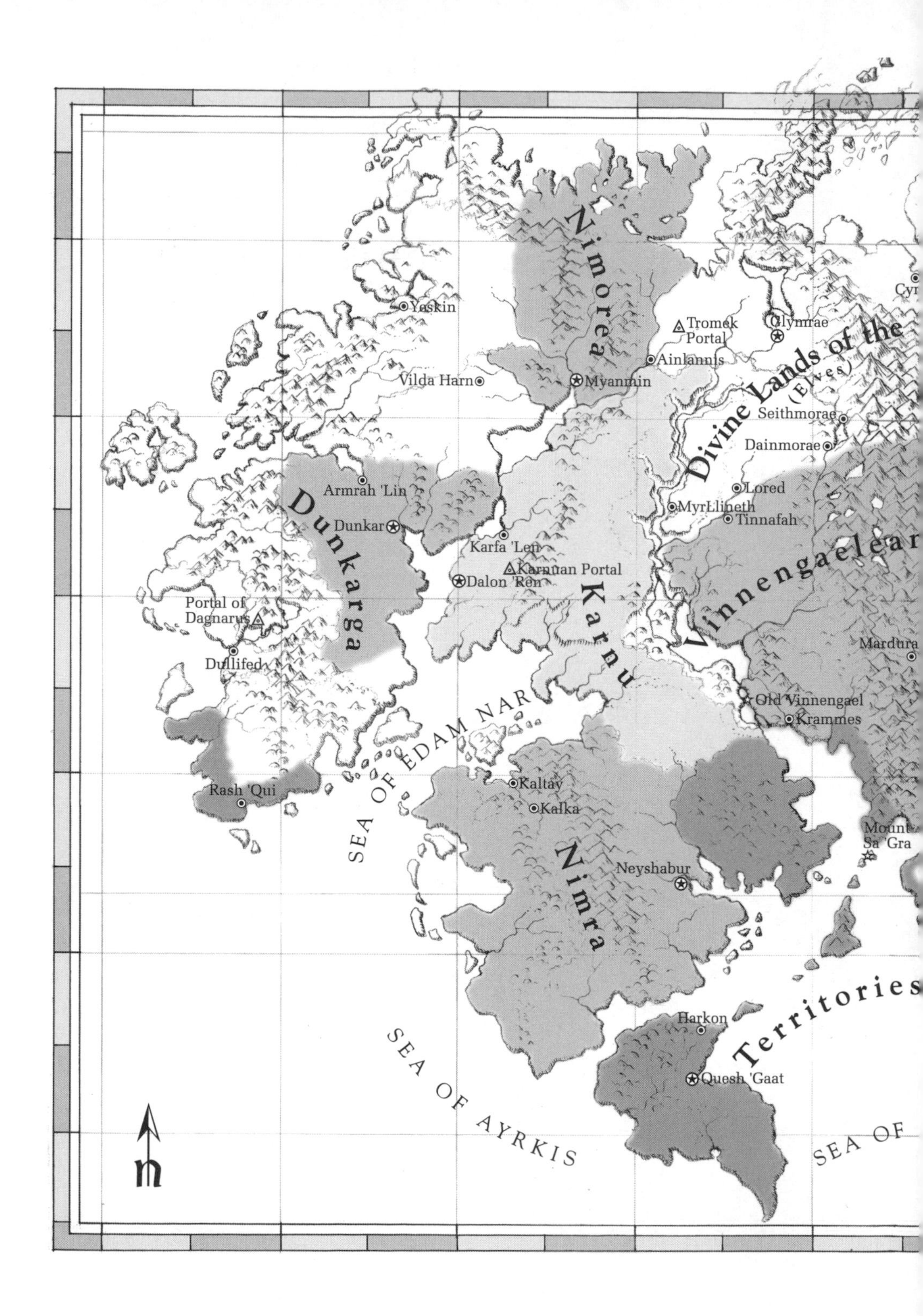

Nimorea
Yeskin
Tromek Portal
Glymrae
Ainlannis
Divine Lands of the
(Elves)
Vilda Harn
Myanmin
Seithmorae
Dainmorae
Armrah 'Lin
Dunkarga
Lored
MyrLlineth
Tinnafah
Dunkar
Karfa 'Len
Karnuan Portal
Dalon 'Ren
Karnu
Vinnengaelear
Portal of Dagnarus
Mardura
Dullifed
Old Vinnengael
Krammes
SEA OF EDAM NAR
Kaltay
Rash 'Qui
Kalka
Mount Sa 'Gra
Nimra
Neyshabur
Territories
Harkon
Quesh 'Gaat
SEA OF AYRKIS
SEA OF
n

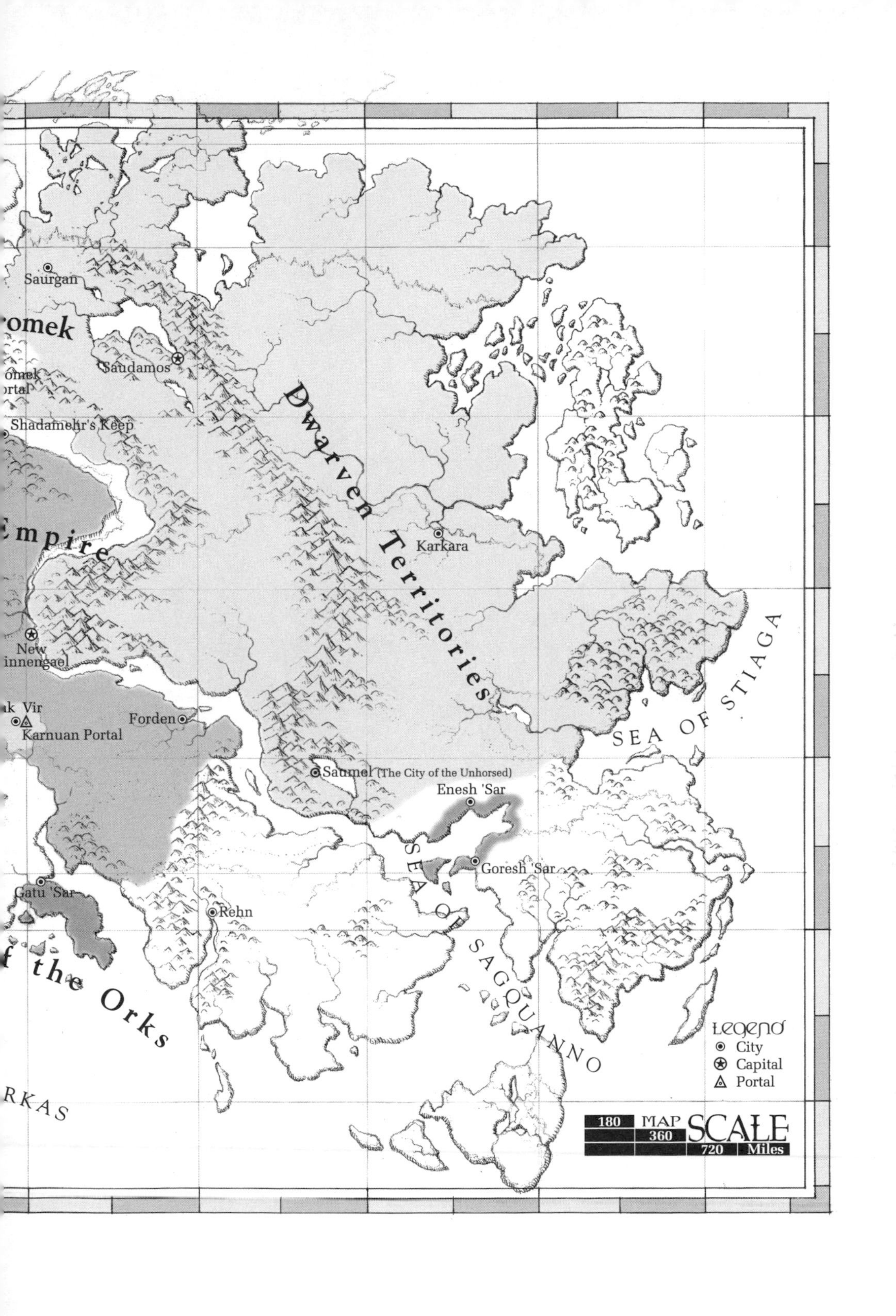

Saurgan
omek
Saudamos
omek
ortal
Shadamehr's Keep
Dwarven Territories
Empire
Karkara
New
innengael
k Vir
Forden
Karnuan Portal
SEA OF STIAGA
Saumel (The City of the Unhorsed)
Enesh 'Sar
Goresh 'Sar
Gatu 'Sar
Rehn
SEA OF SAGQUANNO
f the Orks
RKAS
Legend
City
Capital
Portal
180
MAP
360
SCALE
720
Miles

BOOK
I

SHADOWING THE TWO PECWAE WAS RELATIVELY EASY FOR THE Vrykyl, Jedash. The elderly grandmother and her grandson walked slowly, stopping often to gape at the wondrous sights of the city of New Vinnengael.

A street filled with buildings as tall as giants, full three stories, one stacked atop another, astonished the diminutive, forest-dwelling pecwae. The two spent a whole quarter hour staring at this wonder alone. The gaily painted signs of the guild shops and alehouses were meant to attract attention, and they lured the pecwae with their garish colors and outlandish renditions of animals, objects, and people. The Prancing Porker, the Cocked Hattery (featuring a rooster wearing a hat), the Bishop's Miter Alehouse—drew either a shake of the head from the knowledgeable pecwae (the pig had not been born who could prance), or a laugh.

The two pecwae had no notion they were being followed. They had eluded danger, or so they thought. The moment the Imperial guard had come in sight, bearing down on them and their companions, the instinct for self-preservation that had enabled their diminutive race to survive in a world populated by all manner of predators prompted them to flee. Their companions, including Baron Shadamehr and their Trevinici protector, Jessan, had been arrested. Having no orders regarding pecwae, the Imperial guard had not bothered with them.

Jedash had no orders regarding pecwae, either, but he had seen them arrive in company with a Trevinici. Recalling that Shakur, another Vrykyl, had been searching for a Trevinici traveling in company with pecwae, Jedash had thought this intriguing. He'd reported it to Shakur and taken it upon himself to trail after them. Jedash had been rewarded for his foresight. Shakur sent urgent word through the Blood-knife that Jedash was to capture the two pecwae and bring them to the palace, where Shakur was now residing, having murdered and taken over the body of the young king.

The question for Jedash was how to capture the two without drawing undue attention to himself. And in this, he had rivals.

The sight of pecwae wandering the streets of New Vinnengael was attracting a considerable amount of attention, some of it sinister. About four feet in height, of slender build, with wide eyes and a cheerful smile, the male pecwae had been disguised to pass for a human child, wearing a cap over his delicately pointed ears. The elderly female pecwae, however, had scorned to disguise herself. Small and gray-headed, with a face brown and wrinkled as a walnut, she peered and leered into the faces of everyone they passed; her long, colorful skirt, decorated with beads and bells, clicking and jangling around her ankles. Her walking stick was in itself a curiosity. Carved of wood, the stick was filled with knotholes and every single one of the knotholes was a polished agate, mounted in such a way that each resembled a staring eye.

Most of the citizens who stopped to stare at the pecwae and point them out were simply curious, pausing a moment to gawk at the funny-looking little people. But others were not. Some had a more material interest.

Years past, it had been the fashion among the wealthy of New Vinnengael to keep pecwae as pets. Pecwae children, stolen from their homes, were bought and sold in the marketplace. The wealthy exhibited them as curiosities or kept them as companions, dressing them up like dolls and walking them like dogs. Unused to city life, many pecwae sickened and died in captivity and eventually the Church put a stop to the practice. Dealing in pecwae was now illegal, a crime that could be punished by death.

People found ways around this law, however. Adoption was not only legal but encouraged, and wealthy families could now always "adopt" pecwae children. The Church had no quarrel with this, since introducing pecwae to civilization and the benefits of a Church education could only profit the savage race. The traffic in pecwae was severely curtailed, but a person could still obtain one, if he had the money.

Even on the black market, few pecwae were available, and those that were fetched a healthy price. In order to protect their children, the pecwae tribes had moved out of New Vinnengael and traveled west to the lands of the Trevinici, their ancient protectors. Those unscrupulous merchants who did not fear the Church had a healthy fear of the Trevinici. It was the ancient law of supply and demand.

The sight of two pecwae, alone and unprotected, calmly strolling the streets of New Vinnengael, brought gleams to the eyes of more than one black marketeer.

Jedash understood the danger the pecwae were in better than the two pecwae, and he cursed his ill luck. Quite clearly, he stood a fair chance of having his prize snatched right out from under his nose. He recognized two well-known smugglers among the gawkers, smugglers said to trade in all sorts of contraband, from forbidden books of Void magic to nightshade and baneberry to orks' teeth (thought by some to be an aphrodisiac) to pecwae.

Armed with the magical power of the Void, Jedash was not afraid to fight for his prize. The only weapons he feared—the only weapons that could slice through the Void magic that held his rotting corpse together—were weapons that had been blessed by the gods. Jedash was reasonably confident that neither of those two would have such a weapon in their possession.

That said, Jedash was well aware that the smugglers would not lightly relinquish the chance for such a windfall. If he moved in on his quarry, the smugglers would view him as a competitor and try to stop him. There would be trouble, a commotion, screams, blood. To make matters worse, the city was on edge, the streets unusually crowded, for rumors were circulating that New Vinnengael was about to go to war. Shopkeepers had shut up their stores. The wealthy who had country homes had packed up their valuables and were leaving the city. Soldiers went about looking grim and important, and it seemed that every person who could walk or hobble was out in search of the latest rumor. At the first sight of trouble, some nervous busybody would go haring off for the authorities.

Jedash could have dealt with any number of authorities, but he had orders to keep his true nature concealed. He was not to reveal to anyone that he was a Vrykyl. Dagnarus feared that someone might connect him with the undead Vrykyl, and such knowledge might upset his plans for the conquest of the city.

Traipsing after the pecwae, Jedash mulled over his dilemma, tried to figure out how to deal with the situation. His thoughts were interrupted by Shakur, who was able to speak to Jedash through the magic of the Blood-knives that both carried.

"I have just finished searching the Trevinici warrior. We did not find the Sovereign Stone on him," Shakur stated. "But he was carrying Svetlana's Blood-knife. The Stone must be in possession of the two pecwae. You said you were on their trail. Have you caught them yet?"

"No, Shakur," Jedash replied. "There are . . . complications."

"Another dragon?" Shakur asked, with a sneer.

"No, not another dragon," Jedash muttered, adding sullenly, "If these two pecwae are so blamed important, why don't you come get them yourself?"

"I cannot leave the palace," Shakur returned. "My disguise forbids it. You are responsible, Jedash. See to it that you do not bungle this assignment as you did the last one. Lord Dagnarus was not pleased."

Shakur severed the mental connection, leaving Jedash on his own.

The Vrykyl ground his teeth in anger, but he dared not say or even think a word of defiance. The last assignment Shakur had given Jedash had been foiled by the fact that the dwarf he'd been supposed to kidnap was being guarded by a dragon disguised as a human female. Vrykyl are powerful in Void magic, and there are some who might be able to fight and defeat a dragon—one such as Shakur, for example. Jedash wasn't one of them. He had fled the premises, far more willing to face Shakur's ire than the wrath of a dragon.

Consequently, Jedash needed to prove himself, needed to ingratiate himself to his lord and return to his lord's good graces. Capturing the pecwae would be his opportunity.

Jedash was not brilliant. He was not even particularly intelligent, but he did have the low and desperate cunning of a trapped rat. Shakur's mention of the Trevinici protector gave Jedash an idea, gave him a couple of ideas.

"If I hand over the two pecwae to Shakur, he'll take them to Lord Dagnarus and claim that *he* found them. Why should Shakur be rewarded with my lord's favor?" Jedash asked sulkily. "Why shouldn't it be me? I'm the one who's chasing them down, after all."

Jedash kept on the trail. The crowds that he had previously cursed now worked in his favor. Vrykyl maintain their unhallowed life by feeding on the souls of those they murder. Once they have taken a soul, they have the power of transforming themselves into the victim. Jedash could take on the dead person's appearance, his characteristics, his voice and manner. He could perform the transformation swiftly, as he walked.

There were dangers. Anyone looking at him directly would be startled out of their wits to see a person change suddenly into another person. And there was the uncomfortable moment between the two aspects when the hideous rotting corpse that was the true form of the Vrykyl would be clearly visible. Fortunately for Jedash, those in the streets were more intent on feeding their own fears than noticing a man changing his skin as another might change clothes.

Jedash underwent the transformation.

Settled into his new body, he closed in on his prey.

Bashae noticed the way some of the people looked at him and the Grandmother. He saw the way eyes glittered and fingers twitched, as if counting money, and he was uneasy. He recalled—a bit late—how Arim, the Nimorean kite-maker, had warned him that some unscrupulous people might kidnap them and sell them as slaves.

Bashae tried to explain his worries to the Grandmother, but she refused to listen. She had arrived in her "sleep city," the other world to which pecwae travel in their dreams. Entranced by the sights, which she maintained she had seen in her dreams, she walked the streets and pointed out familiar landmarks, heedless of the stares, heedless of the danger.

Bashae was sorry he'd responded to his instincts and fled when the city guards came in sight. He had the feeling he would have been much more comfortable with his friends, even if they were all in jail, than wandering about the crowded streets, amidst the tall buildings that blotted out the sunlight and these people who stared and laughed and watched them with narrowed eyes.

"I wish we'd stayed with Jessan," Bashae said, after stepping barefoot into some sort of stinking brown gunk.

"Bah!" the Grandmother scoffed. "If we were with them, they would be in more danger, not less." She cast a knowing look at the knapsack

Bashae carried. "We're safer without them, and they're safer without us. So it all works out."

Bashae sighed and clutched the knapsack tightly. He had not known what was in it when he'd accepted the knapsack from the dying knight, Lord Gustav. Bashae had thought the knapsack contained only a family heirloom, meant to be delivered to a dear friend. He knew the truth now, knew that he carried with him the human portion of the Sovereign Stone, a powerful magical jewel. Bashae was not very clear on what the jewel did, but he was clear on two points: the first, that everyone in the known world was searching for it; the second, that most of those searching for it would kill to obtain it.

"Jessan will be worried about us," said Bashae, thinking of his friend and protector, the young Trevinici warrior.

"Of course," returned the Grandmother complacently. "He's supposed to be worried about us. That's why we brought him along. He's probably looking for us right now. If he's not in a dungeon somewhere."

"Do you think he's in a dungeon?" Bashae asked, concerned.

"Anything's possible," said the Grandmother. "Especially in my sleep city." She seemed proud of that fact.

Bashae cast a hopeless glance at the crowds milling about in the street. He'd never seen so many people congregated in one place before in his life. They were thick as ticks on a bear. He didn't see how Jessan could ever find them.

"Maybe it would be a good idea if we stopped somewhere and waited for him," Bashae suggested. "You must be tired, Grandmother."

"I'm never tired," she retorted. A moment earlier she had been footsore, limping, her shoulders sagging. She stood up straight and glared at him. "If *you're* tired, we'll stop and rest."

A door stoop being convenient, the two sat down. The Grandmother gathered her skirt around her ankles so no one would trip over her bells and placed her stick with its staring eyes across her lap. Bashae was somewhat inconvenienced by the stick, which poked him in the ribs, but he managed to find a comfortable position and settled himself to wait for someone to find them. If not Jessan, then Baron Shadamehr or one of his men. Maybe Ulaf, to whom Bashae had taken a liking.

They had run away in the morning, and by now the sun had sailed across the sky and buildings were beginning to cast long shadows. What clouds Bashae could see between the tops of the tall buildings had taken on an orange tinge. Night would be on them soon, sooner in this city than in their homeland.

At least no one will stare at us in the darkness, Bashae was thinking when his thoughts were scattered by the clanging and booming of what seemed to be hundreds of bells.

Every bell in the city gave tongue, droning in deep voices or singing out in higher-pitched tones. The clangor woke the Grandmother, who had fallen asleep with her head on the stick. Bashae stared about in wonderful astonishment. He'd never heard anything like this wild, sweet pealing.

Almost immediately after the bells, a man with a booming voice deeper than any bell could be heard three streets away. "By order of His Majesty the King, curfew has been imposed on the city of New Vinnengael. All people are to be off the streets and in their homes at the hour of Eventide. Anyone caught on the streets past that hour will be subject to arrest and imprisonment."

The man boomed this on one corner, then stalked off down the street to boom it on another. The streets began to empty, with most people heading for their homes. Those inclined to linger were helped along by patrols of armed guards.

"What are we going to do?" Bashae wondered in dismay. "We don't have a home. Where will we go?"

There is nowhere to go, which means that we'll be arrested, he thought. Which means that we'll be reunited with our friends. Darkness seemed to fall, all of a sudden, stranding the pecwae in this strange stone wilderness. He was on the point of calling out to the soldiers, when the Grandmother suddenly cried out, "Evil!" and lashed at something with her stick.

Bashae turned to see a man sneaking up on them, hands outstretched. The agate-eyed stick took the man across the knuckles. He howled and snatched back his hand, but his companion made a lunge at Bashae, seized hold of him by the hair.

"Quit squirming, you little bastard," the man snarled in a rough, deep voice, "or I'll pull your hair out by the roots."

Tears stung Bashae's eyes as he flailed about, struggling to escape his captor. The Grandmother shrieked at the man in Twithil and lashed at him with her stick.

This had little effect, and the man was about to drag Bashae away, when suddenly he gasped. The hand holding Bashae let loose, and he tumbled to the pavement, where he crouched, paralyzed, afraid to move.

Somewhere, close to him, men were fighting.

Bashae couldn't see in the darkness. He heard scuffling sounds, then a splintering crash, as if someone had tumbled through a wooden gate, and a thud. A man slumped to the pavement and lay there staring at Bashae. The man gave a groan, his eyes rolled back in his head, and his body went limp.

Light flared. Bashae peered up, blinking at the sudden brilliance, to see a Trevinici warrior holding a torch.

The warrior was clad all in leather. His reddish brown hair was tied back in the traditional manner. He wore the gruesome trophies of his battle kills around his neck and a long knife thrust into his belt.

"Here you two are," the warrior said, stern and unsmiling. "I have been searching for you everywhere."

"You have?" Bashae said, confused. He did not know this warrior, did not recognize him. "How do you know about us?"

"Your friend sent me," said the warrior.

"Jessan?" Bashae asked eagerly, and scrambled to his feet.

The Grandmother stood nearby, panting for breath, the agate-eyed stick clutched tightly in her fist. She stared at the Trevinici, her black eyes orange in the firelight.

"Jessan sent you?" she demanded, her tone suspicious.

"Yes, Jessan," said the Trevinici. He prodded the bodies of their attackers, who lay in the street. "A good thing I came when I did."

"Yes, it is," said Bashae earnestly. "Thank you for rescuing us. Grandmother," he added in low tones, pinching her arm, "what's the matter with you? This warrior saved us. You should thank him."

"Evil," returned the Grandmother under her breath. "There's evil about. The stick tells me."

"Yes, Grandmother. The evil is lying at my feet," said Bashae, exasperated.

The Grandmother grunted and shook her head.

Bashae gave the Trevinici an apologetic smile. "The Grandmother is also grateful to you, sir. Where is Jessan?"

"He is a long way from here," said the Trevinici. "Outside the city walls. I will take you to him."

"He left the city?" Bashae was troubled. "Without finding us?"

"He didn't have much choice," said the Trevinici dryly. "He was under arrest at the time. They were taking him to their prison that is in the middle of the river, when he managed to escape. That's how we ran into each other. He could not come himself, because they are searching for him. But all this is a long story. Curfew has been declared, which means that everyone must be off the streets. You must come with me now."

"Of course," said Bashae, tugging on the Grandmother's arm.

She ignored him. Staring at the stick, she gave it an irritated shake.

"Bashae! Grandmother!" a familiar voice called out, as a familiar figure came running down the street. "Thank the gods I've found you!"

"Ulaf!" cried Bashae, waving. "He's a friend," he added in Trevini.

"Some friend," the Trevinici grunted, displeased. "To leave you two to wander the streets alone." He took a firm grip on Bashae's arm. "The man is a Vinnengaelean, and none of them are to be trusted. We will leave now."

"Please let go of me," said Bashae, respectfully but firm. Sometimes Trevinici did not know their own strength. "I know you don't mean to, but you're hurting me. I will go with you, but not just yet. Not until I explain to Ulaf. It's not his fault that we're lost. It's our fault. We ran away when we saw the guards coming."

The Trevinici let go of the pecwae, but he didn't look happy. Bashae wasn't surprised. The Trevinici had not been born who had any use for city people.

Ulaf's fair-complected face was flushed from running, his hair tousled. A genial man, with a manner that was invariably friendly and outgoing, he appeared only mildly annoyed at the pecwae for running off.

"I've been looking for you two everywhere," said Ulaf, grinning. If he was startled to find them in company with a Trevinici, he gave no outward sign of it. "Baron Shadamehr was really worried about you. Looks like there's been some trouble." He glanced at the two unconscious men lying on the pavement, then shifted a keen-eyed gaze to the Trevinici. "Who's your friend? Is this his work?"

"I am Fire Storm," said the Trevinici with a scowl. "I did what I had to do to protect the small ones, since others left them neglected. These ruffians meant to make slaves of them, as you must have known would happen if they went wandering alone about the city. I will take charge of the pecwae now. Tell your master that they are safe. Come along, you two. Jessan is waiting for you."

"I'm sorry, but we have to go with Fire Storm, Ulaf," said Bashae, settling the knapsack more comfortably over his shoulder and getting a firm grip on the Grandmother, who was knocking the stick against a wall. "Jessan sent his friend for us—"

"Jessan," interrupted Ulaf in wondering tones. He looked more closely at the Trevinici. "Jessan is with Baron Shadamehr."

"No, he isn't," Bashae explained. "Jessan was arrested and taken across the river. Fire Storm helped him escape or something like that. Anyhow, Jessan sent Fire Storm to search for us and so we have to be going."

"Jessan arrested? And he escaped, you say? How very exiting." Ulaf laid his hand on the Trevinici's arm. "I have to hear this tale! There's an inn nearby called the Tubby Tabby. I'll buy the ale, Fire Storm, if you'll tell your story."

The Trevinici knocked Ulaf's hand aside. Glowering, he turned to the pecwae.

"We have no time for such foolery. Are you coming?" he demanded dourly.

"You won't be able to leave the city," Ulaf remarked cheerfully. "Didn't you hear the bells ringing? They've shut the main gates. No one in or out until morning and maybe not even then. You might as well come to the tavern where it's warm and we can have something to eat."

"What should we do, Grandmother?" Bashae asked in a low voice, speaking Twithil.

"Do about what?" demanded the Grandmother, looking up from the stick.

"Should we go with Ulaf to the tavern or go with Fire Storm to find Jessan? Ulaf says that they've shut the city gates. I want to find Jessan," said Bashae, "but it's a long way to walk, clear back to the river. And I'm really hungry. We haven't eaten anything since morning."

The Grandmother regarded the stick with a look of contempt. "The eyes see something terrible close by us, but they won't tell me what it is or where."

"Grandmother," said Bashae, looking from the gutter that was awash with raw sewage to the two ruffians, who were groaning back to consciousness, "we're in a city. There's evil all around us!"

"This is my sleep city," she snapped.

"I'm sorry, Grandmother. I forgot." Bashae sighed.

The Grandmother knocked the stick against the wall again, as if she'd knock some sense into it, then whispered into Bashae's ear.

"If you must know, I think I made a mistake. My sleep city doesn't smell this bad, and there aren't this many people. I don't think I'll die here, after all," she concluded in a decided tone.

"I'm glad about that, Grandmother," Bashae said. He could see that the Trevinici warrior was growing impatient. "But what do we do? Go to the tavern with Ulaf or go with Fire Storm?"

"Not much of a choice, if you ask me," the Grandmother said with a dark glance for both tall humans. "As for this Fire Storm, he's not telling all he knows. Why didn't Jessan come for us himself? Jessan is not one to shirk his responsibility. He wouldn't have sent another to find us unless something was wrong. As for this Ulaf, he licks us like a playful pup, and all the time he watches us like the cat. Still"—she shrugged—"as you say, it's late, and I'm hungry."

"So we'll go with Ulaf?" Bashae asked.

"Will you find us something to eat?" the Grandmother demanded of Ulaf, shifting from Twithil to Elderspeak.

"I'll buy you whatever you want," Ulaf promised. "But we should hurry. It's almost curfew hour, and the patrols will be coming through the streets, arresting people. You should come with us, Fire Storm. I don't think you want to answer a lot of questions about what happened to these two wretches."

"We had better go to this tavern," the Trevinici said grudgingly. He reached out his hand, took hold of Bashae's knapsack. "That looks heavy. I will carry that for you."

Bashae clutched the knapsack close. Mindful of what the Grandmother had said, he was suddenly wary of this strange Trevinici. All his life, Bashae had been accustomed to trusting everyone. Now it seemed he couldn't trust anyone. It was this city. He hated this city, hated it so much that his hatred made his stomach churn, and he wasn't all that hungry, after all.

"Thank you, Fire Storm, but I can manage," he said.

"Suit yourself," said Fire Storm, shrugging.

"Oh, quit your whining," said the Grandmother to the agate-eyed stick.

LIGHT! WE NEED LIGHT!" ALISE ORDERED, TRYING TO KEEP THE tremor of fear from her voice, trying to hold panic at bay.

She put her hand on Shadamehr's neck, felt for a pulse, and found it. He was still alive. But his skin was cold to the touch, and his breathing was shallow and erratic. He'd been wounded—she'd seen the blood on his shirt as he ran from the palace. He had assured her, with his own jaunty air and self-mocking smile, that it was "just a scratch." There hadn't been time for more.

Having escaped from the palace by leaping out a window in full view of the public and a large number of guardsmen, the baron had caused something of a stir. The alarm raised, the guards set off in pursuit. Alise and Jessan in tow, Shadamehr had thrown off pursuit by dodging down alleys until they came to this tavern. He had made it as far as the back room, then almost immediately collapsed. The room was a storage room with no windows. They had to keep the door shut, in case the guards conducted a search, and no one had thought to bring a light.

"Go back to the bar, Jessan. Grab a candle, a lantern, whatever is available. Bring water and brandywine. And don't say a word to anyone!"

An unnecessary warning, she realized. The taciturn Trevinici warrior had spoken maybe twenty words to her during the weeks she had known him, and those words had been in answer to some direct question. Jessan was not sulky or sullen. Like all Trevinici, he saw no need to engage in idle chitchat. He said what was important to say, and that was all.

Now, for example, he did not waste breath on questions. He simply left to go fetch light. Alise could hear him kicking boxes and barrels out of his way as he stumbled through the darkness. She heard him fumble at the iron door latch, heard the door scrape open.

Light and tobacco smoke and noise flooded the room. Bending over Shadamehr, Alise looked into his face, and fear coiled around her heart, squeezed it so that she very nearly stopped breathing. He was waxen white. No vestige of color remained in his skin. His lips had a bluish tinge, his cheeks were sunken hollows. His forehead was chill and clammy, his long, curling hair damp with sweat. When she put her hand on his forehead, he shuddered and grimaced in pain.

The door shut, the light vanished. Alise was left alone in the darkness. Alone with Shadamehr—the aggravating, irritating, annoying, reckless Shadamehr, generous of heart, noble of spirit, a damned fool. Beloved, detested, a pain in the ass, and dying. She knew he was dying as surely as she knew that he was her lord and she was his lady, whether they admitted it to each other or not. He was dying, and she could do nothing to save him because she didn't know what was killing him.

A scratch, he'd said.

The door opened, light returned. Alise heard a woman's voice asking if there was anything she could do. Jessan said no, and the door closed. The light remained. Jessan came forward carrying a lantern in one hand, a bucket of water in the other, and a pewter flask attached to a leather thong slung about his neck. He set the lantern on the top of a barrel, arranged it so that its light illuminated Shadamehr. He placed the bucket on the floor, handed the flask to Alise.

Squatting beside Shadamehr, Jessan looked at him and shook his head.

Now that she had light, Alise could examine Shadamehr. She ripped open the bloody fabric of his shirt and saw just what he'd told her she would see—a ragged, narrow scratch along his rib cage. The blow had been struck in haste. Aiming to penetrate to the heart, the blade had been turned aside by a rib. Alise ripped a piece from the hem of her linen chemise, dipped the cloth in the water, and washed away the blood.

The scratch appeared to have been made by a blade that was thin as a darning needle. The wound had punctured the skin, but had not gone deep; otherwise, there would have been more blood. Nothing serious, at first glance; nothing to cause such a reaction. Bending nearer, Alise noticed then that the edges of the skin around the scratch were chalk white, almost as if the wound had been packed in snow.

Alise had lived with Shadamehr and his cohorts for many years. She had been involved in numerous dangerous and daring escapades, and she had grown accustomed to working her healing magic on injuries of all types, from knife wounds to bite marks to ghoul clawings. She had never seen anything like this.

Or had she? She suddenly remembered Ulien, Shadamehr's friend, who had been mysteriously slain. She and Shadamehr had gone to investigate. She remembered the sight of the man's body as it lay in the morgue. He had died of a single wound to the heart—a wound that was small, almost bloodless, and ghastly white around the edges.

"Oh, gods," Alise whispered. Her hands began to tremble. Don't do this, she commanded herself. He needs you. Don't fall apart now.

"Jessan," said Alise, "what happened in the palace? Tell me everything. How did Shadamehr get hurt? Did you"—she looked intently at the young man, into his face—"did you see a Vrykyl? You know what one is, don't you?"

"I know," said Jessan, and there was a shadowed, haunted look in his eyes. He shook his head again. "I saw no Vrykyl. As for what happened—"

"You must be brief," Alise interrupted. "I don't think . . ." She swallowed. "I'm afraid the baron is in very grave danger."

Jessan thought back, arranged his thoughts to make his recital as brief and succinct as possible.

"We were arrested and brought before the boy king and the woman who is the person truly in charge of New Vinnengael, or so Shadamehr told us."

"The Regent," said Alise.

"Yes. Shadamehr said that he suspected the Regent of being a Vrykyl, for they can assume the form of any person they have slain. Shadamehr believed that the boy king was the Vrykyl's prisoner, that he was under her control. He planned to rescue the boy king, carry him to safety. The two elves who were arrested with us—Damra and her husband—agreed to help. The guards took the four of us into a room. The Regent cast a spell on me and on the elven Dominion Lord. The Regent said she was searching for the Sovereign Stone. She found the Sovereign Stone on

Damra, but not on me. She seemed surprised and angry at that. There was another wizard, wearing armor and a sword—"

"A battle mage," said Alise. "Hurry, Jessan, please hurry. What *happened*?"

"It was all confusion," Jessan said grimly. "Damra began shouting strange words. Suddenly the room was filled with elves who looked exactly like her."

"An illusion spell," Alise murmured.

Jessan shrugged. The Trevinici have no use for magic, distrust all who cast it. "Her husband spit at the battle mage, and he screamed and fell down. One of the guards attacked Shadamehr. I knifed the guard. Shadamehr grabbed hold of the boy king and suddenly . . ."

Jessan paused, remembering. "Suddenly the baron made a strange sound, sort of a strangled gasp, and dropped the boy to the floor. Then he cried out that we had to run for it. He took hold of me, and the next thing I knew, he was running toward the window, dragging me with him. We crashed through the window. The ground was a long way below us. I thought we were going to die with our brains spattered on the pavement. But we floated down like thistle—"

"Griffith cast a spell on you," Alise said. "Is that all?"

"Yes, we caught up with you then and came here."

Alise gazed long at Shadamehr. Opening the flask, she daubed some of the brandy on his lips.

"My lord!" she called softly. "Shadamehr!"

He groaned and stirred, but he did not regain consciousness. She sighed deeply.

"Did the Regent stab him?" she asked Jessan.

"I don't think so. I didn't see her holding a knife."

"You say that Shadamehr picked up the boy king and then he made an odd sound and he dropped him. Then he said to flee. No more talk of kidnapping the boy." She recalled Shadamehr's words, spoken to the elves as he sent them away.

There is no one to help Vinnengael. Not even the gods.

A thrill of horror raised the hair on Alise's neck and arms.

"My gods! The young king is the Vrykyl!" Alise said softly. "The Vrykyl murdered the king, then murdered his son, and took the boy's place. No wonder Shadamehr said there was no help for Vinnengael.

"I see now what must have happened. Shadamehr grabbed hold of what he thought was the young king, but, instead, he grabbed hold of the Vrykyl."

Alise couldn't help herself. She began to laugh. "What a shock that must have been to the creature. No wonder he stabbed you! Oh, Shadamehr, how very like you. One Vrykyl in the room, and you grab it and try to carry it off!"

Her laughter gave way to tears. She buried her face in her hands for a moment, long enough to regain control of herself. Resolutely, she drew in a deep breath, wiped her eyes, and began to consider what to do.

"You mean that the Vrykyl stabbed him?" Jessan asked.

"Yes, that's what happened," Alise said.

"The knight Gustav was wounded by a Vrykyl's knife," Jessan stated. "There was nothing the Grandmother could do to save him. He fought the Void for several days, but, in the end, he died. The spirits of our heroes battled the Void and saved his soul, so said the Grandmother."

Alise flinched. Trevinici-like, Jessan was accepting of death. He spoke no lying platitudes, did not try to blunt truth's sharp dagger. He had no idea that he had pierced her to the heart.

"Move the bucket closer," she said, dipping the cloth in the water.

"I will summon the spirits of the heroes to fight for Shadamehr," Jessan offered. "When his time comes."

"His time isn't coming," Alise returned sharply. "Not yet."

Jessan glanced at her. When he spoke next, his tone was more gentle. "Perhaps the Grandmother can save him. The knight was old. Shadamehr is young. I will go find the Grandmother and bring her back."

Alise managed to work her stiff, chill lips into a smile. "I don't think there's anything she could do. But you are right, Jessan. You should go find your friends. The pecwae are lost, wandering about the city. Our people are searching for them, but the pecwae know you and trust you and might come to you when they would shun others. You should be with them. Your duty is to them. I will stay here with my lord."

"I will bring back the Grandmother," Jessan said, rising to his feet.

Alise saw it would be useless to argue. She was fast running out of time, and she needed to be rid of him.

"Our people are supposed to meet at a tavern called the Tubby Tabby. It's not far from here. Go back to the main road. Follow it until you come to a chandler's shop. You'll know it by the sign of a candle that hangs in front. Turn left down that street. The Tubby Tabby is at the end of the alleyway. It will be the only building with lights blazing this time of night. If Ulaf is there, send him to me. Tell him to come quickly. No one else, though. Tell no one else about Shadamehr but Ulaf."

Jessan gave an abrupt nod. He repeated the directions back to her and departed, without wasting time in useless well-wishes or lengthy farewells.

When he was gone, Alise blinked back her tears.

"I have to be strong," she said to herself. "I'm all he has!"

She rose to her feet, looked around the room, making her plans. Picking up the lantern, she carried it with her to the door, dropped the latch, and made certain it was locked. Confident now that she would not be disturbed, she went back to Shadamehr and knelt beside him.

Alise was trained in Earth magic, the magic of healing. But she was also trained in another, deadly magic. Alise was one of the few wizards the Church deemed capable of handling the powerful and destructive magic of the Void. The Inquisitors taught her Void magic, intending that she could become one of their Order, who actively seek out Void practitioners with the intention of bringing them to justice. Alise soon found that line of work distasteful, for it meant spying on friends, family, even on fellow brethren.

A former tutor, a mage named Rigiswald, had introduced her to Baron Shadamehr. A wealthy noble, independent thinker, and adventurer, Shadamehr was the only person in history, so far as it was known, to have passed the Tests to become one of the powerful and magical Dominion Lords and then refuse to undergo the Holy Transfiguration, earning the ire of the Church, his king, and, most likely, the gods.

Shadamehr would never tell his age, but Alise guessed him to be in his middle thirties. He had a nose like a hawk's beak, a chin like an ax blade, eyes blue as the skies above New Vinnengael, and a long, black mustache of which he was inordinately proud.

Alise smoothed back Shadamehr's hair with her hand, noted a few silver threads among the curling black, and gray hairs in the mustache.

I will have to tease him about that, she thought, settling herself beside him.

Reckless and daring, Baron Shadamehr had peculiar ideas. He held that the various races of the world should stop killing each other and learn to get along. He maintained that men should quit whining to the gods to better their lives and start working toward betterment themselves.

How like him to come up with such a wild plan to kidnap the young king out from under the nose of a Vrykyl! How like him to convince a wise and sensible elven Dominion Lord to go along with him.

"Maybe this time, you've learned your lesson," she said to him, although she was not very hopeful. Nor, on second thought, did she want to be.

She glanced back toward the door. If only Ulaf would come!

Alise could not use her healing magic on Shadamehr. She had cast a Void spell in order to rescue him and his companions from the palace guards, and now she was tainted by the foul essence of the magic that can only destroy, can never be used to save or create. If she tried to heal him using her Earth magic, the spell would crumble beneath her fingers like a burnt biscuit.

Ulaf might be able to help Shadamehr, for he was also a skilled Earth mage. She couldn't count on him, though. He was out searching for the pecwae and, even if Jessan found him in time and sent him to her, she doubted if Ulaf could heal this wound.

The magic of the gods could not save Shadamehr, but the magic of the Void that had wounded him might.

Alise brought to mind the loathsome spell.

Void magic is dangerous and destructive, not only for its victims, but also for the magi who casts it, for the magic of the Void demands a sacrifice—a bit of a magi's own life essence to power the spell, making the spell-casting painful and debilitating to the user. Even the simplest spell causes lesions and pustules to erupt on the skin, while more powerful spells can inflict such pain that the sorcerer falls unconscious or dies.

Prohibited from using the healing arts by the terrible nature of their magic, Void sorcerers had developed spells that could transfer a bit of the sorcerer's own life essence into the body of another in order to save him. The spell was said to have been perfected in ancient Dunkarga, a land where Void magic is widely accepted. The spell was not often used, and then only under the most dire circumstances, for if the spell was badly cast or the sorcerer made a mistake, the result could be fatal for both caster and patient.

Above all, the textbooks cautioned, "The spell should never be cast by a sorcerer who is by himself, without someone else on hand to assist him. For in order to cast the spell, the sorcerer must place himself in physical contact with the person who is to receive the benefits. When the spell is cast, the Void magic drains the life essence from the sorcerer, sends it flowing into the body of the patient.

"The caster must know when to halt the spell and break contact, and this is where an assistant is necessary. As the life drains from him, the caster grows weaker and weaker. If the caster falls unconscious, while still touching the victim, the spell will continue to drain the caster until it steals away his life. Thus, this warning: Never cast this spell alone! Two sorcerers at least should be present—one to cast and the other to break contact should the spellcaster fall unconscious."

Alise had never used this spell. She had studied it, of course, but she had not committed such a terrible spell to memory. She loathed the use of Void magic. She did not mind so much the pain of the spell-casting, although that was bad enough, or the disfiguring pustules and lesions. She hated the way the magic felt inside her, as if maggots were feeding on her soul.

But she didn't have any choice. Shadamehr's skin had gone gray. His breathing had altered from rapid, shallow breaths to struggled gasps. He shivered with the cold, his body writhed in pain. His nails were blue, his flesh chill, as if death had already claimed him.

Alise looked over her shoulder toward the door.

Never cast this spell alone!

She saw the words printed large in the books, heard her tutor warn her over and over. If only Ulaf would come!

But he wasn't going to. She admitted that to herself. Ulaf was out searching for the pecwae, perhaps facing his own dangers. She could not wait. Shadamehr was very far gone.

Adjusting the lanternlight, Alise reached into a hidden pocket she had sewn into her dress and removed a small, slim volume bound in nondescript gray leather. The book appeared quite harmless on the outside. Even when it was opened, one would have to be a student of magic in order to recognize that this small book was worth the price of her life. If the Church discovered her with this book of forbidden spells, she could be sentenced to hang.

Even as she turned the pages, Alise could feel the heinous magic start to crawl under her skin.

She read over the spell, felt her stomach roil, and was forced to cover her mouth with her hand, so as not to retch. Simply reciting the words in her mind brought on nausea, made her so weak and dizzy she could barely concentrate. She couldn't imagine what horror and pain would come with speaking them.

Alise bent down and kissed Shadamehr gently, tenderly on the lips. Clasping his hand, she pressed his hand to her breast and began to speak the horrible, maggot-ridden words aloud.

THE ORIGINAL TUBBY TABBY HAD BEEN A FAMOUS TAVERN IN THE city of Old Vinnengael. Two hundred years later, stories were still told of the tavern and its fat owner and his fatter orange cat, in whose honor the tavern was named. The stories had passed into popular legend, and almost every minstrel tale of long-ago heroes always began with a fortuitous meeting in the Tubby Tabby.

When the city of New Vinnengael was in the planning stages, several would-be tavern owners came to blows in the desire to name their businesses after the legendary tavern. Then one stated that he could prove that he was the ancestor of that same fat owner, and he even produced a fat cat that he claimed was the descendant of that same famous cat. His proof was accepted. On the day the king moved into the palace of the newly constructed city of New Vinnengael, the man opened the Tubby Tabby Two. The tavern had remained in the family, and now the owner's children's children ran it. A descendant of the same orange tabby snoozed in the sunshine by day and lounged on the bar by night.

The tavern had always been a favorite of the members of the Shadamehr family, one of whom had, years ago, secretly helped the owner out of his financial difficulties. The tavern had a back door that led into a very dark alley bounded by a wall that was easy to climb and another door that led to the roof, with other roofs within easy jumping distance. Since the Barons Shadamehr—an eccentric and independent bunch—were tireless champions of the weak and downtrodden, they tended to be the targets of the strong and powerful, who weren't at all pleased with Shadamehr meddling and took action to stop it, with the result that such means of hasty egress had proven most welcome to the various barons down through the years.

Ulaf was quite familiar with the tavern, for he found it an ideal place to meet with the people who kept him informed of what was going on in the world beyond the walls of New Vinnengael. The tavern was also the place where Shadamehr's people would gather if there was trouble.

Having found the pecwae, Ulaf shepherded them to the tavern, moving as fast as he could, all the while keeping a watchful eye out for the patrols. The bells rang curfew just as they turned into the block on which the tavern was located.

The streets were mostly empty. The patrols were already on the march, looking for violators. The patrols were also looking for Baron Shadamehr, but Ulaf had no way of knowing this. He guessed that something had gone wrong, for he'd heard the blowing of the penny whistles used by Shadamehr's people to alert each other in times of crisis. Ulaf had been about to go find out what was up, when he'd caught a glimpse of the pecwae, disappearing around a corner, and had instead gone after them.

He was certain to discover what had happened when he reached the meeting place. In the meantime, he had the two pecwae, and Bashae had the Sovereign Stone in the knapsack. Ulaf meant to keep hold of all three.

Ulaf would have been glad to rid himself of the Trevinici warrior, who had suddenly arrived on the scene.

"What a strange coincidence," Ulaf muttered, "that in a city that never sees a Trevinici or a pecwae, they should both suddenly bump into one another."

And then he remembered Shadamehr saying once that, "There are no such things as coincidences, only the gods' practical jokes."

So if this was a joke, who was getting the last laugh? Bashae and the Grandmother came from a land far from New Vinnengael, a land where the sight of a Trevinici—the pecwaes' ancient protectors—was as common as a sparrow. They could not know that seeing a Trevinici in New Vinnengael was tantamount to seeing a whale floating in one of the city fountains. Ulaf supposed that Jessan was the first Trevinici to have set foot in New Vinnengael in the past twenty years—if not longer. For there now to be two Trevinici in New Vinnengael stretched credibility to the utmost limits.

And for that Trevinici to have "stumbled" upon the two pecwae . . .

Ulaf had been warned that Vrykyl were in pursuit of the pecwae—or rather, the Vrykyl were in pursuit of the Sovereign Stone carried by the one pecwae, Bashae. Ulaf was unfortunately all too familiar with the Vrykyl. He'd encountered them before, much to his regret. They could take the form of any person they had killed, and he guessed that the strange Trevinici, walking down the street alongside him, was one of the powerful and terrifying Vrykyl. Ulaf had no way of knowing for certain, short of forcing the Vrykyl to reveal himself, and he had no intention of doing that. If this Trevinici was a Vrykyl, then they were in extreme danger.

"On the other hand," Ulaf argued with himself, "if this Trevinici is a Vrykyl, why didn't he use his Void magic to turn me into a pile of greasy ash and take the pecwae and run? Why is he coming along tamely?

"The obvious answer," Ulaf replied to himself, "is that the Vrykyl is under orders to keep himself and his magic hidden."

This surmise was not much comfort, for it opened up another box of terrible suppositions and surmises, the main one being that there were more Vrykyl working on behalf of their master, the Lord of the Void, Dagnarus, whose armies were even now marching down on New Vinnengael from the north.

Ulaf decided that his wisest course was to take everyone—pecwae, Trevinici, Vrykyl, and all—to the tavern, where he hoped he would find Baron Shadamehr and the rest of the Baron's people. Together they could figure some way to deal with this deadly situation.

The Tubby Tabby was located at the end of a block on Chandler's Street. As they turned into the street, the raucous laughter could be heard a block away. The sign featuring a painting of the famous slumbering orange tabby swayed and creaked in the evening breeze.

The heat and noise from inside the tavern burst on Ulaf with the force of a dwarven fire spell as he yanked open the heavy wooden door. On the lower floor was the tavern proper and two large common rooms, where travelers could find a pallet for the night. An enormous fireplace at one end of the tavern provided light and warmth. Seeing a number of his friends and comrades among the crowd, Ulaf breathed a sigh of relief.

Ulaf took firm hold of the pecwae, who stood frozen like terrified rabbits on the door stoop, and shoved them inside. The Trevinici hesitated in the doorway, and Ulaf hoped that he might be intimidated by the crowd and decide to depart. The warrior scowled darkly at the sight of so many people, but he followed the two pecwae inside and hung on to them like grim death.

An unfortunately apt analogy, Ulaf thought to himself.

He scanned the crowd hastily for Shadamehr. He did not see him, and that was a bad sign. Either the baron was still under arrest, or something worse had happened. None of Shadamehr's people gave any outward sign that they knew Ulaf, who gave no sign that he knew any of them. The tavern owner, who knew Ulaf well, looked right past him, and the busy serving wenches cast him harassed glances, as if he were just another customer. All knew that Ulaf might be there on some important business, that he might be using any one of his assumed identities, and that if he wanted to be recognized, he'd give them the signal.

The tavern was crowded. Visitors to New Vinnengael had been caught by surprise by the curfew. They'd be sleeping four to a bed. In addition, some of the locals who lived nearby and who figured they could sneak home before the patrols caught them, were here to talk about the rumors of war. Every table was filled, but Ulaf was not concerned, and, indeed, shortly after his arrival, a table near the door opened up. He steered the pecwae in that direction. The two men who had been sitting there passed by him without a glance, although one did rub his nose in a peculiar manner.

Ulaf knew the man, knew that his signal meant that something dire had happened and that they had to talk. The man walked up to the bar. Ulaf didn't dare leave the pecwae, not with the strange Trevinici hanging about, but he needed to know what was going on.

He settled the Grandmother in her chair, thinking as he did so that the normally feisty elder pecwae was unusually subdued. Every so often, the Grandmother lifted the agate-eyed stick, turned it this way and that. Then, looking grim, she would shake her head and the stick at the same time.

Some of the patrons were gawking at the pecwae and the Trevinici. Shadamehr's people studiously avoided looking at them and did what they could to distract the attention of the rest. The man at the bar rubbed his nose again, and this time gave a loud sneeze.

The Trevinici did not sit down but stood leaning against the wall, his arms folded, his dark gaze fixed on the two pecwae.

"Bashae," said Ulaf, "come with me—"

"Look, it's Jessan!" cried Bashae. He waved his hand. "Over here, Jessan!"

Jessan entered the room, extremely pleased and relieved to see his friends; so pleased that his usually stern expression relaxed into a smile. He halted a moment to stare in astonishment at the strange Trevinici. He was about to greet this fellow warrior, then recalled his urgent message. Jessan turned aside, spoke in a low, urgent tone to Ulaf.

"I need to talk to you. Alone."

Ulaf nodded and the two moved back toward the door.

"I have just left Alise and Shadamehr," Jessan said. "The baron has been wounded. Alise wants you to come right away."

"Wounded?" Ulaf repeated, shocked. "Is it bad?" It must be, he thought, for Alise to send for him.

"He's dying," Jessan said bluntly. "He's in the back room of a tavern down that way." He jerked his thumb. "Alise is with him, but I don't think there is much she can do for him. He is in a very bad way."

"Oh, gods," Ulaf said, feeling his own life drain out of him.

His first impulse was to dash off immediately, but he forced himself to think the situation through rationally. He had the pecwae under his care, the pecwae and the Sovereign Stone. They were his responsibility, and he couldn't abandon them. He glanced at the man at the bar, who returned his glance with an urgent look and an even louder sneeze. Jessan, meanwhile, had gone back to staring at the Trevinici.

"Jessan," Ulaf said. "Do you know that man?"

"No," said Jessan. "I've never seen him before. By his markings, he belongs to a tribe that lives far from my tribe, somewhere near Vilda Harn."

"That's strange," said Ulaf, "because he claims to know you. He told the pecwae that you sent him to find them. He used your name to try to lure them out of the city."

Jessan's brow furrowed. "Why would he say that? I've never seen him before. I've been with Baron Shadamehr."

"Jessan," said Ulaf swiftly, "I'm going to tell you something that you won't like to hear, and you must remain calm. You can't react. I think that Trevinici is really a Vrykyl."

Jessan stared at him for a moment. His eyes darkened, his frown deepened, but he said nothing.

"Don't expose him," Ulaf cautioned. "Not in here. I believe he's after the Sovereign Stone, and he won't hesitate to kill everyone in this place to get hold of it."

"What do we do?" Jessan asked.

"You go over and talk to the Trevinici. Look at how nervous he seems. He knows something's up. Allay his suspicions."

"And then what?"

"All chaos is going to erupt in a moment. When it does, you grab the Grandmother and Bashae and hustle them out of here. Take them back to Alise and Shadamehr."

"What about the Vrykyl? He'll try to stop me."

"Don't worry about the Vrykyl. I'll deal with him. Your only concern is the pecwae. Understood?"

Jessan gave an abrupt nod and walked over to talk to the strange Trevinici. Ulaf lingered a moment, expecting the worst and preparing to deal with it. Jessan knew what he was about, however, and the two were soon conversing. Bashae munched contentedly on bread and cheese and listened to the two warriors. The Grandmother sat staring into space, her mouth gaping slightly, her gaze glassy-eyed and vacant.

Ulaf didn't like the looks of her. The thought came to him that perhaps she was having an apoplectic fit, as sometimes occurs with the elderly; but, if so, there wasn't a damn thing he could do about it. He pushed his way through the crowd, heading for the bar. As he walked, he nonchalantly lifted the penny whistle that he wore on a silver chain around his neck, brought the whistle out into plain sight. He toyed with it, but didn't put it to his lips.

Reaching the bar, Ulaf took his place next to the man who had been rubbing his nose.

"What news, Guerimo?"

"There was trouble in the palace. Shadamehr and the Dominion Lord had to jump through a window. Now there are battle magi after him!"

"Battle magi!" Ulaf groaned.

"They're probably on their way here now. They know this is where he holds court when he's in the city. Do you know where the baron is? We need to warn him."

As Ulaf listened, he kept his gaze fixed on the pecwae and Jessan and the false Trevinici.

"Strange as this may seem," Ulaf said, "we have worse problems. I need to create a diversion."

"The usual?" Guerimo grinned.

"The usual," said Ulaf.

Jessan had made the decision to leave New Vinnengael before he had ever reached the Tubby Tabby. He'd thought it all out on his way to the tavern, which he'd managed to locate more by accident than design. He would retrieve the two pecwae and go back to their homeland, to a place where he could see the sun and breathe the air. Once there, he was certain he would be able to think things through and find again the answers that he seemed to have lost along the way.

In Jessan's former life—the life he'd lived before he had set out upon this journey with the Sovereign Stone—he'd been a child. In this life, he had left childhood behind. He had fought and vanquished a powerful foe. He had taken his warrior's name—Defender. He had been faithful to his promise to the dying knight, Gustav. He had visited strange lands, met strange people. He'd come to admire some of them, come to loathe and fear others. He had learned much, or so people kept telling him. On thinking it over, however, Jessan realized that they were wrong. In his previous life, he'd had answers to everything. Now, he had only questions.

He needed to be rid of this city, where he started out in the right direction, but always seemed to take a wrong turn and wind up in a blind alley or a dead end. He could not see the sky for the tall walls, he could not feel the sun for the shadows they cast, he could not breathe the air for the stench.

His arrival at the tavern, with its confusion of heat and noise and bright light, confirmed him in his decision. Nor was he particularly surprised to hear that the strange Trevinici was a Vrykyl. In Jessan's other life, he would have scoffed at such a notion. In this life, he was suspicious of everything and everyone. He knew that evil could lurk in a friendly form and he hated the knowledge.

He was glad to see Bashae and the Grandmother, glad to see them safe and glad to see that they looked as lost and friendless and forlorn as he felt. One obstacle remained and that was the Sovereign Stone. They had fulfilled their promise to the dying knight, Gustav. More than fulfilled it, in Jessan's opinion. Bashae had tried to give the Stone to Damra, then he tried to give it to Baron Shadamehr. Neither would accept it, leaving the enormous responsibility to Bashae. Looking at the small and frail-seeming pecwae, ringed round by large, ham-fisted humans and shadowed by the Vrykyl, Jessan burned with anger.

"This Stone is their worry. Let them take it," Jessan said to himself. "We have done our part. We have done enough."

Bashae scooted over on his chair, offered Jessan half of the seat and more than half of the bread and cheese.

"I'm glad to see you, Jessan," Bashae said. "I was worried about you. Fire Storm said you'd been arrested."

Jessan looked intently at Fire Storm, who was watching him warily. Was this man truly a Vrykyl? Jessan couldn't tell. Fire Storm looked as a Trevinici warrior should look, right down to the fringe on his leather breeches.

"I am glad you came to the aid of my friends, Fire Storm," Jessan said. "They are not used to the dangers of a city. But I am curious as to why you claimed to know me, when this is the first time we've met."

Jessan felt that was a natural question, one that either a Vrykyl or a Trevinici would expect him to ask.

Fire Storm's tense expression relaxed. "I must admit that I exaggerated the truth, though not perhaps as much as you might think. The fame of Jessan and his quest has spread among our people."

"It's my quest, too, you know," Bashae pointed out, offended. "We're in this together, Jessan and I. And the Grandmother."

"Of course," said Fire Storm politely. "My mistake."

He might be telling the truth, Jessan conceded. My people would have shared the story of the dying knight and those who set off to take his "love token" into eleven lands with every other Trevinici they met. But that doesn't explain what Fire Storm is doing here in New Vinnengael—a long way from our homeland.

On the other hand, no Trevinici warrior ever stoops to flattery. He is much more likely to insult you than fawn over you.

"Bashae," Jessan said blandly, "I need to use the privies. Come along with me, so that you don't get lost again."

"I'm not the one who managed to get myself arrested," said Bashae, indignant. Switching to Twithil, he went on to describe just exactly what Jessan could do with himself in the privies.

Twithil being a very descriptive language, Jessan couldn't help but grin. He gave Bashae a look, nodded ever so slightly at Fire Storm.

Bashae slid a sidelong glance at the Trevinici. The pecwae's right eyelid flickered.

"All right, Jessan. I'll come," he said.

"I will come, as well. Strange customs these city people have," Fire Storm added with a shrug. "Building houses for people to crap in."

Jessan was about to say that he'd changed his mind, he didn't need to go that badly, when the Grandmother gave a screech that nearly lifted the hair off his head. Glaring at Fire Storm, the Grandmother struck him in the chest with the agate-eyed stick.

Ulaf heard the Grandmother scream, an eerie, primal sound like the shrill scream of the mouse caught in the hawk's claws or the rabbit pierced by an arrow. The awful sound sliced through the noise of the tavern, caused a startled serving maid to drop a mug, and stopped the conversations of every person in the room. Shrieking in fury in her own language, the Grandmother struck the Trevinici, Fire Storm, in the breast with the agate-eyed stick.

The stick shattered in her hand, broke asunder. Agate eyes rolled and bounded across the floor, but no one paid them any attention. The Trevinici began to undergo a hideous transformation. The leather breeches and leather tunic he wore disappeared. The reddish hair and the stern, unsmiling face of the Trevinici warrior dropped off, the flesh rotting, revealing a horribly grinning skull. Armor, black and fell as the Void, flowed over his body. A black helm slid over the bony skull. Black gauntlets covered skeletal hands.

I was right, Ulaf thought. The gods help us!

The people in the tavern sat for a moment in stunned silence, then pandemonium ensued. Few knew what this evil creature was, but all knew that it was born of the Void and that where it walked, death and destruction followed. Some tried to flee, others tried to hide. Everyone cried out or screamed, leapt up or shrank down, fell over chairs or tried to dive under tables. Shadamehr's people looked at the Vrykyl, then at each other, then at Ulaf.

He had a split second to make a decision. He was competent in magic, but he could never hope to fight the deadly Void magicks of a Vrykyl.

"Throw things at him!" he roared above the chaos. "Keep him occupied!"

Ulaf brought the words of the spell he'd been planning to cast to mind, spoke them aloud. The magic tingled in his blood. He pointed at the floor beneath the Vrykyl's feet and magic flowed from him. The floorboards began to heave and buckle. The Vrykyl lost his balance, crashed to the floor.

Shadamehr's people picked up crockery, bowls, plates, bottles, jugs, whatever came to hand, and hurled them at the Vrykyl. Plates smashed on the black breastplate, ale sloshed over his helm. The crockery barrage would not do him any harm, but it might rattle him, keep him from casting his own magic.

Ulaf was not a tall man. He couldn't see above the heads of the crowd, most of whom were on their feet, either fleeing or fighting. He had lost sight of Jessan in the chaos, couldn't see what was happening to him or the pecwae.

Ulaf dared not waste time searching for them. Commending them all to the gods, he ran behind the bar, thrust open a door and dashed up the short flight of stairs to the second floor. He crashed through another door and ran out onto the roof. Several patrons were already in the streets, shouting for the guards. Men-at-arms would be no match for the Vrykyl. Ulaf searched the darkness, straining his eyes.

And there they were. Six battle magi in full regalia—the most feared wizards in New Vinnengael, perhaps on the continent of Loerem. Only the best and strongest and most disciplined wizards were chosen by the Church to become her champions. Skilled in wielding both steel and magic, they were not only formidable wizards, but among the best swordsmen in the military. They fought as a unit, pooling their magical skills to forge spells that had the power to decimate a regiment.

A white aura surrounded them, for they were using their magic to light their way through the dark city streets. The magical light glinted off their swords and helms and their chain-mail halberds, illuminated the tabards of their high office that they wore over their armor. They were thorough in their search, taking their time, inspecting every building.

"Vrykyl!" Ulaf cried aloud. Investing the word with the wings of magic, he sent it flying off. "Vrykyl!" he said again. "The Tubby Tabby!"

He waited a tense moment, then had the satisfaction of seeing the heads of the battle magi jerk up, see them whip around, searching for the source of the voice that seemed to explode in their ears.

"Hurry!" Ulaf urged them.

The battle magi didn't need the urging. They were already running through the streets.

Ulaf turned and dashed back down the stairs. He had gone about halfway when he heard an agonized cry—the shrill, high-pitched cry of a pecwae.

SHADAMEHR CAME SLOWLY TO CONSCIOUSNESS. HE KNEW NOTHing except that he felt weak and nauseated. He was lying flat on his back on a hard, cold surface, with flickering yellow light glowing somewhere above him. He wondered what had happened to him, and started to try to remember. Fear stopped him. He was afraid to go back there. Afraid to remember. Something horrible had happened. The shadow of the horror lay across his heart, and he did not dare try to look into the past.

A strange and unpleasant warmth suffused his body, as though the blood had been taken out of his veins, heated in a cauldron, then poured back in. A sickening, metallic taste burned in the back of his mouth and it made him gag. His stomach roiled and cramped. He retched, but not having eaten since breakfast, there was nothing in his stomach to purge. He lay back, shivering and weak.

Memory returned, unwanted, unbidden. He reached out to pick up the young king, to save him from the Regent, who had been taken over by a Vrykyl. He had his hands on the child, was lifting him off his feet. Terrible, searing pain flashed through his body. He looked into the child's face and saw a skull. He looked into the child's eyes and saw the Void.

The young king of Vinnengael was the Vrykyl.

Shadamehr could feel again his sense of helpless horror and revulsion, but he couldn't remember much else, for the ice-cold fire of the wound had started to spread through his body.

As for where he was now, he couldn't have said if his life depended on it.

"And maybe it does," he mumbled, trying to push himself up to a sitting position. "The Vrykyl will be searching for me. I know his secret. He can't let me live. Ugh! Blast!"

Shadamehr collapsed back onto the floor, lay there gasping, chill sweat running over his body. He heard a moan; murmured, broken speech. Shadamehr's vision was blurry, his eyes dazzled from staring into the lanternlight. He turned over, managed to prop himself up on one elbow, searched for the voice.

He let out a shivering breath. "Alise!"

She lay next to him, her hand—limp and motionless—on the floor. She seemed, in her last moments, to have reached out to him.

His own fingers trembling, he brushed aside the vibrant red curls that trailed over her face. His breath caught in his throat.

Alise was a beauty who made nothing of her beauty. She scoffed at the notion that she was beautiful and would laugh heartily at the sonnets and songs written in her praise, much to the discomfiture of many an earnest young swain. She had a sharp tongue, a temper to match her fiery hair, a quick wit, and she used all these as a porcupine uses its prickles to hide a loyal, compassionate heart.

Her beauty was gone, destroyed. Lesions split the soft skin of her cheeks, oozed blood that trailed down her neck. Hideous pustules covered her forehead and one eye, which was swollen shut. Her lips were cracked and blackened. The hand, reaching to him, clenched in pain, the nails digging into her flesh. She moaned again, a sob of agony.

"Alise!" Shadamehr gasped, appalled. "What happened? Who did this to you?"

He knew the answer the moment he asked the question.

"Oh, gods!" He shut his eyes. "I did."

He lifted her hand, unclenched the stiff, cold fingers and pressed her hand to his lips. Tears burned his eyelids.

Shadamehr was not a magus, but he knew magic. A magus named Rigiswald, who been his tutor, had once tried to teach Shadamehr a few rudimentary spells. Not only did Shadamehr prove inept at magic, it affected him in a perverse way. Any spell he tried to cast, even the most mundane, ended in disaster. Shadamehr himself emerged unscathed from carnage, but others were not so fortunate. After a week of suffering, which included a concussion and a sprained ankle, Rigiswald burned the spellbooks and forbade his pupil even to so much as think a word of magic.

Shadamehr had maintained an interest in magic, though he was careful not to try to cast it himself. He and Alise, Ulaf, and Rigiswald often held lengthy discussions concerning magic, including Void magicks.

Void magic could not heal a dying man, but it could save one by transferring some of the life essence of a Void magus into the dying man's body. The spell was dangerous, for in saving the victim, it could kill the spellcaster.

Shadamehr put his hand on Alise's neck. He could barely feel a pulse. She was in terrible pain, for she cried out, and her body wrenched and twisted. The pain could not rouse her from the deep darkness in which she struggled. For his sake, she had given herself to the Void, and the Void was laying claim to her.

Alise was going to die. Unless he did something, found help for her, found some way to stop the Void from dragging her away from him, she was going to die.

She was going to die, without ever knowing that he loved her.

Shadamehr gritted his teeth and, through an enormous effort, managed to lift his arms, reach up, and seize hold of the top of a barrel. He paused a moment, gasping for breath, then, with another effort, he pulled himself upright. He stood hunched over the barrel, shaking and shivering uncontrollably.

He managed to focus his bleary eyes long enough to find the door. It seemed miles away. He didn't know where he was, for he had no recollection of coming here. He could hear nothing. No sounds came from beyond the door. Now that he thought of it, he seemed to remember hearing someone banging on the door and calling out, but that had been eons ago.

He tried to call for help, but the shout came out a cracked yelp. He let go of the barrel, took a step, took another step. His head throbbed. The room began to tilt and wobble. His stomach heaved, his knees buckled. Feeling himself start to fall, he tried desperately to save himself by grabbing for the barrel. He upended it, sent it crashing to the floor, along with himself and the lantern.

Fortunately he did not set fire to the cellar. The lantern's flame went out, drowned in lamp oil.

Shadamehr cursed himself and his weakness and his failure, which was going to cause him to lose the one person he would have given up his life to save.

"You should have let me die, Alise," he said.

Managing to crawl back to her, he took her hand in his own, kissed her hand, her dear, tortured face. He gathered her in his arms, cradled her head on his chest, and held her shivering, chilled body pressed against his.

"You should have let me die. No great loss," he murmured. "Nothing but a conceited, heedless, reckless fool, who meddles in affairs that aren't any of my concern simply for the sheer fun in meddling."

He rested his cheek against her soft hair.

"Oh, I tell myself I'm doing good. I'm benefiting mankind, and maybe I have managed to do that, now and then. But I do it only because it is fun. It is an adventure. Always an adventure. Just like this mess we're in now. What a bloody, stupid, reckless thing to try to do—save the young king from a Vrykyl. I put the lives of my friends in peril. I put our mission to save the Sovereign Stone in jeopardy. All for my own selfish thrills. If I had just given it a rational moment's thought, I could have figured it out.

"The king suddenly dead. His son the last person with him. Nobody would suspect a child, of course. Nobody suspects now that the boy is anything other than he appears to be. And who would believe me if I told them? Who will believe a profligate adventurer, who never spoke a serious word in his life? A man who was granted the right to become a Dominion Lord and refused, not because I was protesting the politics, not out of any philosophical compunctions or any moral convictions. The truth was that I refused because, plain and simple, I didn't want the responsibility.

"Alise, Alise," he whispered, holding her close. "If I were a Dominion Lord, I could save you. I could have saved myself. Through my own damn, selfish laziness, I have lost the only thing I ever held dear. And you will leave me never knowing that I love you. For I do love you, Alise," said Shadamehr, kissing her gently. "You are my lady."

She had ceased to moan. Her body was growing colder, her breathing labored. Holding her close, he breathed each breath with her, as if he could breathe each breath for her.

"If you die, Alise, I do not want to live. If you are not part of life, I have no care for this empty gift you have given me. But though I have no care for life myself, I will not waste it. I will make you proud of me, Alise. I will. I swear it to the gods."

THE VRYKYL JEDASH FOUGHT TO RETAIN THE ILLUSION. FIRE Storm returned for an instant, but by then people were screaming and pointing. He realized that his mask had slipped and people had seen through his disguise. He abandoned the useless Trevinici illusion, called upon his magic. The Void protected him, covered him in its own black armor, gave him deadly magicks and the power to wield them.

The power of the Void affects not only the mind, but the heart. The Void's weapon is fear. The Void's shield is terror, its armor despair. The best and bravest find it difficult to battle the Void, for it forces a person to battle two foes simultaneously—the terror within and the horror without.

The pecwae stood frozen, helpless. The Vrykyl made a grab for the two, and he nearly had the Grandmother, when some bastard cast a magical spell that caused the floorboards to lurch and roll. He lost his balance, stumbled backward, and crashed up against the wall.

"Throw things at him!" a voice yelled, and the tavern's patrons began their crockery assault.

Plates and bowls smashed against the Vrykyl's armor, mugs struck his helm. The missles could not harm him, but they were an irritation, kept him from thinking clearly so that he could cast a spell of his own.

The air around Jessan grew chill and dank as the air in a burial mound. He smelled the sweet, sickening stench of decay. Fire Storm's face dissolved. The illusion of flesh vanished, revealing the reality of a hideously grinning, gap-toothed skull.

Jessan had only one weapon, the Blood-knife. He had fought a Vrykyl before and, though he had very nearly died, he remembered that this small bone knife had done a great deal of damage to the undead creature. Jessan grabbed hold of the Grandmother and thrust her behind him, putting himself between her and the Vrykyl, who was floundering amid smashed bowls and coagulating stew. A badly aimed mug struck Jessan in the back, between his shoulder blades. He hardly felt it.

"Where is Bashae?" he yelled, glancing over his shoulder.

The Grandmother shook her head.

Keeping one eye on his foe, Jessan searched about frantically for the pecwae. He shouted his friend's name, but if Bashae answered, Jessan couldn't hear him above the roars and hollerings and screams erupting all around. The Grandmother pulled violently on his leather breeches. She jabbed a pointing finger. Jessan followed it and saw Bashae, crouched, trembling, beneath the table, his eyes level with those of the fallen Vrykyl.

Bashae was trapped, fenced in by chairs and table legs. A span of only a couple of feet separated him and the Vrykyl. Jedash covered that distance in the space of a heartbeat.

Frantic as a cornered animal, Bashae tried desperately to escape. He might have managed it, for pecwae are lithe and nimble, their bones supple as willow branches. Dragging the knapsack with him, Bashae slithered backward, scrambling to fit his body between the rungs of a chair leg.

The Vrykyl seized hold of the knapsack's leather straps.

For many months, Bashae had been the guardian of the Sovereign Stone. He might not have known that when he started out, but he knew it now. The knapsack was his pride, his responsibility. The knapsack had taken him on a wondrous journey, taken him places and shown him sights that few pecwae had ever seen. He'd come to feel beholden to the knapsack and possessive of it. Bashae was horribly afraid of this ghastly creature of death and despair. He wanted only to get away from it, as fast as possible. But he was going to take the knapsack with him.

As the Vrykyl tugged on the knapsack. Bashae gave an angry and instinctive tug back and managed to jerk the leather strap out of the Vrykyl's clutching grip. Bashae wriggled backward and was soon lost amid a tangle of table legs, human legs, and human feet. The Vrykyl could not follow.

Furious, he clambered to his feet. Lifting up the table, the Vrykyl hurled it into the crowd. He found Bashae, crawling beneath another table. The Vrykyl made a lunge for the knapsack, which was tangled up with the pecwae, and caught hold of both of them. The Vrykyl gave a violent tug on the knapsack that nearly tore off Bashae's arm.

The leather strap broke loose. Bashae felt it give. Turning, he seized hold of the knapsack, kicked wildly at the Vrykyl.

Jessan tried frantically to reach Bashae, but the Vrykyl was between him and his friend, and chairs, tables and panic-stricken patrons were between Jessan and the Vrykyl. Jessan hurled aside chairs, knocked down anyone who got into his way. He had a fleeing glimpse of staring eyes and wide-open mouths, but they had no meaning, were as leaves blown away on the winter wind of fear for his friend. Jessan cried out a challenge, hoping desperately that the creature would forget about the pecwae and turn to face this new foe.

The Vrykyl had only one thought, and that was to retrieve the knapsack. He paid no more attention to Jessan than to a mewling kitten. The Vrykyl dug his taloned nails deep into Bashae's body. Blood flowed down Bashae's rib cage. He cried out in pain, writhed in anguish. The Vrykyl grabbed hold of the knapsack and hurled the screaming pecwae to the floor.

Like Jessan, the Grandmother had also been trying to reach Bashae. Blocked by the crowd, she dropped to the floor and crawled toward him. When the Vrykyl hurled Bashae to the floor, the Grandmother flung her body protectively over his and glared up defiantly at the Vrykyl.

The Vrykyl drew his sword, prepared to slay both of them and take his prize. He raised the weapon. The Grandmother snatched up one of the agate eyes and threw it into the Vrykyl's helmed face.

The agate eye burst with a flash of pure white. The magical light was horrible. Flaring inside Jedash's head, the light illuminated the Void, leaving the Vrykyl naked and exposed to the gods. He could feel his undead spirit start to shrivel in their blessed gaze.

Coming up behind the stunned Vrykyl, Jessan plunged the Bloodknife into the Vrykyl's back.

The slender, fragile-looking knife sliced through the Void armor, penetrated the Vrykyl's corrupt and rotting flesh. Born of the Void, the knife began to shred the Void magic that held together the Vrykyl's existence.

Pain that burned like hot, molten metal seared through Jedash, as the

Blood-knife weapon severed the dark threads spun of death that bound the Vrykyl to this existence.

Screaming in fury, he whipped around to face his new attacker.

Jessan tried to recover the Blood-knife, but his sweat-wet fingers slipped off the handle. The bone blade remained embedded in the Vrykyl's black armor.

The Vrykyl thrust his hand through the black armor of his breast-plate. He groped about inside his own cadaver and, with a howl of agony, seized hold of the Blood-knife embedded in his decaying flesh and ripped it out.

The Vrykyl had what he'd come for. He had the knapsack, and he was certain that inside was the Sovereign Stone. He crushed the Blood-knife in his black-taloned hand and hurled the remnants at Jessan. His prize in hand, the Vrykyl headed for the door.

The shards of the bone knife struck Jessan. Those that hit flesh drew blood, but Jessan paid them scant attention. Bashae lay in a crumpled and bloody heap on the floor. The Grandmother knelt over him, her face wet with tears and with blood, speaking the ancient pecwae magical spells of healing, her words broken by her sobs.

Fury, white-hot, exploded in Jessan's brain, burning away all instinct for self-preservation. He had one goal, and that was to retrieve the knap-sack his friend had fought with such uncharacteristic valor to keep.

Jessan caught hold of the leather strap that dangled from the Vrykyl's hand. With a strength born of rage and anguish, Jessan wrenched it loose. Astonished, the Vrykyl tried to recover his prize. Jessan jumped backward, to escape the Vrykyl's furious swiping hand, and fell over a chair. He crashed to the floor.

Clutching the knapsack to his breast, protecting it with his body, Jessan tried to stand, but he was starting to grow dizzy. The floor began to tilt and twist underneath him. His bare arms and legs burned with pain, and he was horrified to see that wherever the remnants of the bone knife had struck him, the bits had turned into hideous black leeches that were devouring his flesh.

"Jessan!" Ulaf shouted and his voice seemed to come from a great distance.

Knowing he was trapped, guessing he was about to die, Jessan flung the knapsack as far from him and the Vrykyl as he could manage, flung it in the direction of Ulaf's voice.

The Vrykyl roared in anger and made a desperate grab for the knapsack, but it flew far beyond his reach. The Vrykyl struck at Jessan. The sharp talons of the Vrykyl's gauntlets raked across Jessan's back.

The pain struck to the young man's very soul. His body jerked, he cried out in agony, and collapsed onto the floor at the Vrykyl's feet.

The leather sack landed with a dull plop on the floor in front of Ulaf, who made a diving grab for it. He thrust the sack with its precious contents inside the folds of his loose-fitting shirt.

By now, most of the patrons had exited the tavern, leaping through windows or battling each in an effort to escape out the front door. Those left behind were Shadamehr's people and the tavern's owner, trying gamely to assist in the battle.

The battle magi had arrived, but they didn't immediately storm the tavern. A voice outside the window could be heard calling out commands. The leader of the battle magi deployed his troops to the front and the rear, posting his people at all the exits with orders to keep the Vrykyl inside the tavern, prevent him from escaping. Heavy booted footsteps thundered overhead. Magi with Air magic skills had flown up onto the roof. They were on the second level, and they'd be coming down the stairs at any moment, prepared to attack the Vrykyl from the rear, while others fought him from the front.

The Tubby Tabby was about to become a swirling storm of magic. Vrykyl were known to be the most powerful and most heinous of all Void creatures. The battle magi could not allow him to escape, for he would immediately change form, and they would lose him among the city's populace. Faced with this powerful threat, the battle magi would not be overly concerned about inflicting casualties on a few unlucky tavern-goers, two pecwae, and a wounded Trevinici.

Lifting his voice, Ulaf shouted, "Everyone get out! Now!"

His comrades didn't need to be told twice. They had guessed what was about to happen, and most were already hastening for the nearest exit. The tavern owner rose from behind the bar. He gaped at the Vrykyl, his face white as a fish's belly. He turned pleading eyes to Ulaf.

"Your family is safe!" Ulaf yelled, racing toward Jessan. "Get out now! Go, go!"

"My tavern!" the man cried pitifully.

Ulaf shook his head. "Go! Get out!"

The Vrykyl's fell voice rose in a chant. Ulaf recognized the cold, dark words of Void magic. He had no idea what spell the creature was about to cast, but he knew its effects would be dire.

Jessan lay on the floor, his body covered with blood. He was conscious, gasping and writhing in pain. Nearby, the Grandmother was feverishly placing stones on Bashae's limp body.

Two battle magi, a man and a woman, appeared in the doorway. Both wore plate and chain mail that glittered silver in the firelight and swords at their sides. Striding fearlessly into the room, both of them cried out words of magic, their voices blending as they cast the same spell simultaneously.

"Foul creature," the woman called out. "Return to the Void that spawned you!"

She pointed at the massive fireplace on the north side of the building and made a summoning motion with her hand.

An arc of flame leapt from the fireplace and soared across the room, flaring so near Ulaf that the searing heat singed his bangs and eyebrows.

The fire smote the Vrykyl, dancing across the surface of the Vrykyl's armor as if it were black oil. Flames swirled around the Vrykyl in a vortex that set the wooden furniture to blazing. Smoke filled the air.

Ulaf let go of his spell. His weak magic wouldn't be needed now. The Vrykyl was in good hands. The knapsack containing the Sovereign Stone was safely in Ulaf's possession. His priority was to rescue the pecwae and the Trevinici, take them far away from both the Vrykyl and the battle magi.

Ulaf made his way through the smoke to Bashae and the Grandmother.

"Jessan!" he called. "Jessan! Over here!"

Jessan lifted his head, gazed blearily in Ulaf's direction. Gritting his teeth, Jessan staggered to his feet. He cast a wary glance at the Vrykyl, but the creature was preoccupied, fighting to preserve his heinous existence.

Ulaf pressed his sleeve over his mouth to protect himself from the thickening smoke. He dropped to the floor, where the air was clearer, and crawled toward the two pecwae. The battle magi chanted their spell. Swirling fire enveloped the Vrykyl, raced along his arms, flared from his hands. Flames cloaked him in a fiery cape, his head seemed helmed with fire, but the flames did not consume him, because there was nothing to consume. Fire could not cause him any real harm. The Vrykyl turned to face his enemy.

Darts forged of the Void shot out from the breastplate of his black armor, tore through the smoke-filled air and struck the female battle magus in the chest. The tabard she wore dissolved, the cuirass melted. She gave a strangled gasp, staggered backward, and slumped to the floor.

Well disciplined, her companion did not miss a single word of his chant, but continued his spell-casting. Footfalls clattered on the stairs. An explosion from the rear warned Ulaf that the battle magi were coming in from the back.

Ulaf kept low to the floor and managed to reach the pecwae. Bashae was alive. His eyes were open, and he was breathing, but a glance told Ulaf that the pecwae was in very bad shape. Blood trickled from his nose and mouth. His skin was ashen. His breath caught in his throat from the pain. Turquoise and other stones rested on his chest and his forehead. The Grandmother hovered over him, muttering incantations and coughing in the smoke.

A hand touched Ulaf's shoulder. Turning his head, he saw Jessan squatting beside him.

"Are you all right?" Ulaf demanded.

Jessan nodded. He was bloody and disheveled, with oozing sores on his arms and chest. He must be in agony, but if so he kept his pain to himself. His lips tightened and compressed, his hand clenched, but he said no word of complaint.

"We have to get them out of here!" Ulaf said, gesturing to the pecwae.

Jessan looked at Bashae, and his face darkened. "He is hurt badly. He can't be moved."

Ulaf glanced around. Five battle magi had entered the tavern. They had the Vrykyl surrounded and were slowly closing in on him, herding him into a position where they could concentrate their destructive magic on him. The Vrykyl was trying to cast Void magic, but not having much luck, apparently, for no more magi went down. Ulaf was thankful to note that the battle magi were concentrating solely on their prey. None had so much as glanced in their direction.

"Jessan, listen to me," Ulaf said in low, urgent tones, knowing that the Trevinici was the only person the pecwae would heed. "These people are going to bring down the wrath of the gods on that fiend. If we don't get far away from here by the time the magic goes off, we're all dead!"

Jessan glanced at the magi and the Vrykyl and gave an abrupt nod. "How do we get out? They have blocked off all the exits."

"I'll deal with that. You guard Bashae and the Grandmother."

Ulaf stood up, placed both hands on the wall, and began to chant. He was an experienced magus, but there was always a horrible moment of doubt for any magus, for with every casting there was the possibility the spell might fail. He added a swift prayer to the gods along with the magic and gave a heartfelt sigh of relief when he felt the wall beneath his fingers start to crackle.

He glanced back over his shoulder, saw Jessan conferring with the Grandmother. She shook her head. Jessan said something more. She looked at Ulaf, bleak questions in her eyes. He made a helpless gesture that said, "We have to get out of here!"

The Grandmother gathered up the stones that rested on top of Bashae with a flick of her hand.

"Bashae," said Jessan, "I'm going to pick you up. This may hurt—"

"Jessan," Bashae whispered, struggling to speak. "The knapsack!"

"It is safe. Ulaf has it," said Jessan.

"Let me see it!" Bashae gasped.

Ulaf pulled the knapsack out from his shirt, held it up.

Bashae sighed, relieved. "That's good. I need to talk to Shadamehr, Jessan. Quickly. Before I die. Can you take me to him?"

"You are *not* dying," Jessan said angrily. "Don't talk. Save your strength for getting well."

He lifted his friend gently, trying not to jar him. Bashae moaned. His body shuddered. He went limp, his head lolled back on Jessan's arm.

"He is not dead," the Grandmother said in a trembling voice. "He has fainted. That is good. He will not feel anything now."

Jessan rose to his feet. Pallid from his own wounds, he staggered when he stood.

"Are you all right?" Ulaf asked.

Jessan's tight lips pressed together even tighter. He grunted an assent.

Ulaf turned back to his work. The chanting behind him was rising in volume and intensity. It wouldn't be long.

"Stand back," Ulaf warned.

Flinging the knapsack over his shoulder, he adjusted it securely, then backed off a few paces in order to get a good run at the wall. He braced himself for the impact, which would be bone-jarring if his magic hadn't worked. He couldn't think about that. Turning his shoulder, he ran at top speed straight for the wall.

Wincing, anticipating the impact, Ulaf smashed through the wall with ease, creating a gaping hole in the wood and plaster. His momentum carried him out into the street, where he nearly collided with a startled battle magus.

Seeing a ghostly apparition (Ulaf was covered head to toe in plaster dust) come bursting through the wall, the battle mage brandished his sword, the words of a spell crackled on his lips.

"Friend!" cried Ulaf, raising his dusty hands into the air. "Don't harm us! We were caught in there with these children! We just want to get away from here!"

Keeping his hands raised, he jerked his head toward Jessan, carrying Bashae. The Grandmother stumbled along at Jessan's side, clutching Bashae's hand.

What with the darkness, the smoke, and the flames, the battle magus would not be able to see clearly. As it was, he barely cast them a glance.

Ulaf caught hold of the Grandmother and, ignoring her outraged protests, hoisted her onto his back.

"We have to run for it, Grandmother, and you won't be able to keep up. Put your arms around my neck!"

The Grandmother obeyed, clasping her arms around his neck with a grip that nearly strangled him. Ulaf broke into a run, heading for the tavern where Jessan had told him they could find Shadamehr. Fortunately, the battle magi had illuminated the surrounding area in order to provide a clear field of vision in case the Vrykyl managed to escape. Their spells had lit up half the city, filling the streets and alleys around the Tubby Tabby with a cold, white radiance. Battle magi, stationed at every street corner, could be heard chanting the spell.

The streets were empty. City guardsmen were posted nearby to keep order. The streets around the tavern had been cordoned off, but that didn't stop the citizenry from trying to find out what was going on. People stood in doorways, craning their necks, or peering out the upper-story windows of their houses, trying to see what was happening.

No one stopped Ulaf or the Trevinici, carrying the "children" to safety. One guardsman asked if they needed help. Ulaf shook his head and kept running.

Bashae moaned in pain, his head rocking from side to side.

"How much farther?" Jessan demanded anxiously.

"Only a block or two," said Ulaf. "How is he doing?"

"He's going to be fine," said Jessan.

Ulaf looked at the small, deathly white figure Jessan held so easily in his strong arms, then glanced over his shoulder at the Grandmother, who clung to him tightly. She didn't make a sound, but Ulaf could feel the wetness of her tears soaking through the fabric of his shirt.

Five battle magi had the Vrykyl surrounded. Moving cautiously, they backed him into a corner, all the while chanting the words to a powerful spell. Jedash was still holding his own. He still kept them at bay, but he was growing weaker. The wound made by the Blood-knife had done its damage. He could feel it draining him, siphoning off his energy.

The magi came at him from all directions, half-blinding him with their foul, dazzling light. Jedash retreated. He would have surrendered to them if he could have. He didn't want to fight. He'd never been much of a fighter when he was alive. The armor of the Void could keep his rotting corpse intact, but it had no effect on what he was. The Void could not grant him courage. Jedash might appear ferocious on the outside, but inside the black helm, his eyes darted about the room, searching for a way out. A craven coward in life, Jedash was a craven coward still.

Trampling furniture beneath his feet, Jedash fumbled for his own Blood-knife, which he wore at his side. He closed his hand over it.

"Shakur!" he wailed. "Five battle magi have me surrounded! I am able to hold them off for the time being—" he stumbled against a table, nearly fell, but kicked it asunder and managed to save himself—"but I am wounded and can't hold out for long. Shakur! Are you there? Answer me!"

"I am here," was Shakur's churlish response. "Your orders were to keep your true nature secret. What did you do to provoke this?"

Inspiration struck Jedash. He knew perfectly well that Shakur would not come to his aid, but Shakur was bound to come to the aid of the Sovereign Stone.

"I have it!" Jedash yelped. "I have the Stone! That is why they are attacking me! They're trying to take it from me. You have to come, Shakur! Come now!"

Jedash heard another voice, not Shakur's. The voice that answered was the voice of Dagnarus.

"You lie," said Dagnarus, and his voice was empty and dark as the Void. "You had the Sovereign Stone in your possession, but you disobeyed orders. You were told to bring it to Shakur. Instead, you were greedy, and you lost it."

"I know who has it!" Jedash whimpered. "I can get it back! Please, my lord, please save me!"

"I have better things to do with my time," said Dagnarus.

"My lord!" Jedash cried, clutching the Blood-knife that was made of his own bone. "Shakur! Help me!"

Silence was his answer. The silence of the Void.

The magi backed him into the massive fireplace. Terrified, Jedash tried to use his magic, tried to cast again the deadly spell that had slain the first battle magus. He sought for the words to the spell, but the chanting and praying of the battle magi confused him, so that he couldn't think.

The spell failed. He tried another, only to have it fail.

The chanting of the battle magi reached a crescendo. The blessed magic of the gods flashed and blazed in the air, bright and burning as the sun. The magi held the magic fast. Feeling the destructive force building around him, Jedash turned his back and tried to burrow his way through solid brick.

The battle magi let loose the magic.

The wrath of the gods struck Jedash. The explosive force of the spell ripped apart the armor forged of the Void, pulverized it, smashed it into fragments that disintegrated in the heat of the magic. The blast tore through the fireplace, blew out the wall, and leveled the chimney. Bricks and mortar and wooden beams crashed down on top of the Vrykyl.

The building shuddered, and for a moment it seemed as if it might come down on them all, burying Vrykyl and magi alike. The magi were prepared for that, for they are trained to face the possibility that they might be called upon to sacrifice themselves in the destruction of their foe. The tavern was well built, however, and, after one final shiver, as though the Tubby Tabby was itself horrified by the event, the building settled and held firm.

Other magi moved in. Those skilled in construction magic came to shore up the weakened structure, while the Inquisitors, those magi who made a study of Void magic, came to search the rubble for remnants of the Vrykyl. The battle magi who had cast the spell departed the field. Drained of energy, two were so exhausted that they could not walk, but had to be carried by their fellows.

The blast that had leveled his chimney nearly leveled the poor tavernkeeper as well. Having taken Ulaf's advice, he had fled the premises. Huddled with his family at a safe distance from the scene of the battle, he heard the explosion and imagined the worst. He was on the verge of collapse, when his practical wife pointed out to him that the Church was bound to recompense them for their loss and provide them with money to rebuild. And once that was accomplished, the fame of the Tubby Tabby as the scene of a battle between the Church and a Vrykyl would draw customers from all over the continent.

"We will put up a plaque," she said.

Comforted and reassured, the tavernkeeper took his family to the home of his brother-in-law, there to regale him with tales of his own courage in the face of frightful danger.

The Inquisitors worked throughout the night, removing and sorting through the rubble themselves, permitting no one else to enter the building. When they finally left, sometime near dawn, it was observed that they carried with them a small sack, which they treated with great care. What was in the sack, if it contained pieces of the Vrykyl or his armor, was never revealed. The Inquisitors informed the Regent, who then informed the young king—in case he'd been frightened—that the Vrykyl had been destroyed.

It was said that the young king was extremely pleased to hear the news.

THE LIGHT FROM THE BLAST THAT DESTROYED THE VRYKYL ILLUminated the night sky and shook the cobblestone streets for blocks around the Tubby Tabby. The blast shattered windows, set fire to a neighboring roof, and caused widespread alarm. The fire was soon doused. The city guard and town criers hastened up and down the streets, reassuring the populace that the Revered Magi were dealing with the situation. Everything was under control. People should go back to their beds.

At the sound of the blast, Jessan halted and looked back over his shoulder.

"That could have been us," said Ulaf, as the ground shook beneath their feet.

Jessan nodded, then glanced around in confusion. "I think the tavern where I left Shadamehr is somewhere around here."

"It's down this alley," said Ulaf, turning off the main street.

The magical light cast by the battle magi didn't penetrate as far as the alley. Everything was dark and silent. Too dark, for Ulaf's liking. There were no lights in the tavern's windows.

"How's Bashae?"

"Breathing," said Jessan. "Bashae wanted to talk to Shadamehr. The baron was in a bad way when I left him. I didn't tell Bashae that he might be dead."

"The gods are not in a great hurry to have Shadamehr join them in their heavenly pursuits, so I wouldn't assume the worst just yet," said Ulaf, trying very hard to follow his own comforting advice.

The Crow and Ring, the tavern in which Shadamehr had sought refuge from the Imperial Cavalry, was known to Ulaf. Located near both the Temple and the palace in an alley off Bookbinder's Street, the Crow and Ring catered to tradesmen in the printing and binding profession and minor government functionaries. Small and snug, the Crow and Ring lacked the amenities of the Tubby Tabby, having no back exit, but it did boast a storage room filled with empty ale casks that were about the right size for hiding a full-grown human—as Ulaf could testify from experience—and a proprietor who, though she talked a great deal, knew when to keep her mouth shut.

Ulaf was having difficulty adjusting his eyes to the darkness of the alley, after the eerie white glow of the light spell. Jessan had better eyesight, apparently, for he said, "Someone is there, standing in the doorway."

Ulaf squinted, but it wasn't until they were practically entering the door that he saw the proprietor—a stout woman in her middle years who'd inherited the Crow and Ring from her late husband.

"Who's that?" she asked in a tremulous voice.

Light flared. She had removed the cover from a dark lantern, and now flashed it directly into Ulaf's eyes.

He cried out, raised his hands to shield his face.

"It's me, Maudie," he said testily. "Close the shield! You've near blinded me!"

"It *is* you, Ulaf," she said, peering at him intently. "Thanks be!"

She obediently slid shut the panel on the dark lantern, hiding the light. "Are the guards after you? Where did you come from? What have you got there? Children? Poor dears. Come inside and be quick about it. Did you hear that blast? They say that fiends of the Void are inside the city, going on a rampage and killing innocent, gods-fearing people. I thought that might be what you was, when I heard you coming down the alleyway. I was ready for them. I have a crowbar right handy here by the door. Did you happen to see them? The fiends, I mean? They weren't after the children, were they?"

Still talking, not giving Ulaf a chance to answer, Maudie hustled them inside the tavern and shut and latched the door behind them. She removed the cover on the dark lantern again, taking care this time to keep it from shining in their eyes. A fire burned low in the fireplace, giving off a warm glow.

The Grandmother slid off Ulaf's back and went immediately to Bashae.

"Put him down by the fire," she ordered Jessan.

"I have a bed upstairs," Maudie offered, hovering around them and getting in the way. "The poor child might rest better there. What's wrong with him? Oh!" She gave a little gasp. "He's . . . he's not human! What is he? Not a fiend?"

"He's a pecwae, Maudie," said Ulaf soothingly.

He drew her to one side to let Jessan pass. The Grandmother laid out a blanket on the floor. Jessan lowered Bashae gently onto the blanket, as the Grandmother took out her stones and began arranging the stones on Bashae's head and neck and shoulders, muttering to herself. Jessan sat back on his heels, helpless and concerned.

"What happened to him?" Maudie asked.

"It's a long story. Where's Baron Shadamehr? How is he?"

"I'm that glad you're here," she continued on, talking over her own question, as well as his. "There've been strange going ons in that room. I guess you know that Baron Shadamehr is in there. Oh," she added, blinking at Jessan. "I recognize that barbarian now. He was with him."

"Where is the baron, Maudie?" Ulaf asked, his fear growing. He looked about the tavern, saw no signs of him. "Jessan said he was wounded."

"Aye, the poor baron didn't look good," Maudie said, shaking her head dolefully. "His shirt all soaked in blood. He went in there"—she nodded toward the storeroom—"and a beautiful woman and that barbarian fellow went in with him. Then the barbarian came out and ran away and—"

"How is the baron?" Ulaf demanded. "Where is he? The guards didn't find him, did they?"

"You needn't shout. As far as I know, he's still in there." Maudie said, offended. "As to his health—"

"Didn't you check to find out? Honestly, Maudie—"

Angrily, Ulaf shoved his way around her.

"The door's locked," Maudie told his back. "I beat on it and shouted 'til I was hoarse and there was no answer. *That's* what I was trying to tell you," she added, following him over to the door. "I heard a woman's voice and it sounded to me like it was talking magic and it wasn't healing

magic. I should know. I had the healers in this place day and night when my Sam was dying, chanting their heads off, though it didn't help him none. Because his aura was fighting the magic, they said. The growth ate him up. Then everything went quiet in there. An uncanny quiet, if you know what I mean. I banged on the door, but there was no answer. And then, just when I figured that maybe the woman was a witch and she spirited them both out into the night, there came a dreadful crash and a cry that sounded like demons was in there, then silence again."

Ulaf put his hands on the door, chanting the magic. He'd cast his spell by the time she paused for breath.

"Sorry about your door," he told her.

Ulaf smashed apart the wood, leapt through the remnants.

"Ulaf! Thank the gods!"

"Is that you, my lord?" Ulaf asked uncertainly. The voice was so weak and altered that he barely recognized it. He couldn't see anything in the pitch-dark room. "Are you all right? Wait—I'll fetch a light."

He swung around to grab a lantern, found one thrust into his hands. The Grandmother stood right behind him.

"Shouldn't you be with Bashae?" Ulaf asked her.

"Bashae wants to talk to him," the Grandmother said firmly.

"I'm not sure—" Ulaf began.

"Bashae's dying," said the Grandmother, her voice creaking. "He wants to talk to Baron Shadamehr."

Ulaf did not know what to say, and so said nothing. Taking the lantern from her, he entered the storage room. He flashed the light around, searching among the crates and barrels, casks and bottles.

"My lord?"

"Here," said Shadamehr.

Ulaf followed the sound of his voice. He found Shadamehr resting against a wooden beam, Alise cradled in his arms.

Ulaf gasped softly at the sight.

The baron's eyes were dark and shadowed, his cheeks sunken, his skin ashen. He glanced up at Ulaf, then looked back down at Alise, who lay limp and motionless in his arms. Her head rested on his breast, her vibrant red hair covered her face. She stirred suddenly, her body twitched and she cried out incoherent words. Shadamehr gently smoothed the rampant curls, murmuring softly, soothing her.

Hastily Ulaf set down the lantern, knelt at the baron's side. "My lord! What happened? Are you all right? What's wrong with Alise?"

In answer to his last question, Shadamehr wordlessly drew back her sweat-damp red hair. The lanternlight illuminated her face.

The Grandmother sucked in a hissing breath.

"Gods have mercy," Ulaf whispered.

"What's ails her?" the Grandmother asked.

"Void magic," said Ulaf quietly. "The Void demands a toll of the person who uses it, although I've never seen anything this bad. She must have cast a powerful spell."

"She did," said Shadamehr bitterly. "She gave her life in exchange for mine."

"I know the spell," said Ulaf. "At least, I know of it."

"You can help her," Shadamehr said. "You can heal her."

"I'm sorry—"

"You have to!" Shadamehr cried harshly. He grabbed hold of Ulaf's arm, squeezed it painfully. "You must, damn you! You can't let her die!"

"My lord, there's nothing . . . I can't . . ." Ulaf faltered. He sighed deeply. "There is nothing I can do. Nothing anyone can do, my lord. The gift of healing comes from the gods, and they will not bestow that gift on any who practices the magic of pain and destruction."

"Not even if it is used for good?" Shadamehr demanded angrily.

"Not even then, my lord."

Alise cried out, her body twisted and writhed. Her fists clenched spasmodically.

Shadamehr clasped her tightly, bent his head over her.

"Baron Shadamehr?" Jessan's urgent voice came from the door. "Bashae needs to talk to you."

"Not now!" Shadamehr said impatiently.

"You should go to him. The pecwae is dying," said Ulaf.

Shadamehr stared at Ulaf, then over at Jessan, who shook his head in grim confirmation.

"A Vrykyl," Ulaf said. "There was a fight . . ."

"Oh, gods!" Shadamehr said, closing his eyes. "What have I done?"

"He saved the Sovereign Stone," said Jessan, his voice gruff. "He is desperate to talk to you, my lord. Will you come?"

Shadamehr looked down helplessly at Alise.

"I will stay with her," offered the Grandmother, adding bluntly, "I have said my good-byes to my grandson."

"Yes," said Shadamehr, his heart wrenched with pain and pity. "I will come."

He laid Alise gently down on the floor and wrapped her warmly in her cloak. Painfully, he staggered to his feet. Ulaf saw the blood that covered Shadamehr's shirt.

"My lord, what—"

"Not now!" Shadamehr gasped. He grimaced in pain. "Here, young man, give me your shoulder to lean on."

Jessan put his strong arm around the baron, aided his weak steps. Ulaf hurried around to the other side, and, between them, they helped Shadamehr from the storage room. Glancing behind, Ulaf saw that the Grandmother had her stones out and was placing them at various points over Alise's shivering body.

"Should I run for the healers?" Maudie asked, all in a twitter.

"No!" said Ulaf sharply. "The last thing we need now are Temple magi poking about."

Alise was already considered an outlaw by the Church, for she had been an Inquisitor who had left the holy orders without bothering to tell anyone she was leaving. If they found out that she'd been using Void magic, they would immediately place her under arrest. They would heal her, but only to make certain she was well enough to face her executioner.

"Are you sure?" Maudie persisted, staring at Shadamehr. "He looks to be in a bad way."

"Do you know what we need, Maudie?" said Ulaf. "Hot water. That's what you can do. Go fetch some boiling water. We need lots of it. Buckets."

"Well . . ." said Maudie hesitantly.

"Hurry, woman!" Ulaf ordered, his tone stern. "There's no time to waste!"

"I'll just go put the kettle on." She headed for the kitchen, and they could hear the banging and clattering of iron pots.

Bashae lay on the floor in front of the fire. He appeared to be resting easy, no longer suffering. His face was smooth, free of pain. His skin was so pale as to be translucent, his eyes were clear. A single stone, a bright, glittering ruby, lay on his chest.

Jessan eased Shadamehr down, so he could kneel on the floor beside the pecwae.

"Ulaf," said Shadamehr, "has everything been done for him?"

"The Grandmother used her magic on him, my lord," said Ulaf.

"But is that enough? These folk remedies of hers—"

"My lord, I am a child in magic, compared to the Grandmother," said Ulaf. "His injuries are severe. He should have died of them instantly. The fact that he is still alive to speak to you is a testament to her skill and her faith."

"You have the Sovereign Stone?" Bashae asked Ulaf. "You have it safe?"

He could not speak above a whisper, but his words were distinct, his tone, calm.

"I do, Bashae," said Ulaf. He drew out the knapsack, held it for the pecwae to see.

Bashae's gaze shifted to Shadamehr.

"I asked you once before to take the Sovereign Stone, my lord. You said that the knight had given it to me and that I should keep it." Bashae gave a little shrug. "I would, but I don't think it would go with me to my sleep world. My sleep world is a very peaceful place. They won't want it there."

"I will take the Sovereign Stone, Bashae," said Shadamehr. He reached out for the knapsack, held it fast. "I will fulfill the knight's quest. I should have done so in the first place. If I had—" He shook his head, unable to go on.

"Come closer," said Bashae, "and I will tell you the secret of the knapsack. It's magical, you know." Motioning Shadamehr near, Bashae whispered the secret that the knight had told him. "The Stone is hidden by magic. Speak the name of the knight's wife, and you will see it. The name is 'Adele.' "

"I understand," said Shadamehr. "And I am sorry that I did not take on this burden sooner," he added remorsefully. "I might have spared you this."

"It was better that I had it," said Bashae. "If you'd taken it with you, the Vrykyl in the palace would have found it."

"That is true," said Shadamehr. "I hadn't thought of that." He managed a wan smile. "You have done your part, Bashae. Go to your sleep world with the knowledge that you are a true hero."

"Jessan said that, too," said Bashae, and his dimming eyes went to his friend. "Tell me again, Jessan."

"You will be buried in the mound with the Trevinici warriors," said Jessan, who knelt at his friend's side, held his frail hand in his strong one. "No other pecwae has ever been so honored."

Bashae gazed at him, never taking his eyes from him.

"Your body will be carried by the bravest warriors in the village in a grand procession," Jessan continued. "You will be laid to rest in a place of honor beside the knight, Lord Gustav."

"I like that. No other pecwae . . . ever so honored. Good-bye, Jessan," Bashae whispered. "I'm glad you found your name. Defender. I'm sorry I made fun of it. It's not very exciting—not like Ale Guzzler—but it suits you."

Jessan held his friend's hand tightly. Drawing in a deep breath, he said, "Ever after, when a Trevinici warrior is in need, your spirit will rise to come do battle along with the spirits of the other heroes."

Bashae smiled. "I hope . . . I'm not in the way."

He gave a little sigh. His body stiffened, then relaxed. The hand that Jessan held went limp. The bright life drained from the pecwae's eyes.

Ulaf bent over the pecwae, listened for the beating of the heart, then gently passed his hand over the staring eyes.

"Bashae is gone," he said quietly.

SHADAMEHR SLUMPED DOWN IN ONE OF THE CHAIRS, RESTED HIS head on his arms. He had another farewell to say, this one that would tear out his heart, leaving bleak emptiness, guilt, and bitter regret. Floundering in that dark water, he felt himself caught in a deadly riptide dragging him under. He lacked the energy to fight. It seemed easier simply to give up and let the dark water close over his head.

He stared with envy at Bashae's corpse, at the face smoothed of all pain and worry. Shadamehr longed to find that same blessed peace, but could not afford the luxury. He had made a promise to Alise, a promise to Bashae. He had the Sovereign Stone. The responsibility had been passed to him, and he had to decide what to do with it.

The Council of Dominion Lords had been disbanded by order of the new Regent.

That collection of doddering old fools wouldn't be able to do anything anyway, Shadamehr thought, then reproached himself. He could not very well blame them for not bringing in fresh young blood. He had been offered the chance, and he had carelessly tossed it away.

The Lord of the Void and his armies of fiendish taan were setting up camp outside the city of New Vinnengael. The king was a Vrykyl in a child's body, a Vrykyl who had murdered both the king—a dear friend—and his innocent son in order to steal the throne. Shadamehr knew the truth, but how was he to convince anyone? He was a wanted man, who had dared lay hands on the young king. There was undoubtedly a death sentence on his head, for the Vrykyl would have sent out the order that he be slain on sight.

And in just a few moments, he would have to bid good-bye to Alise—the woman he'd loved for years, the only woman he could ever love.

"I don't have the strength," he said despondently. "I can't do it. Bashae . . . Alise, you put your trust in the wrong person. You've paid for it with your lives. I don't know what to do. I don't know where to go. . . ."

"Shadamehr!"

He reared up his head, opened his eyes. Ulaf stood beside him, shaking his arm.

"I'm sorry to wake you," he began.

"I wasn't asleep," said Shadamehr.

"My lord," said Ulaf, "it's Alise."

Shadamehr blenched. He had to be strong. He owed her that much. "Is it time?" he asked.

"I think you should come," Ulaf answered quietly.

Shadamehr pushed himself up from the table. He refused Ulaf's help, made his way on his own. He was growing stronger. The horrors of the Void remained, floating atop the dark water with the rest of the wreckage of his life, but his body's strength was returning. He entered the storage room, noticing, as he did so, that Ulaf hung back.

Making his way among the barrels and crates to where he'd left Alise, he saw a very strange sight.

Alise seemed to have been swallowed by a circus tent.

Spread over her shoulders and torso was a mass of gaily colored cloth decorated with stones and bells. Shadamehr had some vague recollection of having seen this before and then, looking at the Grandmother, he remembered. The Grandmother had removed her bell-ringing, stone-clicking skirt and draped it over Alise's body.

Shadamehr wondered if it was some pecwae ritual for the dead or if the Grandmother had gone mad, her mind overthrown by the death of her grandson. Holding fast to his own sanity with both hands, Shadamehr didn't think he could cope with this.

He could not see Alise's face, which was shrouded with her own shimmering hair. She was no longer in pain. Her body was relaxed, the limbs still and calm. It seemed that she slumbered, and he was thankful that he would be able to remember her this way.

He knelt down beside her. Lifting her hand, he brought it to his lips. "Farewell, my love—"

The Grandmother reached out, drew Alise's disheveled hair back from her face.

Shadamehr gasped.

Alise's face was smooth, unscarred. At the Grandmother's touch, Alise opened her eyes. Seeing Shadamehr, she smiled drowsily, then closed her eyes and sank back into sleep.

"You did this!" he exclaimed, staring at the Grandmother, whose nut-wrinkled face was suddenly the most beautiful face in all of Loerem.

The Grandmother shook her head and shrugged. "Perhaps I helped. But the gods did the work." She sighed, then looked up to ask quietly, "Bashae?"

"He has gone, Grandmother. I am so sorry." Shadamehr exhibited the knapsack. "He gave me the Sovereign Stone. I will see to it that his quest is fulfilled. I made him that promise."

She nodded and fussed about with the skirt, smoothing the folds, re-arranging some of the stones. She was clad only in a chemise that was frayed and worn. The bells of the skirt jingled faintly.

"She will sleep a long time," said the Grandmother. "When she wakes, she will be good as ever." She looked back at Shadamehr, bright eyes glittering in the lanternlight. "She loves you very much."

"And I love her," said Shadamehr, keeping hold of Alise's hand, as if he would never let go.

The Grandmother held up two clenched fists. "Two lodestones," she said. "They both have powerful attraction, but put them together and what happens?" The two fists bounced apart. "The gods mean them always to be separate."

"I've never had much use for the gods," said Shadamehr. He ran his hand through Alise's sweat-damp curls.

"You should." The Grandmother grunted. With a deft movement, she plucked the skirt off Alise and slid it back on, dropping it down over her head. She gave a wriggle, and the skirt settled atop her bony hips, fell in folds around her legs, bells clanging wildly. "The gods brought her back."

"But the gods didn't bring back Bashae," said Shadamehr. "You asked the gods to heal him, and they refused."

The Grandmother said nothing. Her hands darted to her face, made a swipe at her eyes.

"Why aren't you angry about that?" Shadamehr demanded. "The gods saved this woman, a stranger to you, and they took Bashae, your grandson. Why don't you rage and shout, scream at them until your voice stuns the heavens?"

"I miss him," she said simply. Her face told of her grief and anguish, but her voice was calm, almost serene. "I have buried all my children and many of my grandchildren. Bashae was my favorite of them all. He was so young, his life barely started. That was why I asked the gods to bring him back. I even asked them to take me instead. I had thought I was to be the one to die on this journey. Here, in my sleep city. But"—she shrugged, and the bells rang softly—"the gods decided otherwise.

"A newborn baby screams and cries when it comes into this world. It wails on seeing the light. If you gave the babe a choice, he would go back into the warm, safe darkness. Yet, we say that life is a gift." The Grandmother shook her head. "Perhaps death is a greater gift. Like that baby, we are afraid to leave what we know."

Shadamehr said nothing, for he did not want to argue with her. In his opinion, the gods—if there were gods—were capricious and callous, acting on whim.

The Grandmother smacked him on the forehead with the palm of her hand.

"What was that for?" Shadamehr asked, startled.

"You are a spoiled child, Baron Shadamehr," said the Grandmother sternly. "You have been given everything you want, and yet you roll around in the dirt shrieking and wailing and kicking your heels for more. I don't know why the gods put up with you."

She shoved past him, her stones clicking and bells jangling. Pausing at the door to the storage room, she looked back at him. "They must love you very much."

Shadamehr had his doubts about that, and, for the moment, he didn't care. The gods loved Alise, as he did, and that was all he needed to know.

He lifted her in his arms, held her close, reveling in the renewed warmth that flowed through her body.

"My lord," said Ulaf, coming to crouch down beside him. "We must—"

"She's going to live!" said Shadamehr, hugging Alise close.

She murmured in her sleep and nestled near him—an action she would never have taken if she were conscious.

"Thank the gods!" said Ulaf fervently. "But, my lord, we need to think about what is to be done now. If Dagnarus's taan army is not here, they soon will be. We don't want to be caught in a besieged city." Knowing his lord's unpredictability, Ulaf thought it best to add, "Do we?"

"No, we don't," said Shadamehr emphatically. His mind was working once again. He felt strong enough to swim, even against that dark tide that had been trying to suck him under. "There's an ork ship waiting for us in the harbor. I sent the elven Dominion Lord and her husband there already. The orks have orders to wait until dawn before they sail. I'll take Alise and the Trevinici and the Grandmother with me on board the ship. Meanwhile you and the others will travel overland, carry messages to the Dominion Lords, tell them what has happened and that we will meet them in the city of Krammes. The Imperial Cavalry School is there. We have the human part of the Sovereign Stone. That must count for something. We can raise an army and return to take back New Vinnengael from the Lord of the Void."

"You think the city will fall, then?"

"Yes," said Shadamehr shortly.

"How will I find the Dominion Lords? I know one of them, Lord Randall, but—"

"Rigiswald knows them all. He's in the Temple, reading up on the Sovereign Stone. He's probably still there. You know how he is when he has his nose in a book. Take him with you."

"Now, really, Shadamehr. I think I'd rather travel with a Vrykyl!" Ulaf protested earnestly. "That old man is the most cantankerous old man who ever lived. He has a tongue that could fell small trees."

"Then you'll never want for firewood," said Shadamehr soothingly. "I'm sorry, dear boy, but Rigiswald is the only one who can help you in this. He knows the Dominion Lords and where they're likely to be found."

"Very well," said Ulaf gloomily. "I'll go round up the others. You do remember that there is a curfew, don't you, my lord?"

"That's why the gods invented sewer systems," said Shadamehr. "That's my travel route. What about you?"

"I'll never get Rigiswald down a sewer, and you know it. There's a gatekeeper who owes me a favor," Ulaf added with a wink. "Take care of yourself and Alise, my lord. I'll take care of the others, including Rigiswald."

"Excellent. Now go ask that good woman for some blankets. I'll want to wrap Alise up warmly." As Shadamehr glanced into the tavern's main room, his expression softened. "You'll need a shroud for the body, too. I am taking them home."

"Bashae is my responsibility," Jessan said tersely. "Bashae and the Grandmother."

Shadamehr and Ulaf exchanged startled glances. Neither of them had heard the warrior come up behind them.

"They could travel with me and the rest of our people, my lord," Ulaf offered. "My comrades and I are traveling east," he said to Jessan. "As my lord says, the road may be dangerous. We could use another sword. Will you come?"

Jessan's expression darkened distrustfully.

"I have ample proof of your valor, Jessan," Ulaf added. "We may be walking straight into the arms of the taan. In that case, I can think of no one else I'd rather have at my side."

Satisfied, Jessan nodded. "Then I will come with you, if the Grandmother agrees."

Ulaf persuaded the distraught Maudie, who could not look upon Bashae's body without succumbing to tears, to pull herself together and bring him warm blankets in which to wrap Alise.

"I'm worried about what to do with Maudie," Shadamehr said, accompanying Ulaf to the door. "This city will be besieged or worse in a day or two."

"She's safer here than she would be anywhere else," said Ulaf practically. "Tell her to invite her brawniest customers to help her defend her property."

"I suppose you're right," said Shadamehr. "I should be doing something, anything, to help. Instead, I'm running away."

"You have the Sovereign Stone," Ulaf reminded him. "You need to think of that. I've told Jessan and the Grandmother to be ready to leave by morning. Farewell, my lord. A good journey to you."

"And you," said Shadamehr, shaking his friend's hand. "With luck, the city guards are still preoccupied with the fracas at the Tubby Tabby. You should be able to reach the Temple without being stopped. Give Rigiswald my best when you see him."

Shadamehr returned to find that the Grandmother had swathed Alise snugly in a blanket, folding it around her and tucking in the ends as a mother swaddles a newborn babe. Alise slept soundly through the entire procedure. The hard time came, the time for farewells.

Jessan knelt beside Bashae, keeping silent vigil over the body of his friend. The Grandmother sat staring into the flames of the fire that danced and rollicked without heed or care.

Shadamehr rested his hand on Jessan's shoulder. The young man rose to his feet, and the two moved away, toward the back of the room.

"Ulaf told me of the battle. He told me that you attacked the Vrykyl at peril of your own life. No one doubts you did everything you could to save your friend. You have nothing to regret."

"I have nothing to regret," said Jessan simply. "Bashae died a warrior's death. He will be greatly honored by my people. To blame myself for his death would be to take away his victory. I will miss him," he added more gently, "for he was my friend, but that is my loss, and I must deal with it."

"I wish it were that simple," Shadamehr murmured. He started to bid the young warrior a safe journey, then remembered in time that one did not wish that for a Trevinici.

"May you fight many battles," said Shadamehr. "And be victorious over your foes."

"I wish the same for you, my lord," said Jessan.

Shadamehr winced. "I'm not keen on the fighting part," he admitted. "But I'll take the victory over the foes portion of that wish."

He walked back to say good-bye to the Grandmother. He had grown very fond of her in their brief time together, and he was going to miss her. He touched her gently upon the shoulder.

"Grandmother, I came to tell you good-bye and to say how truly sorry I am for your loss. I will always honor Bashae as one of the bravest people I have ever known. If we all come out of this alive, I will make the story of his courage and loyalty known to the world."

The Grandmother looked up, the flames seeming still to flicker in her eyes, the smoke of the fire dimming them. "So long as you keep his story here," she said, placing her hand over her heart, "that is all I ask. The rest of the world would not care much about it, except perhaps as a curiosity."

She fumbled about her skirts and her pouches, searching for something, and eventually brought out a turquoise. Eyeing it expertly, to make certain it was free of flaws, she pressed the stone into Shadamehr's hand. The gift was a valuable one, for the pecwae believe the turquoise to have special powers of protection. He knew she used them for protection herself, and he didn't want to rob her of it.

"Grandmother, I thank you, but I can't accept this—"

"Yes, you can," she said. She gave an emphatic nod toward the fire. "I've seen where you are bound. You're going to need it."

Shadamehr looked down at the turquoise, sky-blue, streaked with silver. It might come in handy, after all. Secreting the stone in the knapsack that held the Sovereign Stone, he bent down and kissed the Grandmother on her wrinkled cheek.

"Thank you, Grandmother. Have a safe journey."

"I would wish the same for you," she stated, shaking her head, "but it would be wasted."

Very probably, Shadamehr thought.

Lifting Alise, wrapped warmly in the folds of the blanket, he slung the knapsack over one shoulder and Alise's inert body over the other. Clasping her by her legs, he felt extremely grateful that she was comatose, for, had she been awake, she would have protested loudly and indignantly at being hauled about like a sack of flour.

Shadamehr accepted Maudie's offer of a dark lantern. Keeping the lantern's shutter closed, blocking off the light, he opened the door to the inn and peered out into the night. He estimated that he had about three hours until dawn. The street was empty. A fiery glow lit the sky not far away. The Tubby Tabby was still ablaze. Most of the patrols would be concentrated in that area, trying to put out the blaze.

Calling a soft, final farewell, Shadamehr took firm hold of Alise and the knapsack containing the Sovereign Stone and slipped into the darkness.

STANDING IN FRONT OF THE CROW AND RING, ULAF COULD SEE the fiery orange glow lighting the sky like a premature dawn, except that this glow meant sunset for the Tubby Tabby. The city guardsmen and magi would be fighting this magically induced blaze all night, effectively clearing the streets of patrols. Ulaf remained cautious, keeping to the shadows and staying clear of bright pools of light, for the Temple of the Magi was located near the Royal Palace, and the Imperial Cavalry would most certainly be out in full force. Ulaf ran down back roads and dashed up alleys, approaching the Temple from the rear. If caught, he had his story ready and would probably not be in any trouble, but he didn't have time to waste arguing with dunderhead cavalry officers.

Ulaf anticipated no difficulty in entering the Temple itself, even in the middle of a most unsettled night. He was a member of the Ninth Order, an Order dedicated to the study of the magical Portals that permitted swift travel from one part of Loerem to another. Of all the Orders of the Church, the Ninth Order was the least respected.

Two hundred years ago, wise and powerful magi had come together to create the four Portals. Centered in Old Vinnengael, the Portals went into the lands of the Tromek elves, the orks, and the dwarves, carrying merchants and their wares, goods and information back and forth. The fourth Portal purportedly communicated directly with the gods. When Dagnarus launched his attack on Old Vinnengael, he and his sorcerer, Gareth, used powerful Void magicks to defeat the city's defenders. The use of these powerful magicks, combined with the magicks cast by the city's defenders, caused such a disruption in the elemental magic that it blew apart, leveling much of the city and shattering the Portals.

Originally, it was thought that the Portals had been totally destroyed, for none could be found around Old Vinnengael. The Church created the Ninth Order with the intent to try to re-create the magic of the Portals. Their attempts proved futile. The secrets of the creation of the Portals had been destroyed in the blast. The magi worked for years, but were unable even to come close to re-creating the spells. They prayed to the gods, but their prayers went unanswered. The gods, it seemed, wanted no more Portals leading to heaven.

Much to the chagrin of the Church, reports began to come in that Portals were being discovered in various places around the continent, including a major Portal in the elven lands and another in the land of the Vinnengaelean's bitter enemy, the Karnuans. The Church realized that the Portals had not been destroyed. Dislodged, unmoored, the shattered Portals had drifted off to other locations.

The Church had been on the verge of disbanding the useless Ninth Order, but instead determined that it might have some value after all. Its members were sent out across the continent to find and map the errant Portals.

Centuries later, the members of the Ninth Order persisted in their task. Underfunded and ridiculed, members of the Ninth Order traveled extensively throughout Loerem to confirm, verify, and map every reported Portal.

Thus, Ulaf found this a very convenient Order to join. As a member of the Ninth Order, he was able to travel freely, come and go as he pleased. No one cared enough to ask where he'd been or was at all interested in hearing reports about his journeys. So long as he submitted a map with a new Portal every now and then, they were happy.

Matters might have different had he asked the Church for money. Since Shadamehr always funded Ulaf's travels, such requests were unnecessary. He passed himself off as independently wealthy, dedicating his own time and money to this venture. Church officials considered Ulaf obsessed, probably deranged, but harmless.

The Temple of the Magi was not, as its name suggested, a single building. The Temple was the main building, a magnificent structure of marble with stained-glass rose windows and elegant spires designed to sweep men's thoughts upward to heaven. This building housed the Hall of Worship, containing the altars to the gods. The hall was open to the public day and night, with priests on duty at all hours. In this building were also the offices of high Church officials.

The other major buildings in the complex included the university, with its dortours, classrooms, and a library that was famous throughout the continent; and the Houses of Healing, run by the Order of Hospitalers. Surrounded by gardens, the Houses of Healing were long, low, and airy buildings, with enormous windows to admit the sunlight, which was believed to be conducive to health.

Ulaf went immediately to the university building, a cylindrical structure supported by flying buttresses that extended from four freestanding towers. A veritable warren of convoluted corridors, the building's interior was dark and windowless, designed to keep the minds of students focused on their studies, not gazing out into the world beyond. Because of the powerful and possibly dangerous texts housed within its walls, the university was not open to the public and was surrounded by a wall through which a single gate provided entrance and egress. The gate was closed at sunset. All entering after that had to pass through—or attempt to pass through—a small wicket located to one side of the main gate.

The porter at the small wicket was startled, wary, and highly suspicious of a brother demanding entry at this ungodly hour, especially a brother wandering the streets in violation of curfew. Ulaf had only to show his credentials and explain his mission for the porter to shake his head in resignation and remove the magical spell that guarded the door.

Ulaf was given a choice of using his own magic to cast light or taking a lantern. He thankfully accepted the lantern. He'd spent four years studying here and could have walked the maze of halls in his sleep. He went first to the kitchen. He washed his face and hands, splashed cold water on his face to wake himself up. He couldn't remember when he'd last eaten and was thankful to find the bread and cheese left out for those who might be up late studying. Ulaf devoured a loaf of bread on the spot, cut himself a large wedge of cheese, and filled his pockets with apples. Munching the cheese, he made his way to the dortour, where lived the students and the Revered Brethren who worked in the Temple and its environs.

Ulaf noted that there was more activity than normal in the Temple at this late hour. Revered Brethren strode purposefully through the halls, their expressions grim and preoccupied. Loitering in a hallway, Ulaf waited until he saw a brother leave his room. Ulaf slipped into the room (few doors were ever locked in the Temple), dressed himself in clean robes, transferred his apples to a leather scrip, then set off in pursuit of Rigiswald. Ulaf made a bundle of his dirty clothing and deposited it in the receptacle set aside for those novitiates whose duties included laundry.

The library occupied an entire wing of the building, housing the most extensive collection of books on the continent. Here were thousands of books on magic, including books on the theory of magic, the religion of magic, and the practical uses of magic as practiced by every race under the sun. The library also contained books on a wide variety of other subjects ranging from books describing the rigging for a sailing vessel to manuals detailing the proper care for a horse with colic or the fine art of embroidering tapestries or how to prepare pickled swan's tongues.

The library never closed. Dwarven stone-lights—rocks magically enhanced to give off a warm, soft light—allowed scholars to pursue their researches far into the night. Access to the library was strictly regulated. Any of the Revered Brethren in good standing could obtain access simply by exhibiting credentials. Novitiates were permitted inside if they were accompanied by a tutor or if they had a letter from their tutor, then they were restricted to certain areas. Magi of other races were welcome, provided they came with references from the Church attesting to the fact that they used magic responsibly and that they were serious in their pursuit of knowledge. The king and the Dominion Lords were also permitted access to the library, the only laypeople to be so honored.

At this late hour, the library would ordinarily be a quiet, sleepy place. Ulaf was therefore startled to find that this night, the library bustled with activity.

"What's going on?" he asked a brother, who had nearly run him down in his haste.

The brother glanced at him askance, but seeing that Ulaf was wearing the robes of a Revered Brethren and thinking that perhaps he owed him some apology for nearly knocking him over, the brother deigned to respond.

"We've been ordered to move the most valuable books in the collection to a safe location," said the magus in a low voice.

"So the rumors of war are true," said Ulaf.

"You didn't hear that from me, Brother," said the magus grimly, and left upon his urgent errand.

That explained the battle magi standing guard in the halls, watching as the members of the Order of Scribes carried heavy wooden boxes filled with valuable books and scrolls to a protected location. Most of these valuable texts were the rare and ancient books that dated back to the time of the founding of Vinnengael many hundreds of years ago. Some, however, would be books that were considered dangerous, books on forbidden magicks that should not fall into the wrong hands.

A battle magus eyed Ulaf darkly, as he entered the library, and he was glad he'd thought to change his clothes and wash away all traces of the fight at the Tubby Tabby. Keeping his eyes lowered, he meekly entered the library and went straight to the head librarian. Ulaf presented his credentials, chalked his name on the board, and went in search of Rigiswald.

He found the irascible old man in a state of indignation, arguing (in whispers) with one of the Scribes, who appeared to be trying to wrest a book from him. Ulaf hung back, not wanting to get involved. He moved into Rigiswald's line of sight, made a motion with his hand, hoping to attract the elderly magus's attention. Rigiswald saw him and glared, but otherwise didn't take any notice of him. Ulaf sighed deeply and collapsed into a chair. He must have immediately fallen asleep, because the next thing he knew, someone was shaking him. He looked up to see Rigiswald, looking down.

"Why are you here?" Rigiswald demanded in a low, irritated whisper.

Ulaf snapped his head up and blinked his eyes. He couldn't for a moment think where he was. Then memory returned.

"I've come to fetch you, sir," Ulaf said, standing up. "Shadamehr has ordered us to leave the city. And there's more."

Quickly, Ulaf whispered the news of the night's events. He was grateful that the library was a place of enforced silence, for he and Rigiswald could confer in quiet tones and not raise suspicions.

Rigiswald listened closely. He had been Shadamehr's tutor since the baron was a child. A sleek, dapper gentleman, vain of his appearance and fond of creature comforts, Rigiswald was much more interested in the study of magic than the practice of magic. He claimed that spell-casting ruined his clothes. He was a skilled wizard, when he wanted to be, but he took care that he was not often driven to that extremity.

His face held no expression. His only reaction to the dire news that the young king of Vinnengael was a Vrykyl, in league with the Lord of the Void, whose armies were at this moment marching on the city, was to lift an eyebrow, and say, "I see."

Rigiswald smoothed his black beard, which was always neatly combed, trimmed close to his sharp jawline. "So that's why they took away my book. Why didn't the fool just say so in the first place!" He glowered at the back of the Scribe, who was walking off in triumph, book in hand. He turned back to Ulaf. "And why are you here?"

"Shadamehr asked me to come, sir," said Ulaf, striving to be patient. "I'm rounding up our people. We're planning to leave the city tomorrow morning before it comes under siege."

"Where are you bound?"

"To Krammes, sir. Shadamehr's going round by ship. He said that we were to travel overland—"

"Out of the question," stated Rigiswald. "That trip here in the company of the orks was bad enough. Now you propose that I walk a thousand miles to Krammes."

"It's not that far. We have horses. I'm supposed to talk to the Dominion Lords and Shadamehr says that you—"

Rigiswald gave a delicate snort. Turning his back on Ulaf, the elderly mage selected a goose quill from one of the jars placed at intervals around the library for the convenience of those needing to take notes. He took a small ivory scroll tube from his belt, removed the scroll rolled up inside, glanced at it, then turned it over and began to write. When he finished, he tucked the scroll into the tube and handed it to Ulaf.

"Here is where you may find those Dominion Lords who may be of use to you," Rigiswald said. "Use this as your introduction."

"This means you're not coming with me," Ulaf said in loud and frustrated tones that won him a dour look from the librarian. He lowered his voice. "You did hear me say that the city was going to come under attack soon, didn't you, sir?"

Rigiswald shrugged, unconcerned. He began to sort through a pile of books he had stacked up on a table beside him.

"I trust they left me something," he muttered. "Ah, here it is."

Deftly abstracting a slim volume bound in worn red leather, he settled back down in a chair, opened it, and began to read. After a moment, he glanced up at Ulaf.

"You may go on about your business," he said.

"But Shadamehr—"

Rigiswald raised a neatly manicured finger. "Tell the baron I will be of far more use to him here in New Vinnengael than I would be traipsing about the countryside."

He went back to his reading.

Ulaf opened his mouth, shut it again. Shaking his head, he tucked the ivory tube into a pocket, then, muttering imprecations, stalked out of the library.

Glancing up from his book, Rigiswald watched Ulaf depart and smiled to himself. Closing the book, he leaned back in the chair and was soon absorbed with his own thoughts, grim ones, to judge by his expression.

Back at the Crow and Ring Jessan kept vigil over the body of his friend. The night was quiet—the sort of soft and heavy quiet that oppresses the spirit and deadens thought. Ulaf had been gone for some time. Maudie had tried to remain awake to keep an eye on these strange visitors, but the excitement and shock of events had worn her out. She was asleep in her chair.

Jessan was grateful to Ulaf for having provided him with an occupation, a means of being of service, of use to someone. He could not have accepted Ulaf's offer to travel with them otherwise, for he would not be beholden to anyone, not even to this friend of the baron's. Many Trevinici hired themselves out to travelers to serve as guards in return for food and shelter along the way. Jessan might have suspected that this job was being offered him out of pity, but he had seen respect in Ulaf's eyes and heard it in his voice.

Jessan knew himself to be valued for his courage and his skill, and the thought brought a modicum of comfort and warmth to him as he stood alone in the howling, frigid, darkness of his grief and his desperate desire to return home.

Jessan had been eager to go out into the world, eager to prove himself as a warrior. Bored with his humdrum life in the village, as the young are often bored, he could not understand the joy felt by his uncle and the other warriors on returning home after a long absence. How could they trade a life of adventure, danger, and excitement for a life of digging in the fields and minding children? Jessan's thoughts winged to those same ordinary and oft-despised comforts with a longing that ached and burned in his heart.

Jessan remembered even his crazy aunt Ranessa with compassion. He wished that he'd been kinder to her, more understanding. She was family. She was part of the tribe, and that made her welfare important to him, a sacred trust, as Bashae had been a sacred trust.

Jessan did not blame himself for Bashae's death. His conscience was clear. He had done all he could to protect his friend and save him from the Vrykyl. As he had said, to blame himself would take credit from Bashae. The pecwae could have dropped the Sovereign Stone and fled, but he'd made the choice to fight for it, valiantly overcoming all his instincts to remain loyal to the task given him by the gods.

"I honor your courage, Bashae," said Jessan softly. "But part of me wishes you *had* run away. That same part is angry that you didn't. You left me here alone and friendless. I am sorry for my weakness. I hope you understand."

"He does," said the Grandmother. "Where he is, he understands everything."

The time passed, long and heavy. The Grandmother stared into the fire. Jessan's thoughts retraced the footsteps of the remarkable journey that had carried him into foreign lands, introduced him to a kite-maker, the Nimorean Queen's daughter, an elven Dominion Lord, and a madcap baron.

Jessan was thinking how each had made its mark upon his life when he heard the creaking sound of door hinges. He jerked around, his hand going for the weapon that was no longer at his side. He realized then, seeing the gray light outside the door, that dawn was near.

"It's me," said Ulaf softly.

He crept across the floor, not wanting to disturb the slumbering Maudie.

"I have found most of our people," he said. "I've left messages for the others. They'll catch up with us on the road. I have the horses—mine and

Alise's and Shadamehr's. He'd never forgive us if we left his horse here to be eaten by the taan. Are you ready? . . ."

He glanced askance at the body of the pecwae, lying with limbs composed, eyes closed, before the fire. But for the whitish blue pallor of the skin, Bashae might have been asleep.

"We should wrap the body in something," Ulaf suggested uncomfortably. "Otherwise . . ." He fell silent, not certain what to say.

Jessan looked to the Grandmother, who roused herself from her reverie. Rising to her feet, she smoothed the folds of her skirts, setting the bells to tinkling softly. Closing her eyes, the Grandmother began to sing.

She sang an ancient song, a song taught to the pecwae in a time when elves were newborn creatures wandering the continent with wonder in their eyes, a time when the orks left their brothers who swim in the vast oceans to live upon the land, a time when the dwarven young rolled on the ground with wolf cubs, a time when humans used their magic to wrench stones from the earth and fashion them into weapons.

As the Grandmother sang, she spread out her hands. Strands of silk flowed from her fingers. The silken threads wrapped around Bashae, spun a cocoon around his body. Every so often, at set intervals in the song, the Grandmother would tear one of the stones from her skirt and toss it among the twining threads. Her tears flowed at the song's beginning, but the ancient mantra that sped the soul of the dead upon its journey to the sleep world also brought comfort and solace to the living. With the end of the song came an end to tears.

"We are ready to go," the Grandmother said to Ulaf. She was dry-eyed, stiff-chinned. "His soul is departed, and the cocoon will keep his body safe until we place him in the burial mound."

"I have kept the warrior's watch," Jessan added. "I introduced Bashae to the fallen heroes of our tribe and told them of his valor, so that they will accept him among them and honor him."

Ulaf had a momentary picture of the diminutive pecwae walking into the halls of heaven, to be greeted as a hero by the likes of such Trevinici legends as Bear-Mauler, Skull-Basher, and He-Who-Dines-on-the-Brains-of-His-Foe. Ulaf added his own silent prayer, hoping that Bashae would be honored by them, but also trusting that the pecwae would soon be able to make good his escape and go running freely in the meadows, to bask in heaven's eternal sunshine.

"We should hurry," Ulaf said. "No sign of the taan yet, but it's just as well to be away from here."

Removing some coins from his pouch, he laid them on the table beside the sleeping Maudie. Jessan wrapped the small, cocooned body in a blanket and carried it out to the waiting horses, where Ulaf helped him lash the body onto Shadamehr's steed. The horse was usually restless and ill-tempered, but the Grandmother spoke to the animal, told it the nature of the burden it bore. The horse stood quietly, with head lowered.

That done, the Grandmother looked around at her sleep city, at the tall buildings, just starting to emerge from the shadows of night, and smiled sadly.

"When it is my time, I will come back," she promised.

Jessan picked her up, set her on the back of his horse. "When it is your time, you will join the heroes, Grandmother."

She heard the sorrow and loneliness in his voice, felt it echoed in her own heart. Each was all the other had left now.

"Bah!" she said briskly. "They'd just want me to cook for them."

Jessan smiled, as she had hoped he would. Mounting the horse, he made certain that the Grandmother was securely settled, then they rode off through the gray dawn, following Ulaf's lead.

AFTER FLEEING THE ILL-FATED FIASCO IN THE PALACE, DAMRA and her husband Griffith had made their way through the slumbering city without difficulty. A member of the Wyred, that mysterious sect of elven wizards, Griffith had the ability to transform himself into an airy being who could pass through the streets as lightly as a breath of wind. Damra was not a wizard, but she could call upon the magical power of the armor of the Dominion Lords to cloak herself in the black wings of the raven. Thus the two elves were able to escape the vigilance of the Imperial Cavalry, who had orders to arrest them, along with the outlaw Baron Shadamehr.

Damra had been to New Vinnengael before, on those rare occasions when the Dominion Lords were summoned to conference. She recalled that all streets in the city bore names that had to do with their location. They had only to find River Street, which would lead them to the docks. Since it was a major thoroughfare, it was not hard to locate. Patrols passed them by without a glance, a tribute to their powers of magic. On reaching the docks, the elves were just starting to search for the orken ship they'd been told would be waiting for them when they heard a blast and saw a lurid, orange glow light the sky.

"A building has caught fire," said Griffith, his voice seemingly coming from thin air, for he remained concealed by his magic. "I wonder if that means the taan have entered the city?"

Damra watched a moment, waiting for more fires to break out, waited to hear screams and shouts. All was silence, except for some noise made by a nearby patrol, who had seen the flames and were wondering if they should go find out what was going on.

"I don't think so," Damra replied. "Why do I have the feeling it has something to do with Baron Shadamehr?"

"Because trouble follows him like a stray dog?" suggested Griffith.

Damra smiled and looked in the direction of her husband's voice. "I wonder how we're supposed to find that ship? There are undoubtedly several ork ships in port. I'm not sure how we figure out which one is the one we're looking for. In all the excitement, I forgot to ask the baron the ship's name."

"Would there be that many?" Griffith asked dubiously. "I thought the orks and humans were practically at war."

"Orks never let politics stand in the way of profit," Damra replied. "There are always several orken ships moored at the docks of New Vinnengael, and a good many orken traders to be found in the city markets."

"I hope we locate the right ship quickly," said Griffith somberly. "My strength is giving out. I'm not certain how much longer I can hold on to this spell."

"And I hope that the orks will help us," said Damra, sounding dubious. "I do not like having to rely on creatures who are so unpredictable."

"They are not 'creatures,' dear," said her husband, mildly rebuking. "They are people, the same as us."

"Orks are *not* the same as us," returned Damra severely.

Griffith said nothing, wanting to avoid a quarrel. Damra kept silent for the same reason.

Arriving at the docks, the weary elves were astonished to find only one ork ship in port, swinging at anchor in the middle of the dark river.

"That's strange," said Damra.

"Not really," her husband replied. "The orks have warned their brethren of the approach of the taan. The rest of the orks have fled."

The orken ship was distinctive for her painted sails, featuring crude images of whales, dolphins, sea serpents, and seabirds. The ship was the *Kli'Sha*, orken for "seagull," and she was aglow with light, her nervous crew keeping watch.

The rest of the harbor was quiet, except for the occasional patrol. The orks were not the only sailors to have word of the enemy, apparently.

Those Vinnengaelean merchant ships who could put out to sea had done so immediately, taking with them family and friends.

"Where is the Vinnengaelean fleet?" Damra asked suddenly. "Vinnengael is known for its navy. I am surprised that they are not here to defend the city."

"The king ordered them out to sea about a month ago in response to a rumor that a Karnuan fleet would attempt to attack New Vinnengael from the south. The fleet has not been heard from since," Griffith said. "The baron believes it possible that they were lured to their doom by the Lord of the Void."

"Speaking of that fell lord," said Damra, "look there, on the far shore."

Narrow and swift-flowing at this point, the Arven River glimmered darkly in the half-light of a waning moon. Damra pointed across its rippling surface to where pinpricks of bright orange light could be seen ranging up and down the riverbank.

"Bonfires," said Damra.

"Yes," Griffith agreed. "Dagnarus's troops are massing on the riverbank."

"He will attack with dawn."

"I am not so certain he will attack," Griffith said. "Dagnarus is a cunning man, a genius when it comes to warfare, according to legend. He went to the trouble of insinuating his Vrykyl into the Royal Palace. Why would he do that if he meant to level the city. I believe he has other plans for New Vinnengael."

"The gods help them," said Damra, "And us. Here comes another patrol. Try to hold your spell a little longer, my husband."

They needn't have worried. The soldiers paid little attention to their duties. They stared across the water toward the flaring bonfires, every man knowing well what they meant.

Once they were gone, the two elves made their way to the pier, where the ork captain paced and muttered to himself in orken, occasionally saying something to a companion, who lounged at his ease on a coil of rope.

Griffith ceased his spell-casting, letting go of the magic with relief. Damra threw off her magical raven's cloak.

The orken captain gave a violent start at the sight of two elves materializing out of the night almost under his nose. He grabbed his sword.

The first mate leapt up from the ropes and Griffith found the point of a long, curved-bladed sword at his throat while Damra stared down the blade of a wicked-looking dagger.

"Baron Shadamehr sent us," Griffith said hurriedly, using Elderspeak, for he knew very little Pharn 'Lan, the orken language. "He told us we could gain passage on your ship. You must recognize me, Captain Kal-Gah. I am Griffith. I've lived with the baron the past month. This is my wife, Damra, a Dominion Lord."

The orken captain lowered his sword, but only to Griffith's chest. Lifting a lantern, he thrust the light into Griffith's face, peered at him intently, then shifted his penetrating stare to Damra.

Tall and slender, his movements graceful, Griffith wore the traditional black robes of the Wyred, which set them apart from all respected members of elven society. He wore his black hair smoothed back from his face, bound in a long braid at his back. Damra had discarded the magical armor of the Dominion Lord, so as not to look intimidating. She wore a blue silken tunic, bound around her slim waist with a crimson sash and over that the tabard of the Dominion Lord. Since she, too, was considered outside the pale of proper elven society, she eschewed the restricting dress of elven women, choosing instead to wear long, flowing silk trousers. She cut her hair short, wore it tied back in a club.

The orken captain took all this in, stared at them long and hard.

"You know my name," he grunted. He frowned, seemed to think this suspicious.

"Yes, Captain Kal-Gah," said Griffith politely.

The ork captain, who stood seven feet tall and was built on the order of Shadamehr's Keep, was hard to forget. Clad in leather breeches, he stood bare-chested in the teeth of the chill wind blowing off the river. His huge underslung jaw jutted forward, two protruding lower fangs gleamed in the lanternlight. His voice boomed in the night's stillness as though he were roaring over the howl of a gale. His eyes were small, but his gaze forthright and intense. He had shaved his head to reveal some remarkable tattoos. All that was left of his hair was a scalp lock that trailed down his back in a tar-covered braid. A large conch shell hung around his neck, suspended on a length of twined leather.

"We were introduced by Baron Shadamehr at his castle," Griffith continued. "Your shaman, Quai-ghai, also knows me. She and I had a most fascinating discussion about certain Air magic spells she was interested in learning from me." Griffith glanced about. "If she is here—"

"She is on board ship," said the captain. "She sleeps. We sail with the morning tide. Where is the baron?"

"We don't know," Damra replied. "We thought he might be here—"

"He's not," said Captain Kal-Gah.

Damra and her husband exchanged glances. "There was trouble at the palace—"

Kal-Gah grunted again. "I am not surprised. The omens were bad. Very bad. So bad that I might have raised anchor and left with last evening's tide, but I gave the baron my oath. I would not have stayed even then, but the moon is on the wane, which makes oath-breaking unlucky. Then again, I might have stayed anyway. I like the baron. He thinks like an ork."

He eyed the elves. "So you want to board my ship."

"Yes, Captain, if—" said Griffith.

"I will have to consult the omens," Captain Kal-Gah stated decisively. "The shaman is asleep. She will wake in the morning. Until then, sit there." He pointed to a coil of rope.

Damra and Griffith again exchanged glances.

"Captain," said Griffith, "there are soldiers looking for us. As I said, there was trouble. We are elves in a city of humans—"

"Disappear," said Kal-Gah, waving his hand. "Turn yourself into smoke, or whatever is you do."

"I would, Captain," said Griffith, "but I am very tired, and I'm not sure I have the strength. Please—"

"You demean yourself, my husband," Damra snapped, shifting to Tomagai, the language of the elves. "Don't beg him. This was a mistake from the beginning. There is nothing for us to do in human lands. We should return to Tromek. I will take the Sovereign Stone to the Divine. It is what I should have done in the first place. We will go north into the mountains, travel to Dainmorae. I have some money, enough to purchase two horses."

"Perhaps you are right," said Griffith.

Hearing the exhaustion in his voice, she regarded him anxiously, raised her hand to touch his cheek, which was pale and wan. "Can you keep going a little longer?"

"I can manage," he said with a smile. Capturing her hand, he kissed her fingers, then, holding fast to her hand, he turned to the ork. "I thank you, Captain Kal-Gah, but we have decided to—"

"Wait!" The captain had been staring out at his ship. He raised his hand, cutting off Griffith's words. "Look there."

"I don't see—"

"There!" The ork jabbed his finger. "The birds!"

Two seagulls, attracted by the lanternlight, were flying among the rigging, probably searching for food. One bird settled on the jibboom. The captain looked from the seagull to Griffith.

"Ah," said Kal-Gah.

The other seagull landed next to the first. The captain looked from the seagull to Damra. "Ah," he said again.

The seagulls perched there, ruffling their feathers. An ork advanced, lantern in hand, and offered food that was graciously accepted. One bird lifted its head, craned it backward, and let out a raucous caw.

Captain Kal-Gah lowered the sword. Deftly flipping the enormous blade as if it were an eating knife, he thrust the blade into his wide leather belt. "The omens are good. You can both go aboard. I will tell the crew you are coming."

He lifted the conch shell he wore around his neck, put it to his lips, and gave a bellowing blast. One of the crew members waved his lantern back and forth in response.

Captain Kal-Gah jerked his thumb at a shore boat moored to the dock. The six crewmen were asleep, slumped over the oars. Some twitched and grumbled at the conch shell blast, but continued to slumber. It took the captain's shouts and the first mate's oaths and kicks to wake them. Yawning prodigiously, they sat up and peered around, bleary-eyed.

"My boys can sleep through anything," the captain stated proudly. "Help these lubbers aboard," he told his crew, speaking Pharn 'Lan.

The orks obeyed with alacrity. Two strong orks grabbed hold of Griffith and, before he knew what was happening, they swept him off his feet and tossed him bodily into the boat. Two more orks caught him as he landed and hustled him to the back, plunked him down unceremoniously on a benchlike seat, and grunted orders to stay there.

Damra drew herself up stiffly. "Thank you, Captain," she said, "but I can manage on my own."

The captain grinned, shrugged, and motioned his crew to stand back. Damra walked down the pier, looking at the boat that floated in the water below, and suddenly she was not so certain of herself. The boat rose and fell with the waves, and at the same time, it rocked back and forth, bumping against the sides of the dock. She would have to jump down into it, and she must time her jump just right or fall into the water. Damra was not afraid of drowning. She was a good swimmer. But she would look extremely foolish, and elves are very sensitive about their dignity.

She hesitated on the pier, watching the boat bob up and down, seeing the leering grins of the ork sailors gazing expectantly up at her. Then she heard her husband's voice reciting the words to a spell. The wind caressed her, soothed her, and lifted her up in its strong arms. Damra floated on her husband's magic and drifted down into the boat as lightly as a feather falling from a seabird to land gently among the amazed orks, who fell all over themselves and each other to get out of her way.

The first mate howled in dismay, but Captain Kal-Gah only laughed.

"The elf has the wings of a gull, as well as the beak and the squawk," he chortled.

Since the beak reference was to Damra's rather prominent nose, it was just as well she did not understand the language. All the crew members chuckled obligingly—the captain had made a joke, after all—but their chuckles had a halfhearted sound.

The captain himself released the rope that held the boat to the dock, then went back to waiting and watching for Baron Shadamehr.

The orks bent to the oars before Damra had a chance to make her way through the press of bodies. The boat shot out from the dock so swiftly that the motion threw her off-balance. She lurched forward, stumbled into her husband's arms. He lowered her safely onto the bench beside him.

"Thank you, my dear," she said, huddling thankfully into his embrace, adding remorsefully, "I'm sorry I was cross with you back there."

"We're both tired," he said, holding her close. "Tired and hungry. And I could not bear to see you hauled out of the river like a drowned cat."

"Speaking of being hungry, I don't like to think of what we'll find to eat on board," Damra said with a shudder. "Whale blubber, like as not."

"Orks don't eat whales, my dear. They consider the whale sacred. I believe that bread is a staple of an ork's diet."

By the time the elves reached the ship, however, neither of them was

She dipped a finger in the paste, brought it to her lips. The smell was not unpleasant, seemed to have a soothing effect. She nibbled a bit of the paste. Her stomach heaved, but she managed to gag it down.

Griffith shared the paste with her. "At least when we die, we'll be together," he said to her.

Quai-ghai handed them the mug of cool, clear water. She insisted that they drink it down, for, she said, the sickness drained their body of fluids. She stood watching them, the gold tooth thrusting up over her upper lip.

"Either she's waiting for us to drop dead or get better," Damra said. "I can't tell which."

Griffith did not answer. He had fallen asleep. Damra felt sleep steal over her, sleep so soft and heavy that it was like sinking into a thick, feather mattress.

"Damra of Gwyenoc," said a soft voice.

"What is it?" she answered drowsily. "Who is there?"

"I must speak to you. Can you hear me, understand me?"

"I'm sleepy," she mumbled. "Let me sleep."

"This is important. Time flows by swiftly. I must speak to you now or not at all."

The voice was familiar. Damra felt a thrill at the sound of it and the thrill roused her. She opened her eyes.

The room was dark, for the elves were far belowdecks, and there were no windows. She could not see the speaker, but she knew his voice.

"Silwyth?" Damra was more confused than astonished. The sickness dulled her mind, or perhaps the drug. Anything seemed possible, even the unexpected appearance of the old elf on an ork ship in the middle of the Arven River.

A hand, strong and supple, closed over her wrist.

"It is Silwyth," he said.

Lifting her hand, he guided her fingers to touch his face. She could feel the leathery skin, the folds and creases of the myriad wrinkles that were a testament to his age and the hard life he had led. She noted that his face was wet, as was his hand.

She called to mind the last time she had seen Silwyth, in the house of the Shield of the Divine. He had saved her life, then, prevented her from eating the poisoned food given her by the Vrykyl, the Lady Valura.

He had saved the elven portion of the Sovereign Stone from capture by the Vrykyl and placed the Sovereign Stone in her care. He had, by Griffith's account, saved her husband's life.

All this he did, so he claimed, to try to make reparation for the sins he'd committed during the time he was servant to Prince Dagnarus.

Feeling as this were part of a dream, not certain that it wasn't, Damra said confusedly, "What are you doing here? How did you find me?"

"As I told you in the house of the Shield, my life is devoted to following the Lady Valura. She meets on the other side of the river with her master, Lord Dagnarus. They discuss their plans for Tromek."

"Their plans? What are their plans?"

"The Lady Valura has seduced the Shield, drawn him into the Void. He has become a Void worshipper, a fact he keeps secret from the living. He cannot keep such a loathsome secret from the dead, however. His own ancestors have repudiated him, will no longer come to aid him. Nor can he keep such a thing secret from the Wyred. They work against him. He has no need of them," said Silwyth. "The Shield has the Void. Void cultists from Dunkarga and Karnu and Vinnengael work their foul magicks for him. Not openly, of course. Not now. That may soon change."

Damra shuddered, sickened, but not surprised.

"He was ever an evil man, scheming and calculating," she said. "The Void was already inside him."

"The Void is inside each of us," said Silwyth. "Thus the gods warned King Tamaros, when they gave him the Sovereign Stone. Do not split it open, the gods said, 'for inside you will find a bitter center.' Yet, impatient and eager to bring this gift of the gods to the world, he refused to heed their warning. Once I thought him arrogant, and I blamed his arrogance for the disaster that he brought down upon his realm, upon his own family. Now that I am older, I believe that he truly thought he was acting for the best. If there was pride involved, it was the pride of believing that he knew what was best."

Damra paid little heed to Silwyth's words. It is the way of the old to ramble. She cut him short.

"Who cares for this ancient history. What of the Tromek? What of my people?" she demanded. "What is happening to them?"

"The Shield and the Divine wage war against each other. Their troops have met in two separate battles. Victory has not yet been determined, either way, but with each meeting, the Divine loses a little more ground. It is only a matter of time."

"What horror is this?" Damra was dismayed. "Are you saying that the Divine will lose this war?"

"The Void is ascendant in the world," said Silwyth. "The Void's power is on the rise, as the power of the elements wanes. 'The center is bitter,' the gods warned Tamaros. So long as the Sovereign Stone remained intact, the Void was contained. When the Stone was split, the Void was unleashed. The Dagger of the Vrykyl surfaced after lying long hidden, and now the Void dominates. When the Shield wins—and he will win, for the Divine is not strong enough to stop him—he will hand Tromek over to Dagnarus, and the Shield will publicly worship him as Lord of the Void."

"This is monstrous!" Damra cried.

"What is?" Griffith murmured sleepily. "What's wrong?"

"Sleep, dear one," she said soothingly, sorry to have wakened him. "Nothing is wrong. Go back to sleep."

He sighed deeply and rolled over.

Waiting until she heard his breathing even out, she said softly, "I must return to Tromek. I must bring the Divine the power of the Sovereign Stone—"

"No!" Silwyth exclaimed. His hand closed over her wrist with bruising force. "Tromek is the last place you must go, Damra of Gwyenoc! Valura expects that you will do just this, and she plans to lie in wait for you. You have earned her enmity, Damra. Valura blames you for her failure to bring her lord both the elven and the human parts of the Sovereign Stone. She has vowed to kill you and drag your soul to the Void.

"She and Dagnarus know you are here in New Vinnengael. They know you visited the palace. The young king is a Vrykyl named Shakur, one of the eldest and most powerful. You fought him at the Western Portal. He recognized you. The Vrykyl are searching for you even now. Valura is searching . . ."

"How do you know all this?" Damra demanded, her suspicions of Silwyth returning. "How do you know what this Valura thinks and what she and her evil lord plot? How did you find me? How do you come to be on this ship? Perhaps the answer to these questions is that you are Vrykyl yourself."

"If I were a Vrykyl, Damra of Gwyenoc, you would already be dead.

I gave you my reasons in the house of the Shield. As for Valura, I have been following her, as I told you. I have listened to them plotting together. They take care to keep their voices soft, but I hear the very whispers of their souls. How not? Once, our souls were intertwined, tangled in a knot that they cannot now unravel. The Void is ascendant. But it has not yet won. The gods and other forces continue to fight against it."

"But how can I fight if I am not to return to my homeland?" Damra asked, exasperated. "What good is the elven portion of the Sovereign Stone if it remains hidden away? Where am I supposed to go, and what am I supposed to do?"

"I have thought on this long, Damra. For many hundreds of years, in fact. The only way to reduce the power of the Void is to return the Sovereign Stone to those who made it."

Damra blinked at him. Sick and weary, she was finding it hard to follow his reasoning. "The gods made the Sovereign Stone. You want me to return the Stone to the gods? Now, when humans have just found their part of the Stone? They would grow strong, and we elves would dwindle. Is that your idea?"

"I do not speak of returning only the elven portion. All four parts of the Stone must come together in the location where the Stone was given to Tamaros—the Portal of the Gods."

Silwyth is an old man, Damra said to herself, and old men have strange fancies, harking back to the days of their youth. It would be impolite to challenge him, and I don't want to start an argument. I am too tired.

The medicine the ork had given her was working. She was no longer nauseated. She could endure the gentle rocking of the ship without feeling her stomach rock with it. Weak and wobbly, she wasn't going to be going anywhere for a while, and neither was Griffith. They would not be in fit shape to travel until tomorrow or the next day. By then, Shadamehr would be on board and she could explain matters to him and perhaps even obtain his help to return to her homeland. For that was where she intended to go, back to Tromek. And she would take the Sovereign Stone with her.

"The decision is yours to make, Damra," said Silwyth, reading her mind. "But I ask you to think of this. The Void grew in power because the Sovereign Stone was split asunder."

"Meaning that if the four parts are put back together, the Void will once again be contained." Damra shook her head. "One cannot put baby spiders back inside the egg sack."

"Yet, perhaps one should try," said Silwyth, releasing her wrist, "before the spiders grow large enough to devour the world."

An old man's fancy.

"I will think on it," she said.

There was no answer.

"Silwyth?"

Damra stared into the darkness, listened for the sound of breathing, padding footfalls, wood creaking.

Nothing. Night embodied could not have been more quiet.

Night embodied.

Thinking of that, Damra fell asleep.

THE SEWER SYSTEM OF NEW VINNENGAEL WAS NOT EXTENSIVE. ITS network of tunnels ran from the Temple and the palace—the two major building complexes in the city—and emptied into the Arven River. The sewers had been built by those Earth magi who possessed engineering skills, using their magic to burrow through the bedrock. There had been some talk of extending the sewer system to serve the entire city. The expense of such a massive building program was deemed to be too great and, after considerable argument, the project was abandoned. The rest of New Vinnengael followed the ages-old practice of dumping their slop into gutters that ran down the center of the streets and were flushed out naturally with rainwater during the wet season or with water pumped from the river if the rains did not fall.

Rain had not fallen for almost a week, which meant that it was time for the pumps to be put into action. But the sudden appearance of an enemy army camped on the river's western shores drove all thoughts of street-cleaning from the heads of city officials. River water was being pumped, but it was flowing into barrels and buckets, meant to be used to put out the fires of war.

"Lucky for us," Shadamehr said to the slumbering Alise. "Otherwise, we'd be hip deep in gunk. Whereas now it's only wetting my toes."

Shadamehr was familiar with the sewer system. As a child, he and the late king, Hirav, had sneaked out of the palace on numerous occasions to go cessrat-hunting in the sewers. Taking along their slingshots, they had pretended they were chasing wild boar or trolls or other monsters. The hunt always ended with a swim in the river—jumping in clothes and all—to rid themselves of incriminating evidence, or so they fondly thought. Then they would lie in the sunshine to dry off before returning to the palace, happy and tired and stinking to the high heavens.

"We couldn't have fooled anyone but dear old Nanny Hanna," Shadamehr confided to Alise, the memories of those carefree times returning to him forcibly as he once more walked the twisting, turning tunnels. He fed on the memories, using them to take his mind off the fact that he was growing weaker with every step. And they were a long way from their destination.

"Nanny Hanna," he said, pausing a moment to rest. "Sweet woman, but none too bright."

He looked at Alise, hoping for a response, but she remained asleep. Nothing roused her, not the stench, not his voice, not the flaring lantern light, not even when he'd accidentally bumped her head while trying to climb down a ladder with her slung over his shoulder. He wondered, with a pang, if she would ever waken. He'd known people to fall into such deep slumbers that they could not be wakened to take food and slowly starved to death. So even though the Grandmother had said Alise might sleep for a day or more, Shadamehr talked to her, hoping for some sign that she heard him.

"Hirav always told her he'd slipped and fallen in the privies," Shadamehr recalled. "She always believed him."

Shadamehr settled Alise more comfortably over his shoulder, or at least tried to. The muscles in his neck and shoulder, arms and back and legs throbbed and ached. Sweat rolled down his face and neck. He would have liked to stop longer to rest, but he feared that he if stayed still too long, he might not have the strength to continue.

"I often think now," he said, flashing the dark lantern at a place where two tunnels branched off from the main sewer, "of the danger we were in. Once we were nearly caught in a flash flood. Why we both weren't drowned is a mystery to me. Fortunately, we were near a maintenance ladder and managed to escape. We thought it a great lark. Didn't have brains enough to be scared.

"I wonder which way to go?" he asked himself, staring thoughtfully at the two tunnels. "I seem to remember one way leads back toward the

Temple. The other is the one we just came down. It leads to the palace, while the third leads down to the river. That way"—he flashed the lantern light—"looks as if it goes uphill, so that must lead to the Temple. We'll take the tunnel to the right. I seem to remember that right is the way."

He took a step, felt his legs start to tremble. Breathing heavily, he lurched against a wall.

"I just need to stretch," he told himself. "Work out the kinks. Then I'll be fine."

He placed the dark lantern on the floor of the tunnel and doused the light. He would ever after wonder why he did that—shutting off the light. Instinct? The teachings of his youth? Keep to the dark in dark places had always been an old dictum of his father's. Or was it squeamishness? Shadamehr's stomach was still a bit unsettled, and he didn't want to look at what he was stepping in. Or was it the charm of the Grandmother's turquoise? He would never know. All he knew was at that moment, he doused the light.

Gently, he lowered Alise down to the floor, propped her up against the curved and slimy wall, and tucked the blanket snugly around her.

"Sorry about the filth, dear. I'll buy you a new dress."

Straightening as best he could—he didn't remember the tunnel ceilings being this low—he massaged his aching leg and shoulder muscles.

"Not much farther," he encouraged himself. "Not much farther."

"Skedn?" hissed a voice, and it wasn't Alise.

Shadamehr froze in the darkness. The voice had come from the direction of the right-hand tunnel. Harsh and guttural, it sounded like no voice he'd ever heard before. He waited, breathless, unmoving. Although he couldn't understand the words, he could guess at the meaning: *Did you hear that?*

The owner of the voice also waited, unmoving. Then another voice spoke, in response to the first.

"No skedn."

The language had the sound of jagged rocks being tumbled down a mountainside. The creatures didn't appear to be slow-witted, didn't mumble like trolls. There was a note of command in the first voice and deference in the second that was indicative of structure, discipline, organization.

"Taan!" Shadamehr guessed with an inward groan.

He recalled what his scouts had told him of the taan—fierce monsters, they walked upright like humans and used weapons as well or better than most humans. The taan were fearless in battle, fought with intelligence and skill.

His first wild notion was that he might be facing the entire taan army planning on taking the city by attacking from the sewers. More rational thought prevailed. Thousands of warriors could not march through the sewers. These were advance scouts, searching for weak points in the city's defenses.

"And, by the gods, they found one," Shadamehr said to himself. "And we're trapped like cessrats."

He dared not retreat. The taan had heard something, perhaps him talking to himself, and they were on the alert. His only weapon was a dagger he had concealed in his boot. The palace guards had taken his sword and his other weapons from him, but they'd missed the dagger. He might have asked for Ulaf's sword, back at the inn, but he'd had too many other things on his mind to think of it. Thanks to either his father, the love of the gods, or his own good sense, he'd doused the light that would have given away their presence.

Crouching, moving slowly and silently, he pressed himself close to the wall, made himself as small as possible, and quieted his breathing. He cursed the loud thudding noise of his own heartbeat, which seemed to echo through the tunnel. After some quiet fumbling in the muck, he discovered a good-sized rock. He slid his dagger from his boot. His other hand closed over the rock.

The taan remained stationary, still listening. Shadamehr was quiet. They were quiet. All of them were so quiet that he could hear the clicking of cessrat claws along the stone floor.

One of the taan made an explosive sound, a cross between a grunt and a hoot, that nearly did the trick of silencing Shadamehr's heartbeat by stopping it cold. He braced himself for a rush, but then came the sound of shrill, terrified squeaks, a scrabbling sound, the stomping of feet, and the squeaks ended.

"Rtt," said the first voice, and laughed.

Amid scattered chortles, the taan resumed their march.

Shadamehr breathed again, felt chill sweat trickle down his shirt.

Torchlight flared. The taan had arrived at the junction of the three tunnels and stopped to confer. Shadamehr had his first good look at the creatures.

He was impressed and dismayed. Any hopes that he might have harbored for New Vinnengael holding out against thousands of these warriors washed away like so much sewage.

The taan were five in number. Their faces were savage, bestial, with protruding snouts and large mouths filled with razor-sharp teeth. Their hair was long and ragged. Small, squinting eyes glared out from beneath overhanging foreheads. The eyes glittered with the same intelligence he'd heard in the voices. Their bodies were humanlike, but far more muscular and powerfully built. They were festooned with weapons of every type—some human, some elven, some of their own creation, perhaps. Their armor was the same bizarre assortment, probably stolen from the corpses of their victims.

They would occasionally lift their heads and sniff the air, by which Shadamehr gathered that the taan relied on scent for much of their information about the world around them, and he blessed the stench of the sewer.

The taan appeared puzzled over which route to take. They spent some time discussing the matter. Since the taan used their hands as much as their voices for talking, Shadamehr was able to follow the argument.

One taan wanted to split the group, apparently, for he pointed up Shadamehr's tunnel, then pointed to himself. Indicating another tunnel, he pointed to the leader. The leader considered this, but was dubious. He shook his head and jabbed his finger emphatically at the tunnel that led to the Temple.

Shadamehr naturally sided with the leader and mentally urged him to stand firm. The discussion continued. Either out of boredom or fear, the taan who was holding the torch took it into his ugly head to flash the light around. The light lit up Shadamehr, so that his white shirt and Alise's white blanket glowed like the eyes of a girl at her first dance.

The taan drew in a hissing breath, gave a hoot. The leader whipped around. The taan pointed straight at Shadamehr.

"That's torn it," he said to himself.

He rose to his feet, stood protectively over Alise, dagger in one hand, the rock in the other.

"The last stand of Shadamehr," he remarked. " 'Died in a sewer, devoured by rats.' Terrible song. Not a bad rhythm, but where do you go from there? Nothing rhymes with sewer."

"Derrhuth," said the lead taan, sneering.

Drawing his sword—an outlandish-looking blade with a serrated edge—the beast-man strode forward. The other taan held back, grinning and waiting for the show.

"Deer hoot, yourself!" said Shadamehr loudly.

The taan warrior drew near, his teeth bared, snarling. He sniffed the air and then, suddenly, the taan halted. He stared, his squinty eyes opening wide. The taan gulped. He dropped his sword into the muck.

The taan who had been arguing with the leader barked out a question.

The lead taan half turned. "Kyl-sarnz!" he hissed, over his shoulder.

The four taan stared at Shadamehr. The torchbearer took a step backward. "Kyl-sarnz!" he repeated, awed.

"Kyle Zarnzzt," said Shadamehr, having no idea what was going on, but determined to take advantage of the situation. "That's me. Kyle Zarnzzt. Remember that name." He gestured with his dagger toward the tunnel that led to the Temple. "Go that way. Kyle Zarnzzt commands it."

The blade caught the light, flashed brightly. The taan cringed and bowed low.

"Nisst, Kyl-sarnz," he said in reverent tones. "Nisst, Kyl-sarnz."

Rejoining his group, the taan jerked his head and his thumb in the direction of the tunnel that Shadamehr had indicated. All five of the taan bowed low, intoning the phrase, "Kyl-sarnz" over and over. Then, with a rush of feet, they turned and dashed up the sewer.

"I'll be a double-damned dingo dog," said Shadamehr.

He had no idea what was going on and no intention of staying around to find out. Gathering up Alise in his arms, he hastened down the tunnel in the direction of the river. His aches and pains were gone. He had never felt so strong.

"Gut-wrenching terror is a wonderful tonic," he commented to Alise. "Someone should bottle it."

The wonderful restorative powers of fear carried Shadamehr clear to the sewer's end. A huge iron grate blocked off the outlet where the sewer emptied into the river. The gate had been placed there to prevent an enemy from doing just what the taan had done—using the sewer to sneak into the city.

The heavy iron grate, which took three strong men to lift, had been torn by brute force from its moorings and flung aside. Shadamehr thought back to the taan, to their muscular arms. He thought back to himself, standing there facing them with a knife and a rock.

"Shadamehr," he said, "you are one lucky bastard."

The river ran dark and sluggish about three feet from the sewer's outlet. A maintenance ladder led up from the tunnel. Refuse too large to pass through the grate had piled up at the bottom. Shadamehr did not look too closely at the heap. Flashing the dark lantern over the floor, he could see wet footprints leading away from a crude boat, drawn up on the narrow stone outcropping that formed the lip of the sewer opening. He recalled Rigiswald saying something to the effect that all taan are afraid of water.

"Hah!" Shadamehr stated. "So much for that theory. Wait until I tell him! It's not every day I can prove that old man wrong. Now, my dear, one last haul up this ladder."

He paused at the bottom, wondered if he could make it. At least there was fresh air to breathe here. He drew in several deep breaths, then, clasping Alise firmly, placed his hands and feet on the rungs of the ladder.

" 'Girding his loins, the gallant knight climbed her hair to reach the maiden fair.' " Shadamehr sang the old minstrel lay beneath his breath, trying to ignore the pain that was shooting through his legs. "How does one gird one's loins. I've often wondered . . ."

He paused, bit his lip, and sucked in another breath. Sweat poured down his face. His arms trembled, and his legs burned. He could see the top, but it was at least as far away as the moon. Maybe farther.

"Whether my loins are girded or not, they hurt like the blazes," he muttered. "I wonder if that gallant knight chap had this much trouble climbing her hair. Of course, he was going to see the maiden fair. He wasn't hauling her up a ladder, so that probably made the difference."

Shadamehr reached the opening, to find that it was covered by an iron plate meant to keep pedestrians from tumbling down and breaking their necks. Those small boys who had played in the sewer so long ago had been able to lift up the iron plate without too much trouble, crawl out from underneath it. Shadamehr hoped with all his heart that some energetic city official had not decided to bolt the plate in place.

To his vast relief, the plate shifted when he touched it. It moved so easily, in fact, that he wondered if the current crop of small boys had taken up the cessrat hunt. That made him think of the stories he'd heard—how the taan tortured, then ate their prisoners. He thought of all the children who lived and played in New Vinnengael, and he cursed bitterly those adults who would bring childhood to such a terrible end.

"I wonder if Dagnarus was ever a little boy?" Shadamehr asked Alise, as he maneuvered her out the opening. Once she was safely on firm ground, he pulled himself up and out and collapsed onto the street. He lay there gasping for breath and blinking up at the stars, feeling tiny pinpricks of pain jab his calf and thigh muscles. He had no idea what time it was.

"Dagnarus must have been a little boy," Shadamehr mused dreamily. "He wasn't born Lord of the Void. He must have hunted cessrats, played truant from his tutor, thrown sugar buns . . . at servants, just like . . . poor little king . . . murdered . . . 'Void take him' . . . already has . . . keep him, then . . ."

Shadamehr jerked himself awake. " 'Ods bodkin! There's a lark. Escape taan only to be discovered taking a snooze by the Imperial Cavalry. Got to wake up. Madness and folly."

He tried to stand, but his legs wobbled, and pain gripped him in the back, so that he bit his lips to suppress a cry. Tears stung his eyes.

"You have to keep going," he told himself angrily.

"I can't," he answered himself. "I have to rest. Just a few moments." He patted the slumbering Alise on the shoulder. "I'll just rest for a few moments. We'll be safe here."

Shadamehr leaned back against a stone wall. "No, we won't. The taan will come back. The guards will come by. It will be dawn soon. Unless it's only just turned night. Maybe we were down there a whole day. Maybe we were down there six whole days. I'm sorry, Alise. Gods, I'm sorry. I'm sorry about everything . . ."

"Grum'olt," said a deep voice.

Shadamehr opened his eyes, peered up. He couldn't see much in the darkness, just two large, bulky shapes blotting out the stars. Shadamehr tensed, his hand strayed to his dagger. Then he sniffed.

The air was redolent with the scent of fish oil.

Shadamehr smiled and relaxed.

"Gods love you," he murmured, and passed out cold.

One of the orks picked up the baron in his strong arms and slung him effortlessly over his shoulder.

"Phew! Stinky!" said the ork to his fellow, who was gathering up Alise.

"Humans," the second ork grunted, wrinkling his nose in disgust.

Concerned to hear that patrols were out searching the city for Baron Shadamehr, Captain Kal-Gah had posted his people all along the waterfront, with instructions to keep watch for the baron. The captain chuckled to hear that his men had found the baron crawling out of a sewer. His men tossed the baron and Alise in the shore boat. The captain climbed in and ordered the sailors to pull hard for the ship.

Once on board, the captain consulted the first mate in regard to the tide and his shaman in regard to the omens. The first mate reported that the tide was almost at the flood and they could lift anchor and sail at the captain's pleasure. The shaman reported that the omens were good for leaving, bad for staying. The captain wasted no more time.

As dawn filled the skies with pink flame that set the lake afire, the orks sailed down Arven River. Everyone in the ship could see the taan forces massing on the riverbank across from the city of the New Vinnengael. The taan saw them as well and fired a volley of arrows that fell short of their mark. One arrow actually made it as far as the deck. Captain Kal-Gah smashed the black-feathered bolt to pieces with his bootheel, then picked it up what was left of it and tossed it overboard.

The orks bore Shadamehr and Alise below decks, bedded them down in the same small cabin where they'd taken the elves. Alise slept soundly, so soundly that the shaman pinched her to make certain she was not dead—a corpse aboard ship was the very worst luck possible. Seeing her flesh turn red and noting that the patient flinched, the shaman was satisfied.

She turned to Shadamehr. He slept fitfully, at one point shouting something unintelligible and flailing about with his arms. The shaman eyed him, but let him be. Dreams are the bearers of powerful omens and orks are careful not to waken a dreamer, even if he is in the throes of a nightmare.

When the baron quieted, the shaman felt it safe to approach. Holding the lantern over him, she saw the dried blood on the baron's shirt. Quai-ghai was pleased. She enjoyed practicing the healing arts, and she rarely had the chance.

Orks have no skill in healing magic and are thus thrown back to remedies of their own devising. Quai-ghai had developed a marvelous unguent that she used on all occasions, claiming it capable of healing all injuries, from arrow punctures to compound fractures. While the unguent was successful in fighting infection, it burned like fire when applied to the wound, giving the patient the sensation of being roasted alive. Once this side effect passed, the unguent caused the patient to break out in a ferociously itchy skin rash that completely incapacitated him for days. Rather than scratch themselves raw, most of the orks aboard ship preferred to take their chances with natural healing and ran for their lives when they saw the shaman approach.

Here, Quai-ghai was pleased to see, was a patient who did not have to be strapped down like those other cowards.

She ordered her loblolly boy off to the ship's surgery to collect a jar of her special unguent and was waiting impatiently for him to return when she noted something odd about her patient. She stared down at Shadamehr and frowned and growled in her throat. Moving to the other bed, she shook the male elf by the shoulder.

Griffith roused with a start and looked around in bewilderment, unable to remember where he was. The sight of the ork shaman standing over him brought back his memory. He sat up gingerly, expecting his stomach to heave and roll with the pitching of the ship, whose movements were much more lively now that they were under way. His head was clear, however, his stomach at peace.

Griffith smiled his grateful thanks. "Your remedy worked, Quai-ghai."

"Of course it worked," she flared, insulted. "What did you expect?"

Griffith flushed, embarrassed. "Truly I did not mean—"

The ork brushed his apology aside.

"You told me when we met in the baron's keep that you had made a study of Void magic," Quai-ghai stated. "Was that the truth or a lie?"

"I do not lie, Quai-ghai," said Griffith mildly.

"And right there you have told a lie," she said complacently. "All elves are liars. All know it. No harm in that. Orks lie, too, when there is need. Was that the truth or a lie?"

"I have studied Void magic," said Griffith, thinking it best not to argue the matter further. "Why do you ask?"

Noting her grave expression, Griffith realized that this was not idle curiosity and he was alarmed. "Do you suspect the presence of Void magic somewhere?"

Quai-ghai grunted. "Come here."

She led him from his bed across the narrow cabin to another bed. Because of the gloom of the ship's interior, he could not see the bed's occupant until Quai-ghai held the lantern over his face.

"Baron Shadamehr!" Griffith exclaimed. "Is he all right?"

"You tell me," said Quai-ghai. "He smells bad."

"He does, that," agreed Griffith, covering his nose and mouth with his hand, feeling his stomach lurch.

"No, not that way." Quai-ghai was irritated. "Worse. You say you know Void magic. Find out."

"I think I understand what you mean." Griffith looked intently at his slumbering patient, then glanced at Quai-ghai. "I will have to cast a Void spell to find out."

She backed well out of range. Turning away her head, she stopped up her ears with her hands.

Griffith murmured the words that were like spiders crawling around his mouth. He spit them out as quickly as he could, cast the spell.

Shadamehr flinched and cried out in his sleep.

"How very strange," Griffith murmured.

He intoned soothing words, and the baron relaxed, sank back onto the hard bed, and sighed deeply.

Griffith touched Quai-ghai on the shoulder. She gave a violent start, unstopped her ears.

"You were right," he said. "Look there."

The baron's body gave off a faint glow, as can sometimes be seen with bodies that lie too long unburied.

"He reeks of the Void," said Griffith.

SHADAMEHR'S BODY MIGHT HAVE SLUMBERED, BUT HIS MIND WAS active. He walked and walked, traveling through a landscape that was brown and gray and barren, flat and rock-strewn. He had no apparent destination, yet he held to a course and was frustrated and angry when an obstacle blocked his way. He plodded slowly down a road for hours on end, never seemed to be getting anywhere, only to skip over mountaintops as if he had the legendary boots of the giant, Krithnatus, that gave him the power to hop about the world in seconds.

He was in a city where he knew his way. He moved rapidly, with only a fleeting impression of his surroundings. He was aware of destroyed buildings and streets that were broken, shattered. The entire city was empty and deserted. He was alone, and the knowledge saddened him, but didn't surprise him.

He came to an enormous pile of rubble, that had once been a magnificent building, or so he seemed to remember. Next moment, he was underneath the building, with no idea how he came to be there, but that didn't surprise him either. Although he could see nothing for the darkness, he knew that he was in a large round room, standing beneath a domed ceiling.

He was very close to the gods. If he reached out his hand, he could touch them.

Shadamehr resolutely kept his hands at his side.

Someone else was in the room. Someone who seemed to have been waiting for him. How Shadamehr saw him, he couldn't say, for the room was pitch-dark. The man was young, and he might have been considered comely, but for the fact that his face was marred by a birthmark.

"You are Baron Shadamehr, the bearer of the human part of the Sovereign Stone," said the young man.

Shadamehr didn't answer yea or nay. He was uncomfortable and wanted to leave. Believing this to be a dream, he tried to wake himself, but that didn't work.

"Dagnarus is searching for the four portions of the Sovereign Stone," the young man continued. "Once he has them in his possession, he will join them together, at which point he will become so powerful that no person, no country, no nation will be able to rise up against him. He has the Dagger of the Vrykyl to grant him innumerable lives. He will rule Loerem for centuries. This is his plan. He needs only the four portions of the Sovereign Stone to bind all races to him."

"That is a big 'only,' " said Shadamehr. "You have the advantage of me, sir. You know my name, and I do not know yours."

"I am Gareth," said the young man.

"Gareth," Shadamehr repeated. "Why do I know that name?"

"Hark back to the legends and the lore you have heard about Dagnarus, and you will find me among them. I was the whipping boy. After that, I was his sorcerer."

"A sorcerer of the Void, if I remember my legends. You helped to bring about the destruction of Old Vinnengael. Excuse me for speaking bluntly, Master Gareth, but you are dead. And I am dreaming."

"I am dead. You are not dreaming, however. You are the bearer of one part of the Sovereign Stone, and that is why I have summoned your soul to this place. When the gods gave Tamaros the Sovereign Stone, the stone was intact. He was warned not to split it apart, for he would find that the center was 'bitter.' He did not heed the warning of the gods. He split the stone asunder and gave a portion of it to each of the races: human, dwarven, elven, orken. What he did not know was that there was a fifth portion—a portion none of them could see, for they were not looking for it.

"One person saw that portion, however. He was only a child, but he was looking for it, and it was looking for him. The fifth portion of the Sovereign Stone was the Void. Dagnarus accepted it, when it was offered, and he has served the Void ever since. He has served it well, and now the Void grows in power, as the power of the gods wanes.

"To enhance that power, Dagnarus seeks the four portions of the Sovereign Stone. He will find them. For two hundred years, the human part of the Stone remained lost. Then Lord Gustav found it and within moments of its discovery, Dagnarus was aware of it. His Vrykyl, Svetlana, came very close to seizing it. The gods protected the Stone, and it has escaped him thus far. The power of the Void grows stronger by the minute, however, and the Stone cannot remain hidden for long. Dagnarus never sleeps. He searches for it, day and night. He can see even in the darkest darkness. You scurry about, hither and thither, but where will you hide, Baron, that he cannot find you?"

Shadamehr shrugged and smiled. He very carefully did not look at the knapsack he wore slung about his shoulder.

"It makes a good ale story," he said, "but I have no idea what you're talking about."

Gareth smiled and pointed at the baron's heart.

Glancing down, Shadamehr saw that he wore the Sovereign Stone around his neck and that its radiant light blazed in the darkness like a beacon fire.

"Damnation," he said, and wrapped his hand about the Stone to quench the light.

The light welled through his fingers, so that beams of it shot through the dusty room in which he stood, shone clear to heaven.

"Suppose I concede that you have a point, Master Gareth," Shadamehr said, embarrassed. "Just suppose, mind you. What do you suggest I do with the bloody thing? I assume you have a suggestion. Otherwise, why bring me here?"

"You must undo what King Tamaros did. You must return the Sovereign Stone to the gods. In order for that to happen, the pieces must come together here, in the Portal of the Gods."

"All four pieces?" Shadamehr asked, incredulous.

"*All* the pieces," Gareth repeated.

"Why not throw in the sun, the moon, a couple of stars, and the eyetooth of a dragon while you're at it," Shadamehr muttered.

Gareth had no reply. He began to dissolve, like an oil portrait over which someone has passed a wet rag.

"I have said all I have to say."

"No you haven't," Shadamehr said loudly. "I have a question. If you gods didn't want Tamaros to split open the damn Stone, why did you give it to him? If I hand a child a fragile vase and he drops it and breaks it, do I punish the child? *I*"—Shadamehr struck himself on the breast—"*I* am the one at fault, for I am older and wiser than the child, and I should have known what was going to happen."

He shouted into the heavens, trying to make someone hear him. "You gods gave Tamaros this vase, and he dropped it—there's a big surprise—and now we're left to pick up the pieces and try to glue the damn thing back together! Does this make sense to you? What purpose does it serve?

"Or, here's a thought, maybe it was a test? A test for King Tamaros. He failed! Hey, he's human. What did you expect? You must have known he would fail. You gods know everything. If you don't, you're no better than we are, and why should I worship you? If you did know, then that means you were just playing with him. That means you're just playing with us. And that makes you worse than us!

"And you wonder why I didn't undergo your Transfiguration to become a Dominion Lord! Listen to me, damn you. Don't you walk away! I'm not the one who is supposed to have charge of this Stone!"

Shadamehr strode forthrightly into the gray nothingness and woke to find the ork shaman picking him up in her powerful arms with the avowed intention of tossing him into the sea.

After much earnest pleading, Griffith persuaded Quai-ghai that she should not immediately heave the groggy and disoriented baron over the taffrail. Griffith argued strenuously with both her and the captain, trying to persuade them that Shadamehr had *not* been dabbling in Void magic, as Quai-ghai believed. Shadamehr was "tainted by Void," a condition that did afflict those who cast Void magic, but which could, on rare occasions, happen to those unfortunate enough to have been on the receiving end of an extremely powerful Void spell.

Orks fear and detest Void magic, and Griffith might not have succeeded in persuading them, had not the ship's cat—an enormous gray-blue male with golden eyes—rubbed his head against Shadamehr's leg, looked up at him, and meowed.

Kal-Gah looked speculatively at Quai-ghai. Orks are very fond of cats, and every orken vessel has several.

"Nikk likes him," said Kal-Gah, petting the cat.

"True," said Quai-ghai. "A good omen. He may stay."

The question of how Shadamehr had come in contact with powerful Void magic intrigued Griffith. He would have liked to question him, but the baron was obviously in no condition to be discussing anything. Griffith assisted the stumbling, groaning Shadamehr back to his rest. The baron fell into bed facefirst. He reached out his hand to touch the knapsack reassuringly and, after that, did not move.

Griffith cast a spell over Alise, as she lay sleeping, and found that she was also tainted by Void. He knew from gossip around the baron's keep that Alise had once been a member of the Order of Inquisitors, the only members of the Church permitted to learn Void. He recalled that Alise had cast a Void spell in order to rescue them from the palace guard. Even such a simple spell as reducing iron bars to iron shavings would have left her tainted by Void, plus given her the nasty side effects that come with the use of Void magic.

Here was the mystery. Alise was tainted by Void to such an extent that he found it difficult to understand how she had managed to survive. Her skin should be covered with welts and pustules, the toll required of those who wield the magic that is powered by one's own life energies. Alise's skin was smooth and unblemished as fresh milk.

Griffith could find only one possible explanation for such a phenomenon. Tucked carefully in the bodice of her chemise was a large, polished turquoise, blue as the sky and glittering with silver striations.

Griffith would have liked to talk all this over with Damra, but she had spent a restless night, talking and muttering in her sleep, and he had no thought of waking her. He himself was feeling rested and well. The ork medicine had settled his stomach, but he did not yet have his sea legs, as the orks termed it. They walked the rolling deck with ease while he stumbled about like a drunkard. He even found himself wondering what there might be to eat.

He was directed to the galley, where he nearly pitched headfirst down a ladder. An ork grabbed him in the nick of time, saving him from breaking his neck. Griffith was given some brown bread, which he took back with him up top, to stand in the bright sunshine and watch the distant shore slide past.

"We are making good time," said Captain Kal-Gah, and he eyed Griffith approvingly. "The wind is from the north. An 'elf wind.' I am glad now I brought you on board."

Griffith could have told the captain that the wind blew generally from the north this late in the year and that the elves had nothing to do with it, but he kept silent on that score. Knowing the orks from having lived among them at Shadamehr's, Griffith was confident that he would be blamed for something before the day was out. He didn't mind, therefore, taking credit for the wind.

"How far are we from New Vinnengael?" he asked.

"Far enough," growled the captain, "to be safe from the foul snar-ta." He grimaced as he spoke, his lip curling in disgust.

Snar-ta. Orken for "eaters-of-flesh." Kal-Gah was referring to the rumors that had circulated among the baron's people that the taan were known to eat the flesh of their enemies. They were supposedly particularly fond of ork.

"Have they attacked New Vinnengael yet, do you think?" Griffith asked, trying to look northward, into the wind, and finding it difficult.

Captain Kal-Gah shrugged. "We have seen no smoke of burning. But that doesn't mean much, since the city is made of rock."

He turned back to his sailing, obviously not interested in the fate of a city and a people he considered his enemies.

The wind was crisp and biting and blew right through Griffith's woolen cloak and the robes he wore beneath. He made his staggering way to a part of the deck out of the wind and warmed by the sun. He munched on his bread, taking care to share with some of the seagulls in thanks for their assistance with the omen, and looked up to the white mass of sails spread above his head, the intricate tangle of ropes, and the tall, straight masts that seemed to brush the heavens. He marveled at the skill and dexterity of the orken sailors and thought to himself that this was truly wonderful.

He was happy and relaxed, and he knew the reason why. For the first time in many years, he wasn't responsible for anything or anybody, not even himself. True, an evil force searched for them, but, for the moment, the eyes of the Void were focused on New Vinnengael. The orks had the running of the ship and would not welcome his interference. His friends were safe and seemingly well; the taint of Void would wear off in time.

His dear wife had been troubled during the night, but she slept easily now. He had nothing to do, nowhere to go, except where the wind took him. The last time he'd known such peace as this was in his childhood, after the Wyred had come to claim him.

Griffith had been four years old at the time. A precocious child, one of seven boys born to a minor noble. Griffith had known from the time he'd developed the ability to reason that he was different from his siblings. Quiet, introspective, he took no part in the games of competition and combat in which his brothers delighted. He stood apart, watching from the sidelines.

His brothers badgered Griffith constantly to join in their mock battles, and grew angry when he refused. Griffith detested noise and rows. He moved and spoke quietly, so quietly that his mother complained that she often forgot he was around and was startled to find him underfoot. His father, a warrior born, sided with his brothers and accused his mother of coddling the boy, while his mother accused the rest of bullying him.

Lonely, miserable, Griffith remembered well the night the Wyred came to take him away from his home, to take him to freedom.

Most children are terrified of the black-clad figures who creep into their rooms at night and steal them from their beds. Such children must be calmed with spells, lulled into a magical sleep. Not Griffith. He knew the moment he woke and found the black-masked figures bending over him who they were and why they had come. He never spoke a word, but lifted up his arms to the man, who gave a smothered chuckle.

"We were right about you, I see," he said, his words sliding softly through the black silken mask he wore over his face.

Strong arms clasped Griffith securely, bore him out of the bed he shared with his brothers, and took him to Ergil Amdissyn, the so-called floating castle that is the fortress of the Wyred. Griffith would not see his family for over eighteen years. When he was finally permitted to return, his elder brother told him bluntly that his father had been relieved to find that the Wyred had stolen away his effeminate son. This same elder brother, who was now head of the family, arranged a marriage for his younger sibling, but made it clear that Griffith was not welcome in the family home.

Griffith did not miss his family. They had given him two precious gifts: life and Damra, and he had repaid them for both by saving this very elder brother from assassination. His family did not know the truth, of course, for the Wyred work their magic in secret. Griffith was glad they didn't. It was so much more fun to listen to his brother's tale of his heroic exploits and smile in secret, smug in the knowledge of what had really happened.

Griffith could still remember his first sight of Ergil Amdissyn. He did not know how long he rode, clasped in the strong arms of the Wyred mage, whose task it was to steal children gifted in magic. He remembered sleeping and waking and sleeping again, but whether it was one time or a hundred, he could not recall. The Wyred and his companions never spoke to the child, after that first comment, for one of the first teachings for a young mage is to learn to listen to the silence. Then, one morning, the Wyred roused Griffith from his slumbers and pointed a black-gloved hand.

The location of Ergil Amdissyn is a closely guarded secret of the Wyred, who swear never to reveal it on pain of dishonor, death, and imprisonment: dishonor for the House, death for the wizard, and eternal imprisonment of his soul in the terrible prison house of the dead. But it is not fear that has kept the tongues of the Wyred sealed for centuries. It is pride. Pride in themselves, pride in their work.

Ergil Amdissyn is a fortress built into the peak of a mountain of white granite. According to their history, the fortress was built for the Wyred by the legendary dragon Radamisstonsun, who, in return for a favor done for her by the Wyred, used her powerful Earth magic to carve the inside of the mountain into a fortress, hidden and impregnable.

Ergil Amdissyn does not truly float, but only appears to do so, as on the morning Griffith first saw it with the coming of a brilliant dawn. The mountain rose up from out of the cloud-covered waters of a lake fed by hot streams, so that steamy mists drift perpetually over the lake. It seemed to Griffith that the fortress floated on a fiery red-and-gold-tinged cloud. He stared in awe with the feeling that, at last, he had come home.

Griffith thrived in the strict and studious atmosphere of the Wyred schools, unlike some children, who could never get over their longing for home. Such children usually sickened and died, to be buried in the vaults beneath the mountain. Other children died during the schooling, for the training sessions were arduous and dangerous, meant to weed out the weak, both in mind and body. Those boys and girls who survived went on to become some of the most powerful and skilled magi in Loerem.

Unlike the Revered Brotherhood of the Temple of the Magi, the Wyred do not prohibit the use of Void magic. Although the elves abhor the Void, they understand that it has its place among the four elements, and they encourage their members to study it in order to be able the better to fight it. Some Wyred, such as Griffith, are allowed to choose to make the Void and those things pertaining to it a serious study. Griffith's area of expertise was centered on the Vrykyl, and his thoughts naturally drifted from nostalgic reminiscences of his years spent at Ergil Amdissyn to his studies of the Vrykyl and Shadamehr's dire news that the young king of New Vinnengael had been murdered and his body stolen by one of these foul creatures of the Void.

Griffith was musing on this, and, recalling that Shadamehr had been wounded in the palace, the elf thought that he could at last explain the cause of the Void taint that afflicted both Alise and Shadamehr. Feeling a soft touch upon his arm, he turned to see his wife.

"Do I interrupt you?" Damra asked.

"My thoughts were dark," he said. "I am pleased to have them dispelled. How are you this morning? You spent a restless night. Were you troubled by disturbing dreams?"

"One might say I was troubled by a disturbing awakening," said Damra ruefully. She did not stand close to the railing, as did her husband, but kept a wary distance, casting an uneasy glance at the rushing water that spread out in a wide V-shape from the bow.

"I wish you would step away from there, my love," she added nervously. "I do not think it is safe."

Griffith smiled to himself, but did as his wife asked. He walked back with her to the very center of the ship, drew her over to sit beside him on a wooden chest.

"Silwyth came to see me last night," said Damra.

"Truly, that must have been a disturbing dream," said Griffith.

"It was not a dream," said Damra. "He was here, onboard the ship."

"My dear—" Griffith began.

"I know it sounds crazy. I thought I was dreaming at first, but he spoke to me and put his hand on my wrist. He was as close to me and as real to me as you are right now."

Griffith was dubious, perplexed. "I do not doubt you, my dear, but how—"

Damra shook her head. "His skin and clothes and hair were wet, so I assume he must have swum from the shore, but how he managed to elude the orks or find his way to me is a mystery I cannot explain. But then, Silwyth himself is a mystery. He was once Dagnarus's most loyal servant. If it were not for the fact that he freed you from the Shield's prison and gave into my keeping the elven portion of the Sovereign Stone, I would not . . . I do not . . . And yet . . ."

She halted, unable to express herself, and shrugged helplessly. "I know I'm not making any sense, but then nothing involved with Silwyth makes sense. And yet, it seems that I am supposed to trust him."

Damra cast a sidelong glance at her husband.

Griffith smiled ruefully, and he shrugged. "What can I tell you, my dear? That he might be part of some elaborate conspiracy? That he has done all this to earn our trust with secret plans to destroy us?"

"The last seems most likely," she said grimly.

"Why, what did he say to you?"

"That the power of the Void is ascendant," said Shadamehr. "That no one can stop Dagnarus from gaining the Sovereign Stone, and when he does, he will rule the world as a demigod. That the only way to prevent this is to bring all four parts of the Sovereign Stone to the Portal of the Gods and there join them together. Am I right?"

Damra and Griffith looked up at him in astonishment.

"How did you know that?" Damra gasped.

"Because another of Dagnarus's servants told me the very same thing," said Shadamehr gravely.

WHO SPOKE TO YOU?" DAMRA ASKED, HER ASTONISHMENT increasing.

"Dagnarus's Void sorcerer, Gareth."

"Last night?"

"Yes, while I was asleep. I kept thinking it was a dream, but my dreams very rarely make sense. I show up naked in the royal court, tumble off bridges into ravines, or I'm chased by hordes of beautiful women, that sort of thing."

"Are you never serious, Baron?" Damra demanded coldly.

"I'm serious about this," said Shadamehr. "Or trying to be, at any rate. This dream—if that's what it was—was very realistic. We had a conversation, Gareth and I. At one point, I told him he was dead and at another point he informed me that I was the bearer of the Sovereign Stone. We conceded both points. I was in the ruins of a city that I knew immediately was Old Vinnengael, although I have never before been there, and I was in what I believe to be the Portal of the Gods."

"And Gareth told you to bring the four parts of the Sovereign Stone together—"

"—in the Portal of the Gods," said Shadamehr.

"Strange," said Damra, staring out at the sun-sparkled water. "Very strange."

"You *were* heavily tainted by Void magic, Baron," Griffith pointed out.

"What?" Damra stared back at the baron, her gaze dark and suspicious. "What do you mean, he was tainted by Void?"

Griffith appeared sorry that he had spoken.

Shadamehr glanced at him, glanced away.

"It is a long story," he said briefly. "And it has nothing to do with what we are discussing."

"It might," Damra persisted, her tone severe. "A servant of the Void came to speak to you while you were tainted with Void. You expect us to give credence to what he said?"

"A servant of the Void came to speak to you, and you believe him," Shadamehr returned. "Or does Silwyth not count because he is an elf?"

Damra jumped to her feet. "You had no right to eavesdrop on our conversation," she said angrily.

"Then don't hold your conversations in the open air in the middle of the deck," Shadamehr retorted. "Orks aren't deaf, nor are they stupid. They travel all over the world, and some speak fluent Tomagai."

Griffith put his fingertips and the tips of his thumbs together to form a V-shape.

"What is that?" Shadamehr demanded impatiently.

"A wedge," said Griffith, "being driven between the two of you, the bearers of the Sovereign Stone." He looked from one to the other. "A wedge of Void make and design."

Damra's pale cheeks flushed. She lowered her long lashes, but kept her gaze fixed on the baron.

Shadamehr's lips compressed. Shifting his stance, he stood staring out at the rushing river water. The first mate ordered a couple of orken sailors, who had lingered near, hoping for a fight, to quit gawking and go on about their duties.

"I am sorry," said Shadamehr at last. He rubbed his hand over his face, scratched his chin, which was dark from a day's growth of beard. "Yesterday was probably the worst day of my life, and last night managed to top it. That's my only excuse for being rude, and it's not a very good one."

Turning to Damra, he made a formal bow. "I should not have been listening in on your talk with your husband, Damra of Gwyenoc. I apologize."

"And I am sorry, Baron," said Griffith, bowing. "I should not have said anything about the Void taint without discussing the matter with you first. Please accept my apology. I should explain to you, Damra," Griffith added, "that the baron came by the taint of Void innocently. He was the recipient of a spell that saved his life, or so I believe."

Damra remained unconvinced. "I do not understand what you mean, Griffith. How can a Void spell save a life? Void magic kills!"

"Any magic can be used to kill," said Griffith. "A mage can transfer a portion of his own life essence through the Void into the body of another. The spell is quite dangerous, for it can completely drain the life of the wizard, if he is not careful. Or, I believe in this case, I should say, 'she.' "

Shadamehr's face had gone gray and haggard. He gave another abrupt nod of his head, rubbed his chin, and turned away.

"Alise?" asked Damra, amazed. "But I saw her down belowdecks before I came up. She sleeps as peacefully as a babe—"

"The Grandmother," said Shadamehr. "Grandmother Pecwae festooned her with rocks and brought her back. Alise was dying. I held her in my arms and felt the life seeping out of her. Poor Bashae *is* dead. And it is my fault. All my fault."

"We are all of us weary and wounded, in spirit, if not in body," Damra said remorsefully. She rested her hand gently on Shadamehr's arm. "I am sorry for my part in our quarrel." She hesitated, then added, "Sometimes speaking of the night's shadows in the daylight helps to dispel them."

"True enough," Shadamehr responded. "But it is also true that dark things belong to the darkness and should be kept there. We will talk of this, but below, in our cabin. Besides, I don't want to leave Alise alone."

The three made their way across the rolling deck, holding on to ropes or any solid object that came to hand to keep their balance. The orks grinned and nudged each other, laughing at the lubbers.

"Because of your courage, Baron, both portions of the Sovereign Stone have escaped Dagnarus," said Damra, after Shadamehr had concluded his tale.

"Because of my tomfoolery," he returned ruefully. "And dumb, stupid luck."

"Say, rather, the intercession of the gods," Griffith said gently.

"Then why didn't the gods intercede for Bashae?" Shadamehr demanded. "Never mind. It's my own private quarrel."

He sat on a rickety stool near Alise's bed, holding her hand fast in his own. Griffith stood propped up against a bulkhead. Damra was curled up on the bed that was tucked inside a recessed cubbyhole. The four of them were a tight fit. In order to leave the cabin, two had to squeeze up against a bulkhead while the third climbed over them.

At least they had light. By clearing off the grime, they had uncovered a small porthole that could be opened to admit fresh air and the occasional splash. Shadamehr had obtained clean clothes from the orks, and he had taken a bath beneath one of the pumps. But the sewer smell still lingered unfortunately, making them all glad of the fresh air and the small patch of sunlight.

Damra frowned, clearly not amused. Sacred subjects are not matters for joking. Before she could say anything, however, Alise sat up in bed and cracked her head on the low ceiling.

"Ouch!" Alise clapped her hand over her forehead. "What the—" She peered around in the gloom. "Who is that? Where am I?"

"You are with me, Alise . . ."

"Shadamehr? Is that . . . Are you . . ."

"I am, my dear. I shouldn't be, but I am."

Alise flung her arms around him, clasped him tightly. "Thank the gods!" she breathed, holding him fast.

"Devil take the gods," said Shadamehr fiercely. "Thank *you,* Alise. You saved me. I—"

"No!" she said, suddenly recoiling. "No, don't say that. Don't say anything. If you're not dead, why am I alive? That spell I cast . . ."

She shuddered, huddled away from him, pressed her body up against the bulkhead. "What happened to me?"

He tried to calm her, but he could feel her body tense, go rigid at his touch, and he drew back reluctantly. "Alise . . . the Grandmother . . . do you remember anything?"

"The Grandmother . . ." Alise repeated gently. "Yes, I do remember. I remember sunshine and turquoise skies and lying in sweet-smelling grass and the gods came to me. They said . . . they said . . ."

"What?" Shadamehr asked tersely.

"They said, 'Why did you waste your time trying to save that wicked Baron Shadamehr?' " Alise spoke in a whispering, ghostly monotone, adding softly, " 'The baron who smells like a sewer.' "

"They didn't say that," Shadamehr protested, hurt. "Did they?"

"No," said Alise, relaxing at his touch. But very gently, she pushed his hands away. "That's not what they said."

"What *did* they say? That you are a hero for saving the life of the handsome and wonderful Baron Shadamehr?"

"No, they didn't say that either. Our conversation was private." She squinted. "Damra, is that you? Griffith? What are you two doing here? Why is my bed rocking? And why do *I* smell like a sewer?"

"We're on board an ork ship," Shadamehr explained. "We're fleeing New Vinnengael. And about the sewers—"

"That's a relief, leaving New Vinnengael. I suppose we're on the run, two jumps ahead of the palace guard who are determined, as usual, to hang you or behead you or maybe both." Alise pushed back a few straggling red curls from her eyes, swung her feet over the bed.

"Don't you remember?" Shadamehr asked.

"I find I am hungry, my husband," said Damra hurriedly. "Did you say something about bread in the galley?"

"Yes, I'll show you," Griffith offered. "If you two will excuse us—"

"I'll come with you," said Alise. "I'm ravenous."

Shadamehr caught hold of her wrist.

"Alise, we need to talk."

She lifted her head, shook back her red hair, and looked him in the eye. The two of them were alone in the cabin. The elves, deeply embarrassed, had fled.

"No, we don't. There's nothing to say."

"Alise—"

"Shadamehr." She took hold of both his hands in hers, held them fast. "I know what I need to know. I remember what I need to remember. Nothing has changed between us."

"But it has," Shadamehr said quietly.

"Then it shouldn't," she said, refusing to look at him.

"Alise, you saved my life," said Shadamehr, drawing her close. "Because of me, you nearly died—"

"And so now you are in love with me," she stated, trying to wriggle away. "Now you want to spend the rest of your life with me. Have baby Shadamehrs. Grow old together."

"Yes!" he cried rapturously.

"What?" She stared at him.

"Yes to all that. But not baby Shadamerhs. Baby Alises. Six girls with red hair, like their mother, to plague me and torment me and never do what they're told and . . ." He paused. "We'll have to deal with a few small matters first, of course, such as the Sovereign Stone, which is now in my possession and which a dead man told me to take to Old Vinnenagel and the Lord of the Void, Dagnarus, seizing New Vinnengael and the fact that we're on the run for our lives, but once this is all sorted out—"

"I knew it!" Alise struck him in the chest. She started to push him away, then stopped, looked up at him earnestly. "I don't think it will work, Shadamehr."

"Of course, it will work. The dead man told me—"

Alise smiled, a lopsided smile, held up her hands, made two fists. "I don't mean that. I mean us. Lodestones," she said, hitting them together, bouncing them apart. "You see? I do remember. Now if you'll excuse me, I'm going to go wash the sewer out of my hair."

"Alise," he said, holding her fast. "I don't blame you for not trusting me. I never spoke a serious word in my life before last night and now listen to me. You can't shut me up. I love you, Alise. And not out of gratitude for saving my life," he added sternly, halting the words on her lips. "I calculate that saving my life this one time makes us even for all those other times you put my life in danger."

"I never!" she said indignantly, trying unsuccessfully to wrest her hands from his grip.

"Oh, but you did. There was that time with the trolls. 'Don't ride across the bridge' I warned. But, no, you wouldn't listen and out come three of the biggest trolls I've ever seen in my life, and trolls are damn hard to kill—"

"I'll think about it," Alise promised hastily.

"You'll think about marrying me? Truly?"

"Yes," she said. "Anything not to hear the troll story again. Now will you let me go wash my hair?"

"I was going to suggest it," said Shadamehr. "Quite frankly, my dear, I think it's proof of my love that I even let you get close to me, the way you smell . . ."

Alise gave him a shove that knocked him backward into the bulkhead, kicked his shins for good measure, then turned and marched out.

Alise was an experienced sailor, having accompanied the baron on more than one expedition. Before the day was out, she would have the sailors rigging a pump for her to wash her hair. She would have her chemise hanging from the yardarms and, dressed in clothes borrowed from the orks, be dancing hornpipes at the midnight watch.

"We will work," said Shadamehr, fondly rubbing his bruised shin.

He stood alone in the cabin, smiling at the small, round patch of sunlight. But even as he watched, the sunlight faded away with the passing of a cloud.

Always a cloud. And this time, enormous clouds, masses of clouds. So many they might never see the sun again. He lifted the knapsack containing, presumably, the human portion of the Sovereign Stone. The knapsack looked very ordinary, its leather worn, its stitching frayed. Holding it to what light remained, he opened it up, peered inside, saw nothing except lint. According to Bashae, the knight Gustav had claimed the knapsack to be magical. The Sovereign Stone was hidden in folds of magic and could be revealed only by a secret word.

"Wouldn't it be a great joke," said Shadamehr to himself, "if all this time we've been risking our fool lives for an empty knapsack."

The word he was supposed to speak, "Adele," was on his tongue. He would see this Sovereign Stone. He would see what Bashae had given his life to protect. He would see with his own eyes what all the fuss was about. He was not going to take this on faith. . . .

You are the bearer of the Sovereign Stone.

Gareth's words. That was why Gareth had come to him.

I wasn't dreaming. Shadamehr knew that as certainly as he knew that he loved Alise and that—would miracles never cease—she loved him. She might not know it yet, but he'd convince her. There was just the small problem now of keeping them all alive.

The word "Adele" went unspoken. He could hear, over the creaking of the ship, the voices of Damra and Griffith talking to Alise. He could hear her voice, her laughter.

He draped the worn leather strap over his shoulder. Better get used to carrying it. He didn't dare leave it anywhere for the Void to find. So long as it was his responsibility, he would guard it with his life. As for what happened to the Stone in the future, that was a decision for others to make. He wasn't a Dominion Lord, a blessing for which he was certain the gods must be grateful.

"It's early in the day. Let's see what else I can screw up," he said cheerfully to himself, as he went on deck.

RIGISWALD FROWNED DOWN AT HIS BOOK. THE VOLUME WAS NOT nearly as informative as he had hoped. He shut it with an irritated snap.

"You're a dolt," he told the long-dead author.

Rigiswald sat in his chair, wondering what time it was. Thinking of time made him wonder what day it was. He lost track of time in the library, where there were no clocks, no windows, no town criers insisting that it was noon and all was well. What day was it? Had Ulaf been here last night or the night before? Had a whole day truly passed since then?

Yes, it had, Rigiswald decided. He'd gone to bed, after Ulaf's departure, and slept most of the day. Then he'd eaten a bad supper in the mess hall, then come back to his reading. It had to be close to dawn. He wondered whether or not he should bother going to bed or simply move on to breakfast. He had just decided on the latter, when he felt a touch upon his shoulder.

He looked up to find the head of the Order of Battle Magi looking down.

"They told me I would find you here, sir," Tasgall said in the low tones that were always used in the library. "I would like a word with you."

"I've been expecting you," said Rigiswald, setting aside the book.

A hovering novitiate pounced on the volume and bore it away to whatever safe haven they were using these days.

"The taan won't have any interest at all in the books, you know," said Rigiswald, accompanying Tasgall out of the library. "Few taan can read.

They have no written form of their own language. They wouldn't know what to make of books. Neither would Dagnarus," Rigiswald added.

Tasgall made no response, beyond a flickered glance.

Leaving the library, they walked down a large corridor that smelled of oiled leather and wood and vellum. Off the corridor were meeting rooms furnished with ornately carved tables surrounded by high-backed chairs of dark wood and classrooms. He and Tasgall were the only two in the corridor. The rooms were empty and dark. With the coming of day, this part of the university would be filled with activity, but none walked here at night.

"As a child, Prince Dagnarus often played truant," Rigiswald continued. "We have the account of his tutor, who wrote that Dagnarus preferred hanging about with the soldiers to studying his lessons. Your precious books would be safe enough from him, I should imagine."

"Prince Dagnarus died two hundred years ago," said Tasgall. He spoke in a heavy voice, with no intonation, as if reciting the words by rote.

Rigiswald smiled and ran his hand over his beard, smoothing it.

They walked the length of the corridor before the battle mage halted. He looked back down the hall, the way they had come and, seeing no one in sight, he gestured abruptly to Rigiswald, led the way into one of the meeting rooms.

The room was dark, smelled of chalk.

Tasgall muttered the words to a spell, and the room was filled with a soft gray light. Tasgall glanced about the room, made certain that it was empty. He motioned Rigiswald to seat himself in one of the high-backed chairs, then walked over to look out into the hall, before he shut the door.

Rigiswald settled himself in the chair. Resting his hands upon the arms, he crossed his ankles and waited.

Tasgall pulled out another chair, but the battle mage did not seat himself. He remained standing, his hands clasping the carved slat that adorned the chair's back.

Tasgall in full battle regalia was an impressive sight, a force comprised of a deadly combination of steel and flame. Tonight he was dressed in the soft woolen robes generally worn by the Brethren in their hours of study or relaxation. Devoid of his armor, he was just another human—a middle-aged man in his late forties, the sharp lines of his square-cut, clean-shaven face blurred with fatigue, his dark hair going gray at the temples, his brow furrowed. Tall and powerfully built, he dwarfed his former teacher—the slender, dapper Rigiswald.

Rigiswald had known even then that the dark-eyed, brooding, and intense Tasgall would make an ideal battle magus, and he had advised him to pursue his studies with that goal in mind.

"Where is Baron Shadamehr?" Tasgall demanded abruptly.

"That is not how you speak to someone considerably your elder, Tasgall. Even if you *are* head of the battle magi," Rigiswald returned.

Tasgall's hands tightened their grip on the chair back. "I have been up for two nights. Night before last, I had to deal with your baron, who tried to kidnap the king, then promptly vanished. Then there was the battle with a Vrykyl in a tavern, a Vrykyl who killed one of my people before we sent it back to the Void that spawned it. Yesterday and today I've been dealing with the probability of an enemy invasion. You have only to look across the river, and you will see the fiends camped on the shore! You will forgive me, therefore, sir, if I am somewhat deficient in tact."

Rigiswald raised an eyebrow. Placing the tips of his manicured fingers together, he tapped them gently.

Tasgall let out an exasperated breath, then said, "Do you know where to find the Baron Shadamehr, sir?"

"No, I do not," Rigiswald replied.

"I think you do," said Tasgall.

Rigiswald rose stiffly to his feet. "Then you are calling me a liar. I bid you good morning—"

"Wait, wait! Damn it!" Tasgall moved to block the path of the elderly mage. "We know you are part of the baron's household, that you were his tutor, and you are now his friend and confidant."

"I have that honor, yes," said Rigiswald, still standing.

"The baron rode into the city two days ago—"

"Was I riding with him?" Rigiswald interrupted.

"No, sir, you were not, but—"

"I arrived here several days ago. I have spent my time in the library, as I am certain you know from your spies. I have left once to go to my bed, six times to eat, and eighteen times to go to the privies—my bladder isn't what it used to be—and I met once with the Nimran ambassador, as I am certain your spies have also told you. Did your spies inform you that the Baron Shadamehr came to speak to me on any of those occasions?"

"No, sir," said Tasgall grimly. "He was inside the palace trying to abduct the young king."

"Indeed? And how came he to be in the palace?"

"The Regent wanted to see him."

"What about?"

"I am asking the questions, sir," said Tasgall.

"You asked me one, and I answered it. You didn't like my answer, but that's not my fault. If you have other questions, I will be happy to answer them, but you will probably not like any of those answers either. Therefore, I see no need to continue this fruitless conversation. I am quite weary, and I would like to get what sleep I can before the city comes under siege. Good morning to you, sir. Again."

Rigiswald circled around Tasgall, who did not try to stop him. The elderly magus had nearly reached the door before Tasgall spoke.

"Whatever else the Baron Shadamehr may be, he is no coward. I served with him on the field of battle, as you yourself know, sir. I have seen for myself his tenacity, his resolve, and his courage, and I do not agree with those who say that he refused to undergo the Transfiguration out of cowardice."

Rigiswald halted, turned to look over his shoulder. "Well, sir, and what of it?"

"I have seen Baron Shadamehr in his tomfooleries, I've seen him in his cups, I've seen him in battle, and I have never before seen him afraid. Not until the night he was in the palace. I saw his face, and I saw fear. Something happened to him inside the palace that scared him so that he lunged through a crystal window to a five-story drop onto stone pavement. I want to know what it was."

Rigiswald shook his head, took another step.

"Tell me this, then," said Tasgall. "Does Baron Shadamehr have in his possession part of the sacred Sovereign Stone?"

Rigiswald took another step and another.

"Sir," Tasgall said in tightly controlled, level tones, "I am responsible for the lives of several thousands of our people, not to mention the life of the young king. If you have information that might be useful to me in helping to save those lives, and you withhold that information, then the blood of innocents will be on your hands."

Rigiswald glanced around. "You have no need to concern yourself with the life of the young king. The young king is dead."

"Impossible!" stated Tasgall impatiently. "I just left him. He is sleeping soundly."

"Very soundly," said Rigiswald. "At the bottom of the river. The young king you left slumbering in his bed is a Vrykyl."

Tasgall's jaw worked. His dark eyes flared in ire.

"Where is Baron Shadamehr?" he demanded, his voice taut.

"Ah, we're back to the beginning," said Rigiswald, sighing. "I will tell you that I don't know where he is. You will call me a liar. I will start to walk out—"

"No, sir," said Tasgall. "*I* will walk out." He stalked past Rigiswald, out the door and into the dark corridor beyond.

"I told you that you wouldn't like my answer," remarked Rigiswald.

Tasgall did not look back.

"Gods help us," Rigiswald muttered, as close to a prayer as he'd ever come in his life.

Dagnarus, Lord of the Void, stood on the banks of the Arven River and stared across it at the city of New Vinnengael, a city he planned to conquer. He stood alone and unseen, cloaked in the magic of the Void. Night had fallen. Some distance away, his taan troops were gathered around the campfires, telling stories of the brave deeds they would do when the signal was given to attack.

Dagnarus did not see this city, however. He saw another city, built on the banks of a different river. He saw a city of white marble, towering cliffs, a city of waterfalls and rainbows. His city, Vinnengael, the city of his birth, the city he had been born to rule.

Truth to tell, when Dagnarus had lived in Vinnengael, he'd never noticed the white marble or the rainbows. He'd never paid much attention to the waterfalls, and when he looked at the white cliffs on which the city was built, he saw them as part of the city's defenses. Only after the destruction of Vinnengael did he look back on that city and see it through the colored prism of his longing. Only then did he remember the rainbows, and that only because Gareth had once made mention of them.

Thinking of the old city and looking at the new that had been built to honor the old (and also to outdo it in splendor), Dagnarus at last understood what he found so galling, standing on the riverbank and contemplating tomorrow's battle. An obsessed lover, he could take the object of his love by force, but he didn't want her that way. He wanted her to come to him. He wanted her to want him, to humble herself before him and swear that she had always loved him and that she would love no other. He would not achieve his dream by sending in an army of taan to clap her in chains, repeatedly rape her, and leave her to die in her own blood on the roadside.

He could go to his adored and try to woo her. But what was he to do with ten thousand taan, thirsting for her blood?

Dagnarus put his hand to the Dagger of the Vrykyl.

"Shakur," he summoned his second-in-command, one of the Vrykyl, a creation of the Void and the Dagger that Dagnarus had used to take Shakur's life, giving him living death in return.

Long minutes passed. Shakur did not respond.

Dagnarus repeated the summons irritably. He might go days or months without communicating with his Vrykyl, but when he spoke, he commanded their immediate attention.

"My lord," Shakur responded.

"You kept me waiting," said Dagnarus.

"Forgive me, my lord, but there were people with me."

"Send them away," said Dagnarus. "You are king, after all."

"I may be king, but I am also a little boy, my lord," Shakur returned. "These fools hover over me like clucking old hens. Especially now, with an army of monsters camped outside the city gates."

"What is the mood in the city?" Dagnarus asked.

"Fear, panic," Shakur replied. "Martial law has been declared. The battle magi rule the city. Soldiers fill the street. The gates are closed. No one comes in or goes out. The harbor is empty."

"Has anyone else discovered you?"

"No one, other than the baron, and he is likely dead by now."

"*Likely* dead? You don't know for certain?"

"The palace guard continue to search for him, my lord, but they have yet to find him. I stabbed him with the Blood-knife. Nothing could have saved him."

"For your sake, Shakur, I hope that is true."

Dagnarus was extremely displeased by this lapse on the part of the Vrykyl. The oldest of his Vrykyl, Shakur had once been the best, the strongest, the most ruthless. He'd made several mistakes lately, mistakes that had cost Dagnarus dearly. Obviously, the Vrykyl was starting to deteriorate. Not surprising. Shakur had been around two hundred years. The Void alone held his rotting corpse together. He was forced to kill more and more often to drink the souls he needed to sustain his horrible existence. He was growing sloppy, careless. Dagnarus fingered the Dagger that had given Shakur this dreadful life. He could always take it.

"When do you launch your attack, my lord?" Shakur asked, thinking it best to change the subject. "Tomorrow morning?"

"I'm not attacking," said Dagnarus.

"*Not* attack, my lord?" Shakur was understandably amazed. For two hundred years, he and his master had worked and planned for very little else.

"When day dawns, I will ride into New Vinnengael under a flag of truce. I will demand to see you—the young king. You will make certain that I am granted an audience."

"My lord, I don't like this plan. The city is ripe for the fall—"

"I don't give a damn what you like, Shakur." Dagnarus's fist clenched over the dagger's hilt. "I find that I am beginning to detest strongly this habit of yours of constantly questioning my decisions. You will obey me in this as in all else."

"Yes, my lord."

"Oh, and you needn't bother to keep searching for the Sovereign Stone. I have taken charge of that matter, as I should have done from the beginning."

"Are the other Vrykyl to continue to hunt for it, my lord?"

"No, Shakur. There is no need to waste resources chasing after it. I have arranged for the Sovereign Stone—all four parts of the Stone—to come to me. Two of them are already on the way."

"Very good, my lord. We can make use of the Vrykyl who have been on the hunt. I suppose you know that Jedash is dead?"

"No great loss," said Dagnarus.

"No, my lord. Now about the attack on New Vinnengael, it occurs to me—"

"Isn't it past your bedtime, Shakur?" Dagnarus interrupted. "Shouldn't your nursemaid be coming to tuck you in and kiss you on your curly little head?"

Shakur seethed in silence, struggled to contain his anger.

Dagnarus, amused, let him fume.

"My lord, what is your plan for tomorrow?" Shakur asked finally, humbly.

"To become King of Vinnengael," said Dagnarus.

THE WAITING TOOK ITS TOLL ON THE PEOPLE OF NEW VINNENGAEL. Yesterday morning, the soldiers had stared out over the walls into the ranks of the monstrous enemy and felt their blood burn with hatred and loathing and the fury that comes to men facing battle. As the day passed, hot blood cooled, fury and hatred chilled to doubt and dread. With the coming of night, the blazing bonfires of the enemy lit the night sky with an orange glow; their bestial shrieks sent shivers down the spine. Officers ordered their men to try to sleep, but every time the soldiers dozed off, one particularly horrible shout would jolt them from dreams that hadn't been all that pleasant anyway.

This morning, the soldiers who stared down at the enemy were grim, bleary-eyed, and hopeless. Officers did what they could to rally their troops, but the cheers they had been met with yesterday were grunts and halfhearted mumbles today.

Rigiswald woke with the dawn, wakened from a sound sleep with the gnawing, tingling sensation in his belly that always presaged some dire event. Some called it premonition and claimed it came from the gods. Rigiswald believed it came from the brain, which had passed its night in diligent work, while the body slept. He had spent days reading all that he could find on the Sovereign Stone, which included information on King Tamaros, Prince Dagnarus, and the doomed and tragic King Helmos. Of all of the documents, the one that had proven most helpful was the account written by Evaristo, who had been Dagnarus's tutor.

Although a resident of Old Vinnengael, Evaristo had not been in the city when Dagnarus—then Lord of the Void—led his forces against it. Evaristo maintained it was good fortune that had led him and his family to make the two-hundred-mile journey to visit his wife's uncle, who dwelt in the city of Krammes. Rigiswald guessed that Evaristo had been warned of the coming attack by his former pupil Gareth, who had by then become a powerful Void sorcerer, credited with having formed the plan to cast the spell that drained the water from the River Hammerclaw, destroying one of the palace's main defenses and allowing Dagnarus's forces to take the city by surprise.

In his memoirs, Evaristo made no secret of the fact that he had always been fond of Gareth and had done what he could to try to break Dagnarus's fell hold on the young child, who had been Dagnarus's whipping boy. Evaristo had failed. Gareth loved Dagnarus and had remained his friend, steadfast and loyal. That the friendship would prove fatal to Gareth, Evaristo had no doubt, for Dagnarus, blessed with the charm of an adder, was also possessed of the viper's conscience.

From Evaristo, Rigiswald had learned a great deal about the personality of Dagnarus, and thus he alone, in all of New Vinnengael, was not surprised that Dagnarus was holding off his attack. Nor was he surprised when one of the battle magi hunted him down in the dining hall, where he was making up for having missed his dinner.

"The Most Revered High Magus's compliments, sir," said the battle magus, who were not usually sent to run errands. "Her Grace asks if would you come to the palace as quickly as possible."

Rigiswald continued calmly eating a bowl of chicken *en casserole.* His appetite was the envy of several young and badly frightened noviates.

"Am I under arrest?" Rigiswald asked.

The battle magus looked startled. "No, sir. You are one of several of the Temple's respected elders who have been summoned to the palace to meet with the Regent and His Majesty."

Last night I was a criminal. Now I'm a respected elder, Rigiswald reflected with an inner chuckle. He said that he would come, finished his chicken, returned to his room to change to his finest robes, then walked across the plaza that separated the Temple from the palace.

The day was gray and overcast, with a light mist falling. The streets were deserted except for the patrols and a few stray dogs. The clouds, the drizzle, the empty streets, and the knowledge of what he feared was coming oppressed him, a feeling that was unusual for him.

Rigiswald was a pragmatist. He saw his fellowmen for what they were: often stupid, generally good-hearted, occasionally sublime. Since Rigiswald did not expect a lot of his fellowmen, he was not disappointed in them. He had come to the conclusion that there was about as much true evil in the world as there was true good, and that most everyone fell somewhere in between.

Take Dagnarus, for example. How much easier it would be, Rigiswald reflected, if he were evil incarnate—some sort of monstrous aberration, like a troll, that thrives on inflicting pain and torment.

"But he is not a troll," Rigiswald remarked to himself. "For all he is Lord of the Void and has used the power of the Void to extend his life beyond that of any normal person, Dagnarus is still human. He is still a man, as we are men. Because of that, he can see into our hearts, which gives him the advantage, for we cannot see into his. If we could see into his heart, what would we find? Much that would shock us, I daresay. And much that would be familiar to us."

Rigiswald shook his head. "Perhaps that is the real reason we do not look. We're afraid of seeing ourselves. Yet someone has to. Someone must."

Arriving at the heavily guarded main gate, Rigiswald was passed through by a battle magus, who was armed with a list of those who had been invited to the palace to confer with the Regent and His Majesty. Always the Regent first, the king second. The young king was an afterthought.

How very frustrating that must be for the Vrykyl, Rigiswald considered, following one of the palace servants through the golden-filigreed, velvet-tapestried, marble-floored halls. The Vrykyl must retain the form of the child and do nothing that might cause those around him to suspect him. Yet, at the same time, the Vrykyl must manage to control events so that they benefited his master.

If nothing else, Rigiswald thought, it will be interesting to observe the Vyrkyl's attempts to manipulate the proceedings.

The Regent had commanded that the meeting be held in the Hall of Past Glories, called thusly because of its four enormous murals that portrayed scenes from Old Vinnengael. Rigiswald wondered if the Regent had considered the extreme irony of holding a meeting to discuss Dagnarus's siege of the city of New Vinnengael in a room that celebrated his siege of the old.

Rigiswald doubted it. Clovis had a hammer-and-tongs sort of intelligence that beat imagination into shape and then doused it in cold water to freeze it forever. She probably thought this room would inspire them. Rigiswald felt exactly the opposite. The gray gloom outside was less oppressive than this room dedicated to defeat, destruction, and death.

The large round table that usually stood in the center of the hall had been removed. Chairs were placed around the walls of the enormous room. Most everyone remained standing, clustered in the center. Candles burned in the chandeliers, which could be lowered by a system of ropes and pulleys for the servants to light. Rigiswald stood beneath one of the chandeliers, until he saw that a spot of melted wax had fallen on his cassock. Frowning, he moved to a different location.

The tension in the room was palpable. People entered hurriedly, out of breath, their expressions grim. They would pause a moment in the door, search the crowd, then head straight for friends to converse in low, urgent tones. Nerves stretched taut, people shifted restlessly from one group to the other. Occasionally one voice would rise above the others, ring out in anger, only to be hushed by companions.

The heads of each of the Orders of Magi were here, along with the knights who held command posts in the Imperial Cavalry and the city guard. Here were several barons who had property in or around New Vinnengael and the Keeper of the Purse, the head of the Royal Treasury. Rigiswald knew most of them. There were others he did not recognize, including one portly gentleman in the rich but unostentatious clothing of the upper middle class. Someone said he was the head of the Association of Merchants' Guilds.

Notable by their absence were the Dominion Lords.

Several of the heads of the Orders of Magi nodded to Rigiswald, but none came to speak to him. He was not quite approved. He preferred it that way, preferred keeping to himself, stayed out of the gloom-laden conversations. He drifted about the room, listening in here, eavesdropping there. He noted, in passing, that another person was doing the same—the head of the Order of Inquisitors.

Rigiswald soon became aware of discord in the hall. The barons and the knights were not pleased over the fact that the Church had stepped in to seize power following the king's death. The barons believed that one of their own number should have been named Regent, and they were backed by the knights, who blamed the Church for the sad state into which the Vinnengaelean military had fallen over the years. True, the Church had its own militia with the battle magi, but these people were answerable only to their superiors and, while they were well trained and diligent in their desire to work with the military, they were not trusted. The barons and the knights spoke in strident tones of a conspiracy by the Church to overthrow the true monarchy. This attack by the enemy was either a ruse or part of the plot and so on and so forth.

Wandering over to where the magi were gathered, Rigiswald heard similar talk, except with the demons reversed. The magi spoke of the barons as being in a conpsiracy with rebels who wanted to destroy the Church. The enemy army was part of their plot or a ruse and so on and so forth.

Rigiswald had no use for the Regent. He knew Clovis to be obtuse and hidebound, but he also knew that she was a gods-fearing woman who, whatever her faults, was loyal to her king and her country. The barons and knights were also gods-fearing, loyal men. When their blood cooled a bit, they would look back on what they'd said with deep chagrin. But for now, the Void was very active in this room, using fear and mistrust to drive apart those who should be standing united.

Rigiswald agreed with only one comment, and that came from a baron who looked around at the murals portraying the glories of Old Vinnengael and muttered that the choice of the room was "god-awful."

Presaged by a ceremonial horn call, members of the king's house guard marched in to the chamber. Taking their places at the head of the hall, they slowly and solemnly struck the butt ends of their spears on the floor to quiet the crowd.

"His Majesty the King."

Conversation ceased as everyone in the room bowed low. The young king, looking very small and fragile and sleepy, walked between the ranks of his guards. The Regent entered behind him, accompanied by Tasgall, who wore his full regalia.

Rigiswald had known Clovis many years, dating back to when they were students. He was slightly her elder, but not by much. She looked the same now as she had looked fifty years ago, only a bit grayer. Heavyset, she had gray eyes, as colorless as her mind. She had no imagination and no sense of humor. She considered laughter offensive to the gods, who intended that mankind take life seriously.

The young king walked to a throne that had been placed beneath a gold-fringed canopy on a raised dais. The chair was much too large for the child. He perched his backside on the throne and slid into it, having been taught that kings never looked behind them. The Regent took her place at the right hand of the king. Tasgall stood on his left. The king's chamberlain, who was one of the Revered Brethren and who doubled as his tutor, stood behind the throne. The household guard ranged around the king, while others took up positions at the door.

What would they say if I told them that the very evil they are trying to guard against is already inside the room? Rigiswald thought to himself. He might have been tempted to laugh, if he not been so much closer to weeping.

The Regent stepped forward. She intended to speak, but before she could open her mouth, the hall exploded with a barrage of questions, demands, and angry accusations. The tumult was deafening. Stunned, the king shrank back in his chair. His guards closed in around him. The Regent's face flushed an ugly red. Tasgall sent a warning glance to the battle magi.

Taking advantage of the commotion, Rigiswald moved to stand where Tasgall could see him and he could see Tasgall.

Tasgall held Rigiswald's gaze, then, his lips tightening, he looked away.

Rigiswald began to understand why he'd been summoned. At first, he'd hoped that Tasgall had thought things over and was ready to believe him. Now, Rigiswald realized, Tasgall had brought him here to discredit him. Rigiswald was disappointed. He'd figured Tasgall to have more sense.

"His Majesty understands your concerns," stated the Regent, when she could be heard over the tumult. "And we will be listening to them and addressing them. First I want to welcome a distinguished visitor, the monk Nu'Tai, who has traveled here from Dragon Mountain."

At this announcement, silence fell.

A stooped, wizened, dried-up old man entered the too-quiet hall, accompanied by two enormous humans, clad all in furs. The small old man was the monk. The two large beings accompanying him were members of the Omarah, a race of people who lived on the mountain and whose lives are dedicated to guarding the monks' sacred personages.

The monks of Dragon Mountain record all important events on their bodies, tattooing them onto their skin. When the monks die, their bodies are preserved in special vaults in the monastery for future generations to study. Everyone in the room was thinking the same thing: was the monk there to record the fall of New Vinnengael, as his long-dead predecessor had recorded the fall of Old Vinnengael?

The monk bowed to the king, who slid forward on his throne and bobbed his head. The Regent welcomed the monk and introduced him to certain important personages, calling them to come up to be introduced. Rigiswald was not one of them. He kept his eyes on the king.

Little Havis's feet did not touch the floor. He swung his legs back and forth and then, nervously, he began to kick the sides of the throne. He was halted by another whisper from his chamberlain.

Tasgall slid a glance at Rigiswald, who could perfectly read the man's thoughts as though he'd spoken.

"This child is a malevolent creature of the Void?"

Rigiswald clasped his hands together, rocked back on his heels, then forward onto the balls of his feet to keep the circulation in his legs going, and wondered how all this would end. Badly, he thought.

The Regent announced that the monk had come to New Vinnengael in order to bring them sad news. Gustav, Lord of Knowledge, a noble and honored Dominion Lord, was dead. He had died in far-off lands and had been buried in a mound of dirt by the barbarous Trevinici. The Regent proposed that a delegation be formed to travel to Trevinici lands to recover this noble lord's body and bring him back for a proper burial.

The crowd grew restless during this harangue. Surrounded by ten thousand fiends of the Void, the Vinnengaeleans were thinking fearfully of their own deaths, not some elderly knight who'd been half-mad anyway. With his insane quest to find the Sovereign Stone, Gustav had been an embarrassement to the Council of Dominion Lords. The only real emotion felt on hearing of his death was relief.

Rigiswald wondered if the monk had told the Regent that Gustav had found the portion of the Sovereign Stone intended for the humans.

If so, Clovis did not mention it to the assembly. Rigiswald couldn't blame her. She couldn't very well tell this volatile crowd that the Sovereign Stone had been found, but that no one had any idea where it was. Most of them would immediately leap to the conclusion that the Church had hidden it, storing it to use later for its own purposes.

The monk retreated into the background, taking a seat in one of the chairs that ranged along the wall. The Omarah loomed over the wizened old man. All eyes turned to the Regent. Everyone waited tensely to hear what she had to say, most of them prepared not to like it.

Clovis once again opened her mouth, but her speeches were apparently doomed to go unheard this day. One of the Temple novitiates who served the Regent came racing breathlessly into the hall. The novitiate was making straight for the Regent, when he realized by the sudden humming that everyone in the room—including the king—was staring at him. Abashed, he froze midway. The Regent's sharp tone commanded his attention. Recalling himself, the young man hastened over to speak to her.

The Regent's eyes widened. A baffled look came over her heavyset, jowled face. Confounded by whatever news she had just heard, Clovis would have probably given a great deal to have been told that news in private. As it was, she could not leave the room. The crowd had begun to comment on the novitiate's arrival, and some of the barons demanded to know what was going on.

"Your Majesty," Clovis said, turning to the king, "the enemy commander has asked that he be permitted to enter New Vinnengael under a flag of truce. He has no wish to attack us, he says, and suggests that we try to find a peaceful solution. We must decide whether or not he is to be admitted."

In the stunned silence that followed this pronouncement, the young king's high shrill voice rang out clearly.

"We say 'yes,' " said Havis III. "Permit him to enter our city and have speech with us."

Clovis gave a little gasp. She had spoken to the young king out of a politic desire to silence the clamorous barons. The king was supposed to say that the matter was up to her. She had certainly not intended for the king to make his own decision, and she was startled and displeased that he had done so.

"Your Majesty, we should discuss this matter privately—"

The king slid from his throne, stood facing her. "We say that this commander should be permitted to enter the city. We wish to see him and hear him. That is our will, and you will obey."

Cunning, that Vrykyl, thought Rigiswald. He looked at Tasgall, to see what he made of his kinglet now, but couldn't catch the man's eye. The battle magus was intent upon the Regent.

Clovis was "in a pickle," as the saying went. She clasped her hands together over her ample stomach and glared down at the king, trying to cow him. She did not succeed and was forced to speak.

"Your Majesty, as your Regent, appointed by the Church and sanctified in the eyes of the gods, it is my duty to guide your decisions. Everyone knows of your concern and care for your people, and we know that you want to do what is best for them. To that, I impute the earnest desire of yours to speak to this evil man, and I will take your wishes under advisement. A matter this serious, however, should not be decided lightly. I propose that we take some time to consider."

Clovis turned to the chamberlain. "His Majesty will retire."

His Majesty didn't look at all pleased about that. He frowned, and one small fist clenched. He seemed on the verge of arguing, but on second thought, decided against it. He would look like a petulant child and lose ground in consequence. As it was, men and women who had formerly regarded him with pity were now eyeing him with respect. He could only gain by behaving graciously. The chamberlain and the house guards escorted the king out of the hall.

The Regent spoke briefly to the novitiate, who left the chamber in haste, then said loudly, "This assembly will adjourn. We will reconvene in an hour. At that time, we will give this man our answer."

If she thought she was going to be able to leave without further talk, she was mistaken. Clovis might have been Regent, but the Regent wasn't the king. She was immediately surrounded by the clamoring barons and knights. Even the head of the Association of Merchants' Guilds put himself forward, shouldering his way into the crowd to express his opinion.

The Regent, her face grim, her cheeks flushed, tried to force her way through, but without success. Tasgall and his battle magi finally cleared a path. The Regent summoned the heads of the Orders to her side, and they left the room, guarded by the battle magi.

Abandoned, the barons and the knights and the other courtiers clustered together in their own groups, their voices raised in ire, sprinkled with threats that the Church wasn't going to have its way in this.

Rigiswald made good his own departure, gliding out of the room just in time to see the heads of the Orders walking to the far end of a long corridor lined with portraits of past kings and queens of Vinnengael. The Regent stopped at the end of the corridor. The heads of the nine Orders gathered in a huddle around her. Several battle magi formed a cordon across the corridor to give them privacy for their hasty meeting.

Rigiswald wandered a short distance down the corridor, affecting to be absorbed in admiring a portrait of young Havis's deceased mother. Standing in front of the painting, his head tilted to one side, he estimated the distance between himself and the gathering of magi.

Approximately two hundred feet. Removing a vial of water he had stuffed up the tight-fitting cuff of his gown, he pulled out the stopper with his teeth and shook a few drops onto his fingers. He whispered the words to the spell, then flicked the water in the general direction of the crowd around the Regent. The spell worked. Within moments, he was able to hear their conversation quite clearly.

"Of course," the Regent was saying, "this man who calls himself Lord Dagnarus has taken a good, hard look at our defenses, and he has come to the realization that he has no chance of defeating us. The best he can do is besiege us and, so long as our ports remain open, this will be naught but a minor inconvenience. I am not about to negotiate with him."

"A siege would be more than a minor inconvenience, Regent," stated Tasgall bluntly. "Their siege towers are armed with orken jelly. This Lord Dagnarus could create a firestorm that would wipe out half the population of this city and reduce homes and businesses to charred ruins.

"However," he added, his voice grim, "that is preferable to surrender. I heard what horrors these fiends inflicted on Dunkar when that city surrendered. I agree that we should fight, but we should know the worst that can befall us before we commit ourselves, and prepare for it."

"Revered Brother Tasgall speaks wisely, Regent," said the head of the Order of Inquisitors. "According to our sources, the enemy army is made up of taan, a race skilled in the use of Void magic. And it is not just their shaman who can make use of this foul magic. The ordinary soldier has the ability to use Void magic whenever he likes, without suffering any debilitating consequences."

The Inquisitor was a tall man, big-boned, and so excessively lean that he seemed almost cadaverous. He had lank, gray hair and the large, protruding eyes of those afflicted with a goiter. His bony jawline and high cheekbones gave his face a skeletal look, and the current joke among the novitiates was that he had summoned himself from the graveyard. Devoid of warmth, sarcastic, and ill-tempered, the Inquisitor had not been well liked before he was named to head the Order of Inquisitors, and now he was universally detested.

The Regent was clearly shocked by his news. "How is that possible?" she demanded. "And why wasn't I informed of this before?"

"Indeed," Tasgall agreed angrily. "The battle magi should have been told about this before now!"

"Before now, you would not have been interested," countered the Inquisitor.

"Void magic by its very nature takes a toll upon the bodies of those who cast it," stated the Regent. "I think you have been misinformed, Inquisitor."

"What we have learned we have learned at great peril from those of our Order who have risked their lives to walk among these creatures," the Inquisitor returned, his tone cold with anger at being doubted. "The taan are able to achieve this by the use of stones embedded beneath their hide. We do not know for certain how these stones work, but we theorize that the taan draw on the energy of the stones to power the magic, rather than being forced to draw on their own life energy."

"However they do it, Regent," Tasgall stated, "if what he says is true—and I suppose we must believe him—this means that there is a possibility that every single one of the enemy coming over our walls is a Void sorcerer, capable of wielding spells of death and despair as well as steel."

The Regent looked appalled, then her lips tightened. She shook her head.

"I am not suggesting we surrender," Tasgall added, reading her thoughts. "We will win, of that I have no doubt. The gods could not allow it otherwise. But the battle will be bloody and destructive."

"Is there anything else you have learned about these taan that you haven't told us, Inquisitor?" the Regent demanded.

"Several of the undead knights of the Void known as Vrykyl are among the army of Lord Dagnarus," said the Inquisitor, unperturbed by her accusation. "Vrykyl that are far more powerful than the one that was slain two nights ago by the heroic actions of our battle magi. The Vrykyls' command of Void magic is immense. Witness how many of our battle magi were required to bring down one of them, and one of the weaker. No disparagement on your gallant actions, my lord."

The Inqusitor bowed to Tasgall, who bowed back, but said nothing.

"If our Dominion Lords were present, they would be able to face these Vrykyl on equal terms, but as I undestand it, Regent, you disbanded the Council and sent the Dominion Lords away from the city."

"I followed the will of the gods," Clovis returned through gritted teeth. She was rattled, losing control of the situation. "These Dominion Lords were created by imperfect means and thus are themselves imperfect. Mad Lord Gustav was a prime example."

" 'Mad' Lord Gustav was wise enough to find our part of the Sovereign Stone, which had been missing for two hundred years," said the Inquisitor.

Gasps of astonishment came from most of the assembled heads of the Orders, who turned their startled eyes on the Regent. Tasgall, head of the Order of Battle Magi, and the Seneschal, head of the house guard, were the only ones to whom this news did not come as a shock.

"Is this miracle true, Most Revered High Magus?" demanded the head of the Order of Diplomacy.

"Praise the gods," said the head of the Order of Scribes.

"I wouldn't be too quick about that," said the Inquisitor dryly. "Lord Gustav recovered the Stone, but he died before he could deliver it. The Stone has since gone missing. Unless you have been successful in locating it, Regent?"

"No, I have not," the Regent answered in dour tones. "And I will thank you to keep your voice down, Inquisitor."

"A pity," said the Inquisitor. "The Stone might be of some use to us in repelling these Void monsters."

"As a matter of policy—" the Regent returned angrily.

"The Void is at work here," Tasgall intervened. "I trust you are all aware of that."

The argument ceased.

"And now, what is to be done?" Clovis asked. She turned to Tasgall. "Do you actually recommend that we negotiate with this Lord Dagnarus?"

"His Majesty has decreed it," Tasgall stated.

"His Majesty is a child," the Regent retorted.

"A child who has put us in an untenable situation," Tasgall returned. "The barons are already unhappy with the fact that the Church has gained control over the monarchy, or at least that's how they see it. If we go against the king's wishes in this matter, we will further alienate the barons and the knights whose support with troops and money we will need if we are attacked."

He hesitated, then asked, "Do you know why His Majesty took it into his head to intervene in this matter, Regent?"

Ah, thought Rigiswald, pleased. You're thinking now, Tasgall. You're starting to wonder if I am right. Very good, sir. Very good.

"His Majesty is a little boy and, as such, he is extremely interested in the prospect of battle," said the Regent. "He spends all his time in his room, staring out the windows at the enemy army across the river. When he isn't looking out the window, he's fighting mock battles with his toy soldiers. It is no wonder that he wants to meet the man who has launched this attack on the city."

"He is interested in battle, you say," said Tasgall. "Not frightened?"

"He is not in the least frightened," said the Regent, with almost maternal pride. "His Majesty is not a coward."

The head of the Order of the Arts spoke up. A serious, taciturn man, he was noted for his extreme deliberation of thought.

"I do not think we have much choice in the matter, Regent. I think we must hear from this man, though there is no doubt that we must refuse any terms for surrender."

"I agree," said the Inquisitor. "I am curious to see this Lord Dagnarus. Strange rumors circulate about him."

"I suppose we must meet with him," said the Regent in ill-humored tones. "Are we all agreed?"

The nine assembled murmured their assent.

"I will make the arrangements." Clovis paused, then said in a soft voice, "I suppose, Tasgall, that His Majesty must be present at this meeting?"

"I fear so, Regent. The barons would be angered otherwise. But I suggest that you speak to His Majesty first. Remind him that he is supposed to follow your guidance and that he is not to make any decisions without consulting with you first. And I would bring him to the meeting late, so that his appearance is merely a matter of formality."

"Yes, a good suggestion," said Clovis. "And you may be assured that I will have a long talk with His Majesty."

The Regent stalked off, her ceremonial robes rustling around her thick ankles.

"Truly," Rigiswald muttered, shaking his head as he returned to the Hall of Past Glories, "Tasgall is right. The Void is at work here."

NO FANFARE, NO TRUMPET FLOURISHES, NO GRAND CEREMONY introduced Dagnarus into the city he hoped to make his own. He was hustled in secret through a wicket located in a side gate near the dockyard, then blindfolded and taken to the palace in a closed carriage. It was remarked, by those battle magi who guarded him, that he was not in the least offended by these proceedings, but seemed to accept them with good-natured amusement.

Dagnarus was not what they expected. Leader of an army of monsters, he had been viewed as a monster himself. Instead, he was a charming, handsome man, self-assured and confident. He was well dressed but not ostentatious in a woolen cape and high boots, embroidered doublet and snowy white shirt. He wore his clothes with an air of elegance. He brought with him a fine sword, which he gave into the hands of the battle magi with orders to take care of it, for the blade had once been his father's. He was like a fine blade himself—ornately decorated, polished to a high gloss, and possessed of a sharp edge.

Men of war could tell at a glance he was one of them. During the carriage ride, he spoke to his guards of certain recent battles fought by the Vinnengaeleans against dwarven raiders, during which he made it clear that he had studied the battles, speaking knowledgeably about the strategies and tactics used by both sides. The hardened battle magi found themselves drawn into the conversation against their will and, by the end of the carriage ride, were prepared to give Dagnarus their grudging respect. He knew what he was about, when it came to war, that was certain.

Who he was, where he had come from, how he came by this monstrous army, and why was he attacking Vinnengael—these were questions the battle magi sought to answer. He was human, and appeared to be about thirty-five years of age, with auburn hair and intense green eyes. He was clean-shaven, with an ingratiating smile and a hail-fellow-well-met aspect. He spoke fluent and idiomatic Elderspeak, which seemed to indicate that he was Vinnengaelean, but there was something rather old-fashioned about his speech. He called a "halberd" a "haubert," a term that, as one man put it, "had gray hair and a beard on it when my grandfather was a lad." The battle magi could not penetrate Dagnarus's defenses, for he would either counter their verbal thrusts or use his wit to turn them aside.

The battle magi kept Dagnarus blindfolded as they led him through the corridors of the palace to the Hall of Past Glories. He bore this indignity with good humor, grinning beneath his mask and complaining that he could see none of the beautiful women for which he had heard the city was famous. Upon detecting an odor of perfume as he walked past one of the startled ladies of the court, he paused to bow to the unseen woman in a courtly manner.

He was taken into the Hall of Past Glories, where his blindfold was removed. He blinked at the light a few moments until he could see, then, smiling, looked at the crowd gathered around him. He was met with hostile stares, curled lips, growlings, and mutterings. Their obvious enmity did not appear to bother him one whit. He remained calm, relaxed, and confident.

The Regent stood on the dais, her hands clasped, her head thrown back, magnificently offended. If by this attitude, the Regent hoped to intimidate Dagnarus or inflict upon him a sense of his wrongdoing, she failed utterly. Paying absolutely no attention to her, he stared intently at one of the murals depicting Old Vinnengael. He turned to Tasgall, who stood, armed and ready for trouble, at his side.

"Is that supposed to be the Royal Palace, Magus?" Dagnarus asked.

Tasgall answered warily, not trusting even this seemingly innocuous question. "Why do you want to know, sir?"

"Because if that's the case, you've got it all wrong," Dagnarus returned, laughing.

Before anyone could stop him, he strode across the room, scattering the barons and the courtiers and the heads of the Orders, who scrambled to get out of his way. The battle magi leapt after him, weapons drawn and spells ready. He paid them no heed, but continued on his way and came to stand in front of the mural, not far from the chair in which Rigiswald happened to be sitting, ostensibly reading a book.

The Regent glowered after Dagnarus and glared at Tasgall, who shrugged his shoulders to indicate that he had no idea what was going on, nor, so long as this man was not posing a threat, was there anything he could do about it.

Dagnarus studied the mural. "The artist has the waterfalls right. But he's mangled the palace." He placed a finger on the painting. "This wing extended out this way. The entrance was over here, not where he has put it. He's added an extra tower and, because of that, this balcony, where my father used to walk, faces too far to the west. Before I leave, I'll draw you a picture, to make certain you get it right."

Hearing nothing behind him—the silence was such that everyone in the room might have been struck down dead—Dagnarus turned around to face them. A smile played on his lips.

"Well, well," he remarked. "Perhaps now is not the time for fond remembrances."

He glanced back at the painting, and Rigiswald noted a shadow darken the handsome features. "Still, I would like for it to be right."

The shadow was soon gone, replaced by charming *bonhomie.* Rigiswald was one of the few to have noticed the look or heard the murmured words that chilled him to the marrow.

The Regent stiffened and exchanged grim glances with Tasgall and the Inquisitor. They were both thinking the same thoughts as Rigiswald except, unlike him, they didn't believe Dagnarus. They didn't believe he was the person he claimed to be.

You will come to, said Rigiswald silently. He will see to that. The gods help us!

The Regent drew in breath to launch into her speech, her bosom swelling like the sails of a ship in a high wind.

Dagnarus forestalled her.

"Where is my young cousin, Havis?" he asked, glancing around.

The Regent said coldly, "I do not know of whom you speak, sir. I was not aware that you claim relation to any in this room. Or that any would claim relationship with you."

"His Majesty the King," said Dagnarus, smiling and choosing to ignore the insult. "Havis III. My little cousin. I say 'cousin,' although I'm sure that the relationship is probably much more complex—second cousins by marriage twice removed or some such nonsense. I have traveled a long distance to see him, and I would not be denied the pleasure."

"Pleasure!" The Regent gave forth one of her snorts. "You hold a dagger to our throats, and you speak of pleasure!"

"You refer to my army. I was not certain of my welcome in this city," Dagnarus replied, his smile engaging. "I deemed it best to come prepared."

"Prepared for what, sir? War?" Clovis's voice shook with rage.

"No, Regent," said Dagnarus. His tone was earnest, serious. "I am here to establish my rightful claim to the throne of the Vinnengaelean Empire."

"Silence!" the Regent thundered, to quiet the assembly.

The guards slammed the butts of their spears on the stone floor. The confused hubbub came to an abrupt end, but not through any action of the Regent. At that point, either by accident or design, the young king made his entrance. Accompanied by his guards and his chamberlain, he strode into the room. As he paused to acknowledge the bows of the assembly, his eyes went immediately to Dagnarus. Rigiswald watched closely, to see if any sort of sign passed between them. The child's eyes were wide with a very natural curiosity. Dagnarus regarded the king with a kind of patronizing benevolence.

The Regent clucked the king onto his throne, gave a look meant to remind him of his manners, then turned away in response to the Inquisitor, who had stepped to the dais and was speaking to her with obvious urgency. Rigiswald could have cast his eavesdropping spell, but he didn't need to expend the energy. He could easily guess what the two were discussing. The Inquisitor had recognized the danger, and he was undoubtedly warning Clovis not to proceed further, urging her to stall for time, meet with this man in private. Perhaps he was telling her more "rumors" he'd heard.

"You do not want to hear his explanation about his right to the throne," the Inquisitor was undoubtedly saying to her emphatically. "Above all, you do not want to give him a public forum."

Tasgall hastened over to join them, to add the weight of his argument.

The Regent was skeptical. Rigiswald could read her lips form the word, "Flummery!" The Inquisitor pressed his point, and Tasgall apparently sided with him, for he nodded whenever the Inquisitor opened his mouth. Outnumbered and outargued, the Regent was forced to back down. She had to figure out how to extract herself from this situation and remove Dagnarus from the room without affronting the barons. She might have saved herself the trouble, for by then it was too late.

They had forgotten the king.

Havis III leaned forward, and said loudly, "I heard you state, sir, that you have a rightful claim to the throne. I would be interested to hear the nature of your claim."

The Regent tried to hush him. "Your Majesty, this is not for you to worry about—"

"I want to hear him," said the king, with a look. "Please, sir, go ahead."

"Certainly, Your Majesty," said Dagnarus, responding to the child with becoming gravity. "I am Prince Dagnarus, second son to Tamaros, late king of Vinnengael. My elder brother, Helmos, being dead, I am Tamaros's only living heir and the true and rightful King."

During the ensuing tumult, the Regent shouted at the guards to remove His Majesty to a place of safety—an excuse to get rid of him, of course. The king was in no danger. The raised voices and fierce words were not aimed at him, although the Regent came in for her share of outrage. Some called for the imposter's head, while others called for the Regent's. Some shouted that Dagnarus be allowed to tell his tale, others that he be thrown into the Arven. The king, with the obstinate stubbornness of a child, refused to leave the hall, and the Regent, under the glaring eyes of the barons, could not very well order His Majesty carried out bodily.

The guards took up position around the throne, stood with weapons drawn. Young Havis looked solemn and subdued, but certainly not afraid. His gaze was fixed on Dagnarus, which was perfectly natural. Dagnarus looked once at the child, as if to assure himself that Havis was safe, then, with calm nonchalance, turned his attention to the assembly and stood at ease, a very slight smile on his lips.

The disruption in the hall gave Rigiswald a chance to observe closely the Lord of the Void. Rigiswald tried very hard to see some outward signs of the Void at work, some physical indication that this man's life had been extended by means of the foul magic that never gives freely but demands a price.

Dagnarus's skin was fair and unblemished, his hands callused and scarred, as would be the hands of any warrior, for the calluses were made by the pommel of a sword and the scars were battle scars, not the scars of lesions and pustules. His body was firm, well muscled. He stood straight and tall. He was comely in appearance. Certainly he did not look two hundred years old.

Rigiswald's view of Dagnarus was from the side, and he was thinking that he would like very much to get a close look into his eyes when Dagnarus turned his head to look at Rigiswald.

"Would you take my likeness, old gentleman?" Dagnarus asked with a teasing grin, raising his voice to be heard over the uproar.

"I would," said Rigiswald, "and add it to the painting."

He gave a nod toward another part of the mural that depicted Helmos following his Transfiguration. King Tamaros stood together with Helmos, who wore the shining armor of a Dominion Lord. The faces of both were exalted, happy—artistic license, for history recorded that Helmos was made Lord of Sorrows, the only time such a woeful title had been bestowed by the gods on a Dominion Lord. Dagnarus, the second son, was nowhere to be seen.

Dagnarus flicked a glance in the direction of the mural. He gazed long at the two figures, father and son, forever bound in a moment of shared pride and exultation that forever excluded the younger son, the wild son, the son who had not measured up. Dagnarus looked back, and Rigiswald had his chance. He looked into the eyes.

He expected to see the nothingness of the Void. Instead he saw the shadow of pain that two hundred years could not ease and the fire of a blazing ambition that two hundred years could not quench. Rigiswald saw in those eyes humanity, and he was sorry, deeply sorry. To see the hollow emptiness of death would have been awful, but far preferable to seeing emotion, intelligence, longing—the fullness and warmth of life.

"You believe me, then, old gentleman?" Dagnarus asked, with a playful air that was feigned, according to the eyes.

"I believe you," said Rigiswald, adding bluntly, "to my sorrow."

Dagnarus did not take offense. He appeared to find the conversation an interesting one and seemed ready to continue, but by then order had been restored in the hall. The Regent was speaking, and Dagnarus turned to give her his full attention.

"Your claim is ridiculous," stated the Regent. "I should not even dignify it with attempts to refute it, but I will state some of them for the record: The real Dagnarus would be over two hundred years old, the real Dagnarus was most certainly killed in the destruction of the city brought about by himself, the real Dagnarus—"

"Pardon me, Most Revered High Magus," Dagnarus interrupted. "If I could offer proof of my claim—irrefutable proof—would that be sufficient?"

Rigiswald looked from Dagnarus to young Havis, and suddenly he knew their plot, knew it as surely as if they had revealed it to him. He knew it, and he could do nothing to stop it, for no one would believe him.

The Regent opened her mouth.

Don't do it, Clovis, Rigiswald mentally warned her. Don't play his game. Ask him for his terms, then refuse him and throw him out on his ear. Better we all die and this city be leveled than that you hand us over to the Void.

"Let us see your proof, sir," the Regent said, with cold dignity.

Rigiswald sighed deeply and sat back in his chair, arms folded and his head bowed.

"I call upon the monk from Dragon Mountain," said Dagnarus.

The Regent looked startled, but, after a moment's discomfiture, she drew herself up. "I don't see—"

"Please, Regent," said Dagnarus gently. "You asked for proof."

The monk, whom everyone had forgotten, rose to his feet and tottered forward to stand between his gigantic, silent bodyguards. He made a bobbing bow to the assembly, then regarded Dagnarus with an interested, scholarly air.

"Reverend sir," said Dagnarus in tones of immeasurable respect, "I am aware—as are we all—that the monks of Dragon Mountain do not make history, they observe history."

The monk bobbed his hairless, tattoo-covered head to indicate that such was true.

"I ask you, Reverend Monk, to bear witness to an historical fact. Am I in truth what I claim to be? Am I Dagnarus, second son of King Tamaros, born to him and his lawful wife, Queen Emillia, daughter of Olaf, King of Dunkarga, in the year 501?"

The monk clasped his hands together, made another bobbing bow. "You are that Dagnarus," he said.

He spoke without emotion, his words clipped and precise. Everyone was stunned by what he'd said, shocked and amazed, but not a single person in that room doubted him.

"Then there is evil at work here!" proclaimed the Regent, in a strangled voice. "The evil of the Void."

Too late, Clovis, said Rigiswald to himself, leaning back in his chair and staring up at the ceiling. You opened the barn door, and now the horse is careening merrily down the hill.

"As to that, Regent," said the monk with yet another bob of his head, "I can make no comment, for I have no information pertaining to that subject."

"All know he was made Lord of the Void," the Regent continued, casting the monk a furious glance, which did not discommode the monk in the least. "Let this Dagnarus deny that, if he will. Let him deny that if he *is* Dagnarus, son of Tamaros, his life has been extended by evil means!"

"I do deny it," stated Dagnarus calmly. "I will tell my story, since you ask it. If His Majesty will hear it." He made humble obeisance to the young king.

"We will gladly hear your story, sir," said Havis, his childish voice sounding clear and bell-like in the shocked silence.

"Your Majesty, I most strongly protest—" the Regent began.

"Please relate it to us," Havis went on, refusing even to look at the Regent, much less heed her sputterings. "I ask you all, gentlemen and ladies, to give Prince Dagnarus your full attention."

That was unnecessary. No one was looking anywhere else. The roof could have sailed off the hall, thought Rigiswald, and no one would have noticed.

"It is true that I was made Lord of the Void," said Dagnarus forthrightly. "The fault was mine. I sought to cheat the gods, and I was punished for it. For years, the Void twisted my heart and shadowed my thinking, led me to question the wisdom of the gods who had made my elder brother king. I could not bear to see him ascend the throne of my beloved Vinnengael. I was her true king—by courage, by valor, by wit, by everything except the accident of my birth. I sought to remove my brother by force. I attacked the city of my birth and, in my wild rage, brought about its destruction."

Dagnarus sent a flashing glance around the assembly. "I did not kill my brother, as history reports. Helmos was slain by Gareth, a Void sorcerer who sought to purchase my loyalty by killing the king. I did not wish Helmos's death. I grieved over him and promised the gods that if I were spared, I would make reparation for my fault and be a true king of Vinnengael. I slew Gareth, but I was too late. The forces of Void magic that he had let loose could not be controlled. They clashed with the magic of the gods and tore out the heart of Vinnengael.

"I should have died in the ruins of Old Vinnengael, died beside the body of my brother. I wanted to die there beside him, for—at that moment—I saw the enormity of my crimes. I did not die, however. The gods were not yet finished with me. They reached down their hands and plucked me from that city and cast me into the wilderness. Broken in body and shattered in spirit, I came to know that the gods had not abandoned me, that they believed that I could yet be saved, for I held in my hands the Sovereign Stone.

"The gods had granted me the power to save the blessed Stone from the destruction of Vinnengael. I held it in my hands—wet with my murdered brother's blood—and I wept. I begged the gods' forgiveness. I promised I would redeem myself. Then and there I renounced the Void. The gods required tests of my loyalty, however. They took the Sovereign Stone from me and gave it into the hands of a monster that nearly killed me. When I recovered, I found myself in another world, a world of terrible creatures of the Void. A race of savages, the taan were little better than animals when I found them. They would have slain me, but I managed—with the help of the gods—to overcome their suspicions and their hatred. I gained their respect and came to be a leader among them.

"Time lost all meaning for me while I was in the land of the taan. I worked hard to civilize them and train them with one thought in mind—to return to my own world and do what I could to make amends. In order to achieve that, I prayed to the gods that they would extend my life.

The gods granted me my wish, and thus you see me here before you today, the same age as I was when I was exiled from all that I loved.

"During my years of exile, I saw Vinnengael fall in men's esteem. I saw her held up to derision, saw her despised and ridiculed. I saw the Church grow in power, saw the monarchy become weak and ineffectual, her nobles ground down beneath the heel of the clergy."

Some low-voiced mutterings of agreement came from the barons.

"I saw her military dwindle, its numbers decline, morale plummet," Dagnarus continued. "Thus, when Karnu attacked Vinnengaeleans at the city now named Delak 'Vir, the Vinnengaelean army was defeated, forced to retreat in shame. Worse than that, Vinnengael did not act to take back the Portal the Karnuans stole from us.

"Years go by, and Karnuans walk our soil with impunity. They demand fees from us to use what was once our Portal. They sneer at us and call us cowards. Are the Vinnengaelean soldiers cowards?" He looked directly at several members of the Imperial Cavalry, whose faces were flushed.

"No!" Dagnarus said, biting off the words. "Vinnengaelean soldiers are the bravest, the best, the most loyal soldiers in the world."

He was interrupted by shouts of angry agreement.

Dagnarus raised his voice. "I should know. I led them into battle myself on many occasions. But even the bravest soldiers need training, they need money, they need the best in weaponry and armor. More than that"—he paused—"they need respect."

Several of the knights cheered. The soldiers lifted their heads. Their eyes gleamed, their hands clenched into fists. Some nodded emphatically, while others exclaimed "yes!" and nearly all cast dour glances at the Regent and the other Church officials.

How clever, Rigiswald thought, admiring in spite of himself. How very clever.

"Yes, I came back to Loerem with an army!" Dagnarus cried. "An army that has conquered Dunkar and brought it low! An army that has taken on Karnu and will soon conquer that proud land." He pointed directly at the knights. "Because of my assault on their homeland, the Karnuans have been forced to pull back many of their troops from Delak Vir. If you attack them now, they cannot withstand your might. You will recapture your Portal and with it regain the respect that is your due."

Cheers met each of his statements.

Dagnarus paused again, then said, quietly, "I give you Dunkarga, its wealth, its people. I give you Karnu, its wealth, its people. I give these to Vinnengael as my gift. With these two great nations now under her control, Vinnengael becomes the most powerful nation in Loerem, more powerful than she was under the rule of my father, King Tamaros, the gods assoil him."

Dagnarus held out his hands, as though he held those countries within them. "Take them. They are yours. All I ask is that you grant me what is mine by right. Make me king. Or rather, emperor. For Vinnengael will become the greatest empire in the history of Loerem."

No one spoke. No one even seemed to breathe. The Regent blinked at him, dazed. Of all the demands he could have made, she had not expected this one. The Inquisitor's face was impassive, he gave nothing away. Grim and glowering, Tasgall looked often at Rigiswald, trying to meet his eye. Rigiswald refused to answer that mute appeal. Tasgall was too late. This had gone too far.

Like all successful liars, Dagnarus had cunningly based his falsehoods and half-truths on a few solid facts. He had grown up amid palace intrigue. His Vrykyl must have told him of the growing enmity between the Church and the barons and the military. For too long, the complacency of the Church had beamed like strong sunshine on a frozen, snow-packed mountain of problems. It had taken but a single shout to start the snow to sliding, and now no one could halt the coming avalanche.

"What about that army of fiends?" the Regent demanded suddenly. "What will you do with them? We heard what happened to Dunkar. We heard how its women were carried off, its children were butchered. Will the same happen to our people? Even if we agree to your terms, which, at the moment, we do not, I do not think it likely that those savages of yours will give up and go back meekly to their homeland."

Dagnarus was ready with his answer. "Half my forces I will send to Delak 'Vir to fight the Karnuans and regain our Portal. The rest, as King of Vinnengael, I will destroy."

"Will you destroy troops who are loyal to you?"

The question came from the young king, and he sounded disapproving.

Rigiswald saw Dagnarus's eyes flicker with a dangerous light. Bowing to the king, to acknowledge his question, Dagnarus replied, "The farmer does not speak of loyalty when he butchers pigs, Your Majesty. The taan are not men. They are animals. They have been well fed, well treated by me. If I demand their lives, it is no more than what they owe me in return."

Dagnarus turned to the assembly. "I do not require that you give me an immediate answer. I will withdraw for a short time to give you a chance to consider my proposition. When the sun sets, I will return for your answer. Is that satisfactory?"

"Yes," said some of the barons loudly.

The Regent exchanged glances with the Inquisitor and with Tasgall.

"We need far more time than that," stated the Regent.

"I don't see why," said Dagnarus with a charming smile. "You either accept my proposal or refuse it. Until sunset." He made his obeisance and was about to withdraw when Rigiswald, impelled by some inner demon, spoke up, "And what of the Vrykyl, Your Highness?"

Dagnarus turned, his cloak falling around him in graceful folds. His expression was one of baffled confusion.

"I beg your pardon, old gentleman?"

"The Vrykyl," said Rigiswald. Clasping his hands behind him, he rose to his feet. "Foul and undead creatures of the Void created by the one who wields the Dagger of the Vrykyl. I am certain you must have heard of them."

"From my nursemaid when I was little," said Dagnarus, his lips twitching with suppressed laughter. "I know nothing more of them, I assure you, sir."

"One was slain last night in the city," stated Tasgall. He might have added more, but Dagnarus interrupted him.

"If that be true, and such evil creatures do walk the earth, then all the more reason Vinnengael needs a strong king to protect her. Until sunset."

Dagnarus departed. Such was his majestic demeanor that those who had been guarding him looked to Tasgall to see if they should continue. He gave them a furious glance, and they hastened out after Dagnarus. Rigiswald bet that they would not try to blindfold him this time.

Havis III, at a stern glance from the Regent, slid off his throne and, taking time to adjust the crown, which had slipped over one eye, stepped with carefully taught dignity off the dais. Halfway across the room, he stopped and faced the assembly.

"I think he should be king," said Havis.

The adults glanced at each other, discomfited, embarrassed. Some looked pitying.

"Your Majesty!" The Regent came bustling over. "You have no idea what you are saying."

"I do," said Havis. He pointed to the monk from Dragon Mountain. "This man said Dagnarus was the true king. All know the gods hold the monks sacred. He wouldn't lie, would he, Madam?"

The Regent blanched, nonplussed. "No, Your Majesty," she finally said.

"I will pray to the gods," said Havis III. "I will ask them for their counsel. But I think I know what I must do, and that is to abdicate"—he brought out this hard word after a struggle—"in favor of my cousin, Prince Dagnarus."

He left the room, walking between his guards with the childish dignity that was so becoming and so utterly and heartbreakingly convincing.

When he was gone, the hubbub of voices rose. The barons took their leave, and with them went the soldiers and knights. The head of the Association of Merchants' Guilds left in haste, jowls quivering, presumably to report back to his fellow merchants. Courtiers and functionaries fluttered about like gaily colored birds, prepared to fly to whatever hand held the food. The Regent gathered the heads of the Orders around her, like so many chickens. They all looked stunned, as though they'd been struck by falling debris. Tasgall started to join them, then changed his mind.

Rigiswald picked up the book he had been reading. Tucking it under one arm, he walked toward the door.

"I need to speak to you. Where are you going?" Tasgall demanded.

"To my dinner," said Rigiswald.

"But we aren't finished," Tasgall protested.

"Oh, yes, you are," said Rigiswald. "You just don't know it yet."

Paying no attention to Tasgall, who called stridently after him, Rigiswald left the palace and walked alone through the sodden, gray streets of New Vinnengael.

RIGISWALD ATE A CHEERLESS DINNER ALONE. THE HOUR FOR sunset drew near, although one could tell only by a gradual deepening of the grayness. The sun could not be seen for the heavy clouds that dragged curtains of rain over the city.

Of course, word spread. The barons and knights retired to a tavern to discuss the matter and, although they took a private room, their raised voices could be heard by everyone who crowded inside the tavern in search of news. The head of the Association of Merchants' Guilds summoned his members to an emergency session. They met in the Guild Hall—an enormous, imposing building of dark timber and whitewashed walls located at the end of a street known as Guild Hall Row. Horse holders and carriage drivers crowded into the doorway to hear the proceedings, passing on what they heard to the guards who were supposed to be patrolling the streets.

Rigiswald stood on the steps of the Temple, watching the large crowds beginning to gather in front of the palace. All thought of curfew was abandoned. The city guards, who should have been keeping people off the streets, were among those pressing against the wrought-iron fence that encircled the palace grounds, craning their necks to get a view of the man who claimed to be the long-dead son of long-dead King Tamaros.

The barons and knights came out of their meeting to find their way back to the palace blocked. The moment the crowd became aware of their presence, they clamored for news. Eventually, finding that they could not enter the palace otherwise, the barons hastily chose one of their number to speak. Someone rolled forth a large dray used by one of the local breweries for hauling kegs. The spokesman climbed into the wagon; the crowd was hushed, attentive.

The baron began by relating everything that Dagnarus had said. The baron's recounting was accurate, as far as it went. He was sympathetic to Dagnarus, that much was clear, and he soon had the crowd on his side. There were emphatic nods in many places and a rousing cheer when he came to the part "Vinnengaelean soldiers are the bravest, the best, the most loyal soldiers in the world!" for there were many in the crowd who had served in the city militia and who, even now, had friends and relatives standing duty on the walls.

When he spoke of the young king, his voice softened, and the crowd murmured in sympathy, particularly the women.

"But as much as we love our young king," the baron proclaimed, "he *is* young—only a child. He will not be of age to rule for many years. Meanwhile, we all know who is the true power behind the throne."

He cast a grim glance at the Temple. The crowd followed his gaze, and a low rumble, like a growl, swept the multitude.

"Hypocrites," Rigiswald told them from his vantage point in the Temple. "There is not a one of you who has not run bleating to the Church at some time in your life. You want to be healed, you want magic to lift the stones that build your homes, you want to be protected. Yes, we've made mistakes, the gods help us. But you're about to make the biggest mistake of your lives."

"We support Prince Dagnarus!" cried the baron.

The crowd let out a cheer that shook the ground and sent the pigeons flapping skyward in alarm. The barons and knights climbed into the wagon and were escorted by the crowd in a grand procession to the gates.

Rigiswald, disgusted, turned on his heel and went back inside the Temple. There he found some of the novitiates and acolytes huddled together in the foyer, listening with wide eyes and shocked expressions.

"Is it true, Revered Brother?" asked a young woman with a snub nose who wasn't in awe of anyone, let alone an elderly master. "Are they truly siding with the Lord of the Void?"

"Go back to your studies," Rigiswald advised her. "You will have need of them."

Outside, he could hear the crowd shouting: "Dagnarus! Dagnarus!" Someone scrounged up a kettledrum, and they began chanting the name to its rhythmic beat, separating the name into three parts with the drum in between.

"Dag-nar-us!" Boom. "Dag-nar-us." Boom.

"Well, that should make him feel at home," Rigiswald reflected as he went back to his room in the dortour. "He'll think he's back among his savages."

Once in his room, he slammed shut the door, to block out the noise, and bolted it. The resulting silence was soothing, gave him a chance to think. He pondered what to do. He intended to report to Shadamehr, but should he make his report now or wait until the matter of Dagnarus was final? Rigiswald decided that there was no hurry. The baron was out in the middle of the ocean somewhere, hopefully sailing as fast and as far away from New Vinnengael as possible. As for Dagnarus, his coronation was a given, as far as Rigiswald was concerned. He was curious to know how their new king planned to rid himself of ten thousand slavering monsters thirsting for Vinnengaelean blood though.

And how would Dagnarus deal with the Church? He couldn't hope to find support there. Or could he?

"He will," Rigiswald decided, lying down on his bed, worn out by the rigors of the day. "He'll win them over, and those he doesn't he'll remove. If I were you, Clovis, I'd watch my back."

The thought occurred to Rigiswald, as he was drifting off, that he had better watch his own back. He'd been foolish to mention the Vrykyl. Dagnarus had been none too pleased, and there had been a look in his eye that jolted Rigiswald out of his slumber when he recalled it. He fumbled about his robes, drew out his vial of earth, tossed some beneath the door, and muttered a few words of magic.

The warding spell would not stop the Lord of the Void, but Dagnarus could hardly be expected to come deal with an annoying old man himself, and it might stop one of his minions. Either that, or give Rigiswald time to defend himself.

Keeping hold of the vial, Rigiswald rolled over and went to sleep.

Prince Dagnarus did not leave the palace. He was escorted to a private chamber, where he was furnished with food and wine. Since he dined on the Void, Dagnarus had no need of sustenance, and, in fact, the sight of food sickened him. But he had learned over the years to pretend to eat for the benefit of those watching, learned to force down a few mouthfuls, shoving the food around on his plate, sharing delicacies with his guests. He could drink, and he did drink, often to excess.

Wine closed the staring, accusing eyes of Gareth and Shakur and all the rest of those he'd murdered. Wine made the foul Vrykyl Valura—the woman he had once loved, the woman he now loathed almost as much as he loathed himself—beautiful again. Wine gave him the patience to put up with Shakur, kept him from slaying a servant who was rapidly growing to be more trouble than he was worth. Wine gave Dagnarus the ability to stomach the taan, a deadly weapon he himself had forged, a weapon he despised and had recently begun to think might come to be pointed at his own throat.

Dagnarus did not drink deeply this evening. He needed his wits about him. Looking back over his performance that day, he was pleased with it. He was particularly impressed with his decision—formed in the moment—to destroy the taan. Once he was Emperor of Vinnengael, he would have no need for such a large military force. He would send half to retake the Portal at Delak 'Vir, then ship those taan back through the Portal to continue the fight in Karnu—a fight that was going badly, but one he had not yet lost.

All was proceeding according to plan. He had won over the barons, the knights, and the military. He had not won over the Church, nor would he ever, but he could deal with that. He had been planning to have his Vrykyl replace certain key people—the Regent, for one. But he'd been forced to abandon that idea as too dangerous. The battle magi knew of the Vrykyl; they'd actually managed to slay the inept Jedash. Dagnarus blamed Shakur for that lapse. The battle magi would be on their guard against them and, much as Dagnarus hated the Church, he had a healthy respect for the brains and abilities of her magi.

"I will dispense with the Regent's services," Dagnarus decided, pouring himself another goblet of the excellent wine that came direct from the royal cellars. "I will make her a nonentity. Too bad she cannot meet with an accident, but that would look suspicious. The key is to win over the battle magi. Once I have them on my side, they will keep the heads of the Orders in check. The most dangerous to me is that blasted Inquisitor, always sniffing about in search of Void magic."

Dagnarus turned the goblet in his hand, stared into the ruby depths. "I will see to it that his Order is disbanded. That should be easy enough. No one trusts them. I'll wager that most in the Temple will be happy to see them gone. As to the battle magi, they are warriors, and I understand warriors. We understand each other. They will help me destroy the taan and, after that, there will be no question of their loyalty to me."

That decided, he sent the servants away and spent the remainder of his time pacing the room and thinking. He heard the cheers of the crowd outside, heard them chanting his name, and he smiled. He ignored Shakur, who wanted to speak to him through the Blood-knife. Shakur's impertinent question about the king destroying those loyal to him had angered Dagnarus, and he intended to make his anger felt. Let Shakur stew a bit, reflect on the fact that he hung suspended over the Void by a rope thin as a hair, a rope Dagnarus could sever at whim. Dagnarus shut out Shakur's whinings and pleadings and concentrated on more pleasant prospects—his plans for the future, both long-range and short.

His long-range plans were very long-range. Dagnarus's ambition did not stop with Vinnengael. The Shield of the Divine was under his control; the elven nation was practically his for the asking. All that was left was finally to subdue Karnu, then go after the orks and the dwarves and, once they were conquered—which they would be, when he had control of all four parts of the Sovereign Stone—he would rule over all of Loerem. Since his life span was extended every time he used the Dagger of the Vrykyl to steal another's life, Dagnarus planned to rule Loerem for a very long time indeed.

All he required was the Sovereign Stone. Too long it had eluded him. He saw the gods at work, but that did not daunt him. Dagnarus wanted the Stone, had wanted it for two centuries, and he intended to have it. He'd devised a means of thwarting the gods. Even now his agents were working to bring the Stone into his grasp.

Prince Dagnarus returned to the Hall of Past Glories at the hour of sunset, which, with the overcast skies, was almost dark as midnight. He was greeted by barons and knights, merchants and the military, who formed a double line through which he walked, welcomed by their applause. The representatives of the Church stood huddled together, off to one side, surrounded by armed guards. The wizened old monk from Dragon Mountain was present, dwarfed by the enormous Omarah. The young king, looking sullen and pouty, sat upon his throne and kicked at the legs with his feet.

Dagnarus grinned inwardly at the sight. "So, Shakur," he said mentally, his hand clasping the Dagger of the Vrykyl that he wore concealed beneath his flowing cloak, "what has been going on?"

Shakur sounded aggrieved. "I tried to speak to you earlier, my lord—"

"You are speaking to me now, and we don't have much time." Dagnarus moved slowly along the line, bowing to the left and the right, stopping occasionally to shake someone's hand or receive someone's blessing.

"There was a frightful row, my lord," Shakur reported. "The barons and the military and the merchants side with you. They have never liked the power the Church has wielded, and they see this as a way to overthrow them. The Regent argued, as you might expect, that you were a liar, a foul creation of the Void, who will drag them all into the Void. She was hooted down and, after much shouting, the barons eventually ordered that the Church officials be forcibly expelled from the palace. It seemed for a moment as if there was going to be a fight, but the battle magus Tasgall intervened. He said that so long as he breathed, the day would not come when Vinnengaeleans shed the blood of Vinnengaeleans, especially with an enemy at their gates. He asked for time alone with his fellow Church members.

"They spoke together in private for about an hour; the result was that they agreed to accept you as ruler of Vinnengael, on condition that you fulfill your promise to get rid of the taan who threaten the city. In truth, there was not much else they could do, not without starting a civil war. I am certain they are plotting against you, my lord."

"Of course they are, Shakur." Dagnarus had very nearly reached the end of the line, was drawing close to the dais.

"They could be removed . . ."

"No, Shakur, I intend to use honey on these flies."

Dagnarus reached the dais. He stood in front of little Havis, who returned his lord's smile with innocent charm and dead, empty eyes.

"One question, my lord, before we commence this charade," said Shakur. "What is to become of me? I cannot remain a child locked up in this prison forever."

"I rather like you as a child, Shakur," said Dagnarus playfully. "We could have such fun together, you and I—play stickball and king-of-the-mountain."

"My lord—" Shakur was seething.

"Come now, Shakur," Dagnarus said, "give us a 'cousinly' kiss."

Bending his knee, Dagnarus knelt before Havis, who rose from his throne. Walking forward, the king gave Dagnarus a kiss on the cheek.

The resulting cheers thundered up and down the corridor and could be heard by the waiting populace outside, who joined in lustily, though they had no idea what they were cheering.

"Well, my lord?" Shakur demanded dourly, as Dagnarus straightened to his full height.

"Don't worry, Shakur," said Dagnarus. "I will see to it that you are set free. I have need of you elsewhere, in fact."

"Very good, my lord," said Shakur.

Havis reached out his hand, took hold of Dagnarus's hand, and turned so that they faced the multitude. The boy raised his voice.

"Let it be hereby known by all assembled and let it be proclaimed to the citizens of Vinnengael that I, Havis III, king of Vinnengael, do freely abdicate the throne bequeathed to me by my father, Havis II, in favor of my cousin, Prince Dagnarus, son of King Tamaros, rightful heir to the throne of Vinnengael."

Havis removed the crown (which was much too large for him and required padding to prevent it sliding down his nose), and handed the crown to Dagnarus with a bow.

He held the crown for a moment, staring at it, his expression somber and grave. The crown dated back about 180 years, and was modern in make and design. The old, heavy crown of Vinnengael, with its one hundred magnificent star sapphires, each surrounded by diamonds, had been lost in the destruction of the city. Dagnarus had searched for that crown, as well as the jewel-encrusted orb and scepter and other valuable pieces of royal jewelry, on his perilous journey into the ruins, but had not been able to find them. He guessed that Helmos had hidden them away for safekeeping when the city came under attack. Dagnarus intended to find them, but that would come later.

For the moment, he held in his hand two hundred years of dreams and desires, tears and blood. He looked out into the crowd. He saw the fat barons smiling and exchanging glances and nods. They thought they had him in their pockets. He saw the courtiers prepared to fawn over him as they had fawned over the Regent, ready to shift allegiance whenever the wind changed. He saw the magi—rebellious, smoldering with anger and probably already plotting his downfall. All would bend their knees and proclaim him king, but they would do it with winks and nudges, or glowering looks, or simpering snickers.

No! by the gods or by the Void, whoever would accept his vow. He wanted them prostrate before him, all of them crushed and humbled, the arrogance bled out of them, the fight kicked out of them. He wanted them to bathe his feet with grateful tears. He wanted their ungrudging blessings.

They needed a whipping.

"I thank you, Your Highness," said Dagnarus. "I accept this crown, but only in trust—"

The people began to murmur. The barons looked uneasy, the magi wary.

"—until I have proven myself worthy of being your ruler. And that will not happen until I have led the fight to crush the enemy that threatens you."

Dagnarus walked over to the elderly monk, who was watching with eyes that were bright with curiosity and interest on the surface, dark and inscrutable beneath. He handed the crown to the monk.

"I ask you hold this for me, Keeper of Times, until the day has come when I am victorious over my enemies, have ground them to dust beneath my feet."

Those in the room thought he was speaking of the taan. What the monk thought or knew was anyone's guess.

The monk gave a nod, and said something to the Omarah, in what was presumably their own language. The Omarah grunted. One reached out and took hold of the crown. Engulfing the precious object in a huge and none-too-clean hand, he thrust it unceremoniously beneath his sheepskin vest, then resumed his protective stance. His impassive expression did not alter. He might have been harboring a plucked chicken, not the symbol of the most powerful kingdom on Loerem.

Behind Dagnarus, the hall was abuzz, few knowing what to make of his action, everyone speculating eagerly with his or her neighbor.

Dagnarus ignored them. He looked across the room to the mural, to the painting of his father, Tamaros, standing proudly next to Helmos.

Dagnarus looked long at his father, long at Helmos, the child beloved.

Not anymore.

Dagnarus beckoned to a courtier.

"Send for the artist who painted that mural."

"At once, Your Majesty," replied the man, with an elaborate bow. "If I could perhaps give him some hint of the nature of Your Majesty's wishes—"

Dagnarus smiled. "He is to plaster over that picture and paint my portrait in its place."

THE BARONS AND THEIR COHORTS WERE UNDERSTANDABLY EAGER to hear how Dagnarus planned to defeat the taan army. During the day, the enemy army was swallowed by the gloom, and there were some who hoped that they might all march off. When night fell, their campfires could once more be seen as orange smudges in the murk. Dagnarus assured the Vinnengaeleans that he had a plan. He intended to put it into effect the very next day.

His first order as king was that a lavish banquet be prepared that night in his honor, with plenty of food and drink, and that all present were to be invited. He included the monk in his invitation. The monk politely declined. Dagnarus asked if the monk found his chambers in the palace suitable. The monk replied that he did, and he and his Omarah went off to them. Dagnarus reveled in the knowledge that what he had done that day would be recorded on the old monk's wrinkled skin, then he returned to business.

The heads of the Orders declined his generous offer to join him at the banquet. The Regent asked coldly if they might be allowed to return to their duties in the Temple, and Dagnarus permitted them to do so. The barons growled at that, said loudly that the churchmen should be kept under guard, perhaps even arrested. Dagnarus turned to them.

"Gentlemen," he said, his tone severe, "I take offense at that kind of talk, which is an insult to the cloth. You will show the same respect for the Church that you show to me."

The barons looked startled, some even sullen, at this rebuke.

"Come now, gentlemen," Dagnarus added, his smile returning, "we have much to rejoice about. Proceed to the banquet hall. I will join you there shortly and we will drink to my coronation and the discomfiture of our enemies."

The barons departed, sounding the new king's praises. The room emptied, until only the Church members remained.

"I know that you do not trust me, Revered Sister," Dagnarus said to the Regent, "and that is understandable. But I hope that in time we can become friends. I assure you that I have the utmost respect and veneration for the gods, who have so greatly blessed me."

The Regent, gray-faced and ill-looking, made no reply. Bowing stiffly, she asked, "Do I have your leave to depart, Your Majesty?"

"You do not need my leave, Regent," said Dagnarus gently. "You and any other member of the Church are welcome in the palace at any time. You may come and go freely."

"Thank you, Your Majesty," she said, and stalked out of the hall. The others, bowing, followed after her.

"Battle Magus," Dagnarus called.

Tasgall, grim and wary, glanced around.

"I would speak with you concerning my plan for dealing with the taan."

The battle magus returned and came over to stand before the throne. Tasgall faced Dagnarus, looked him straight in the eyes. He said nothing, waited expectantly.

Dagnarus dismissed the servants. When he and Tasgall were alone, Dagnarus stepped down from the throne.

"Come take a turn about the room with me, Revered Sir," Dagnarus said. "I find it easier to think on my feet."

The battle magus fell into step beside him.

"What is your name, sir?" Dagnarus asked. "Forgive me. I know we were introduced, but I have no head for names."

"Tasgall, Your Majesty."

"Surname?"

"Fotheringall, sire. My family comes from a small village in the foothills of the Ork Mountains."

"There is a pass through those mountains, as I recall. Do the orks ever come through that pass?" Dagnarus asked, with evident interest.

"The occasional raiding party, Your Majesty," Tasgall replied. "Nothing more."

"I understand that the orks have threatened to go to war against us, because of what they believe is our complicity in the matter of the Karnuan seizure of their holy mountain. It occurs to me that they might come through the pass in force. Do we need a garrison there?"

Tasgall did answer immediately, but gave the matter thought.

"I do not think I would waste the manpower, Your Majesty," he said at last. "The orks have little stomach for ground warfare. That much is apparent from the fact that they have not yet tried to retake their mountain."

"I knew it was so in the old days," said Dagnarus. "I did not know if their customs and habits had changed in the intervening time. I plan to turn to you, Tasgall, for advice and information of this sort. I trust I will be able to rely on you?"

"I am glad that I will be able to be of service to Your Majesty. It's good that finally someone is—" Tasgall paused, shut his mouth.

"Good that finally someone is taking an interest in military affairs? No, you do not need to answer that. I understand."

"Now about the taan, Your Majesty . . ." Tasgall hinted.

"Always one to get down to business, aren't you, Tasgall? I like that in a man. I have a plan for dealing with the taan. To pull it off, I require the help of your battle magi—all of them, as many as you can assemble within twenty-four hours. It is essential that they be familiar with Void magic, that they know how to recognize it and counter it. I will meet with them tomorrow, to explain my plan. You will bring them to me here at the palace when the sun is at its zenith."

Tasgall, who had slowed his pace during their conversation, finally came to a halt. He regarded his new monarch in speculative silence.

"I know," said Dagnarus. He had continued walking, and now he rounded to look back at the battle magus. "I know what you are thinking. That this would be a fine way for me to dispose of some highly dangerous individuals who have no reason to love me."

Tasgall made no reply, continued to stare intently at his new ruler.

"I am not a good man," Dagnarus admitted. "I have done terrible things in my life. Things I bitterly regret. I could offer as my excuse that I was young and heedless, and that would be the truth. I could say that I was ambitious and fond of power, and that would be the truth."

He shrugged. His smile twisted, his eyes darkened. "I could say that the gods have punished me, that I have suffered in consequence of my acts, and that would also be the truth. But know this, sir."

Dagnarus lifted his gaze, opened his eyes, so that Tasgall could see deep inside him, see the darkness and the tiny spark of light.

"I did what I did for one reason, Tasgall. In all the evil acts I committed, I was motivated by one desire that was pure and untarnished, one desire that has guided everything I have done since the time I was old enough to understand myself. To be the King of Vinnengael, to guide her to greatness and glory, to place her in a preeminent position in this world, to see her rule unchallenged over all other nations, that is and has always been my dearest wish. I swear to you, Tasgall, that all I have done and all I will do is for Vinnengael.

"Tasgall," said Dagnarus earnestly. "I know you believe that I am king because I held a knife to your throat. I know that you do not trust me. I plan to earn that trust, but that will take time. Time we don't have. I say only this—if I truly meant harm to Vinnengael, I would have used that knife. I would have unleashed ten thousand taan upon her. The taan are fierce and terrible warriors, whose greatest hope in life is to meet death gloriously in battle. They would have taken New Vinnengael. You did not stand a chance. I did not do that. I ask you, therefore, to give me the opportunity to prove myself by saving the city and the nation that I love."

Tasgall was moved. Dagnarus could see it. He pressed home his advantage.

"I will make you this promise, Tasgall. I give my life into your hands. If a single Vinnengaelean dies because of my treachery, you will slay me."

Tasgall shook his head. "Your life already spans two hundred years—"

"By the will of the gods! Yet, I am mortal!" Dagnarus said eagerly. "Give me your sword."

Never taking his eyes from Dagnarus, Tasgall removed his sword from its sheath and handed it, pommel first, to his king.

Holding the hilt in his right hand, Dagnarus wrapped the left hand around the naked blade, clasped it tightly, and then slowly and deliberately slid his hand along the razor-sharp edge.

"Your Majesty!" Tasgall gasped. He took an instinctive step forward, hand reached out to stop him.

"Stand back!" Dagnarus ordered. He winced slightly at the pain, but that was all. Letting loose the sword, he opened his palm.

Blood smeared the steel blade. Blood, red and gleaming, filled his cupped hand and dripped from his hand onto the floor of the Hall of Past Glories.

"You see, I *am* mortal," Dagnarus said.

Tasgall stared at the blood on his king's wounded hand, on the blood that continued to drip onto the floor.

"The battle magi will be assembled and ready for you to command by morning, sire."

"Excellent," said Dagnarus. Using the sword, he carelessly sliced a long strip of cloth from his cloak and bound it over the wound.

"I could heal that for Your Majesty," said Tasgall.

"Come now, sir," said Dagnarus, smiling, "what would be the point of this exhibition if I permitted you to heal me? No. The wound will be a constant reminder to us both of my promise to you."

Dagnarus wiped the blade clean of blood with the tail of his maltreated cape, then returned the sword, with a flourish, to Tasgall, who received it solemnly and thrust it back into its sheath.

Certain of Tasgall's admiration, if not yet his complete trust, Dagnarus proceeded to explain his plan for the annihilation of the taan army. As Tasgall listened, he became more and more intrigued. Forgetful of time, they remained talking in the Hall of Past Glories until one of the barons came to carry Dagnarus off to feasting and celebration.

As for the taan, instead of the battle they had been promised, they watched their god, Dagnarus, Lord of the Void, ride alone into the city they had come all this way to attack. The taan knew of this strange custom of the derrhuth, that they must talk before a battle, "to try to prevent bloodshed," or so their god had told them, but they did not understand it.

Since taan live to shed their blood in battle, they saw no need to waste time bandying words. The fact that these derrhuth would do anything to avoid a fight further convinced the taan—who needed little convincing—of the inherent weakness of the species. The taan returned to their campfires and their topaxi and their stories of brave warriors. The topaxi was stronger than usual, and the celebration grew rowdy. Needing a vent for the aggression, the taan started to take it out on each other. The fights were not good-natured. They were brutal and ugly and more than one nizam had to wade in to break them up.

Nb'arsk stalked about the camp, watching the morale of her people dip lower and lower, and she could not imagine what Dagnarus was up to. This was not the first time he had showed that he had no real understanding of the taan, for all he claimed to be their god.

The other derrhuth in the camp—the human mercenaries, who served Dagnarus—were not bothered by this lack of action. The humans spoke laughingly of sieges that lasted months, even years, during which time enemy armies did nothing but take an occasional potshot at one another from over the walls. Nb'arsk had thought at first they were telling her falsehoods that were meant to be funny—joking was another mysterious aspect of the derrhuth—but she at last became convinced that they spoke the truth. Derrhuth really did fight that way.

Nb'arsk watched the humans laughing and cursing over their games of chance, watched them roll about in the bushes with some of their females, or lie on the ground, wrapped in their blankets, snoring. She watched them with loathing, despised them for cowards. She wondered that her god could stomach being around them, and, not for the first time, Nb'arsk wondered about her god.

Dagnarus fought like a god of the taan, he had the courage of a taan, the ferocity of a taan, the cunning of a taan. For all this, Nb'arsk revered him. Yet, there was a mystery about him she could never understand. When he was not wearing the miraculous black armor that marked him as Lord of the Void, Dagnarus the god chose to walk about in the skin of a derrhuth.

Now he had gone off to the city of derrhuths—a fat city, he said, with stores of steel armor and steel weapons, with treasure chests filled with the gemstones the taan first enchant with Void magic, then place beneath their hides, and with many derrhuth to be taken into slavery and used for food. All that, their god had promised them. Better, though, he had promised them war against a well-armed foe, the chance for the young warriors to prove themselves and advance in rank, and for the older warriors to achieve glory.

Three times the sun had risen on this city and three times it had set, and there was no talk of battle. There was just talk.

Nb'arsk was a kyl-sarnz, a Vrykyl. Three taan had been "god-touched," as the taan knew it—transformed into Vrykyl. The eldest of these, K'let, an albino taan, had been among the first taan to meet Dagnarus when he entered their world. Dagnarus had slain K'let with the Dagger of the Vrykyl, transformed him into the undead, soul-stealing fiends of the Void.

The Vrykyl are bound to Dagnarus through the Dagger, forced to do his will or face banishment into the emptiness of the Void. All Vrykyl were constrained to obey Dagnarus, but not K'let. When Dagnarus sought to exert his control over K'let, the Vrykyl defied him. K'let saw then, as Nb'arsk was beginning to see now, that Dagnarus had no care for the taan, but was merely using them for his own ends.

K'let broke with Dagnarus—the first and only Vrykyl ever to do so. K'let left Dagnarus's army, taking with him taan loyal to him. K'let's goal was to prove to the taan that Dagnarus was not a god, that he was nothing but a derrhuth playing at being a god.

Nb'arsk knew because she was in touch with K'let through the Blood-knife—something Dagnarus did not know.

Nb'arsk did not believe K'let. She was pleased and honored to be among the "god-touched," and was proud to serve Dagnarus. Nb'arsk should have told Dagnarus that she was in contact with K'let. Yet she did not. She did not speak to K'let either, but kept her misgivings to herself.

Her misgivings had grown during their march through the land of the gdsr—the elves, a race of derrhuth so weak and spindly that they did not even make good slaves. The cities of the gdsr were fat and filled with jewels and steel, and the taan looked forward to conquering them. Dagnarus forbade it. The taan swept through the lands of the gdsr by means of a magical hole-in-the-air. They fought one battle, and that was over one of these holes.

No cities, no slaves, no armor, no jewels. Only talk. The gdsr, Dagnarus announced, were going to surrender to him. He would be their ruler and, because of that, he wanted their cities left intact, their people unmolested.

After that, the taan had marched into the land of the xkes, the humans, and it was then that Nb'arsk contacted K'let. She did not agree with all his views—in her mind, Dagnarus was still her god—but her doubts were beginning to grow.

Dagnarus did not return to his armies that night. Nb'arsk had no fear that something might have happened to him—he was a god, after all. When she heard shouts and cries coming from the city, she was pleased. She expected that any moment the taan would be summoned to battle. The taan hastily caught up their weapons and waited for the call.

The call did not come.

Nb'arsk rounded up one of the half-taan, a miserable race, yet one that was useful, for they could speak the language of both the taan and the xkes. Commanding the cringing half-taan to accompany her, Nb'arsk entered the camp of the mercenaries and searched for their leader, a human named Klendist. Klendist had taken command of the army, following the execution of the former mercenary leader, Gurske, following the ill-fated battle of the elven Portal.

"What is going on?" Nb'arsk demanded through the translator. She pointed toward the walled city. "What is the meaning of all that noise? Has our god started the killing without us?"

"Hardly!" Klendist began to laugh, then clamped his mouth shut. He was not afraid of the Vrykyl, as were most of the other humans. But he didn't like her, didn't like being around her. "That's cheering you hear. I don't know what's going on, but it must be good. Likely the city has surrendered."

The half-taan translated as best she could, for the taan have no word for "surrender." Nb'arsk had come to understand it, however.

Nb'arsk glared balefully at the city, which smelled so strongly and sweetly of human flesh. "So again we are not to fight."

"Who knows?" Klendist said, shrugging. "His Lordship will tell us, one way or the other."

"I don't like this," Nb'arsk growled.

"It is not your place to like it, Vrykyl," Klendist returned. "You will do what your god tells you."

The half-taan sank to his knees before translating Klendist's words, begging that the Vrykyl would not think they were his own words. Nb'arsk knew well enough that they were not.

She turned on her heel, about to depart, when a sudden thought struck her.

"Dagnarus is not your god, is he?"

Klendist was first startled by her question, then amused.

"No," he answered shortly.

"Who is your god?"

"I don't believe in gods," Klendist returned. "A man does for himself in this life."

Nb'arsk considered this. "None of you xkes believe Dagnarus is a god. Why is that? He is as powerful as a god."

"I guess because he was born human," Klendist said. "Whatever may have happened to him after that, he started out the same as us. Likely his old man walloped him on his backside, same as my old man did me. So, no, I don't consider him a god."

The human walked off, shaking his head at the stupidity of the "savages."

Nb'arsk stared after him. She had wondered about the humans' impiety before now, but she had always put it down to the fact that they were an impious race. They held nothing sacred, unless it be their physical pleasures. She was often angered by their lack of reverence around Dagnarus; but now that she looked back, she saw that he did nothing to encourage reverence for himself among the xkes. Not as he did among the taan.

"What if K'let is right?" she muttered, chilled. "What if he is not a god? What does that mean for us?"

Nb'arsk walked among the taan, who slept soundly, after their revels. She pondered such questions all the rest of the night.

She had her answer in the morning.

Dagnarus returned to his forces as the sun's light illuminated the eastern sky. Darkness still lay upon the land; the taan warriors slept. The taan taskers were up and about, preparing the meal that would break their fast. Cloaked in the Void, Dagnarus emerged from the mists rising off the river, seemed to materialize right in front of Nb'arsk.

She was startled and impressed and uncomfortable. He seemed godlike, shredding the mists that clung to him with ghostly hands. The black armor of the Void gleamed in the predawn gray light. Catching sight of Nb'arsk, he motioned her to walk with him.

She could not tell what he was thinking, for she could not see his face. He wore the bestial helm of the Lord of the Void, kept his face concealed. The faces of the derrhuth were weak faces, soft and pliable, revealing every emotion, every thought. Dagnarus always wore the helm when he spoke to the taan, well aware that when he came before them in his human form, he lost something.

He turned the bestial metal face toward Nb'arsk. She saw dark eyes and inner fire, and for a moment she cowered, for she feared that he might have seen her rebellious thoughts. She very nearly sank to her knees, to beg him to forgive her, but then he spoke, and his demeanor was brisk, businesslike. They communicated through the Dagger of the Vrykyl, thought to thought, thus sparing the need for a translator.

"I have orders for you, Nb'arsk. You will take five thousand taan and march south to a city known as Delak 'Vir. I will send one of the taan sages to you with maps. You will attack and seize the city and the Portal that is there. Once you have conquered the city and slain or enslaved all the inhabitants, you will leave one thousand taan to guard the city. The rest of you will enter the hole-in-the-air. The Portal will take you to the land of Karnu, where you meet up with the other taan Vrykyl, L'nskt, and you will reinforce those taan already fighting there."

Nb'arsk was pleased and relieved. No derrhuth-talk of negotiating or surrender. This was talk a taan could understand: seize, conquer, slay, enslave.

"You will leave at once," Dagnarus continued. "Rouse the taan and get them started. I want the army on the road by first light."

The taan were always prepared to pick up camp and move, so a swift departure did not present a problem. But why were they splitting forces? What were the remainder of the taan going to be doing?

"Tomorrow at first light, we enter New Vinnengael," he replied.

"Enter, Ko-kutryx?" Nb'arsk asked, displeased. "Not attack?"

"There is no need to attack," he returned. "The city has surrendered to me. The people have made me their god."

"I am pleased for *you,* Ko-kutryx," said Nb'arsk. "But for the taan this means no slaves. No gemstones, no armor."

"On the contrary," said Dagnarus. "These city people are an arrogant people. They need to be humbled in both spirit and body. They need to understand that *I* am their god and that my word is law. I plan to use the taan to teach them what it means to respect my authority."

Nb'arsk was skeptical. "How will this come about, Ko-kutryx? How will we gain entry to the city without battle?"

"The city people think, in their arrogance, that they are preparing a trap for the taan, a trap into which the taan will walk blindly because the taan are ignorant beasts."

Dagnarus laughed at this, as did Nb'arsk.

"In reality, of course," he continued, "it is the taan who will be setting the trap for the humans—a trap I will spring once the taan are inside the city."

"I would like to be a part of that trap, Ko-kutryx," stated Nb'arsk eagerly. "So will all the taan." She made a dismissive gesture. "We will conquer this hole-in-the-air another day."

"I gave you an order, Nb'arsk," said Dagnarus. "I am not accustomed to having my orders questioned. You will march at first light, as I have commanded."

"Yes, Ko-kutryx," Nb'arsk replied, chastened. "I did not mean to question you."

"I will not be here to see you leave, for I must return to the city. Remember, you must be on the road with first light. Glory in battle, Nb'arsk."

"Glory in battle, Ko-kutryx."

Nb'arsk roused the taan and gave the order to march. The taan worked swiftly to dismantle their camps, and in less time than it would have taken the humans to have crawled, bleary-eyed, out of their tents, the taan were packed up and ready to go. The prospect of more slaves, more armor, and a grand battle lay before them. Their spirits high, the taan cheered Nb'arsk as she took her place at the head of the column and gave the order to move out.

Glancing back at the city, Nb'arsk was sorry and ashamed of her previous feelings of doubt and disloyalty. The taan Vrykyl and half the taan army headed south for Delak 'Vir.

ONE OF THE FIRST LESSONS GIVEN A MAGUS IS A LESSON IN SLEEP. Since the ability to sleep is inherent in all living creatures, the notion that one must be taught to sleep seems ludicrous to those who do not have to rely on the use of magic for either their lives or their livelihood. Magic is termed a "gift" of the gods, and so it is—a power akin to that of the gods given to mankind for his use. But the term "gift" does not imply, as some laymen mistakenly believe, that magic may be used without cost.

Wielding magic is hard work, drains the strength of the magic-user. The only means of renewing that strength is through sleep; deep, peaceful, restful, uninterrupted sleep. Thus, all magi must know how to leave behind them all worldly thoughts and cares and find strength and renewal in sleep.

Battle magi, in particular, must learn to find peace and relaxation under circumstances that are far from peaceful or relaxing. Thus Tasgall was able to banish all his mental turmoil, his worries, anxieties, fears, and doubts with a few moments of silent prayer. He slept well and deeply, woke with the dawn feeling refreshed, to find that his worries, anxieties, fears, and doubts were exactly where he had left them the night before.

The bell that woke the inhabitants of the Temple and sent them about their daily chores had barely rung before the knocking started on Tasgall's door. He was summoned to meet with the Regent. He was summoned to meet with the Inquisitor. He was summoned to meet with both the Regent and the Inquisitor.

He sent back word that he would meet with the heads of the Orders, that the meeting would be brief, and that he would do all the talking.

They didn't like that, of course. He'd known they wouldn't, but he could not afford to spend the time required for them to hear his plan, discuss it and debate it, view it from all sides, turn it inside out, then try to decide whether and how to proceed with it.

He planned to talk privately to only one person that morning, and that person was Rigiswald. Tasgall sought out his old teacher in the library.

Entering, he searched among the tables and their silent readers doggedly pursuing their studies even in the midst of turmoil and war, to find Rigiswald seated near a stone-light. Tasgall rested his hand upon the magus's shoulder.

Rigiswald glanced up. Seeing who it was, he immediately closed his book and accompanied Tasgall to the room where they had talked earlier.

"I do not have much time," Tasgall said. He did not sit down, and neither did Rigiswald. "I have to meet with the heads of the Orders in a few moments to explain the course of action we are going to take tomorrow against the taan. The heads are not going to like it," he added grimly. "I don't like it. And yet, this course is our only way to live through this, that I can see."

"What do you want of me?" Rigiswald asked.

"You know this man, Dagnarus."

"I wouldn't say that," Rigiswald replied.

"You have studied him—"

"As best one can. I have studied what has been written of him, but he is, as are we all, a very complex individual."

Tasgall brushed all that aside with an impatient gesture. He then proceeded to outline Dagnarus's plan for dealing with the taan. When he had finished, he looked intently at Rigiswald.

"Well?" Tasgall demanded.

"Well, what?" Rigiswald returned irascibly, unwilling to be drawn into that matter. "You have obviously made up your mind to go along with him, Tasgall. I don't understand what you seek of me. My approval?"

"No," said Tasgall. "From what you know of him, is this a trap—"

"Certainly it is a trap."

"But a trap for whom?" Tasgall asked tensely. "For the taan? Or for us?"

s silent, thoughtful, then he asked, "Do you now believe
ng is one of Dagnarus's Vrykyl?"

what to believe," Tasgall returned impatiently. "At one
terday, yes, maybe I did. But now I'm not sure, and, anyway, does it really matter? The young king is no longer king."

Rigiswald could have said that it mattered a great deal, but, of course, it didn't. Not to Tasgall, who held the lives of thousands in his hands. Rigiswald sighed deeply.

"Dagnarus pledged his faith with his life," Tasgall argued, seeming to try to convince himself as much as Rigiswald. "He has given himself as hostage. We are to slay him if he betrays us."

"If he is the wielder of the Dagger of the Vrykyl, he has as many lives as there are Vrykyl in this world, for everyone of them bequeaths a life to Dagnarus when he dies. You might have to kill him forty times over in order to truly slay him," Rigiswald said dryly.

"He is mortal!" Tasgall stated. "He cut himself. The red blood flowed."

"And did he permit you to heal his wound?"

"No. He said . . ." Tasgall paused.

"Of course, he didn't. He didn't let you heal him because you couldn't. Dagnarus is the Lord of the Void, and, as such, he is tainted with Void. All the Earth magic in the world could not have healed him. If it is any comfort to you, Tasgall, I myself found Dagnarus to be quite charming, engaging, even sympathetic. We both know what he is, yet we both feel drawn to him. He is like one of the bitter potions the healers must mix with honey so that patients will swallow it. Except that he is poison."

"And is this honey-coated poison meant for us?" Tasgall asked. He looked worn, suddenly, weary.

Rigiswald hesitated. "It is not so much the lies that trouble me, as it is the multitude of truths."

Tasgall snorted, exasperated.

"I believe Dagnarus when he claims that this trap is a trap for the taan," Rigiswald said. "I believe him when he says that he will not turn against us and hand us over to those monsters. From my studies on Dagnarus and from what I saw of him yesterday, his dearest wish in this life is to be what his father was—the beloved and honored ruler of Vinnengael. He won't accomplish that by betraying us to the taan."

"That is how I read him," said Tasgall. "But I have one more question for you: Why have the taan entered New Vinnengael at all? He promised to send away half his force and, from reports I received this morning, he has done so. Five thousand taan marched off to the south at first light. Why not just send them all away?"

"He wants us to view the taan in action. He wants us to see how vicious they are, how well they can fight. Yes, we may defeat them now, but the battle won't be easy. He wants us to know that at any time he chooses, he can unleash this vicious dog and send it leaping for our throats."

"That was my take, as well," said Tasgall. "I will have to cram it down the throats of the heads of the Orders. Thank you for discussing the problem with me. I needed to be sure that I have made the right decision."

"I am not certain that you have, Tasgall. I think we'd all be better off in a taan stewpot. But then, you don't have much choice."

"You say yourself that he has the good of Vinnengael at heart. It might not be such a bad thing to have a strong monarch for a change," Tasgall returned testily. "One who is determined to raise Vinnengael in the world's regard and restore her to her former place of glory."

"On top of a charnel heap?" said Rigiswald.

Tasgall eyed the elder magus. "As you say, sir, I don't have much choice."

He left Rigiswald, glad for his advice, yet sorry he'd asked. Tasgall was put in mind of his dreams. Not the substance, for that continued to elude him, but the spirit that left him with a disquieting sense of defeat, loss, and impending doom.

The council meeting went as he'd expected. Tasgall presented Dagnarus's proposal, stated that he was in favor of it, and then stepped back to wait for the breaking storm. The others were convinced that Dagnarus meant to destroy them, that by opening the gates to the taan they might as well be opening the gates to their own doom. Tasgall stood fixed and immovable in the midst of the howling winds that raged at him, ignoring the aspersions and recriminations that buffeted him, answering their arguments by restating his position over and over. He won by being the last man still standing. Over and over he asked if anyone had a better plan and, finally, they were forced to admit that none of them did.

By the end of the meeting, the Regent was suffering from heart palpitations and had to be assisted from the room. She was taken immediately to the House of the Hospitalers. Tasgall permitted the others to depart only after he'd received their sworn promises that each would assist him or at least not get in his way. The head of the Order of Hospitalers had the most to do, for the Houses of Healing would have to be made ready to receive large numbers of casualties.

The one upshot of the meeting that Tasgall found most disconcerting was the fact that the Inquisitor came out on Tasgall's side. Tasgall had never liked the Inquisitor, not even when they were in school together. Tasgall guessed that the only reason the Inquisitor was siding with him now was so that the man would have the opportunity of insinuating himself into his meetings with Dagnarus. Tasgall had seen the Inquisitor and the Regent whispering together. He had no doubt that he was now suspect.

Fine. Let them suspect him of being drawn into the Void. Upon becoming a battle magus, he had sworn an oath to the gods to defend Vinnengael and its people with his life. He would do as he had vowed, though he made enemies of his fellows.

Though his very heart misgave him.

Tasgall brought his battle magi to the palace at the appointed hour. There were fifty in all, a number that included some of the most powerful magi then living. All were highly trained, highly skilled. Most were veterans, having fought the Karnuans at Delak 'Vir and the dwarves on numerous occasions, for the dwarves constantly raided Vinnengaelean territory. Most wielded both Earth and Fire magic, which was the preferred weapon of battle magi because of its extremely destructive nature.

Tasgall was proud of his people. His men and women met Dagnarus with cool detachment and a professional demeanor. They had a job to do, and, whatever their thoughts and feelings about Dagnarus and this sudden shift in power, they kept those thoughts to themselves. As Tasgall had foreseen, the Inquisitor asked politely to be permitted to sit in on the meeting. The asking was a formality. Tasgall could not deny him. His only hope was that the Inquisitor had enough care for the people of New Vinnengael not to do anything that might put them in danger. Knowing the Inquisitor's fanatic adherence to duty, his hope was a faint one.

Dagnarus was in an excellent humor and why not? He had achieved his dearest wish, at long last. He came to greet the magi all personally. He insisted on shaking hands with each and every one of them, asked their names, then escorted them to the meeting room himself. All this he did with a regal air, remaining friendly, but keeping his distance, managing to be at once both king and comrade.

Tasgall could see his magi warming to the man, and he could not blame them. He had to work very hard not to fall under Dagnarus's spell—a spell that had nothing to do with magic.

Dagnarus led them to a meeting room furnished with a round table on which was spread a detailed map of the city. The magi stared at the map in amazement, for none had ever seen anything like it.

"I had a team of mapmakers work on it all night," said Dagnarus. "I knew we would need it, you see. Pure folly to go into battle not knowing the terrain. Is it accurate? Can any of you find fault with it?"

He appeared anxious for the commendation and was pleased as a child by their praise.

"Thank you. Or rather, thank your mapmakers. Excellent fellows, every one of them. I sent them home with a bag of silver tams each. Now"—Dagnarus rubbed his hands—"down to business." He leaned over the map. "The taan will enter here—"

Dagnarus continued talking, pointing to various locales as he explained his plan. The magi focused on his discussion, intent upon the map. Suddenly Dagnarus lifted his eyes, looked straight at the Inquisitor. The king continued to talk, never missing a word, and Tasgall was perhaps the only one who noticed, with the exception of the Inquisitor. His bony face did not change expression. He did not flinch or move. Yet some word passed between the two, of that Tasgall was certain.

Dagnarus smiled slightly, then lowered his eyes to the map. He proceeded with his plan. The Inquisitor stood in silence, his emotions unreadable, except that a muscle twitched in the man's jaw, his hands clenched, knuckles whitened. Tasgall would have given a bag of silver tams himself to know what had occurred. He would ask, of course, but the Inquisitor might not be inclined to answer. By the look of it, whatever had happened between them had not gone the Inquisitor's way.

The discussion and development of the battle plan went on for another two hours without a break. Dagnarus had many good ideas, but some that weren't so good, arising mainly from an imperfect knowledge of the capabilities of a battle magus. He was willing to listen, quick to understand, asked intelligent questions, and glad to give way to superior knowledge.

At the end of two hours, he called a break. He ordered the servants to prepare food and drink for his guests in the dining hall, after which they would resume their discussion. He was pleased with the way the plan was shaping up, had no doubt that they would be victorious on the morrow. He was sorry to hear that the Inquisitor would not be with them during the upcoming sessions, but knew that duty called. The king led the way to the dining hall, conferring with several of the battle magi as they walked.

Tasgall excused himself and managed to catch up with the Inquisitor before the man exited the palace. He fell into step beside him.

"What happened back there, Inquisitor?" Tasgall asked.

"Nothing happened," said the Inquisitor.

"Oh, yes, it did. I saw the exchange. Whatever it was, I need to know. Listen to me," Tasgall added in exasperation, grabbing hold of the man's sleeve and forcing him to halt and face him. "*I* am not the enemy."

"Aren't you?" said the Inquisitor coolly. "You seem very cozy with your new king. Very quick to laugh at his witty remarks and praise him to the skies."

"I laughed because what he said was funny," Tasgall growled. "As for praise, his plan of battle is a good one, and I told him so. I don't trust him, any more than you do. I made that clear in our meeting this morning, if you'd been listening. I thought I also made clear that now is not the time for the left hand to wonder what the right hand is doing. We're all in this together, or should be. What happened?"

The Inquisitor gazed out into nothing for long moments, then his overlarge eyes met Tasgall's.

"I cast a magic spell on him, one intended to disrupt Void magic."

Tasgall was impressed. No slouch at magic himself, he'd had no clue that the Inquisitor had been spell-casting, and he'd been standing right beside him.

"With what intent?" Tasgall asked.

"Experimental," said the Inquisitor. "If he is Lord of the Void, as history claims, I thought perhaps the spell might force him to reveal his true nature, expose him for what he is."

"What your spell exposed was a very comely, intelligent, charming man," returned Tasgall. "Either your spell failed, or perhaps he has been redeemed as he has claimed."

"Balls!" the Inquisitor said, his tone sharp. "My spell did *not* fail. My spell struck a wall and shattered."

"So what are you trying to say, Inquisitor?" Tasgall demanded, growing impatient at having to drag out every scrap of information. "Or not say, as the case may be."

"The spell I cast was a Void spell," the Inquisitor replied in chill tones. "The only way it could be countered was by another Void spell, a very powerful one. Think of that, Battle Magus, the next time you laugh at his jokes."

"And what do you propose I do?" Tasgall demanded of the Inquisitor's back. "Do I allow the taan to come in and slit our throats? Do I cry: 'Ha-ha, sir, the laugh is on you! We're all going to die out of spite.' Is that what you would have me do?"

The Inquisitor paused, turned slowly around. He spoke in low tones, his gaze abstracted, turned inward. "All my life, I have fought against the Void. I have done the gods' work. Good work, too, or so I believed. In order to do my work, I had to learn Void magic." His brow furrowed. He shook his head. "You will not understand this, Tasgall, but I never saw the paradox in that. I never saw, until now, when I looked into his eyes, that I had become what I most loathe.

"As long as Dagnarus rules Vinnengael, Tasgall, so it will be with us all." He shrugged. "Do whatever you think is needful. It won't matter. Not in the end. We lost this battle two hundred years ago."

Tasgall fumed his way back to the meeting room. It was all very well for Rigiswald and the Inquisitor to be so blamed high-minded and speak so eloquently of martyrdom, but what would the twenty-five-year-old Vinnengaelean mother with three little children clinging to her skirts have to say on that subject? She would probably be pretty damned eloquent herself!

Rounding a corner, he very nearly collided with Dagnarus, who was coming from the other direction. A flotilla of courtiers sailed along after him, plying him with compliments and flatteries. Sighting Tasgall, Dagnarus made a leap at him, seized hold of him by the arm, and dragged him off for a private talk. The courtiers remained behind, bobbing in the water, until such time as His Majesty should once more sail in their direction.

"Tasgall," said Dagnarus, "I wanted to let you know that I'm sending young Prince Havis out of harm's way. For his own safety, of course, and to ensure that Vinnengael still has a king, just in case—the gods forbid—our plans go awry. The prince tells me his father has a hunting lodge in the Illanof Mountains. I think he will be safe there, don't you?"

"I don't know, Your Majesty," said Tasgall, troubled. "There is the matter of the taan army—"

"I know the disposition of that army, Tasgall," said Dagnarus, smiling. "They are massed along the river. None have ventured west. I will provide a safe route of travel for His Highness. He will have his own personal retainers with him, and as many men-at-arms as we can spare."

"That will not be many, Your Majesty," said Tasgall.

"Nor will many be required. The prince will be in no danger. I guarantee it. Now, let us return to our work. I am much impressed with your battle magi, Tasgall. I think we are off to an excellent start, don't you?"

"Yes, Your Majesty," said Tasgall.

THE VRYKYL, VALURA, ANNOUNCED TO THE TAAN THAT DAGNARUS had conquered the city of New Vinnengael single-handedly, that its people had declared him to be their god. She proclaimed that the taan would celebrate this occasion with a god day.

Although the taan were again disappointed that there would be no fighting this day, they did not grumble, as they had on previous days. They had been promised that on the morrow they would enter this city and take what they wanted.

The taan loved nothing better than a god day. There would be storytelling and strong food, washed down with copious quantities of topaxi. The highlight of the day would be the kdah-klks—ritual fights between tribal members that had once been used to determine leadership of the tribe, but which were now used to test the skill and courage of young warriors and to enable older warriors to advance in rank.

To mark this Day of Triumph, calaths would be pitted against calaths. This meant that entire battle groups would fight each other, with valuable gifts of weapons and armor going to the winners. The taan were elated.

"You must fight well," the kyl-sarnz told them, "for the xkes of the city will be witness to your prowess."

Valura pointed to the city walls, as she said this, where the taan could see the humans lined up on the battlements, staring across the river at the taan encampment. The taan jeered at them and clashed their weapons.

Her task done, as Dagnarus had commanded, Valura handed over the responsibility for making the arrangements for the god day to the members of the Black Veil, an elite group of taan shamans. Valura was under orders to return to Tromek, the elven kingdom, to support the Shield in his battle against the Divine. She was being sent away, and she knew she would never be allowed to return.

Valura wanted to be with Dagnarus. She wanted to share his victory, to be with him when he gained the prize for which he'd worked and fought and sacrificed so much for so long. She wanted to be present to see him crowned King of Vinnengael. She begged to be allowed to attend the coronation, to take her place among the Vinnengaeleans, to assume the guise of the beautiful and enchanting elf woman he had once loved.

Dagnarus refused her pleas. The time was not right, he told her. She would come to New Vinnengael, but not now. When the Shield came to Vinnengael to hand over to Dagnarus the rulership of the Tromek nation, Valura could come with him. At that time, Dagnarus would be glad to welcome her to his court.

Valura knew he was lying to her. She knew, even if he didn't know himself.

"I will never be permitted to enter New Vinnengael. My presence would ruin the day for him. Everyone else in the world would see the illusion of a beautiful elven woman, with skin that is petal-soft and lips that are rose-hued and almond eyes of wondrous brilliance. When he looks at me, he sees the fleshless skull, the empty eye sockets, the rictus grin. I am a constant reproach to him. I gave up my soul to be with him, and now he loathes the very sight of me. Every time he looks at me, he sees the truth of what he is—the Lord of the Void."

Dagnarus no longer wanted to be Lord of the Void. He wanted to be King of Vinnengael. He did not want her love, which was dark and tainted with evil. He wanted the love of the living, he wanted their adoration. Banish her, and he would banish that part of his life.

So he trusted. So he hoped. But his trust was misplaced, for it was in himself. His hopes were doomed, for hope also depended on himself. For the time being, he was pleased with this shiny new toy. He was content to play gently with it, lest he break it. But, over time, the toy would grow shabby, the paint would peel, and the wheels would keep falling off. The toy would disappoint him, no longer fulfill his voracious ambition. He would tire of it. He would toss it aside and seek out another and yet another after that.

Woe betide those who put their faith and trust in him, such as these pitiful taan, such as she. He drank their blood and stole their souls and gave nothing in return.

She summoned her mount, a beast known as an equis, a demon horse, spawned of the Void. Seating herself on its back, she grasped the reins, but she did not immediately give the command to leave. She took a moment to look at the taan, feasting and cavorting and capering about their fires, making gleefully ready to celebrate their god's victory. She looked at the walls of New Vinnengael, lined with soldiers, making grimly ready to defend their city and their new king.

"Poor bastards," she said with cool pity, then she turned her mount's head north, toward Tromek.

Dagnarus meant to frighten and intimidate the people of New Vinnengael into obedience by having the taan perform what might be described as military maneuvers, and he succeeded. The soldiers on the wall watched in shocked amazement to see the taan rush eagerly into battle, shouting and screaming with joy, fighting each other with a ferocity that left many lying on grass stained red with blood. And this was only practice.

Dagnarus also meant to weaken the taan, wear them out, reduce their numbers and dull their will to fight, and he succeeded in that as well. By nightfall, most of the warriors were either dead tired or just plain dead.

The taan slept well that night, in their tents or in the arms of Lokmirr, goddess of battle. The only Vinnengaeleans who slept were babes too young to know fear and those who tried to drown fear with brandywine. Fortunately, the latter were few in number, for Dagnarus had placed the city under King's Edict. One of its provisions was to close all the taverns and inns and brewery houses until the end of the current crisis.

Battle magi, civilian volunteers, and the military worked through the night to make everything ready by the morrow. People were evacuated from businesses and houses located near the main gate, moved to safer ground. They put up barricades blocking off all the major streets, overturning drays and wagons in the middle of the roads, tossing on furniture, wooden chests, ale barrels, even removing heavy wooden doors from their hinges and adding them to the growing pile.

Clothiers contributed bolts of cloth to the Hospitalers, to be turned into bandages. Extra beds were set up in the hospital. Those patients who were not in critical condition were sent home to make room for the anticipated casualties.

Soldiers and archers moved into the empty houses and shops, to take up their hiding places and get what sleep they could before morning. Novitiates climbed onto the roofs, making necessary preparations for the battle magi, bringing with them stores of candles, to be used by those casting Fire magic, hauling up waterskins and food to help them keep up their strength.

The work was accomplished by moonlight or torchlight, with as little noise and commotion as possible, for the taan must not suspect that anything untoward was happening in the city. Dagnarus ordered all the sewers blocked off, their entrances flooded with river water, in order to halt any taan who might take it into their heads to enter the city by that route.

Dagnarus came out to inspect the work and more than one good citizen was startled that evening to find his new king working alongside him, cheerfully bending his back beneath sacks of flour or lending his strength to help in overturning a wagon. Confident, cheerful, exuberant, Dagnarus lifted the hearts of all who came in contact with him.

Rigiswald roamed the streets, observing the preparations, and as he watched and listened to Dagnarus, the elderly magus grudgingly marveled and grudgingly admired.

Rigiswald walked away pensive and sorrowful. He had never known any man so well suited by nature to be king. Had he been born the eldest son, Dagnarus might this moment be slumbering peacefully in death, honored and revered as a good and wise monarch. Truly, the most tragic words in all the languages of all the races were: "what might have been."

Several hours after midnight, most of the preparations were ready. Dagnarus made a show of going to his bed. Then, cloaked in the Void, he left New Vinnengael, slipping out of the palace by one of the several secret tunnels that had been built in order to protect the king during an attack or popular uprising. He had a horse waiting for him, and he rode to a prearranged site north of the city.

Dagnarus went over his plans in his mind as he rode, searching for some flaw he might have missed.

He had rid himself of Valura and Shakur, who were both embarrassments to him.

As for the Vinnengaeleans, he was pleased with them, for the most part. Oh, there were some who were dangerous and would have to be removed—that gimlet-eyed Inquisitor, for one. The fact that the fellow was skilled in Void magic would make removing him a bit more difficult, but not even the most skilled wizard could protect himself from a fall from a horse or an unfortunate tumble down a flight of stairs. Then there was that shrewd-looking old gentleman who had so disconcerted Dagnarus by asking about the Vrykyl. Dagnarus had endeavored to find out who he was, but none of the courtiers seemed to know. He had meant to ask Tasgall, but had forgotten about the matter in their discussions yesterday. After this battle was over, he would find out who this old gentleman was and determine whether or not he should be concerned about him.

As for the taan, Dagnarus hated losing five thousand troops but it could not be helped. Their deaths would not be wasted. Their blood would anoint him king. And, in truth, he was doing them all a favor. A taan's dearest wish was to die in battle. He was going to see to it that five thousand of those wishes were granted.

"Just as my wish has been granted," he said to himself with a grin.

He could not really believe it. He had worked for over two hundred years for this day, and, finally, it was about to dawn. He would be crowned King of Vinnengael.

There was just one problem, one annoying fly who had landed in his precious ointment, one flaw in the otherwise flawless jewel.

K'let.

Once Dagnarus had blessed the day he'd met K'let. Now he rued it. Of all the people Dagnarus had known throughout his life, K'let came the closest to being considered a true friend. K'let was a taan, but Dagnarus had always possessed the ability to understand the taan, probably because he was a warrior himself. He and K'let had much in common: both were ambitious, both ruthless in obtaining what they wanted, both courageous and skillful warriors.

Dagnarus had made one mistake in dealing with the albino taan. He had underestimated K'let and overestimated himself. K'let was no longer merely an embarrassment like Shakur. The rebellious taan Vrykyl had become a danger. Many thousand taan were now on Vinnengaelean soil.

Thus far, most were loyal to Dagnarus, but if K'let were to succeed in uniting them—as he was attempting to do—they could be a very serious threat.

Arriving at the meeting place, Dagnarus found Klendist, the leader of the mercenaries, awaiting him.

Dagnarus had recruited Klendist, a former bandit and sometime guerrilla leader who had been making a good living raiding towns along the Vinnengael-Tromek border. Klendist brought about eight hundred men with him, all seasoned veterans, some of them war wizards.

Klendist was a taciturn man, short in stature, on the wrong side of fifty, tough, and sinewy. He feared nothing this side of the Void and not much beyond. He greeted the Lord of the Void, as Dagnarus came riding through the darkness, with a curt nod and a broad grin.

Dismissing his bodyguard, Klendist waited for orders.

"Where are your men?" Dagnarus asked.

"Over that hill," Klendist replied with a jerk of his thumb.

Dagnarus glanced in that direction. The night was still and silent.

"You won't see them or hear them, my lord," Klendist added. "But they're there, all the same."

"I take it you left the taan camp without rousing any suspicion."

"You don't see the gigs or hear them, either, do you, my lord? We slipped out of camp quietly, as you ordered. Some of their pickets were awake, but we told the gigs we'd lost our stomach for fighting and that we were heading back home."

"They believed you?"

"Of course. The gigs think all humans are cowards. What are your orders, sir?"

"You will ride west to a city called Mardurar, located in the central part of Vinnengael—"

"I know it."

"Good. Once there, you will meet up with Shakur."

"Where?"

"He will find you," said Dagnarus.

Klendist shrugged. "And after that?"

"He'll have further orders for you. You will obey him as you would obey me. I can't give you specifics because the situation is fluid. It changes moment by moment. I can tell you this much. Some of the taan have rebelled against me and struck out on their own. Their leader is a taan Vrykyl. I want them destroyed."

"I trust that Shakur will deal with the Vrykyl," Klendist said, frowning.

"Yes," said Dagnarus, smiling to himself in the darkness. "Shakur will deal with K'let."

If all went as Dagnarus hoped, he would be freed of two problems. He fully intended that a battle between the two powerful Vrykyl would end in the destruction of both.

"You have only to fight the taan, Klendist."

"We look forward to that, my lord. We've seen what the gigs do to our women. As it is, I've had trouble keeping my boys from slitting some gig throat."

Dagnarus thought it amusing that Klendist, who had committed more rapes and other brutal acts of abuse against females in his blood-soaked career than he could probably count, should suddenly become the sworn avenger of womankind. Dagnarus said nothing, however. He bade Klendist ride with haste.

Taking his lord at his word, Klendist departed then and there, without ceremony. Dagnarus left as well, riding in the opposite direction, heading toward the taan camp, to the place where he had established his command center.

He summoned to him the powerful taan shamans, who were known as the Black Veil and were the leaders of the taan army in the absence of the kyl-sarnz, the Vrykyl. The Black Veil were not all present. Several had ridden with Nb'arsk, to be in on the attack of the Portal at Delak 'Vir. Those who were present greeted Dagnarus with awed reverence and respect, far different from the curt nod given to him by Klendist.

Dagnarus gave the Black Veil their orders, which were not complicated: when the horns sounded at sunrise, the taan were to mass in front of the main gate, there to await entry. All the taan were to enter the city, including the taskers and the children, not just the warriors. The Black Veil were surprised at this, for generally the taskers remained behind in camp to make ready for the warriors' return.

"This time," Dagnarus told them through his interpreter, "all the taan will celebrate the day, the taskers included. There is enough wealth in this fat city for all. And it will be instructive to the young taan, to see victory firsthand."

Once inside the city, the taan were free to take what they wanted—slaves, jewels, armor, whatever they could find.

"Thus will I subdue the proud hearts of the Vinnengaeleans and give them cause to fear me," Dagnarus said.

He asked that the Black Veil and the taan nizam be among the first to enter, to walk at the head of the taan army, dressed in their full regalia, in order to strike fear into the human hearts and destroy their morale. The Black Veil agreed with pleasure. Making their obseisances, they left Dagnarus's presence and went to rouse the slumbering taan.

Having planned the attack, Dagnarus hastened back to Vinnengael to defend against it. He felt not unlike the Punch-and-Judy puppeteer, who, armed with a puppet in each hand, gives battle to himself.

20

DAY DAWNED. THE WORD TO ATTACK CAME TO THE TAAN, FINALLY.

Led by the six shamans of the Black Veil and the nizam who were in command of the battle groups, the taan surged across the river on floating bridges that had been ready and waiting for days. Hooting and shouting, they massed in front of the city gates and around the city walls. The taan were not in prime fighting condition—most of the warriors were feeling sluggish and stupid after the previous day's battles and the night of carousing.

They would have never been permitted to go to war in that condition, but then, they were not going to war. They were going to enter a fat city of derrhuths, seize the strong for slaves, slaughter the helpless, and burn and loot.

Tasgall and Dagnarus watched from the battlements. They were the only two up there, or so it appeared from below. The battlements were manned, but the archers and swordsmen lay flat on their bellies, their weapons in their hands, awaiting the signal.

Wrapped against the morning chill in a heavy cloak of black velvet, Dagnarus said he'd slept well that night. He was rested and ready for the day. He made a final inspection of the city, expressed his pleasure in the hard work that had been done during the night, and took time to speak personally to many of the soldiers and battle magi. He then climbed the stairs leading up to the battlements to join Tasgall, who had been waiting there since long before dawn.

Tasgall looked down with grave mien at the taan army, whose warriors could be seen shoving and pushing, jostling and elbowing, and in some cases fighting each other in order to be among the first to enter the city. He was reminded of squirming maggots consuming a rotting corpse. The stench was like that of a rotting corpse. It twisted his stomach. He was sorry he'd eaten breakfast.

"Do not let your magi or the soldiers fall into complacency," Dagnarus lectured him. "A taan warrior at half his fighting strength is a match for any human warrior fully rested and prepared. And these taan, once they realize that they are trapped, will fight with the ferocity of a cornered dragon."

"I assumed as much, Your Majesty," said Tasgall. "I have warned my people and the commanders of the military."

"As we have planned, the battle magi will take out the Black Veil and the nizam first, depriving the taan of their leaders. That will not help much, however, for the taan have never relied on their leaders in battle anyway, each taan seeking to earn glory for himself."

"Yes, Your Majesty," Tasgall replied.

Dagnarus had told them this in the meeting yesterday, but Tasgall had not truly believed it, not until now.

He looked down at the snarling, shouting, jeering taan, waving their gruesome battle standards, some of which bore human heads or other body parts, and he felt the hair prickle on his spine. He had never known fear before battle, but he knew fear now. He feared the taan. He feared his new king. Had Dagnarus betrayed them? Were they to be given over to these savages? Were ten thousand more taan warriors massed somewhere beyond the horizon, waiting for the city gates to be opened to them, waiting to swarm inside?

"Your Majesty," said Tasgall respectfully, "you should return to the palace now, to a place of safety. I have posted guards—"

Dagnarus smiled, shook his head. "I sent my guards off to fight, Tasgall. They will be of more use in the battle. I have never been one to command from the rear, and I will not start now."

Dagnarus twitched aside a fold of his cloak to reveal a splendid breastplate, made of steel inlaid with gold, worked into an intricate knot pattern. The workmanship was exquisite; no one did such fine work these days. Tasgall had seen such pieces of armor, but only in the palace armory or in some noble house, where they resided on stands and collected dust and spiders.

"This was my father's armor," said Dagnarus with fond pride. "I have never worn it before. I swore I would not wear it until I could once more stand with my people and wield my sword to defend them. So I swore on his tomb, where I found it lying amidst the ruins."

"You went back to Old Vinnengael?" Tasgall asked, amazed.

"I did," said Dagnarus, and his eyes were haunted, shadowed. "I went there as part of my penance. It is not a place to which I would willingly return."

"Are the old stories about it true?"

"I do not know the old stories," Dagnarus returned, his voice grim. "But if they speak of a place whose evil has drawn every loathsome creature that crawls upon Loerem, then, yes, the stories are true. I do not know if the evil can be driven out and the city reclaimed, but I would like to try. I would like to make it a fitting memorial for those who lost their lives, including my mother. She was in the palace that night. She was mad, quite mad. My doing—I drove her to madness. Someday, I'd like to make it up to her. To her and to my father."

Tasgall knew himself forgotten. Dagnarus spoke to shades hovering somewhere on the verge of his memory, shades whose accusing eyes were always fixed on him, shades whose accusing fingers always pointed at him. Tasgall might have thought this a deceit, a lie meant to cozen him, but the pain he saw twisting the handsome face and heard aching in the voice was too real to be assumed.

"Are you ready?" Dagnarus asked.

"Yes, Your Majesty," said Tasgall, trusting at last. "All is in readiness."

"Give the signal to open the gates."

The great wheels turned. The gates of New Vinnengael, a marvel of engineering, slid up into the double archways that divided the enormous road leading into the city—one side for egress, the other for entrance. The taan entered through both of them.

The members of the Black Veil came first. Eager as the taan were to start their rampage, the taan held the shamans of the Black Veil in such fear and awe that they dared not surge ahead of them. The Black Veil walked in silence, wrapped in the black robes that concealed the ritual scarring of their bodies and the valuable gemstones buried beneath their hides. These gemstones powered the Void spells of death and destruction that each shaman could taste upon his tongue. The Black Veil turned their heads, looked at Dagnarus, also wrapped in black, who stood upon the battlements. They bowed to him and appeared to think that they were supposed to join him, for they prepared to start climbing the stairs up to the battlements.

Dagnarus made a sweeping gesture, pointed to the heart of the city. The Black Veil bowed and went on. Tasgall let out a low whistle. He could feel the power of the Void rolling off those shamans, flooding the city like dark water. He hoped his magi were up to the task.

After the shamans came the nizam, the elite taan warriors who had earned their rank through heroism in battle. They surged through the gates, jeering and clashing their weapons together, shouting challenges to the xkes to come out from their hiding places and fight them and die. Looking up at Dagnarus, the taan cheered and whooped and promised him that they would slay many thousands this day and dine on their hearts in his honor.

Dagnarus understood them. Tasgall did not, which was just as well, or his faith in his king might have been shaken. Dagnarus said nothing, merely gestured, indicating that the taan were to proceed as planned.

The rest of the taan warriors came rushing in after their leaders. They surged forward eagerly, pushing and shoving, each taan fearing that another would beat him to the prize.

The city was silent, seemingly deserted. But the taan could smell the xkes, smell succulent flesh and the warm blood. The humans were nearby, hiding behind their walls like the sweet meat of the zarg nut hides behind its shell.

The city of New Vinnengael was a planned city, not one that had grown up from a village. As such, Vinnengael's streets were straight and wide, not twisting and narrow. Prominent buildings such as the palace and the Temple were located in the center, with residential areas in certain locations, shops and businesses in others, and it was even predetermined which businesses should go where.

The buildings nearest the gate contained shops that catered to those first entering the city, selling everything a visitor might need from maps to cunningly designed purses guaranteed to thwart pickpockets to candied ginger for a sweet tooth. The shops were empty, for the plan was that the taan were to be lured farther into the city. The first taan to reach these buildings kicked down the doors and ran inside. Finding nothing of value, they left in disgust.

The taan continued to pour through the gates, a floodtide of bodies that soon spread down every street. Tasgall waited tensely for the first sounds of fighting. This was the critical part. As many taan as possible must be lured into the heart of the city.

"I fear, Your Majesty, that the moment fighting breaks out, the taan will realize that they have fallen into a trap, and they will flee," said Tasgall.

Dagnarus laughed. "That will never happen. A taan warrior who flees battle would be disgraced. The tribe would strip him of his possessions, torture and kill him. He would not permitted to enter the afterlife. His soul would be consumed by the Void. No, I guarantee to you that will not happen."

"Even if they know it is a trap?" Tasgall asked.

"Especially then," Dagnarus said carelessly. "The more hopeless the battle, the greater the glory."

Voices began to speak in Tasgall's ears; the battle magi communicating to him magically what they were seeing. The taan warriors had been given leave to rush ahead of the nizam and they were now running down the major streets, searching for a fight, and becoming increasingly frustrated. Several began kicking in doors and ripping the shutters off the windows. Inside some of those buildings were Vinnengaelean archers with arrows nocked, ready to fire, backed up by soldiers prepared for hand-to-hand combat.

The nizam spread out, joining in the rampage, not taking any sort of leadership role that the magi could see. The shamans of the Black Veil remained together, and it seemed to those watching them that they were starting to grow concerned. They huddled together in deep discussion, ignoring the taan who flowed around them.

Tasgall reported all this to Dagnarus, who nodded and said, "Be patient. Now is not yet the time."

Last to enter the gate were the taskers, holding small children by the hands, carrying the youngest on their backs. Tasgall looked down at the taan children, skipping and dancing and laughing like any child on a holiday. The thought had not occurred to him that he would be slaying children. He told himself that they were children who would grow into savage beings, but he still felt an aversion to slaying those weaker than himself, those who couldn't fight back, those who had no understanding why they were dying.

"Do not fool yourself, Tasgall," said Dagnarus. "Those children have already developed a liking for human flesh."

The question "And who gave them their first taste of it, Your Majesty?" was on Tasgall's lips, but he swallowed it. Now was not the time to go mucking about in politics. He had a job to do. He cleared his mind of all emotion, all doubt, so that it held nothing but the clean-burning fire of the magic.

The last group of taan taskers was crowding inside the gates when shrieks and fierce howls arose from within the city proper.

"The taan have broken into one of the buildings, Your Majesty," Tasgall reported. "The archers are firing into their midst. And, Your Majesty, it appears that the shamans of the Black Veil have turned around. They are heading back this way."

"Give the signal," Dagnarus ordered.

Tasgall motioned to one of the novice battle magi who had been crouched in the shadow of the wall. Rising to her feet, she spoke words of magic and passed her hand through the flame of the fire burning in a nearby brazier. Her hand seemed to scoop up the flame into a ball and, in one sweeping motion, she hurled the fiery orb into the sky, where it blazed a brilliant orange. The bright ball of flame would be visible to all those on the rooftops, who were waiting and watching for it. Selecting their targets, the battle magi began to chant their spells.

The men manning the wheels that lowered the gates jumped up from their hiding places. Guarded by men-at-arms, the men turned the wheels, and the gates began to lower.

The taan taskers heard the rattle and the creaking and turned to see what was going on. Those near the gates, who could see what was happening, looked alarmed and cried out. Unlike the warriors, taskers do not fight unless hard-pressed. Their role was to ensure the survival of the tribe, and many of them had just come to the realization that such survival was imperiled. Grabbing the children, several taan began running toward the gate, shouting out warnings as they ran.

"The gates fall too slowly!" Dagnarus cried, watching the ponderous descent of the heavy gates. Leaning over the wall, he bellowed, "Cut the ropes!"

The men working at the wheels stared stupidly, not understanding. One astute young soldier heard the command, saw the danger. Leaping forward, he sliced through one of the ropes with a single stroke of his battle-ax, all the while calling for his comrades to assist him. Knights and men-at-arms fell on the ropes with a will. The gates came thundering down, but not before several taan taskers and their charges had managed to escape. The archers rose from their hiding places, fired a volley of arrows after them. Every shot told. The taan stumbled and fell to the ground. Some stayed where they had fallen, but others leapt up and kept going.

The archers stared. They could see the feathered shafts protruding from the backs of the fleeing taan, but nothing seemed to stop them. Their officers shouted orders. The archers fired again and again. At last, all the taan were stopped. Almost every corpse had at least three arrows sticking out of it. The archers were round-eyed and amazed.

They had no time for rejoicing. The taan taskers realized that they had been betrayed, that this was a trap. They raised their voices in unearthly howls that were not wails of despair, but were warnings, meant to alert the other taan to their danger. Grabbing up anything that came to hand for a weapon, the taskers and even the children launched a furious assault on the battlements.

Preparing to face them, Tasgall saw movement out of the corner of his eye. He glanced back out to see a taan, with arrows sticking out of her back, stagger to her feet and run off. Tasgall started to shout a command to bring her down, then kept silent. He did not have the stomach to shoot a fleeing enemy in the back. Let her go. What harm could one do, after all? He turned back to the battle.

Young, unblooded warriors, who had been relegated to the rear while their elders and betters invaded the city first, heard the cries and came rushing back. The young warriors, accompanied by taskers, attacked the barricades that had been piled up around the stairs. In minutes, the taan tore apart what it had taken the Vinnengaeleans hours to erect. The barricades fell. The taan stormed up the stairs, shrieking and wielding strange and fearsome-looking weapons: spears with three sharp heads; enormous curved-bladed swords; a V-shaped weapon formed of two blades, each sharp enough to cut off a man's arm. The archers had no need to aim. They were sure to hit something by simply firing into the mob.

Unlike the elder warriors, the young taan fighters wore almost no armor. Arrows thudded into their bare hides, but had little effect. Sometimes the young warriors would halt and yank them out and toss them away in irritation, but more often, they would simply leave them and carry on, too caught up in their battle lust even to notice.

Tasgall's magic and that of his fellow battle magi proved more effective. Balls of flame exploded among the taan on the stairs. The fiery blast killed several immediately, and many more were set ablaze when the flaming corpses fell among the crowd of taan below.

The fiery deaths of their comrades did not stop the taan. They surged up the stairs again, kicking aside the still-blazing bodies of their comrades, climbing over them, or stepping on them in order to reach the enemy above. Those who reached the top crashed into the knights and soldiers waiting to halt the advance. Knights and soldiers who had never seen anything like this.

Overwhelmed by the strength and savage ferocity of the taan, the defenders began to fall back. Tasgall dared not use his magic, for fear of hitting his own men. He and Dagnarus exchanged glances and simultaneously drew their swords and ran forward to halt the retreat.

Tasgall was an adequate swordsman, not a great one. He wielded a two-handed broadsword and depended on the sheer force of his blows to kill. Dagnarus was a superb swordsman. He set upon the taan with such skill that few came close to touching him. He had obviously fought them before. He was familiar with their methods and their strange-looking weapons.

Tasgall was curious to see how the taan would react to their "god" attacking them, and was surprised to see that none apparently recognized Dagnarus. Tasgall would have liked to watch Dagnarus's sword work, but he was battling for his life.

Having discounted the taan as unskilled savages, he was now being forced to reconsider that idea. Their weapons looked strange and outlandish, but they were incredibly lethal, and the taan wielded them with skill. One taan came at him, twirling a multibladed sword in both hands, the blades moving so fast that they blurred in Tasgall's vision. The taan defended with one weapon, attacked with the other. The sharp steel sliced through the metal-studded glove Tasgall wore, cutting open the back of his hand. The other blade trapped his sword, halting its deadly downward stroke.

The taan's snarling face thrust close to Tasgall's. He could smell the foul stench of the creature, look straight into the small eyes glaring with rage. The taan was tall and barrel-chested and seemed made of nothing but muscle and sinew and bone covered by a hairy hide tougher than leather armor. The taan was not above using his feet as weapons. He kicked at Tasgall, trying to knock him off-balance, all the while slashing at him with his deadly blades.

The two shoved and heaved and grappled, neither making any headway, then suddenly the taan gave a grunt and arched backward, falling away so suddenly that Tasgall was overset and almost tumbled off the battlements. The taan slumped at his feet, dead, the blade of a sword protruding from his belly. Dagnarus caught hold of Tasgall, steadied him, and pointed below.

The taan had gained the stairs leading to the battlements and more were coming up every moment. Another fiery blast from one of his battle magi cleared the bottom of the stairs, but only momentarily. More taan ran to take the place of those who were being roasted alive.

"Look out for the shamans!" Dagnarus shouted to Tasgall. "Void magic-users!"

Tasgall looked down among the taan to see several taan shamans, some almost naked, others wrapped in robes that looked like winding sheets, pointing up at him. He was forced to shift from the use of steel to the use of magic, which meant that he had to clear his brain of the blood-dimmed rage that comes with hand-to-hand combat and find within himself the clear, cold logic required for the casting of magic. He was trained to refocus his thoughts, but even so, he needed a few moments to concentrate and bring the words of the spell to mind.

Four black darts erupted from the chest of one of the shamans. The darts soared upward, trailing hideous black ooze behind them. The darts moved with incredible speed. Tasgall only had time to realize that one was aimed at him before it struck his cuirass.

Tasgall's armor was enchanted to repel magical attacks and it dissipated the Void magic. The dart burst harmlessly on his cuirass. The man beside Tasgall was not so fortunate.

The dart struck the knight in the center of the forehead, slammed through his metal helm. His skull exploded, splattering those around him with blood and gore.

Tasgall was too far from the brazier to be able to use Fire magic. He had with him several vials of blessed earth. Drawing out one of these, he hurled it to the stone floor, stamped his foot upon the stone, and spoke the words of the spell.

The ground beneath the taan shamans began to quake and buckle. The jolt threw them off their feet. Tasgall took a spear from the hand of the dead knight and hurled it with all his force at one of the shaman, who was struggling to regain his feet. The spear impaled the taan. The body twitched for a few moments, then went limp. Tasgall shouted commands, ordered archers and spearmen to turn their fire on the shamans. Within moments, all of them were dead.

Wiping blood and brains off his face, Tasgall looked about hastily. Dagnarus was leading a charge that was sweeping the taan off the stairs. Most of the taan warriors were dead or dying. The taskers milled about, uncertain and disorganized. The archers fired at them, like shooting ducks in a barrel. The battle magi flung spells at them. Now it was just a matter of slaughter.

When Dagnarus returned, grinning and unscathed, he asked gaily, "How goes the rest of the battle? What are you hearing from your magi in the field?"

"Very little now, my lord," Tasgall replied. His magi had fallen silent, and he was worried. "Of course, they should conserve their strength for fighting, not waste it talking to me. But the reports indicated that the fighting in the city was fierce."

"The taan have a saying," said Dagnarus, sobering. " 'Derrhuth are in love with life. The taan are in love with death.' "

"Which means?" Tasgall asked.

"That those who fear death will always be at a disadvantage," Dagnarus replied.

"Maybe, my lord," said Tasgall. "Or maybe not. For those of us who fear death will fight to survive."

That day, the Vinnengaeleans fought to survive.

The taan knew now that they had run headlong into an ambush. Enraged, the taan meant to kill as many humans as they could before they died.

The Vinnengaelean soldiers were completely taken aback by the ferocity of the taan warriors, who fought with a raging joy that came near to demoralizing their opponents.

Dagnarus had tried to warn the Vinnengaeleans, tried to prepare them for what they would face. It is doubtful if they could have ever been prepared for the sight of taan warriors, their bodies smeared with blood, slavering and raving, smashing bodily through lead-paned glass windows and charging headlong into a barrage of arrows.

Elite taan warriors wore armor, much of it taken from derrhuth they had slain. They disdained wounds; most would fight on even after losing a limb. They used magic to shield themselves from weapons of steel or sorcery, emerging unscathed from the firestorms of the battle magi. Outnumbered, trapped, the taan hit their enemy with such shocking force that for a moment it seemed the taan might yet win the day.

Although trained as a battle magus, Rigiswald was too old and out of practice to participate in the fighting. He had instead volunteered to use his magic skills in healing the wounded. At dawn, he walked over to the hospital along with a cadre of other magi who had forgone their own various areas of specialization to take up healing magic. Rigiswald walked side by side with magi skilled in engineering or architecture, stonemasons (who used their magic to shape, lift, and lay building blocks), Portal-seekers, librarians, members of the Order of Inquisitors, alchemists, cooks, and tutors. Most carried spellbooks, some magi actually reading as they walked, trying hastily to bone up on magic they had not used since they were novitiates. Even young magi had been pressed into service, for they could at least cast simple cantrips designed to treat minor wounds and ease pain.

Rigiswald had just entered the Houses of Healing—a sprawling building reminiscent of elven design, surrounded by green lawns and trees and blooming shrubs, with many areas that could be opened to fresh air and sunlight—when he heard and felt the boom of the falling gate. He and everyone else turned to look out the windows in the direction of the north part of the city, where the battle would take place. The Houses of Healing were located on a natural rise, and although their view was blocked by tall buildings, the magi could catch glimpses now and then of small figures (battle magi, perhaps, or men-at-arms) prowling about atop the buildings.

The howls of the taan—inhuman and ghastly—pierced the still morning air. Rigiswald's stomach clenched, and he was not a man easily disturbed. Faces around him went pale. People exchanged grim glances. The Hospitalers put their volunteers immediately to work, had them moving beds, rolling bandages, helping prepare and bottle poultices and salves, ointments and potions, or comforting frightened patients.

The howls and shrieks grew louder. Rigiswald, who was scooping ointment into stone jars, had managed to position himself near a floor-to-ceiling glass pane that faced in the direction of the battle. He saw a sheet of blue-white flame rise into the air, a wall of fire that would incinerate anything in its path. The screams of taan being burned alive were horrible to hear. At the dreadful sound, a young novice sitting next to Rigiswald gave such a violent start that she dropped the vial she was filling, sent it crashing to the floor.

Rigiswald said what comforting words he could, which weren't many, advised her to drink some water, take deep breaths, and move away from the windows. A second glance outside showed a huge column of black smoke spiraling into the air. Those in the hospital continued their duties in silence. Then the wounded began to come.

The first casualties were those who could walk under their own power. They came singly, or in groups of two or three, helping each other. They had been sent on by healers present at the site of the battle, who were dealing with more critical wounds.

"They need more litter bearers up there," were the first words out of the mouth of one soldier, gesturing wearily with his head toward the front lines.

The strongest magi went off with litters. Healers descended on the wounded, giving them shoulders to lean on and helping them into the hospital. One woman slumped to the ground, unable to go farther. Recognizing by her armor and her tabard that she was a battle magus, Rigiswald went to see to her himself, for he was familiar with the types of wounds these magi tended to receive.

Several young novices hung around her, clearly uncertain what to do, for she was clad in armor and they had no idea how to unfasten it. Rigiswald ordered one to remain with him, in case he needed help, and sent the others off to help someone else.

The young man ran over to inspect what appeared to be a stream of dark water running down the broad highway known popularly as "Fine Day Way," for on fine, sunny days, the populace would turn out to walk the road, greet friends and family, show off new finery and hear the latest gossip.

The stream running down Fine Day Way was gradually widening to a steady flow. The young man bent down to stare at it. He gasped, backed away, his face livid. Clapping his hand over his mouth, he staggered off into some bushes.

The dark stream was not water, but blood.

Rigiswald shook his head and bent over the battle magus, who was regaining consciousness.

"Where are you hurt?" he asked crisply.

Her limbs were sound. She had taken no blow to the head. She was covered with blood, but it might not be her own. Her pulse was weak, but strengthening. She had no fever. He thought he knew what was wrong, but he wanted to make certain.

"I have taken no wound," she said, her voice weak. "A spell went awry."

He'd guessed right. Sometimes a spell will not work properly. The reasons for such an occurrence are various. Perhaps the magus misspoke a word or left out a sentence or recited the words in the incorrect order. Perhaps she lost concentration, went blank in the middle of the spell. Or, perhaps, the magus had done everything right but, for some reason beyond the understanding of mortal man, the magic simply did not work the way it was supposed to work. In those instances, as the textbooks metaphorically described it: "The magic behaves like a fiery steed. With the casting of the spell, the magus puts his spurs to the horse's flanks. If the spell is successful, the horse proceeds at a canter, the rider remains in control. If the spell goes awry, the horse bolts. The rider has no control and is either pitched off the horse's back or dragged along to his doom."

"Unbuckle her armor," Rigiswald ordered the novice. "Then run and fetch me some brandywine and water. Be quick!"

The novice did as he was told, his slender, quick fingers making short work of the leather knots that held the magus's cuirass in place. Once this was removed, the magus breathed easier.

"Go tend to the others," she said, closing her eyes. "I will be all right. I just need rest."

"The others are in good hands," said Rigiswald. "I will wait here with you until you feel strong enough to walk."

The novice returned with two flasks and a cup. Taking the flask of brandywine, Rigiswald mixed in a small amount with the cool water. He lifted the magus, helped her to drink.

"Ah, brandy," she said, and smiled up at him. "The soldier's restorative. You must be an old campaigner."

"I've been in my share of battles. How goes it up there?" Rigiswald asked.

She shuddered and averted her eyes. "I've been in my share of battles, too," she said in a low voice. "And I've seen no horrors to compare to this. They have Void sorcerers among them—powerful sorcerers, wearing long black veils, who use Void magic in ways that are completely unknown to us. Tasgall had warned us to target these sorcerers, and we were prepared to do so, but before the words to the spells were even on our lips, these sorcerers covered the streets in darkness so black it seemed that they must have stolen away the sun. I could not see the man standing next to me. I could not see my own hands! We were on a rooftop, and we were afraid to move, for we could not see our footing.

"We could not see them, but the Void sorcerers could see us. The magus next to me suddenly sank to his knees. He cried out that his heart was being torn from his chest. Another man, a dear friend named Grims, went into convulsions so severe that he toppled off the building. He did not die from the fall. I could hear his screams . . ."

She shivered. Her voice trailed off. Rigiswald gave her some more brandy.

"Talk it out," he said to her. "Free yourself of it."

"That will never happen," she replied. "I will carry the horrors of this day to my death."

"What happened to the Void sorcerers?" he asked.

"I do not know. There was a blast of flame and the darkness ended. The flame did not destroy the sorcerers, however, or, if it did, we could not see any bodies. I think it likely that they took advantage of the darkness to flee. I did find Grims, or what was left of him. The monsters had ripped him apart with their bare hands."

Rigiswald looked up to see a steady stream of wounded coming from the city, among them litter bearers carrying the more seriously injured.

"I have to go now," said Rigiswald. "Will you be all right?"

She did not seem to hear him. Her eyes stared back into the fearful darkness.

"We kill and we kill and we kill," she said. "And still they keep coming."

He patted her hand and left her the brandy flask. Rising to his feet, he stared out at the wounded, the dead, the dying.

Rigiswald looked at them. He looked at the river of blood flowing down the street, and in that moment, he looked into the heart of Dagnarus and saw his true plan.

His trap was set for all.

VINNENGAEL WAS VICTORIOUS. THE TAAN WERE DEFEATED, ANNIHILATED. Dagnarus gave orders that not a single taan was to be left alive, and his orders were obeyed. The taan were destroyed, but at a terrible cost. The Arven River was contaminated by the blood flowing into it. The water turned a horrible murky brown color and smelled of death.

Taan corpses clogged the streets. Guardsmen loaded the bodies onto carts and hauled them away, but it took days to remove them all. Cessrats and pinktails poured out of the sewers to feed on the dead, bringing with them diseases exacerbated by the lack of clean water. The corpses were burned on a gigantic pyre built south of the city to take advantage of the prevailing northerly wind flow to carry the smoke away.

The Vinnengaeleans who had died in the battle were buried in a mass grave outside the city walls, for there was neither time nor strength nor material to build so many coffins and tombs, or give them individual rites.

At first, the north wind blew the smoke of death away from Vinnengael, but on the second day after the battle—the day Dagnarus was to be crowned king—the wind shifted to the south, carried noxious smoke and ash into the city. The ash coated every surface with a layer of black soot that had a horrible, greasy feel to it. The citizens wore strips of cloth tied around their noses and mouths and forbade their children to play outside. The ash covered the gleaming white facade of the palace's marble walls and burrowed into the nooks and crannies of the Temple's ornate stonework. The citizens scrubbed and scoured, but water had little effect on the soot, only served to smear it.

The streets and stones were stained with blood that could not be removed. People worked for days to scrub the stains from the stones of Fine Day Way, but the task proved impossible. The blood had seeped into the cracks between the cobblestones and nothing, it seemed, could get rid of it.

Having seen the taan and witnessed the savage bestiality with which they had fought, the Vinnengaeleans could only shudder and consider themselves fortunate beyond measure that their city and people had not suffered a worse fate. They had their new king to thank and were prepared to do so with all their hearts. Everyone, from the highest-born noble in his palatial town house to the young scamp who mucked out the stables of the shabbiest hostelry in the city, pitched in and worked with a will to clean up New Vinnengael in time for Dagnarus's coronation.

The gruesome stains that could not be removed were covered over with plaster. The foul smells that could not be eradicated were masked with flowers.

Seven days after the victory of Dagnarus over the enemy army that he himself had led, he was crowned King of the Vinnengaelean Empire. She would be majestic and revered and honored. All nations would bow to her. All peoples would bow down to their king.

On the dawn of his coronation day, Dagnarus walked alone in the Hall of Past Glories. He had dismissed the servants and the courtiers, sent them off to continue their preparations.

The Church would preside over the coronation. Dagnarus had worked long and hard to ensure their participation—their willing participation, and Tasgall had ensured his success. Dagnarus was pleased with Tasgall. The battle magus reminded the king very much of the captain of his father's guard, a man who had taken an interest in the young Dagnarus when no other adult had bothered, a man who had—in essence—helped to raise him.

Captain Argot had deserved a better fate. He had died in the battle of Old Vinnengael, and Dagnarus had been truly grieved to hear it. The king resolved that Tasgall should be rewarded. He was not yet a suitable candidate for a Vrykyl; Tasgall was not initiated into the ways of the Void.

But that might come in time. Meanwhile, he named Tasgall Most Revered High Magus—upon the resignation of the former Regent, Clovis, because of health concerns.

Since it was required that all heads of the Orders submit their resignation when a High Magus is chosen, the others had done so. Customarily, the new High Magus would simply refuse to accept them. Tasgall, acting on the advice of Dagnarus, had accepted every one of them and replaced them with people loyal to himself.

Tasgall had a conscience, and that conscience was giving him painful jabs, for he had taken the post of Most Revered High Magus only with the greatest reluctance. He did take it, for he had seen what harm can come when the Church and the crown stand opposed to each other, or when one becomes too powerful and dominates the other. Tasgall fancied that he and Dagnarus were working in tandem for the good of Vinnengael. Dagnarus had yet to disabuse Tasgall of that notion. Dagnarus had learned patience, during his two hundred years, and he had also learned subtlety.

All was progressing nicely, even as to the recovery of the Sovereign Stones. There were problems, admittedly, but once he was emperor, those would be solved.

Valura reported from the elven kingdom of Tromek that the civil war had ground to a standstill. The forces of the Divine were still stubbornly holding certain key areas of Tromek, including the western end of the Portal, defended by the warriors of House Kinnoth, who were especially tough and tenacious and had proved impervious to all attempts to cause them to shift their allegiance.

Consequently, some of the Houses currently supporting the Shield were starting to waver in their support, but Valura expressed confidence that an assassination here and a scandal there would bring the Houses back in line. Dagnarus ordered her to remain in Tromek until the war had ended and the situation was resolved to his satisfaction. After that, he had plans for Valura that would keep her in Tromek—and away from him—forever.

She would not be happy, but she would obey. She was bound to obey.

In the throne room, located on the ground level, the people were gathering: the high-ranking members of the Church, the barons, minor nobles, knights and their ladies, the wealthy and influential merchants, ambassadors of those governments who were still allied with Vinnengael (few in number), the royal musicians and honored guests, such as the quick-thinking young soldier who had acted with such dispatch to cut the ropes that lowered the gate.

Young Havis would not be there. He had been sent away. Word would reach Vinnengael in about six months that the poor child had succumbed to some illness, measles perhaps. No one would care much, by then.

They would all be assembled in the throne room, waiting for their king, the conqueror. The Vinnengaeleans had been victorious. Unfortunately, in their victory, they had suffered their greatest defeat. They might try to wash away the smoke and the blood, but they could never wash away the memory. From that day forth, no Vinnengaelean could walk the roads of New Vinnengael without seeing those gruesome stains. No Vinnengaelean would be able to sleep at night without hearing the screams of the dying echo in their ears. No Vinnengaelean would be able to forget the mounds of bodies piled up in the marketplace or the stench of the smoke from the funeral pyres.

By bringing the war into New Vinnengael, Dagnarus had forced war's horrors upon every man, woman, and child in the city. He had done so for a reason. When he was crowned, he would promise the grieving and devastated populace that if they promised to be loyal and obedient, he would promise to keep them safe, keep them secure.

They would promise humbly. They would promise gladly. Kneeling in blood, they would swear their fealty. They would never forget.

Dagnarus would never let them.

He lifted the crown of Vinnengael from the velvet pillow on which it rested, ready to be carried by the Most Revered High Magus down to the chapel, where he would beseech the gods' blessing on their king.

The gods might give it or not, as they chose. Dagnarus really didn't care. He didn't need the gods. He had the Void. He wanted only one blessing.

Dagnarus walked over to the portrait that had once portrayed the two kings of Vinnengael, father and son, Helmos and Tamaros. The portrait had been redone. The artist and his assistants had worked day and night to have it ready for this historic occasion. The room reeked of fresh paint and linseed oil.

In the portrait, King Tamaros stood next to his son, Prince Dagnarus. The father's face was aglow with pride. Dagnarus, handsome, charming.

Clothed in his royal finery, prepared to descend to the throne room and receive the accolades of his people, Dagnarus sank down on his knees before the painting.

"I have done it, Father," Dagnarus said. "I am King of Vinnengael. I will make you proud, Father. I swear it. You no longer need be ashamed of me."

His father seemed so close to him. Dagnarus waited an instant, half-dreading, half-hoping for some whisper from the grave.

No word came, but Dagnarus felt sure of his father's approval. Rising to his feet, Dagnarus left the room to be greeted with resounding cheers from the assembled knights and barons, waiting to provide him with an honor guard.

All through the lengthy and sometimes tedious coronation ceremony, the newly crowned king imagined he could feel his father's gaze rest proudly upon him—Dagnarus, the child beloved.

Rigiswald had not attended the coronation ceremony, although he had received an invitation. Tasgall had told him that Dagnarus had wanted very much to meet the "old gentleman" who had taken an interest in the Vrykyl.

"Thank you," Rigiswald had said, "but I'm going to be busy."

"Doing what?" Tasgall had asked.

"I haven't decided yet," Rigiswald had replied.

Tasgall had frowned, but he'd said nothing more.

The sounds of revelry could still be heard in the streets. The celebrations had lasted all night and were still going strong after sunrise. Rigiswald carefully folded his best lamb's wool robe, preparatory to rolling it up and inserting it into a leather satchel. He was interrupted by a knock on his door.

He opened it to find a smart-looking young page boy, all dressed up in ruffles and gold embroidery. The page boy held out a wafer-sealed packet.

"For you, sir."

Rigiswald accepted the packet, handed the page boy a coin for his trouble. The boy departed, gaily flipping the coin in the air and catching it backhanded.

Rigiswald started to close the door, then he saw Tasgall, standing on the opposite side of the corridor, watching him. Rigiswald gave a brief nod and turned away. Tasgall, taking the nod for an invitation, followed Rigiswald into his room.

Rigiswald tossed the packet on the table. He slid the robe into the satchel, smoothed it and sprinkled it with oil of cedar to keep away the moths.

"That is a summons to the Royal Palace," said Tasgall, with a glance at the packet.

"Yes," replied Rigiswald. "I suppose it is."

"You're not going to attend?"

"No, I am not."

"His Majesty will be displeased."

Rigiswald began to roll up his stockings into neat balls. "His Majesty has so many hundreds waiting for his notice that one elderly gentleman will not be missed."

"I know what this is about," said Tasgall.

"As it happens," said Rigiswald, "so do I."

"You will do no good by staying away."

"I will do no good by going."

"His Majesty was disappointed that Baron Shadamehr was not present for the coronation," said Tasgall. "Shadamehr was the only baron not in attendance. His absence was noticed."

Rigiswald slid the sock balls neatly into the bottom of the satchel. Holding up a small, polished, silver disk, he examined his reflection. He combed his clipped beard and hair, then slid both the disk and the ivory comb into the satchel.

Tasgall watched him in exasperation. "If Baron Shadamehr does not come immediately to swear his homage and fealty to his new king, he will be judged a traitor. He will be exiled on pain of death if he returns to Vinnengael. His lands and castle will be forfeit to the crown. His Majesty requires some assurance that the baron will come."

Rigiswald added to the satchel several books, some he had newly purchased and some he had brought with him. He inserted them carefully, arranging them so that they did not wrinkle the robe or crush his stockings. His packing finished, he lifted the satchel, closed it, and adjusted the straps. He put on his traveling cloak.

"I am not Baron Shadamehr's social secretary," said Rigiswald as he fastened the gold clasp that held the cloak securely in place. "I do not plan his engagements."

"You are his friend, sir. You should advise him that paying homage to his king is something he must do."

Rigiswald hefted the satchel. He did not offer to shake hands. "Good-bye, Tasgall. Congratulations on your elevation in rank."

He started toward the door.

Tasgall picked up the packet, toyed with it.

"The baron's family has held that land for generations. His income derives from the produce of that land and from the fees he collects on those who travel downriver. If Shadamehr loses his barony, he will be an impoverished exile, with nowhere to go, no friends to speak up for him, no refuge."

Rigiswald halted, turned around. "I hear that the head of the Order of Inquisitors died yesterday."

Tasgall did not immediately reply.

"He died of . . . what was it? Heart failure?" said Rigiswald.

Tasgall stared down at the packet. "He has been in poor health for some time. An inquest held that he died of natural causes."

Rigiswald smiled, tight-lipped. "I should watch out for those natural causes, if I were you, Tasgall. I hear they are going around."

Tasgall crossed the room in three steps, caught hold of Rigiswald's arm.

"Tell the baron that all he must do is bend his knee and swear his loyalty to King Dagnarus."

"That is all?" Rigiswald regarded him mildly. "My friend, that is everything."

Rigiswald walked alone down the city streets, which they were still scrubbing, and exited the city gate, which they were still repairing. Glancing back over his shoulder, he saw Vinnengael's new flags, featuring a golden phoenix rising up from the blood red flames, fluttering in the smoke-filled air.

BOOK
II

WOLFRAM THE UNHORSED HAD NOT PLANNED ON STAYING LONG at the monastery on Dragon Mountain. Because of the reward, given to him by the late Lord Gustav, Wolfram was a lord himself. He was lord of a manor house—a human manor house in human lands—and he was looking forward to entering that house as its owner, there to astonish and dismay the steward and servants by announcing that they now had a dwarf for a master.

He told himself every day that he was leaving. Every day, he found some excuse to stay. Weeks passed, and the dwarf still hung about Dragon Mountain. The truth was, Ranessa was learning how to be a dragon, and she was having a hard time of it. Wolfram didn't like to leave her.

He didn't know why he should be surprised. Ranessa hadn't been a rousing success as a human. She had alienated her family and the entire Trevinici tribe into which she'd been born. After that, she had managed to insult or offend nearly every single person she'd met on their journey. Wolfram conceded that some excuse could be made for her misanthropic attitude. Ranessa had spent all the years of her life up to this point thinking she was human (and hating it), only to suddenly realize in one overwhelming and catastrophic moment that she wasn't human. She was a dragon.

After he himself had recovered from the shock (a recovery that had required numerous mugs of the monks' good nut brown ale to sustain him), Wolfram had hoped that the discovery of her true nature would transform Ranessa from an irritable, irrational, and half-mad human female into a relaxed and easygoing dragon. As it turned out, Ranessa was still irritable and irrational. The only difference was that before becoming a dragon, she had used her sharp tongue to snap off a man's head. Now she had the sharp teeth to go along with it.

The monk, Fire, who was Ranessa's dragon mother, assured Wolfram that Ranessa's behavior was normal. All freshly "hatched" young dragons experienced similar problems growing accustomed to their new shape and form and the new way they must learn to look at themselves and the world around them.

"After the first euphoria in realizing her true nature wears off, the young dragon is confused and upset. She may feel angry and betrayed and find it difficult to adapt to such a completely new way of life. The reaction is not dissimilar to that seen in newly Unhorsed dwarves," Fire added coolly.

Being an Unhorsed dwarf himself, Wolfram understood exactly what she was talking about, but he perversely maintained that he didn't.

"It seems a rum way of doing things, ma'am," he argued. "Unnatural. Why don't you dragons raise your children yourself, instead of palming them off on us poor unsuspecting mortals? Raising babies isn't easy, what with all the crying and puking and messing their drawers, if you know what I mean. Still, we put up with it. We don't go handing off our kids to you. No offense, ma'am."

"None taken, Wolfram," Fire replied, and he was relieved to see that she was amused, not angry.

A shape-shifter, Fire had gone back to her dwarf form, and she walked along beside him as any right and proper female dwarf would walk along beside him. Since she could change into her true dragon form at any moment, Wolfram didn't want to make either form mad at him.

The two strolled through one of the gardens that surrounded the monastery. Five dragons guarded the monastery, kept the monks safe from harm. Four of these dragons were representative of the world's elements: Fire, Water, Earth, Air. The fifth dragon represented the absence of the elements, the Void.

The people of Loerem were aware that dragons guarded the monastery, but few knew that the dragons also ran the monastery, for the dragons disguised themselves as monks when dealing with the other races. Wolfram had discovered the truth quite by accident, having inadvertently witnessed Fire transform from a female dwarf into a magnificent red dragon.

Lies, that's what it is. All a pack of lies, Wolfram thought indignantly. Not that he himself was above telling lies. A lie or two came in handy on occasion. This wasn't the same, though. These lies affected people's lives.

"People come to care about people," said Wolfram gruffly. "People come to care about people as people, then they find out they're dragons. Some people might get hurt. That's all I'm saying, ma'am."

"I understand, Wolfram," said Fire.

The garden was built on the edge of a steep cliff and provided a wonderful view of the land spread out beneath the tall mountain peak. The two came to a halt at a stone wall placed there to prevent anyone from taking a tumble off the side of the mountain. Wisps of clouds scudded below them. Far below, the river was a blue thread winding among red rock.

Ranessa was out there among the clouds, practicing her flying. She loved flight, she told Wolfram. Loved soaring on the thermals or diving down upon some panic-stricken goat. She loved circling the tall, snow-capped peaks, knowing herself high above the world and its problems.

But Ranessa couldn't fly forever. She had to land, had to come back down to solid ground. For some reason, Ranessa just couldn't seem to get the hang of landing. The first time she'd tried, she'd flown in too fast, skidded, put her head down too soon, flipped nose over tail, coming at last to a crashing halt up against the monks' stables, wrecking the building and killing two of their mules.

Wolfram had been certain Ranessa had killed herself in the process. She'd come out of the disaster with most of the scales scraped off her nose, a torn leg muscle, and an avowed determination never to fly again. Blue sky and clouds and freedom called her forth, however. Daily, she practiced her landings (in a large, empty field). She claimed she was getting better. Wolfram didn't know. He could not bear to watch.

Wolfram rubbed his nose, scratched his beard, and looked out to see Ranessa flitting restlessly among the peaks. Her red scales glittered orange in the sun. She was a graceful and sleek winged beauty. He wished, suddenly, that she could see herself as he saw her. Perhaps that would help.

"Our reasoning for placing our young among people is not completely selfish," Fire stated. "We discovered that living among people gives some of the young an understanding of you, how you think and act."

"Too bad the reverse isn't true," Wolfram said grumpily. "I've been wondering about something. Ranessa felt compelled to come here. She saw the Dragon Mountain in her dreams. Does that happen with all your young?"

"Only to a few," Fire replied. "It happens to those dragon children who are dissatisfied with their lot in life. To those who are searchers, seekers. Those who do not fit in. Like Ranessa. They know that life holds something special for them, and they do not rest until they find out what that is. Her search led her here, to me."

"And what happens to the rest? Those who like being human or dwarven or elven?"

"They live and die as humans or dwarves or elves, never knowing that they were anything else. Thus, we lose some of our children. We know this is a danger, and we accept it."

Gazing out at Ranessa, Fire smiled with pride. "Ranessa needs a friend now."

"Good luck finding one," Wolfram remarked. "I'm leaving tomorrow."

"Have a safe journey," Fire replied, and departed, walking back into the monastery.

Wolfram stood watching Ranessa, his hands jammed into the pockets of his leather breeches, a scowl on his face. He could see she was growing tired, for her head was starting to droop. She was probably putting off landing as long as possible.

Wolfram shook his head, then went inside the monastery, telling himself he was going to see to his packing. Instead, he ended up heading out to that barren field.

He found Ranessa lying amidst a heap of boulders, beating her wings in a fury, sending up clouds of dust.

Fanning away the dust with his hand, Wolfram walked around to where she could see him.

"What are you doing here?" Ranessa demanded. "Come to have a good laugh?"

"I came to see that you didn't break your fool neck," Wolfram returned. "You're improving."

"Meaning what?" Ranessa glared at him.

"Meaning . . . you're improving," said Wolfram. "You didn't land in the lake."

The dragon glowered. "If you must know, I was aiming for the lake. I missed."

Ranessa heaved her massive body out of the jumble of rocks, kicking aside boulders with her feet, lashing her long, scaly tail in irritation. One of the boulders bounded very close to Wolfram, sending the dwarf scrambling to escape being crushed.

"Sorry," Ranessa muttered.

She spread her wings in the sunlight. The late-afternoon sun shone through the transparent red-orange membrane, making it seem as if the dragon was lit by an inner fire. Red scales blazed. Her elegant head, set on the sinuous neck, arched and dipped, as she forced herself patiently to search the membrane to make certain there were no minute rips or tears, for even the smallest hole in the wing can expand rapidly during flight, causing severe damage if left untreated. Not being much given to patience, Ranessa had learned this lesson the hard way.

"Why did you want to land in the lake?" Wolfram asked.

Sometimes, when he saw her like this, shining in the sunlight, he was moved to tears. He cleared his throat and glanced with a shudder at the icy blue water of the snow-fed lake.

"I thought landing in the water would be easier," Ranessa replied sulkily. "Softer."

She shook herself all over, scales rattling, then folded her wings at her sides. Heaving a sigh, she lowered her head to the rock-strewn ground, her nose on a level with Wolfram. She jerked her head off the ground. She'd set her chin down on a small pine tree. Breathing an irritated gout of flame, she reduced the pine to cinder. Sighing again, she lowered her head, nestled comfortably into the sun-warmed earth.

"I like doing that," she said.

"Setting things on fire," said Wolfram.

"Yes. That and the magic. Except I'm not very good at either."

"Fire says you're doing fine," Wolfram tried to reassure her. "It takes time, that's all." He paused a moment, then said nonchalantly, "Maybe you'd like to go back to the way you were? You can, you know. You can change back to your old human self."

The dragon's slit eyes were green, glittered with the brilliance of emeralds in contrast to the fiery orange scales. Wolfram looked into the eyes, searching for the Ranessa he'd known: the wild, untamed human woman. A small part of that Ranessa was there—the part that was frustrated, impatient, afraid. That part was receding, however, growing more distant every day. The dragon part, the part he couldn't understand, was taking over.

"No," she said.

Wolfram rubbed his nose, stared gloomily down at his boots, which were worn with the road. He was leaving tomorrow. Most definitely.

"I don't know if you can understand this or not," said Ranessa, and, from the way she spoke, it seemed she was trying to understand it herself. "But I was never comfortable in that body. Once, when I was little, I saw a snake shed its skin. How I envied it! My own skin felt so small and tight and constricting. I wanted nothing more than to rip open my back and slough it off. Now I have, and I don't ever want to crawl back inside that skin again. But I don't expect the likes of you to understand."

"As a matter of fact," Wolfram stated with dignity, "I do understand. I shed my own skin once."

"What? How? Tell me," Ranessa urged, her green eyes widening.

"Never you mind," said Wolfram. "It's a long story, and I just came up here to tell you I'm leaving tomorrow."

"You said that yesterday," Ranessa pointed out. "And the day before."

"Well, this time, I'm leaving," Wolfram returned.

He waited for her to say something to try to stop him, but she didn't. The air was freezing cold. He was starting to lose all feeling in his toes, and he stamped his feet to warm them.

"Good-bye, then," he said, adding stiffly, "Thank you for saving my life."

That done, he turned away, started the long walk back down the mountain peak toward the monastery below.

He heard the dragon's tail restlessly smashing against the rocks. A small avalanche of crushed stone cascaded around his feet, nearly tripping him. When he was about halfway down the mountain, Ranessa called after him.

"Thank you for saving mine."

Wolfram ducked his head, pretended he hadn't heard.

Circling the west side of the monastery, heading for the front entryway, Wolfram walked around the side of the building and came to a dead stop. For a moment, he stared, doubting his eyes. Then he ducked hastily back around the side of the gray stone building.

"Damn!" He cursed his luck. "I knew I should have left before now!"

A party of dwarves—about twenty of them—were setting up camp outside the front of the monastery. He couldn't tell, from this distance, what clan they belonged to. Every clan has some sort of marking by which they identified themselves and, in the dimming twilight, he couldn't make out any distinguishing markings. He would have to move closer to get a better view and Wolfram had no intention of moving closer.

He might tell himself—he did tell himself—that with a couple of million dwarves roaming the plains of the dwarven lands, the odds that any one of these twenty might know him by sight was remote, odds made better by the fact that he hadn't been back to his homeland in twenty years. These were Horsed dwarves, too, and Wolfram was Unhorsed. He came from Saumel, the City of the Unhorsed, and while some clan dwarves did occasionally visit Saumel on business, they never stayed long. If they had seen him, they probably wouldn't remember him.

The "probably" was a chance he couldn't take.

Watching the dwarves unpack their horses, Wolfram was suddenly extremely curious. What were they doing here? He had never in his life known dwarves to travel all the way from their lands to the monastery on Dragon Mountain. Few Clan dwarves even knew of the existence of the monastery or Dragon Mountain, for that matter. The journey must have been long and arduous; dangerous, too, for the dwarves would have been forced to pass through the lands of the Vinnengaeleans, their ancient foe.

The sun slid down behind the mountain. The sky turned a brilliant gold, the land took on shades of night. Keeping in the shadows of the fir trees, using them as cover, Wolfram crept nearer.

The party was made up of twenty dwarves and double that number of horses: the small, shaggy, sturdy horses bred by the dwarves and honored among all those in Loerem who know horseflesh. The dwarves were heavily armed—customary for dwarves traveling into hostile territory, which was any territory outside dwarven lands. Their arms and weapons were not the crude sort made by most clan dwarves. Wolfram recognized in astonishment the exceptional work of the Karkara Unhorsed, who lived on the eastern side of the Dwarven Spine Mountains. Such marvelous weapons were extremely difficult to come by, even among the dwarven clans, and were highly prized and very expensive.

This must be the escort for a clan chief, and no ordinary clan chief at that. Perhaps the exalted Chief Clan Chief. Scraps of conversation he managed to overhear confirmed this. The dwarves spoke of one called Kolost. Judging by their respectful tones, he was an important personage among them. Whoever this Kolost was, he was inside meeting with one of the monks. Wolfram still couldn't make out the clan, though, and this puzzled him.

Some of the ponies had markings on them, but others did not. Some ponies sported horse blankets of similar make and design, but not all. Several of the dwarves wore red beads dangling from the ends of their mustaches, while the others wore no beads at all. Another oddity about this group was that the dwarves, while they all acted in concert, treated each other with stiff, marked respect. When not engaged in some task, they separated, clustering together in smaller groups of three or four.

Suddenly, Wolfram figured it out, and he cursed himself for being the world's greatest dullard. These dwarves were not high-ranking warriors from one clan. This group was comprised of high-ranking warriors from several clans.

Wolfram might be excused for not having reached this conclusion earlier by the simple fact that he had never in his life witnessed such an occurrence: this many clans coming together under the leadership of one clan chief. Even the Chief Clan Chief, who was nominal leader of all the clans, customarily traveled with warriors from his own clan.

The Unhorsed were an exception to this rule, but then, they didn't have much choice. The Unhorsed were those dwarves who, because of injury or law-breaking or some other mischance, had been thrown out of the clan. Exiles, they had been forced to band together in order to survive, and thus the four cities of the Unhorsed were established.

Having figured all this out, Wolfram recognized Steel Clan by the red beads, Sword Clan by their horse blankets, and Red Clan by the zigzag mark on the rumps of their ponies. These clans had been bitter enemies in the past. What had brought their high-ranking warriors together to make a dangerous journey across half a continent?

Who was this Kolost? What was he doing here at Dragon Mountain of all places? What business could a dwarf possibly have with the history-recording monks? So intense was Wolfram's curiosity that he was tempted to make himself known to his fellows and find out what was going on. He fought the temptation, however, reminding himself that he was an outlaw, a criminal, and that he risked being dragged back to Saumel in ignominy and chains.

Meanwhile, his gear was inside the common room, and he was outside, with twenty dwarves between him and the entrance. He glanced up at the wall behind him. The windows were open to the crisp mountain air. He considered trying to crawl inside, then remembered that the giant Omarah were always roaming the halls, and they would view with ire any dwarf caught shinnying unceremoniously through a window.

Wolfram had no choice but to hunker down behind the fir trees and wait until the dwarves wrapped themselves in their horse blankets and went to sleep. Then he could sneak inside, grab his pack, and depart before anyone saw him.

Night closed in around the firs and around Wolfram. The clan dwarves built the nightly fire sacred to the dwarves, one of whom, the Fire magus, is given the responsibility of building the fire every night and carefully extinguishing the fire every morning. The dwarves cooked their evening meal, roasting rabbits on spits.

When they were done, the dwarves wrapped themselves in their horse blankets, set the watch, and bedded down for the night. Wolfram figured that any moment this Kolost would return to camp, for no clan dwarf would ever consider spending the night inside a building if he could help it. The clan chief did not appear, however, and, eventually, hunger and the fact that his knees were aching from squatting in the fir trees impelled Wolfram to action.

He rose to his feet, wincing at the pain of his stiff joints, and made his way quietly through the darkness to the main doors. Wolfram waited until the dwarf on watch had turned his back and was strolling in the opposite direction, then Wolfram scooted along the back edge of the firs, dashed up the stairs, and raced inside the front doors.

He came face-to-face with an imposing-looking dwarf and Fire, the dragon, in dwarven guise.

"Ah, Wolfram," said Fire imperturbably. "We were just coming to look for you. Wolfram, this is Kolost, Chief Clan Chief. Kolost, this is the dwarf I told you about. The one who can assist you. He is Wolfram, the Dominion Lord."

YOU ARE WOLFRAM, THE DOMINION LORD?" KOLOST ASKED.

"Wolfram's my name," said Wolfram. "But I'm not a Dominion Lord."

"So the monk is lying?" Kolost stared very hard at Wolfram, who found he couldn't meet the dwarf's piercing gaze.

"Not lying," said Wolfram, ducking his head. "Mistaken. She's mistaken, that's all."

"How could she be mistaken?"

Wolfram shrugged, kept his head down, muttered something.

"What did you say?" Kolost demanded.

"Same name. Common name, Wolfram. . . ."

His words fell into a well of silence, went spiraling down into the darkness, and landed with a thud. Kolost stood with his arms folded across his chest, regarding Wolfram with a frown. Clearly, the clan chief couldn't understand what was going on and, with customary dwarven tenacity, he was determined to find out. The monk Fire watched Wolfram with a patient smile, like a parent indulging a child in bad behavior, aware that eventually the child will improve on its own.

Wolfram could look forward to endless hours of badgering from Kolost and endless hours of that damned patient smile. He capitulated.

"All right! I am that Wolfram. Or rather, I was. I was once a Dominion Lord. We all make mistakes when we're young and foolish. But then I came to my senses. I quit, resigned." He ripped open the front of his wool shirt, bared his chest. "You don't see a medallion on me, do you? Right, you don't. Because I don't wear one. Because I'm not a Dominion Lord. Not anymore. So, if that's all, I bid you both a good night. I'm going to get something to eat."

He stalked off, his head high, to the table where the monks had laid out the nightly collation. In truth, Wolfram had lost his appetite, but he made a show of being hungry. He piled the wooden bowl high with bread and cheese and smoked meat and took it off to a corner of the common room. Plunking himself down on the flagstone hearth, he began to chew bread furiously. He watched Fire and Kolost out of the corner of his eye.

The two stood with their heads together, conferring. Wolfram could hear parts of the conversation, guessed the rest. Kolost asked about the medallion Wolfram had mentioned. Fire explained that the medallion was a gift of the gods to all those who undergo the painful Transfiguration to become Dominion Lords. The medallion provided magical armor that protected the Dominion Lord from attack and also gave him certain magical powers.

Wolfram had to work to swallow the bread. He managed, with the help of some ale, to bolt it down, and started grimly on the meat.

The conversation ended. Fire departed. Wolfram hoped that Kolost would leave, as well. To his dismay, the clan chief came walking toward where Wolfram sat with his back to the fire. Wolfram groaned inwardly.

He eyed Kolost, trying to get the feel of his enemy. This was the first chance he'd had for a good look at the clan chief, and Wolfram was both surprised and puzzled by what he saw. Kolost was about standard height for a dwarf, but he was on the lean side, which made him appear taller. His hair and thick eyebrows and long mustaches were black, his eyes a deep brown. His face was so sunburnt and wind-ravaged that it was hard to tell his age. From a distance, Wolfram had figured him for a middle-aged dwarf. Now, viewing him close-up, Wolfram was startled to see that Kolost was still a relatively young man. Far too young to be a clan chief.

What was most puzzling was that Kolost wore no clan insignia or markings of any sort. His only ornament, if one could call it that, was a battle-ax that he wore strapped onto his back. A connoisseur of weaponry, Wolfram had taken note of this ax when Kolost was talking to Fire. The ax was of Karkara design and workmanship and was one of the finest Wolfram had ever seen.

Kolost veered off toward the table, and Wolfram's heart rose. The clan chief was merely helping himself to a mug of ale. Kolost paused to take a long drink, gave a belch of satisfaction, then came over and squatted down on the hearth beside Wolfram.

The two were the only visitors to the monastery this night. Wolfram sat in tense and sullen silence, waited for the accusations, the denunciations, the fight.

"Good ale," said Kolost. "For humans."

Wolfram said nothing, chewed his food.

"It might help you to know that I was once one of the Unhorsed," said Kolost. He did not look at Wolfram, but gazed out over the common room, the trestle table, the baskets of bread, pitchers of ale. "I was born and raised in Karkara."

At this startling pronouncement, Wolfram nearly choked on his meat. His head jerked up. He stared at Kolost.

"But you're a clan chief." A thought occurred to Wolfram. "Those men out there. They don't know, do they? Don't worry. I'll keep your secret."

"They know," Kolost said. His dark, thick brows came together in a frown. He glanced sidelong at Wolfram. "I would not live my life a lie."

Wolfram snorted. "That sounds very fine, but you can't expect me to believe any of this. An Unhorsed would never be accepted into a clan, much less rise to clan chief. If you're trying to trick me—"

"It is the truth," said Kolost sternly. "Not only am I a clan chief, I am Chief Clan Chief—the ruler of the dwarven nation."

Having made this pronouncement, Kolost relaxed, grinned wryly. "Of course, there are those among some of the clans who dispute my claim, but that is to be expected. They will come around."

He was not bragging. He was supremely confident, and, looking at him and hearing him, Wolfram could no longer doubt that what the dwarf said was true.

"My parents were Unhorsed," Kolost continued. "My mother was a cripple. She'd been crushed by a horse during a raid. Her legs never healed properly, and her parents took her to Karkara. She was only eight years old when they abandoned her. The other Unhorsed raised her and eventually she met and married my father. He was an outlaw who'd been banished from his clan for coupling with another man's wife. He worked as a blacksmith's assistant. That would have been my job, too, but the Wolf told me that my destiny did not lie in Karkara. The Wolf did not intend for me to be a soot-covered smithy all my life. The Wolf advised me to leave my parents, to cross the Dwarf Spine Mountains and find a clan who would accept me. This I did. I was twelve years old at the time."

Wolfram gave up any pretense of eating. He stared, and he listened.

"The journey was long and hard. I starved, I went thirsty. I lost my way. But whenever I was hungry, the Wolf fed me. When I was lost, the Wolf guided me. He led me to the Steel Clan. At first, they drove me away, would not permit me even to enter their camp. I was persistent. I followed them day and night. I had no horse, but I kept up with them as best I could on foot. Whenever I lost them, the Wolf showed me how to find them. I did my own hunting and gave them gifts of meat, to show I would not be a burden.

"And then came the day the clan chief left the camp and walked out to meet me. He said that because of my courage and my stubbornness, the clan had agreed to take me in. He gave me to a couple who had lost their only child to sickness and said I was to be their son. And so I was taken into Steel Clan. By the time the clan chief died, I had proven myself a strong warrior and a skilled hunter. I held my own in contest and battle and, against all precedent, I was made clan chief.

"I traveled back to Karkara. I purchased and bartered for weapons, and these I carried over the mountains and gave to the warriors of Steel Clan. Under my leadership and with our fine weapons, we proved our prowess in battle to both Sword and Red Clans. They agreed to accept me as Chief Clan Chief, as have the Unhorsed of Saumel and Karkara. The other clans will soon join them."

Wolfram stared in wonderment. Kolost spoke in matter-of-fact tones about his past, but Wolfram could see through the words to the reality. He could envision the terrible hardships endured by the boy, the loneliness, the fear. Wolfram could admire the nerve and determination that had overcome all these obstacles, led Kolost this far. Where did Kolost plan to go in the future?

The clan chief read his thoughts. Kolost smiled and took another pull on his ale.

"I have no small ambition in mind, as you might imagine. I plan to rule the dwarven nation, to bring all clans under my control. Once I have done that, I will extend our territory, seize back the lands the humans and elves and orks have taken from us. And I do not mean raiding cattle pens. I mean take back the land, force them to give it to us, with perhaps a little extra into the bargain."

"So why did you come here?" Wolfram asked, feeling dazed and dazzled, as though he brushed up against the blazing sun. "You surely didn't come looking for me."

"No, I did not," said Kolost. "Not you specifically. I had no idea that a dwarven Dominion Lord even existed." He paused, then said, musing, "Although in a way, perhaps I did come looking for you. The Wolf told me that here at Dragon Mountain I would find the help I needed. Perhaps the Wolf meant you."

"Perhaps he didn't," said Wolfram shortly. He cast a sly glance at the clan chief. "You don't seem the type to need help anyway—mine or the monks'."

Kolost frowned into his empty ale mug. "I know myself, my strengths and my limits. I know dwarves, the Horsed and the Unhorsed. I know how they think and how they will react to what I do and say. I know battle and I know peace. I know the ways of nature—wind and flood and fire. But my problem does not concern any of those, and I am baffled. That is why the Wolf sent me here for answers."

"So what is this burning question that has led you over hundreds of miles into the land of your enemies?" Wolfram asked, relief making him bold. It didn't seem likely he was going to be hauled back as a criminal, after all.

"The dwarven portion of the Sovereign Stone has been stolen," said Kolost. "I came to ask the monks if they had any information about the thief."

"Stolen?" Wolfram was amazed. "Are you sure?" His voice hardened. "Perhaps it was just misplaced. No clan dwarf and few of the Unhorsed ever gave a damn about the Stone anyway." He marveled that even after all these years, the anger was still hot inside him. "Why do you even care?"

"It is true that, in the past, none of them cared," said Kolost, his tone grim. "But now they do. The Sovereign Stone was given to the dwarves by the Wolf. The Stone is ours. None has the right to steal it from us."

"The truth is, you think you might need it," said Wolfram cunningly. "Do you know who took it? Surely, someone must have seen the thief."

Kolost shook his head. "It was done by stealth in the night. No one saw or heard anything."

Wolfram scratched his head. For two hundred years, the dwarven portion of the Sovereign Stone had resided safely in the Unhorsed city of Saumel. No dwarf would ever steal it. This Kolost was the first dwarf Wolfram had met who even seemed to know or care about the Sovereign Stone. Saumel was a center of trade for the dwarven realms. Members of other races were permitted entry into the city, although they were supposed to keep their movements confined to certain sections. The dwarves set no watch on the Sovereign Stone, other than the children.

"What did Fire say?" Wolfram asked. "Did she know who the thief might be?"

"I do not think so," said Kolost, a puzzled frown creasing his forehead. "That woman is very strange. Not like a true dwarf at all. I am not certain that I trust her." He eyed Wolfram, as he said this.

"Oh, Fire's all right," Wolfram said, passing it off. "And if she knew, she'd tell you. What did she say?"

"She said that she had no help to give me, but that there was a dwarf visiting here who has knowledge of the Sovereign Stone, for he is a Dominion Lord."

"*Was* a Dominion Lord," said Wolfram testily. "*Was*. I'm not anymore. I gave it up."

"That is not what Fire says," Kolost stated.

"And what does she know about it?" Wolfram huffed.

"She knows that although you may have given up on yourself, the Wolf will never give up on you."

Wolfram grunted. He occasionally swore by the Wolf, but that was about as close as the relationship between them went these days.

Kolost rose to his feet. "We will speak more of this in the morning. Will you share my fire with me this night?"

To be invited to share a dwarf's fire is a great honor, a mark of friendship. Wolfram saw the trap, though, and congratulated himself on cleverly dodging it.

"I thank you, Clan Chief," he said. "The moon is full, and the road beckons. I have already stayed in this place too long. I must be off."

He expected Kolost might be angry or insulted. Wolfram was prepared to deal with either or both.

"The Children were murdered," said Kolost.

Wolfram flinched, as though someone had jabbed him with a needle.

"What do you mean?" he asked, prevaricating. "What children?"

"The Children of Dunner. The Children who are the Stone's self-appointed guardians. Whoever took the Stone murdered them. The Children fought to defend it. They died heroes. I bid you smooth grasslands, Wolfram."

Meaning, have a safe journey. Kolost walked out of the monastery. Wolfram stood staring into the fire long after Kolost had left. Wolfram stared so long that his eyes began to water from the bright light.

At least, that's what he told himself.

Kolost and his escort were up with the sunrise, dousing their fire and packing up their meager belongings. Kolost had completed his task. His question had been asked and answered. Never mind that the answer wasn't the one he wanted. He accepted that with the stoic fatalism that had carried him through life. He prepared to move on.

Wolfram watched the dwarves from the shadows of the doorway. He had slept badly that night, troubled by strange dreams. He decided he might at least ask Kolost a few more questions.

The dwarves knew by his long beard and lack of clan markings that Wolfram was Unhorsed, and they regarded him with pity. Wolfram ignored them. He'd seen that look before, all too many times. He walked straight up to Kolost, who was bent, peering beneath his horse's belly, checking the tightness of his saddle girth.

"Kolost," said a dwarf, warningly. "One comes."

The clan chief straightened, turned to face Wolfram. If Kolost had been smug or smiled knowingly or looked triumphant in any way, Wolfram would have turned on his heel and walked off that instant. The clan chief's expression was grave, calm, gave nothing, expected nothing, and so Wolfram stayed.

"How long ago did this theft take place?" he demanded.

Kolost gave the matter thought. "The full moon has shone on our journey three times since then."

Wolfram gaped. "Three months?"

"It has taken us that long to travel this distance," said Kolost. "We are not elves. We cannot fly."

"Neither can elves," Wolfram muttered.

"I would not know," said Kolost politely. "I have never met an elf."

"You're not missing much." Wolfram stood in thought, wavering, undecided. He looked back at Kolost. "I don't know what you expect me to do about this theft. By the time we travel back, three more months will have passed. Or longer. The thief could be on the other side of the world by then. He might be there now, for all we know."

He shook his head. "No, it's hopeless. There's nothing I can do. Nothing anyone can do. I get around a lot, though. I'll keep my ears open. If I hear anything—"

"Hello, Wolfram," said Ranessa, walking up from behind. "Who are your friends?"

Wolfram's toes curled. His hair rose. He could have cheerfully thrown himself off the mountain and, for a brief moment, actually considered it.

She was in her human form, the first time he'd seen her that way since she'd become a dragon. He'd forgotten just how strange she looked with her black, uncombed hair straggling down over her face; her well-worn and none-too-clean leather pants and tunic; and that wild, half-mad glint in her eyes.

Dwarves have no use for humans. The clan dwarves exchanged dour glances. Kolost looked stern and disapproving.

Wolfram had been speaking Fringrese, the language of the clan dwarves. He shifted to Elderspeak.

"Now is not a good time, Ranessa," he growled. "You can annoy me later. What are you doing here, anyway? And in that getup?"

"I came to see if you'd gone," Ranessa returned coldly. "And, of course, you hadn't. As for this 'getup' as you call it, Fire won't let me use my dragon form around the monastery. She says I might break something."

"Who is this human, Wolfram?" Kolost demanded, in Elderspeak.

"Nobody important," said Wolfram, shifting back to Fringrese. "A human who latched on to me. I can't get rid—"

"I am Ranessa," said Ranessa, drawing herself up and regarding Kolost with disdain. "And I am a dragon."

"A dragon!" Kolost repeated.

"She's mad as a mistor," said Wolfram in low tones. "I know you want to get an early start, so I'll just say my good-byes. Have a safe journey—"

"I am not mad!" cried Ranessa in a towering rage. "I am sick and tired of people thinking me mad!"

"Don't, Ranessa," Wolfram begged, realizing he'd made a terrible mistake. "I'm sorry."

"I'll show you who's mad!" Ranessa stated.

Her human form flowed into that of the dragon. Her arms became wings. Her head glistened red as the scales sparkled over her flesh. Her black hair transformed into a black, spiky mane that quivered with indignation and triumph. Her green eyes glinted. Thick, heavily muscled back legs supported a massive body. Her red shining tail lashed moodily across the ground.

Catching one sniff of dragon, the horses stampeded, some galloping off down the mountain, others dashing around the eastern wall of the monastery.

The dwarves stared in horrified, frozen shock for a single moment. Then Kolost shouted out orders. He grabbed his battle-ax and held it, braced. The other dwarves snatched up sword or ax or bow and prepared to attack.

Wolfram yelled himself hoarse, trying to calm the dwarves on one hand and Ranessa on the other. The dragon gave out a roar and bared her glistening fangs. Startled from their studies by the horrendous noise, the monks looked out the windows and peered out from the door. The Omarah came pounding across the compound, brandishing their huge staves, intent on quelling the disturbance.

Suddenly, Kolost pointed.

"Another one!" he cried. A second dragon came flying out of the east, winging her way over the mountains.

At the sight of her mother, Ranessa collapsed back into her human form. She huddled behind Wolfram, trying to hide. Since she was tall and he was short, this was not a great success.

The red dragon swooped low over the monastery.

"Put away your weapons, gentlemen," said Fire, circling above them. "My daughter means you no harm. Do you, Daughter?"

Ranessa, crouched behind Wolfram, shook her head.

"Forgive my child, sirs," Fire continued. "She is newly hatched and has not yet learned proper behavior. I am sorry about your horses. The Omarah will round them up and see to it that they are returned to you."

Kolost gazed upward in dazed awe, too stunned to react. Wolfram touched the clan chief's shoulder.

"You better do as she says," Wolfram advised. "Put away your weapons. Now."

Kolost lowered his battle-ax and gave orders for his escort to do the same.

"This is all your fault!" Ranessa cried, and smote Wolfram between the shoulder blades, a blow that knocked him to his knees. She stalked off, leaving him to pick himself up.

"Again, sirs, I apologize," said Fire.

Lifting her wings, she sailed among the clouds, vanished around the side of the mountain.

The dwarves shifted their stares from the dragon to Wolfram. Let them stare. He didn't care.

"They'll bring your horses back."

Wolfram turned on his heel and walked off, headed for the monastery to retrieve his pack. He was worn-out from lack of sleep, but he figured he could put several miles between himself and Dragon Mountain before he collapsed.

He snatched up his pack, put on his new fur-lined hat. He was on his way out the door and off Dragon Mountain—this time, for good—when the heavy hand of one of the Omarah engulfed his shoulder.

"Fire wants to see you."

"I don't want to see her," said Wolfram. "I'm leaving."

"Fire wants to see you," the Omarah repeated. The hand tightened its grip.

Wolfram found Fire staring out the window, her hands clasped behind her back. When she turned, she had a worried, anxious expression on her face that reminded Wolfram forcibly of his own mother, who had often worn just such an expression. He felt suddenly and unreasonably guilty.

"Ma'am," he said, snatching off his hat. "I'm truly sorry—"

"It's not your fault, Wolfram." Fire smiled ruefully. "If it's anyone's fault, I suppose it's mine. Ranessa is my first child, you see. I have fallen into a trap common to parents with their firstborn. I have been overprotective of her. Too indulgent. She is willful and headstrong, much as I was when I was a young hatchling. In other words, I've made a hash of motherhood. I'm going to send Ranessa out into the world, Wolfram. And I want you to go with her."

Wolfram tried to protest, but all he managed was a strangled gargle.

"This could be the solution to all your problems," Fire continued, pretending not to notice his discomfiture. "Ranessa will have a chance to see the world through her dragon eyes. You and Kolost will travel swiftly and safely to the city of Saumel. The disappearance of the dwarven portion of the Stone is extremely serious, Wolfram. You understand that, don't you?"

"I . . . I suppose so, ma'am," said Wolfram, dazed. "It's just . . . I don't know who could have taken it. Who would even want it . . ."

"Don't you, Wolfram?" Fire asked quietly. Reaching down her hand, she toyed with a small silver box, adorned with turquoise.

Wolfram stared at the box that had once been in the possession of the dead Dominion Lord, Gustav. Memories came flooding back. Gustav had died defending that box, which had once held the portion of the Sovereign Stone given to the human race. Gustav had bequeathed the box to Wolfram. Perhaps the Dominion Lord had bequeathed something else along with it.

Horrible suspicions flooded Wolfram's mind. He'd had two encounters with Vrykyl, and he didn't want a third. The memories alone were enough to shrivel his private parts. But then he thought about the children.

Wolfram cleared his throat. "I'll go back to Saumel, ma'am. Though I'm not a Dominion Lord, I'll do what I can."

"Why aren't you a Dominion Lord, Wolfram? You underwent the Transfiguration—"

"The gods made a mistake," he said, feeling the heat rush to his face. He waited tensely for Fire to say something more, but she remained silent. Taking a deep breath, he went on. "And Ranessa can come with me. She's a pain in the butt, no offense, ma'am, but, well, I think I understand her now. I know what she's feeling . . ."

"That the gods made a mistake with her, too?" Fire asked, with a sad smile.

Wolfram put his hat on his head. "I don't know about Kolost. Dwarves are fine riding horses, but dragons . . . I don't know, ma'am. I don't think he'll do it."

"I have seen into his heart. He is eager to return to the dwarven lands. He fears that while he is away, his rivals are working against him. I will speak to him. I do not think he will raise any great objection," said Fire. "And I will speak to Ranessa."

Wolfram had ridden a griffon before—on a dare—and he'd enjoyed it. Flying was an exhilarating experience, like galloping full tilt over a sun-lit meadow. He had a sudden vivid image, though, of riding on the back of the willful, wayward, and awkward young fire dragon. He recalled her inept, clumsy, and bone-jarring landings, and he wiped his forehead with the sleeve of his shirt.

"Uh, ma'am, if you could have a word with her about carrying riders. How it wouldn't be wise to suddenly decide to flip over in midair and how she might want to watch where she's setting down and not make it a lake, for example, or an ocean or the pit of a volcano . . ."

Fire smiled. "I think you will find that Ranessa has more sense than you give her credit for, Wolfram."

"Yes, ma'am," said Wolfram politely, dubiously, and he bowed his way out.

TIME PRESSED ON THE OTHER PEOPLE OF THE WORLD, HOUNDED them with its steady, unrelenting pace. Time for Dagnarus was measured in centuries, yet he heard its ticking clock.

Time had slowed for Shadamehr and Damra and Griffith. Time for them was measured in the ringing bells that announced the changing of the watch on board the orken ship. Blessed with fair weather and a fast wind, they left the Sea of Sagquanno, sailing west for the Sea of Orkas. Their days were filled with leisurely strolls on the decks, serious discussions of the future, less serious stories and songs, and, always, ork omens. Yet every four hours they heard the bells, reminding them that even in the stillness of the night, time rode the waves that flowed beneath their bow.

Time beat with steady wings for Wolfram and Kolost. Ranessa managed, for the most part, to take seriously the responsibility for the safety of her riders. Her landings improved to the point that Wolfram could now almost keep his eyes open. As for Kolost, he was enchanted with flight, saw immediately how useful it could be in battle. He began to consider seriously how he might import griffons, who were not native to the dwarven lands.

Time galloped on swift horses' hooves for the Grandmother and Jessan and Ulaf, riding west, riding home. Time cantered for Rigiswald, who had fallen in with a wine-merchant's caravan traveling to Krammes. He exchanged his services as a healer for protection and companionship and wine enough to wash away the bitter aftertaste left by his experiences in New Vinnengael.

Time shoved at the backs of all those who had come into contact with what might be called Lord Gustav's Sovereign Stone, with one exception. For Raven, traveling with the taan, time was a long day's march, the breaking down of one camp and the setting up of another, and more marching.

The Trevinici make some attempt to count the passing of days, for a warrior home on leave needs to know how many sunrises he can remain with his people before he has to return to his post. But for Raven, time had essentially stopped. There was nowhere he had to be, nowhere he needed to go.

Raven looked back across time to see his past life receding in the distance. He watched without regret as it dwindled and faded away. He could never go back to that life—a life of dishonor for a Trevinici who had been captured in battle and dragged off a prisoner, while his comrades fought and died.

The killing of his captor, Qu-tok, was the bright beacon fire that now lit Raven's way. He had taken revenge on the enemy who had brought shame on him. He had taken his revenge on the enemy who had mocked him, laughed at him, made sport of him. In slaying his enemy, Raven had earned a dubious honor—he'd attracted the notice of one of the hideous, undead Vrykyl, an albino taan called K'let, who had made Raven his bodyguard. Raven had attained another honor, one that meant more to him. He had gained favor with the taan tribe.

No longer a prisoner, Raven was a warrior among the taan, granted full warrior status. He had been given Qu-tok's weapons, his tent and its place of honor in the outer circle of warriors, and all of Qu-tok's possessions, which included a half-taan slave called Dur-zor. Raven had no use for most of Qu-tok's possessions. Qu-tok had some fine armor, which had been presented to him as a reward for his bravery in battle, but it wouldn't fit Raven, and so he gave it away to some of the other taan in the tribe, further gaining in goodwill. The very finest piece—a helm that had been presented to Qu-tok by the hand of their god, Dagnarus, himself, Raven gave to Dag-ruk, the nizam, leader of the tribe.

Dag-ruk was pleased with the gift and pleased with the giver. If Raven had known how pleased the female taan was with him, he would have buried the helm in the deepest hole he could dig and crawled in after it. He had no notion, however. Dur-zor knew, for she saw the way Dag-ruk looked at Raven, and she understood the true meaning that lay behind Dag-ruk's flattering remarks. It was not for Dur-zor to stand in the way of Raven's glory, and so she said nothing.

The days passed, mostly unnoticed by Raven, who found it easier to live from moment to moment, refusing to think of the past and ignoring the future. He had work to keep him occupied, for which he was grateful. Dag-ruk's tribe had made the decision to join with other tribes under the rebellious taan, K'let.

Dag-ruk's tribe had met K'let's tribes in battle, but the Vrykyl had not wanted to fight his fellow taan. He had wanted to convert them to his cause. He had spoken to Dag-ruk and her people, told them that this god they worshiped, this Dagnarus, was not a god at all, but a mere human. A human who cared nothing for the taan as he claimed, but who was using them to gain ascendancy over the soft and sniveling races of Loerem. When he was through with the taan, K'let claimed, Dagnarus would not reward the taan, as he had promised. He would turn on them and try to destroy them.

K'let urged the taan to break with Dagnarus, to go back to their worship of the old gods, who were taan themselves, and who cared for and understood the taan. K'let's words were persuasive, and Dagnarus was not around to refute them. Dag-ruk had been taught to worship the Vrykyl, or kyl-sarnz, as the taan know them—the "god-touched." She admired K'let, as did all taan, who knew the story of his rebellion against Dagnarus, and she felt in her heart that he spoke the truth. She had agreed to follow him and brought most of her warriors along with her. Those who did not agree had either kept their mouths shut or left the tribe.

K'let and his taan supporters, including Dag-ruk and her tribe, traveled east, heading for some unknown destination. What that was, K'let would not say, but they were apparently in a hurry to reach it. He commanded the taan to march long hours every day. They made no stops, but that was nothing out of the ordinary for the nomadic tribes. All the taan felt the urgency of their travel, and many speculated at their destination, including Raven.

What with the long marches by day, the evenings spent in practicing how to use the strange taan weapons that he'd inherited and teaching

Dur-zor the ways of human lovemaking in the night, Raven had all he needed to keep his mind occupied.

He enjoyed most of it, even the marches, for he was accustomed to roving and liked the freedom of the road. The exception was the time he spent around K'let. The very sight of the Vrykyl gave Raven the horrors, reminded him of that terrible ride he'd made to Dunkar, burdened with the accursed armor of the dead Vrykyl who had slain Lord Gustav.

Raven liked learning the use of a new weapon—the tum-olt. Similar to a greatsword with a serrated edge to the blade, the tum-olt required two hands to wield. He also enjoyed his nights with Dur-zor, whose only idea of lovemaking up to now had been the brutal treatment of human females or the almost-as-brutal coupling of taan mates.

Dur-zor lived for the nights when the two of them could be alone together, shut out the rest of the world. She yearned all through the day for the touch of his hands on her body, the touch of his lips on hers. She had come to learn the word "love" from him. She knew what it meant—the wonderful, terrible feelings she had for him. She never spoke the word to him, though, for Dur-zor knew that he did not love her, and she did not want to give him pain.

After their lovemaking, they would lie together, and she would teach him words in the taan language. Raven could never speak taanic, the guttural language of the taan. The human throat is not capable of making the sounds. He was learning to understand it, however. Because of their years of serving among the armies of other countries, Trevinici had developed an affinity for language. Raven was a quick study, and he rarely needed Dur-zor to translate what he was hearing, though he still needed her to give his replies.

This night, Raven had just returned to the tribe after spending two hateful nights standing guard duty for K'let. Several taan tribes had come together under K'let's leadership. Dag-ruk's tribe had set up camp about five miles from the main tribe, where K'let had tented. Raven came back late at night. He was ravenously hungry and disappointed to see the cook pot empty.

"What is this?" he asked Dur-zor.

She dropped down to her knees. "I'm sorry—"

Raven took hold of her hands, lifted her up. "I've told you, Dur-zor, you don't kneel to me. I'm not your master. We're equals, you and I." He gestured to her, then to himself. "Equals."

"Yes, Raven," said Dur-zor hurriedly. "I'm sorry. I forgot. Dag-ruk has sent—"

But Raven wasn't interested in Dag-ruk. He glanced around the camp, his frowning gaze going to other half-taan, most of whom were down on their knees, doing the menial jobs that were beneath the taskers, or accepting the blows they received on a daily basis.

"I can't believe they treat you and your kind like dogs," he said, his anger growing. "Worse than dogs. I've a good mind to speak to Dag-ruk about it."

"Please, Raven," said Dur-zor, pleading. "Don't start this again. I've told you before. You cannot help us. You will only make trouble for us and for yourself." She cast a fearful glance at the tent of the nizam. "Dag-ruk wants to speak to you, Raven. You should not keep her waiting."

Raven set his jaw. His expression grim, he left his tent and walked through the camp toward the tent of the nizam. Dur-zor hurried after, worried and fearful. She had come to know that stubborn look. Nothing she could say would deter him. He'd worn that same look when he'd challenged Qu-tok in the kdah-klk.

Dag-ruk stood in front of her tent, laughing at something with several taan warriors. Tall and strong Dag-ruk bore her battle scars with pride. She had won the favor of the shaman, R'lt, and her arms were lumpy with the magically enhanced stones he had inserted beneath her leathery hide. She was a fearless warrior and a powerful nizam. At Raven's arrival, Dag-ruk turned from her conversation. She frowned, and the warriors grinned. Although the taan admired Raven for his defeat of Qu-tok, the warriors—particularly the young ones—were jealous of him and did not mind seeing him take a fall.

"You have kept me waiting, R'vn," said Dag-ruk, her tone severe.

Before Raven could respond, Dur-zor intervened.

"It was my fault, great Kutryx," she said, dropping to her knees, humbling herself before Dag-ruk. "I forgot to tell him."

"I might have known," said Dag-ruk with a sneer.

She started to kick Dur-zor. The half-taan braced herself for the blow, but before Dag-ruk could strike, Raven stepped between the two of them.

"If you want to kick someone, Kutryx, kick me," he said. "Only know this—I kick back. Tell her what I said, Dur-zor."

"Raven, please!" said Dur-zor, trembling. "Don't do this."

"Tell her!" he said coldly.

Dur-zor repeated the words in taanic, although she said them so brokenly and softly it is doubtful if Dag-ruk heard them. Dag-ruk didn't need to hear them, though. She understood Raven perfectly.

So did the watching warriors. Their grins vanished. They stared, appalled and shocked at his audacity. Most expected to see him die on the spot, for no one defied the nizam.

Dag-ruk's hands clenched to fists. Raven stood his ground, ready, waiting.

Word of the confrontation spread as the shaman, R'lt, hastened to the scene. He said nothing, moved silently, glided along the fringes of the crowd. Dag-ruk was aware of him. Although she did not acknowledge him, her hands relaxed. Her lips parted in a bestial grin, revealing rows of yellowed teeth.

"You are very bold, R'vn, to speak this way to your nizam," said Dag-ruk.

"The nizam knows my great respect for her," answered Raven, astonished, as was everyone else in the crowd, that he was not flat on his back. "The nizam is fair and just. The fault was mine, not Dur-zor's."

"She is a half-taan," said Dag-ruk dismissively. "The fault is always hers."

Raven opened his mouth, but he heard, behind him, Dur-zor make a soft, pleading whimper, and he kept quiet. He had yet to find out why Dag-ruk had summoned him.

"You are bold, R'vn," Dag-ruk continued. "And you are brave. You have proven yourself in the kdah-klk and in the calah. You please me, R'vn. You please me so well, in fact, that I am going to take you for my mate."

A gasp went through the ranks of the warriors. No one dared say a word, however, except R'lt. He made a hissing sound. Dag-ruk glanced at him disdainfully, ignored him.

Dur-zor had to swallow twice before she could translate the hateful words, the words that would take Raven away from her forever. She wished in that moment that Dag-ruk had crushed her skull. The pain of death would be nothing compared to this.

Raven understood, though he could not believe it. He waited for the translation to be certain.

"Tell the nizam that I thank her for this great honor," said Raven. "But I must refuse. Tell her I already have a mate. You are my mate, Dur-zor."

Dur-zor stared, her breath stolen away. At last she managed to whisper, "Is that true, Raven? Am I . . . yours?"

"Of course, Dur-zor," he said. "I would not lie with you otherwise. To do so would dishonor you."

"A half-taan has no honor, Raven," said Dur-zor, though her heart sang within her. "Still, I thank you for that. You have made me very happy. I will remember always. Now I will tell Dag-ruk that you will be proud to be her mate."

"What? No, you won't," said Raven. Catching hold of Dur-zor's arm, he dragged her up to stand beside him. "I thank you, Dag-ruk," he said, speaking loudly and distinctly, as though that would help her to understand his words. "But I have a mate. Dur-zor is my mate." He raised Dur-zor's hand in the air.

"Furthermore," Raven called out, turning to face the crowd, "I expect all of you to treat my mate with the same respect you treat me."

Dur-zor tried to shrink into nothing. She was terrified, though not for herself. She was terrified for Raven. Still, even as she cringed, she could not resist casting one, small, triumphant glance at the furious nizam.

Dag-ruk made a swift gesture with her hand, a gesture that commanded everyone to get out. The taan fell all over themselves in their haste to obey, all except R'lt, who remained standing motionless. Dag-ruk glared at him and, finally, he turned slowly and walked off.

Dag-ruk thrust her face close to Raven's, who took care not to fall back or give way, knowing that to do either would be a sign of weakness.

"There is one reason I do not kill you for this insult, R'vn, and that is because you have found favor in the eyes of K'let, the kyl-sarnz. You had best hope that the shadow of his hand continues to protect you, for if it is ever removed . . ." Dag-ruk snatched the tum-olt from its leather sheath, held the blade to Raven's throat. "I will feast on your heart."

Raven remained still. He did not flinch, though the sharp blade drew blood.

Dag-ruk thrust the sword back into its sheath. With a last, enraged snarl, she entered her tent.

"I will give you time to reconsider your refusal," she said.

Raven felt burning pain on his neck. He touched the wound, his hand came away covered in blood. He put his arm around Dur-zor, who was so weak from fear that she could barely stand. Holding fast to each other, they made their way through the ominously silent camp. The other taan avoided looking them in the face, fearful of raising Dag-ruk's ire. Raven could feel the burning eyes stare at him as he passed. A few of the half-taan did meet his gaze, though they lowered their eyes quickly afterward. He saw in them a dawning respect and admiration, and that gave him an idea.

Raven had not realized before then that being selected as one of K'let's bodyguards gave him both status in the tribe and provided him with a certain amount of protection. He guessed immediately that K'let's favor was behind Dag-ruk's desire to take him for a mate, and that led him to an intriguing thought. Raven had cursed the hours he was forced to stand in close proximity to the Vrykyl. Perhaps, instead of cursing them, he might make use of them. As a soldier, Raven had always scorned those who ingratiated themselves with their commanders to try to obtain a promotion. Raven didn't want a promotion. He wanted something else, something more important. What could it hurt?

All that could wait, however. His idea was only half-formed, and he was too tired to think about it now. He drew the trembling Dur-zor inside their tent, took her in his arms, and held her close. He began to kiss her, but she stiffened and slid out of his grasp.

"You must go to her, Raven," said Dur-zor. "You must tell her you are sorry, and you want to mate with her."

"But I don't, Dur-zor," said Raven. "You are my mate. I pledged myself to you. Let Dag-ruk do what she likes to me."

Dur-zor looked at him sadly. He would never understand, nor did she want him to. Her life had already been so blessed—that was another word he had taught her. She had no right to expect more. With a sigh and tremulous smile, she nestled into his arms.

Taan tents, even those that belong to the great among them, are small structures, designed to be broken down rapidly and carried away on the taan's back. The nizam Dag-ruk could not stand upright in her tent. She could not pace about, could not walk off the fury that burned so hot in her blood it seemed to blister her guts. She crouched on the dirt floor, seething and gnashing her teeth, digging her sharp talons into the palms of her hand so that they ran red with blood.

Hearing a sound, she looked up to see R'lt.

"Who gave you permission to enter?" she snapped, foam flecking her lips. "Get out!"

"Not until I have had my say, Dag-ruk."

Although the nizam rules the tribe, the shaman holds the power of life and death over its people, and so he is often the more feared of the two. It is the shaman who places the magical stones beneath a warrior's hide, the shaman who grants the warrior the gift of Void magic, the shaman who can withdraw that gift or even turn the gift against the warrior.

Dag-ruk glared at him.

He stared back, his gaze cold.

She thrust out her lower lip, sullen, defiant.

"Say what you must, R'lt, then get out."

"Why would you mate with an xkes? Would you shame us all?"

"I have my reasons," she said. "And I don't need to explain them to you!" She made a dismissive gesture. "You are jealous, that is all."

"As if the day would ever dawn when I would be jealous of xkes!" said R'lt with a sneer. "What will the taan think of you the day you bring forth his babe—a mewling, puking half-taan . . ."

Dag-ruk's lips curled in a smirk.

"Ah, I understand. That is why you choose him," said R'lt, his voice hard with anger. "You could rid yourself of his babe. You could not do so with mine!"

"I am a warrior!" Dag-ruk flashed. "I am nizam of my people. How long would I be nizam if I were not able to join the battle because my belly is swollen with your brat? There are other reasons, though. R'vn stands high in K'let's favor. The shaman Derl told me in private that K'let has great things planned for this xkes."

Dag-ruk lowered her voice. "K'let plans to make this R'vn a Kyl-bufftt."

"A Vrykyl? Pah!" R'lt spit on the ground in a show of defiance. He was uneasy, however. The aged shaman Derl was known to be K'let's closest friend and confidant. "Why would K'let choose to so honor an xkes?"

"Ask K'let," said Dag-ruk, with an unpleasant smile.

R'lt cast her an angry glance, but said nothing. Dag-ruk realized, somewhat late, that it might be dangerous to thwart such a powerful man. She adopted a conciliatory tone.

"You understand, R'lt, that I do this for the tribe. For you, for us. In order to be one of the gods-touched, R'vn must be killed. His corpse will not need a mate. By then, I will be elevated in rank, perhaps even made the commander of a calath. Then I would consider having a child."

"My child?" said R'lt.

"Your child," said Dag-ruk.

R'lt eyed her. He did not trust her. She was lying, trying to placate him. He saw that she feared him, and he was pleased. She would bear him a child. He would see to that. He dared not touch her now. But the day would come when she would be humbled and glad to take him for her mate.

He left her tent, left her smirking, thinking she had won. He spoke softly the words of his magic and cloaked himself in shadow, so that he was one with the gathering night. He waited outside Dag-ruk's tent. He did not have to wait long. She emerged from the tent, shouted in a loud voice for Ga-tak, one of the warriors.

The summons passed through the tribe and, within moments, Ga-tak came hurrying to her.

"I have a task for you, Ga-tak," said Dag-ruk.

The warrior nodded, looked at her with a gleam in his eye.

"You know the half-taan, Dur-zor?"

Ga-tak hesitated, not wanting to admit to anything.

"You know her," Dag-ruk growled. "I want you to kill her."

"Yes, Nizam," said Ga-tak, and he would have dashed off on the instant, but Dag-ruk stopped him.

"Not now, you grolt! You must be subtle. I do not want R'vn to know. He might cause trouble with K'let. You will do this when he is on duty with the kyl-sarnz. You will take Dur-zor far from here, slay her, and hide her body where it will never be found. I will tell R'vn that she has run away. Do you understand?"

"Yes, Nizam," said Ga-tak.

"Good. Be off with you. Let me know when the deed is done."

Dag-ruk ducked back inside her tent. Ga-tak departed, pleased with his task. R'lt lingered, but Dag-ruk did not leave her tent, nor did she invite anyone else to come in. He departed. He now had his own plans to consider.

THOUGH THE SUN WAS HIGH IN THE SKY, THE SHAMAN DERL WAS asleep when he received the summons to attend K'let. Any other taan caught slumbering during the hours meant for work would have been driven from the tribe with rocks and curses. Derl was in no danger, however. The most powerful Void sorcerer ever to have walked on Loerem, he was revered only slightly less than K'let, the god-touched, and was feared as much.

Derl spent much of his time sleeping. Having extended his life through the use of Void magic, he had not been able to extend the vitality of youth. He was an ancient taan. He had lived so long he had forgotten how old he was. His body was frail, and he was forced to conserve his strength. He would need strength in the times that he saw coming. Derl had vowed to the old gods, to Iltshuzz and Dekthzar and Lokmirr and to Rivalt, his patron goddess, that he would live long enough to see Dagnarus destroyed, thereby proving to the taan that this xkes was no god.

Derl's body had grown feeble. His hair had turned white, his hide a mottled gray. He slept more than he was awake these days, but when he was awake, his mind was sharp and keen as the blades of a sut-tum-olt. A young shaman touched Derl on the shoulder.

"K'let summons you, Master," said the danhz-skuyarr in tones of reverence and respect.

Derl blinked at the bright daylight, then rose painfully from his bed.

The young shaman assisted by rubbing the elderly taan's muscles to restore the circulation.

"Something has happened," Derl said, eyeing the young taan sharply and noting her air of disquiet. "What is going on? Are we being attacked?"

"No, Master," the young shaman replied. "But you are right. Something dire has happened. Did you . . ." she hesitated. "Did you not hear K'let?"

"You know that I am deaf in one ear," he said testily. "I heard nothing. What about K'let? What did he say?"

"He 'said' nothing, Master," the shaman replied, her voice hushed with awe. "He gave a terrible shriek that pierced the heart. A shriek that echoed through the camp and caused all the warriors to drop what they were doing and grab their weapons and come running. All thought the scream was his death cry. His bodyguards came out to tell us that nothing was amiss, the kyl-sarnz was safe. They did not say what had happened. They said only that K'let wanted to see you immediately."

"Hand me my robes," said Derl. "Any of them. It doesn't matter. Make haste."

With the aid of the young shaman, he wrapped himself in the heavy garments that were not heavy enough to keep out the chill he felt in his bones even on the hottest summer day. He walked through the camp, moving slowly, but under his own power. Daily routine had come to a halt. The warriors stood about with their weapons in hand, wary and tense. The taskers gathered the children near, just in case.

The bodyguard, one of whom was the xkes, R'vn, stood aside to allow Derl to pass.

K'let's tent was built on a larger, grander scale than the tents of most taan. Dagnarus had gifted K'let with a tent such as those used by human kings and commanders, a tent large enough that a taan could stand upright. Derl was grateful. Bending and stooping to enter the small taan tents was starting to wreak havoc on his old bones.

He entered the tent to find that K'let had abandoned his Void armor. He had taken his taan form. Derl stopped to stare. K'let rarely used his taan form, preferring to encase himself in the shining black armor of the Void that set him above and apart from his people. Born an albino, K'let had been shunned by his people, treated little better than a half-taan. Though he had, even in life, risen to an almost godlike status among the taan, the pain of those memories was so acute that they spanned the gulf of death. Rarely did K'let adopt the guise of what he had been when he was alive—a taan male, strong and muscular, ferocious and formidable, with clay white hide and lizardlike red eyes.

K'let paced back and forth in the tent. His expression was unlike anything Derl had ever seen, and he had known K'let for close to a hundred years. His bestial face was twisted in a snarl of scowling fury, but there was a gleam of fierce joy in the red eyes.

"K'let," said Derl, "I come in answer to your summons. I fear you have had dire news—"

"Your fear right," said K'let, halting his pacing and rounding on Derl. "Dismiss the guard."

Mystified, Derl lifted the tent flap. "You and the rest of the guard are dismissed."

The human, R'vn, might not understand the words, but he could hardly fail to miss the gesture. He walked off, heading in the direction of his tribe's encampment.

"Yes, my friend, what is it?" Derl asked, dropping the tent flap.

K'let motioned the shaman to come near. The taan's red eyes burned. "I have been in contact with Nb'arsk."

Nb'arsk was also a Vrykyl, a taan Vrykyl like K'let. The two communicated through the Blood-knife.

"Five thousand taan are dead at the battle of the God City," said K'let.

Derl stared, shocked speechless.

"They were murdered," K'let continued, grinding the words beneath his sharp teeth. "By Dagnarus."

Derl did not know what to say. The appalling news left him paralyzed, shaken. His legs started to prickle and tremble, the blood left his head. He was forced to sit down or fall. K'let assisted the aged shaman, squatted beside him.

When the dizziness passed, Derl felt better. Now he understood the scowling fury . . . and the triumph.

"Tell me," was all he said.

"When the taan came to the God City, Dagnarus rode into the city by himself, telling the taan he wanted to talk the xkes into surrendering."

Derl shrugged, made a face. He had never been able to grasp this strange concept, but he let the matter pass.

"Dagnarus told the taan to wait for him before they launched the attack. Days passed, and Dagnarus did not return. Then one morning he came to the taan to say that the xkes had not only surrendered, they had agreed to accept him as their king and their god. There would be no attack on the human city. He ordered Nb'arsk and five thousand taan to march south, to take one of the magical holes-in-the-air, and proceed from there to reinforce the taan fighting in the human land of the xkes, Nesskrt-tulz-taan (Those Who Die Like Taan)."

"Nb'arsk captured the magic hole-in-the-air?" Derl asked with interest.

"Of course." K'let dismissed this as nothing. "She did not immediately enter the hole, however, for the taan had taken many slaves, and she knew that they would fight better if they were permitted to enjoy their spoils before going on. They had been there four days when a tasker came stumbling into camp. The tasker was half-dead from her wounds. She reported that Dagnarus had led the remaining taan into a trap. Once the taan entered the walls of the God City, the gates closed behind them. They were attacked by powerful wizards wielding foul magicks and by archers and swordsmen. Our people fought bravely and took many xkes with them into death, but no taan survived. Lokmirr gathered to her five thousand taan that day. All died, including the taskers and the children. Yet, even though they were ambushed, they died heroes, and they will be honored by our people. I will see to that."

Derl saw K'let's expression, and he understood why K'let chose to relate this to him in his taan form. Taan usually did not honor warriors who had gone down to defeat. In this instance, however, these taan had died nobly. In their defeat, they had won a great victory for K'let and for all the taan people.

"The day that I predicted would come *has* come," K'let said with fierce elation. "Dagnarus has proven that he is no god of the taan, that he cares nothing for the taan. As he murdered these five thousand, so he means to murder all the rest of us—once we have gained him his great victories, of course."

"Where is Nb'arsk?" asked Derl.

"I ordered her to travel through the magic hole. She will continue to fight the humans, but now she fights for the glory of the old gods and for the glory of the taan, not for Dagnarus. The taan will keep all slaves and loot for themselves, not give them to him. Eventually, she will bring her armies to join up with us."

Derl considered this a good plan, but he was skeptical. "Nb'arsk lacks your strength, K'let. I fear she will not be able to break with Dagnarus. He will continue to control her through the Dagger of the Vrykyl."

"On the contrary, my friend," said K'let, "she and Lnskt have already broken with him. He let them go. He said he had no need of them anymore and he bid the Void take them."

"Is he such a fool?" Derl asked in wonder.

"Whatever else he is, Dagnarus is no fool," K'let growled. "I see his plan now, as I have seen it all along. He will go to the other derrhuth of this fat land and tell them that the taan have slipped the leash and are now a threat to all derrhuth. He will admit that it is his fault, and he will make amends. He will lead the battle against us, and he will need all derrhuth to join him."

"But, if we continue to fight the derrhuth, we are doing Dagnarus's bidding," Derl argued.

"We will fight only long enough to provide our warriors with strong food and many slaves, jewels for our hides and armor and weapons. Then, when the Dagger of the Vrykyl is mine and Dagnarus is my slave, we will return through the magic hole-in-the-air to our old land."

"A pity to leave this place," said Derl. "Such a fat land."

"Bah! Too many trees and too much water for my liking," K'let returned. "Our gods do not like it here either. They will be happy when we come back home. Besides," he added offhandedly, "we can always return through the magic hole anytime we want."

"True," Derl agreed. "What is to be done now?"

"We will send all the scouts we can spare to carry tidings of this to the other tribes. I have ordered Nb'arsk and Lnskt to do the same. They will tell those taan who already side with us to come out of hiding, to begin to speak openly of the old gods and urge the people to renounce Dagnarus and return to the old ways. They will proclaim that I am the new leader of the taan."

"That will cause discord among some of the tribes," Derl predicted. "Some will remain loyal to Dagnarus. Blood will be spilled."

K'let shrugged. "All the better. Let us purge our ranks of any who continue to view this filthy xkes as a god. The Void take them."

K'let assisted Derl to stand. "Summon the tribes to come together. I will speak to the people, tell them what has happened, and send out the scouts."

"I will go forth to prepare to give thanks to the gods," said Derl. "Tomorrow will be a day of celebration."

"Add one more matter to your prayers, Derl," advised K'let, as the shaman was leaving. "I heard yesterday from our eastern travelers."

"And?" Derl paused, looked back.

"Their mission was successful," said K'let, grinning hugely. "They have arrived safely at the meeting place and await me there."

"All went well?" Derl asked.

"All went very well," K'let answered.

Unnerved by the memory of K'let's horrific shriek, Raven was glad to go back to camp and do what he could to try to cheer Dur-zor. He was still rattled from that terrible yell, when he had another unpleasant surprise.

The shaman, R'lt, stepped out of the shadows and stood blocking Raven's path.

Raven brought himself up short, so as to avoid touching R'lt. Like all Trevinici, Raven had an inborn repugnance to magic and those who wielded it. He had no use for human magi, and this taan shaman, who stank of the Void, turned Raven's stomach.

Raven eyed R'lt warily. "What do you want?"

"I came to warn you, R'vn," said R'lt, speaking through a half-taan translator. "Your wretched Dur-zor is in danger."

Raven stared at him, wary and suspicious.

"Dur-zor!" R'lt repeated, then he drew his finger across his throat in a slashing motion. "Dag-ruk's orders." He turned and jabbed a finger back at the camp.

Raven understood everything in a moment and took off running. He cursed himself for a fool. This was why Dur-zor had been so unhappy. This was why she had insisted that he mate with Dag-ruk. Thinking selfishly about himself, he had never given a thought to her. Dag-ruk would not punish him. He was a warrior and valuable to her. He was favored of K'let. Dag-ruk would punish Dur-zor, remove her as an obstacle.

Raven dashed into camp, his untoward haste and wild looks raising the alarm. Warriors shouted at him, demanding to know what was going on. Raven ignored them, ran straight to his tent, and thrust open the flap, peered inside.

Dur-zor was not there.

He searched throughout the camp, but did not find her. The warriors, understanding at last, went back to their work. Raven noted that many exchanged glances, and his suspicions were confirmed. Everyone knew what was going on.

He accosted the first half-taan he found.

"Where is Dur-zor?" he shouted.

The half-taan shrank away from him. He grabbed hold of her, shook her. "Tell me, damn you! Where did they take her?"

Accustomed to obedience, the half-taan raised a trembling hand, pointed east.

Raven flung the woman away from him, turned and ran in the direction she had indicated. He had not gone far before his trained eye saw signs that someone had gone ahead of him. Grass stalks were crushed and bent. He could see the talon marks of taan toes in the dirt. He followed the signs, his heart in his throat, expecting at any moment to stumble across Dur-zor's body.

He continued tracking, making what haste he could, but fearful of going too fast and losing the trail.

But this trail would be hard to lose. The taan had not taken any care to hide their tracks. Whoever had snatched Dur-zor was not bothering to shake off pursuit. Her captor must be confident that Raven was back guarding K'let.

Either that, Raven thought suddenly, or this is an ambush.

"That's why R'lt is suddenly so friendly," Raven said to himself. "He wants to mate with Dag-ruk. Everyone in the tribe knows that. This way, he rids himself of a rival."

Well, it is as good a day as any to die, Raven reflected.

He ran over the ground, glancing only now and then at the trail. He'd traveled about a mile when he came to a small rise. The country was made up of rolling hills and valleys, an ideal place for an ambush. He had the warrior's instinct that he was getting close, and he slowed his pace as he ran up the next hill, preparing himself for the danger that lay ahead. He had almost reached the rise, when he heard Dur-zor scream.

She did not scream out of fear. Her scream was that of a warrior, and it came from just over the rise. Raven sped up the hill, his tum-olt in his hand. Topping the rise, he saw a taan warrior and Dur-zor struggling. In former days, she would have accepted her death as her due, but now she fought for her life, kicking and clawing and biting, trying to grab the dagger he had been about to use to stab her to the heart.

Raven gave a fierce, challenging bellow.

The warrior, Ga-tak, lifted his head, but he did not shift his attack from Dur-zor to the Trevinici.

Ga-tak knew he wasn't in any danger. At Raven's shout, two fellow taan warriors leapt up out of the tall grass in which they'd been hiding.

Raven was not fool enough to think he could defeat three veteran taan warriors, and, even he if managed to, Dur-zor would die. Her strength was already failing. She cast him a pleading look.

Raven had only one chance. He flung down the tum-olt, so that it stuck, quivering, in the ground. Raising his hands, he cried out in a loud voice, "In the name of K'let, I command you to stop!"

To Raven's shock, it worked. The taan understood only one word, but that was the most important word—K'let, a taanic word even a human could pronounce. Raven wore the ceremonial armor he'd been given when he joined K'let's guard: an ornately etched breastplate of steel; a steel collar ringed with spikes worn over chain mail, with a snow-white cloak symbolzing the albino. He wielded a tum-olt that was a gift from K'let.

"I am K'let's servant," Raven continued. "If you harm me, you harm K'let."

A bit grandiose and not precisely true, but it impressed the taan.

Ga-tak hesitated. That was all Dur-zor needed. She twisted out of his grasp and ran to stand beside Raven.

Ga-tak and the other taan warriors looked at each other uncertainly. They had orders from Dag-ruk to kill the half-taan and orders from R'lt to kill the xkes, but they also had a healthy fear of the Vrykyl K'let. Dag-ruk and R'lt would be furious. They might kill their bodies, but K'let could shrivel their souls, cast them into the Void, and prevent them from ever joining the battle of the gods that would one day determine the rulership of heaven.

The souls won out.

The taan sheathed their weapons. Ga-tak threw down the dagger. One by one, they walked past Raven, who dared not give in to his relief. He maintained his show of outraged indignation until they had departed.

The taan cast him cool glances as they left, as much as to say, "You may have won now, but where will you go from here?"

Raven wondered that himself. When he was certain that the taan were gone and that no more were going to leap out at him, he sighed deeply. Then he turned to Dur-zor.

"Oh, gods! What did they do to you?"

Ga-tak had struck her repeatedly, by the looks of it. Her face was bloodied and bruised, her nose broken, both eyes starting to swell shut. One wrist was purple and swelling, probably broken, and she had slash marks on her arms from where she'd fought to avoid the dagger. The knuckles of her hands were cracked and bleeding.

Raven was sorry at that moment that he hadn't chosen to fight. He put his arms around her, held her close.

"Forgive me, Raven," she mumbled through her bleeding lips. She spit out a tooth.

"It's not your fault."

"Yes, it is. I should have let him kill me. I am a burden to you." She hung her head. "If I had died, you would live in honor. Now, we will both be hunted. I have caused your death. I am a coward."

"You are not a coward," said Raven. "Do you remember the word I taught you—hope? So long as we are alive, we have the hope of making things better."

He kissed her gently, so as not to hurt her wounded flesh. "If I had found you dead, I would have let them kill me. I would not want to live without you."

Dur-zor looked up at him as best she could through her swelling eyelids. "Truly, Raven?"

"Truly, Dur-zor," he said. "You are my mate. As long as I live, I will have no other. I love you."

Dur-zor hated herself for asking, but she could not help it. "Do you love me as you would love a human woman, Raven? A human woman like my mother?"

"I love you for you, Dur-zor," he said.

"I love you, Raven," Dur-zor said. "But, then, you already know that.

Unfortunately," she added, with taan practicality, "love does not help us much. If I go back to the tribe, Dag-ruk will kill me—"

"And if I go back, R'lt will kill me," said Raven.

"We could run away . . ." But even as Dur-zor said the words, she fell silent.

Both looked out at the bleak plains, brown and barren. A human and a half-taan alone, without shelter or any idea of where they were, would either perish from the elements or die at the hands of human or taan raiders.

The idea that had been in the back of Raven's mind for days surged to the forefront.

"I hate to ask it of you, after that mauling you took, but we have to hurry. We have to reach K'let before the others do."

"K'let?" Dur-zor repeated fearfully. "Do you run toward death now, Raven?"

"No, I run toward life. Every taan around here seems to imagine that I have some sort of influence with the Vrykyl," said Raven grimly. "We're going to see if they're right."

RAVEN CAREFULLY AVOIDED GOING BACK TO HIS OWN CAMP, FOR fear Dag-ruk would challenge him. He set a brisk pace, and Dur-zor managed to keep up with him, nursing her broken wrist and peering through her swollen eyes. Raven was worried about her, but he didn't have time to coddle her, not that she would have expected coddling anyway. Raven did not think that Dag-ruk would go to K'let to complain about him, but there was always that chance. As for R'lt, there was no telling what he might do.

Arriving in K'let's camp, Raven was startled to find the tribe in an uproar. The taan were stirred up, shouting and yelling, making wild gestures and brandishing their weapons. Shamans were huddled together, conversing in low tones, while young shamans hovered near, waiting for orders. Taskers bustled about, making ready—or so it appeared—to strike camp.

"What has happened?" Dur-zor wondered, staring about.

Taan are nomads, and pulling up stakes was not that unusual, except that Raven had been told K'let intended to remain behind for several days, to await the arrival of another taan tribe. He recalled K'let's hideous shriek. Now was not the time to start asking favors. Yet now was the only time he had.

He headed for K'let's tent. Hauling Dur-zor with him, he walked up to the taan guards, saluted, and said that he had an urgent message for K'let.

He counted on the excitement of the camp working for him in this instance, and he was not mistaken. The taan guards knew Raven. They sent him through to see the Vrykyl. He entered to find K'let in a meeting with all his nizam, including Dag-ruk.

She took one look at him, one look at Dur-zor, and knew the whole story. She glared at him. He glared back and had the satisfaction of seeing her lower her eyes. She slid one uneasy glance at K'let, then pretended to ignore Raven. The nizam stood in a line before K'let, awaiting their orders. K'let glanced at Raven and motioned him to join them.

Raven took his place at the end of the line. Dur-zor crept behind Raven, tried to make herself as small as possible.

"What's going on?" Raven asked her softly. "What is K'let saying?"

He listened in amazement to the story of the ambush and murder of the five thousand taan in a place called God City. Raven squeezed her hand when she had concluded.

"Good," he said softly.

K'let issued his orders, briefly and succinctly. Scouts would be sent to spread the story among other taan. Those tribes with K'let would now travel east with all possible speed, to join forces with other taan moving up out of the south. The nizam had no questions, and K'let dismissed them to go about their duties. After loudly expressing their outrage and their fury, they departed. Dag-ruk flashed Raven one burning glance as she passed him, but she said nothing. Raven concentrated on K'let, thankful that the Vrykyl had retained his taan form. He was not so intimidating in his own hide.

Assuming that all his nizam had left, K'let turned to say something to Derl. The aged shaman nodded in Raven's direction.

"One remains, K'let. Your pet human."

K'let turned, frowning. He looked Raven up and down. His frown increased when he saw Dur-zor. She started to sink to the ground, but Raven held her up.

"I need you to translate," he said.

"What do you want, R'vn?" K'let snarled.

"A chance to speak to you, great Kyl-sarnz," said Raven.

"I am not in the mood to talk to xkes now," K'let said. "I let you live out of a whim."

"I am here to see that you don't regret that whim, great Kyl-sarnz," said Raven. "I have a proposition." He thrust Dur-zor forward into the light. "Look at this. Look at what the taan have done to her."

K'let shrugged. "She is an abomination. They may bash in her skull, for all I care."

"Yet were you not once considered an abomination, mighty K'let?" Raven said boldly, to make up for the fact that his heart thudded in his chest. He was taking a terrible risk.

Dur-zor stared at him, afraid to repeat his words. There was no need. Having been around Dagnarus for over two hundred years, K'let understood well enough.

His eyes narrowed.

"Say what you have to say, R'vn, before I slay you."

"Only this, great K'let. That once you were considered worthless by your people and yet the tales of your triumphs in battle, the stories of your bravery and courage are legend. I say that these you call abominations, these half-taan, are being wasted. The taan use them as slaves, to haul drinking water and wipe the backsides of children, when they might be taught to wield spears in your army. The taan kill them for sport, when they might be dying for your cause in battle. Look at her. Look at the beating she has taken. Yet she stands before you, brave and uncomplaining. You have seen her skill in battle, and she is self-taught. What might she do with training?

"I propose to you that I take the half-taan and form them into a tribe of their own. I will train them to be warriors to fight for you."

Derl said something in a soft voice. K'let listened and gave a brief nod. He did not take his red eyes off Raven.

"Why would you, a human, agree to fight other humans? For that is what it will come to, you know," said K'let.

Raven paused, trying to understand his own feelings, trying to explain himself to himself as much as to K'let.

"Like the taan, my people are warriors. Like the taan, we believe that those who die in battle are blessed in the afterlife, given a chance to fight heaven's battles. I heard your stories of the taan who were massacred. I would not want to die like that, trapped inside the walls of a city. I would not want to die at the hands of wizards—cowards who hide behind their magic and dare not fight a man face-to-face. Because I understand, I want to avenge the deaths of those taan."

As Dur-zor translated this, her own voice grew stronger. She caught some of Raven's fire.

"The taan use the half-taan as slaves, as you say. They will not be pleased to lose them," said K'let.

"It seems to me that you have given the taan much more important things to think about now, great K'let, than the loss of a few slaves who are easily replaced," said Raven.

Derl gave a cough that might have been a chuckle. The shaman muttered something. K'let muttered back, their words soft and indistinct.

"I will be forced to pay the taan for the loss of their slaves," K'let grumbled.

"If I can turn your slaves into a fighting force, then your wealth will be well spent," Raven answered.

A glint shone in K'let's eye. "How do I know I can trust you? I would not want it to be said later that I raised up the young bahk who then bit off my head."

"I pledge my honor to you, Kyl-sarnz. Your fight is my fight."

"One other human made that vow to me once," K'let said softly. "And he betrayed me."

"I will not betray you, Kyl-sarnz," said Raven proudly. "You have my word."

K'let grunted, unimpressed. He eyed Raven craftily. "Correct me if I'm wrong, R'vn, but at the moment your life is worth less than a cracked stewpot. Oh, yes, I know all about Dag-ruk and R'lt. I am kept well informed."

"That is true, Kyl-sarnz," Raven said, seeing no reason to deny it.

"Then I will make you the same bargain Dagnarus made with me. I will give you what you ask for. I will make you nizam of your own tribe of half-taan. You will be under my protection. No taan will harm you or yours in peril of my wrath. In exchange, when I demand your life, you will give it to me."

Raven thought this over. Dur-zor murmured a protest, but he silenced her.

"I agree, Kyl-sarnz."

"It will be done, then," said K'let. "I plan to speak to all our people before we start. I will make the announcement then. When we set up camp this night, you will make your own camp, and the half-taan will join you." He made a dismissive gesture.

Raven saluted and departed. Once outside the tent, he drew in a gulp of fresh air, a gulp that rid his lungs of the fetid stench of the Void. He looked in triumph at Dur-zor, expecting to see her happiness reflect his own. Instead, she was worried and thoughtful.

"What is wrong now?" he demanded, irritated. "You have what you always wanted—freedom for you and your people."

"I know," she said, smiling as best she could with her split lip. "And I am very proud of you, Raven. Still"—she sighed—"it will not be easy. There are some who find comfort in being a slave."

"I don't believe that," he said shortly. "You didn't."

Dur-zor could not explain herself, and so she dropped the subject. She moved close to him, snuggled near him. "I do not like it that you were forced to sell your life to K'let."

"Bah!" Raven shrugged. "I got the best of the deal. As K'let said, my life is worth nothing now, so I have nothing to lose. I intend to make myself so valuable to K'let that he won't want to collect on his debt. Besides, I'll probably cheat him and die in battle anyway."

"I hope so, Raven," said Dur-zor earnestly.

He pretended to frown at her. "That's a fine thing for a mate to say."

"Oh, not that I hope you die!" she cried, aghast. "It's just—"

"I know," he said, laughing and hugging her. He felt good with the world. "I was teasing. One of the first things I'm going to teach the half-taan is how to laugh."

"The first thing you are going to have to teach them, Raven, is how to live," said Dur-zor solemnly. "Right now, all they know is how to die."

THE DRAGON FLIGHT TO THE CITY OF SAUMEL HAD A STRANGE, dreamlike quality to it for both dwarf passengers and the dragon who carried them. The dwarves, wrapped in warm sheepskin coats given to them by the Omarah, sat huddled together for warmth on the dragon's broad back, holding fast to a leather harness that Kolost had fashioned from the harness of his horse and attached firmly to the dragon's spiky mane.

Neither dwarf nor dragon spoke during the time they were airborne. As they soared over the land, the only sounds that could be heard were those made by the dragon—the creaking of tendons and the slow swish of her wings—and even these were stilled when Ranessa drifted upon the air currents. The dwarves marveled at the sights—towering trees sliding smoothly beneath, the dragon's shadow gliding across the ground below, the bright flash of sunlight reflecting off the smooth surface of a small lake.

Each dwarf was absorbed in his own thoughts. Kolost's were of conquest. He looked at the land of Vinnengael below and saw it teeming with dwarves. His ambitions were as broad as the horizon, and he was not daunted by the vastness of the world viewed beyond the tip of the dragon's wing. In his mind, Kolost galloped over his enemies, his dwarven troops riding to victory behind him.

Wolfram's thoughts were not as pleasant. He saw little of the land below, took no notice of the sky above. His gaze turned inward, to the reason he wasn't a Dominion Lord. And no one could convince him to go back to being a Dominion Lord. Not even Kolost, no matter how often he spoke of it. As on this night.

After they landed, the dragon left them to go seek food and shelter. Bad enough, Ranessa told Wolfram, that she had to bear their company during the day. She needed to be alone at night, and so she often went off on her own, seeking out some cave or hollow or grotto where she could rest by herself.

Kolost had a way of ferreting out a man's deepest thoughts. He was that rare object—a good listener. He took an interest in all he heard. He did so for a reason. Not only did he learn by it, but, snared by his interest in them, people were inclined to share a bit too much of themselves.

Kolost, like any good hunter, spotted his prey from a distance, circled in on it, then pounced.

"Tell me of this Dunner," said Kolost. "I know about the Children of Dunner, those children of the Unhorsed who are self-appointed guardians of the Sovereign Stone. But who is Dunner?"

Wolfram did not want to talk about Dunner or anything to do with the Sovereign Stone. But Wolfram was hoping to learn more from Kolost about the clan chief's plans, and in order to get, Wolfram had to give. Tit for tat as the saying goes among combatants, a blow for a blow.

"Dunner was the first dwarf ever to become a Dominion Lord," Wolfram replied. "He was an Unhorsed. He lived in Old Vinnengael, spent most of his time in the Royal Library."

Wolfram had to make a detour in order to explain to Kolost the concept of a library. Dwarves have about as much use for books as orks do.

Once libraries were established to his satisfaction, Kolost asked, "What did Dunner do in the library?"

"He read the books," said Wolfram.

Kolost pondered this. "You say he was Unhorsed. Was he one of the mad ones?"

"Dunner wasn't mad," Wolfram replied, defensive of his hero. "He was like you—interested in people. He learned a lot about people through book reading. All sorts of people: humans and elves and orks. He later put his lessons to good use."

Kolost seemed struck by this. He pondered in silence for several moments, then said, "These books . . . What did they tell him?"

Wolfram gestured with a rabbit bone. "Oh, lots of things: books about warfare, about strategy and tactics; books about plants, which ones are poisonous and which ones can be used to heal; books about the history. Because he read so much and gained more knowledge than any other dwarf who had ever lived, Dunner was chosen to receive the dwarven portion of the Sovereign Stone. He brought it back with him to the city of Saumel. Unfortunately—"

Kolost stopped him. "These books . . . Can you read them?"

"I can," said Wolfram. "All the Children of Dunner are taught to read. Dunner taught the first, and they taught those who came after."

"Go on," Kolost said. "What happened to Dunner? Why did he become a Dominion Lord?"

"No one knows for certain," said Wolfram cautiously. "One of the stories is that he hoped the Transfiguration would cure his crippled leg, and he could go back to riding again."

"The Trans-fig-ur-a-tion," said Kolost, sounding it out slowly. "This is the ceremony where the Wolf gives the Dominion Lord the magical armor. Tell me about it."

"I can't," said Wolfram. "We're sworn to secrecy."

That wasn't quite true, but he wasn't about to relive that wrenching, searing pain.

"So what happened to Dunner?" Kolost asked.

"He became a Dominion Lord and his leg was cured, but he remained one of the Unhorsed. No one knows why. He had some great disappointment in his life. It was said that he befriended the young prince, Dagnarus, and was horrified when the prince turned to evil, became Lord of the Void. Dunner left Vinnengael and took the Sovereign Stone to the dwarven realms. He hoped that the Stone would help the dwarves grow strong, but"—Wolfram shrugged—"since it came from the hands of a human, our people didn't trust it."

Kolost grunted, frowned, and shook his head at the stupidity of the dwarves.

"Dunner built a shrine for the Stone in Saumel," Wolfram continued, "but few dwarves ever paid any attention to it. One day, Dunner found some children playing with the sacred Sovereign Stone—or so he thought. He was angry, until they told him that they were not playing with the Stone. They were the guardians of the Stone. Dunner was pleased by this, and it was then he left Saumel, never to return. It is said that when the first Children of Dunner came of age, those who were called to be Dominion Lords went in search of him. Are you thinking you might become a Dominion Lord?" Wolfram asked slyly.

"Me? No," said Kolost, looking shocked. "I mean no offense, and I hope you will take none, but in order to lead the people, I must win their trust and their loyalty, and I couldn't do that if I were a Dominion Lord. As you say, dwarves do not trust any gift that came from the hands of a human king."

"But it didn't," Wolfram argued. "The Sovereign Stone was a gift of the gods . . . er . . . the Wolf."

"You know that, and I know that," said Kolost, his eyes glittering in the firelight. "The Wolf told me that I must find the Stone and bring it back. Even though I will not become a Dominion Lord, I want dwarven Dominion Lords riding beside me. I want their strength, their wisdom—"

"Dominion Lords are not warriors." Wolfram felt compelled to point out. "They are bound to peace."

"Just so," said Kolost. "After war comes peace. You dwarven Dominion Lords will help me keep what I gain."

Wolfram scratched his beard, amazed and bemused by this remarkable man. Most dwarves never see beyond this night's sunset, as the saying goes. Here was one who saw beyond a lifetime of sunsets to a bright sunrise.

He had to correct a flaw in Kolost's thinking, though.

"You said 'you' Dominion Lords," said Wolfram. "Don't count me among them."

"Why not, Wolfram?" Kolost asked. "What happened? Why did you give it up and flee?"

"I don't want to talk about it," Wolfram muttered.

"But you already have. In your sleep. I know it has something to do with Gilda—"

"Stop!" Wolfram roared. He glared at Kolost.

"Who is she, Wolfram? Your mate?"

Wolfram shook his head. The pain ached, throbbed.

"Who then?" Kolost said softly.

"My twin sister. Gilda."

Kolost was silent. If he'd said anything, Wolfram would not have spoken. But he had to fill the silence. Otherwise, he would hear her voice. He had worked hard to banish the sound. He had filled his life with other voices so that he wouldn't have to hear it. Now, in the silence, he could hear her voice alone, and though it was far distant and he couldn't understand her, he knew that she wanted him to tell her story, their story.

"We were Children of Dunner. That's what you call us." Wolfram gave a snort. "Children of wretchedness is more like it. You know what it is like to be the children of the Unhorsed. Their lives are empty and desolate, and that is the legacy they hand down to their children. You had the guts to refuse that legacy. You had the guts to leave."

"You also refused the legacy, Wolfram," said Kolost.

"I thought so," Wolfram admitted. "When I first saw the Sovereign Stone, saw how beautiful it was, shining crisp and clean like a star on a bitter-cold night, I thought I'd found my calling. I told Gilda about it and took her to see it. We pledged ourselves to the Stone. We served it, guarded it, along with the other Children of Dunner. No one else cared about it, but it meant something to us—hope of a better life. We used to talk about becoming Dominion Lords, like Dunner, and traveling to all those wonderful, magical places we'd heard so much about from the traders who came to our city. And now I've seen 'em all," he added softly, almost to himself. "Every one of them."

He sighed deeply and remembered.

"All the Children start out wanting to become Dominion Lords, but few do. Most lose interest in the Stone when they reach their teen years. They think more of taking a mate, earning their way. But some are called. We were, she and I. Dunner came to us in a fire-vision and told us to seek his gravesite. The way was hard and long. Our trials were many. We succeeded because we were together. Neither of us could have done it alone. I knew we would be Dominion Lords together . . ."

He paused, swallowed, but that was only to moisten his throat. The words, the memories crowded thick on his tongue. Gilda was right. It was a relief for him to speak of this. He'd never done so, not until now.

"We wondered what the Tests would be, if they would be very difficult, for we'd heard stories from the human traders about the Tests their lords underwent. As it turned out, the search for Dunner's grave was the Test. He told us that. His spirit told us, that is. He spoke to each of us, alone, and asked us if we were ready to undergo the Transfiguration. It was the proudest moment of my life . . . and of hers."

Wolfram rubbed his aching forehead.

"I'm not a Dominion Lord."

"You passed the Test . . ." Kolost prompted.

"The Wolf won't forgive me. I renounced the gods. I said terrible things to them. And I meant them, every one," added Wolfram with a flash of ire. "After what they did . . ." He fell abruptly silent.

"What did they do?"

He didn't answer, at first. When he did, his voice was soft with fury. "Gilda wanted to be a Dominion Lord. She worked hard at it, twice as hard as I did. She was more worthy than I was. I went along with it mostly because of her. And they killed her for it. She died in the flames. I can still see her . . . still hear her cries . . ."

He could say no more. He bit his lip to keep the bile from bubbling up out of his throat. When he was in command of himself again, he looked up, defiantly.

"I gave her my medallion. It was hers by right. I placed it in the coffer with her ashes and buried it beneath the long grass of the plains of our homeland, beside Dunner's grave. Then I left, and I haven't been back."

Kolost began to bank the fire, reverently performing the parts of the nightly ritual that are allowed to those dwarves who are caught benighted without a Fire magus present. That done, he wrapped himself in his blanket and went to sleep.

Wolfram dreamed that night that he heard Gilda calling to him to wake up, as she had done when they were children. When he did wake up, it was dawn, and she was not there.

The dwarves knew they had arrived in dwarven lands when they flew across the river the dwarves call the Arven, a name that was adopted by humans and is now found on human maps. The dragon flew over the city of New Vinnengael, giving Kolost the unique opportunity of gauging its defenses from the air. At his request, Ranessa even circled the city once, dipping her wings. Her appearance brought people running out of shops and houses to stare. Guards atop the battlements craned their necks to see. Ranessa claimed that she did it to give Kolost a good view, but Wolfram suspected that she was enjoying the attention.

Dragons were a rare sight on Loerem. Ranessa was probably the first most of these people had seen. So enchanted were they that some of the humans raced along the battlements, trying to keep them in sight. Wolfram amused himself by waving, though he knew that they couldn't see him.

"A large city," Kolost announced. "With strong walls."

Thinking he sounded daunted, Wolfram glanced back at him.

"The trick is to lure them out of those walls," said Kolost with a wink and a grin.

Wolfram rolled his eyes, shook his head.

Once across the river, Ranessa turned south. She was not yet confident enough to fly over the high ridges of the Dwarven Spine Mountains, so she followed the Sea of Sagquanno, intending to come up on Saumel from the south.

Saumel was built into the side of a mountain gorge that overlooked Lake Saumel. Located near the Sea of Sagquanno, Saumel became the center of trade for the dwarven realm. Saumel was the only dwarven city with a harbor and the only dwarven city to welcome visitors of other races (although welcome might be too strong a word).

Members of other races were not permitted to dwell in Saumel, but tradesmen were allowed to keep temporary residences on the city's outskirts. Saumel was the only dwarven city where one could see humans and orks and elves walking the streets, although the outsiders were now supposed to keep to certain restricted areas.

Because Saumel's Unhorsed dwarves interacted with people of other races and actually got along with them (for the most part), Dunner had believed that the dwarves of Saumel would be more open to new ideas, and so he had brought the Sovereign Stone to the city of Saumel. He had been disappointed in his belief. The Stone had been there for over two hundred years, with no one but a group of ragged children to pay any attention to it.

"Trust the dwarves to want the Stone only after it is gone," Wolfram told Kolost.

Ranessa set them down without incident in the foothills of the mountains. Her landings had improved on the flight, as had her disposition. Fire had been right. Away from Dragon Mountain, alone with her thoughts, Ranessa was finding her dragon skin much more comfortable.

Still and all, she was Ranessa. Wolfram had a sinking feeling that this good behavior must be putting a strain on her and that it couldn't last. He was right. No sooner had they set down than Ranessa shifted her form to that of her disheveled and wild-looking human self and announced her intention of coming to Saumel with them.

"No," said Wolfram flatly.

"And why not?" Ranessa demanded, bristling.

"Because where we must go, humans are not allowed," said Wolfram. "If you tried to enter those parts of the city, you would be turned back, maybe even arrested."

Ranessa gnawed her lip and regarded Wolfram with deep suspicion. "I think you're lying. I'm going to go ask Kolost about this."

"Go ahead," said Wolfram.

Ranessa marched over to Kolost, who was repacking his gear. After speaking to him, Ranessa returned, her steps slow while she thought through her next ploy, which turned out to be flattery and charm.

She brushed back her untidy hair from her face to smile at Wolfram. "You will tell them to let me through. You're an important person. A Dominion Lord. Kolost says so. They'll listen to you."

"Girl, dear," said Wolfram, "I left Saumel twenty years ago, and I haven't been back since. No one knew me before I left. No one will know me now. Besides, the law is the law, and not even the Wolf himself could break it. What if I had walked into the village of the Trevinici, alone and uninvited? What would your people have done?"

Ranessa glowered at him. "You expect me to stay here, alone, with nothing to do and no one to talk to while you're out enjoying yourself?"

"I'm not going to be enjoying any of this," Wolfram growled. "Besides, dragons are solitary creatures, so Fire tells me. You're supposed to enjoy being alone."

"I do," she said haughtily. "I much prefer my own company to the likes of you. I just thought you might need help. Considering that you're always getting into some sort of difficulty."

Wolfram ignored her last remark. "There is one possibility."

Ranessa eyed him warily. "What's that?"

"You could shape-shift into a dwarf."

"I will not!" she stated with indignation.

Wolfram shrugged. "Well, then, I guess there's not much to say."

Ranessa realized too late that she'd walked into his trap. "I've a good mind to fly off and leave you stranded here."

"I do thank you for bringing us here, girl," said Wolfram in mollifying tones. "Kolost and I both thank you. I wish you could come, I truly do, but you see that it's impossible. If you feel the need to go back to Dragon Mountain, I understand. But I'd like you to stay. If you do," he added, struck by inspiration, "I'll bring you a gift."

"You swear by this Wolf you're always talking about?" Ranessa eyed him suspiciously.

"I swear by the Wolf," said Wolfram.

"Very well," said Ranessa loftily. "You may go. I will wait here for you and for my gift. But you better not be long about it."

"Trust me," said Wolfram. "I don't plan to linger."

Wolfram and Kolost entered Saumel on foot, passing through the Dwarf Gate, that took them into the heart of the city, as opposed to the Outsider Gate, that led into areas reserved for members of other races. Kolost had told Ranessa that Wolfram was an important personage among the dwarves, but, in truth, the important personage was Kolost. Knowing the customary reserve of the Unhorsed, Wolfram was surprised to see Kolost greeted with smiles and the backslaps that are the marks of respect among dwarves, and even a few brotherly handclasps.

Wolfram was amazed at this, for the Unhorsed were usually withdrawn and reticent around clan dwarves. Watching Kolost walk the streets crowded with dwarves, many of them afflicted with some sort of handicap, Wolfram saw that in the City of the Unhorsed, Kolost was an Unhorsed. He knew their language, he knew their customs. He knew and shared their pain.

"And when he rides the plains, he is a clan dwarf," said Wolfram, impressed. "He knows *their* ways. He understands *their* problems. He can live in both worlds without offending either. I think I have underestimated him. He may well conquer the world."

As he had figured, Wolfram was looked upon as an oddity, a dwarf who deliberately chose to live life apart from his own people, to live life among the Outsiders or, as some termed them, the Outlandish. He found his name recorded in the census book, however, though they had to flip through a great many pages to find him. His name was written in alongside the names of his mother and father, both of whom were now dead. Gilda's name was next to his. He saw the notation beside her name, written in his own hand.

Dead.

He turned away.

Because he was in the census book, all areas of Saumel were open to him.

Although Wolfram had deliberately pushed all memories of the city of his birthplace out of his mind for twenty years, he still knew his way around. The city had grown, of course, and changed, but the old part was carved into the side of a mountain, and it had not changed.

Saumel was a city built by Earth magic, human magic, a gift of some long-dead Nimorean Queen in return for a forgotten favor done for her by the dwarves. The old city was like a honeycomb, with houses and shops built into the rock. With the numbers of the Unhorsed constantly growing, Saumel had been forced to expand. The city now spread into the bottom of the gorge and ran up the sides, spilled out into the river basin and meandered around the lake.

Wolfram had been born and raised in the old part of the city. The faces he saw as he walked the familiar streets were the same faces he'd seen when he left. Or rather, their expressions were the same: grave, solemn, without joy. Joy was galloping freely over the plains, something these dwarves would never know. The wonder was that more of the children of the Unhorsed did not seek their fortune out on the plains, as had Kolost. But dwarves have a strong sense of duty and family. Most know and accept their lot in life.

Like Kolost, Wolfram had rebelled against his lot. Unlike Kolost, Wolfram had turned his back on his people. Comparing himself with Kolost, Wolfram felt ashamed.

He trudged along the stone streets, worn smooth by generations of dwarven boots, his eyes roving here and there, seeking out familiar sights. He opened the gates and let memory flood through him. The memories weren't the bitter torment he'd feared. They left him feeling warm and softly saddened.

"I'm sorry," said Wolfram, glancing at his Kolost. "What did you say?"

"I asked if you would like to share my dwelling," said Kolost.

Wolfram shook his head. "No, thank you. I know where I must spend this night. It is the least I can do for them."

Kolost understood. "You want to go there now?"

"Yes," said Wolfram. "Enough time's been wasted already."

"I see you know the way," said Kolost, as they turned into a little-used side street.

"I am not ever likely to forget it," said Wolfram.

THE DWELLING PLACE OF THE SACRED SOVEREIGN STONE WAS A tent in the old part of the city. Most of the homes and shops of this part of Saumel were built cavelike into the mountain, following the natural shape of the mountain, so that some dwellings and businesses wandered up the mountainside and tumbled down.

Dunner had pitched the tent in a large plaza intended to be a recreational area by the human builders, who did not know that recreation was something unknown to any dwarf—clan or Unhorsed. The plaza was unique in that no dwelling places or businesses were built near it. The plaza was surrounded on three sides by rock; the fourth looked out over the lake.

Dunner had hoped that the dwarves would build a permanent temple for the Sovereign Stone, but that had not happened. The tent was the same tent Dunner had pitched there over two hundred years before. The tent was a bit more worn than Wolfram remembered, with new patches sewn crudely into the leather. He couldn't imagine what was holding the tent together.

All in all, the tent and the plaza were just as he remembered it, except for one thing—the number of dwarves gathered in the plaza.

Wolfram regarded the crowd in amazement. This had always been a quiet, out-of-the-way corner. He wondered what they were doing here.

"They come to pay tribute to the Children," said Kolost, answering Wolfram's unspoken thoughts.

"A little late," Wolfram remarked bitterly.

"They know that now."

Wolfram halted on the outskirts of the crowd. The dwarves stood in silence, giving the dead the gift of their respect before going back to their daily lives. The sight of all these people standing around the tent, so different from what he was used to, made Wolfram uneasy. Then it made him angry.

"They are trying to make amends," Kolost explained.

Wolfram snorted. Walking up to the tent, he listened to the stillness that came from inside. He didn't have the heart to enter. Not yet.

"Tell them to leave, will you?" he said to Kolost. "I can't think with all these people about."

Kolost seemed about to say something, then changed his mind. He went to the dwarves, spoke to them in quiet tones, and, after a few curious glances at Wolfram, the dwarves left the area. All except one. A female dwarf remained behind, holding her ground with stubborn tenacity. She wore her hair loose, unbraided—a sign of mourning among some dwarves. She said nothing, either with her mouth or her eyes. She watched in silence, not venturing near, but not leaving either.

"She is the mother of one of the murdered Children," said Kolost in a low voice. "She was the one who found them."

Wolfram glanced at her, then looked away. "She can stay."

He paused another moment outside the tent, then, taking a deep breath, he plunged inside. Kolost followed after.

The tent was typical of those used by the clan dwarves. Made of hides, it had an opening in the top that was used for both light and ventilation. The interior of the tent was cool and shady, and it took a moment for Wolfram's eyes to adjust from the bright sunlight gleaming off the rocks outside. When he could see, he stood confused, for images of what had been overlaid what was and, for a moment he couldn't tell one from the other. So much was the same and, at the same time, so much was horribly different.

"All is as it was," said the woman standing at the entrance. "I wouldn't let them touch anything. Except they took away the bodies. My child runs with the Wolf now."

"I'm sorry," said Wolfram gruffly.

"You are one of the Children, aren't you?" the woman said.

"How did you know?" Wolfram asked, too startled to deny it.

"You're not like the rest of us," said the woman. "You don't look guilty. You look angry. I knew one of the Children would come back, sooner or later. That's why I made them leave everything the way it was. That's why I waited."

"Am I the only one to come?" Wolfram asked.

"That I have recognized," the woman answered. "If others came, their anger did not burn the way yours does."

Wolfram could recall them all. There had been six in his time, counting him and Gilda. He wondered what had happened to the rest, decided he didn't want to know.

Kolost held back, staying out of the way, keeping quiet. The woman remained outside.

Wolfram walked closer to the altar—a horse blanket spread atop a wooden box. The horse blanket was worn and threadbare from long exposure to the elements. It had been worn in Wolfram's day, but no one ever thought of replacing it, for legend had it that the blanket had belonged to Dunner himself. The Sovereign Stone had been given the place of honor atop the blanket. Placed directly beneath the opening in the tent, the Stone sparkled with myriad rainbows when the sun was overhead, rainbows that skipped and danced with the children.

The wooden altar had been smashed to splinters. The horse blanket lay trampled on the floor. The crude iron firebox had been overturned. The Sovereign Stone, suspended from a thong made of braided horsehair, was gone.

Wolfram knelt beside the blanket, lifted it to the light. The blanket was covered in reddish brown stains that had soaked deep into the fabric, stiffened it. Even after three months, there was no mistaking the smell of blood.

Wolfram glanced around. The walls of the tent, that had once danced with rainbows, were splattered with same brownish red stains.

Wolfram let the blanket fall from his hand. He searched halfheartedly through the debris, knowing he wouldn't find the Sovereign Stone among the broken bits of wood, but thinking he should at least make the effort. Whoever had murdered the Children had taken the Stone. That's why they had come.

He left the tent. Kolost came out after him, his face solemn.

The woman stood outside the tent, huddled in her shawl. "I am Wolfram, one of the Children of Dunner. Kolost has asked me to help him locate the Sovereign Stone and avenge the deaths of these Children."

The woman nodded. "My name is Drin. I will tell you what I know. My boy was one of the Children of Dunner. I didn't think much of it, at the time. I didn't care where he went, so long as he wasn't up to mischief. I am a weaver by trade. I work at home, and he was out from underfoot. That's all I cared about."

As she spoke, a tear slipped out of one eye and trailed down her face. "His father is a bootmaker, and he was very strict with Rulff. He wanted him home at supper, and he would send me to fetch him if he was late. When I would come here, I'd find him and the other Children sitting inside the tent, telling stories or some such thing."

Another tear, the mate of the first, slid down the other cheek. "When I came to fetch him, they would playact like I was an enemy, trying to steal the Sovereign Stone. They would grab up the sticks they used for swords and surround the Stone, ready to defend it."

She gazed up at Wolfram. "When I found his body, he had a stick in his hand. He lay right inside the entrance, the first to be struck down."

Wolfram wiped his sleeve over his nose.

"After supper, Rulff would go back," the woman continued, her voice soft. "Some of the Children had no homes, he told me, and they slept here. He always came home, though. We waited until midnight. His father was furious. I went to find him . . ."

"I am sorry, Drin," said Wolfram, clearing his throat.

"There is one odd thing," she said. "There were nine Children of Dunner. There were only eight bodies."

"Maybe one of the children stayed at home that night," said Wolfram.

"No." Drin was positive. "This girl was one who had no home. She'd been recently abandoned by her clan. I had her to supper sometimes. Her name is Fenella, and no one has seen her since that night. I've asked around."

Wolfram rubbed his chin. "Well, now, I'll take that into consideration. Do you have any idea who did this?"

Drin shook her head. "I paid a Fire magus to cast a scrying spell to try to see what had happened. He said his vision was blocked. He couldn't see anything. But there was something strange about it. He gave me my money back and told me not to try again."

Wolfram glanced at Kolost, who nodded.

"Is there anything else you want to know?" Drin asked.

There was, but not from the boy's mother.

"No," said Wolfram, "thank you for your help."

"I can go home now," Drin said heavily and, hugging her shawl close, she turned and walked away.

Wolfram watched her depart, then turned to Kolost.

"How did the Children die? What sort of weapon was used?"

"Her boy, Rulff, had been stabbed with a sword. The others suffered similar wounds, from what I was told. One little girl had her skull crushed."

"No one heard anything?" Wolfram demanded, frustrated. "No screams or cries for help?"

Kolost shook his head. "I asked those who live near here. If anyone did hear cries, they said that the Children were always shrieking and carrying on. No one paid any attention to them. What do you make of this missing child?"

"Likely she'll turn up," said Wolfram. "Why would anyone murder eight children and carry one off? She probably ran away and is too terrified to come back."

"That was my thought," Kolost agreed.

"This Fire magus. I take it you know him?"

"I already talked to him. He was no help."

"Still, I'd like to hear what he has to say."

"He lives not far from my dwelling. We will talk to him, then you will be my guest for dinner. Are you sure you don't need a place to spend the night?"

Wolfram glanced back at the tent. "I'm sure."

The Fire magus was an elderly dwarf, who made his living selling his scrying skills.

"In eighty years of scrying," he said, "I have never encountered anything like it. Do you know about casting, sir?"

Wolfram did, but he pretended he didn't to hear what the old man had to say.

"To cast a scrying spell, I have to do it in a place where a fire has burned in the past. I build a new fire where the old one burned, and I can see in the flames what happened in the area. The Children generally built a fire for warmth at night, so there was no difficulty with that. I went to the tent and I built my fire and I looked into the flames. I saw the Children sitting around the fire, their faces glowing in the light. One said something about hearing a noise. He went to the tent entrance and"—the magus spread his hands—"that was all."

"What do you mean, that was all?" Wolfram asked.

"A blackness rose before my eyes, as if the entire tent was filled with a thick, choking smoke. I could see nothing through it. I could hear nothing. I could not even see the flames of the fire. I felt as if the smoke were suffocating me. The feeling was a horrible one and very real. I lost my concentration, and the spell ended."

"Did you cast another?"

"I would not," said the Fire magus grimly. "I gave her back her money. It was the curse," he added in dire tones.

"What curse?" Kolost demanded. "You said nothing of this when I talked to you before."

"Ask him," said the magus, and slammed his door shut in their faces.

"Did you try some other Fire magus?" Wolfram asked Kolost that night over their shared supper.

"I spoke to some others, but by then the old man had told his hair-curling tale, and no one was willing to risk it. Thus, my trip to Dragon Mountain."

Wolfram pushed aside a half-full trencher and reached for his mug. He had a terrible thirst, but no appetite. Kolost's dwelling, like that of all dwarves held only his gear and a few cooking utensils. He and Wolfram squatted on the floor. The cook fire was their only light.

"What did the old man mean about the curse?" Kolost asked. "He didn't mention that before."

Wolfram took a long pull at his ale. Reaching for the pitcher, he filled up his mug again.

"I suppose he means," he said, wiping foam from his lips, "the Curse of Tamaros. You never heard of it?"

Kolost shook his head.

"Trust some old graybeard to recall it. It seems that when King Tamaros split the Sovereign Stone, he made the recipients swear an oath that should any one of the four races ever be in need, the members of the other three should come to the aid of the one, bringing with them their portions of the Sovereign Stone. You know of the fall of Old Vinnengael?" Wolfram cocked an eye at Kolost, who nodded.

"What you probably don't know is that when the Lord of the Void threatened to attack Vinnengael, King Helmos sent to Dunner for his aid, required him to bring the Sovereign Stone to Old Vinnengael. According to legend, the Children of Dunner refused to hand over the Stone, saying that dwarves had naught to do with the wars of humans."

"Nor should we," said Kolost grimly.

"True, but it broke the oath," said Wolfram. "The elves did not send their portion, nor did the orks. Old Vinnengael fell. And thus many believe that the oath-breakers were cursed by Tamaros from the grave and that they will be called to account someday."

Kolost frowned. Dwarves are not as superstitious as orks, nor are they as bound up in their own honor as elves. Dwarves do have a strict moral code, however, and to break one's sworn word is a very serious misdeed, one that had often resulted in a dwarf being cast out of his clan.

"If the human king did curse us, it was his right," said Kolost.

"I suppose so," said Wolfram, unconvinced. He took another pull at his ale.

"Do you think we are cursed?" Kolost asked.

"Yes," said Wolfram after a moment's thought. He waved his hand. "I don't believe that rot about Tamaros cursing us from the grave. From what I've heard, he was a good man who wouldn't have cursed a flea for biting him. What I do believe is that we have inherited the problem. The living should have dealt with the Lord of the Void two hundred years ago. Just like those who heard the screams of the Children," he added bitterly. "Instead of crawling out of their warm beds to go to find out what was wrong, they pulled the blankets over their heads and went back to sleep."

"This Dagnarus, the new King of Vinnengael, is he the one they call the Lord of the Void?"

Wolfram nodded.

"But what has he to do with us?" Kolost demanded.

"He has a great deal to do with us," said Wolfram. "If you want the Sovereign Stone back."

Kolost's eyes widened in astonishment, then narrowed in anger. "He stole our Sovereign Stone!"

"I think his minions stole it," said Wolfram. "And murdered the Children."

"Are you sure?"

"No," said Wolfram bluntly. "I don't see how we can ever be sure."

"Then how do we get the Stone back?"

"You can't," said Wolfram, draining the last of his ale. "Call it Tamaros's curse, if you like, or the dwarves' own curse. They should have cared for the Stone while they had it, not after it was gone."

He rose to his feet. "I bid you a good night and good fortune, Kolost."

"You're leaving Saumel?"

"In the morning."

"But aren't you going to help us?"

"There's nothing I can do," said Wolfram shortly.

Kolost walked him to the door and opened it for him.

"I wish you'd—" Kolost stopped in midsentence. His gaze shifted to a point behind Wolfram.

"What?" demanded Wolfram irritably, whipping his head around to look. "What's out there?"

"Nothing. My mistake," said Kolost, shrugging. "Have a good journey."

"I intend to," stated Wolfram.

He peered intently up and down the street, but the hour was late, and most dwarves were in their beds. The street was empty. Wolfram glanced back suspiciously at Kolost.

The clan chief stood in the door, watching him.

Wolfram was not looking forward to spending the night in the bloodstained tent, but it was the least he could do for them, the murdered Children of Dunner. It was his punishment, his penance. With a parting wave at Kolost, Wolfram trudged into the night.

Kolost smiled to himself as he watched Wolfram depart.

Trotting along behind the dwarf, as he wended his way through the dark city streets, was the shimmering form of an enormous silvery gray wolf.

WOLFRAM RETURNED TO THE TENT THAT HAD ONCE HOUSED THE Sovereign Stone and made ready for the long night. He did not build a fire in the firebox, though the air was chill. He wanted to keep the darkness. He'd seen too much for comfort already. Before he slept, he sat on the floor of the tent and gathered the souls of the murdered Children around him. He'd never seen them before, so he gave them the faces of the Children he'd known, of those who had been his friends and companions. He wondered what had become of them. Dead, he thought, like Gilda. Guilt-ridden, like himself.

"You must not blame yourselves," Wolfram said, speaking to the Children. "That darkness the Fire magus talked about. The one that choked him. That was the Void. The creatures who took the Sovereign Stone were creatures of the Void. They're terrible beings, these creatures called Vrykyl. I've seen two of them, and I never want to see any more. They have the power of the Void behind them. Maybe if every dwarf in the city had risen up against them, they could have stopped them. But maybe not. You didn't stand a chance."

Wolfram sighed, sat in silence for some time. At last, he said, "You may have lost the Sovereign Stone, but you kept the most important treasure. You kept your souls. Because you stood up to the Vrykyl, because you fought back, the Void couldn't take you. We'll get on without the Stone. We've gone for two hundred years without it. We'll manage two hundred more. I want you to go to sleep now. There won't be any more bad dreams. I promise. Go to sleep and when you wake up, you'll run in the sunshine. Run forever. The Wolf will be with you."

The faces of the Children were solemn. He didn't know if they understood or not. He hoped they did. He made himself comfortable, a bit too comfortable, seemingly, for the next thing he knew he had fallen asleep and was dreaming. He knew he was dreaming because the tent flap opened and Gilda stood there.

Wolfram had banished her memory a long time ago. He had not brought her face to mind for twenty years. Seeing her, he regretted that. He realized how much he'd missed her. He found a comfort in her. The pain was still in his heart, but it was no longer a torment to him. The pain was sad and softened, warmed with the happiness of their childhood days together.

"Gilda!" he said softly. "I'm glad you've come back to see me. It's been a long time."

"Too long," she said.

"I don't understand, though. Why did you come to me now?"

"I came when you called, Brother," Gilda answered with her own mischievous smile. "Don't I always when you call?"

"No. Hardly ever, as I remember. Yet," he added, his tone softening, "we were never far apart for long."

"We've been apart for twenty years. I was beginning to think you would never call me, Wolfram."

"I don't remember calling you now, Gilda," he said, embarrassed. "I'm glad you came, but I don't remember—"

"But you did remember," she said. "You summoned the memory that you buried in the long grass with my ashes."

"I had to forget," Wolfram said. "I couldn't have gone on otherwise. I buried part of myself in that grave."

"I know," she said gently. "And that is why I have walked with you all these years, though you never knew it."

"You have walked with me?" He was astonished and yet he wasn't. Part of him seemed to have known this already. He looked at her closely. "What are you wearing, Gilda? It looks like armor."

"It is armor," she said, smiling. "The armor of a Dominion Lord."

The armor was of dwarven design, not the full plate and chain-mail armor of a human Dominion Lord. Gilda wore the leather armor favored by dwarves, the type of armor Wolfram had worn for the few, brief, anguished moments he'd been a Dominion Lord. The leather was hand-tooled and adorned with silver, with silver buckles. She wore silver bracers on each wrist and a silver open-faced helm. A silver battle-ax hung at her side. She wore on her breast two medallions, both adorned with the head of a snarling wolf.

"I don't understand," said Wolfram, just for something to say. Reaching beneath his shirtsleeve, he pinched himself, hard. He was ready to wake up now.

"This is not a dream, Wolfram," said Gilda. "I am here, and I have the two medallions. Our medallions. The ones Dunner gave us when we became Dominion Lords."

"But you didn't!" Wolfram protested angrily. "You died! They killed you!"

"I can explain, if you are ready to hear," Gilda said. Removing the second medallion from her neck, she held it out to him. He glowered at it, did not touch it.

"When I underwent the Transfiguration, Wolfram, the Wolf appeared to me. He said that the time was coming when the power of the Void would be on the rise, and the power of the other elements would wane. In that dark time, the Dominion Lords of all the races would be called upon to fulfill their oath and bring the pieces of the Sovereign Stone together. The choice would be theirs, and upon their choices would hang the destiny of the world.

"You were the Wolf's chosen, Brother. You would be a Dominion Lord, the only dwarven Dominion Lord, for after us, the power of the Void would grow strong, and no others would come to seek Dunner's grave."

"It should have been you, Gilda," Wolfram said. "You should have been the Dominion Lord. Not me. You wanted it more."

"I wanted it for the wrong reasons. My heart was filled with hatred and vengeance. I wanted to be a Dominion Lord in order to get back at our people, to punish them for what they had done to you and me and the rest of the children. I wanted to punish them for the suffering of our parents and for the hardships we endured. The Wolf saw into my heart, and he made me see the Void that was inside me. He gave me a choice. I could fail the Test and live out my life as I was—bitter and vindictive and filled with rage. Or I could be your guide as you walked into the darkness.

"I chose the latter, Wolfram," said Gilda. "I have walked with you a long time, though you have not known it."

"What do you mean—you've walked with me?"

Gilda grinned. "Do you recall the bracelet the monks gave you? The bracelet that would grow warm when you met someone you were supposed to follow? The bracelet grew warm when you met Jessan and Bashae, didn't it?"

Wolfram nodded, perplexed.

"The bracelet's warmth led you to Lord Gustav and the Sovereign Stone."

"Yes," said Wolfram.

"The warmth did not come from the bracelet, Wolfram," Gilda told him. "The warmth you felt was the warmth of my hand."

"I wish you had told me," he said, blinking back tears.

"I thought you would understand without the need for words. We always understood each other before."

Wolfram looked into his own heart and saw the truth.

"I did understand, Gilda. But I was angry. I pretended to be angry at the gods, but I wasn't. I was angry at you. You were all I had left in the world, and you chose to leave me."

"I didn't leave you. You know that now. Take the medallion, Wolfram. Be what you were meant to be. The Wolf has need of you."

"I don't know . . . It's been so long . . ."

Wolfram woke with a start to find the half-light of early morning filtering in through the hole at the top of the tent. He had fallen asleep under the bloodstained horse blanket and, with a shiver, he threw it off. His dream was fresh in his mind, so fresh that he looked around the tent in the hope that he might see Gilda again.

The tent was empty, except for himself. Still, he felt a peace he had not known in many years, a peace he hadn't found in all his restless wanderings. He stood up, stretched to get the kinks out. Leaning down to pick up his pack, preparatory to departing, he felt something thump on his chest.

He looked down to see a silver medallion, adorned with the head of a snarling wolf.

The medallion of a Dominion Lord.

"You're back," said Kolost, opening the door to Wolfram's knock.

Wolfram stumped inside. "You don't seem surprised."

Kolost smiled. "I saw the Wolf follow you last night. I knew the Wolf would reason with you."

Wolfram grunted, not inclined to explain. "I've had an idea. I'm going to do a fire-scry myself. I think I may be able to see through the darkness."

Kolost opened his mouth to protest that Wolfram was not a Fire magus and thus could not cast such a spell. He closed his mouth in time, before the words came out. One does not question the mysteries of the Wolf.

"I think you might want to be there," Wolfram continued. "I'd like to do it while it's early yet. And we should seal off the area. Keep everyone out. I'm not sure what might happen."

"That can be arranged. I will meet you at the tent," Kolost promised.

Wolfram nodded and trudged back to the temple, as the Children of Dunner knew it. He clasped the medallion in his hand as he walked. The morning was cold, and the metal was warm. He felt, when he touched it, as if he were touching Gilda's hand. He thought of her remark about the bracelet on his wrist, and he shook his head wryly. He might have known. She was always getting him into trouble when they were kids. She was the adventurous one, forging ahead. He, the more cautious, lagged behind. He wished he had kept the bracelet, but he returned it in a fit of pique to Fire.

Reaching the plaza, Wolfram ducked into the tent and halted, alarmed. Someone had been here in his absence. He didn't know how he knew, but he knew. He poked and peered around, but could find nothing missing, nothing rearranged. He emerged from the tent, walked around the plaza, staring intently into any recessed area, where someone might be hiding. He found no one. He did not discount his feelings, however. Instinct had saved his dwarf behind more than once. He'd be sure to tell Kolost to keep a sharp lookout.

Wolfram had brought with him some wood and kindling, enough to build a small fire. Returning to the tent, he picked up the maltreated firebox and placed the wood inside. Then he sat back and stared at it, bemused. Wolfram was no magus. He'd never cast a magic spell in his life, had never wanted to cast one. Now he was going to attempt a grand spell, one that even experienced magi find difficult.

Wolfram wasn't worried about casting the spell. He was worried because he wasn't worried. He felt a warmth inside when he thought about the spell, a knowledge that he could do it, even though he had no idea how. And that bothered him.

Kolost peered inside the tent. Wolfram stepped out to meet him. The plaza had been sealed off. Dwarves stood guard at the entrance, waved away the curious.

"Someone's been in the tent," said Wolfram. "Tell your people to keep a sharp lookout."

"They're good men. They know what to do," said Kolost. "Who was it? Do you have any idea?"

Wolfram shook his head. "Just a feeling, that's all. Come inside. Sit there." He gestured to a place near the firebox. "If the spell works, we'll see everything just as it happened that night, as if we were there ourselves. But, of course, we won't be. It's just visions of the past."

Kolost nodded to show he understood and took his place where Wolfram indicated. Kolost sat down with knees akimbo, placed his hands on his knees, and looked expectantly at Wolfram.

"I'm going to . . . uh . . . change," Wolfram said, his face flushing with embarrassment. He didn't want Kolost to think he was trying to show off or that he was putting on airs. "It's part of being a Dominion Lord. The armor, that is."

Wolfram eyed Kolost askance, waited tensely for him to ask questions. Kolost said nothing, however, merely indicated that he was ready to begin. Wolfram was relieved. He was liking this dwarf more and more.

Clasping his fingers tightly around the medallion, Wolfram brought to mind the remembered image of Gilda in her magical armor and, the next thing he knew, he was clad in armor of his own: fine, supple leather with silver buckles and a silver helm.

Kolost's eyes widened at the sight, but he kept his mouth shut.

The wondrous armor was as familiar as Wolfram's own skin, made him feel secure and protected. He knew immediately what he had to do to cast the fire-scry spell. The magic flowed from him at will. He had only to think it and it was done. The wood in the firebox burst into flame.

Wolfram stared into it, his thoughts concentrating on the night another fire had burned in this box.

Images of myriad nights flooded into his mind, so many that he was overwhelmed. He needed something to connect him to the one particular night. Reaching out his hand, he grabbed hold of a corner of the bloodstained horse blanket.

Fire swirled in the firebox, and the tent was filled with smoke, thick and choking. Wolfram couldn't breathe. He heard Kolost coughing and gagging.

"Get out!" Wolfram ordered the Void.

The smoke roiled furiously. Then there came a wolf's howl. A gust of wind shook the tent, sent the edges to flapping. The wind sucked the smoke out of the tent, carried it away. Wolfram could breathe again. He heard Kolost gulp air in relief.

Looking into the flames, he saw the Children . . .

The Children of Dunner each took turns being the bearer of the Sovereign Stone. Every day, a different Child wore the stone. This night, Fenella was the bearer. A sickly child, Fenella had been abandoned in the city of Saumel. In leaving her behind, her parents were obeying the decree of the clan chief, who maintained that the weak child placed the entire clan in danger. Fenella had been given into the care of an elderly dwarf female. Her caretaker had just recently died. The ten-year-old girl was on her own.

By now, Fenella had outgrown the childhood illnesses. She was strong as any young dwarf. But that didn't mean she could go back to her clan. She had no idea where they were, and they probably wouldn't take her back anyway. Fenella took over the basket-weaving business of the dead woman and, though her life was hard, she was making do.

Weaving baskets all day left her only the nighttime hours to pay tribute to the Sovereign Stone. She never missed a night, however. She looked forward to the day when she would be called to go on the quest for Dunner's grave and ask his blessing to become a Dominion Lord. Fenella knew this was her destiny. Dunner himself had told her in a dream.

This night, Fenella lifted the Sovereign Stone from its place of honor in the tent that was a temple and watched it sparkle in the firelight. Every time she touched the Stone, she was awed, humbled. She felt as if she could draw a straight line from herself to Dunner and from Dunner to King Tamaros. The hundreds of years intervening were as nothing, when she wore the Stone. The difference between a dwarven orphan child and a human king was nothing.

Fenella was a storyteller, and on those nights when she was the bearer of the Stone, she entertained the other Children with stories of the Stone and those whose fates were bound up in it. Although the stories were old, having been handed down from Dunner himself, Fenella breathed new life into them. The Children never tired of listening to her.

Fenella sat on the box that was an altar and made herself comfortable. Seven Children of varying ages ranged themselves around her. One, a boy named Rulff, was put in charge of guarding the entrance to the tent against intruders. The post was honorary. There had been only one intruder, in all the history of the dwarven Sovereign Stone, and that had been two hundred years ago, when a Dominion Lord, sent by King Helmos had invaded the sanctity of the temple-tent to ask for the Stone's return. Still, the Children were always on the lookout for someone to try to steal the Stone. Rulff took his place proudly, a sharpened stick in hand.

Fenella had been feeling sad all that day, and she chose for her story one that always made the Children laugh.

The tale had been a favorite of Dunner's. It dealt with a human child called Gareth, who was companion to Prince Dagnarus, and told of the first time Gareth had attempted to ride a horse. The tale was amusing to dwarven children, for, although some had never ridden a horse, they were all born to the saddle. They laughed heartily when Fenella came to the part where the horse bucked and the human boy Gareth went sailing out of the saddle, head over heels, to land in a hayrick.

Rulff turned his head. "Hush," he said. "I think I heard something."

He opened the tent flap, stared into the darkness.

"Someone's out there," he reported, and he sounded puzzled, for few people ever came this way during the day and none at all after dark.

"Maybe it's another knight come to try to take the Stone from us," said one of the Children hopefully.

"Maybe it's your mother, Rulff," said another, and he snickered.

"You get up on the box, Fenella," said a third. "We'll stand guard."

Fenella, feeling proud and only a little nervous, took her place on top of the box. The other Children lined up in front of her, sharpened sticks in their hands. Fenella rested her hand on the Sovereign Stone and found reassurance in the feel of the crystal that always seemed to her to be humming to itself, as though the jewel had an inner life of its own.

She was listening with her heart to the Stone's song, when Rulff gave a scream that was so horrible she froze up inside. The blade of a sword, smeared with blood, thrust out of Rulff's back. A beast-man tore open the tent flap, barged inside. As the beast-man entered, it kicked impatiently at Rulff, impaled on the sword. His body slid off the blade and landed in a heap on the ground.

Two more beast-men shoved into the tent. One of the older boys made a desperate lunge at the beast-men with his sharp stick. The beast-man made a kind of gurgling sound that might have been a laugh and brought his club down on the boy's head, smashing it open, spattering the tent wall with blood and gore.

Some of the other Children fought. Some screamed and tried to escape. Some stood staring, frozen in terror. The wicked swords of the beast-men flashed in the firelight. Bodies fell, some of them headless, others stabbed to the heart. The floor was red with blood.

Fenella was the only child left alive. She couldn't move. She stared at the slavering beast-men, their arms bloodied to the elbows, and she waited to die. One raised his sword, and Fenella shut her eyes.

A voice said something in a commanding tone, and Fenella did not die.

She opened her eyes to see the beast-men pointing at her and arguing. Their language was as horrible as they were.

The beast-men reached a decision. One walked toward her, his bloody sword in his hand. Fenella felt a hideous warmth wash over her, and she was afraid she was going to faint. She grasped hold of the Sovereign Stone, and the cold of the crystal helped brace her.

The beast-man knocked her hand aside. He grabbed hold of the Stone.

A flash of white light blinded Fenella. She could not see anything for long minutes except the blue afterimage of that flash. When that cleared, she saw the beast-man who had tried to take the Stone lying on his back on the ground, wringing a blackened hand.

Fenella was proud of the Stone for fighting the monsters, and her pride gave her courage. She stood straighter and stared at them defiantly.

Another of the beast-men tried to seize the Stone. Fenella was ready and she squinched her eyes tight shut. Even then, she could still see the blinding light.

The beast-man lay on the ground, shaking his head and groaning.

The beast-men glared at her and at the Stone, at a loss for what to do. One of them shouted something, and a fourth beast-man entered. This beast-man was apparently some sort of slave, for he walked with his head bowed and stood, cringing, before the other beast-men. This creature looked like one of the beast-men, and he didn't, for he didn't have the beast-man's snout. His nose was more like the nose of a human.

The beast-men and the newcomer held another conversation. Fenella knew that the conversation involved her, for they constantly pointed at her and pointed at the Stone. The beast-man pointed at her hand, then held up his own burnt hand.

The beast-man said something in a tone of finality. He kicked at the slave and pointed at Fenella.

The slave picked up one of the sharpened sticks and approached Fenella. She thought that he was going to kill her with the stick, and she braced herself to die. Instead, he used the tip of the stick to gingerly catch hold of the horsehair rope from which the Stone dangled and carefully slide the Stone around so that it now hung down Fenella's back.

Dropping the stick, the slave took hold of Fenella. He hoisted her onto his back, grasped her wrists around his neck, and, giving the nod to his companions, carried her piggyback out of the tent.

The slave's nails dug painfully into Fenella's arms. His strong grasp bruised her flesh. The smell of the beast-men, mingled with the smell of the blood of her friends, made her sick and dizzy. She felt the hideous warmth come over her again, and this time she let herself sink into it.

Wolfram watched the vision in the flames, and his rage burned hotter than the fire. Calming his fury, he paid close attention to all that was happening, listened closely to the beast-men's talk, in the futile hope of hearing anything that might be useful.

The three spoke briefly in a language that was as ugly as they were. Wolfram could make out only a couple of words amid the hoots and whistles. He found, though, that he could understand the slave, who spoke the beast-man's language, but the words came out clearer, not as clotted. One word this slave repeated several times, always with a show of awe, was the word, "K'let." The word was easy to understand, although Wolfram had no idea what it might mean.

As the slave carrying Fenella left the tent, one of the beast-men accompanied him, probably to keep an eye on him. The other beast-men stayed behind to ransack the tent, searching for more treasure. They smashed the box and even searched the small bodies. Finding nothing, they snarled their displeasure and departed. Wolfram tried to keep track of them, but once they passed out of the tent, he lost them in the darkness. The fire in the firebox dwindled and died. The spell ended.

Wolfram gave a deep sigh. Neither he nor Kolost said anything. The sight had been too awful for speech.

When Kolost finally spoke, his voice was harsh, almost unrecognizable. "What were those creatures?"

"They are called 'taan,' " said Wolfram. "I heard about them at the monastery. These are the same creatures who sacked Dunkar, killed many hundreds, and enslaved hundreds more."

"What was that other creature, the one that looked human."

"He was a half-human. A gods-cursed mixed breed."

"I have never heard of these 'taan' before. Where do they come from?"

"No one knows. The Void, maybe. Dagnarus, Lord of the Void, brought them to this land, or so I have heard. They serve him."

"Then this Dagnarus is the one who has stolen the Sovereign Stone, the one who is responsible for the deaths of the Children."

"So it would seem," said Wolfram.

"At least we have found out why there were only eight bodies. They carried off the ninth child. What will they do with her, do you think? Why didn't they kill her?"

"You saw what happened when they tried to take the Sovereign Stone," said Wolfram. "The magic of the Stone prevented them from touching it. They could see that the girl touched it and that it wouldn't hurt her. My guess is that they think she has some power over the Stone, and that's why they took her. Hopefully, if they believe that, they'll do their best to keep her alive. And that gives us a chance," added Wolfram, grimly determined.

"A chance for what?" asked Kolost.

"A chance to rescue her and recover the Stone."

Kolost gestured to the embers that flickered in the firebox. "But this happened months ago. They could be anywhere—"

His words were cut off by a shrill shriek of anger and an all-too-familiar voice.

"I will go where I please! Keep your filthy hands off me. Wolfram! Come out here this minute! I said don't touch me, you dwarf, you. If you do, I'll swear you'll be sorry. You don't want to see me angry—"

"The Wolf save us. It's Ranessa!" Wolfram groaned, and raced out of the tent.

RANESSA! DON'T!" WOLFRAM SHOUTED, HAVING VISIONS OF her shifting into a dragon right there in the middle of the plaza. "Ranessa?"

He looked around, bewildered. He heard her voice, but he couldn't see her. Then a dwarf female with long, untidy black hair came storming toward him, brandishing her fists at the other dwarves, who were attempting to stop her and pausing every now and then to kick at them or take a swing.

At the sight of Wolfram, she cried, "Thank goodness!" and shifted to her human form.

The sudden transformation of the dwarf female into a human female achieved one objective. The dwarves who had hold of her let loose and fell back, muttering among themselves. Several raised weapons, and those who were not armed picked up stones and sticks.

"Girl, you mustn't—" Wolfram began.

She brushed his words aside. "One of those things was here! I saw it." She pointed. "It was standing right over there, near that tent you came out of."

"One of what things?" Wolfram asked, thinking she might mean a beast-man.

"Like the thing that tried to carry you off," she said, her eyes dark with anger. "Like the thing that killed Lord Gustav. What did you call it—"

"A Vrykyl?" Wolfram gasped, the hair pricking the back of his neck beneath his helm. He still wore his Dominion Lord armor, but armor hadn't helped Lord Gustav. The Vrykyl had stabbed him right through it. "Do you still see it?"

"No. I was going to go after it, but these nincompoops wouldn't let me pass. I tried to reason with them"—Ranessa rounded on the dwarves, who were slipping up on her from behind—"but the thing must have heard me shout, because when I looked for it again, it was gone."

"Let her be," Wolfram ordered, waving his arms at the approaching dwarves. "She's with me. I'll answer for her."

The dwarves eyed him askance, none too certain of him either, this strange dwarf in his fancy armor. Kolost came to back up Wolfram, assured the dwarves that he had the situation well in control. The dwarves retreated, but they kept a suspicious watch on Ranessa and on Wolfram.

"What is she upset about?" Kolost asked.

"There was a Vrykyl here," said Wolfram. "One of those Void knights I was telling you about. He was listening at the tent."

"If Void creatures walk the streets of Saumel," Kolost said grimly, "we will find them."

"No you won't," said Ranessa. "He was disguised as a dwarf. I could see through it, but that's because I'm a dragon."

"Keep your voice down!" Wolfram said sharply. "We're in enough trouble already."

"So how do we find this Void knight?" Kolost asked.

"You don't want to," said Wolfram earnestly. "Trust me, Kolost. There's nothing you could do to harm it. Just hope it got what it came for and that it went away."

"But what did it come for?" Kolost demanded. "The Sovereign Stone is gone."

The unpleasant thought occurred to Wolfram that perhaps the Vrykyl had come for him.

"You didn't get a feeling that Vrykyl was following us, did you?" he asked Ranessa. "You know, the way you felt the last time the Vrykyl followed us?"

"No," she said positively. "We were not followed. Besides, Vrykyl can't fly. Can they?"

Wolfram didn't think so, but he didn't know that much about their habits, and he didn't care to find out.

"What was it doing by the tent?"

"Eavesdropping," Ranessa answered readily. "The Vrykyl had his head plastered against the side. He was listening to what you were saying."

"Now that's damned odd," Wolfram muttered.

What possible interest could a Vrykyl have in his fire-scry? Wolfram couldn't figure it out, and he decided he wasn't going to let it bother him. He had a task ahead of him. He would concentrate on that.

"It sticks in my craw to think of that child in the hands of those monsters," Kolost stated, his dark eyes shadowed with anger.

"Mine, too," said Wolfram. "Not to mention the Sovereign Stone."

"Yes, the Sovereign Stone, of course," Kolost agreed, almost as an afterthought. He looked back at the tent, his brow furrowed.

Wolfram regarded Kolost with amazement. The clan chief continued to astonish and impress him. Any other clan leader's first thought would have been of the valuable jewel, not the orphan child.

"Well, girl, we'd best be off, before you start a riot," Wolfram stated. "We're *walking,*" he added with emphasis, thinking he detected by the gleam in her eye that she was planning to shift into her dragon form on the spot.

Ranessa looked sullen, and he knew he'd guessed right. "I don't like this place," she said, casting a disparaging glance around through the tangles of untidy hair. "And I don't like these people. And I don't like being a dwarf," she added accusingly, as if it was Wolfram's fault. "You are all so . . . so short."

Kolost fell into step beside them. "You're going after the beast-men, aren't you?"

"Yes," Wolfram said.

"The trail will be cold now. How will you even know where to start looking?"

Wolfram shrugged. He was busy keeping an eye on Ranessa.

"It seems hopeless," said Kolost. "Still, the Wolf walks with you. The Wolf will show you the way."

At the edge of the plaza, Kolost came to a halt. "I wish I could come with you, but I am needed here. In my absence, Sword Clan and Red Clan have started a war. I'm going to have to go knock a few heads together."

"Good luck," said Wolfram.

"You, too," said Kolost.

As they separated, each man said silently to the other, "You're going to need it."

The Vrykyl, Caladwar, had been an elf when he was alive. He would have agreed with Ranessa, in that he found wearing the guise of a dwarf to be tedious in the extreme. To an elf fond of licentious living, the self-denying lifestyle of the Unhorsed was incredibly dull. Caladwar came to hate the dwarves so much that he couldn't even take pleasure in killing one, for that meant he'd have to crawl into the dwarf's skin and be filled with a flood of depressing memories. Caladwar feared he was going to have to go on being a dwarf for the rest of his undead life, but, fortunately for him, the dwarven Dominion Lord turned up, and Caladwar was able to secure the information his master had been so desperate to acquire.

It was not the appearance of the dragon that had sent Caladwar running off. Caladwar had been a member of the Wyred before he turned to the Void. He held a high opinion of his own prowess in magic—an opinion that was not unjustified. Caladwar could have fought the young and inexperienced dragon, and probably defeated it. Caladwar wasn't interested in fighting dragons, however. He wanted only to get out of this horrible dwarf skin and back into his own. He left the plaza because he was eager to relay the information to his lord, and then leave this godsforsaken place.

Dagnarus had sent Caladwar to Saumel to secure the dwarven portion of the Sovereign Stone. Caladwar had arrived only to discover that someone had beaten him to it. He'd reported that to his lord, who had been furious and ordered Caladwar to remain in Saumel until he found out the identity of the thief.

Caladwar had tried casting his own fire-scry, hoping to use his magic to reveal the culprit. His plans were thwarted by the Void, which was supposed to be their ally, a fact that Caladwar found extremely perplexing. Someone out there was challenging Dagnarus for mastery of the Void. And now Caladwar knew who.

Reaching his dwelling place, Caladwar placed his hand on the Bloodknife and sent forth an urgent summons to Dagnarus.

The Lord of the Void was not quite as prompt to answer as he had been before he became the ruler of Vinnengael, and Caladwar fumed in impatience. He reminded himself that Dagnarus was in the public eye, surrounded by people most of the day and well into the night.

"Be quick," Dagnarus said, his voice coming suddenly and unexpectedly. "I don't have much time. What have you discovered?"

"I know who stole the dwarven Sovereign Stone, my lord," said Caladwar smugly.

"You had better, or I would not thank you for bothering me," Dagnarus returned coolly. "Dispense with the dramatics and tell me."

"The thief is K'let, my lord."

Silence as empty as the Void met his words. When the silence continued unbroken, Caladwar grew worried. He needed to obtain permission to leave the dwarven city, and he'd not yet received it.

"My lord?" he questioned. "Are you there?"

"Are you certain?" Dagnarus demanded.

"I am, my lord. A dwarven Dominion Lord performed a fire-scry in the tent where the dwarves kept the Stone. I could not see the vision, but he and another dwarf spoke of it afterward. The Stone was taken by three taan warriors and a half-taan slave. You would have found this amusing, my lord. The taan were not aware that the magic of the Stone would punish them for touching it, and so they—"

"I find none of this amusing." Dagnarus cut him short. "Tell me this—do these taan have the Sovereign Stone?"

"They left with it in their possession," said Caladwar.

"By K'let's command?"

"The taan spoke of K'let often. But how could K'let know the whereabouts of the Stone?"

"Side by side we fought many times," said Dagnarus, quietly, remembering. "I saved his life. He saved my dream of conquest. We were different races, yet of one mind. Of all the Vrykyl I ever created, he alone understood me. I forgave his defiance, because it is what I would have done myself. I could not forgive his rebellion. I would have taken care of his people. He should have trusted me . . ."

In other words, Caladwar thought, Dagnarus himself had told K'let how to find the dwarven part of the Sovereign Stone. If Dagnarus had not told K'let directly, he'd been careless of his thoughts, and the cunning K'let had read them through the Blood-knife.

"Yes, Caladwar, this is my fault," said Dagnarus, and Caladwar cringed.

"My lord, I did not mean—"

"Enough," Dagnarus said. "This may yet work to my advantage. The Stone means nothing to K'let. He cannot make use of it. He cannot even touch it. He has taken the Stone because he knows I will come for it. And so I shall. And so I shall . . ."

"What are your orders for me, my lord?"

Please let them be far away from here, Caladwar pleaded silently.

"You will return to Tromek and assist Valura and the Shield in his war against the Divine."

"Yes, my lord! Thank you, my lord. I will leave at once."

Caladwar was halfway out the door, the Blood-knife still clutched in his hand, when his lord's parting thoughts came to the Vrykyl's mind. Caladwar tried not to hear, for he was fearful that Dagnarus might change his mind and order him to remain in Saumel. The Vrykyl could not very well help hearing, however. He realized, with a sigh of relief, that the Lord of the Void was not speaking to him, but to the rebel.

"You have made a mistake, K'let," Dagnarus said, and his calm was more frightening than his rage. "I would have overlooked much from you, but not this."

Hastily, Caladwar thrust the Blood-knife back into its sheath. He took care not to touch it again until he was safely out of dwarven lands and on his way back to Tromek.

Wolfram and Ranessa spent three days flying around and about the southern tip of the Dwarven Spine Mountains, searching for the trail left by the taan. Three months had passed and the trail was as cold as yesterday's porridge. But all Wolfram needed was a campsite or the remnants of a fire. Once he found that, he could determine by his scrying if the fire had been built by the taan, and from that he would know which direction they were headed. Find one fire and it would be easier, so he reasoned, to find the next.

He figured, logically, that the taan would travel to the west. They had come from the west, from Dunkarga. The taan were still fighting in the west, in Karnu. The taan would naturally head back in that direction with their prize. If Wolfram had known of the taan's fear of water, he would have not wasted his time searching along the shores of the river. He did not know, however, and so he assumed that they had crossed over by boat. He and Ranessa spent several days gliding slowly up and down the riverbanks, searching for the remnants of a campfire. They found several, but each time he did the scrying, he saw only parties of dwarves.

Ranessa thought the search boring. She complained during the day, sulked through the night. She threatened every hour or so to return to the monastery, with or without Wolfram.

The third night, after another day of searching that turned up nothing, he and Ranessa sat around their own fire.

"I want to talk to you," she said abruptly. "We've wasted another whole day flying up and down this blasted river, and I'm sick to death of it."

"You didn't have to change out of your dragon form to tell me that," said Wolfram, poking the fire. "Why do you bother?"

"Because we're going to have an argument," said Ranessa, her dark eyes glinting.

Wolfram snorted. "We're always having arguments, girl! What's that got to do with shifting your form to a human?"

"Because," Ranessa said loftily, "dragons don't argue with the likes of you. It's demeaning."

Wolfram heaved a sigh. "I don't suppose I'll be able to get any sleep until you've had your say."

"No," said Ranessa.

"Very well, girl. Get on with it."

"Two days ago, you'd never heard of this dwarf child," stated Ranessa. "No one cared for her before this happened. I don't see why you should start caring about her now. No one cared about that blasted Stone, either, for that matter."

"I'm doing this for that very reason," said Wolfram.

He muttered the ritual prayer over the night fire, began to bank the coals.

"For what reason?"

"For the reason you said. That no one cared about her." Wolfram stood up, wiping his hands. He looked at Ranessa, looked at her hard and intently. "You of all people should understand that."

He walked off to his bedroll. Wrapping himself in his blanket, he saw her still standing there, staring after him. Wolfram drifted off to sleep with a warm glow. He'd finally managed to have the last word.

The next morning, Ranessa was gone.

Wolfram searched the area around their campsite, but there was no sign of Ranessa in any form—human or dragon. He told himself that she was hunting; her dragon form required an enormous amount of meat, and she often left to go after deer or mountain goat. Depending on her mood, she would sometimes bring him back a haunch to roast.

The nagging thought persisted that this time she'd carried through on her threat. He'd made her angry enough last night that she'd left without him. He wandered about the shoreline of the river, wondering bleakly what he would do. With her, the quest had been just short of hopeless. Without her . . .

"I'll go on," Wolfram said to his reflection that wavered in the water at his feet. "I've committed myself. It will take years, maybe. The rest of my life."

He smiled ruefully. "I'll be like Lord Gustav and his mad quest. They'll be singing songs of *me* next."

A shadow glided over him, the shadow of vast wings. Wolfram looked up in joy and relief. Ranessa flew above him, wheeling about him in tight circles.

"You're looking in the wrong place!" she called down to him. "The taan traveled north of here. Far north. They crossed the Arven River near New Vinnengael."

Wolfram gaped at her. "How do you know?"

"What?" Ranessa bent her head. "I can't hear you."

"How do you know?" he bawled.

"Oh," she said. "I asked."

"Asked what?" Wolfram demanded. "Asked who?" He waved his arms to indicate the vast and empty wilderness. "There's no one around here to ask!"

Ranessa muttered something.

"What did you say?" he shouted.

"If you must know, I asked a seagull."

"Come down here!" Wolfram commanded, pointing at the ground. "I'm losing my voice!"

Ranessa circled down slowly. Finding a clear place to land, she settled down on the sun-warmed rocks.

"I thought you said you asked a seagull," said Wolfram, coming over to stand near her snout.

"I did," said Ranessa. "I asked a seagull if he had seen any of these taan, and he told me all about them. It's been the talk of the bird community for months," she added disparagingly. "They have so little to occupy their tiny minds."

"I didn't know you could talk to seagulls," Wolfram said, amazed.

"Well, I can," said Ranessa. She didn't seem inclined to elaborate.

"Is that something all dragons can do?"

"I suppose so. Look, now that we know their direction, shouldn't we be going?"

"Just a moment," said Wolfram. "Do you mean to say that during this time we've been flying hither and yon, searching for the trail of these taan, all you had to do was ask a passing bird?"

Ranessa stared straight ahead.

"Girl," said Wolfram, in exasperation, "why didn't you?"

Ranessa glanced down at her nose at him. "Talking to birds is just so . . . pecwae."

"Pecwae?"

"Yes, pecwae. Are you coming?" she demanded irritably.

"I'm coming," said Wolfram. He climbed up on her back, careful to keep his chuckle to himself.

THE VOYAGE OF THE ORKEN SHIP CARRYING SHADAMEHR AND HIS companions was idyllic, a journey of bright sunshine and rushing winds and foaming water. The ship sailed rapidly, thanks to the remarkably fine weather and the magical talents of Quai-ghai, ship's shaman, and Griffith, ship's passenger. One used her magic to calm the waters. The other used his magic to summon the winds. The ship sped through the Sea of Sagquanno, rounded the Cape of Bad Omens safely, and entered the Sea of Orkas in record time.

Captain Kal-Gah was impressed. He'd never realized how valuable an elf who worked Air magic could be. Taking Griffith aside, the captain offered him a permanent job as Ship's Second Shaman. Griffith expressed his appreciation and honor, but was forced to refuse.

"Since the Wyred paid for my training," he explained, "they would not look kindly upon me selling my skills in magic to anyone else."

Captain Kal-Gah understood. He offered to cut the Wyred in for a small share of the takings, if that would make them happy.

Griffith said he was afraid that it wouldn't.

Captain Kal-Gah did not give up on his scheme, however. Orks have long been prejudiced against the magic of other races, considering that any orken shaman who uses magic other than the magic of water is the next best thing to a traitor. Captain Kal-Gah began to think that this was narrow-minded of his people, and he hinted broadly to a shocked Quai-ghai that she should broaden her horizons.

While Griffith spent his time with Quai-ghai, learning Water magic spells, Damra was relaxing for the first time in her life. Lulled by the beauty of the sea and the knowledge that she was cut off from the world and that no one could make demands of her, she passed her days in quiet, spiritual meditation and reflection. At night, she found comfort in her husband's arms.

Shadamehr spent the voyage improving his knowledge of the art of sailing. He was already familiar with navigation, having learned that on a previous voyage. Now he was intent upon learning all he could about the ship. He climbed up the rigging and descended into the hold. He burned all the skin off his palms sliding down a rope and nearly broke his neck in a fall from a mast. Fortunately, he landed in the water. The orks were able to fish him out. He came dripping wet on board, laughing and claiming that he'd enjoyed the swim.

Seeing that he was serious in his study, the orks were glad to teach him. They said he was lucky, for there had not been a bad omen since he came on board.

Shadamehr didn't feel lucky, or even very content. For some inexplicable reason, Alise was not happy, and he couldn't understand why. He went out of his way to play the perfect lover, but romantic words brought sarcastic responses and his melting looks caused her eyes to raise to the heavens. She was by turns snappish and sharp-tongued or silent and aloof. Sometimes, he would catch her regarding him with a look of sadness that was mingled with frustration.

"I don't understand women," Shadamehr complained plaintively to Griffith. "I'm trying to be what she wants me to be, and yet she will have none of me. Which rhymes, by the way."

"Are you?" Griffith returned. "Or are you trying to be what you want her to want you to be?"

Thinking gloomily that he would never understand elves either, Shadamehr went back to the rigging.

The ship left the Sea of Orkas, turning north to sail up the Straits. One day—the day after the day the orks hauled Shadamehr out of the sea—he was standing at the railing, practicing with the sextant, when Alise walked up and stood beside him.

She had been avoiding him as if he'd adopted the orken habit of slathering himself all over in fish oil and he was surprised to see her, surprised and pleased.

"So, where are we?" she asked.

"By my calculations, somewhere north of Tromek," Shadamehr replied blithely.

Alise looked at him in astonishment, and he saw the ghost of a smile play on her lips. The smile vanished swiftly, however, and she turned her gaze back out to sea.

"You're working very hard at enjoying yourself," she remarked. "So hard you nearly broke your fool neck."

"If it comes to that," Shadamehr replied. "You're working very hard at *not* enjoying yourself. Alise, we have to settle this between us—"

She gazed out over the sun-sparkled waves. "It is settled. I don't want you to love me. I want things to go back to the way they were between us. As if nothing had happened."

"I don't think that's possible, Alise," said Shadamehr.

For a minute she looked defiant. Then she sighed. "No, I don't suppose it is."

"You are afraid," he said suddenly.

She bristled. "I am not."

"Are, too!" he returned mockingly. Seeing her color rise in her cheeks, he added, "You're afraid that if we're lovers, we can't be friends. That we'll lose what we have together."

"Well," she said to him, challenging. "Haven't we?"

"No, I—" Shadamehr paused. He stood there with his mouth open. For, by the gods, they had lost it.

She walked away, left him standing at the taffrail, staring unseeing at the rolling waves and their foaming wake.

The joyful spirit of the passengers evaporated as the *Kli'Sha* sailed into what the orks knew as the Blessed Straits. In order to reach Krammes, the orks would have to sail past the isle of Mount Sa 'Gra, their sacred mountain that was now in the hands of the detested Karnuans. The orks avoided sailing in this direction if they could help it. It was not that they feared attack. Land-bound warriors, the Karnuans knew better than to fight the orks at sea, where the orks would have all the advantages. The orks could not bear to look at the peaks of the revered mountain and imagine the humans defilers walking the halls of their temples.

The orken lookouts sighted a few ships flying the Karnuan flag, but those turned tail the moment they saw the orken pennant and sailed away, to jeers and challenges from the orken crew.

Mount Sa 'Gra, with its plume of smoke streaming from the snow-whitened top, came into sight. The captain ordered all hands on deck. The orks lined the rails and climbed into the rigging. Taking off their caps, they gazed longingly at the mountain. Quai-ghai, their shaman, recited an orken prayer in low, solemn tones.

Although Damra could not understand the words of the chant, she could hear the grief and aching pain in the shaman's voice and see it reflected on the faces of the orks. The chant ended in a fierce, strong shout. The orks shook their fists in the direction of their mountain, their voices joining that of their shaman in a thunderous roar.

"They vow to return," said Captain Kal-Gah, translating. "And on that day, the Blessed Straits will run red with Karnuan blood."

"Given your anger," Griffith said, "I am surprised that you haven't tried to take your mountain back by now."

"The Captain of Captains is wise," stated Kal-Gah. "We are gallant warriors on board our ships, hopeless bunglers on land." He grinned suddenly. "Being an ork, I can say that though I would cut your throat from ear to ear if you said it, Baron."

Kal-Gah clapped Shadamehr on the back, a blow that propelled him halfway across the deck.

"We have heard," Kal-Gah added more solemnly, "that the Captain has a secret force of orks assembled in Harkon. They wait for the right omens to attack."

"Is that true?" Alise asked, interested.

"Whether it is or it isn't, it keeps the Karnuans from sleeping well at night," said the captain. He gazed back at the mountain, dwindling on the horizon, and his smile tightened to a grim line. "We will come back. Someday."

The elves and humans took their meals in their cabin, away from the orks, mainly because the sight and smell of orken food was too much for them to stomach. That night, the orks had captured a large squid and were anticipating a grand feast.

The mere thought of eating the squirming, slimy creature was enough to ruin Damra's appetite, and she only picked at her meal, which wasn't all that great to begin with. The ship had stopped at one of the towns along the coast to take on supplies, so the elves were able to add nuts and dried fruits to the menu of hard-baked biscuit and cheese. Having eaten nothing else for days on end, Damra thought that if she never saw another fig for as long as she lived, it would still not be long enough.

To add flavor to the meal, the four discussed the orken political situation.

"I can't imagine what it would be like to lose someplace that you love and revere so much," said Alise. "To know that people who care nothing about it are probably writing nasty words on the walls of the temple where your god resides."

"And where they toss their sacrificial victims into the bowels of the sacred mountain," said Shadamehr cheerfully.

"Do they?" asked Damra, amazed.

"Yes, I'm afraid so. The orks consider it a great honor, actually, to be given to the god of the mountain. And thus most of the victims they sacrifice are orks, who presumably think a leap into molten lava leads to heaven."

"But to take life, which is sacred, is not right," Damra argued.

"According to your gods. Not according to the orken god. Would you impose your beliefs on the orks? That's what the Karnuans did, you know. That was the excuse they used to capture the sacred mountain. They claimed that offering living sacrifices was offensive to the gods."

"It is," said Damra.

"And slaughtering thousands of orks and enslaving thousands more *isn't* offensive to the gods?" Shadamehr asked, with a wink at Griffith.

"Don't encourage him, Damra," said Alise. "My lord Shadamehr will argue that the ocean is dry and the sun shines at midnight, if you let him."

"Still—" Damra began.

She was interrupted by the arrival of one of the cabin boys, the son of Captain Kal-Gah, brought along on this voyage to learn the trade.

"Sir," said the boy, thrusting his head in through the door, "the shaman said for you to come right away. She's doing her daily water speak, and it seems that someone is trying to contact you."

"May I come along, my lord?" asked Griffith eagerly. "I've never seen this spell performed. Unless you think this message might be private."

"No, no," said Shadamehr gaily. "I have no secrets. So long as Quai-ghai does not mind your presence, I have no objection. Ladies? Would you like to come along, too? Although her cabin is small, and I suppose all of us would be rather a tight fit."

Alise said she was going to bed, and Damra wanted to meditate. Griffith and Shadamehr were on their own.

"I'll wager I'm not going to like whatever it is I'm about to hear," Shadamehr predicted gloomily, as they followed the cabin boy belowdecks to Quai-ghai's quarters.

"What makes you say that?"

"Because no one goes out of his way to tell you good news, yet people fall all over themselves to tell you the bad stuff."

The cabin boy shushed them as they approached Quai-ghai's cabin. He did not knock on the door, but gently opened it to admit the two men. They slid quietly inside, trying their best not to disturb the shaman's concentration.

Quai-ghai sat at a table in front of a large bowl fashioned out of an enormous quahog shell. Seawater in the bowl moved gently with the motion of the ship. Quai-ghai was talking to the water, asking questions and receiving answers. Cocking her head, she listened, then replied.

"Wonderful!" Griffith breathed softly, as he took his place opposite the table. "Have you ever seen this done before?"

Shadamehr shook his head. Quai-ghai flashed them both an irritated glance, and Griffith lowered his voice to a whisper.

"She and another shaman can communicate directly with each other with this magic. All that is required is that each have a bowl of water and know the proper spell. Wyred who are permitted to study Water magic find this spell to be invaluable for rapid communication over long distances."

"I should think so," said Shadamehr, intrigued.

"The two people must establish a certain time of day when both will be present," Griffith continued. "According to Quai-ghai, almost all orken shamans choose sunset as the time they will be at their posts, in order to receive or send messages."

Quai-ghai lifted her head. "The spell is ended. You no longer have to whisper. Do you know someone named Rigiswald?"

"Crotchety old geezer? Bad-tempered, but a snappy dresser?"

"I didn't see him," said Quai-ghai with dignity. She frowned at the baron. "This is a serious matter."

"Sorry," said Shadamehr meekly. "Please go on."

"The Rigiswald person hired a shaman to contact you through me. The shaman has been trying for a week, and finally managed to speak to me this day. The Rigiswald person says to tell you that Dagnarus, Lord of the Void, is now King of Vinnengael."

"At which news, I am sure, there was much rejoicing," said Shadamehr dryly.

"The Rigiswald person says to tell you that Dagnarus has the support of the people, for he led the battle against the taan army and slaughtered them."

"The taan army that he brought himself?" said Shadamehr, lifting an eyebrow. "That was good of him. What else?"

"The Rigiswald person says to tell you that Dagnarus has ordered all his barons to New Vinnengael to do him homage and swear their loyalty to him. If they decline, their property and assets are forfeit to the crown. According to this Rigiswald," Quai-ghai added, her voice softening, "the king has seized your lands and your keep and all your revenue. The Rigiswald person warns that if you go back, you are in danger. Your keep is not all that you will lose."

"I see," said Shadamehr quietly. He could feel Griffith's gaze on him, but he chose not meet it. He stared unseeing at the bowl of water. "Anything more?"

"An attempt was made on the life of this Rigiswald while he was on the road, but he survived, and he will meet you and Alise in Krammes."

"Tough old bird," said Shadamehr, smiling. "An assassin would have to get up pretty early in the day to do in Rigiswald. Any other cheerful news? The world about to come to an end?"

"No, that is all," said Quai-ghai. "Is there anything you want to tell this person?"

"Just to take care of himself," said Shadamehr. "And we will see him in Krammes.

"Well, well," he said to Griffith, after they had both thanked Quai-ghai and taken their leave, "it seems I am pfenningless."

"I am so sorry, my lord," said Griffith.

Shadamehr gave a lopsided smile. " 'Easy come, easy go,' as the Dunkargan thief said when they chopped off his head. Still, I was fond of my keep, even though it was a tad drafty in the winter."

"What will you do?" Griffith wondered.

"I rather think I'll have to get it back."

"But, my lord," exclaimed Griffith, appalled. "Dagnarus is King of Vinnengael, with thousands of troops at his command, and he's also—"

"Lord of the Void, with Vrykyls and ravenous taan and Void sorcerers ready to satify his every whim? Yes, I know. But I have my health. That must count for something."

"I don't see how you can joke about this, my lord."

Griffith could not imagine a greater calamity. To be exiled was the worst possible fate that could befall an elf. Death was far preferable.

"It's either that or sit down and sob uncontrollably," said Shadamehr. "And sobbing always makes my nose swell. Don't worry. I'll think of something. I always do."

Shadamehr put his hand on the elf's shoulder. "Brace yourself, my friend. Now comes the really hard part."

"What's that?"

"Telling Alise. You won't need to summon any winds this night, Griffith," Shadamehr predicted. "The blast of her fury will propel us along so that we'll be lucky if we don't end up in Myanmin by morning."

The blast of Alise's fury didn't quite propel them to the Nimorean coast, but it came close. She was enraged at Dagnarus and the fools of New Vinnengael for having fallen victim to his treachery, and she was equally as enraged at Shadamehr for taking the disastrous news with such apparent calm.

"My dear," he said in response to one of her tirades, "would you feel better if I hung myself from the yardarm?"

"Yes," she retorted. "At least you'd be doing something constructive. You spent this morning fishing."

"Since we're stuck on a ship in the middle of the Blessed Straits, I'm not certain what constructive thing I could be doing, other than catching our dinner."

"You could be making plans," Alise said, with a wild gesture. "Deciding what to do, where to go—"

He leaned back against the rail, regarded her with a cool, insufferable smile.

"Damn you!" she said. Doubling her hand into a fist, she punched him in the arm.

"Ouch!" Shadamehr said, startled. "What was that for?"

"To make you stop smirking. You knew this would happen," she said accusingly. "You knew this would happen, and you didn't tell me. You knew before we even left the keep—"

"I wish I could claim that I had foreknowledge that I was going to be exiled and stripped of my lands and titles and made a target for assassination, but I'm afraid I can't, dear heart."

"Hah!" she said. "You chose Krammes for our destination because it is on the other side of the continent from New Vinnengael and because you have friends among the officers at the Imperial Cavalry School. Friends you can recruit to help you take back your keep . . ."

Shadamehr rolled up his sleeve. "Look there. Look at that mark you made. I bruise easily, you know."

"You always said that the best-trained officers in the world came from that school," Alise went on. "They won't be willing to follow Dagnarus, nor will the people of Krammes. We'll form an army and march on New Vinnengael. You have the Sovereign Stone. You'll have to become a Dominion Lord, of course, but I'm sure the gods will overlook the defects in your character and not fry you to a crisp during the Transfiguration—"

"What would you say the odds were, exactly?" Shadamehr interrupted. "On not frying me to a crisp."

"Oh, seventy/thirty," said Alise.

"Seventy which way and thirty which way?"

"Seventy they fry you."

"Not great," he pointed out.

"I don't honestly see how you can expect better."

"I suppose you're right."

"You could always do something to improve them," Alise said.

"Do you think that's possible?"

Alise was about to make a witty retort. Looking at him closely, she changed her mind. "Shadamehr, I believe you're serious!"

"I think about it sometimes," he said. "About Bashae, giving his life to protect the Stone. And for what? To hand it off to me. What good am I doing with it? Precisely nothing. I don't know what to do," he added, frustrated. "Do I summon the Council, as Damra wants? Or do I take the Stone to Old Vinnengael, as Gareth told me in the vision."

He turned away, stared moodily out to sea.

"You know I was joking, don't you?" Alise rested her hand on his arm, massaged the place where she'd hit him. "I don't think there is a man on this world who is better suited to be a Dominion Lord. The gods would be crazy not to snap you up."

"That's the rub," said Shadamehr. "The gods. All my life, I've been in control of my own destiny. I may have bungled things here and there, but, if I did, I had no one to blame but myself. To give myself into the hands of fate or destiny or whatever you want to call it—that's what truly frightens me, Alise."

"I don't think it's like that, exactly," she said.

"What do you mean?" He turned to her, interested to know what she was thinking.

Shadamehr stood silhouetted against the backdrop of rolling blue waves touched here and there by white froth. Seabirds skimmed the tips of the waves, either in search of fish or because they loved the adventure of flying through the foam. The wind ruffled his long hair. His face was tanned from the sun, and that made his eyes blue as the ocean. The laughter that usually danced in his eyes, like the sun glinting on the water, was gone. Understanding that he was opening his heart to her, laying bare his fear and his doubt, Alise pondered long before she replied, trying to explain what was for her the inexplicable.

"There is a spell that some Earth magi are taught," she said, her words coming slowly as she went over each in her mind, to make certain it was the word she wanted. "A spell that we know as Earthen Killer. With it, we can summon into being a shambling mass of rock and order it to do our bidding. The Killer has no mind. It has no will of its own. It gives no thought to what it's doing. The magus has to keep this thing in control, for it would just as soon kill him as his enemies."

Alise looked into Shadamehr's eyes. "The gods don't want an Earthen Killer. The gods want men and women who can think for themselves and make decisions and act on those decisions. Sometimes those decisions will be wrong, but the gods understand that. I don't believe that those who become Dominion Lords act at the direction of the gods. I believe that they act on their own. I think that what makes Dominion Lords special is that they are given the chance to look into the minds of the gods. Not far, perhaps. Just a tiny glimpse. But even that tiny glimpse helps them to judge what to do."

"Or perhaps," said Shadamehr thoughtfully, "Dominion Lords are given the chance to look inside themselves."

"Maybe it's the same thing," said Alise.

He reached out with his hand and smoothed back the red curls that blew across her face. "We can never go back to what we were, Alise," he said.

"I know," she replied.

"So where do we go from here?"

Smiling at him, she kissed him on the cheek. "To Krammes, my lord," she said.

THE CITY OF KRAMMES HAD BEEN THEIR DESTINATION FROM THE start of their voyage and, as they drew nearer, their expectations for this city shone as brightly as the beacon fires the orks built nightly to serve as guide for the ships sailing the treacherous shoals of the Blessed Straits. Time had been suspended while they were at sea, but now the pendulum was swinging again, the ticking resumed.

Shadamehr was eager to see if any of the Dominion Lords, warned by Ulaf, had arrived. He would at last be able to hand over to them responsibility for the Sovereign Stone. And he was also looking forward to talking with Prince Mikael, ruler of the city, and the officers of the Imperial Cavalry School, to find out what they thought of their new king, Dagnarus. Alise was looking forward to seeing Ulaf and their friends. Damra and Griffith were both hoping and dreading to hear news of their homeland. Captain Kal-Gah had cargo to sell in Krammes. The crew smacked their lips when they thought about the ale houses. Everyone was looking forward to fresh food and water and walking on dry land.

Orken vessels were generally to be found in this part of the world, so near their homeland, and so it was no surprise when the shout of "sail, ho" came from the lookouts.

An orken ship appeared on the northern horizon. The ship did not run down to meet them, but hove to and waited for them to come up to her. Once within hailing distance, the orks bellowed across the waves at one another. After some moments of this, Captain Kal-Gah, his expression grim, ordered a boat to be lowered to carry him across to the other ship.

"I don't like this," said Shadamehr, looking grave. "Something's wrong."

"I hope whatever it is doesn't prevent us from going to Krammes," Damra said. "I cannot eat another dried fig. They're starting to stick in my throat."

The four of them hung over the rail, watching the other ship and waiting anxiously for the captain's boat to return. Griffith questioned Quai-ghai, but she knew no more than they did. The omens, she said, had been particularly good that morning. Griffith took that as a hopeful sign, until Shadamehr pointed out that good omens for orks didn't necessarily mean good omens for humans and elves.

Captain Kal-Gah returned to his vessel, coming aboard to the blast of a conch shell. He barked sharp orders that sent the crew racing to their duties, then summoned his passengers to his cabin.

"We are not going to sail into Krammes," he announced.

"Why not?" Shadamehr asked, as the others stared bleakly at the captain. "What's wrong?"

"The city is under attack," the captain replied.

Alise gasped. "Dagnarus! I knew it!"

"No," said the captain, and his face split into a grin. He slapped himself on the chest. "Orks!"

"Orks are attacking Krammes?" Shadamehr repeated in dazed tones.

"The Captain of Captains is here," said Captain Kal-Gah proudly. "And her entire fleet. They are laying siege to the city now."

"But . . . why?" Alise asked, bewildered. "The orks and the Vinnengaeleans aren't at war. Are we?"

"We are now," said Captain Kal-Gah fiercely. "The Captain has long been angry at the Vinnengaeleans for helping the Karnuans seize our mountain. The Captain summoned the fleet, and now they are laying siege to Krammes."

"The Vinnengaeleans didn't help the Karnuans," Alise protested indignantly. "Not willingly. Our fleet was tricked."

"So you claim," said Captain Kal-Gah, with a wink.

"But it's true—" Alise began.

Shadamehr seized her hand, squeezed it.

"Can you take us closer?" he asked. "So we could see the battle."

"Yes, I can do that," stated Kal-Gah. He brightened up. "It should be a wondrous sight. I expect that half the city is ablaze by now."

He went back to the deck to shout orders. The four friends returned to their quarters, where they stared at each in blank dismay.

"This doesn't make any sense," said Shadamehr thoughtfully.

"They're orks," stated Damra, as if that explained everything. "They probably read it in this morning's fish entrails."

"Orks may be superstitious, but they're not stupid," said Shadamehr. "They have a reason for everything they do and, I repeat, this doesn't make sense. True, the orks are angry with the Vinnengaeleans, and they had reason to be. We were fools to let the Karnuans trick us and steal our ship. But that happened long ago. Why didn't the orks attack then? Why suddenly decide to attack Krammes now? Unless . . ."

He paused, then said quietly, "Maybe they do have a reason."

"Dagnarus," Alise said.

"Our new king," Shadamehr agreed. "He's allied himself with the orks. Makes perfect sense, of course. He seizes control of eastern Vinnengael and the orks conquer western Vinnengael for him. They attack Krammes by sea. He has taan forces ready to move in by land."

"I see one problem with that," Griffith protested. "The orks have no love for Void magic."

"They probably have no idea Dagnarus has anything to do with Void magic," Alise pointed out. "The Vrykyl was able to fool all of you into thinking he was a human child. As Lord of the Void, Dagnarus would find it much easier to hide his alliance with the Void."

"Alise is right," said Shadamehr. "All Dagnarus would have to do is promise the Captain of Captains he would help her gain her sacred mountain back, and the orks would be only too happy to comply. Especially if it meant they had a chance to avenge themselves on Vinnengaeleans in the process."

"Promises he has no intention of keeping," said Damra.

"He might," said Shadamehr speculatively. "Dagnarus might well be interested in taking the sacred mountain from the Karnuans. Not that he'll give it to the orks."

"Why would he want it?" asked Alise. "The island has some strategic value, I suppose, but—"

"I know why. Because the orken portion of the Sovereign Stone is rumored to be hidden there," said Griffith.

"Precisely," Shadamehr replied.

"The orks would die before they told him where to find it," said Damra.

"He's Lord of the Void," said Griffith grimly. "He wouldn't find death much of an obstacle. He can drag the truth from their corpses."

The four regarded each other in dismay.

"Very well. Now that we have this all figured out, what do we do to stop him?" Damra asked. "I suppose we could try to talk to this Captain of Captains, but why would she believe us?"

"Because of my honest face and stunning good looks?" said Shadamehr.

Alise snorted in derision. "What would be really helpful is a bad omen. Something that would frighten the orks into fleeing Krammes." She cast Shadamehr a withering glance. "There, you might be useful."

"A bad omen," Shadamehr repeated. He looked speculatively at Griffith. "It would have to be something more spectacular than fish entrails."

"I think that could be arranged," said Griffith, smiling back.

"I don't like this," said Damra frowning. "It's tampering with the works of the gods."

"Have another fig," said Shadamehr, holding out a basket of dried fruit.

Captain Kal-Gah's ship joined the orken fleet, whose ships were taking turns lobbing flaming jelly at the city of Krammes. Captain Kal-Gah had exaggerated when he said the city would be ablaze. The orks had barely begun their bombardment. The city was not yet in flames, although smoke could be seen rising from some buildings along the wharf.

The history of Krammes proved the old adage that it is an ill wind that blows nobody good. Two hundred years earlier, Krammes had been the orphan child begging for crumbs at the table of the wealthy city now known as Old Vinnengael. Krammes was located south of Vinnengael, at the mouth of the estuary that led to Lake Ildurel and the city itself. The Vinnengaeleans had built a fortress at Krammes, intended to guard that estuary. A trading post had grown up around the fortress, but it struggled to survive. Few ships bound for the lucrative markets of Old Vinnengael cared to stop at the smaller, poorer markets of Krammes.

With the fall of Old Vinnengael, the fortunes of Krammes changed almost overnight. Survivors of the disaster fled downriver to Krammes, swelling the population and bringing in what wealth they had managed to salvage. Krammes continued to grow and now, two hundred years later, it was a thriving city, second only to New Vinnengael in size and importance. Markets teemed with customers. The city was home to foreign traders. Black-skinned Nimrans could be seen rubbing shoulders with olive-skinned Dunkargans and pale-skinned Vinnengaeleans. Elven merchants traveled to Krammes via the trade route that ran south from Dainmorae. Weapons of dwarven make could often be found in the markets, brought by the orks from the dwarven lands to the east, or sometimes by dwarven traders.

The fortress that guarded the entrance to the estuary stood on a promontory overlooking the Blessed Straits. The fortress had been strengthened down through the years, for Krammes was always wary of her Karnuan neighbors, one reason for the founding of the Imperial Cavalry School. The fortress was equipped with the most recent developments in weapons technology, and the orks were angered to discover that this included the orken specialty—flaming jelly. The fortress could heave enormous boulders that would tear through sails, smash holes in the bulkheads, or fling red-hot metal that would set fire to a ship's decks and the rigging.

Fearful of the fortress's weapons, the ork ships could not sail as close to Krammes as they would have liked. Thus the orks were doing little damage to the city itself, although the siege was bound to have a devastating effect on the city's economy. So long as ork ships blockaded the harbor, no other ship dared enter.

At least, that was Captain Kal-Gah's thinking, explained to Shadamehr, as they sailed toward the battle. Shadamehr agreed with the assessment. He did not mention his suspicions that taan forces might well be on their way from the east.

"If the orks can be persuaded to retreat," Shadamehr told his companions, "I can enter the city, reach the prince, and alert him to this danger. That's where your bad omen comes in. We have to cause the orks to retreat."

"You'll have to make certain that Quai-ghai doesn't see me," Griffith warned. "She would know immediately I was casting a spell, and that would prove disastrous. Captain Kal-Gah may be your friend, Baron, but orks take their omens very seriously and if they were to discover that we were cooking one up, they would kill us."

"You could do the spell in the cabin," Shadamehr suggested. "Or do you have to be on deck?"

"For the spell I have in mind, so long as I have line of sight, I can cast the spell from the cabin."

"Fortunately, the battle should keep everyone distracted," said Shadamehr. "We'll make sure they stay that way. If anyone asks, Griffith, we'll say that you are indisposed."

"And that I have my own cures," Griffith emphasized hastily. "I don't want Quai-ghai down here lathering me with fish oil and banging drums."

"Agreed. Especially about the fish oil. When do you—"

An orken cabin boy banged on the door and opened it simultaneously, causing all of them to start guiltily. Fortunately, the youngster was too excited to notice. "Captain says the battle is in sight, Baron." The youngster grinned, hopping with excitement. "You can see flames and smoke and everything."

"Glorious!" said Shadamehr heartily. "We'll be straight up."

He and Alise ascended to the deck, leaving Damra and Griffith below. Damra kept watch at the door. Griffith groaned pathetically in his bed.

Shadamehr headed off Quai-ghai's offers of leeches and stewed fish heads. Fortunately, Quai-ghai was interested in watching the battle, and so she did not press her attentions on the sick elf. Shadamehr and Alise took up positions where they could see the proceedings and keep an eye on the ladder leading to their quarters.

According to Kal-Gah, the battle had reached a stalemate, with neither side able to gain the advantage over the other. One orken ship was aflame. Her crew worked frantically to douse the fire and had not yet been forced to abandon ship. Smoke rose from the dockyards of Krammes, but only a few thin trails. The orks could not sail closer to attack the city proper. The Krammerians could not sail out to drive away the orks. So they blazed away at one another, flinging great globules of flaming jelly through the air, along with anything else that seemed likely to do harm.

All the while, Shadamehr speculated, Dagnarus's forces might be drawing closer.

"Stop fidgeting!" Alise ordered him. "And quit peering down the ladder. Someone's bound to notice."

"What's taking him so long?" Shadamehr demanded impatiently. "I—"

"Look!" Alise whispered in excitement, tugging on his sleeve.

The orken sailors posted up among the rigging "hallooed" out for the deck, several of them pointing. All eyes turned that way, diverting their attention from the battle.

The ocean this day was relatively calm, with only a light breeze that barely ruffled the flag. That made the sight they witnessed all the more strange. It seemed to Shadamehr's startled gaze as if the seawater in one small part of the ocean suddenly lifted, not in a wave, but a vast circle that had a smoky gray hue. A long, sinuous tendril of gray snaked out of the darkening heavens, twisting with deadly grace as it slid over the surface of the foaming water.

"A waterspout!" breathed Alise.

"By the gods!" said Shadamehr softly. "I've never seen one."

To judge by their clamor, the orks had seen waterspouts before and knew them to be erratic and sometimes lethal, if they caught a ship in their spinning turbulence. A worse omen could not be imagined. Quaighai shouted at the top of her lungs; her bellows coinciding with the captain's orders to up anchor and set sail. His commands and the shaman's cries echoed from every orken ship in the fleet.

The waterspout slid over the ocean waves, churning up water in its path, kicking up the clouds of sea foam and spray. The spout moved slowly toward the fleet's position, too distant to threaten any ship, but clearly visible to all.

Shamans aboard the ship of the Captain of Captains used their magical skills to shout orders that carried over the water to all ships of the line.

"They're being ordered to break off the attack," said Shadamehr with satisfaction.

The waterspout continued to snake over the ocean. Several ships were already sailing away.

"You realize," said Alise suddenly, "that our ship is going to go haring off along with all the rest. How do you plan to enter Krammes when we're five hundred miles away?"

"Damn!" Shadamehr swore. "I never thought of that. And my plan was so exceedingly brilliant! Strange I never noticed this minor flaw. Captain? Where's the bloody captain?"

Shadamehr went bounding across the deck, bumping into the rushing sailors, who muttered apologies and shoved him out of the way. Alise shook her head and smiled and sighed simultaneously.

A thundering shout came rolling across the water and slammed up against the ship. The mate responsible for communicating ship to ship answered with his own magically enhanced "halloo" and turned to report to Kal-Gah, just as Shadamehr came running up on the other side.

"Captain!" the mate said, with a salute. "We have orders to heave to. The Captain wants to speak to us."

(The word "Captain" is the same for the captain of the ship and the great Captain of Captains, the leader of the orken nation. The manner in which the title is inflected indicates the difference.) Captain Kal-Gah shot a glance at Shadamehr.

"That is a very great honor," Shadamehr said, relieved. They would not be leaving Krammes yet, apparently. "Or is it?" he asked, noting that the captain did not appear to be wildly enthusiastic.

Kal-Gah grunted. "Take your friends and get below. Keep out of sight."

He began to shout orders so fast that his words clotted on his tongue.

"Seems a sound idea," said Shadamehr.

Collecting Alise, he hastened back to their quarters, where he found Griffith in bed. He was not shamming now. He was exhausted after his spell-casting.

"Remarkable, Griffith!" said Shadamehr, going to shake hands. "Scared the bejeebers out of everyone, myself included. The orken fleet is fleeing hither and yon."

"With one exception," said Alise in ominous tones.

The elf lifted himself up on one elbow. "What's wrong? Did somebody suspect something?"

"Not that *I* could tell," said Shadamehr.

Alise rolled her eyes.

"Then what's happening?" Damra demanded. "What's all the commotion."

"We're heaving to. The Captain of Captains wants to have a word with our captain," said Shadamehr.

"What does that mean?"

"I'm not sure. Kal-Gah thought it best if we removed ourselves from the premises."

"Maybe she suspects our omen was a hoax," Griffith said grimly.

"If that was the case, she wouldn't have let the other ships of the fleet leave," Alise pointed out.

"Does she even know that humans and elves are on board?" Damra asked.

"Kal-Gah had a little chat with his fellow captain aboard that other ship when we first arrived," said Shadamehr. "He might have kept the fact that he carried passengers secret—"

A knock sounded on their door.

"Captain's respects, and you're wanted up top," said the cabin boy.

"Or he might not," Shadamehr conceded.

"I have spoken to the Captain of Captains. She wants to meet you," said Kal-Gah. "She is sending a boat to take you over to her ship."

"You told her about us?" asked Damra.

"Of course," said Kal-Gah, shrugging. "She is the Captain."

The four looked at each other.

"I don't like this," said Alise. "What if she is in league with Dagnarus? She might know all about us *and* what we carry!"

"I don't see that we have much choice," Shadamehr said quietly.

As if to make his point, the orks on board the Captain's ship could be seen lowering a boat into the water.

"We could refuse to go," Griffith suggested. "Kal-Gah likes us."

"Kal-Gah could love me like a brother, but if the Captain told him to slit my throat, he'd be sharpening his knife."

"An all-too-apt analogy," said Alise.

"Sorry, but it's the best I could do on short notice. No ork would dare disobey the Captain of Captains," said Shadamehr with finality. "I think we have two choices: We either climb into that boat or we try to swim to Krammes."

The boat bumped alongside the ship. At Kal-Gah's order, his crew lowered rope ladders.

"What about the Sovereign Stone?" Damra asked softly, speaking in elven. "Will you take it with you or leave it here?"

"Take it with me, of course," said Shadamehr. "I trust Kal-Gah, but orks have their own code of ethics that sometimes don't agree with ours. What about you?" he asked Damra.

"My part of the Stone is always with me," she replied with a smile. "Safely hidden."

"As is mine," said Shadamehr. "Stuffed somewhere into the folds of time and space, according to Bashae."

Kal-Gah came up to them. "The boat is here. You must not keep the Captain waiting."

"We're eager to meet her, but I have to go back to the cabin to fetch something. A—a present for the great Captain," said Shadamehr.

Captain Kal-Gah started to frown at the delay, but his frown cleared at the mention of a gift.

"A good idea," he said.

"Now what am I going to give her?" Shadamehr muttered as he went clattering down the stairs that led belowdecks. Snatching up the knapsack, he grabbed one of Alise's pearl hair combs and was ready to toss it inside, when he saw something glittering at the bottom of the sack.

"Lord Gustav's amethyst ring," he said, drawing it out. "The ring he told Bashae to take to his true love: I hope you won't mind, sir," said Shadamehr, speaking respectfully to the spirit of the gallant knight, "but your true lover is going to stand six-foot-five and have fangs. I'd almost forgotten it was in there."

He held the amethyst to the waning light. The sun glowed deep in the purple heart.

"Oh, no, you don't!" said Alise, bounding into their quarters. She snatched up her comb and thrust it defiantly in her hair. "I know the way your mind works. The minute Damra told me what you were up to, I knew you'd give my pearl comb to the ork."

"I stand wrongfully accused," said Shadamehr, wounded. "I'm going to give the Captain this." He held up the ring.

"It won't fit," said Alise. "Except maybe through her nose."

"Still, I think she'll like it. I seem to recall hearing that orks value the amethyst, because they believe it protects them from the intoxicating effects of strong drink." He thrust the ring back into the knapsack.

"She can always wear it on a chain around her neck," suggested Alise.

"Excellent idea, my dear. It's why I keep you." He kissed her on the cheek, swiftly, before she could evade him. "That and for love of your red hair."

"And my pearl comb," she said, pushing him away. "Ulaf brought this comb all the way from Nimra and, no, you're not giving it to some ork."

"Always best to have a fallback position, though," Shadamehr muttered under his breath.

"I heard that!" said Alise.

Damra stared at the rope ladder dangling over the side of the ship and wondered how she was ever going to manage to descend the fragile-looking thing, especially with the ship riding up and down in the waves and the small boat bumping up against the hull. She was relieved to find out that she and the others would ride down in what was known as the "lubber's chair," a contraption that looked very much like a child's swing attached to ropes.

She did not enjoy the ride, however. The lubber's chair twisted in the wind. The boat was far beneath her, and the orks who stood ready to catch her laughed and snickered and made crude jokes at her expense. They knew their business, however. The moment the chair came near, they grabbed her, hoisted her out of the chair, and flung her into the boat, leaving her gasping for breath and staring at the waves that had looked small from aboard the ship, but appeared mountainous now that she was down among them.

Alise came next and then Griffith, who caused the orks much amusement by riding down with his eyes tightly shut. He was unconcerned by their sneers, however. Shadamehr was last.

"Take away your lubber's chair," he said with dignity, and, before Kal-Gah could argue some sense into him, Shadamehr was over the side and climbing down the rope.

Falling down the rope proved more accurate. He managed a few feet and then a wave came from out of nowhere, slapped against the hull, drenching Shadamehr and causing him to lose his grip. He tumbled backward into the arms of the orken sailors, who shook their heads and rolled their eyes and hustled him onto a seat. They began to row back to the Captain's ship.

"Must you always play the fool?" Alise demanded.

"I thought I would impress them with my seamanship," said Shadamehr plaintively.

"You impressed them with something, that's for sure. Shadamehr," she said, her voice changing. "What is Kal-Gah doing?"

Kal-Gah had been standing at the rail, watching them depart. Now, after a wave, he turned around and began shouting orders. Sailors ran up the lines, began to unfurl the sails and shake them out to catch the wind.

"He's leaving," said Shadamehr.

THE GREAT CAPTAIN OF CAPTAINS WAS IN HER FIFTIETH YEAR. Big-boned, with iron gray hair that she wore in one long braid, she looked to be part of the sea on which she'd spent her life. Her eyes were the color of the waves on a gray morning in winter. She rolled in her gait as the waves rolled onto shore. She wore around her neck a strand of seashells and shark's teeth. Golden earrings hung from her earlobes. She was dressed as any other orken sailor, in leather breeches and a loose-fitting shirt that bellied out with the wind like a sail. She was barefoot and bare-armed. All of her flesh that was visible was covered with tattoos of dolphins and seagulls, whales and starfish.

The trip in the small boat—sliding up waves and diving down into them—had been unsettling to elven stomachs. Both Damra and Griffith once again became seasick and could barely stand by the time they staggered out of the lubber's chair.

"Time for my notable charm," said Shadamehr, rubbing his hands.

"It's worked so well so far," said Alise caustically. "As I recall, in the past few weeks, you've been slapped, stabbed, and thrown overboard."

"I fell overboard," said Shadamehr with dignity.

"You might try to find out if we're guests or prisoners," Griffith suggested. He was pale, but composed, feeling more at ease now that he was out of the small boat.

"You may not want to the know the answer," said Shadamehr. "Shush, here she comes."

The Captain of Captains strode across the deck, approached them without ceremony. She towered over them by a head and shoulders, stared down her nose at them. Her expression was stern, and the hard gray glint in her eye did little to make her guests feel at ease.

"Baron Shadamehr at your service," he said, bowing. "Meeting the Captain of Captains is a very great honor."

The Captain eyed him up and down and grunted. The feeling was obviously not mutual.

"Captain Kal-Gah told me about you," she said. Her gaze flicked to the elves. "And them."

"I have the pleasure of introducing Damra of Gwyenoc," said Shadamehr. "Her husband, Griffith. This is Alise."

The Captain eyed each in turn, her gaze long and penetrating.

"You are a wizard," she said to Griffith.

"I have the honor to be one of the Wyred," he replied.

The Captain switched the gray glint to Alise. "And you, as well."

"I have some small skill in Earth magic," Alise replied.

The Captain glanced from Alise to Shadamehr and back to Alise again. "Are you his woman?"

"No, I am not," said Alise in frost-rimed tones.

"You are wise," said the Captain.

Her voice was deep, but well modulated, not harsh, as are some orken voices. She spoke Elderspeak fluently, with a trace of an accent that Shadamehr recognized as Nimran. According to Kal-Gah, the Captain of Captains had grown up on a ship that sailed the trade routes between Nimra and the orken territories. Kal-Gah had provided little other information, except the fact that Captain was a widow, with grown children who were now sailing ships of their own. She had been Captain of Captains for twenty-five years. She was an orken hero, having sunk two Karnuan vessels and captured three more.

"Now that everyone has been introduced," said Shadamehr, "I brought you this in honor of our meeting."

He presented the Captain with the amethyst ring.

She took the ring—it seemed small as a child's christening ring in her huge hand—held it to the light and watched it sparkle.

"A good omen," she said and deposited the ring in her capacious bosom.

"You're welcome," said Shadamehr. "Now I was wondering if you could tell us why Captain Kal-Gah has departed in this sudden manner—"

"He left because of the bad omen," said the Captain, frowning. "The waterspout."

"Oh," said Shadamehr, discomfited. "I see."

The Captain's eyes narrowed. "The omens were good until you came among us. You brought a bad omen with you. Why is that?"

"Uh, no, you've got that wrong," protested Shadamehr. "I didn't bring the bad omen. My omens are all good, as you can plainly see with the ring there. You could ask Kal-Gah. Well, you can't since he's left. But I didn't have a bad omen to my name the entire voyage. Same with my friends. Lucky, very lucky. All of us."

"Perhaps I can provide a reason for the bad omen," Griffith interjected smoothly. Now that he was on the ship's deck, which was far more stable than the cockleshell boat, he and Damra were starting to feel better. "It seems to me that it came because the gods are trying to tell you that you are attacking the wrong people. You should not be attacking Krammes. Your war is not with Vinnengael. Your war is with Karnu."

"We would go to war against them," the Captain growled. "If the sons-of-weasels would fight us on the open seas, ship to ship and man to man. The vermin hide behind the walls of their forts far inland, so that we have to march for days to reach them and then, instead of fighting a fair and honorable battle, they form into squares and columns and march this way and dash that way and come at us from all directions. We do not know how to fight on land."

The Captain nodded in the direction of the city of Krammes, where thin tendrils of smoke could still be seen rising into the air. "I have heard that some of the best generals in all of Loerem are in Krammes. What do they call that place—a horse school?"

"Imperial Cavalry School," said Shadamehr. "But 'horse school' pretty well sums it up."

The Captain glowered at him. "I was planning to ask them to help us learn how to fight our foe on land. How to deal with these columns of pikemen and hordes of archers and horses. We go to war to fight humans, not horses, yet that's what we're up against."

She thrust her lower fangs—that had been filed to sharp points—over her lip and nodded again toward Krammes. "As I said, I was going to ask for their help, then you came, bringing your bad omens."

"But," said Alise, confused, "you weren't asking for help. You attacked them. Set buildings on fire."

"Yes?" said the Captain. "So?"

"You don't pummel someone you're going to ask a favor of—" Shadamehr began. His voice petered out, as he realized that it might, in fact, be an orken custom.

"Answer me this, Baron." The Captain jabbed Shadamehr in the chest with her forefinger. "If I limped into this wonderful horse school of theirs, showing off my wounds and begging the horse teachers to help me, what would they say?"

"Well—" Shadamehr began.

" 'Wounded ork,' they would say in pity. 'You are bleeding on our carpet. Please go away.' "

"I don't think—"

"I come to them wielding a fiery sword," said the Captain with a fierce snort. "I want them to say, 'These orks are fighters! Worthy of our teaching.' And then you come along," she grunted, "and ruin it."

"Could I confer with my colleagues for a moment?" Shadamehr asked. "Explain this to them? They don't speak orken."

The Captain waved her hand, walked a few paces off.

"She does have a point, in a twisted sort of way," Damra said.

"If you believe her," said Griffith skeptically.

"I find it impossible to see how anyone could have thought up a lie like that," Shadamehr said, sighing. He scratched his head. "I may have mucked up things rather badly."

"Don't worry, dear," said Alise, in soothing tones. "It's not the first time, and I'm sure it won't be the last."

"My woman!" cried Shadamehr heartily, putting his arm around her and hugging her. "Such a comfort! I think I have a remedy, though.

"Captain," Shadamehr called out. "I know many of the officers at the . . . er . . . horse school, and I think I could persuade them to help you. You and I could go ashore under a flag of truce and speak to them. Explain about the fiery sword and all that."

The Captain eyed him narrowly. "Do you think they would listen to you?"

"I've donated quite a lot of money to the school over the years," said Shadamehr. "I think they might listen to me. And to the great Captain of Captains, of course."

"Humpf," said the Captain, sucking her lower lip. "I will think on it."

She folded her arms across her ample bosom, tilted back her head. "Captain Kal-Gah said he was taking you to Krammes. What business did *you* have there?"

"Sea voyage," said Shadamehr promptly. "Good for our health."

To his surprise, the Captain gave a great guffaw of laughter.

"So Kal-Gah said," she said and, still laughing, she walked off.

The orks escorted the four to their quarters belowdecks, similar in all respects to their quarters aboard Kal-Gah's ship: four small cubbyholes built into the walls; a table on which some dried-out bread had been placed along with a slab of cheese, a bowl of water, and several crockery mugs.

"So what do you suppose Kal-Gah really told her about us?" Damra asked.

"Kal-Gah is a loyal friend, but an ork's first loyalty is to the Captain. We can safely assume he told her everything he knows," said Shadamehr. "Which would include finding Alise and me half-dead and tainted with Void in the sewers of New Vinnengael. Cheese anyone? I think it's goat."

"And he would have told her everything that happened at the keep," Alise observed. She stood leaning against the door, glancing out every so often to make certain no one was eavesdropping. "Some of the orks on board the ship were with us at the keep. The arrival of Damra—an elf—traveling in company with a pecwae and a Trevinici was the talk of everyone there."

"And we've never made a secret of the fact that Damra is a Dominion Lord," said Griffith, exchanging glances with his wife.

"A lackwit could reach the conclusion that Bashae was carrying something of value in this knapsack," said Shadamehr, throwing the knapsack on the bed and throwing himself after it. "Something so valuable that a Dominion Lord was guarding him. And while orks have their own way of thinking, they're certainly not lackwits. I don't trust this Captain." He glanced at Damra. "Do orks have Dominion Lords these days? I know they did years ago."

"If they do, I haven't met any. They stopped attending the Council meetings after the fall of Mount Sa 'Gra. The trouble began when they petitioned the Dominion Lords to assist them in recovering their mountain, and the Dominion Lords refused."

"Why did they think they would help?" Shadamehr asked, propping himself up on his elbow.

"Because the orken portion of the Sovereign Stone is in Mount Sa 'Gra," Damra replied.

"I see." Shadamehr looked grave.

"Supposedly the Stone is safe and well hidden," said Damra. "At least, that's what the orks told the Council."

"But they still refused," said Alise.

"We had good reason to," Damra stated. "The duty of a Dominion Lord is to try to bring about peace between the races, not to join in a war with one race against another. We tried to explain that to the orks, but we didn't get very far. Their Dominion Lords walked out, and they haven't been back since."

"Meanwhile, Dagnarus is exerting all his efforts to find the four parts of the Sovereign Stone. His Vrykyl have infiltrated governments of other races. I don't see any reason why the orks should be different. Which brings us back to our original theory that he has offered them to help take back Mount Sa 'Gra in return for attacking Krammes from the sea, keeping them busy while he marches overland."

"I have to admit that makes more sense than giving the people of Krammes a bloody nose with one hand and offering to shake with the other," said Griffith.

"Still," argued Shadamehr, "there's a certain wonderful logic to that which I like."

"So what do we do?"

"Nothing we can do," said Shadamehr. Leaning back on the bed, he rested his head on his arms. "Keep the two Sovereign Stones safe and secure until we manage to reach Krammes—"

"Griffith," said Alise suddenly, "wouldn't you like to wash your face?"

"Do I have dirt on it," asked Griffith, startled. "Where—"

"Yes, it's filthy. Wash your face in that bowl of water," Alise said urgently, pointing. "That nice, refreshing *bowl of water* . . .

"Ah!" cried Griffith. "Thank you for pointing that out to me."

He grabbed hold of the bowl and hurled it to the deck. The bowl broke into pieces. Water splashed over his shoes and the hem of his robes.

Shadamehr sat up on the bed, staring. "Are you generally in the habit of smashing up the crockery?"

Griffith ignored him.

"I fell for that same trick when I was a student," he said bitterly. "I had to live on nothing but water for a week to teach me the lesson. Obviously a week wasn't long enough."

"If someone would explain—" said Shadamehr.

Alise bent down, picked up a piece of the bowl. "Do you remember that message Rigiswald sent to you? Quai-ghai looked into a bowl of water and she could hear—"

"—everything that other ork said to her," finished Shadamehr. He came over to view the wreckage. "Well done, Alise, though you might have been a bit quicker on the uptake."

"It looks harmless enough," said Damra, carefully picking up another one of the crockery shards. "Maybe we're letting our fears run away with us. Is there any way you can tell for certain if they were using this to spy on us?"

"Not now," said Griffith. "The spell has been dissipated."

"What do we do?" Alise asked.

Shadamehr shook his head. "Nothing much we can do. We talked a lot about the Sovereign Stones, let any number of cats out of the bag. It's too late to go chasing after them. Are you positive it was you who created that waterspout, Griffith?"

"Yes, why?" he asked, startled.

"Just checking," said Shadamehr, adding gloomily, "I don't know about you, but this is the last time I ever dabble in bad omens."

They had a small porthole in their cabin. The sunset was spectacular, the sinking sun spreading a trail of blazing purple-orange across the surface of the blue-gold water, but none of the four had the heart to enjoy it. Griffith swept up the shards of the broken bowl and piled them on the table, prepared with his apologies if the orks asked what had happened to it.

The orks did not. The orks did not disturb them. The elves lay on their beds, trying vainly to sleep. Shadamehr—bent double—paced restlessly about the cabin, listening to the creaking of the ship and the shipboard sounds of running feet, flapping sails, and the chants that accompanied every part of shipboard life. Alise sat and watched him.

"At least," said Shadamehr, peering out the porthole, "they're not sailing off."

"True," said Griffith. "They haven't raised the anchor."

"That's not such a hopeful sign," said Alise. "If your theory is correct, the Captain could be waiting for the taan army to show up."

"You're right," said Shadamehr somberly. "I'd forgotten that."

A knock thundered on the door, then a large ork thrust his shaved and tattooed head inside. "Captain says you're wanted for dinner."

"Not the main course, are we?" Shadamehr asked.

"Naw," said the ork, grinning. "We got squid!"

At that, Damra, who had risen to her feet, sank back down. "No, thank you. I'm not hungry."

The ork's grin was gone in a moment. "You will come," he said. "You will all come. The Captain commands it."

"At least it's not dried figs," said Shadamehr in her ear as they walked out.

The Captain's quarters were located in the ship's prow and were quite splendid, by orken standards. A large window provided a stunning view of the ocean. The table, made of a slab of wood resting on top of trestles, could accommodate ten orks or fourteen humans. An enormous map of the continent of Loerem and all the surrounding seas hung on a wall. Another map—this one smaller and more detailed, featuring the Blessed Straits, the estuary, Krammes, and Old Vinnengael—was spread out on a desk, anchored in place by various navigational instruments. So interested was Shadamehr with the maps that he had to be persuaded to leave them to take his place at the table.

The Captain of Captains sat at the head of the table, with her guests ranged along either side. Joining them were two other officers. The rest of those in attendance were shamans.

The food had been prepared for orken and human and elven palates, with fried squid and fish chowders for them and a purple soup for the elves. The orks drank ale. The Captain provided wine for the humans and the elves, a treat they had not tasted since they had left New Vinnengael. Orks do not drink wine, considering it a drink suitable only for very young children, and sickly children at that.

Shadamehr accepted the generous mugful the orks poured for him. He tasted it, rolled it on his tongue. The wine was the heady, spiced red wine from southern Dunkar, and it tasted wonderful, especially after weeks of drinking stale water from barrels. He hesitated a moment before drinking, thinking things through. He thought he knew now what was going on. Smiling to himself, he lifted the mug to his lips and drank the spiced wine. He drank it all and asked for more.

Conversation flowed with the wine. The Captain spoke of the political situation in the world. Shadamehr was impressed with her knowledge. He had the feeling he should be uneasy about certain things she said, but the wine was too good to ruin by arguing. She knew about Dagnarus. Shadamehr tried to get some sense of how the Captain felt about him, but she proved noncommittal, with one exception.

"If it had been left up to the orks two hundred years ago," said the Captain, tearing off a hunk of bread and using it to sop up the remains of her soup, "Dagnarus would not be a problem for you humans."

"What do you mean?" Shadamehr asked politely, feeling a story coming on.

"When King Tamaros was given the Sovereign Stone, he invited all the representatives of the four races to come to share in it. He held a great ceremony. Our Captain of Captains was invited to it. He didn't know whether to go or not, for the omens were very bad. His shaman assured the Captain that the bad omens were for the humans, not the orks, and so the Captain went. During the ceremony came the worst omen of all for the humans. The young princeling, Dagnarus, was given one of the pieces of the Sovereign Stone to give to his elder brother, Helmos. When he handed the stone to his brother, the stone slipped and cut Helmos, so that he bled."

The orks were silent—solemn and serious in the presence of such a terrible sign from the gods.

"King Tamaros went on with the ceremony," the Captain continued. "He could do nothing else, I suppose. The Captain of Captains and the shaman waited around, to be witness to the slaying of the young princeling, for, of course, with blood spilled between brothers, Dagnarus could not be allowed to live. Nothing happened, however, except a party. The Captain wanted very much to return to his ship, and so he asked King Tamaros when he planned to kill the prince, expressing his hope that it would be before the next tide. He even offered to do it himself, if it would speed up the proceedings. Imagine the Captain's shock when he heard Tamaros say that he had no intention of killing Dagnarus. That it had all been 'an accident.' "

The shamans shook their heads over the criminal stupidity of humans.

The Captain chewed vigorously on her bread. "Blood spilled between brothers. We were not surprised when war broke out. If Tamaros would have listened to the orks, his kingdom would not now lie in ruins."

"This calls for another glass of wine," said Shadamehr. "Change the subject," he ordered under his breath.

"Is it true, Captain," said Griffith, "that you have orken shamans who are skilled in all forms of elemental magic?"

The Captain nodded. "It is true."

"Most orks consider any magic except Water magic an abomination. Yet, you have orks who practice Fire magic and Earth magic."

"And Void magic," said the Captain.

"Indeed," said Griffith uneasily. "Void magic? But you orks despise the Void."

"Some orks despise elves," said Captain. "Some elves despise orks. Yet here you are. The Void is the center of the great circle of life. Without nothing, there cannot be something. The Void has its uses," she added complacently. "As do elves. Or so I am told."

"More wine," said Griffith.

Shadamehr poured out the ruby red wine for himself and his friends. He lifted his glass in a salute to the Captain of Captains. Drinking the wine, he listened to the ship's bell ringing the changing of the watch. He looked at Alise, whose red hair glowed like flame in the light of an oil lamp that hung above their heads. The lamp swayed with the gentle rocking of the ship . . .

The lamp swayed round and round . . .

The walls swayed round and round . . .

A cry and a crash.

Alise on the floor. Damra on the floor.

Griffith on his feet, reaching out . . .

Griffith on the floor.

Round and round. In a circle.

In the center was the Void.

ALISE AWOKE WITH THE WORST HEADACHE SHE'D EVER EXPERIenced in her life. Her head felt as if it had been stuffed with rocks, whose sharp and jagged edges jabbed her painfully when she tried to move. She would not have moved if she'd had a choice. She would much rather have remained still until death took her, which she felt certain would not be long. But beneath the pain and the nausea ran a nagging sense of danger that impelled her to open her eyes and try to lift her head from the pillow.

She groaned and lay back down. Bright sunlight, streaming in through a window, lanced straight to the back of her head. Lying there, trying to understand what was wrong, she finally figured it out.

The bed wasn't moving.

Wincing, she shaded her eyes with her hand, looked about the room. The objects in her vision swam about, and only after intense concentration could she manage to make objects stop wiggling and crawling. Her suspicions were confirmed. The window was a window—it wasn't a porthole. She was in a room with whitewashed walls and nothing much else, except crude beds and a single chair.

An elderly man sat on the chair beside her bed. His beard was clipped and smooth. He wore robes of finely combed wool and he regarded her without expression.

"Rigiswald . . ." Alise said dazedly. She tried to sit up.

"Take it easy," Rigiswald counseled. "You've had a rough night. And your day isn't going to be much better, I'm afraid."

Fear cleared her head.

"Shadamehr!" Alise said thickly. Moving her swollen tongue was difficult. She looked around the room, could not find him. "Where is he? What has—"

"Not here," said Rigiswald. "He and the elven Dominion Lord are both gone."

"Griffith?"

"He's here. He's in the next room, sleeping it off."

Alise looked down at herself—her red hair bedraggled, her dress disheveled and filthy.

"Where are we?" she asked, dazed. "This isn't the ship . . ."

"No," said Rigiswald. "You're in Krammes. An inn. The Merry Tippler."

Alise sat up. "Where is Shadamehr?" she demanded firmly.

"I believe, my dear," said Rigiswald, "that the orks have both him and the elven woman. I forget her name."

"Damra," said Alise. She rose to her feet, lurched unsteadily across the floor, and grabbed hold of the window ledge to steady herself. She stared out to sea. She stared until her eyes ached and the tears streamed down her face.

"The ship . . . The Captain's ship . . ."

"Gone," said Rigiswald crisply. "Sailed off. You should come back to bed. Lie down before you fall down."

Alise turned away, but she did not go back to her bed. "Tell me what happened. How did you find me? Us?" she amended, remembering Griffith.

"I've been keeping a watch," Rigiswald replied. "The ork's message stated that the ship was nearing Krammes. I have friends among the orks here and put the word out that I would appreciate being informed when my friends arrived. I gave them descriptions of you and Shadamehr.

"Last night, an ork came to my room about midnight. He said that I should come with him right away. That one of the persons I'd been inquiring about was in trouble. He brought me here, to this establishment. Are you certain you won't sit down?"

"I feel better standing up. I am standing up, right?"

Rigiswald nodded.

"I hoped that was the case. I wish the floor would quit moving," Alise said.

"You don't have your land legs back yet," said Rigiswald. "When I arrived, I found four orken sailors. One had you slung over his shoulder. The other was carrying the elf. They were in an argument with the owner of this place that terms itself an 'inn.' The orks stated that arrangements had been made to leave you and the elf here for the night. Money had been paid out, as I understand it.

"The owner stated that the money wasn't enough. That he ran a respectable business and he didn't want anything to do with 'drunken hussies.' I should add here that the orks had wrapped a scarf around your friend Griffith's head. With his ears hidden, he makes a rather attractive-looking female."

"Oh, gods!" Alise groaned. She made a feeble attempt to shove her hair back out of her face and gave up. "I wake up feeling like something that's been run over by a wagon and left to die in an alley, to find you here, Griffith dressed like a woman, and Shadamehr gone."

Her voice trembled. "I think I will sit down," she said, and staggered back over to the bed. "What happened after that? Did you question the orks?"

"I did. They claimed that they had met you two in a bar on the waterfront. That you had all been having a 'good time' until you and your friend passed out from too much drink. They were told to bring you here. I asked who told them, who paid the money, and so on and so forth. In answer, they handed me this, said I was to give it to you."

Reaching into a leather pouch, Rigiswald drew out a ring, held it out to her. The amethyst glittered in the sunlight. Alise took it, her fingers shaking.

"Did they say anything else?" she asked.

"They said the ring belonged to 'Shadamehr's woman.' " Rigiswald smiled slightly.

A tear slid down Alise's cheek.

"It does," she said softly, to herself. "It really does."

She clasped her hand tightly over the ring.

"Where do you think the orks have taken them? To . . ." She swallowed, trying to force the words past the lump in her throat. "To Dagnarus?"

"I don't know," said Rigiswald gravely. "But I fear so. Both were carrying portions of the Sovereign Stone, after all." He patted her hand.

"Still, we must keep up hope. All is not as bleak as it seems. The message they sent you about the ring doesn't sound as if it came from someone with evil intent."

Alise made another shove at her hair. "I don't know. They knew we had the Sovereign Stones with us. The orks knew who was carrying them, and they've kept those two people. What other reason could there possibly be except to turn them over to Dagnarus?"

Sighing, she sat silently a moment, holding fast to the ring.

"Have you heard from Ulaf? When do you expect him and the others?"

"I haven't heard anything," Rigiswald replied. "As to when he'll arrive, I have no idea. He was meeting with various Dominion Lords along the way."

"I don't suppose any of them have shown up here in Krammes?"

"No," said Rigiswald curtly. "I don't expect them to. I doubt if he found any alive. Dagnarus and his Vrykyl would have seen to that."

"So, what are we going to do?" Alise asked.

"Move you and the elf to a different inn," said Rigiswald, casting a disparaging glance about the room.

"And after that?" Alise couldn't help but smile. At least some things in her life remained the same.

"I plan to finish reading my book," said Rigiswald, unperturbed. "You are the energetic one. You should probably hang about the waterfront, see what information you can pick up among the orks. They won't tell you anything, but at least you'll feel useful."

"Thank you," Alise said dryly. She put her hand to her throbbing head. "I can't believe we let them drug us! We should have known. It was so damn obvious. The orks didn't drink the wine. That alone should have tipped us off that something was wrong."

"Sometimes we pull the wool over our own eyes," said Rigiswald sententiously.

Alise stared, appalled. "Are you saying that Shadamehr knew he was being drugged and he let it happen? But why?"

Rigiswald didn't answer. He regarded her intently. "Think of the message, my dear."

"Oh, no!" Alise cried. "He wouldn't. That—That—"

"He knew where he had to go, didn't he?"

"Nonsense! He couldn't have figured all that out," said Alise with a toss of her head, a move she immediately regretted.

"He knew where he had to go. He knew he alone was responsible for the Stone. He must have been fairly certain that no Dominion Lords would come to Krammes. And he knew that you would be in danger if you came with him. And he also knew that if he tried to insist that you leave him—"

"He knew, he knew, he knew," said Alise impatiently. "He doesn't know anything. He doesn't know me like he thinks he knows me. He had no right to send me away. I hate him," she added, sitting up straight and wiping her eyes. "I hate him with every fiber of my being. I have hated him from the first moment I met him. I have hated him in the past and I intend to hate him in the future. He's the most expasperating man in the universe."

She held the amethyst ring tightly, very tightly.

"And now," she said, "I'm going to go wake Griffith, and the two of us will set about finding out what has happened . . . what has happened . . ."

She stood up or tried to. The room tilted. The floor slid out from beneath her feet. Fully intending to walk to the door, Alise landed facedown on the pillow. She moaned softly. "Oh, Shadamehr, how could you go and get yourself kidnapped by orks."

"I'll be here when you wake up," said Rigiswald, pulling another book from his pouch.

"Tell Shadamehr . . . when you see him . . . that I hate him," Alise mumbled, closing her eyes.

"I'll do that," said Rigiswald.

The Captain of Captains sat in the stern of the shore boat, her hand on the tiller, guiding the boat that was slowly, silently crawling up the estuary. The boat's oars had been muffled. The six orken sailors who rowed the boat took care to lower the oars into the water quietly, with only the smallest splash, so that their presence would not be detected. The orks traveled by night, gliding past the fort that had made such a nuisance of itself during their bombardment of Krammes.

The Captain was not particularly worried about being discovered. The omens had been exceptionally good this night, as the omens had been good all week. She did not count that pitiful attempt at omen-faking performed by the elf. The Captain chuckled every time she thought about the waterspout, forming out of a clear blue sky with not a cloud in it. A goony bird could have seen through that!

Tonight's omens foretold the cloud cover that hid the moon and stars and promised the rain that obliterated the sounds of a boat sneaking underneath the humans' very noses.

And the rain came, dancing across the water in sheets. An ork stood at the prow, staring into the darkness, watching for obstacles in the estuary. The Captain did not expect any. The orks had sailed this estuary in their tall ships for centuries. They had mapped and charted every eddy and snag. The orks rowed with ease, making good time, chanting their rowing chant beneath their breaths, instead of booming it aloud. The Captain's shaman sat nearby. At her feet were two largish lumps, covered in tarps to keep them warm and dry.

One of the lumps began to snore loudly. The shaman glanced at the Captain in concern.

"Turn him over on his stomach," said the Captain.

The shaman did so, with the result that the snoring ceased.

"Even in his stupor, he holds on to that knapsack," said the shaman in admiration.

"Yes," said the Captain, "he does."

"Is that where he hides the Sovereign Stone?" the shaman asked.

"It is," said the Captain.

"And the other?"

"She is a Dominion Lord. It will be protected by her armor."

The shaman nodded his understanding.

"How long will they sleep?" the Captain asked.

"As long as you want, Captain," the shaman replied. "All I have to do is cast the spell again."

"Good." The Captain grunted. "Let them sleep a long time. They will need their rest . . . where we're going."

The shaman nodded, and the rest of the night passed in silence as the boat glided unseen up the estuary.

LOCATED IN THE ILLANOF MOUNTAINS, ABOUT FIVE HUNDRED miles northeast of Krammes (as the dragon flies), Mardurar was a mining town, noted not only for its gold and silver mines, but also for the fiercely independent spirit of its citizens. "Independent" was how the Mardurs viewed themselves. Others had another word for them: "outlaws."

The mines belonged to the crown and were run by crown-appointed ministers. A posting to Mardurar had one great advantage—the person who supervised the removal of vast quantities of wealth from the mountain could do very well for himself in the process. A posting to Mardurar had one great disadvantage—it was in Mardurar.

The first problem the pampered royal official from the sunny climes of New Vinnengael had to face was the weather. The cold was unbelievable, and the snow was worse. The snow began falling in the autumn, stopped for a brief time during the three sunny months of summer, then started all over again. The natives were not the least bothered by snow or the cold. Earth magi kept the mountain passes open, so that the wealth from the mines flowed down the mountain all year long. The natives strapped sticks to their feet and slid down the mountainside or hitched up teams of dogs or elk to pull them about in sleds. The royal official sat shivering in his log house, unable to get warm.

Mardurar was home to a great many magi, far more than any other town of comparable size. Most of the miners were Earth magi, who used their talents to drag the ore from the mountain. One might think that a large number of magi would lend an air of refinement and graciousness to the town.

One would be wrong. These magi were not the bookish scholars of the Temple. Few of the miners could read or write. Most had learned their craft from their parents, who had learned it from their parents, and so forth, going back generations. The spells they used were often sung or chanted as the miners went about their daily tasks of forcing the mountain to give up her wealth. Big and brawny, hard-living and hard-drinking, quick with their fists and glib with their tongues, the magi of Mardurar considered themselves the rulers of Mardurar, and woe betide those who thought otherwise.

One group who did think otherwise were the soldiers of the Royal Army. Posted in the city to ensure that the wealth of the mountains actually made it down the mountain and not into the pockets of corrupt officials or bandit lords, the soldiers of the Bastion of Mardurar, known disparagingly among the miners as the Bastion Bastards, were as tough as the miners and just as quick and skilled with their fists.

The two had a healthy hatred for each other, but also a certain grudging respect. Brawls were a daily occurrence. But whenever there was a tunnel collapse in the mines, soldiers and miners worked side by side to dig out the unfortunate victims. As might be expected, the other large group of Earth magi located in Mardurar were healers.

Mardurar was also famous for the Meffeld Cross-road.

Located about ten miles outside the city, on the east slope of the Illanof Mountains, the Meffeld Cross-road was the junction of two major highways. One highway led west through the famous Meffeld Pass, the only route known at that time through the Illanof mountain range that split the country of Vinnengael down the middle. The other highway led to the city of Mardurar itself. The crossroads was a well-known meeting place, despite the fact (or perhaps because of it) that crossroads were known to be cursed.

Earth magi kept both highways open throughout the winter. They used their magic to create huge beings made of stone known as Earthen Killers. Animated mounds of rock, the mindless monstrosities stood twenty feet tall and were completely under control of the Earth magi. At their commands, the Earthen Killers went thundering down the road, their huge "arms" flinging snow in great clouds to the left and right, their boulder "feet" stomping the road smooth. The magi had to keep careful control over their magical creations, for the Killers were aptly named and would wreak havoc if they once got loose, stomping and pummeling any living being they could catch.

On the day that Ulaf and his band arrived in Mardurar, the highways had been newly cleared, the latest snowfall tamped down and shoved aside. Its services no longer required, the Earthen Killer was once more an inoffensive pile of rock and boulders heaped up in a mound near the crossroad, waiting to be reanimated with the next snowfall.

The stones resembled a gigantic cairn, and were a startling and sometimes unnerving sight to newcomers, particularly due to their proximity to the crossroad. Although the royal officials of Mardurar stoutly maintained that no unfortunate suicide had ever been buried at this important crossroad, few believed them.

Ulaf and his band came to the crossroad in the late afternoon. A light snow was falling, just enough to cause the horses to twitch their ears and blink their eyes when the cold flakes hit them. The snow was not going to last. The clouds were thin. Sometimes the sun would actually break through, causing the snowflakes to sparkle, dazzling the eye.

At the crossroad, Ulaf reined in his horse.

"The rest of you ride ahead into Mardurar," he instructed. "You'll find rooms at the Hammer and Tongs. I'll see Jessan and the Grandmother off, then join you."

The others departed, taking the road to Mardurar, their thoughts on a warm fire and the mulled wine for which the Hammer and Tongs was famous. Ulaf turned to his companions.

"Here is where we part, Jessan. That road"—Ulaf pointed—"leads down the western face of the mountain to the plains below. Once you are out of the mountains, keep your face toward the sunset and you will eventually reach Karnu. You will not have difficulty traveling in Karnuan lands?"

Jessan shook his head. "Many of my people serve with the Karnuan army. The Trevinici are well respected and highly prized. No Karnuan would be so foolish as to attack me." He glanced behind him, at the Grandmother. "Or those under my protection."

"No Karnuan, perhaps," said Ulaf gravely. "But who knows if Karnu even still rules its own lands? We've heard stories that the taan have been fighting to conquer Karnu. They may well have conquered it by now."

Ulaf went on to urge Jessan to continue traveling with him and his men, even though he knew he would waste his breath, and he was not surprised that the young Trevinici refused. Jessan was determined to return to his homeland, as was Grandmother Pecwae. No matter that the journey would be long—perhaps a year or more—or that they would be traveling through dangerous territory. Wounded in body and in soul, both Jessan and the Grandmother longed for the healing powers of home.

"Very well, if you insist on going, at least accept this. I have drawn up a rough map." Ulaf handed over a square piece of leather. Unrolling it, Jessan spread it out on his horse's neck. "You do not want to travel too far to the north. You will run into the lands of the elves, and that would not be wise."

Jessan nodded. He'd seen enough of elven lands to know that he wanted to keep clear of them. Ulaf went on to provide advice as to the best routes and how to avoid places where there might be fighting. Although impatient to be on his way, Jessan forced himself to pay attention. There are different types of warriors in this world, Jessan had come to learn. Not all of them need to brandish a spear and charge the enemy headlong in order to prove their courage or their worth. He had grown to respect Ulaf on their journey, and he was grateful to the man for his advice.

"I would travel with you into the pass," Ulaf added, handing over the rolled-up map. "But I want to stop at Mardurar for a couple of days to catch up on the latest news and to replenish my supplies at the Temple of the Magi."

"Then this is good-bye," said Jessan. "Good luck to you. Give my greetings to the baron. I often think of him, traveling with the Sovereign Stone. He is the one who is truly in danger. I hope he fares well."

"He will," said the Grandmother. "He is one of the god's favored, that one. Although—"

The Grandmother did not finish her thought. She turned her head around to stare back down the road they had just ridden. Lifting her newly carved agate-eyed stick in the air, she twitched it this way and that, so that all the eyes could take a good look.

"Evil," she said suddenly. "Coming this direction." She gave the stick a shake. "At least now you have sense enough to warn me ahead of time."

Ulaf glanced down the road. He could not hear or see anything, but that meant nothing. The sound of hoofbeats would be muffled in the snow.

"A Vrykyl?"

The Grandmother shrugged. "I don't know. Maybe."

"Could the Vrykyl be following us still?" Jessan asked, alarmed.

"I don't think so," said Ulaf. "You no longer have the Blood-knife or the Sovereign Stone, so I don't see how it could. Still, it will be best to find out. You and the Grandmother ride on ahead. I'll wait around and see who comes along. If it's trouble, I'll catch up with you and let you know."

"Agreed," said Jessan, relieved. This would spare them both a long and uncomfortable good-bye. "We had best hurry." Waving his hand, he and the Grandmother rode on.

Ulaf turned his horse's head and guided the animal among the rocks of the fallen Earthen Killer toward a pine forest that rose up behind the rock pile. Hidden among the trees, he tethered his horse, counseled the animal to silence, then crept back on foot to the rock pile. Ulaf crouched behind the rock, choosing a position where he could see through the chinks in the stones.

Jessan and the Grandmother proceeded up the road, riding pillion. The horse bore a litter carrying Bashae's body, wrapped in its soft cocoon. The litter dragged along the road, leaving a distinctive trail that would be difficult to miss.

Ulaf waited a long time, so long that his feet began to grow numb with the cold. He was beginning to regret having trusted in a stick. Then, just as dusk was falling, a lone rider came into view. The rider, like most travelers, was heavily wrapped in a thick, hooded cloak. If it was a Vrykyl, the creature would be traveling in disguise, so Ulaf did not pay much attention to the person seated on the horse. He was far more interested in the horse's trappings, which were like nothing he'd ever seen, particularly the caparison, red with golden trim around the edges that had been fashioned to resemble flames.

Ulaf would have bet his eyeteeth that the caparison was magical. The rider's cloak was stained with the mud and slush of the road. The caparison was as clean and bright as if it had been new-made that very day.

If the rider was following Jessan, he would halt at the crossroads to study the trail, trying to determine which route the Trevinici had taken.

The rider did halt, but he did not look at the trail. He turned in his saddle and searched the surrounding woods with an intense scrutiny that caused Ulaf to press himself against the rocks and quiet his breathing.

Not finding what he sought, the rider remained seated on his horse at the very center of the crossroads. Obviously, he was waiting for someone.

His curiosity now piqued, Ulaf wiggled his toes in his boots to try to restore the circulation and settled down to wait also. He hoped the meeting happened soon; otherwise, he'd been walking home on blocks of ice. Times like this he wished he'd been born a Fire mage.

The rider appeared as impatient as Ulaf, for just as the sun dipped down behind the mountain, the rider began to shift restlessly in the saddle. Fortunately, neither the rider's patience nor Ulaf's frozen toes were tried too long. He could hear another horseman approaching at a gallop. The rider guided his horse off the road, took up a position in the shadows where he could see the stranger.

Reaching the center of the crossroad, the stranger halted his horse and looked around. He caught sight of the rider by the side of the road and said loudly, "A fine night for travel, is it not, sir. Bright and crisp."

Since the sky was, in fact, overcast, Ulaf guessed that the words were a coded greeting. His guess was confirmed when the first rider emerged from the shadows.

"Is that you, Klendist?" said a deep voice.

"Is that you, Shakur?"

Shakur! The name sent a tingle up Ulaf's spine. Shakur was the most ancient of the Vrykyl and the most powerful. If there was such a thing as a commander among the ranks of the Vrykyl, Shakur would be it. Ulaf forgot his frozen feet.

"You have my orders?" Klendist asked.

"You are to proceed with all haste to Old Vinnengael, there to await the arrival of Lord Dagnarus. You are to arrive there in a fortnight."

"A fortnight! Are you mad—"

Shakur handed over a scrollcase. "Here is the location of a rogue Portal. It will cut the time of your ride to Old Vinnengael. His Lordship wants you there as soon as possible, so I suggest you leave immediately."

"Old Vinnengael," Klendist said in grim tones. "What does His Lordship want us to do in that accursed place?"

"You will find out, but all in good time. You have your orders—"

"Not so fast, Shakur," said Klendist, and there was an edge to his voice. "My men and I didn't sign on to go to Old Vinnengael."

"What's the matter, Klendist?" Shakur sneered. "Afraid of ghosts?"

"Ghosts are the least of my concerns," said Klendist coolly. "I once thought of doing some business inside Old Vinnengael. The treasure of an empire lies buried there. I did some investigating and decided it wasn't worth it. There's bahk living there, for one thing. Hundreds of them. I'm not riding into Old Vinnengael or anywhere near it until I know more about what it is I'm supposed to do once I get there."

Shakur did not immediately answer. Perhaps he was asking Dagnarus for orders, or perhaps he was trying to outwait Klendist. If so, he failed. Klendist hung on with grim determination. Night had fallen. The two were black blobs against the white backdrop of the fresh snowfall. Ulaf tried to warm his fingers with his breath.

At last, Shakur spoke. "His Lordship says that there is no need for you to enter Old Vinnengael. Four Dominion Lords are traveling to the ruined city. He wants you to apprehend them before they reach their destination."

"Dominion Lords?" Klendist laughed. "I didn't know there were any still in existence. Why does he want them?"

"He does not want them," said Shakur. "He wants what they carry."

"What's that?"

"Something they stole from His Lordship. Do not push your luck, Klendist."

Hearing the warning note in Shakur's fell voice, Klendist apparently decided he had all the information he required.

"So we ride to Old Vinnengael in search of these Dominion Lords. How do we know we're all going to arrive there at the same time?"

"The Void is with us. They will be there."

Klendist shrugged. "If you say so. Do we kill them?"

"No, you will take them alive and you will keep them that way. His Lordship wants to question them," said Shakur.

"Catching is more trouble than killing," Klendist said reflectively. "I'll expect to be rewarded accordingly."

"You've had no reason to complain of your treatment in the past," Shakur replied.

"Just tell him that, will you? Now, what do these Dominion Lords look like?"

"The Void will guide you to them."

"It's like squeezing water from a rock, getting any information out of you, Shakur," said Klendist irritably. "We're all on the same side, you know. Speaking of which, what about the gigs? What are they doing here?"

"The what?" Shakur was clearly baffled.

"The gigs. The taan." Klendist made a gesture with his gloved hand. "We've spotted a group of them here in the mountains. They're skulking about in those woods to the north."

"Indeed?" Shakur turned his head in that direction, as if he could see through the night and the pine trees. "How many?"

"A small group by the looks of it," said Klendist. "A hunting party, maybe."

"Did they see you?"

Klendist snorted, insulted. "As if they could. So His Lordship didn't send them here?"

"No," said Shakur, after a moment's pause, "he did not."

"Want us to kill them?" Klendist offered. "Won't take long. We can do it before we leave in the morning."

"You will leave now, Klendist," said Shakur coldly. "Summon your men. There is no time to waste. As for the taan, they are of no consequence. You have your orders."

Turning his horse's head, Shakur rode off, the horse's hooves kicking up chunks of frozen ground. He rode toward the north.

"No consequence, eh?" Klendist chuckled. Then he growled. "An all-night ride for us, after being in the saddle most of the day. The boys will not be happy. Still, when there's His Lordship's reward in the offing—"

Tucking the scrollcase carefully into the breast of his tunic, Klendist turned his horse's head back in the direction from which he'd come.

Ulaf shoved himself away from the rocks and began to hobble on his half-frozen feet toward where he'd left his horse. The pain of the returning circulation was agony, and he stifled a groan. He spent a moment deciding what he was to do, but only a moment. Mounting his horse, he rode off after Jessan.

Ulaf was not worried about locating the Trevinici. He figured that Jessan would be the one to find him and he was right. Ulaf had ridden about five miles west of the crossroads when Jessan stepped out of the shadows of the woods and stood in front of him. Ulaf brought his horse to a halt.

The on-again, off-again clouds had vanished for good. The night was brightened by the light of a three-quarter moon shining on the snow. The fir trees cast eerie moon-shadows in stripes across the road.

"It was a Vrykyl," Ulaf reported, leaning over his horse's neck. "But it's not following you. The fiend was here to meet with a mercenary captain, a man named Klendist. He and his men will be riding this way shortly. They're bound for a rogue Portal. I'm going to follow them to discover the location of the Portal's entrance. I need for you to ride back up the road to Mardurar, alert Shadamehr's people. Tell them to ride after me. I'll wait for them at the Portal. You'll have to make haste. Unfasten the litter and leave it by the roadside. The Grandmother can stay here with Bashae's body while you're gone."

"What is wrong?" Jessan asked. "What did you hear?"

"The baron and Damra are walking into a trap. I've got to try to find them and warn them."

Ulaf smiled grimly. "The Vrykyl said that the Void was working with them. It wasn't the Void brought me to that crossroads in time to hear what they were plotting—"

A stone struck Ulaf in the chest with such force that it knocked him backward off the horse. He was wearing a thick leather vest and a heavy fur-lined sheepskin coat, or the blow might well have stopped his heart. As it was, he lay stunned in the road, unable to move or to react as two figures, dark against the moonlit sky, bent over him.

Lips parted in a horrible grin. Sharp teeth gleamed in the moonlight. A fist struck him on the jaw, and Ulaf went limp.

The Grandmother screeched a warning. Jessan grabbed hold of the hilt of his sword, but before he could draw his weapon, strong hands seized hold of him, pinned his arms to his side. A bestial face loomed in front of him, leered at him.

Jessan smashed his head into the taan's forehead.

The taan let loose and toppled backward. Jessan drew his sword, turned to face his attackers. The Grandmother's screeching abruptly ceased. Two taan stood crouched in a defensive stance, both eyeing Jessan, waiting for him to make the first move. He swung his sword and started to leap forward.

A blow struck him from behind. His brain seemed to explode with pain, but he fought it off, kept upright. He tried to turn to deal with this new menace, but another blow fell, and Jessan slumped into the snow.

The taan stood looking down at him and, although he would never know it, they paid him the ultimate compliment.

"Strong food," said one.

THE LEADER OF THE SMALL BAND OF TAAN WAS TASH-KET, A TAAN scout whose exploits had already made him a legend among his people. None of his achievements equaled this, however. He had crossed a continent teeming with his enemies, located a strange city in a strange land, entered that city unseen, and made off with the prize he'd been sent to acquire.

He and his fellow scouts had found their way with the aid of an excellent map, provided by Dagnarus, though he did not know it. The taan had also reluctantly relied on the help of a half-taan named Kralt. The taan would never have lowered themselves to travel in company with a half-taan, but Derl had ordered them to do so, telling them that they would find Kralt useful. More human-looking than most half-taan, Kralt had proven his worth. He was able to disguise himself well enough to enter human towns and gather information.

Having stolen the "lightning rock" K'let had sent him to acquire from the dwarves, Tash-ket and his troop made their way back across Vinnengael to the rendezvous point, the town of Mardurar, where they were to meet up with K'let. The taan had arrived first. Tash-ket had been here for several weeks with orders to lie low and do nothing that might give away his presence. Tash-ket obeyed those orders—to a certain extent.

The taan scout is a unique individual. Sent out ahead of the tribe by the nizam to search for game, enemies, and good camping grounds, the taan scout lives an isolated and solitary existence and is expected to think and act on his own. Thus he tends to develop an independence not usually found among the majority of taan.

Tash-ket revered K'let and obeyed orders as far as the scout ever obeyed any orders. Tash-ket followed those he agreed with and ignored those he did not. Having been holed up in this godsforsaken wilderness for weeks on end, forced to endure the wet, cold slop that fell from the skies and covered the ground with white, Tash-ket grew bored and extremely hungry. Both prompted him to ignore the order to lie low.

Tash-ket and his band had arrived in the forests of Mardurar to find the woods almost denuded of game animals. They came across the occasional deer or rabbit or goat, but the taan considered those animals weak food. Tash-ket needed strong food, needed it to start the sluggish blood pumping through his veins and bring the fire back to his belly and his heart. His companions needed strong food as much as he did.

Tash-ket did not see the harm in attacking a small party of humans in order to assuage his appetite. His attack was well planned. He and his fellow scouts struck at night, when no one would be around. Once they had brought down their prey—one of whom fought well, which was extremely gratifying—the taan dragged them far off the road, so that their remains would not be discovered.

Tash-ket was pleased with the results of their hunt. One human had proven to be stronger than Tash-ket had hoped to find in the land of the xkes. Tash-ket laid claim to this human's heart. The other xkes would serve well enough for his comrades. The scrawny old female would feed the half-taan. Tash-ket looked forward to torturing the xkes, in order to test their strength further. Kralt argued against torturing them, saying they should be killed at once, their screams might be heard by others, and that would be disobeying K'let's commands. Tash-ket paid no attention to the words of a slave.

As for the dwarf child, Tash-ket didn't worry about her. The taan fed her whatever was left over from their meal, which wasn't often much. Kralt had learned to communicate with the child, and he would sometimes go into towns to steal human food to give her. Kralt was the one who insisted that they keep her alive. She had powers over what they came to call the lightning rock. She could touch it without harm, and they could not. Tash-ket didn't argue. So long as he had nothing to do with either the rock or the child, he didn't care what Kralt did.

Tash-ket sat near the fire, sharpening his knife, his stomach growling with anticipation.

Ulaf regained consciousness to find himself sitting on the ground, ropes wrapped around his arms and chest, binding him to a tree. Next to him, Jessan was also propped up against a tree. He was trussed up in much the same way, except that his wrists were also bound. Ulaf's wrists were free and he managed to wriggle his arms around in the bindings until his fingers could touch the ground.

Jessan was still unconscious. His head slumped on his chest. His face was covered in blood.

The Grandmother lay on her side in between Ulaf and Jessan. She was not tied to a tree, but had been dumped onto the ground. Her hands and feet were bound, but the taan did not seem to worry much about her escaping, rarely even glanced at her. The Grandmother was conscious, her bright, dark eyes gleaming in the firelight. She did not look at Jessan or Ulaf. Her gaze was fixed intently on something on the other side of the taan camp.

"Taan," Ulaf repeated groggily to himself. "We've been captured by taan."

He remembered Klendist telling Shakur that taan were in the area. Ulaf hadn't paid much attention to that part of the conversation, a fact he now regretted.

His head hurt abominably. He needed to be able to think clearly, and he couldn't through the pain. Scraping up a small bit of dirt with his fingernails, Ulaf used the earth to cast a healing spell on himself. He longed to cast one on Jessan, who appeared to be very seriously injured, but the spell required that he be able to touch his patient.

The taan mostly ignored their captives, beyond casting them a hungry glance now and then. They sat around their fire, laughing and talking. One was busy sharpening a knife.

"Grandmother!" Ulaf whispered.

She didn't hear him.

"Grandmother!" Ulaf whispered again, more urgently, keeping one eye on their captors. He nudged her with his foot.

The Grandmother twisted around to face him.

"Jessan's in a bad way," said Ulaf softly. "He needs healing."

The Grandmother shook her head.

"His wounds are the wounds of a warrior," she said. "He would be angry if I took them away."

"Better angry then dead," said Ulaf grimly. "I need him alert and awake, Grandmother, and you're going to have to do it. I can't get close enough to touch him."

"He did permit Bashae to heal the pain of his injured hand once," said the Grandmother. She made up her mind. "Very well."

She scooted and wriggled her small body over to Jessan. Her skirt, with its jingling bells and clicking stones, made muffled sounds, and one of the taan looked over at them. He said something to the others, and they all made hooting sounds and grinned widely. Apparently they found their captives' struggles amusing. The Grandmother managed to touch Jessan's foot with her hand.

"It won't be perfect," she said. "I can't reach my healing stones."

"It will do," Ulaf said, and hoped he was right.

The Grandmother closed her eyes and began to mutter words in Twithil, the pecwae language that was like the shrill twittering of birds.

Ulaf watched Jessan closely. The young man's breathing eased and smoothed. Some color came back to his face. He ceased to groan, and his eyelids fluttered. He blinked and looked around dazedly.

"I left the scars," the Grandmother assured him, then she went back to staring intently at whatever it was that had attracted her attention.

"What is it, Grandmother?" Ulaf asked, peering in that direction. "What are you looking at?"

And then he saw it. Ulaf gasped softly.

Seated some distance from the fire was what appeared to be a child. At first, he thought it might be the child of one of the taan, but on second glance, he saw it was not. Ulaf could not immediately tell what race the child was, for it was bundled up in so much clothing that he could not distinguish the features. Incredibly, dangling from the child's neck, was a dazzling, radiant jewel.

The jewel caught the firelight and transformed it into myriad glittering sparks of rainbow brilliance, so beautiful that Ulaf wondered if he'd been struck blind, not to have noticed it immediately. The jewel was large—as big as his fist—and it was an unusual cut for a gem. The jewel was triangular and smooth-sided, as if it had been sheared from some larger portion . . .

Ulaf gasped again, this time loud enough to attract the attention of the taan, who stood up and glared at him. He changed the gasp into a cough. The taan sat back down again.

"I have never seen a stone like that," said the Grandmother, her voice soft with awe. "Its magic must be very powerful."

"It is," said Ulaf quietly, for now he recognized what the child was wearing. "It is the Sovereign Stone."

The Grandmother twisted around to stare at him. "The same as the rock Bashae carried? Are you sure?"

"I recognize the jewel from the pictures I've seen in the old books. But who it belongs to, what it's doing here, and how it came to be in the possession of a child are questions beyond my ability to answer. Maybe I can talk to her."

The taan paid no attention to the child. In their excitement over their captives, they appeared to have forgotten about her. She sat alone, off to herself. Ulaf tried a smile. He tended to be a favorite with children.

The child rose to her feet and took a tentative step toward him. Then he saw that she had a rope tied around her neck, like a dog's lead. The other end of the rope was tethered to a tree.

The child's movement brought her nearer the fire, so that Ulaf could see her clearly. Because of her short stature, he had taken her for a child of about six. Now, when he saw her face, he realized he had been mistaken. This child was at least twice that age. By her swarthy complexion and dark hair and flat-nosed features, he knew her to be a dwarven child. He motioned again, but the child regarded him with dark, empty eyes and did not come closer.

Ulaf recalled reading that children guarded the dwarven portion of the Sovereign Stone. Children of Dunner, they were termed. That could be the answer to part of this riddle. He wanted very much to find out the answers to the rest, but he didn't see much chance of that happening. His destiny appeared to be the main ingredient in a taan stew.

"What happened?" Jessan's voice was weak, but his words were clear, coherent. "Where are we?"

Ulaf twisted around to look at him. "How are you feeling?"

"Fine," Jessan answered. A pain-filled grimace belied his words. "Who are these beasts that walk like men? What is going on?"

"They are taan," said Ulaf. "Creatures of the Void."

"What are they going to do with us?"

"My guess is that they're going to eat us."

Jessan stared, appalled. The Grandmother blinked, then grunted.

"The taan have a taste for human flesh," Ulaf explained.

"No beast-man is going to eat me!" Jessan's arm muscles bulged. He tried to break free himself of his bonds.

Hearing the commotion, the taan jumped to their feet. Gathering around Jessan, the taan watched him with interest. They gestured and grinned, seemed to be urging him on.

"Taunt them!" said Ulaf swiftly. "See if you can't trick them into cutting you loose."

"Cut these ropes!" Jessan cried, straining against his bonds. "Fight me man to man, you cowards!"

At this one of the beast-men, who looked different from the others, a taan with almost human features, said something to the other taan. They hooted with glee.

"Tash-ket has no intention of fighting a slave," said the human-looking taan, speaking fluent Elderspeak. "But he will honor you by permitting you to fill his belly."

Jessan snarled and threw himself against the ropes. The taan jeered and poked at him with sharp sticks.

Ulaf had a spell in mind, one he called "Ankle Biter" that would shake the earth beneath their feet, causing them to fall heavily, maybe break a leg or perhaps even knock themselves senseless. If they released Jessan, Ulaf could use his spell to take out one or two of the taan, giving Jessan a chance to tackle the rest.

Unfortunately, the taan weren't falling for it. The taan who had been sharpening the knife took a step toward Jessan. By the gleam in the taan's eye, he wasn't planning to use his knife to cut the ropes. Jessan kicked out violently with his legs. In desperation, not knowing what good it would do, but thinking he had to do something, Ulaf prepared to cast his spell.

Then the Grandmother began to sing.

The taan's hide was thickly scarred, he had what appeared to be gemstones embedded in his flesh. The scar tissue had grown partially over the gems, forming bizarre-looking lumps, but enough of the gemstones were still visible to catch the firelight. Ulaf was wondering what the gems were for—it seemed a strange way to wear jewelry—when one of the gemstones in the taan's arm burst out of his hide and fell to the ground.

The taan gave a grunt of astonishment. Lowering his knife, he stared at the bleeding gash in his arm. The Grandmother continued to sing, her song growing louder and stronger. After staring at the stone for a moment, the taan gave a shrug and raised the gleaming knife, holding it above Jessan's heart.

Two more gems erupted from his flesh, one falling out of his forehead and the other bursting from his breast. The taan howled in anger and whipped around to glare at his fellow taan. He lost two more gems, this time from his left arm.

The taan said something in a loud voice, made a motion toward himself, as if demanding to know what was going on.

His fellow taan shook their heads and backed away from him, eyeing him warily. One raised his weapon, held it pointed at him.

Another gemstone popped out of the taan's leg. Furious, he turned his stare on his captives. His gaze went from Ulaf to Jessan and finally to the Grandmother, singing in her shrill voice. The taan thrust his knife at the Grandmother. Jessan gave a roar and lunged helplessly against his bonds. Ulaf started his spell-casting, but before he could utter more than the first words, an eerie darkness came over his mind and he forgot the spell, lost it completely.

The firelight vanished. The moonlight disappeared. The light of the stars, the light of the world was quenched, replaced by vast, empty night. The Grandmother's singing hushed. The taan's snarling fury died away.

The darkness was complete, yet Ulaf could see someone inside it. Black armor gleamed with a dark iridescence, like a crow's wing.

"Kyl-sarnz!" cried the taan. "Kyl-sarnz."

"A Vrykyl!" breathed Jessan, his voice catching in his throat.

"Shakur," thought Ulaf, slumping back against the tree. "And here I was thinking so smugly that other powers were at work against the Void. He's come for the Sovereign Stone, of course."

He looked for the dwarven child, but she was not where he'd last seen her.

"She is here," said the Grandmother softly revealing the child crouched beside her. "She is with me. She came to me when I sang."

"You have the Sovereign Stone," said the Vrykyl, his hollow voice echoing as if it came from a deep and empty well. "Your god, Dagnarus, will be pleased. You there, slave. Translate my words."

The half-taan did as he was told, repeated Shakur's words to the taan in their language.

The taan cast glances at each other. The taan who had lost his stones spoke a word of command. He said something to Shakur, gestured for the half-taan to translate.

"My master, Tash-ket, says to tell the kyl-sarnz that Dagnarus is not our god. Dagnarus is an imposter who will lead the taan to ruin. We serve K'let. We serve the old gods."

"And K'let says that you serve him well," said a taan, walking into the camp.

This taan looked different from the others. He was older, much older, and his white skin glimmered eerily in the darkness. He spoke the language of the taan, but his voice was cold and hard and empty as that of Shakur's. The half-taan translated the words.

"K'let says that we will be rewarded. K'let says that you are old and decrepit, Shakur, and that he has no honor in fighting you. He bids you crawl back to your master—"

Shakur gave a growl of contempt and turned to face K'let. The Void grew and expanded, its darkness immense, consuming. Ulaf felt himself start to slip into the emptiness. A touch on his arms and a gruff whisper in his ear jolted back him back to his senses.

"Don't move," came the whisper, tickling Ulaf's ear. He could hear and feel the blade of a knife sawing through the ropes. "Be ready."

"To do what?" Ulaf asked softly.

"Fight, if you've a mind," the whisper answered. "Run if you don't."

Ulaf freed his hands of the ropes, moving slowly and carefully so as not to draw the attention of the taan. He cast a glance over his shoulder, saw a dwarf with a knife in his hand slipping through the darkness, heading over to Jessan.

"Good to see you again, lad," said the dwarf, cutting the ropes.

"Wolfram?" Jessan tried to twist around to stare.

"Face forward, you daft Trevinici!" Wolfram hissed irritably. "Don't give me away."

Jessan did as he was told. He glanced at Ulaf, to see if he had an explanation.

Ulaf shook his head. He was concentrating on his spell. He didn't know what the dwarf had in mind, but he was ready.

Wolfram dared not try to reach the Grandmother and the child, who were out in the open. He hovered in the trees near them, watched them closely.

"Dwarf!" Ulaf whispered urgently. "How many are with you?"

"One other," said Wolfram.

Ulaf's heart sank. He'd been hoping for an army, and even that might not be enough to halt two Vrykyl, who were still facing each other.

"Don't threaten me with Dagnarus, Shakur," K'let was saying. "He can't touch me. And that should tell you something, Shakur. You could be free of him, as I am free. Don't pretend you haven't dreamed of that day. I know your thoughts, Shakur. I've felt them through the Blood-knife. I know how much you hate him—"

Blazing light split the darkness of the Void. Vrykyl and taan and prisoners stared upward in astonishment to see the tops of the fir trees burst into flame. The fire flashed off glittering red scales. A dragon's enormous wings fanned the flames. Her two dark eyes glared down at them. The firelight shone on her sharp fangs and sparkled in her mane.

Ulaf had a momentary glimpse of something rushing past him. He thought it was Wolfram, but if so, it was Wolfram encased in shining silver.

He grabbed hold of the Grandmother and the dwarven child. Plucking them off the ground, Wolfram tucked one under each arm, turned, and fled back into the shadows of the trees. Ulaf began his spell-casting. Jessan cast off his bonds and surged out to do battle.

Tash-ket was the first to recover from the shock. He grabbed hold of a spear and aimed it at the fleeing dwarf. Ulaf cast his spell. The ground lurched beneath Tash-ket's feet. He flung his spear, but his aim was off and it sailed into the darkness. The taan lost his balance, and Jessan was on him. Grabbing hold of the taan's head by the hair, Jessan jerked the head backward, snapping the neck.

Tash-ket's body went limp.

Another taan, wielding a stone-headed club, leapt at Jessan. He tried to scramble out of the way, but he slipped. The taan raised the club over him.

A fiery blast from the dragon turned the taan into a blazing torch. Screaming horribly, he took off running, panic-stricken, into the woods. Flames trailed behind him, and it was not long before his screams ended.

Jessan ran out of the smoke, his body glistening with sweat and stained with streaks of soot and blood.

"Where are the Vrykyl?" he demanded tensely. He brandished a taan weapon he had grabbed. "Did you see them? Where did they go?"

Ulaf shook his head. Coughing, he covered his mouth with his sleeve. His eyes burned and stung. He peered back into the flaming trees, into the darkness made deeper by the light of the dragon's magical fire. Taan bodies lay on the ground, but there was no sign of the Vrykyl.

"I don't know," said Ulaf.

WITH THE ASSISTANCE OF SEAGULLS AND VARIOUS OTHER BIRDS and beasts, Wolfram and Ranessa had tracked the taan who had taken the Sovereign Stone from Saumel across Vinnengael, had finally caught up with them on the outskirts of the town of Mardurar.

Ranessa had urged rushing in and slaying all of them at once. Wolfram had reminded her curtly that they didn't want to slay them *all*. There was the safety of the dwarven child to consider. He had scouted the taan camp, hoping to find a time when they all slept, so that he might sneak in and make away with the child. But the taan were never negligent about setting the watch, and no taan ever fell asleep at his post.

He had tried to think of some way to rescue the child, but the taan watched her and the Sovereign Stone day and night. Despite being a Dominion Lord and possessing magical powers and wondrous armor, Wolfram had no thought of attacking the taan by himself. The gods may bless the weapon, but they can't guide the hand that wields it, and Wolfram had never received any training as a warrior. He had only a rudimentary knowledge of fighting, just enough to be able to extricate himself from a brawl. He had only to look at the taan, see their strength and their prowess with their weapons—for they practiced daily—to know that he could never hope to fight all of them. He could always unleash Ranessa on them, but he could not do that and guarantee that any of them, himself included, would come out alive.

He had fretted and fumed. He had just gone to sleep after another disheartening day of spying on the taan, when he suddenly sat upright, certain he'd heard someone talking to him.

"Go to the taan camp!"

Wolfram glanced over at Ranessa. He had insisted that she remain in human form, so as not to alert either the taan or the residents of Mardurar to the fact that a dragon was hanging about. Wrapped up in a bearskin, she was sound asleep.

"Probably I dreamed it," he told himself.

He tried to go back to sleep, but he could still hear the words quite clearly. He got up, walked over, and roused a resentful Ranessa.

"You're a fool," she told him, but she went with him to the camp.

They skulked about the shadows of the trees.

"They've got prisoners!" Wolfram said. He had the feeling that the Trevinici looked familiar. He squinted, stared into the firelight, and he gave a great gasp.

Ranessa punched him in the arm. "Shut up! They'll hear you!"

"Look! Look there!" he said to Ranessa, actually reaching out and shaking her to emphasize his amazement. "That Trevinici man. Get your hair out of your eyes and tell me I'm not seeing things."

"I do think I know him," she said, but she sounded doubtful.

"He's Jessan!" Wolfram hissed, scandalized. "Your nephew."

"My nephew." She paused, then said softly, "I had forgotten him. They all seem so far away. I wonder what he's doing here?"

"Never mind about that now. Here's our chance," said Wolfram, rubbing his hands. "I'll run and cut their bonds—"

"Does your plan include Vrykyl?" Ranessa asked, her voice hardening. "Because one just walked into the camp. No, wait. Now there are two Vrykyl. One is disguised as a taan, but I can see through him."

So could Wolfram, now that she pointed it out. He had been so hopeful and now he could have flung himself facefirst into a snowbank and wept.

"We can do it," said Ranessa. She turned to him and smiled. "You can do it. You're a Dominion Lord. And I am a dragon."

Before he could argue, she was gone, racing off into the darkness. Wolfram gripped his knife and slipped into the camp. He cut loose the Vinnengaelean and Jessan, then slipped quickly back into the shadows to await his opportunity to rescue the child.

He heard Ranessa circling above in the darkness. He had come to know the sounds of her, the flap of the wings through the cold, still air. He heard her draw in a deep breath, then let it out with a whoosh.

The treetops burst into flame. Grasping hold of his medallion, Wolfram said a prayer, and the silver armor of the Dominion Lord slid reassuringly over his body. Wolfram dashed into the taan camp. He grabbed hold of the Grandmother and Fenella. Ignoring the Grandmother's indignant screech and her wail about some stick, Wolfram tucked the pecwae under one arm and Fenella under the other and dashed into the woods.

WOLFRAM HEARD THE DRAGON'S ROARING AND THE CRACKLING of the blazing trees, the screams of a dying taan, and Jessan's war whoop. Wolfram ignored them all, continued running.

The moon, shining bright on the snow, lit their way. Unaccustomed to running and carrying a heavy load, Wolfram was growing tired, his hold on the pecwae and the dwarf child weakening. He had just decided that they were far enough from the camp for safety when he suddenly went blind, as blind as if his eyes had been gouged out. Not only was he blind, he was deaf and dumb and had lost the use of his limbs. He could not see because had no eyes. He could not run, because he had no feet. He had no hands to fight or to a keep hold on anything, including his very life. He tried hard to grasp it, but his fingers started to slip, and he felt himself falling into a vast emptiness.

A hand caught hold of him. A hand gloved in silver. The hand drew him back from the Void. Radiant in her gleaming armor, Gilda stood over him. She raised her shield and, by its light, Wolfram looked up to see the Vrykyl. The creature was armored in the Void and wore a helm that was made in the hideous likeness of the taan that they had been following.

Gilda stood over her fallen brother, holding her shield so that it protected both of them. The Vrykyl drew a strange-looking weapon, a huge sword with a serrated edge. He leapt at her, swinging the sword.

The blade struck the shield. The Vrykyl gave a snarling cry and dropped his weapon. He fell back, wringing his hands. Picking up the sword, he glared at her, glared at the shield.

Wolfram found purchase with his hands. Clinging to life, he pulled himself up over the chasm of the Void. He staggered to his feet, went to stand beside his sister.

The Vrykyl seemed to be trying to figure a way around this shining creature of heaven. Raising his sword, he made another rush. He didn't strike the shield. He smote it with his hand and knocked it out of his way. He aimed a blow at Wolfram.

"Foul creature of the Void!" Ranessa cried out from the darkness. "He's my dwarf! You will not harm him!"

The dragon breathed out a huge gout of flame. Catching the fiery ball in her talon, she flung the blazing orb at the Vrykyl.

The fire rippled over the black armor of the Void. K'let absorbed the blaze harmlessly, sucked the flame into the Void, where it flickered and went out. Lifting his helm, the taan Vrykyl gazed up in wonder at the dragon.

"Your kind are not native to the world of the taan," he cried out, though none of them could understand him. "I would like to stay and fight you, for my honor and for yours. But I must decline your offer of battle. A cohort of mine is around here somewhere, and it would be just like Shakur to attack me from behind."

K'let glanced back at the dwarf and the shining creature of heaven who guarded him.

"As for the Sovereign Stone, I'll know where to find it."

K'let slid into the Void himself, became the darkness, became the emptiness.

"Where did it go?" Wolfram demanded, twisting his head in a panic to see. "I can't find it. Is it behind us?"

"The Vrykyl is gone for the moment," Gilda answered. "But so long as the Sovereign Stone is in the world, he remains a threat. Wolfram, you must take the Stone to Old Vinnengael."

"Old Vinnengael?" Wolfram repeated, stunned. "Why? No, don't go, Gilda! Tell me!"

"Wolfram!"

He opened his eyes.

Ranessa, in human form, knelt at his side.

"Wolfram! Wake up! Are you hurt?" She began to pummel him, apparently with the intention of assisting him to regain consciousness.

"If I wasn't, I am now," Wolfram stated, shoving her fists away. He sat up. "Where is Gilda? Where did she go? I have to ask her something. Gilda?" he called out. "Gilda, I don't understand."

The moonlight shone down among the fir trees. The dwarven child, Fenella, sat near him, holding fast to the hand of Grandmother Pecwae. The Sovereign Stone shone brightly in the pale, cold light.

"Dunner," said Fenella. "I'm glad you found me."

Reaching around her neck, she removed the chain on which hung the Sovereign Stone and held it out to him.

"I kept this for you, Dunner," she said shyly.

Wolfram made a swipe at his eyes, cleared his throat. He hesitated a moment, then took the Sovereign Stone, on its braided horsehair thong, and held it fast.

"I'm not Dunner," he said, embarrassed. "My name is Wolfram. I'm trying to follow in Dunner's footsteps and not doing such a great job. But I will take this, and I thank you for guarding it so well. Dunner would have been proud of you."

Fenella smiled, pleased. She did not venture to come near him, but stayed close to Grandmother Pecwae.

The Grandmother frowned at Wolfram, regarded him with deep suspicion. Reaching out a bony finger, she poked at his armor.

"Did you steal that?" she demanded.

"Aren't you going to thank me Wolfram?" Ranessa demanded shrilly. "I saved you from the Vrykyl. That's the second time I've had to do that by the way."

"Ranessa," said Grandmother Pecwae, "I see you found yourself."

Ranessa was ready with a pert reply, but she looked into the old woman's eyes and changed her mind.

"I shed my skin," she said, confused.

"Good," said the Grandmother. "I always knew it was too tight."

Wolfram gazed down at the Sovereign Stone in his hands, watched it splinter the moonlight.

"Someone's coming," said Ranessa in warning tones.

Wolfram stood up, put himself in front of Fenella and the Grandmother, and faced the darkness.

THE DARKNESS COALESCED INTO THE VINNENGALEAN AND JESSAN. Wolfram heaved a great sigh.

"The Vrykyl may still be around," said Ulaf. "We should leave here immediately. We're all in danger—"

"Aunt Ranessa?" Jessan exclaimed, thunderstruck. "Is that you? What are you doing here?"

"Hello, Nephew," said Ranessa coolly. "Did you bring me a present?"

Wolfram stared into the Sovereign Stone, into its bright, pure, clean heart. He hung the Stone around his neck. The Stone melded with the silver armor and vanished. He knew the Stone was with him, though. He could feel its weight on his soul.

Gilda stood beside him.

"Old Vinnengael," she said.

Wolfram nodded.

They heeded Ulaf's advice and left the forest. They returned to the highway, only to find that their horses had bolted and were nowhere in sight. The litter carrying Bashae's body lay off to one side. Jessan said it had fallen off when the horses fled but the Grandmother said, no, the gods had kept hold of it. By the looks of the road—the churned-up earth and muddy snow—a large group of horsemen had ridden this way.

"Klendist. I missed them," Ulaf said glumly. He kicked at a pile of dirty snow with his boot. "Damn it, who said the Void wasn't at work around here?"

"You did, as I recall," said Jessan, smiling. "They left a trail that a blind ogre could follow. Their tracks will lead you to the Portal."

"From what I've heard of this Klendist, he'll take care to cover his tracks," Ulaf returned morosely. "Still, it's the only thing left to do." He glanced around, his frustration growing. "I suppose I must walk, for I see no sign of our horses."

"The taan frightened them, but they did not run far," said the Grandmother. Putting her fingers to her lips, she gave a piercing whistle. Then, lifting her voice, she called out something in Twithil.

"What is she saying?" Ulaf asked.

"She has told the horses that the danger is gone and that it is safe to return," Jessan replied.

"Will it work?"

Jessan pointed.

The horses came trotting down the road, coming from opposite directions. They went straight to Grandmother Pecwae, nuzzling her and nibbling playfully at her hair.

As soon as his horse was at hand, Ulaf mounted and turned to head back in the direction of the crossroad.

Jessan caught hold of the bridle. "You're in no condition to ride, my friend. You're half-frozen, as it is."

"I don't have much choice," Ulaf said. "I have to locate Klendist and see where he enters that rogue Portal. It's the only way to reach Baron Shadamehr in time to warn him that if he takes the Sovereign Stone to Old Vinnengael, he could be walking into a trap."

"Eh?" Wolfram looked up, startled. "What did you say about a trap?"

"I overheard one of the Vrykyl, the one known as Shakur, talking to a mercenary in the pay of Dagnarus," Ulaf explained. "He said that the Dominion Lords carrying the pieces of the Sovereign Stone were told to take them to Old Vinnengael. According to Shakur, they're walking into a trap set for them by Dagnarus." A thought came to Ulaf. He eyed the dwarf with sudden, keen interest. "Why do you ask?"

"No reason," said Wolfram. Shoving his hands in his pockets, he turned away.

Ulaf looked at him in concern, but he was in a hurry. He couldn't stay to discuss the matter further. The dwarf wasn't likely to tell him anything anyway.

"The gods go with you," Ulaf said.

His blessing went to all of them, but his gaze lingered longest on Wolfram, who met it stubbornly.

Ulaf kicked his horse's flanks and galloped down the road.

Wolfram watched him go, gnawed his lip.

"We should be going," said Jessan. "I don't like the feel of this place."

"The Void is very strong," Ranessa agreed. "Where are you going, Nephew?" she asked diffidently.

"Home," said Jessan shortly. He found he could not look at her. It seemed very right, that she should be a dragon. They had always known something was wrong with her as a human. But he still was having trouble understanding.

"The way back to Trevinici lands is long and dangerous," Ranessa said. "I know. I rode it with the dwarf."

She shook her hair out of her face, made her pronouncement. "I will take you, Nephew, and the Grandmother and the body of Bashae back to the lands of the Trevinici."

Jessan looked startled, then dismayed. "No, Aunt—"

"We agree," stated the Grandmother. "The plan is a good one."

"Grandmother," said Jessan. "You don't understand."

"I do understand," said the Grandmother irritably. "I'm old. I'm not stupid. She is a dragon, and she's going to fly us back to our home. A home that may not be where we left it," she added, cocking a bright eye at him. "Did you think of that? What if the tribe has picked up and moved? How will we find them? It would be much easier if we had wings. She"—the Grandmother pointed at Ranessa—"gives us wings.

"I lost the stick, Jessan," the Grandmother said with a little tremor in her voice. "I had to leave it behind. I don't have any way to see the evil now. We should go with Ranessa. She wants to do this for you. She wants to make things right."

"Ranessa is a good soul, lad," Wolfram added. "You can trust her with your life. I've done that, and I've had no reason to regret it."

"You want to go home, don't you, Jessan?" the Grandmother urged softly.

"Yes," said Jessan. "More than anything else, I want to go home."

"Very well, then," said Ranessa. "No more discussion. Jessan, you and the Grandmother—"

"And Fenella," the Grandmother chimed in. "She's coming with us."

"Out of the question," said Wolfram firmly. "Fenella is a dwarf. She belongs with her people."

"How will she travel there? Will you take her?"

Wolfram was caught. He scratched his chin in perplexity. He couldn't take Fenella to Old Vinnengael. And he couldn't very well haul the child all the way back to Saumel.

"It's just . . . Well, I thought maybe I could . . ."

"Were her people good to her?" the Grandmother asked.

Fenella held fast to the Grandmother's hand, her dark eyes fixed on Wolfram. He thought of the shrine, that was now empty. He thought of the Children of Dunner and the child no one had missed. He thought back to two other children, himself and Gilda, alone in the world, except for each other.

"It's up to you, Fenella," Wolfram said. "Where do you want to go, child? Do you want go back to your homeland? Or would you like to live with the Grandmother and her people?"

"Will you be coming back to Saumel, Wolfram?" Fenella asked. "Will the Sovereign Stone?"

"I don't know, Fenella," Wolfram told her honestly. "I can't answer that."

"I would like to be a Dominion Lord someday," Fenella said. "But, until then, I think I would like to go with the Grandmother. I can always go back home, can't I?"

"Yes," Wolfram said. "You can always go back home."

They picked up Bashae's body in its soft cocoon, removed it from the litter. Jessan and the Grandmother and Fenella began to make the body ready for the continuation of its journey.

Wolfram watched for a while. It was time for him to leave, but he was suddenly reluctant to do so. It had been a long time since he'd traveled alone.

He walked over to Ranessa, who stood staring up into the stars as though she could not wait to be among them.

"I'll miss you, girl," he said. "I wish you were coming with me."

"I have an obligation." She glanced over at Jessan. "They were good to me. I didn't do much to deserve it."

"It wasn't your fault."

Ranessa smiled the ghost of a smile. "Even as a dragon, I could have been kinder, I think. Still"—she shrugged—"what's done is done. I will take them to their land and help them find their people. It's the least I can do."

"Where will you go after that?" Wolfram asked, an aching in his heart.

"I need to be on my own for a while," Ranessa answered. "Maybe a long while. Dragons are solitary beings, Wolfram."

"So are dwarves," he answered. "Some of them."

"Then come and find me someday," Ranessa said with a sudden, dazzling smile. "We will be solitary together."

"I'll do that," he promised.

Ranessa leaned down, gave Wolfram a swift, hard kiss on the cheek, a kiss that burned like the touch of flame. She turned away from him, spread her arms and flung back her head. An expression of joy suffused her face, and the dragon's face, the dragon's wings, the dragon's body shone in the moonlight.

"Hurry up, Nephew!" she commanded. "We don't have much moonlight left."

Jessan began to lash the pecwae's cocoon onto the dragon's spiky mane.

"I'm sorry about Bashae," Wolfram said.

"He died a hero," said Jessan. "Not many pecwae can say that."

No, thought Wolfram. And I doubt many would want to. He remained politely silent, however.

"My people will take good care of the dwarven child," said Jessan, adding in a low voice, "I will see to it that she is not raised by pecwae."

"Thank you," said Wolfram, hiding his smile. "It was good seeing you again, Jessan. Or maybe I shouldn't call you that now. Did you find your adult name?"

"That will be up to the elders to decide," said Jessan. "But, yes, I found it." He paused a moment, then added somberly, "It wasn't what I expected."

"It never is," said Wolfram.

Jessan nodded. He lifted the Grandmother to the dragon's back, hoisted up Fenella to sit beside her. He climbed up onto the dragon, settled himself between the wings.

Putting one strong arm protectively around both the Grandmother and Fenella, Jessan grasped the dragon's mane with the other. "We're ready—" He paused, looked back at the dwarf, and smiled ruefully. "We're ready, Aunt Ranessa."

Spreading her wings, the dragon dug in with her powerful hind legs, then leapt into the air.

"Good-bye, Wolfram!" Ranessa called out as she soared toward the stars.

"Good-bye, girl," Wolfram said softly.

BOOK
III

SHADAMEHR HAD THE SENSATION OF BEING A CHILD AGAIN, BEING rocked to sleep in his cradle. He might have enjoyed it, except that for some strange reason, his mother kept flinging cold water into the bottom of his cradle, water that was continually sloshing back and forth. And as if that wasn't bad enough, she covered him with a blanket made of fish.

He tried repeatedly to wake up to complain about this rude treatment, and sometimes he managed to do so. He would wake up just enough to be able to drink water that tasted of fish, eat fish that tasted of fish, and when he was starting to think he was sufficiently awake to sort things out, he would sink back to sleep in the waterlogged cradle.

Shadamehr had no idea how long this lasted. Day blurred into night and back to day again. His sleep was dreamless and peaceful, except for the sloshing water and the smell of fish. No one hurt him. Indeed, they were very protective of him. Just like his mother. Despite that, he felt resentment start to grow inside him, and one day when he had been hoisted out of the bottom of the cradle and carried onto dry land, Shadamehr stared at a cup of water they shoved into his hand and tossed it away.

"No," he said groggily. "I won't stand for this."

His words came out sounding as if they'd been mixed with mush, but apparently the orks understood, for one of them ran off to report. The Captain appeared. She stood over him, glared down at him. Shadamehr roused himself, looked up at her. She seemed to swell in his vision, then recede and swell again, and he spent a few moments blinking until she settled down.

"Whash going on?" he demanded. His tongue felt as if it had got into the wrong mouth.

"You have been asleep for six days. How do you feel?" the Captain asked.

He gave her question a moment's thought. "Well rested," he answered.

The Captain laughed heartily.

The boat had been beached on the bank of a wide, sluggishly flowing river, where willow trees dropped dead yellow leaves into the water. One ork stood guard over the boat. Other orks were fishing or cooking fish. The air was chill. The winter sun shone overhead, danced off the water. Damra lay beside him, slumbering soundly.

"Is Damra all right?" Shadamehr asked.

"She is well," said the Captain. "She sleeps, that is all. We have fed her and given her water. Do not worry."

Shadamehr cudgeled his weary brain, forced himself to try to think. Damra was there, but others were missing. He started to remember.

"Alise and Griffith," he said. "Are they safe?"

"Your fire-haired woman and the elven omen-maker? I left them behind." The Captain chuckled. "I have no need for bad omens on this trip."

Shadamehr winced. "You knew the truth about that?"

"Of course!" The Captain was disdainful. "A shaman who can't tell a god-given omen from an omen made by an elf wouldn't be much of a shaman."

"Why did you go along with it, then?" Shadamehr asked. "Why order the ships to leave?"

"It suited my plans," said the Captain.

One of the orks shouted something. The Captain waved her hand.

"We have to go." She pointed at the fish. "Eat your meal. You will grow weak otherwise. Even in sleep, your body requires food."

"Where are we going?" Shadamehr asked.

He heard chanting and began to feel drowsy. They were casting a spell on him. He fought against it, but it was no use.

The Captain took the food from his limp hands. The last words he heard were those of the Captain.

"You know where," she said.

Again the enforced slumber, the smell of fish, the water sloshing around him in the boat, as he lay at the bottom, covered in an oil-slick tarp. Again the passage of time, slipping past him like the river water, the waking and wondering and eating, all ending with the sounds of chanting. The Captain did not speak to him again, and the other orks stared at him with blank expressions when he demanded answers.

Then the motion of the boat ceased. Strong hands grabbed hold of him. A muscular ork flung him over his shoulder. Once he got Shadamehr properly settled, the ork wrapped an enormous arm around Shadamehr's legs and carried him off as if he were an obstreperous child being hauled away to bed.

His head and arms hanging down behind the ork, Shadamehr could see nothing except orken behind. His brain was still sleep-fogged, and he drifted in and out of consciousness. But the next time he awoke, he awoke fully, without the horrible sensation that someone had stuffed his head full of goose feathers.

He sat up. His hands and feet were securely bound, but, checking himself over, he found that otherwise he appeared to be in good condition.

"About time," came a deep voice from the darkness, speaking Elderspeak. "I'm sick and tired of listening to you snore."

"I don't snore," Shadamehr returned with dignity, then added, "I wonder why it is we always deny that we snore. One would think it was some kind of terrible malady, like the plague."

"Who cares?" the voice said irritably. "Who are you, anyway?"

Shadamehr didn't immediately answer, for a rock was jabbing him uncomfortably in his posterior. He scooted his body into a more comfortable position and looked about. As near as he could make out, he was in a cave. Sunlight streamed in from a large opening about ten paces distant. Outside, he could hear the crash of rushing water—a far different sound than the gentle rippling of the placidly flowing river.

Hearing a groan and a sigh, he wriggled around and saw Damra lying next to him. Her hands and feet were bound like his.

"How very extraordinary," Shadamehr said. "Her magical armor should have protected her. Strange. Very strange."

He wiggled his hands experimentally. Finding that the knots were secure, he gave a shrug. He wasn't going anywhere, not for a while at least.

"I said—who are you?" repeated the voice belligerently.

"Are you a prisoner?" Shadamehr asked.

"No, I'm here for my health!" the voice snapped.

As Shadamehr's eyes adjusted, he could eventually make out a short, squat figure, trussed up with ropes around his arms and legs, sitting with his back against the rock wall. Shadamehr could see nothing of the face, except a pair of eyes that gleamed with indignation.

"You're a dwarf!" said Shadamehr.

"What has that got to do with anything?" the dwarf demanded.

"Look, I'll tell you my name. It's Shadamehr. I was formerly Baron Shadamehr, but now I'm landless, pfenningless Shadamehr. I'd shake hands, but I'm rather incapacitated at the moment."

"I've heard of you," said the dwarf.

"Good things, I hope?"

"I'm trying to remember." A pause, then the dwarf said grudgingly, "The name is Wolfram."

"By the gods!" Shadamehr gasped in astonishment. "I've heard of you myself!"

Something clicked in Shadamehr's mind, like the inner workings of a water clock. It was only a trickle of thought, but enough to start the mechanism moving. He had the feeling that something had clicked for Wolfram, too, for he grew a shade less distrustful.

"Do you know a Vinnengaelean named Ulaf?"

"Do you know a Trevinici named Jessan and a pecwae named Bashae?"

Damra sat up, stared down at her bonds in perplexity. "What has been going on?"

"I was wondering that myself," said Shadamehr. "Your magical armor should have acted to protect you."

"What magical armor?" Wolfram asked suspiciously.

"Who is that?" Damra asked, just as suspicious.

"For that matter, who are you?"

"Damra, this is Wolfram, who was with Lord Gustav when he died, according to Bashae. Wolfram, this is Damra, the person Bashae gave the Stone to. It seems we have come full circle," said Shadamehr. "I know how we got here, Wolfram. The orks brought us. How did you come to be here? Did the orks bring you?"

Wolfram hemmed and hawed a great deal, but eventually his story came out.

"So you ran into Shakur. You travel in exalted company, Wolfram," said Shadamehr.

"And you are lucky to be alive with your soul intact," said Damra.

"Your friend, Ulaf, is looking for you, Baron. He had a message for you."

"We'll get to that later. When did all this happen?" Shadamehr asked.

"Not long ago," said the dwarf evasively.

"If we are where I think we are," said Shadamehr, "Mardurar is a far piece from here."

"If you must know, there's a rogue Portal in the Meffeld Pass," said Wolfram. "I took it. I'm in a hurry, you see. I inherited a manor house in the north—"

"From Lord Gustav," said Damra.

"Never mind Lord Gustav," Wolfram growled. "I was on my way to my manor house. I walked out of the Portal and the next thing I know, a shadow comes alive and looms up in front of me. Then the sun falls from the sky and gives me a blip on the noggin that knocks me cold. And that shouldn't have happened, because—" He halted, clamped his mouth shut.

"Because . . ." Shadamehr prompted.

Wolfram remained silent.

"Because your magical armor should have protected you," said Shadamehr. "Just as Damra's should have protected her."

"What magical armor?" Wolfram groused. "I don't know what you're talking about."

"I'm afraid I don't either," said Damra.

"He is a Dominion Lord," said Shadamehr. "He carries the dwarven portion of the Sovereign Stone. And he's not going to his manor house. He's going to Old Vinnengael."

Wolfram's jaw dropped so that they could practically hear it thunk on the cavern floor.

"Here, now," he said suspiciously. "How do you know all this?"

"Because I carry the human portion of the Sovereign Stone," said Shadamehr. "And Damra of Gwyenoc carries the elven portion. And, unless I am much mistaken," he added, as the Captain of Captains entered the cave, "the fourth part of the Stone is with us as well."

Reaching beneath her shirt and the leather, fur-lined vest she wore over it, the Captain of Captains drew out a silver chain from which hung suspended a jewel, smooth-sided, triangular in shape.

"You told us that the Sovereign Stone was inside Mount Sa 'Gra," said Damra.

"I lied." The Captain shrugged. "But there was a second full moon that month when I said it."

"A lie told under the second full moon in the same month doesn't count as a lie," Shadamehr explained.

"Besides," the Captain continued, her voice hardening, "there was a reason for the falsehood. We discovered that an evil creature, one we call a Soul-stealer, seeks our Sovereign Stone. He thinks it is in Mount Sa 'Gra. He searches for it there. Not here." She thrust the stone back into her breast.

"What's a Soul-stealer?" Wolfram asked, puzzled.

"A Vrykyl," said Shadamehr. The mental waterwheel was turning very fast now. "Dagnarus sent one of his Vrykyl to take the form of an ork to try to steal their Stone."

"But why spellbind and tie us up and make us prisoners?" Damra demanded. "Why bring us here to this cave?"

"I know the answer!" Shadamehr cried, wriggling in excitement, as pleased with himself as any brown-nosing schoolboy. "You had to drug us to separate us from Alise and Griffith. A very wise idea. I had that part figured out. The spellbinding took me a bit longer, but I've solved that, too. You had to keep us spellbound because the person who is behind this was afraid we would try to escape before he could meet us and explain it to us. Right so far?"

The Captain nodded. Summoning two orks, she told them to untie the captive's bonds.

"You had to keep us tied up in the cave," said Shadamehr, wincing and flexing his fingers as the circulation started to return to his hands, "because you were afraid that in our groggy condition, we would wander out and tumble into the Orken Gorge which is where we are. Right?"

"We had to secure the boat," said the Captain.

"Of course you did!" said Shadamehr. "Which meant you had to leave us alone. And you treated our friend Wolfram here in such a rude fashion because the person behind this wants all four bearers of the Sovereign Stone to make this journey together. Am I right again?"

"But the dwarf said that he was stopped by a 'shadow come to life,' " argued Damra, "and struck over the head 'by the sun falling from the sky.' "

"And so I was," Wolfram stated, still wrathful.

"I think I can answer that, too," said Shadamehr. "There is your sun."

He pointed to the orken Captain.

In response, she clasped hold of a medallion she wore on the same chain as the Sovereign Stone. Silver armor flowed over her body. A silver helm, in the form of a dolphin leaping from the waves, adorned her head. Standing in the sunlight in the cavern opening, the orken Dominion Lord did look very much like the sun come to Earth.

"And here is your shadow," Shadamehr added.

An elf, clad all in black, slipped silently into the cavern. Coming to stand beside the ork, he bowed to the group.

"Silwyth," said Damra, understanding at last.

"One night," said the Captain, "as I was out for an afternoon's fishing in my boat, a strange sleepiness overcame me. I dreamed that a human came to me. He said his name was Gareth, and he told me that I must take the orken portion of the Sovereign Stone to Old Vinnengael. The time had come for the oath-breakers to make good the vow that they had taken long ago.

"When I awoke, I went back to shore. I summoned the shamans and told them of my dream. I asked them to perform the omens to see if I should obey this human's command. A strange thing happened. None had seen the like before. The omens were good and bad—both at the same time.

"What did it mean? What was I to do? Who could explain it? My shamans tried." The Captain made a contemptuous gesture. "Those with the good omen said I must go or all would be lost. Those with the bad omen said I must not go, for if I did, all would be lost. The shamans actually came to blows over the matter.

"My great-grandfather was the Captain of Captains who received the Sovereign Stone from King Tamaros. He was the oath-breaker. The orks fell on hard times after that. My great-grandfather came to believe that he had brought bad luck to us because he broke the oath. Our sacred mountain has been taken from us. Many thousands of our people are enslaved. It is time to fulfill the oath and return the Stone. That was what I thought. Yet, what of the bad omens?

"Perplexed over what to do, I went out again in my boat, hoping to find the human in my dream. While I was waiting to fall asleep, I passed the time fishing. I caught nothing. That was very strange, for I am always lucky with my fishing. I began to fear that the gods had turned their backs on me. I cast out my net one last time and that time I caught something."

The Captain pointed. She pointed at Silwyth. "I caught an elf."

"I don't believe it," Damra muttered. "Not even of him."

"But don't you see how clever this is?" Shadamehr murmured.

"Oh, he is very clever," Damra returned.

"The stories of Dunner tell about this one," said Wolfram, joining their conversation. "Silwyth the Serpent, Dunner called him. He claimed it was this Silwyth who lured the young prince to ruin."

"He's watching us," Damra warned. "Look at his expression. Smug, knowing. As if he could hear every word we were saying about him."

It was hard to find any expression amidst the etchings of time that crisscrossed the elf's leathery skin. His dark eyes were on them, and they glittered with what might have been smugness or might have been amusement or might have even been malice. It was hard to tell.

"You still don't trust him?" asked Shadamehr.

"I don't know," Damra replied, troubled. "I just don't know."

The Captain halted her tale, eyed them grimly, waiting for them to be silent.

"Sorry," said Shadamehr in meek tones. "Didn't mean to interrupt. Please go on."

"The elf came up with my net, dripping water," the Captain continued. "He said that the gods had sent him and that he came about the Sovereign Stone. I told him about the two differing omens, and he was able to explain them."

"I'll bet he was," said Damra.

Shadamehr nudged her to be silent.

"The omens meant that taking the Sovereign Stone to Old Vinnengael would be both good for the orks and bad. But that the good outweighed the bad. Which was right," the Captain added. "The shaman with the good omen decked the shaman with the bad one. I decided to take the Stone to Old Vinnengael and fulfill my great-grandfather's oath.

"The elf told me that I should travel up the Darkstream River. I planned to do that, but the sons-of-hop-toads in Krammes refused to give my ship passage—"

"And so you attacked them!" said Shadamehr.

"I did, indeed," said the Captain, her face brightening as she remembered the battle. "Then Kal-Gah came along and told me of his passengers and that they were humans and elves fleeing this Lord Dagnarus in New Vinnengael. The elf had told me that humans and elves and dwarves would all be making the same journey and that it would be wise if we traveled together. When I heard what Kal-Gah had to say, I consulted the omens, and they were good. I found out that you were the bearers of the Sovereign Stone, and I decided to bring you along with me.

"I didn't know about the dwarf," the Captain added, with a nod for Wolfram. "The elf came to me this morning and told me that he needed my help in fetching the last part of the Sovereign Stone. He said that it was being carried by a dwarven Dominion Lord and that only another Dominion Lord could persuade him. That was how you came to be here, dwarf."

Wolfram rubbed his bruised head. "You call that knock persuasion?"

"I didn't have time for a discussion," said the Captain imperturbably. "The river rage was coming."

Wolfram grunted, rubbed his head, then his chin. His gaze, lowering and speculative, went around the group. Outside the cavern came the sound of what the orks called "the river rage" thundering through the gorge.

"I saw the river rage once," said Shadamehr. "A magnificent sight. Unless you're a boat that happens to be caught in it. The water boils and churns as the river rushes headlong to the sea. Twice a day, though, the rage calms, as the tidewaters neutralize the flow. At that time, the river is navigable. Which means we are stuck here until the water settles down again," said Shadamehr. "What is everyone thinking?"

"That Griffith should be with me," stated Damra, accusingly.

"He is not a Dominion Lord," said Silwyth calmly. "Old Vinnengael would mean his death."

Damra looked at him. Then she glanced at Shadamehr. Then looked away.

Shadamehr, for once, had nothing to say.

Uneasy silence fell, then Wolfram spoke, his voice so low that they could barely hear him over the crashing water.

"Your Vinnengalean friend said it was a trap."

"What?" Shadamehr asked, his head jerking up. "My friend? Do you mean Ulaf?"

"That's why he wanted to find you," said Wolfram. "He said that he overheard the Vrykyl talking to a mercenary. The Vrykyl said that Dagnarus is setting a trap for the bearers of the Sovereign Stone, a trap in Old Vinnengael."

"Yet you were headed there anyway," said Shadamehr.

"The person who told me to take the Stone there would never lead me into a trap," said Wolfram firmly.

"But it is a trap," said Silwyth. "A trap within a trap within a trap. The hunter tethers the goat to lure the lion. The lion stalks the hunter. The hungry dragon watches them all."

"Why do I get the feeling we're the goat?" Shadamehr said beneath his breath.

"Were you planning to tell us this?" Damra demanded.

"You already knew, Damra of Gwyenoc," said Silwyth. "You didn't need me to tell you."

Outside, the sound of the churning water began to diminish.

The Captain listened, then rose to her feet. "The river rage has nearly run its course. We must be on our way before it starts again. Those who are going to Old Vinnengael, meet me at the water's edge."

Walking out of the cavern, she began bellowing orders to her crew.

Wolfram rose, cast a defiant glance at the others.

"I'm going. If I have to go alone, I'm going."

He stalked out of the cavern.

Damra stood up.

"I will go," she said. "You are right, Silwyth. I have known all along it was a trap. So sings the minstrel about the faithless lover, 'She has my trust, whom I have never trusted.' "

"May the Father and Mother walk with you, Damra of Gwyenoc," said Silwyth.

"I would say the same prayer for you, Silwyth of House Kinnoth," said Damra gravely, "but I do not know if that would be a blessing or a curse."

She walked out of the cave.

"I'll go," said Shadamehr, slapping his knees and standing up. "I've got nothing better to do—"

He halted, staring. Only a moment before, Silwyth had been sitting calmly on a boulder. Now he stood in front of the cavern's entrance, his staff held before him horizontally, so that the way was barred.

"Here, now. What's the meaning of this?" Shadamehr asked playfully.

"You may not go, Baron Shadamehr," said Silwyth. "You are not a Dominion Lord."

"Oh, for the love of—" Shadamehr bit off the words. He regarded the elf in exasperation. "I have the human portion of the Sovereign Stone. If I don't go, who will?"

Silwyth shook his head. "You do not have the sanction of the gods. You do not have the blessed armor. Without that, you will not withstand the perils of Old Vinnengael. You will die, and the doom of the mission will be assured."

"So what am I supposed to do? Ride back to New Vinnengael and ask Dagnarus to make me a Dominion Lord? Should I do that before or after he has me assassinated? I've made it this far in my life without the benefit of the gods' blessing," Shadamehr went on, his anger rising. "I've fought bahk and dragons, trolls and giants, klobbers and blueroots and Void-spawn and I have overcome them all—"

"All but one," said Silwyth.

"And what is that one?" Shadamehr challenged.

"You know your foe," said Silwyth. "You have met him in the lists many times, and always he has defeated you."

Shadamehr stood glowering, his jaunty mockery gone.

"Think of your comrades," said Silwyth, glancing over his shoulder at the other Dominion Lords. "They will do what they can to protect you, but at great cost to themselves and to the mission."

"I don't want their help," said Shadamehr shortly. "I don't need it."

Silwyth smiled. "Your foe is here now, if you would care to do battle."

"The Void take you!" said Shadamehr.

Knocking aside the elf's staff, he stalked out of the cavern.

LEAVING THE CAVE, SHADAMEHR DID NOT LOOK AT THE DOMINION Lords. He turned his back on them to climb up the rocks and boulders that lay at the foot of the steep gorge through which ran the Darkstream River.

"He is a good man with a good heart," said Damra to Silwyth, both watching Shadamehr as he slipped and stumbled among the rocks. "Once I faulted him for refusing to become a Dominion Lord. I thought him a coward or perhaps one who wanted only to make a mockery of us. Now I have come to know him, and I understand his reasons."

"He does not even understand his reasons," countered Silwyth, his gaze fixed on the solitary figure. "And there are not so many men of good heart in this world that I would lose one for lack of trying."

"You truly believe he would perish?" Damra asked.

"I know he would perish, Damra of Gwyenoc," Silwyth replied.

"I have heard many rumors of the perils to be found in Old Vinnengael. But that is all they are—rumors. Have you been there?"

"I have," said Silwyth.

"And you survived," she returned coolly. "Yet you are not a Dominion Lord."

"I survived because I knew them," said Silwyth softly. "And they knew me."

"Who knew you?" Damra wondered, puzzled.

"The dead," Silwyth replied.

Chilled, Damra stared at him. "Void magic?"

"All manner of magicks swirl about the ruins of that once proud city," Silwyth said. "You must be prepared for them, or they will drag you down to death and worse. The gods' blessing is your lifeline; it will keep you afloat."

"Will you be coming with us?" she asked abruptly.

"I will meet you there," Silwyth replied. "This news the dwarf brought about a trap troubles me. I must see what Shakur is up to. And so, farewell, Damra of Gwyenoc, until we meet again."

"Tell me this, Silwyth," Damra said, halting him. "If we bring the four parts of the Sovereign Stone into the Portal of the Gods, will all this end? Will our homeland be safe?"

"Ask the orks," said Silwyth with a sly smile. "They have seen the omens."

Damra turned to look down at river's edge, where the orks had gathered around the boat. They were in deep discussion, some gesturing up the river, others shaking their heads and pointing back down.

"Silwyth—" Damra turned back, only to find that he had gone.

She made a halfhearted search, not truly expecting to find him among the jumble of boulders and the scrub trees that clung perilously to the sides of the gorge. She thought of his dire warnings, of the peril of her people. The gloom of her dark musings threatened to overwhelm her. From below came the voices of the orks raised in argument. Above her, Shadamehr sat alone on a large outcropping of rock, tossing pebbles down the side of the cliff.

Damra began to climb.

"Would you like some company?" Damra asked.

Shadamehr squinted up at her, shading his eyes from the westering sun. "If by company, you mean yours, yes, I would be grateful." He tossed a handful of pebbles down the cliffside, watched them go bounding and clattering among the rocks. "The company *I've* been keeping is abysmal."

"And what company would that be?" Damra asked, smiling.

He slid to one side to make room for her. She sat down next to him, picked up a handful of pebbles, and began to toss them one at a time down at the water.

"My foe," he said with a rueful smile. "The foe I cannot defeat."

He flung the pebbles away from him with a curse and sat with his elbows on his knees, his head bowed.

"Alise nearly died trying to save my life when the Vrykyl stabbed me," he said, his voice muffled. "Did you know that?"

"No," said Damra. "Neither of you ever spoke of it."

"I wouldn't now," said Shadamehr, a shiver raising the hair on his arms, "except that it has something to do with what I've been thinking. When I regained consciousness, I saw her lying half-dead next to me, her face and body a mass of oozing sores from the Void. She had saved me—unworthy beast that I am—and I couldn't do anything to save her. Just like I couldn't do anything to save Bashae. I told myself then that if I'd been a Dominion Lord, both of them would be alive and well. None of this would have happened."

"It is folly to think like that," Damra said gravely. "If you had taken the path of a Dominion Lord, who knows where it would have led you? Perhaps far from where you were needed."

"Perhaps," Shadamehr said, though he sounded dubious. "Anyway, that's what I believed—that I should have been a Dominion Lord. I thought I had missed the chance. I regretted it, certainly, but—"

"But . . ." Damra said, gently prodding.

"But apparently not enough." He didn't look at her. He stared, frowning, down at his boots.

"Why do you say that?"

"Because I'm being given another chance."

"And . . ."

"And I'm not taking it." Shadamehr sighed, grimaced. "I stink of fish."

"We all do," said Damra.

"I was thinking of taking a dip in the river. Want to join me?"

"So why won't you become a Dominion Lord?" Damra asked. "You've given me reasons before now, but those are reasons you've been making up to fool yourself."

"How very astute you are," said Shadamehr admiringly. "You and Silwyth. I didn't know I was making up reasons. Not until just a few moments ago. And here you knew all along."

"What conclusion did you come to?"

"It's not very pretty," he warned.

"I think I can stand it," she said, smiling.

He paused, then took a deep breath, as if he were about to leap into the river below. He let his breath out slowly, then said, "I don't like having to say 'thank you.' "

Damra stared at him.

"It's very simple," he said with a shrug. "I'm supposed to say 'Thank you, gods' whenever they step in to save my silly neck. Well, I won't do it. I don't want them stepping into my life. I'm in control of my own destiny, and, while I admit that I've pretty much made a hash of it, it's my hash. I made it; I'm the one who has to choke it down. It's not someone else's hash, if you take my meaning.

"And there's another thing," he said, frowning, in deadly earnest. "If I'm attacked by a thug in an alleyway, I don't want to find myself covered head to toe in fancy armor, looking like the Lord of Silver-plated Teapots. I want to be able to deal with the wretch myself—man to man, human to human, human to ork or dwarf or elf. I don't want to lose control of my life," he concluded with finality. "And I don't want to lose my humanity."

"I see," said Damra coolly.

"Oh, blast!" He swore, suddenly stricken with guilt. "I didn't mean that you had lost control of your life. You and your gods have an understanding. Me and my gods—we don't."

He took hold of her hand and pressed it to his lips. Keeping fast hold of her fingers, he looked at Damra intently.

"I am the bearer of the Sovereign Stone. I may not have been the chosen bearer, but I have accepted the burden, and I will carry it faithfully to the end, as I promised Bashae. Whatever courage and brains and skill and luck I've got, they're all at your disposal. I can be nothing more than I am, but everything I am—my life and my honor—I dedicate to you and to the others and to the sacred cause that brings us together."

He kissed her hand again, then stood up.

"I think I will take that bath." He started picking his way among the rocks.

Something glittering caught Damra's eye. She reached down among the pebbles he'd been tossing.

"Shadamehr," she said. "You dropped this."

He came back. "What is it?"

And then he saw what it was. He froze, did not touch it.

"I found this, as well," Damra said. "I think it goes with it." She held up a strip of paper. "There's writing on it."

She read the words, that were in Elderspeak.

"Lord of Seeking."

Shadamehr reached down, slowly, and took from her hand the holy medallion of a Dominion Lord. "I don't understand. What about the Transfiguration—turning to stone, dying to be reborn . . ."

"You did die," Damra said mildly. "You just told me. Alise brought you back."

"Alise . . . not the gods."

"What are the gods, if not love?"

Shadamehr stared at the medallion for a long time, undecided, then, with a shrug and a sigh, he thrust the medallion into a pocket of his breeches.

"Lord of Seeking," he said ruefully. "I guess it beats Lord of Silver-plated Teapots. Thank you, Damra. Thank you very much."

"There now," said Damra, "that wasn't so hard."

JOINING THE OTHERS AT THE WATER'S EDGE, SHADAMEHR SILENTLY and without comment showed them the blessed medallion that marked him a Dominion Lord. Wolfram scratched his chin, twitched an eyebrow. The Captain grunted, as if this were something she'd expected all along, and went back to haranguing her crew for some infraction regarding the boat.

"Feel any different?" Damra asked.

"No," he said bluntly. He tried to put the medallion around his neck. His fingers fumbled at the clasp. "I can't latch this damn thing!"

"Let me," said Damra. Her own medallion had no clasp. The gods themselves had placed it around her neck.

The Lord of Seeking. His way would never be smooth, but that was as he had chosen.

"There you are," she said, patting the chain.

"It itches," he muttered.

"You'll get used to it."

He said nothing, but only rolled his eyes.

"Hold this a moment."

He handed her the knapsack, then leapt off the rocks into the river, landing with a splash that soaked those standing on the bank. He bobbed back the surface, puffing and blowing and treading water.

The orks grinned. Wolfram snorted in disgust. He had little use for water, either for bathing or drinking.

"Is it cold?" Damra called.

"Yes," said Shadamehr, his teeth chattering and his lips turning blue.

He dived beneath the surface, came up snorting, then crawled out onto the bank. He gave himself a luxurious shake, like a dog. Wolfram drew back, scowling and wiping water off his shirt.

"Humans," muttered the Captain of Captains. "They're all mad. No wonder the omens were bad."

She gestured at the boat. "Get in."

One of the orks, still grinning, handed Shadamehr a blanket to use to towel himself down. The others climbed into the boat. The orken rowers took their places. The Captain entered last, manned the rudder.

Damra handed Shadamehr the knapsack. He took it, slung his arm through the straps. He noticed that it felt it different. Heavier than usual. Suspecting Damra of playing a joke on him, Shadamehr opened the sack, expecting to find a rock inside.

The sunlight gleamed on the crystal-smooth sides of the Sovereign Stone.

Shadamehr stared in wonder at the sparkling jewel.

"Maybe I do feel a little different," he said softly. He took it out, held it up to the light.

The jewel was beautiful, remarkable. The stone was heavy in Shadamehr's hands, far heavier than it should have been, to judge by its size. The edges were sharp, so that he was wary of touching them, lest they cut him. The sides were smooth, so that he delighted in running his fingers over them. The stone was cold to the touch, yet warmed as he held it.

He searched for his reflection in the crystalline surface, but could not see himself. Yet, it seemed, he could see the eyes of millions. Turning the stone one way, he could see through the clear crystal to the rocks and water and clouds and the flickering flames of their fire and they were all magnified in his sight, each one close to him. Turning the stone in another direction, all was blurred together, a jumble of grays and greens, blues and orange. He began to understand the mystery of the stone and the wonder of it, and he felt awed and humbled to think that this precious jewel should have come into his hands.

It was as if he held a tiny sliver of the mind of the gods.

"Are they all as beautiful as this?" he asked. "Could I see them?"

One by one, each of the others drew forth the portions of the Sovereign Stone, held them, gleaming, in the sunlight. He knew by their expressions that they all felt his wonder and awe.

"Here's an idea," said Shadamehr suddenly, thrilled and elated. "Let's try putting all the four pieces together!"

The expressions on the faces changed. They were suddenly dark and shadowed, wary and suspicious.

"And who would carry it?" Wolfram demanded. "You, I suppose."

Shadamehr was taken aback. "Why, I don't know. I honestly didn't think of that. I guess . . ."

"No one's carrying my part of the Stone," said Wolfram, his brows lowering.

"I . . . I would not burden anyone with mine," said Damra, her cheeks flushing.

"I carry the ork's portion," said the Captain. "None other."

"I see," Shadamehr said quietly. He dropped the Sovereign Stone into the bottom of the magical knapsack. It vanished from his sight. He felt more secure, now that it was hidden away, but the elation was gone. He was suddenly tired and oppressed.

He climbed into the boat. The others climbed in after, arranging themselves so no one sat near another. They started the trip upriver to Old Vinnengael.

Shadamehr sat by himself, staring into the dark water. He wondered if King Tamaros had also seen the emptiness that was the Stone's heart.

And if so, why hadn't he smashed it into pieces?

Silwyth thought about the Dominion Lords, as night fell. He wondered where they were, wondered if Shadamehr had accepted the gods and vice versa—if the gods had accepted Shadamehr.

Silwyth's thoughts turned from Shadamehr to Shakur and from there to Dagnarus. He wondered what the Lord of the Void was plotting. The mercenary band of which the dwarf had spoken was something new. Silwyth had not figured them into his calculations. Would they disrupt his plans? He needed to find out more about them.

Silwyth made no sound as he walked. He went barefoot, the soles of his feet hard and supple as the finest boot leather.

He had lived so long in the wilderness, lived off it and amid it, that he was part of it. The animals did not stir as he passed. The deer continued to graze. The rabbit slept. The squirrels mistook him for a tree. The snake slid over his foot. The fox hurried past on fox business with never a glance.

Silwyth had seen signs near the Portal that a large band of riders had been in the vicinity. Busy with the Captain and Wolfram, he had lacked the time to investigate. He planned to return to the Portal, pick up Klendist's trail, and follow him. They were all bound for the same place—Old Vinnengael, where he would meet the Dominion Lords. They would need a guide through the ruins, someone who knew the dangers. First, he would deal with this Klendist.

Silwyth came to a shallow stream that flowed among the trees. The stream was lazy, took its time. The water murmured softly to itself as it tripped over rocks and slid beneath willows, its ripples decorated with winter's dead leaves. Silwyth was about to cross the lazy stream when he felt a sudden, strange lethargy seize hold of him.

He sat down on a moss-covered tree stump, suddenly and heavily. The weakness had robbed him of the power to walk. He'd been subject to such attacks before, but never this severe. He knew immediately what was happening.

He was dying.

Silwyth thought of all he had left to do, all that remained undone, unfinished.

"Let me live," he prayed to the Father and Mother. "Just a little longer."

"Lay down your burden," was the answer. "Others will take it up. That is the way of all things."

With a sigh, he let it go.

He sat on the rock and looked at the water, dappled with shadow and sunlight. He saw himself as another of the brown, dried-up leaves, falling onto that rippling surface, carried to the endless sea.

Now that the burden was gone, lethargy brought peace. He was not afraid. He waited for death patiently, as a lover waits for his beloved. The song of the stream, the warmth of the sun made him drowsy. His head fell forward on his breast. He was drifting into the sleep that is the final gift of the Father and Mother, when a shadow fell over him, a shadow cold and empty.

The shadow, the danger, roused him and pulled him back.

Silwyth opened his eyes.

"Lady Valura."

She stood before him in her woman's form, beautiful, young, her skin white and waxen as the petals of the gardenia, her mouth carnelian, her body matchless in its form and grace. The eyes, the empty eyes, stared down at him.

"If you seek revenge, Lady," said Silwyth, "you come too late. I am dying."

"Liar!" She spit the word. Her lips twisted in a sneer. "What have you ever done but lie? You are not capable of speaking the truth!"

"I have never lied to you, Lady Valura," said Silwyth.

She moved closer, watching him warily. He had tricked her before, tricked her and hurt her and humiliated her. She did not trust him, would never trust him, not until she held his chilling body in her arms and sucked his soul into the Void.

Silwyth did not move. In his eyes she saw what she always saw: pity. When he was dead, she would pluck out those eyes.

Valura reached into her bosom and drew out the Blood-knife, the knife made of her own bone.

"You seek to thwart my lord," she said.

"I have done my best," Silwyth replied.

"Why?" she demanded.

"You know why, Lady Valura." He looked up at her, into the empty eyes. Once, long ago, he'd seen in those eyes a lovely garden.

"Dagnarus loves me!" she cried.

"He hates you. He loathes you. He cast you off. He sent you away. He does not want you around him . . ."

She clutched the bone knife, her fingers clenching and unclenching. "He will. When I save him from his peril. When I give him what he has long sought. He will love me. He will! And you will be witness to it. For I will take your body and your soul!"

She stabbed the knife into Silwyth's chest. In her fury, she struck wildly and she missed her target. The knife did not pierce his heart.

Enraged, she jerked it out, held it poised to strike again.

Silwyth saw his own blood glisten on the knife. He saw his blood spattered on the lady's white gown.

"You may steal my body," he said. "But you will not claim my soul. That I have given to the Father . . . and the Mother . . ."

Valura struck again. Her aim was true. She stabbed to the heart.

Her form altered, changed. Valura vanished. Silwyth stood in her place.

His corpse remained seated on the stump, slumped over, blood oozing from the two chest wounds. Valura kicked the corpse, knocked it sideways into the stream. She kicked it again and again, viciously, until at last her rage was spent.

"Curse you!" she said with Silwyth's lips. "Curse you to the Void!"

But that did not happen. He had escaped the fate he deserved. His corpse lay in the stream. The water flowed red with his blood. His dead face stared up at her. In his eyes, the pity.

She had taken his face. His soul had escaped her.

Valura had stabbed a dead man.

ACTING ON K'LET'S ORDERS, THE TAAN TRAVELED EAST. THEY moved rapidly, their strong legs eating up the ground. Their destination was unknown to them.

That K'let had a purpose, none doubted. Taan did nothing without purpose. No moment was ever wasted in frivolity. Even during those rare times when the taan were permitted a day of recreation, their sport consisted of honing the skills of their warriors, the skills that meant their very survival.

Raven continued to lead his tribe of half-taan, a task that was proving extremely difficult. Although K'let had mandated that the taan accept the half-taan as fellow tribesmen, not even the revered kyl-sarnz could force the taan to treat the half-taan with respect. They were shunned and tormented.

K'let had ordered that the half-taan should march with the main body of taan, so that they could be protected. This meant that the half-taan were relegated to the rear of the column, forced to eat the dust of the hundreds of taan ahead of them. The taan had the first pick of camping ground. The half-taan were given the worst. Lately, the taan had taken to raiding the half-taan camp at night, stealing their food, cutting slits in their tents, destroying anything they found.

Raven protested this treatment to Dag-ruk and the other nizam. They laughed at him and jeered. What did he expect? These wretched half-taan could not take care of themselves, could not think for themselves. Even K'let knew that. It was why he had ordered that they march close to their protectors. Half-taan were fit only to serve the wishes of their masters. Raven soon realized that he would never change the mind of the taan. Only the half-taan could do that.

Raven worked with the half-taan, teaching them to use weapons, teaching them fighting tactics, teaching them to think for themselves and respect themselves. The last, the most important, proved the most difficult. Every time a taan walked into their camp, the half-taan cringed and groveled. When Raven berated them, they cringed and groveled before him.

Raven was patient. He had worked with raw recruits during his days with the Dunkargan, and he knew that teaching them self-respect would take time. Fortunately, the taan blood in each of the half-taan ran hot. They were natural-born warriors. And although their half-human bodies lacked the physical power and stamina of the taan, they proved to be quicker and more agile. Every day the half-taan improved with their weapons, and, as they gained confidence in their skills, they began to gain confidence in themselves. Raven only hoped that they managed this before some taan killed them.

Acting on K'let's orders, the taan continued their journey, turning northward. Their destination now had a name, Krul-um-drelt, meaning "City of Ghosts." One of the half-taan told Raven that the human name for the city was Old Vinnengael.

Raven opened his eyes wide on hearing that. The ruins of the city of Old Vinnengael had an evil reputation, not only among his people, but among all peoples he'd ever encountered.

"City of Ghosts," Raven muttered to himself. "K'let will fit right in. I'm not sure about the rest of us."

He tried to find out more about why they were traveling to Old Vinnengael. He spoke to Dag-ruk about it, but if she knew, she would not tell him. She went about openly with the shaman, R'lt, and had proclaimed that she would take him for her mate. Dag-ruk treated Raven only slightly better than a half-taan himself and would deign to speak to him only if she felt like it. Raven redoubled his efforts to train the half-taan in fighting.

The taan were within a day's march of Old Vinnengael when they were ordered to halt and set up camp. K'let had been away from camp for sometime, gone on some mysterious mission. Orders came from Derl, who was in command in K'let's absence. The taan would camp there to await K'let's return.

Raven took advantage of the respite in their constant marching to work with his half-taan. He was pleased with their progress. They were starting to hold their heads up, to look straight ahead instead of constantly staring at the ground. He was so pleased with their advancement in their fighting skills that this day, he sought out Dag-ruk.

"Dur-zor," said Raven, "tell Dag-ruk that I propose a contest between our two tribes."

Dag-ruk burst into laughter. Turning to the taan warriors who had gathered around her, she told them Raven's proposal. The taan hooted and grinned.

"Does she refuse?" Raven asked.

"Of course, Raven," said Dur-zor. "There is no honor for the taan to fight a slave."

"But the half-taan are not slaves," Raven argued. "Not now. K'let has set them free."

Dur-zor looked uneasy.

"What is it?" Raven demanded.

"The taan do not see it that way, Raven," said Dur-zor. She gave him a pleading glance. "I did not want to tell you the truth. You were so pleased with what you were doing."

"Tell me," Raven said grimly.

"The taan believe that K'let gave you all the half-taan as your own slaves."

Raven stared. "Of all the—" He halted, baffled, then said, "Tell them the truth, Dur-zor. Tell them that the half-taan are not my slaves, any more than you are my slave. Tell them that the half-taan are . . . are"—he fumbled for a word—"are my brothers."

"Do you mean that, Raven?" Dur-zor's eyes shone with pleasure.

"Of course I mean it. What do you think I've been doing all these weeks? Training an army of slaves for my own personal protection?"

"No, Raven, of course not," said Dur-zor hastily. "I will tell Dag-ruk."

The nizam was not impressed, however. Her lips curled in a sneer, and she said something that Raven could not understand, then walked off. When Raven asked Dur-zor to translate, Dur-zor would say only that Dag-ruk would not even consider a contest.

As they trudged back to their tribe, Raven was silent and thoughtful. Dur-zor had come to know that look on his face.

"Raven, what are you plotting?" she asked with trepidation.

He glanced at her and smiled. "Am I really so transparent?"

"I do not understand that word, Raven."

"Can you really see through me? Like seeing fish through clear stream water?"

"Oh, yes, Raven," said Dur-zor. Again, noting his look, she said, "Was that the wrong answer?"

He gave a rueful laugh. "We all like to be thought of as mysterious. I guess I'm not. What am I plotting?" His tone grew grim. "We'll have our contest, whether Dag-ruk wants it or not."

Dur-zor sighed deeply, but she took care that Raven did not hear her.

Back in camp, Raven summoned together his half-taan.

"I have been to Dag-ruk, to ask if the taan warriors would compete in a contest with us," Raven announced.

Most of the half-taan looked eager. Some looked startled. Others just looked sick.

"The answer was no. Not only that, but their 'no' was an insult."

He was pleased to see flashes of anger in the eyes of most of the half-taan, and he heard several growl. A few were vastly relieved, but that was only to be expected.

"We're going to shove that 'no' down their throats!" Raven continued, and several of the half-taan grinned and shook their spears. "Tugi, you and Gar-dra and Mok will come hunting with me. We're going to bring down the largest beast we can find and haul it back to camp. Once we've got it, we'll make a fine show of it. We will spread the word among the taan camps that we have strong food for tomorrow night's meal. They will come to our camp to steal it. We will hide in our tents, and when they sneak into camp, we will teach them a lesson."

The half-taan began to grin. One gave a whooping cheer that was silenced at Raven's frown. Only a few appeared fearful. Raven noted these. He'd make sure they were assigned some task that would keep them out of the way, keep them from being harmed. Overall, he was pleased with the response. His half-taan were eager to prove themselves. Thoughts of groveling and cringing were gone.

Raven assembled his hunting party and went out in search of a wild boar that had been sighted in the area. Dur-zor remained in camp, continuing the weapons lessons for those who had yet to fully master the skill. The lessons were accompanied by insults and laughter, as some of the taan warriors came to watch. Taan children threw rocks at them. Dur-zor gritted her teeth and continued on with grim perseverance.

The half-taan killed their boar. Returning to camp, they gutted the animal and hung the meat high in a tree to let the blood drain. They spread the word among the taan that the half-taan would have a fine feast tomorrow. Strong food.

Back in their camp, the half-taan practiced with their weapons and waited eagerly for sundown.

Klendist and his force reached Old Vinnengael at about the same time as the taan, although neither was, for the moment, aware of the other. Klendist rode from the east and made camp south of the ruined city, that was about ten miles distant. The taan were camped about twenty miles to the west. On the morning that Raven asked Dag-ruk about the contest, Klendist formed scouting parties, sending them out to observe the lay of the land. He ordered his men to keep special watch for any small parties, such as this group of Dominion Lords.

The scouts departed. Klendist remained in camp, waiting for Shakur.

The day passed with no sign of the Vrykyl.

Klendist found the wait boring. He had no real idea when to expect Shakur, and the thought came to him that he might be stuck there for days on end without action unless, by some stroke of good fortune, they came across these Dominion Lords.

The scouts returned at sundown with their reports and, at about the same time, Shakur rode into camp. He motioned peremptorily to Klendist to ride with him.

"I see your scouts have returned. What have they found?" Shakur demanded when they were alone.

"A group of bahk have taken up residence outside the ruins of Old Vinnengael," Klendist reported. "My men counted about fifteen of the monsters, but there may be more inside the city."

Shakur eyed him. "That will make no difference to you, Klendist. You have no need to enter the city. Not unless you fail in your assignment."

"We're not going to fail."

"Good. What else?"

"No sign of those Dominion Lords—" Klendist began.

"No, it is early yet."

"But this is a vast area. There are more ways into the ruins than there are holes in a Dunkargan cheese," Klendist stated. "If I had five hundred men, we couldn't begin to cover them all."

"You will not need five hundred men. You probably won't even need five. The Dominion Lords have a guide, who will lead them straight to you."

"Ah, well, that's better," said Klendist. "Who is this guide? We don't want to kill him by mistake."

"Valura is in no danger from the likes of you," Shakur returned coolly. "And you are not to kill anyone."

"Sorry, my mistake. But these are Dominion Lords, Shakur. Powerful warriors who fight with the blessing of the gods. We may not have any choice—"

Shakur's helmed head leaned close.

Klendist was a brute, with a brute's callous courage, but he could not help feeling a clenching in his gut as he stared into those empty eyes and caught a whiff of the rotted flesh beneath the black armor.

"You have a choice, Klendist," Shakur hissed. Drawing out the Blood-knife, he held it in his palm. "This is your choice."

The knife was yellowed with age, stained russet brown with the blood of those whose lives it had drained.

"I understand you, Shakur," said Klendist harshly. "Put that damn thing away."

"See that you do understand me," said Shakur, thrusting the knife back into its sheath. "The Dominion Lords are to be captured alive."

Klendist growled in dissatisfaction. His horse shifted restlessly. "I've been thinking about this. Taking them won't be easy."

"You have war wizards who can deal with them, and Valura will be there to help you." Shakur was fast losing patience. "By the Void, Klendist, there are only four of them! You are two hundred. You can all pile on top of them, if nothing else."

"And what do we do once we have them?" Klendist retorted, undaunted. "They will be difficult to guard. I don't want the responsibility for them."

"You will not have it long, rest assured of that," said Shakur. "His

Lordship is eager to meet with them. Once you have captured them, His Lordship will come retrieve them."

"And he'll pay us?"

"And pay you."

"Very well," said Klendist. "We'll wait until we hear from you. Just out of curiosity, Shakur. While we're dealing with the Dominion Lords, what will you be doing?"

"There is another Vrykyl out there, one who is far more dangerous to my lord than any twelve Dominion Lords. My task is to deal with their rebel."

Klendist gave a whistle. "That powerful, huh? Mind telling me who he is or what he looks like? I wouldn't want to run across him."

"If you did, it wouldn't matter," said Shakur. "Because by the time you figured it out, you would already be dead."

The Vrykyl turned his horse's head, galloped off.

Klendist glowered after him. He remained watching until he was certain that Shakur was gone. Klendist didn't believe this story of a rebel Vrykyl. Shakur was up to something.

"Something private on his own," Klendist muttered. "All that bullshit about dealing with some deadly foe. As if there was any foe a Vrykyl couldn't handle. Well, whoever the rebel is, I wish him luck. I wouldn't mind seeing that Void-cursed monstrosity fall off his high horse."

Returning to the campsite, Klendist found his men in a state of excitement. The last patrol had ridden in, and they came with good news.

"Did you find the Dominion Lords?" Klendist asked, swinging down out of the saddle.

"No, sir, not them," said the scout contemptuously. His face split in a wide grin. "Something better, sir. We found gigs."

"Taan?" Klendist said with interest. "Where? How many?"

"Looks like several tribes of the fiends, sir. They're camped about twenty miles from here, off over there."

He pointed to the west, where the shapes of rolling hills were silhouetted against the twilight.

"How many, do you estimate?"

"Not many, sir. We could take them."

"We figure we could attack them at night, sir," said another. "Catch them off guard."

"Gigs don't like to fight at night, sir," one reminded him.

"They may not like to, but they're still damn good at it," said Klendist. "Did it look like they were expecting trouble?"

"No, sir," said the scout. "They had posted their pickets, but just the usual number. It will be easy enough to shut them up." He drew his finger across his throat.

"We lived with the gigs, Captain," one reminded him. "We endured their stink and their filth for months. Now it's time to get some of our own back. We know their ways. We know where to find their chief's tent, and we know where the big muckety-muck warriors sleep. We can sneak in, take them by surprise."

"We can wipe 'em out, sir. See to it that their little gigs don't grow into big ones."

"By the time they wake up, they'll find our spears in their bellies. What do you say, Captain?"

Klendist was tempted. True, he was working for Shakur, but the Vrykyl himself had said that their quarry was not due to arrive for days yet. Having lived side by side with the taan for months on end, Klendist had come to hate them every bit as much as his men did. He hated their stink, hated their beady little eyes, hated their superior attitude. He thought of what they did to the humans they took prisoner—the torture, the rape, the butchering, and after that . . . Well, what the taan did after that didn't bear thinking about.

"Saddle your horses," Klendist ordered, adding in a shout, to be heard above the cheers, "Try not to kill them all. Let's keep a few for sport. We may be stuck here a long time."

Laughing, the mercenaries rode out into the night, taking along several wineskins to lighten the tedium of the ride and fire their blood for the coming slaughter.

The night deepened. Raven crouched in his tent, his eye to the tent flap. Dur-zor knelt behind him, her kep-ker in her hands. The other half-taan were hiding in their tents, watching, waiting. Raven had taught them an old Trevinici trick used when fighting at night. They had smeared their faces and bodies with mud so that they blended into the darkness.

A half-moon shone, low in the sky. The starlight was bright. Shortly after midnight, Raven saw the hulking shapes of six taan warriors lope into camp. They did not even bother to sneak in quietly, but came laughing and chortling. Roaming carelessly through the half-taan encampment, the taan kicked over drying racks and sent cooking pots rolling. One taan snagged a tent post with his toe, bringing the tent sagging down. The taan chortled.

Raven held his breath, hoping that the tent's occupant—Gar-dra, one of the more militant half-taans—did not spring the trap prematurely. Raven heard a grunt and a muttered curse coming from the tent, but Gar-dra remained inside. The taan did not even hear that much. Their eyes were fixed on the boar meat that hung from the branch of a nearby tree, to keep it from the ravages of coyotes and wolves. The taan smacked their lips and talked of how well they would dine that night.

"Slaves do not deserve such strong food," one said loudly.

"I am amazed the slaves managed to bring down such a fierce animal," said another. "Probably the animal was old and weak, unfit for a warrior's feasting."

"Then we will give it to the children," said a third, and they all hooted with laughter.

The taan headed for the tree that stood some distance outside the camp. In their arrogance, none bothered to look behind. Padding soft-footed, Raven crept from his tent. A wave of his hand brought the half-taan slipping out after him. Gar-dra emerged from his wrecked tent, his face twisted in a scowl, his eyes glittering with anger. The half-taan had heard the insults. Even the meekest were roused.

They were so roused that Raven started to worry. All the half-taan carried weapons. He wanted to show the taan that the half-taan could fight and fight well, but he didn't want any taan killed, and he was concerned that, in their current mood, the riled half-taan might cave in a skull or break someone's neck.

It was too late to halt them now. The half-taan had almost caught up with their former masters, whose eyes were on the boar meat. Something, either a rustle of the grass or a warrior's sense, alerted one of taan. He glanced around. Before he could shout a warning, Raven leapt on him and bore him to the ground.

Dur-zor let out a war cry. The other half-taan joined in and fell upon the taan in a rush. Fists swung, clubs thunked. The air was filled with the sounds of grunts and snarls and gurgling laughter from the half-taan. The occasional yelp came from the taan.

Raven smashed his fist into his taan. The warrior lay on the ground, stunned, but not unconscious. Before the taan could recover, Raven grabbed hold of the taan's wrists, bound them securely with a length of sinew. He did the same with the taan's ankles. By then, the taan had come to his senses. Struggling futilely in his bonds, he glared at Raven with fury.

Raven looked around the field of battle to find that the fight was over. The half-taan had done well. All six taan lay tied up on the ground, snarling and snapping and making impotent threats. The half-taan laughed and poked at them with their clubs or sticks. The half-taan were pleased with themselves, proud of their accomplishment. Raven was pleased with himself. He'd given his people confidence, and he'd also given the taan something to think about.

"Don't worry, friends," Raven said to the angry taan, through Durzor, "we won't let anything happen to you. We'll take you back to your camp."

At that, the taan were so enraged that they began to foam and froth at the mouth. Being hauled back to their camp in ignominy and shame, prisoners of their former slaves, would make them objects of ridicule and shame. The half-taan tied ropes around their chests, preparatory to hauling them bodily over the ground. Remembering how he himself had been hauled in the same way, when he was captured by the taan, Raven basked warmly in his revenge.

With their taan prisoners trussed up like pigs going to market, Raven and his half-taan started their triumphal procession toward the taan camp.

Topping one of the many rolling hills, Klendist could see the taan campfires. His men were keyed up, excited. They'd gone a long time without action and were spoiling for a fight. They laughed and made vows as to what they would do to the "gigs" when they caught them.

They were close enough to see the occasional figure moving about the camp. Most of the taan were asleep in their tents, for the hour was late. The scouts had reported that there were two main camps and one small camp, set off by itself. Klendist figured they would hit the two main camps first, destroy them, then ride down on the small camp.

The sight of the taan whetted the appetites of the raiding party. The men spurred their horses and rode wildly toward the camp, each man wanting to get in the first kill. Klendist rode at their head.

A taan rose up out of the long grass, practically underneath the nose of Klendist's horse. The taan let out an eerie howl that split the night wide open and caused the horse to rear in panic.

All around Klendist, taan leapt up out of the grass, howling and moaning like fiends of the Void in their final torments. Horses bucked and reared. Several ran off with their riders, who fought desperately to bring them under control. By the time Klendist drew his sword, the taan had dashed off into the night, running to warn the camp.

Klendist cursed roundly. They'd lost the chance for a sneak attack. Still, he figured, he and his raiding party were mounted, while the taan were on foot. They would be on the taan before they had time to form an organized resistance.

"Jonson!" he yelled, when all had recovered. "Take half the men, attack that big camp over there. I'll deal with this one. We'll meet back here!"

He galloped forward.

"The taan will have to honor us now," Raven said in satisfaction as they dragged their prisoners to Dag-ruk's camp.

"Either that or they will kill us," said Dur-zor. "It will be worth it, though."

"They won't kill you," said Raven. "They can't. We bested them in a fair fight. Well, an almost fair fight."

"We are slaves, Raven," Dur-zor reminded him. "And to them we will always be slaves—slaves who dared raise their hands against their masters. For that, we must die."

"You're serious, aren't you," Raven said, coming to a stop. "Do they all think this? Do all the half-taan believe the taan will kill them for this?"

"Oh, yes, Raven," said Dur-zor complacently.

He looked back at the half-taan, laughing and chattering happily over their victory.

"And they did this anyway?" he asked.

"As I said, it will be worth it."

"I won't let them—" Raven began angrily.

An unearthly sound split the air. The sound came from far away, echoing among the hills—howls rising from many taan throats.

The half-taan froze, listening. The taan prisoners ceased their cursing and threats. They twisted in their bonds, trying desperately to see what was happening.

"What is it?" Raven demanded. He'd never heard anything like this terrible sound.

"An attack!" Dur-zor gasped.

The ground shook beneath their feet. Raven had been in countless battles against mounted troops, and he recognized the pounding made by horses' hooves. A force—a large force—of mounted men was riding down on them.

The taan do not ride horses. Taan have no use for horses. Taan warriors fight best on the ground, even against a mounted foe. The hoofbeats came closer. Shouts and cries carried on the still night air. Raven could hear other shouts, as well, and recognized the voices—humans.

His heart lurched in his chest. His eyes stung with sudden tears. He could not remember the last time he'd heard a human voice.

This is salvation, he realized. This is rescue. This is a return to my homeland, my people.

"They are human, Raven," she said, her face pale. She knew him so well, knew what he was thinking.

The half-taan looked to him, wondering what to do. The taan prisoners looked at him, crying for him to set them free.

"Cut them loose," Raven ordered, drawing his knife.

The taan were up and running almost before the half-taan had finished slicing through the tough sinews. As they ran off, the taan stopped, looked back.

"Bgrt, taan-helarrs," he said harshly, then he turned and dashed off toward the sound of battle.

Dur-zor's eyes glimmered with tears.

"You will stay, Raven?" she asked.

"I will stay. You are my people," said Raven. "What did the taan say?"

"He said, 'Join us in glory, warriors,' " said Dur-zor proudly.

Klendist galloped into the taan camp—Dag-ruk's camp, though he couldn't know that. Although he had lived in proximity to the taan, he knew nothing about them. He expected to find in the taan what he would find in humans caught in the same situation—panic, confusion, maybe some resistance, but nothing that he and his men couldn't handle. They had the advantage. They were mounted, they had superior weapons. They were humans, not beasts.

Klendist rode his horse over taan tents, smashing them, trampling them. He had hoped to catch taan slumbering in those tents, taan who would be crushed beneath his horse's hooves. He was disappointed. The tents were empty.

He cheered up when he saw a taan with a young child in her arms go running out of another tent. Klendist dug his heels into his horse's flanks and caught up with her in a bound. He sliced off her head and the child's in a single stroke. He laughed heartily. Waving his bloodied sword, he looked back to see if his men had seen this neat trick.

They cheered and laughed. Klendist galloped on toward the center of the camp, where the taan warriors would gather to protect their chief.

One of the men rode up beside him.

"The boys want to know what we do if we find any human women?" the man shouted.

"Kill them!" Klendist shouted back. "They've got taan seed growing in their bellies. We'll be doing them a favor."

The man nodded and rode back to spread the word.

The half-moon had set by then, but they had full advantage of the lambent light of the stars. The taan stood together in a single mass. The light gleamed here and there on a weapon. There were children among them.

Klendist felt the first twinge of unease.

These taan were not warriors. Warriors would not be saddled with the care of children. Much as Klendist despised the taan, he knew that the warriors would not have run off to leave their children to die. Where, then, were they?

A shriek was the answer to his question. The warriors were behind him, all around him. They came running through the darkness, running in for the kill. He'd led his men straight into an ambush.

Taan warriors came out of nowhere, their mouths wide-open in slavering grins, screaming and howling like accursed souls being dragged into the Void.

Klendist turned his horse's head, yanking the beast about so fast that it nearly foundered. He turned just in time to see a taan catch one of his men. Reaching up, the taan caught hold of the mounted man from behind, dragged him off his horse. The taan drove his spear through the writhing body, then set off on foot in pursuit of another rider.

Klendist was not one to fight against overwhelming odds for the sake of honor or heroics. He knew when he was whipped. Wielding his sword with savage efficiency, he fought back the taan who had him surrounded.

"Retreat!" he shouted, striking savagely to the right and left. "Retreat!"

He bent over his horse's neck and dug his heels into the brute's flanks. The horse, already maddened by the shrieks and the smell of blood, charged into the midst of the taan, bowling them over and trampling them beneath its hooves.

Klendist's only thought was to escape the carnage. He was surrounded by tents, surrounded by taan. One of his men cried out to him for orders, but he ignored him. It was every man for himself now.

A few of his comrades caught up with him, and they banded together, trying to fight their way out of the ring of death, slashing at taan faces that loomed, shrieking, out of the darkness.

Klendist saw a way out. He headed for it and at last he was free of the camp, out on open ground. He had maybe ten men with him, and most of them were wounded. He alone was unscathed.

He glanced back toward the taan camp and was relieved to see that the taan were not coming after them. They too busy with their killing. He could hear screams, moans, and the pleas of his men not to be left behind.

He knew very well what would happen to those who remained in taan hands. He'd seen for himself how the taan treated their prisoners. He'd seen living men disemboweled, seen their arms and legs hacked off.

Klendist grunted and rode on. He wasn't about to go back into that fiends' nest. Not with ten men, some of whom were riding dead men, by the looks of them. He galloped on, heading for the meeting place. Perhaps the other half of his force had experienced better luck. He'd join up with them, regroup, come back, and finish off these slimy gigs.

"Captain! Look!" one of his men called.

Klendist turned in the saddle, looked to the north. An orange glow lit the grasslands, coming from the direction of the other taan camp. Klendist smiled grimly and urged his horse toward the fire, hoping to at least arrive in time to slit a few taan bellies before they were all killed. One man, riding beside him, slid off his horse, fell to the ground, too weak to remain in the saddle. Klendist ignored him, rode on.

He was close enough to see black shapes milling about the dancing flames when a figure loomed at him of the darkness. Klendist raised his sword and bore down on the foe.

"Captain! Hold! It's Jonson!"

Klendist arrested his killing stroke, yanked hard on the horse's reins to pull it up.

"Looks like you've had some fun!" he shouted. Then he was close enough to see Jonson's face.

"Fun, sir!" Jonson echoed in a hollow voice. He was deathly pale, his eyes wide and starting out of their sockets. He was covered in blood, and half the hair had been singed off his head.

"We rode into a hornets' nest! Or worse—a nest of Void sorcerers! I've never seen the like, Captain, and I hope to the gods I never see anything like it again. Dick Martle was riding next to me and one of those black-robed fiends came out and pointed at him and he . . . he . . ."

The man choked, leaned over his horse to vomit.

"Well?" said Klendist grimly.

"He turned into a living corpse. Right there in the saddle. They sucked the life out of him, all the juice, the flesh. I saw his skull grinning at me, and then he was nothing but a pile of ashes . . . Gods, sir! It was horrible!" Jonson retched again.

"But who set the fires? Didn't you?"

"They set them," said Jonson with a shudder. "Who would have thought the gigs'd set fire to their own camp? Gives 'em light to kill by, I guess. You hear those screams, sir?"

Klendist was trying hard not to. "I hear them."

"They're tossing our men into the blaze. Alive. Roasting 'em like pigs."

"How many came out with you?"

"I don't know, sir," said Jonson. "I wanted only one thing and that was to get out of that Void pit! I didn't wait around to see what anyone else was going to do."

More of his men were arriving, riding up singly or in groups of twos or threes. Some who'd lost their horses rode double with their comrades.

Klendist made a swift count of about thirty. Thirty out of two hundred. He pondered what to do.

He did not like to be beaten. He was tempted to ride back into the taan camp with his troop and gain his revenge. Some of the men had their blood up, were urging him to do just that. Others sat trembling in the saddle, shaken and stunned, their faces blanched from the horrors they'd witnessed.

Better to cut my losses, he decided. Shakur will be angry enough at it is. At least, I still have men enough left to deal with the Dominion Lords—

A horse whinnied, someone shouted, but it was too late. Klendist thought for a wild moment that the night itself had taken on form and shape, for the darkness came alive. Strong hands grabbed hold of him and yanked him from his saddle.

Klendist landed heavily on his rump. He'd dropped his sword, but he had his fists and his wits. He knew that to lie for long on the ground was to lie forever in his grave, and he scrambled to his feet. He lashed out with his fist at the first face that came near, felt the satisfying crunch of bone.

Death was all around him. He saw Jonson fall, his skull crushed. Something struck him on the head. The blow dazed him, and he reeled backward, stumbled into strong arms.

"I can save you," said a voice in his ear, a human voice, speaking Elderspeak. "But you'll have to keep your mouth shut and do as I say."

Klendist gave a groggy nod.

An arm strong as a steel band wrapped around his chest. He felt the prick of a knife at his throat and any thought of struggling against his captor vanished.

"This one is mine!" said the human in harsh tones. "He is my prize."

Klendist saw that his attackers were half-taan, the accursed offspring of human and taan. He was surrounded by these monstrosities, with their half-human, half-beast faces and their half-human voices. They regarded him with wide grins of glee. Their hands were dark with blood.

"I killed one, Raven!" said a half-taan in excitement. She wore hardly any clothes. Her breasts were bare and smeared over with mud. "I killed him as you taught me."

"All are dead, Raven," said another. "As you ordered."

"You did well," said the human, who had hold of Klendist. "Drag their bodies back to our camp. We showed the taan we could outwit them. We will now show the taan we are warriors!"

The half-taan gave a cheer and shook their weapons in the air.

"Still, it would have been better if we had taken slaves," said one of the half-taan. "The taan would have even more respect for us."

"No!" said the human sharply, his voice rasping in Klendist's ear. "There will be no slaves in our camp. Your own mothers were slaves. You were slaves. You were tortured, tormented. Would you do that to another person? If so, you can leave my tribe. Clear out. I don't want you."

The half-taan hung their heads.

"We are sorry, Raven," said a female, chastened. "We did not think. Of course, you are right."

"We make clean kills," Raven said sternly. "These men were armed, they came to fight and to die. We came to fight and to die. That is war. Death and glory are the fate of the warrior, not slavery. And it is not a warrior's fate for his flesh to fill our bellies. Once we have shown the bodies to the taan, I will teach you how to build a burial mound for these men and how to honor the dead."

The half-taan were bewildered by this concept. Several scratched their heads, but no one protested.

"What about the one you have, Raven?" asked the female. "What will you do with him?"

"He is their leader, their nizam, Dur-zor. I will question him."

The half-taan chuckled. They thought they knew what was coming for the human.

"Could we watch?" asked one eagerly.

"No. He will talk more freely if it is just the two of us."

The half-taan were disappointed, but the human added, by way of distraction, "You can keep the armor and the weapons you captured. Those are the honorable prizes of a warrior. And we will keep the horses. I'll teach you how to ride. No more walking. Walking," he added with a grin, "is for taan. Now they will eat *our* dust!"

The half-taan cheered again, but the cheering was subdued. They were happy about the armor, but they glanced askance at the horses, clearly not enthusiastic about learning to ride the tall, formidable beasts.

The human gave Klendist into the keeping of the half-taan he had called Dur-zor, a female. Klendist had the disgusting impression, from the way she looked at him and talked to him that this half-taan was the human's mate. He wasn't surprised. This Raven was a Trevinici, humans who were little better than savages themselves.

The half-taan bound Klendist expertly, hand and foot, then left him lying on his belly on the ground. From that vantage point, Klendist watched the half-taan fling the bodies of his men over the saddles of the horses and lash them securely in place. This done, Raven showed the half-taan how to lead the horses by their reins, showed them how to calm a spooked horse by rubbing its nose and speaking gently to it. The half-taan had a way with horses, seemingly, for the animals responded well to them. The half-taan began to grow more at ease.

"Will I stay with you, Raven?" Dur-zor asked.

"No, go back to camp. See that my orders are carried out," said Raven. "You are nizam in my absence."

A shadow of fear fell across her face. She looked from him to Klendist, lying on the ground.

"Leave me that horse," said Raven, pointing. "That's your horse, isn't it?" he said to Klendist, who gave a nod.

"Raven . . ." said Dur-zor uneasily. She touched him gently on the arm. "Raven, will you . . ." She couldn't go on. Her courage failed her.

He put his hand on her ugly face, leaned down, and kissed her on the mouth. Klendist thought he was going to be sick to his stomach.

"Go back, Dur-zor," Raven said. "Watch over our people."

"Yes, Raven," she replied quietly.

Rounding up the others, she led them away. She looked back once, as she did so. Raven smiled at her, and she smiled tentatively back. Then she faced forward, continued walking. Her people came behind her, leading the horses loaded with their gruesome cargo.

Raven watched them until they were out of sight, never spared a glance for his prisoner. Klendist had lots of time to think, and he finally had it all figured out.

"You're a free man now, Trevinici," said Klendist. "Cut these ropes, and we'll get out of here before the gigs ever miss you. My horse can carry us both, at least back to my camp."

The sky to the east was gray with the first faint light of the coming dawn. Raven squatted down beside Klendist, looked him in the face.

"That wasn't a ruse," Raven said. "I belong with them. I don't expect you to understand." He shrugged. "I'm not sure I understand myself. But that is the way it is."

Klendist scowled, struggled in his bonds. "I might have known. You're a damn savage. No better than these gigs."

"And you, by your stink, are a Vinnengaelean mercenary," said Raven. "Who hired you to come attack us? Who knows we're here? The Vinnengaelean army? Some local lord? Who?"

"The gigs are damned Void-spawn!" Klendist growled. "No one paid me to attack them. I had to live among them myself for months. I never turned into one of them, though. I never turned traitor to my race! It's a human's duty to rid Loerem of the monsters. It's the duty of every human." He glared at Raven.

"I'd say you failed in your duty," said Raven, grinning. "So you claim you thought up this raid yourself? You are either a great fool or a cunning liar."

Raven gazed intently at Klendist.

"I believe you," Raven said at last. "Which means you are a great fool."

"Cut me loose!" Klendist swore. "I'll fight you with my bare hands."

"I'll cut you loose," said Raven coolly. "But I won't fight. I could never wash away the yellow of your coward's blood."

He sliced through Klendist's bonds. Klendist rubbed his wrists and looked about for his sword. He saw it lying nearby.

"I will take your horse," Raven was saying. "A noble animal, far too noble to bear the likes of you—"

Klendist made a leap for his weapon. His hand closed over the hilt. He swung himself around, swinging the sword at the same time.

Raven ducked the wild, slashing blow. His foot slammed into Klendist's groin, doubled him over. Klendist fell into the dirt, lay there clutching himself, rolling about in agony.

"I would not stay here long," Raven advised. "Taan scouts will be out on patrol. You won't want them to find you."

"You'll be sorry for this," Klendist gasped. "I'll remember you, don't think I won't. There'll be rewards out for your head, Trevinici. Every bounty hunter from here to Dunkarga and back will be on the lookout for you, you damn gig-humper."

"You've already wasted a lot of valuable time," said Raven.

Picking up Klendist's sword, Raven swung himself up onto Klendist's horse. With a smile and a mocking salute, the Trevinici rode off and was soon lost to sight among the hills.

Left alone, lying on the blood-soaked ground, Klendist took stock of his situation. He thought about Shakur. He thought about the taan scouts. Klendist decided that the Trevinici's advice was sound. Gritting his teeth, he pulled himself to his feet. Massaging his burning member, he staggered off, heading northward.

Klendist had a lot of ground to cover this day. Not only did he have to escape the taan.

He had to escape Shakur.

TOWARD MIDDAY, RAVEN, MOUNTED ON HORSEBACK, RODE INTO Dag-ruk's camp. His half-taan tribe followed him on foot, leading horses behind them. All was silent in the taan camp, except for the moans of the dying prisoners, staked out in the tall grass. The taan warriors gathered around Raven, but said nothing, made no move. The warriors eyed the bodies that the half-taan brought with them, eyed the horses that the half-taan led, the bloodstained weapons they carried. They noted that the half-taan walked with heads held high, walked proudly, as would a taan.

Raven did not deign to look at any of the warriors. He kept his gaze fixed on Dag-ruk's tent.

She emerged, as Raven rode up to the front of her tent. He dismounted, stood facing her. Dur-zor came hurrying up to translate. She did not kneel to Dag-ruk, as she would have once done. She stood proudly at Raven's side.

Dag-ruk looked at the bodies of the humans. She looked at the half-taan. She looked, last, at Raven.

"These humans escaped your warriors," Raven told her. "They were going to regroup, attack your camp again. We stopped them."

Dag-ruk's eyes flickered. She seemed uncertain how to respond. She could not deny that some of the humans had managed to escape, nor could she deny that the half-taan had brought them down.

Raven waited for her to say something and, when it became clear she had nothing to say, he remounted his horse. Reaching down his hand, he caught hold of Dur-zor and pulled her up behind him.

"We are returning to our camp now," he said, "to celebrate our victory and to put the dead to rest."

Dag-ruk found her voice. "They are strong food. Your warriors will dine well this night."

Raven understood the compliment, and he was immensely pleased by it. He was careful not to show his pleasure, however.

"We will dine on the wild boar we killed yesterday," he said. His gaze went to the six taan who had tried to steal it. "The dead we will bury."

"That is not the way of the taan," Dag-ruk said coldly.

"No," said Raven, "but it is the way of the half-taan."

K'let returned to the taan camps the morning after the raid. He cast a curious gaze at the human prisoners as he walked through the camp. K'let said nothing, asked no questions until he reached his tent. Immediately on arrival, he sent for Derl.

The aged, wizened shaman had been on the lookout for K'let, and he responded to the summons with eager alacrity. K'let took his preferred form, that of the albino taan he had been in life. He met Derl with a frown, for the shaman had to be assisted into the tent, leaning on the strong shoulder of one of his assistants.

"What have you done to yourself?" K'let demanded.

"I was injured in the battle last night," Derl replied, with a proud glint in his eye. "A twisted ankle, nothing more."

"He was leading the attack, Kyl-sarnz," said the assistant. "He killed many before he slipped in some blood and went sprawling. Fortunately, the warriors found him and carried him to safety."

"That the day should come when I have to be carried to safety," Derl muttered, irate.

"Still, they did well," said K'let. "I cannot afford to lose you, my friend. Now of all times. Leave us, Shaman. I will take care of him."

The shaman deposited Derl gently upon the floor. The elderly taan appeared so frail and fragile that it seemed his bones might snap at a touch. K'let did not make a fuss over him, for that would have disgraced both of them. He ordered that strong food be brought to Derl and encouraged him to eat in order to regain his strength.

Derl had long ago lost any appetite for food of any kind, but he ate a little to do honor to his host.

"What happened here?" K'let asked, when Derl had shoved away his bowl.

"A human raiding party," said Derl, and that was all that needed to be said on the subject. "But what of your mission, K'let? Do you have the Sovereign Stone?"

"No," K'let replied.

"No?" Derl was disappointed. "Did Tash-ket fail in his mission?"

"He did not fail," K'let said. "He obtained the Stone from the gdsk. I could have taken it. I chose not to."

"But, K'let, your plan . . ." Derl was bewildered.

"My plan." K'let chuckled. "Why settle for one Stone when I can have all four and Dagnarus into the bargain?"

Derl stared, amazed.

K'let was pleased with himself. He started to slap Derl on the knee, thought better of it. He might break something. He contented himself with tapping Derl on the chest.

"You have always said that the gods of the taan are with us, even in this strange land. You are right. I was on my way to meet with Tash-ket to obtain the Stone, when I came across Shakur. It seems that Dagnarus discovered that Tash-ket had stolen the Stone in my name. Dagnarus was furious, and he sent Shakur after me."

"Shakur!" Derl spit on the ground. "Did you dispatch him to the Void where he belongs?"

"Shakur is a slave," said K'let with contempt. "What honor is there in fighting a slave? It is his master I seek."

"And you have found a way?"

"I have. The gods brought me in time to overhear Shakur tell one of his human toads that Dagnarus has set a trap for the four Sovereign Stones. Even now, chosen warriors of each race bring the stones to Old Vinnengael. And there, too, comes Dagnarus. The gods are with us, Derl," said K'let, nodding. "The gods are with us."

"We will give thanks this night to L'K'kald and Lokmirr for it is their hands I see in this," Derl said, nodding wisely. "Are you certain that this Stone means so much to Dagnarus that he will come for it?"

"All that he has done in this land, all the blood of our people that he has spent has gone to gain him this one object, this Stone. He will come for it."

"This Stone must have very powerful magicks," said Derl, his watery eyes shining with greed. "Perhaps you do wrong to give it up."

"Bah!" K'let gave a snort. "Xkes magic. Worthless. The Dagger of the Vrykyl, now. That is Void magic. With it, I will create an army of kylsarnz. When we go back to our own land, we will be invincible. None can stand against us."

"What do we do now? What are your orders?"

"You and the tribes will remain here and wait for Nb'arsk and L'nskt and their tribes to meet up with us. I will go on to Old Vinnengael. When I come back with the Dagger and my slave, we will travel to the hole-in-the-air and return through it to our land."

"Your slave!" Derl rubbed his withered hands. "I know who one will be . . ."

K'let gave a hooting laugh. "Dagnarus will serve *me* for a change. Eternity will not be long enough for my pleasure at the sight of him kneeling before me."

"But who will be your other Vrykyl?" Derl asked. He bowed his head. "I hope that one day you will so honor me, yet, I feel that I still may be of some use to you alive—"

"Not you, my friend," said K'let, resting his hand on Derl's shoulder. "Someday, as you say, but not now. You must take us back to the gods, back to the old ways."

"Then who?"

K'let rose to his feet. Going to the tent's entrance, he parted the flap. "Send for the human, R'vn. Tell him to bring food and water and his weapon. I have a journey to make, and he will accompany me. We are going to the City of Ghosts."

Dur-zor and the other half-taan were elated when the messenger arrived with word that K'let had chosen Raven to accompany him on his mysterious mission to the City of Ghosts. Dur-zor could barely contain her glee as she translated the taan's message, and the other half-taan whooped and shouted and chanted Raven's name. The commotion grew so loud that some of the young taan warriors of Dag-ruk's tribe came running over to find out what was going on.

Proudly, Dur-zor told them. The young warriors gazed at Raven with admiration and envy. Some touched him in hopes that his good fortune would rub off on them.

Raven said what he knew that his people wanted to hear. He spoke of the great honor done to him, then he went into his tent to pack what he would need for the trip.

Dur-zor entered the tent. "Raven, the messenger grows impatient— What is the matter?" Alarmed, she caught hold of his arm. She stared at him, her face contorted in horror. "Raven! I forgot! The claim he made on your life . . . you can't go!"

"I have to. This is a great honor. Dag-ruk would give every magic stone in her hide to have this honor."

He smiled at her, shrugged. "I am a nizam, Dur-zor, and one of the responsibilities of the nizam is to look after the welfare of the tribe. If I go with K'let, the half-taan will be honored and accepted by the taan, even if I am no longer here to watch over them." He picked up his pack. "You are nizam while I am gone."

Dur-zor flung herself into his arms. "I will wait for you. I will be here. We will all be here, waiting for you. I will pray to the gods for you. I will pray to your gods."

"I would like that, Dur-zor," he said.

As he left the camp, the half-taan cheered their nizam and, to his astonishment, cheers went up from Dag-ruk's camp.

Raven left the cheers behind, left all that he cared about behind. Looking back, he saw Dur-zor standing in the midst of the tribe, her tribe now. She raised her hand, waved to him. He waved back, then he faced forward. He never expected to see any of them again, and he was startled to find how much that hurt him.

He had gone about two miles when a dark shadow of enormous wings slid over him. Tilting his head, Raven looked into the cobalt blue sky.

A dragon flew among the clouds.

Raven had heard of these wondrous beasts all his life, but he had never been privileged to see one. He stopped walking to stare, entranced by the dragon's marvelous, deadly beauty.

The dragon was far, far above him, but even at that height, he could see the sun shimmer on red scales, so that they flashed with fire. He could see the sinuous curve of the neck, the glistening tail, the slow dip and rise of the enormous wings. The dragon was too high to see him, save perhaps as a speck on the rolling hills.

The dragon flew on. Raven watched until it had disappeared from sight. He would never know that in that moment he had seen his wayward sister, Ranessa. Yet he knew that in some strange way, the sight of the dragon lifted his heart, gave him courage.

THE PEOPLE OF NEW VINNENGAEL WERE MAKING PREPARATIONS for the annual spring festival. They had worked hard to remove all traces of the taan invasion, repairing buildings that had been damaged, scrubbing the exterior walls to remove the black, greasy soot that fell from the skies after days of burning the bodies. They had washed most of the blood stains from the streets. The wounded were healed by now, although they would bear scars of the battle for the rest of their lives. Few would show off there scars or boast about them to their grandchildren. None was proud of what had been done that day. Everyone looked forward to the fragrant spring winds, which would blow away the lingering stench of death, and the gentle spring rains, which would cause flowers to bloom in the blood-soaked ground.

Even though the festival was yet a month away, shop owners sent out apprentices to cover the plaster walls with a fresh coat of whitewash. Sign painters repainted or touched up the colorful shop signs. Dressmakers plied their needles by candlelight, for every gentle lady must have a new gown to wear to His Majesty's Spring Revels.

The sounds of hammer and saw could be heard from dawn to dusk, as the carpenters erected booths on the fairgrounds. Small boys were employed to walk every inch of the grounds, clean them of stones and sticks. The innkeepers and tavern owners and Hospitalers laid in fresh supplies, for this was the busiest time of year for them all. The Spring Faire attracted people from every part of Vinnengael. Merchants would travel from Dunkarga, Nimra, and Nimorea. Even in this time of civil war, elven merchants were expected from Tromek, and a few dwarf merchants would make the trek from Saumel. Ork ships filled with goods had already started to clog the harbor.

The weather might be gray and gloomy, rainy and cold now, but the sun always shone on the Spring Faire. People listened to the rain dripping from the eaves and closed their eyes and imagined warm sun and laughing children.

Times were good for the people of New Vinnengael. They were pleased with their new king, and they had reason to be. Dagnarus might have climbed over the broken, twisted bodies of hundreds to reach the throne, but, once there, he washed the blood from his hands and tried his best to do what he considered right.

"Someday, they will speak of King Dagnarus of blessed memory," he said to himself, standing before the portrait of his father. "Well, perhaps not 'blessed memory,' for I won't be dead. I won't be a memory. I will be their living king, ruling through the ages, leading Vinnengael to eternal prosperity."

He had long puzzled how he was going to explain the fact to his people that he would never age, never die. He could not tell them the truth, of course, that he lived on lives stolen through the Dagger of the Vrykyl. Already, since he'd been king, he'd found two people willing to give their souls to the Void in return for favors from their royal master. The favors they received were not quite the favors they had sought. The Dagger of the Vrykyl had found them both acceptable candidates, and now Dagnarus had two new Vrykyl, one of them a lord who spied on his privy council and the other a Temple magus.

Dagnarus decided to tell his people that the gods would grant him eternal youth in return for the safe recovery of the blessed Sovereign Stone. The Church would be appalled. He'd let them rant and rave, silence those who grew too tiresome. He had his supporters, and they would come through for him. Meanwhile, the people would see their young and handsome king standing with his hand upon the sacred Stone, all four parts together at last, as it was meant to be. In time, the clamor would diminish. His opposition would dwindle away. Those who were babes in arms today would grow old under his kingship and commend their children to him on their deathbeds.

All was in readiness to accept the Sovereign Stone. He'd ordered the carving of a new marble altar on which to place it. Curiosity ran high as to what this altar might be for, but Dagnarus would say only that it was destined to bear the greatest gift the gods had ever given mankind.

Dagnarus was meeting with his privy council when he felt the Dagger of the Vrykyl grow pleasantly warm against his flesh. He carried the dagger with him always, thrust into his belt beneath his silken shirt. The warmth meant that one of his Vrykyl was seeking to contact him. Dagnarus hoped and expected it would be Shakur, for the last report he'd received from Gareth indicated that the four Dominion Lords bearing the Sovereign Stones were drawing near the ruins of Old Vinnengael.

"Gentlemen," said Dagnarus, rising to his feet. "No, please, do not stand up. I must beg your indulgence for a few moments. I hate to interrupt our discussion, but I must make use of the privies. I do not know why it is that happens to me whenever we meet, gentlemen," he added with a grin. "I'm beginning to think that is why it is called the 'privy' council."

The members laughed heartily. They always laughed at the king's jokes.

Dagnarus managed to rid himself of courtiers and servants and hangers-on, who continually dogged his footsteps. He recalled Silwyth, how adept he had been at filling the royal life with courtiers when they were wanted and shooing them away when they weren't. The elven chamberlain had taught him all he knew about the intrigues of court life. Dagnarus supposed that elves had a natural gift for this sort of thing. His current chamberlain was an ass. Dagnarus made a mental note to contact the Shield and ask that he send him an elf to serve in this capacity.

On reaching the royal bedchamber, Dagnarus ordered his chamberlain to shut the door, ordered his guards to refuse entry to anyone. A modest man who was fond of his privacy, Dagnarus had built for himself a water closet for his own personal needs. In this windowless chamber, with its stone walls and stone floor and heavy doors, Dagnarus responded to the Dagger's call.

"There is a problem, my lord," Shakur said. "Klendist did not arrive at our meeting place. I warned you that he was unreliable—"

"What happened to him? Something must have happened."

"I have no idea, my lord. When I went to their camp, it was empty.

They had not been there for several days, by the looks of it. I waited another day, but they never came back."

"And the Dominion Lords? The Sovereign Stone?"

"I have no idea," Shakur said dourly. "I have lost track of them. It was not my responsibility—"

"If you value your tongue, Shakur, you will cease to wag it," said Dagnarus.

"Yes, my lord."

"I should not have left this to underlings," Dagnarus muttered. "Yet how could I leave my responsibilities here? There are certainly disadvantages to being king. It curtails the freedom of one's movement. By the Void! If only I could find a way to split myself in two, be in two places at once."

"Yes, my lord," said Shakur. "What are your commands?"

"I will come take charge of the situation. It is what I should have done all along."

"Yes, my lord. By the way, my lord, K'let has arrived, along with a large force of taan."

"If you think to disconcert me with this news, Shakur, you fail. I know K'let's plan. The taan is clever, but he is not capable of subtlety. I will deal with him, once I have dealt with the Dominion Lords."

"Very good, my lord."

"I will be with you shortly, Shakur," said Dagnarus, and the contact ended.

Fortunately, he had already made arrangements for his absence. He had let it be known that he was fond of hunting. The former king had kept a hunting lodge in the Illanof Mountains. Pleading a need to escape the rigors of court life, Dagnarus was going to go hunting. The dragon of the Void, one of the five who lived upon Dragon Mountain, was already waiting for Dagnarus's call, waiting to bear him swiftly to Old Vinnengael. Once there, he would search for and find the four Dominion Lords.

He ran his finger lightly over the sharp edge of the Dagger of the Vrykyl.

"Where is Silwyth?" Shadamehr asked.

Damra glanced around. "I thought he was helping you and the Captain with the boat."

"And I thought he had gone ahead with you to scout," said Shadamehr. "And now, it seems, he's nowhere."

Acting on the advice of Silwyth, the Dominion Lords left their boat behind on a shore some distance from the ruins of Old Vinnengael. They walked along an old highway running through the Grain Coast, a stretch of rich land nicknamed Vinnengael's "bread basket." Even now the remnants of farming villages could still be seen. Although the villages had escaped the effects of the magical blast, they had not escaped the ravages of war. Dagnarus's troops had raided the farms, stealing the food, slaughtering the cattle, setting fire to anything they had not been able to carry off.

"Good soil here," said Shadamehr. He bent down to pick up a handful of the black earth, let it trickle through his fingers.

"I am surprised that no one has returned to farm this land," said Damra. "It is far from the ruins of the city. They could ship their goods down the river."

"There's the reason," said Shadamehr, and he pointed to the side of the road. "Bahk tracks. Fresh ones."

"Those tracks are enormous," said Damra, awed. "I could lie down full length in one."

"Yes, nasty beasties, the bahk. I've fought one or two in my time. Didn't enjoy it much."

"It figures. What with us hauling around the Sovereign Stones," said Wolfram, returning from a trip to the underbrush, "those great hulking monsters will be drooling all over us."

"Do not worry, Wolf's Son," said the Captain in sonorous tones. "They drool on you only after they rip you apart."

"Wolfram!" the dwarf insisted dourly. "I keep telling you. It's Wolf-ram."

The Captain grinned and shrugged as she always grinned and shrugged when the dwarf corrected her, something he did at least three times a day. The ork had made up names for all of them. Shadamehr was Shadow Man and Damra was Dame Rah. The Captain was quite fond of these names and stuck to them. Only the dwarf was bothered by it. Something about his nickname struck a nerve, seemingly, a fact that did not escape the ork. The only person she had not given a nickname to was Silwyth, and that was because the Captain rarely spoke to him directly, though she spent a great deal of time watching him, her expression grave and troubled.

She read the omens everywhere they went. As the others were staring at the bahk tracks, the Captain left the trail, went crashing through the underbrush. She came back holding the carcass of a dead squirrel. She muttered words over it, then stood gazing at it, her lips pursed.

"What's the outcome?" Shadamehr asked.

The Captain shook her head.

"I can't say. My shaman is not with me," she told him.

She had left the other orks behind with the boat, with instructions to wait for her for a moon's half cycle. If she had not returned by then, the orks were to go back to their people and choose a new Captain.

"I may not be reading these right."

"But are they good or bad?" Shadamehr persisted.

The Captain handed him the maggot-ridden corpse. "See for yourself."

"I can see the omens were bad for the squirrel," said Shadamehr, with a grimace.

The Captain again shook her head.

"Will the bahk attack us?" Damra asked. "I've never encountered a bahk, but I know that they are drawn to magical objects and, as Wolfram says, we have with us four of the most powerful magical objects in the world."

"It depends on where they have their lairs. Silwyth said he knew—"

Shadamehr turned to find Silwyth at his elbow.

"Damn!" Shadamehr took an involuntary step backward. "Don't sneak up on me like that. You took ten years off my life. Provided, of course, that I have ten years to spare, which at this point appears doubtful. You should really make some sort of noise, my dear fellow," he added earnestly. "Belch or sneeze or something. The dead make more racket than you do."

Silwyth bowed and took a step backward. "I am sorry if I have offended."

"No, no, that's all right." Shadamehr mopped his brow with his shirtsleeve. "Did you see the bahk tracks?"

"Yes, Baron. I followed them a mile or so." Silwyth pointed north. "They go north, toward the ruins. A single bahk, probably an elder by the size and depth of the tracks."

"Heading straight for Old Vinnengael?"

"Yes," Silwyth replied. "There are many bahk in the area. The tracks of this one joined several others, all traveling north. My guess is that they make their homes in those cliffs over there to the east. The rock is limestone, and it is riddled with caves."

"Why are they here?" Damra asked.

"There was a part of the city known as the Mysterium, where you could buy magical artifacts from all over Loerem. Hundreds of these artifacts still lie in the rubble. The bahk are drawn to them, seek them out."

"So how do we avoid them? And what do we do if we come across one?"

"Run," said Shadamehr succinctly. "No, I'm quite serious. The bahk are huge, hulking creatures. They move relatively slowly, and most of the time you can outrun them."

"We will not be going into the Mysterium, so I trust that we will not encounter them," said Silwyth. "Still, if we meet one, the Baron's advice is sound."

Old Vinnengael lay due north of them. To the east was the good, rich bottomland, surrounded by limestone cliffs. To the west was Lake Ildurel. The lake water was a deep, deep blue, cool and dark in the early-morning sun. The ruins of the city were shrouded in clouds, a fact that struck Shadamehr as odd, for the day was warm and dry, and no mists rose from the motionless lake.

"Where does that mist come from?" he asked.

"The waterfalls," answered Silwyth. "Once there were rainbows, but not anymore. Now there is only gray fog."

They continued walking in silence, each thinking, perhaps, about the rainbows.

"It was a bahk took the Sovereign Stone from Dagnarus," Silwyth said quietly, almost as if he were talking to himself.

"Eh?" Wolfram said sharply. "How do you know that?"

"So say the legends of my people," Silwyth replied, with a sidelong glance at the dwarf. "I do not know for certain, of course."

"Well, your legends are right," stated the dwarf bluntly. "I was with Lord Gustav when he died. He found the Sovereign Stone on the corpse of a dead bahk."

"Come, Silwyth," said Shadamehr. "Let us hear this legend."

The elf's face darkened. He seemed to regret having spoken.

"According to what I have heard, the magical blast that destroyed much of the city spared the life of Dagnarus. How is that possible, you ask? Only the Father and Mother know."

"Or the Void," said Damra coolly.

Silwyth glanced at her, but did not reply. He continued with his story. "Dagnarus regained consciousness to find himself in a forested land unknown to him. He was horribly hurt, but he was alive, and he had the prize for which he had sacrificed so much, the prize that should have been his by right. He had with him the blessed Sovereign Stone."

" 'That should have been his by right'?" Damra repeated. "I thought you were on our side, Silwyth."

"I relate the legend as I have heard it, Damra of Gwyenoc," said Silwyth.

Damra and Shadamehr exchanged looks.

"I don't much like the sound of that," Shadamehr whispered, his brow puckered.

"I don't either," said Damra. "In fact, I think our Silwyth has been acting very strange lately."

Silwyth continued to talk, his voice soft and empty. "Dagnarus gave thanks to the gods for giving him the Stone, and he vowed he would be worthy of their faith in him. At that moment, a monster of a type that had never before been seen in this land came out of the forest—a bahk. Drawn by the magic of the Sovereign Stone, the bahk attacked Dagnarus. He fought with the very last ounce of strength he had remaining, fought to save what the gods had given him. He was too weak, however. The bahk tore the Stone from his hand and took it away. Dagnarus lost consciousness. He was too weak, too horribly wounded to go after the Stone. Many long years he searched, but in vain."

He looked up at them. "So goes the legend."

"Strange," said Damra. "I've never heard that tale."

"You are not of House Kinnoth," he returned. "We should increase our pace. We have no time to waste. You do not want to be caught in Old Vinnengael after dark."

"Where are we going once we get there?" Shadamehr inquired. "The temple? The palace? Your favorite tavern?"

"We are bound for the Temple of the Magi, or what is left of it," said Silwyth. "To the Portal of the Gods."

"Is that where we're going to meet up with Dagnarus?" Shadamehr asked, offhandedly.

Silwyth remained impassive. His expression did not change, although reading any expression in that wrinkled mass of flesh was difficult. Silwyth's almond-shaped eyes, in their slits of puckered flesh, were always hooded, shadowed. The elf had developed a trick, in later days, of never quite meeting one's gaze full on—a trick Shadamehr found intriguing.

He looked into the eyes, hoping to see a flicker of surprise, annoyance, fear—he wasn't certain what. What he saw astonished him so much that he almost forgot the question.

"I don't know what you mean," Silwyth said, and his voice was calm. He had hesitated a moment too long, however.

"I am . . . um . . . sure you must recall it," said Shadamehr, recovering his wits with an effort. "What we talked about in the cave. How Lord Dagnarus—"

"He is now your king," Silwyth corrected.

"I beg his pardon," said Shadamehr. "How His Majesty King Dagnarus was setting a trap for us. Wolfram told us. He'd had a message from my friend Ulaf. Surely you remember?"

"You must forgive an old man," said Silwyth, "who is often forgetful." He glanced pointedly at the sun, which was starting to sink into the west. "We should be hurrying. We have several more miles to cover before darkness. We will want to enter the city in the morning hours and it will take us all day to reach our goal. We do not want to be trapped there after dark."

"Speaking of traps," Shadamehr said blithely, "I was just wondering if Dagnarus was setting his trap for us in the Portal or somewhere else."

"The others perhaps find your foolery amusing, Baron," Silwyth replied. "I fear that it is lost on me. Each of you has been told that you must take the Sovereign Stone to the Portal of the Gods. I will guide you there or not, as you choose." He shrugged his thin shoulders. "If you think it is a trap, do not go."

He bowed and walked off down the road. The dwarf stumped after him, and the Captain fell into step beside Wolfram. Damra was about to follow, but Shadamehr caught hold of her arm, detained her.

"Look into his eyes!" Shadamehr said softly.

Damra stared at him. "What—?"

"I've looked into eyes like that once before. Back in the palace in Vinnengael. When I picked up the young king."

"Do you mean Silwyth—?"

"He's not Silwyth," said Shadamehr grimly. "Not anymore. He's a Vrykyl."

FOUNDED BY VERDIC ILDUREL IN THE YEAR ONE, THE CITY OF OLD Vinnengael had been built on the shores of the lake that would one day bear his name. Originally a fortress, the city grew quickly and was forced to expand up into the cliffs. Over the years that followed, magi skilled in the manipulation of rock and stone built ramps and stairs that extended from one level to another, providing access for both wagons and pedestrians. Bridges spanned the gorges. Orks constructed marvelous cranes that raised and lowered goods too heavy to be moved by wagon. Wealth flowed into the city by boat from the sea and by land, traveling over the smooth roads built by the Earth magi and guarded by the Vinnengaelean army.

The city was already the center of Loerem when, under the reign of King Tamaros, the magical Portals made it the center of the universe. Forged by magi of all the elements, the Portals extended into the homelands of the other races, bringing elves, orks, and dwarves to Vinnengael. Journeys that would have taken months or years were cut to days and weeks. Traders from all races came to Old Vinnengael. Though they might have small use for humans, they had great use for the glittering silver coins known as tams, in honor of Vinnengael's King Tamaros.

Envisioning a world in which all races could live in peace, King Tamaros encouraged all people to come to Old Vinnengael, and he did everything in his power to make them welcome. The city was at the height of its glory at that time.

The king's magnificent palace, set against the backdrop of the seven waterfalls, was one of the wonders of the known world, and many made the climb up the steep stairs that led from cliff to cliff to gape at it and envy those fortunate enough to live in such splendor. Their envy would have changed to pity had they known the jealousy and malevolence and sorrow that dwelt within those shining walls amongst the glittering rainbows. None could know, and so they went away thinking how great and wise was their king and that his strong rule, as evidenced by the castle, would never falter.

Tamaros's younger son, Dagnarus, decided that he should be king. Defying the gods, Dagnarus was the chosen of the Void. He became Lord of the Void and was given the Dagger of the Vrykyl. Banished from the kingdom by his elder brother, Helmos, Dagnarus returned a year later to lay claim to the throne, bringing fire and death to the city. With the help of Gareth, his childhood friend, who had become a powerful Void sorcerer, Dagnarus dried up the River Hammerclaw, which Vinnengael counted upon for defense of its walls, and marched his troops down the riverbed to enter the city from the rear. Led by the Vrykyl, whom few could withstand, his armies attacked the city from the front. His siege towers hurled flaming orken jelly into the city, and fire soon raged throughout Vinnengael's streets.

Dagnarus's two objectives were to obtain the Sovereign Stone and make himself king. To do so, he had to depose his elder brother, Helmos. Dagnarus looked for his brother in the palace, but could not find him. He determined that his brother must have fled for help to the gods, and so Dagnarus went to the Portal of the Gods, located inside the Temple of the Magi.

According to legend, Dagnarus and his brother, Helmos, met and fought over the Stone. The magical forces unleashed in that terrible battle swirled out of control, snapped like whips. The resulting blast brought down the Temple and the surrounding buildings, sent shock waves through the city. Buildings collapsed and fell into the streets, which were clogged with fleeing people and battling soldiers. Cracks opened in the ramps, sending people plunging to their deaths. The great cranes toppled, crushing many beneath.

Death and ruin came to Vinnengael and her people. The survivors fled. The city was left to its ghosts.

The Dominion Lords and their fell guide entered the outskirts city at dawn. They stood at the edge of the lake, where the turgid water lapped at their feet. The remains of what had once been the bustling docks of that great city stood crumbling around them.

This part of the city had been the farthest from the blast and had been little damaged by the explosion. Fire had been the enemy here. The fires started by the orken jelly set the wooden docks ablaze, destroyed the warehouses, with their rich store of goods, burned down the taverns and the brothels and the homes of sailors and fishermen. The remains of the docks could still be seen—blackened fingers of charred wood reaching out into Lake Ildurel, like the blackened hands of the wretched burn victims, who had flung themselves into the chill water to try to ease the terrible pain. They had found ease, most of them, by drowning.

"People ran from the upper levels to the lake level to escape the flames," said Silwyth, pointing to the cliffs high above, barely visible in the strange gray mist that hung over the ruins. "Those who lost their footing were crushed to death beneath the feet of the panicked mob. Those who reached the lake had nowhere to go, for there were no boats. They were trapped on the shore, the deep waters of the lake before them and the fires behind."

The Dominion Lords stood amidst the rubble, their hearts subdued. They had heard all their lives of the terrible tragedy of that day, but it was a legend, a tale told in the twilight. Now they stood inside the tale. The smell of burnt wood was sharp in their nostrils. The water that lapped on the shore was filthy, littered with debris. The gray mist from the falls congealed on their skin and made everything wet to the touch, so that their clothes felt clammy. The air was chill. The sun shone on the lake, but could not burn through the watery fog that made every object seem misshapen and distorted. The streets had disappeared under piles of debris that had once been buildings. The Dominion Lords stared in shock, overwhelmed by the appalling level of destruction. The thought came to each of them: How do we find our way through this?

The practical and pragmatic Captain put the thought into words.

"If the ramps that lead to the upper levels are destroyed, how do we reach the Temple?"

"I did not say the ramps were destroyed," Silwyth replied. "I said that there were cracks in them. The ramps are still there and can be climbed by those with courage."

"But if we have to crawl and hack and pick our way through all this mess, it will take us days—months maybe—to reach our destination," said Shadamehr.

"And you have warned us not to be caught here after dark," Wolfram stated. He gestured to the rubble, which was stacked up in great heaps. "Hah!"

"Yet there is a way," said Silwyth. "Remain here while I search it out."

"Wait, Silwyth!" Shadamehr said. "I'm going with you—"

Silwyth vanished. Wolfram plunged into the mists searching for him, but returned alone.

"He's disappeared," Wolfram reported. "I lost him in the fog."

"I think he's made of fog, that one," said the Captain.

"Or worse," said Damra. She looked at Shadamehr. "Should we tell them?"

"Tell us what?" Wolfram demanded.

"That Silwyth is no longer Silwyth," said Shadamehr. "We think that the real Silwyth was murdered and that this one is a Vrykyl."

Wolfram reached for his sword. "Then we should kill it."

"What makes you think so?" the Captain asked, laying a restraining hand on the dwarf's shoulder.

"He has changed," said Damra. "When I first met him, I trusted him even though I did not trust him. Now"—she shook her head—"I do not trust him at all."

"I never trusted him," Wolfram stated.

"I agree with Dame Rah," said the Captain. "He has changed. I trusted the Silwyth I caught in my fishing net. But I do not trust the one who brought us here."

"The question is, what do we do?" Shadamehr asked. "Do we confront him and maybe risk his turning on us?"

"Yes," said Wolfram, raising his sword.

"I think we have to," Damra agreed.

"No," said the Captain. She folded arms across her chest. "We don't say a word to him."

"I side with the others," said Shadamehr. "Why should we continue to follow this evil being?"

The Captain shrugged her massive shoulders. "Each of us was told to take the Stone to the Portal. And that is what we must do. Do you know the way to this God Portal, any of you?"

"But the Vrykyl is most probably leading us into a trap," argued Shadamehr.

"All the better," the Captain said.

"Wait!" Shadamehr raised his hand. "I fell off when you went around that curve. Please explain."

"If the elf is a Vrykyl and the Vrykyl intended to kill us, it could have done so anytime," said the Captain. "Instead, the Vrykyl promises to take us to the Portal of the Gods. Probably, as you said, Shadow Man, to fall into the trap of this Void lord. Therefore, the Vrykyl will see it to that we arrive at the Portal safely."

"In order to kill us once we get there," said Shadamehr.

"The fish you have been eating has done your brain good, Shadow Man," said the Captain, nodding in approval. "Once we reach the Portal, then we confront the Vrykyl and this Void lord and do whatever it is that must be done."

"I wish I could be that calm about it. Still, forewarned is forearmed," said Shadamehr thoughtfully. "At least we'll be prepared." He shrugged and kicked at a bit of charred wood at his feet. "I'll stay here and wait for our friend. The rest of you might want to take a look around, see if there are signs of any bahk."

The party split up. Wolfram and the Captain went to investigate the ruins of a large building. Damra walked along the shoreline, which was littered with the burnt-out hulks of ships; twisted, rusted iron, and rotting nets. She stepped on something and, looking down, she saw that she had trodden upon a skull, half-buried in the sand.

Elves revere death, for in death the soul is free to return to the Father and Mother, to dwell with them in the wondrous, glittering realm of heaven. Elven dead are treated with immense respect, the body burned, so that the soul is freed to rise into the heavens, on the breath of the gods. The skull seemed to repudiate everything in which she believed.

There are no gods, the empty eyes revealed. Death is the Void, and there is nothing beyond.

Hearing her cry out, Shadamehr came to her. He took hold of her, drew her close. His arm around her was strong, warm and comforting.

"I'm sorry I frightened you. It's only a . . . skull. But there is so much death here. So much terror and despair." Damra pressed her hands over her eyes. "It is too awful, too sad to bear."

"I know," Shadamehr said somberly, his own heart oppressed. "I understand."

"Do you?" She looked up at him, her brow furrowed. "I don't believe you. You never take anything seriously."

"I'll tell you a secret," said Shadamehr. "The reason I laugh is to keep my teeth from chattering."

He looked up at the cliffs they were going to have to scale, at collapsed buildings, cracked roads, crumbling stairs. In the distance, he could hear the roar of the falls, a roar muffled by the dank mists that shrouded the city.

"I'll tell you something else, Damra," he said somberly. "From here on out, things are only going to get worse."

"I heard something!" said Wolfram. He pointed toward the ruins of the building. "It came from in there."

"I heard it, too," said the Captain. She drew the enormous curved-bladed weapon that she wore thrust into her broad leather belt.

"This used to be a warehouse, maybe," said Wolfram, eyeing the rubble warily.

"Whatever it was," said the Captain, "it's not anymore."

The two moved closer, keeping their eyes fixed intently on the rubble.

"What did you hear?" Wolfram asked in a low voice. "What did it sound like?"

"A board moving," said the Captain. "I don't see anything. Do you?"

Three of the four walls of the warehouse were still standing. Built of brick, the walls had resisted the fire that had destroyed other structures nearby. The roof had collapsed, however, taking down most of the front portion of the building with it. Sword in hand, Wolfram peered through the mist into the darkness. He strained his ears, but could not hear the sound again, nor any sound, beyond the rasping breath of the ork.

"Why don't you orks breathe through your noses, like the rest of us?" Wolfram asked irritably. "I can't hear anything with you huffing away like a bellows."

"Our noses are smaller than our mouths," said the Captain. "We take in more air this way."

Wolfram thought this over. He couldn't very well find a flaw in her argument, and he let the subject drop. He poked at the rubble.

A board shifted. Something moved, and Wolfram leapt backward.

"There!" he gasped.

"A rat," said the Captain, sheathing her sword in disgust.

"What's going on?" asked Shadamehr, coming up with Damra.

"We heard a sound. Turned out to be a rat," said the Captain.

"Maybe it was," said Wolfram, still peering into the rubble. "And maybe it wasn't. It sounded bigger to me."

He took a long look into the mist-shrouded shadows, but saw nothing. Even the rat had fled.

"Smart little bugger," he muttered. "Smarter than us."

"Silwyth's been gone a long time," Damra observed, shivering in the chill, dark air. "Maybe he isn't going to come back."

"I wouldn't, if I was him," Wolfram said.

"But you are not me, dwarf. I am back and I have found a path through the ruin," Silwyth announced, emerging from the mist. "The path will take us to the first of the ramps. From there, we climb. I will show you the way."

He started off, then realized that he was alone. He looked back.

"Are you coming? Or would you rather hunt for rats?"

"We found one already," said Shadamehr. "And one is more than enough. Lead on, Silwyth. We're right behind you."

At a gesture from K'let, Raven left the mist-shrouded shadows of the warehouse in which they'd taken refuge and looked to see if the dwarf and his companions were well away. The Trevinici had been amazed to see the dwarf, Wolfram—but Raven did not need K'let's sharp, warning hiss in order to keep silent. The dwarf was from another world, another time. He had nothing to do with Raven, and Raven wanted nothing to do with him. He'd had his fill of dwarves and humans, orks and elves. Let them go their way. He would go his.

This City of Ghosts was a city of silence, anyway. To give voice in these blackened ruins would be as disrespectful as shouting in a tomb.

Raven noted that K'let was not surprised to see the dwarf and his oddly assorted companions traipsing around the ruins. K'let might have been expecting them, even watching out for them, for he and Raven had kept watch on the city for days before they entered it. The taan Vrykyl had brought Raven to the ruined warehouse, where they crouched in the shadows, watching as the dwarf and his friends entered the ruined dockyards, had their little talk, then went their way.

Certain that they were alone, Raven returned to the warehouse, where K'let was waiting for him.

The Vrykyl was in his taan form, as he had been throughout their journey. Raven had the impression that K'let didn't much like his black, Void-made armor, for which Raven was thankful. The Trevinici could almost fool himself into believing he was with a taan, not one of the hideous Vrykyl.

Their journey together had been a strange one. K'let could not speak Raven's language, although Raven had the feeling that the Vrykyl understood much of what Raven said. Raven could not speak the taan language—his throat could not make its crackling, popping, and whistling sounds, but he had learned to understand many of the words. They managed a communication of sorts.

"They are gone," Raven reported.

He was about to say more, when he felt the ground shiver beneath his feet. The rotting, blackened timbers shook and trembled.

K'let made another hissing sound, his lip curled back from his teeth. He ducked back into the shadows, motioned Raven to follow.

"Bahk!" K'let said and pointed.

An enormous creature, standing some twenty feet high, lumbered slowly along the crumbling street. Raven had heard stories of these monsters from warriors who had fought them, but he had never truly believed the tales. Not until now.

The bahk's hulking head with its small eyes, shadowed by an overhanging forehead, swung back and forth as it walked. The bahk's shoulders were stooped and rounded. Bony protrusions extended the length of its spine. Its huge feet shook the ground as it walked. The bahk halted as it came near the warehouse. Its head shifted in their direction, the small and lackluster eyes turned their way.

K'let snarled low in the back of his throat. Raven held still, not daring to breathe. The bahk gave a grunt and went on its way, continuing into the ruined city. For a long time after its passing, Raven heard the crashing and rending of timbers and the thud of falling rock—the bahk clearing a path through the debris.

K'let sniffed the air, appeared satisfied. He left the warehouse, gestured to Raven to accompany him.

Raven held his ground, shook his head.

"You can understand me, can't you, K'let? You've been around humans a long time and, if you can't speak our language, you know what I am saying. I want to know what we're doing here in this accursed City of Ghosts."

Raven forced himself to stare straight into the Vrykyl's empty eyes, though it was like looking into a well of darkness.

K'let took a step forward and thrust a taloned finger into Raven's chest. At the touch, Raven could see through the façade of taan flesh and taan hide to living death—the bestial skull, marred by the cracks and fissures left by old injuries; the yellow teeth; the empty eye sockets. He smelled the stench of rot and decay.

K'let tapped his finger against Raven's chest. "I made you nizam. In return, you promised me your life."

Raven said nothing. He stared into the dark eyes.

"It is time for you to fulfill your promise," said K'let. He frowned, leered. "Or are you just another oath-breaking xkse?"

"I keep my promises," said Raven.

"Good," said K'let with a grunt. Turning, he walked off into the dark mists.

Raven stood a moment, thinking of Dur-zor, thinking of his people.

"I keep my promises," he repeated, and followed.

THE DOMINION LORDS LOST TRACK OF TIME, FOR THE SUN'S LIGHT was blotted out by the swirling mists. Their way was easy at first. The streets on the lower level had been cleared of debris, the rubble swept aside, pushed into precariously balanced piles along the edges of the street or shoved down alleyways. They marveled, until Shadamehr explained the cause.

"The bahk did this," he said. "They've cleared a path to the inner part of the city."

"But they won't go up top," said Wolfram, tilting his head to try to see through the gray tendrils of mist that dragged across the higher levels of the dead city.

"Not according to Silwyth," said Shadamehr.

Wolfram placed his hand on an enormous iron beam, part of one of the marvelous cranes that the orks had built. Forty feet long, heavy as a house, the huge beam had been picked up and tossed aside as if it weighed no more than a twig.

"A beast that can move this crane," said Wolfram, "is afraid to go up there." Shaking his head morosely, he sighed and moved on.

They followed the bahk-cleared streets through the first level and up into the second, where the way grew more difficult. Silwyth chose to make a wide detour around the central portion of the city that was frequented by the bahk, thus they could no longer rely on the bahk to clear the path.

They climbed over and around and sometimes under piles of debris and were soon weary and aching, wet and filthy. Without Silwyth's guidance they would have been utterly lost, for the mists grew thicker as they drew nearer the waterfalls, and they soon lost sight of cliffs above them. The buildings on the second level had been better constructed than those in the dockyard. Many had survived both fire and the blast. Standing amid the rubble, these sentinels, with their gouged-out windows and scarred faces, stood silent and lonely watch over the dead. Here and there, one had finally tumbled down, its broken stones clogging the streets.

But though the destruction was less, the sadness and sorrow were greater. The houses had once been vibrant with life, and the absence of that life was emphasized by the simple possessions of the living: chairs and tables, pitchers and cups. A spinning wheel in a corner by a fireplace. A kettle on the hearth. A rag doll. A wooden sword. Dust-coated. Cobwebbed. Whole. Broken. Sometimes these objects lay in the streets, as though the owners had taken them with them in their mad rush to flee the devastation, only to drop them by the wayside. Too heavy, perhaps. Too cumbersome. Or maybe the people realized that this bit of their lives to which they clung so desperately meant nothing anymore, was useless.

"How unfair it seems," said Shadamehr, picking up a cup that had rolled out into the street, "that something so inconsequential as this should survive, when the hands that made it perished. Makes you wonder, doesn't it. We work and strive and suffer, and all that remains of us in the end is some pewter mug."

"That is the Void talking," said Damra in a low voice.

"Maybe it speaks the truth," said Shadamehr bitterly, and he tossed the mug aside.

There were bodies on this level, skeletal remains lying where they had fallen two hundred years before. Many of the bodies were those of soldiers who had fought a raging battle in the streets. Some lay on the cobblestones, side by side, the shafts of arrows or rusted sword blades mingling with their bones. Some lay slumped on crumbling door stoops, as if they had grown weak from loss of blood and sat down to rest, only to fall into a sleep from which they never woke. Several bodies carried shields marked with the symbols of elven nobility. They were found lying around a single corpse, probably their commander.

The bodies of ordinary citizens were here, too. Those who waited too long to flee their homes, or who had been caught up in the battle or the firestorm, succumbing to the choking smoke, crushed beneath a fallen building. In one area, they came across the remains of a family: man, woman, child, and the small skeleton of a dog.

The sorrow and the horror of the piteous sights weighed on their hearts and drained their souls.

"I hear their voices," said Wolfram in hollow tones. "And I feel their touch. They don't want us here."

"Stop it," Shadamehr said sharply. "We're scaring ourselves. They're dead. They died long ago."

"Wherever their spirits are, they are at rest," Damra added gently and whispered a prayer.

"The elves do not rest," said Silwyth. "They were traitors, who died dishonored. They lie here unburied; their spirits refused admittance to the blessed presence of the Father and Mother."

For the first time since Damra had known Silwyth, he betrayed emotion. When he said "refused admittance" his tone was one of bitterness, regret.

Is the voice speaking Silwyth's? Damra wondered. Or the Vrykyl who has seized hold of him? Or are they both so close that the living and the dead speak as one?

She was tempted to ask, but Silwyth kicked suddenly, savagely, at the corpse of the elf.

"We must hurry," he said, and led them on.

It was about midday, or so they guessed, when they reached one of the ramps that ran from the second level to the top of the high cliffs, where stood the magnificent Temple of the Magi and the wondrous palace, set against the backdrop of the seven waterfalls. They could hear the thunder of the water, though the falls themselves remained unseen in the fog.

The ramp had been carved out of the cliff by human magi, experienced in Earth magic. The ramp did not lead straight up the cliff, for the grade would have been too steep for wagons and pedestrians. Instead, it made a gentle curve that wound round the face of the rock.

On a bright and sunny day in Old Vinnengael, walking up this ramp would have been a pleasurable experience. One could have looked upon the vast and bustling city spread out below, the blue lake beyond, and upward to the palace, with its glittering towers and dancing rainbows.

The rainbows had gone gray, the glittering towers had fallen to ruin. The mists blotted everything from view except the ramp, which was slick and slime-ridden, pitted and crumbling, with wide, gaping cracks. Each person in the group knew that this ramp carried them to destiny.

What a strange and terrible path to lead us to the gods, thought Damra.

I wish I had brought some rope, thought Shadamehr. A few stout lengths of rope would make all the difference.

"Dunner walked this road," Wolfram said to Gilda, whose spirit he felt near him. "I am walking in his footsteps. I must do nothing to disgrace him."

The shaman read the omens, recalled the Captain of Captains. The omens were bad for the humans, but good for the orks, or so the shaman said. Omens do not lie, but sometimes they do not tell us all the truth.

"Are you here, my lord?" Valura called out silently to Dagnarus. "Do you lie in readiness? I bring you the gift you have long sought. They follow me like sheep, trusting, unknowing. It will be easy to take them by surprise. Tell me that you are here, my lord. Tell me you are here, waiting for me."

No answer came. Only the rushing crash of the water spilling over the falls.

The climb was long and arduous, the rock so slippery and treacherous that in places they had to crawl on all fours. Their hands and knees were soon scraped and scratched, their clothes soaked, torn and covered with slime. They kept away from the ramp's edge, so that a misstep would not send them plunging over the side. At one point, Shadamehr slipped and slithered halfway back down the ramp before he could stop himself. At another, they came to a crack in the ramp so wide that Wolfram, with his short legs, could not jump across. The Captain picked up the dwarf. With a heave of her huge arms, she sent the stout Wolfram flying. He landed with a thud on his stomach on the opposite side, the breath knocked clean out of him.

And as they climbed, a sense of dread fell on them, grayer and danker than the mists.

"What did you say?" Wolfram looked around at the Captain.

"Me? I said nothing," replied the ork. "I need my breath for more important things—like breathing."

"You said something," Wolfram stated. "I heard you clearly."

The Captain shook her head and continued climbing.

"What is it?" Shadamehr asked, alarmed, looking around at Damra.

"What is what?" She stared at him blankly.

"You touched me on the arm," he said. "I thought you wanted something."

"I did not touch you," Damra said. Both her hands clung to a stone jutting out from the wall. "I don't dare let go. If I did, you'd have to pick me up at the bottom."

"Something touched me," said Shadamehr.

"And I heard a voice," said Wolfram.

Then they all heard the voices, distant, indistinct, echoes of shouts or screams from centuries before. They felt the hands, unseen fingers grasping, clutching, pushing. They began to see things, too, glimpses of movement caught from the corner of the eye, only to vanish when confronted.

"Let go of me," Wolfram cried, taking a swipe at something with his fist.

He lost his balance and would have toppled into a crack, if the Captain had not caught him by his belt and dragged him back. They were near the top of the cliff. The path was here steeper and more treacherous, for parts of the ramp had been buried beneath rockslides. The mists closed in. They could not see the ground below, nor could they see anything above them. They seemed suspended in nothingness.

It was hard to move, to keep going. Unseen bodies buffeted them, pushing and shoving.

I can't keep this up much longer, Shadamehr realized, gasping for breath. He shivered with the cold; sweat beaded on his forehead and rolled down his neck. He lost two steps for every step he took forward. Then something struck him, knocked him off his feet. He fell onto his hands and knees on the rain-slick rock. The crowds surged around him. They were carrying him over the edge of the cliff . . .

Stop it! Damra pleaded.

Their voices clamored in her ears, all of them filled with terror or crying out in pain.

Please stop! I cannot help you! She pressed back against the wall, crying for them to stop.

The Captain struggled on, then the unseen force slammed her up against the side of the cliff, held her pinned. Voices shrieked and howled, so that it seemed she must go deaf or mad. Fists pummeled her, feet kicked her.

Walking within the Void, Valura could see what the others could not. She could see the screaming mouths and the panic-widened eyes, the battering fists and the bloodstained hands. The mob caught her up and swept her back in time to the night that should have been a triumph for her lord, but had gone so terribly wrong. Caught in time, Valura could not move. She fought and struggled, but centuries stood in her way.

"My lord!" she cried in silent supplication. "The dead have us trapped. We are within sight of the Temple, but we cannot reach you. Our path is blocked. If you do not come to my aid, I must fail you!"

But if he responded, she could not hear his voice for the terrifying cries of the dying.

Caught in the unseen tide of terror, Wolfram couldn't see for the mobs that surrounded him, couldn't hear for the screams that shrilled in his ears.

I have to get away from here, he thought, his heart swelling with panic. I have to flee the flames and the falling rock and the murderous soldiers. Death stalks me. I have to flee death and no one is going to stand in my way. These are not people who block my way. They are beasts, trying to save their lives at the cost of my own.

With a roar, he turned around and started to run back down the ramp, only to slip and fall. He lay on the ground, cursing and shrieking.

Shadamehr was on his knees, his hand raised in a futile effort to protect himself. Damra huddled in a crack in the wall, her hands covering her ears. The Captain fought unseen foes, lashing out at the gray nothing in a frenzy of panic.

"What is this that blocks our way?" Shadamehr cried.

"Ghosts," said Silwyth. "Ghosts of despair. Ghosts of terror. Ghosts of fear. Held prisoner by the wayward magic, the ghosts endlessly scream, endlessly flee, endlessly try to escape the inescapable. None can withstand them. They carry all before them in a mad rush to an end that for them is nothing but another horrible beginning."

A chill, pale light glimmered before them, burning like ice on wet flesh. The figure of a woman, helmed and armored, took shape out of the mists.

"Did my master send you?" Valura called out.

"I am come," said the chill voice.

"That is no answer," Valura returned.

"It is the only answer you will have from me," was the response.

"You are a Dominion Lord. I can tell by your armor."

"I am."

"What are you, then?" Valura cried. "What are you called?"

"I am the Lord of Ghosts."

The woman stood before them, clad in armor that shone ephemeral and beautiful as moonlight on a cobweb. Her helm was a mask of her face, set in the calm serenity of death. She carried no weapon. The dead fight no battles, know no fear.

When she spoke, the screams and clamoring voices went silent. She raised her hand, and the shoving, pushing, bashing hands fell limp. The ghosts halted in their terrible flight, fell back, gave way. They bowed before her, permitted her to pass.

The Lord of the Ghosts.

She passed the Tests for a Dominion Lord. She underwent the Transfiguration, and she was granted the blessing of the magical armor. But though her spirit was strong, her body was weak. Her heart burst, and she fell down dead before the altar.

The Lord of the Ghosts beckoned to the four Dominon Lords, motioned them to come forward.

"I have watched for you a long time," said the Lord of the Ghosts. "And so have others. They await you in the Portal of the Gods."

"Who is it that waits for us in the Portal of the Gods?" Shadamehr demanded, not moving.

"*You* wait there, Dominion Lord," said the Lord of Ghosts.

"I don't understand," said Shadamehr.

"You are not meant to."

"I will come," said Damra, clasping her hand around the medallion she wore on her neck.

"We will come," said Wolfram firmly. "Gilda and I together."

"I come to fulfill the oath," said the Captain. "And put an end to bad omens."

One by one, they vanished. Only Shadamehr remained. He and the Lord of Ghosts. His ghosts. Ghosts of regret, lost opportunities, past mistakes, failures.

"I will come," said Shadamehr, humbly.

That left Valura, in the guise of Silwyth, standing on the ramp with the Lord of Ghosts. The calm, serene face of hallowed death looked into the hollow eyes of the hideous, rotting skull.

"You cannot pass," said the Lord of Ghosts.

Fear and despair filled the emptiness of the Void. Yet Valura did not falter. She faced her fear. She faced the Lord of Ghosts.

"You cannot stop me. Nothing can stop me," Valura said. "My lord wants me. All this I did for love of him."

"A love that dishonored you," returned the Lord of Ghosts sternly. "A love that gave nothing and took everything. A love that fed on itself, fed on you."

"Nonetheless," Valura answered, staring straight into the cold and burning light, "it was the only love I ever knew."

FOR MANY DAYS, RAVEN HAD WALKED ALONGSIDE LIVING DEATH IN the form of the taan Vrykyl. Perhaps prolonged exposure to that horror inured him to the terrible sights he witnessed in the ruins of Old Vinnengael. Or perhaps his years on the field of battle had hardened him. He felt cool pity at the sight of the innocents who had died, but a warrior knows that the god of war does not bother to differentiate between those paid to bleed and those who stumble unwittingly into his clutches. Raven felt nothing at all when he came upon the bodies of the unburied soldiers, except to repeat the soldier's prayer in his heart, asking that he be spared such a fate or, if he wasn't, that the god of war accept his spirit anyway.

He and K'let traveled a different route from the one taken by the Dominion Lords. He and K'let did not take the ramp. They could see the others climbing it, and K'let, with a gesture, motioned Raven to a stone stairway. K'let ascended it, and Raven followed. He did not know his fate, but he accepted it, made his peace with it.

Their destination was somewhere at the top of the cliffs on which the city had been built. Every time they halted, K'let turned his gaze in that direction. Raven had no idea what was up there. He knew little or nothing about the city. He'd heard tales of its destruction, but he couldn't remember details. Cities under siege hold little interest for Trevinici warriors. Proper battles are fought in wide-open spaces, with armies charging at one another to meet with a resounding clash of arms. Flinging flaming jelly on helpless people trapped behind walls is not a Trevinici's idea of warfare.

Whatever was up there, K'let was in a hurry to reach it. The taan climbed swiftly and eagerly, using both his hands and feet to scale the crumbling stairs. Lacking the Vrykyl's undead strength and endurance, Raven climbed more slowly, with frequent stops to rest and catch his breath. He could feel K'let glowering at him every time he paused, and since meeting the taan's dead-eyed gaze was not pleasant, Raven forced himself to keep up as best he could.

They were about halfway to the top when Raven felt the touch on his arm and heard the scream. He drew his knife, looked swiftly about. He saw nothing. The hair rose in prickles on his neck. Trevinici do not tell ghost stories. Their respect for the dead is too great, and Raven was not one to give way to his imagination.

"Cobwebs," he told himself, and continued on.

The hands pushed at him and shoved him and tried to knock him off the stairs. Their voices dinned in his ears, howled and shrieked so that they nearly deafened him. He sought to ignore the unseen foe and continue climbing, but he was falling farther and farther behind. The battle sapped his strength. He gasped for breath. Every movement was a struggle. The stair seemed endless, the mist-shrouded cliff top high above him.

Raven collapsed, unable to go on. He crouched against the stairs, beating at the unseen fists and feet, cursing and flailing at them.

A hand closed over his arm.

Raven gasped and shuddered and cried out in agony. The hand was the hand of a Vrykyl, and its touch was the touch of the Void. The hand burned with a dreadful chill that struck to Raven's heart.

K'let's talons dug into Raven's flesh. Rivulets of blood trailed down Raven's arm. K'let yanked Raven to his feet.

Raven tried to jerk his arm free, but K'let's grip was strong, and Raven could not break it.

"Let go of me," Raven said through teeth clenched against the painful burning of the Vrykyl's touch. "I can make it on my own."

K'let's dark and empty eyes stared at him.

"I can make it," Raven repeated. "The ghosts are gone."

K'let stared at him a moment longer, then, with a grunt, he let go of Raven and began once again to climb.

Raven looked down at his arm. The flesh was a ghastly white in the imprint of a hand. Raven rubbed it, to try to restore some color. He could not feel his own touch, however. It was like touching the flesh of a dead man. At least, he could still use his hands, and he used them to good purpose. He climbed rapidly, fear lending him strength.

If there were still ghosts around, they held no terrors for him. Not anymore.

THE DRAGON OF THE VOID CIRCLED THE RUINS OF VINNENGAEL. He was enormous, the largest ever to walk upon Loerem, and he had been here once before. Descending on the ruins of what had once been the proud city of Vinnengael, the dragon had lifted the body of the monk of Dragon Mountain from the rubble of the destroyed Temple of the Magi. The monk had come to record the history of hubris and jealousy, treacherous ambition and blinding pride, heartbreaking sorrow, noble self-sacrifice, and the dragon had been sent to bring the dead monk home.

Shredding the gray mists with his black wings, the dragon settled upon the mountainous ruin that was all that remained of the Temple.

The dragon of the Void was the eldest of his kind upon Loerem and the only dragon wholly dedicated to the Void. How many years he had lived, not even he could say, for the passing of the seasons meant very little to him. He had been an elder dragon when King Tamaros was born. He had witnessed the rise of Dagnarus as Lord of the Void. The dragon had watched the fall of Old Vinnengael, had been the one to rescue the body of the monk from the ruined city so that the history of the moment should be preserved.

The dragon generally took no active part in mankind's affairs, except as one of the five guardians of the monks of Dragon Mountain. The dragon of the Void had little care for mankind, but he did find man's struggles as he plodded along life's brief path to be an endless source of amusement, thus he had agreed to become one of the dragons who guarded the recorders of that struggle.

Over the centuries, the dragon had watched another struggle—an eternal struggle, between the gods and the Void for the souls of man. The Void dragon had watched the tide of battle ebb and flow, with now one side coming close to victory and now the other. He thought it likely that neither would ever win (or should ever win, as the elemental dragons were wont to preach). Then Dagnarus looked inside the Sovereign Stone. He saw the Void and embraced it. He claimed the Dagger of the Vrykyl. The Void dragon was intrigued.

He foresaw that Dagnarus's fire would not blaze up only to gutter out like the fires of so many others before him, extinguished by vacuum of the Void. The fire of Dagnarus needed no air. It fed on itself and it had the potential to burn long and bright. Through him, the Void gained power, and the dragon could actually envision a time when the Void might reign supreme in the world.

"The gods marshal their forces," the Void dragon warned Dagnarus, as the Lord of the Void climbed down from the dragon's back. "They have sent their champions to test you."

Dagnarus laughed. "The gods only think they sent them. The champions come at my behest."

The Void dragon was troubled. "Do not trust your friends, Lord of the Void. And do not underestimate your foes."

"I have no friends," Dagnarus returned. "And my foes fall before me. This day, the Sovereign Stone will be mine."

"Eschew the Sovereign Stone," said the Void dragon contemptuously. "You do not need it."

"I do not need it," Dagnarus agreed. "But I want it. Farewell, Wise Master, and thank you for bearing me to my destiny."

The dragon was black as the Void that is the heart of the universe, around which all the other elements revolve. In his eyes was the darkness that surrounds the stars. Everything that is born, even the stars, must eventually fall into that nothingness. There the gods waited, with hands outstretched, to gather up the nothingness and cast it back into the heavens, where it burst into suns.

The dragon spread his black wings. Night fell over Old Vinnengael, so that the mists were only felt, not seen. The rainbows had long ago disappeared.

Yet, for a moment, the dragon paused.

"Lord of the Void," called the dragon, as Dagnarus walked away, "what will you do with the Sovereign Stone, when it is yours?"

Dagnarus stood atop the mountain of ruin that had been the Temple of the Magi. The rubble was unstable and shifted beneath his weight. He had always possessed a feline's ability to keep his footing, no matter how treacherous the path he walked, and he retained his balance.

"I will bring peace to the realm," Dagnarus answered. "I will stop all wars between all nations. I will put an end to strife, so that people everywhere may prosper."

"Your father's dream," said the dragon.

"I will make it a reality."

"Your father was told, when he was given the Sovereign Stone, to beware the bitter center," said the Void dragon.

"You forget," said Dagnarus with his charming smile, "that I was the one who looked directly into that bitter center."

"I do not forget," said the dragon. "But I think you have."

The dragon spread its wings and blended with the darkness.

"You are wrong," said Dagnarus quietly. Standing atop the ruin, he looked around him and saw the destruction that his hand had wrought. He saw the ghosts, rushing endlessly to their doom. He saw the ash and the rubble, the corpses lying in the broken streets.

"I never meant for this to happen," he cried to the gods, trying to pierce the smoking mists, trying to see to heaven. "It would not have happened, if you had given me what I was meant to have! I will take the gift you gave my father, and I will do what you should have done!"

Raven watched in wonder to see the handsome, richly dressed man slide and scramble with catlike grace and surety among the ruins of what looked to have been a Temple.

"Who is that man?" Raven asked.

"Ko-kutryx," said K'let.

"Dagnarus? Your god?"

K'let's lip curled. "Ko-kutryx," he repeated, and spit on the ground.

Raven saw reflected in the Vrykyl's empty eyes the figure of the richly dressed man, bold and fearless.

K'let pointed at the man, then put his finger to his lips.

Raven nodded. They were to follow this Ko-kutryx, go where he led them, keep silent, not alert him to the fact that they were on his trail.

Dagnarus walked with assurance toward his destination. Either he had no thought of pursuit, or he had no fear. He did not bother to look behind him. K'let rose to his feet and motioned Raven to do the same.

"What of the four Dominion Lords?" Raven asked.

K'let grinned broadly, chuckled in his throat, and shrugged.

Dagnarus rounded the corner of the partially destroyed temple, one of the few buildings still standing. K'let and Raven followed after him.

The taan moved rapidly over the cracked and crumbling pavement, using his toes and their long talons to grip the broken flagstones and secure his footing. Raven had to be more careful, watch every step, for fear that a stone would turn beneath his foot, causing him to slip and wrench an ankle.

He did not have to worry about making noise that might alert the man they tailed. The roar of the nearby falls was so loud that it was hard to think over it. Raven risked one quick look, trying to see the waterfalls, but the coming of twilight and the clouds of fog roiling up out of the chasm into which the water plunged blocked his view.

"In here!" said K'let, gesturing to the Temple.

Raven judged that this had once been some type of holy site by the four mandalas engraved on the marble blocks. This part of the building had survived relatively intact, with only a few cracks in the walls and a partially collapsed roof. This temple was similar in design to the Temple of the Magi in Dunkar, only much, much larger and far more magnificent.

Raven did not feel comfortable in temples. The gods of the Trevinici were gods of the trees and the earth, the sun and the moon and the stars, the water and the fire and air. There were gods of life and gods of death and war. Such gods did not reside inside stifling walls, were not held prisoner beneath domed ceilings or locked up behind gates.

As Raven moved deeper into the ruins, his unease increased. He had no light. Apparently K'let needed none, for he forged ahead without pause, following the sound of Dagnarus's boots echoing hollowly through the empty corridors. Raven stumbled along as best he could, bumping into things and making a racket.

K'let growled and muttered, hissed at him impatiently to keep up. Raven did the best he could, but at one point, he tripped over something and lurched forward. He thrust out his hands to stop his fall. His fingers touched cold, smooth stone, and he was face to face with a grinning skull. Realizing in horror that he fallen headlong into a tomb, Raven scrambled out as fast as he could move. He was not one to believe in omens, as did the orks, but he couldn't help wondering with a shudder if this was not some sort of portent. Perhaps the tomb into which he'd fallen was his own.

Gritting his teeth, Raven stumbled after K'let.

Only twice before had Dagnarus walked the corridor that led to the Portal of the Gods—the first time the night he'd met his brother there and the second time when he'd come there in a futile search for the Sovereign Stone.

The first time, he'd found the Portal easily. The second, he'd searched for it for many weary days. The Portal was not some grand chamber, as might have been expected, but a small monk's cell located in a part of the Temple that was out of the way, not easily found. At last he had found it, or it had found him, he wasn't certain which. This time he knew exactly where he was going. He had committed the route to memory.

He also remembered to bring a lamp, for the Portal was in a part of the Temple shrouded in darkness. The lamplight guiding his footsteps, Dagnarus walked the silent corridors and the empty halls. He paused once, hearing footsteps and a scrabbling sound, as if someone had fallen.

"The Dominion Lords," he said to himself, smiling, "stumbling along in my wake. They bring the Sovereign Stone to me, in the Portal of the Gods. At long last, the fulfillment of a dream."

He wore the black carapace that was the armor of the Void, and now he called upon the Void to remove its protection. Let the Dominion Lords come armored and accoutered to the teeth. They would find him in his traveling cloak and silken doublet. He had no fear of them. Let them attack him, stab him, cut off his head, poison him. They could do all that and more, kill him thirty times over. He had but to kill each of them once.

Confident, at ease, Dagnarus knew he had reached the Portal when the light of his lamp shone upon the skeletal remains of his whipping boy, Gareth.

The bones lay huddled in a heap at the base of a wall in a corridor that led to the Portal. The back of the skull was crushed. The smear of blood that trailed down the wall was still there, clearly visible. The sight of the blood irritated Dagnarus, for it called to mind Gareth's murder—one of Dagnarus's life-long regrets. There had been no need to kill Gareth. The fact that Dagnarus had done so, acting out of jealous rage, was a lapse in judgment—marked him as petty, weak, and vengeful.

The sight of the bloodstain brought back too many memories—memories of Gareth, memories of childhood. Those brought memories of his father, and those brought memories of Helmos. Dagnarus felt himself tumbling down a well of memories.

"The first thing I will do, once I have the Sovereign Stone, will be to wash away that blasted stain," Dagnarus promised.

Gareth had died close to the small cell that was the Portal of the Gods. Dagnarus tried to see inside, but failed. He stepped over Gareth's body, held the lamp high, to illuminate the room.

The chamber had the appearance of a monk's cell, small and windowless, quiet and plain, furnished with a bed, a desk, and a chair. Dagnarus felt a sharp disappointment. This was not the chamber he remembered.

His was a careless mind, which did not recall details well—with one exception. He could recall every single detail of that final meeting with his brother Helmos. He could recall every detail about the Portal of the Gods.

"An enormous chamber," Dagnarus said, flashing the light about the room. "With no walls beneath the dome of heaven. The dome was empty, yet the emptiness was filled with light. In the very center the Sovereign Stone—the quarter piece of the Sovereign Stone—sparkled bright against the radiant light, as the evening star shines at sunset."

Only his brother stood between him and his greatest desire.

His brother stood alone.

Helmos's expression was grave, serious. The light that shone in the Portal shone in his eyes.

"All this is your fault," Dagnarus told Helmos. "If you had given me what should have been mine, none of this would have happened. I will finally make it right, but you will never know the pain this has cost me.

And so I say, damn you, Helmos. Damn your soul to the Void, as mine has been damned all these years. These empty, hollow years . . ."

He stood holding the lantern, looking into the small room with four walls and a ceiling and a bed, a chair, a desk.

"When I get rid of the stain, I'll get rid of this Portal, too," Dagnarus vowed. "I don't need an avenue to the Gods. If the gods want to speak to me, they can come to me. I'll raze this temple, raze the palace and all that's left standing in this horrible place. I'll build a new city here, my own city. I'll rid this place of its ghosts."

As Dagnarus took a step toward the Portal, a pale, ephemeral figure rose up from the bones on the floor.

"My prince." Gareth's spirit bowed, but when Dagnarus tried to move past the ghost, he found his way blocked.

Gareth looked in death as he had looked in life. He wore the black robes of a Void sorcerer. His face was marred with the birthmark that inspired Dagnarus to nickname him "Patch."

"I want to go in, Gareth," said Dagnarus. "Stand aside."

"I am not keeping you out, Your Highness," said Gareth.

Dagnarus flicked a glance past the spirit into the Portal. Shrugging, he turned carelessly away. When he had the Sovereign Stone, he would enter. Or maybe he wouldn't. After all, what would be the need?

"Have you done as I commanded? Are the Dominion Lords coming? Do they bring with them the four portions of the Sovereign Stone?"

"Yes, Your Highness," Gareth replied.

"I am king, now," said Dagnarus sharply. "King of New Vinnengael."

"Yes, Your Majesty," Gareth replied. "I'm sorry. I am accustomed to the old way of speaking."

"Never mind," Dagnarus muttered. "You can call me what you want. The other sounds funny when you say it."

"Thank you, Your Highness."

Dagnarus paced the narrow corridor, his hands clasped behind his back, his gaze going to that annoying smear of blood on the wall.

"Will it take them long?" he demanded, rounding on Gareth. "I never liked waiting. You know that."

"The way for them is difficult, my lord," said Gareth. "You remember—"

"I remember too damn much." Dagnarus stared, frowning, at the blotch on the wall. "I am sorry for that, Patch," he said abruptly.

"Sorry for what, my lord?"

"For . . . this." Dagnarus touched the bones with the toe of his boot. "You served me well for many years. You tried to warn me what would happen if I defied the gods. Perhaps I should have listened to you, Gareth. What do you think? Should I have slunk off like a whipped pup, my tail between my legs? Should I have lived out my days in the small, mean room of my brother's charity?"

"I do not know, Your Majesty," said Gareth, quietly.

"Neither do I, although sometimes . . ." Dagnarus turned his head. "Is that you, Shakur?"

The Vrykyl emerged from the shadows of the narrow corridor. "I have been trying to talk to you, my lord—"

"You've been trying to talk to me. Valura's been trying to talk to me!" Dagnarus made an impatient gesture. "I can barely hear myself think for all the yammering in my head. Well, you're talking to me now. What is it you want?"

"I found out what happened to Klendist and his command."

"What in the name of the Void makes you think I give a damn?" Dagnarus demanded impatiently.

"He ran afoul of K'let."

Dagnarus fell silent. Having no orders to the contrary, Shakur went on.

"I told you about the tribes of taan camped near Old Vinnengael. I do not know for certain what happened, for there were no survivors, but my guess is that Klendist and his men found the taan and decided to raid their camp. Unfortunately for them, one of the camps turned out to be K'let's."

"So K'let is near here—" Dagnarus murmured.

"K'let is very near, my lord," said the taan. "K'let stands before you."

"Gareth, Shakur, now K'let. This place is getting crowded. Shakur, leave me."

"Never, my lord!" Shakur protested.

"I said leave me, Shakur. Go find out what is keeping those Dominion Lords and my Sovereign Stone."

Shakur cast a glance of loathing at the taan. "K'let has brought someone with him, my lord. A human warrior." Shakur motioned to the shadows.

"I can handle K'let and his human," Dagnarus said. "Shakur, you have your orders."

Sullenly, the Vrykyl stalked off. Dagnarus placed the lamp on the floor, near Gareth's outstretched, dead hand.

"Come closer, K'let, so that I can see you. Unless you are afraid of me."

"How many times have we fought together, Ko-kutryx?" K'let asked, striding forward. He retained the image of a taan warrior, a proud taan warrior. The scars of his triumphs mottled his white hide. He did not wear the armor of the Void. He wore the armor that the taan fashioned in their homeland, armor made of bone and hide and sinew. "In all those times, did you ever know me to be afraid? Even my last battle, was I afraid, Ko-kutryx? When you stabbed me, did I flinch or cry out?"

"No, K'let," Dagnarus answered. "You did not. Of all those who served me, you were the best, the most courageous. We might have been brothers, you and I. And that is why your treachery hurt me, K'let."

"My treachery!" K'let hissed the words in taanic. "What of your treachery, Ko-kutryx? What of the five thousand taan who fought your battles and gave you victory after victory. Death was their reward. And what of the rest of the taan you have brought to this godless land? Will death be their reward, as well?"

"I promised—"

K'let pointed a taloned finger. "You have promised much, Ko-kutryx! And all that we have seen of that promise is death!"

"Are you listening to yourself, K'let?" Dagnarus asked in contempt. "You whine like a slave! I brought the taan to this fat land. I gave the taan their pick of females and strong food. The taan have grown rich with slaves and steel armor and weapons. Your bellies and your waterskins have always been full. Your children have grown into powerful warriors. Yes, many taan have died, but what better fate for a warrior than death in battle? What fate does he want?

"You did yourself and your people a disservice when you defied me, K'let. I would have made you powerful—a king in your own right. I would have given the taan all the land and slaves they wanted and strong food for every meal. All that and more, I would have done for you, K'let," said Dagnarus. "If you had not betrayed me."

K'let was silent, pondering.

"I did not know, Ko-kutryx," K'let said at last. "You are right. A warrior's fate is death. To be taken by the gods . . ."

"One god, K'let," Dagnarus interrupted. "I am the god of the taan."

"You are the god of the taan, Ko-kutryx," said K'let. His clenched fingers relaxed, his twisted scowl eased. "I am sorry I spoke as I did. I came here intending to ask for your forgiveness, to be taken back into your favor. Anger ran off with my tongue. Will you forgive me?"

"I will," Dagnarus said. "And now, if that is all, you have leave to go. I will have orders for you later. You are dismissed."

He turned to Gareth. "Where are the Dominion Lords?" he demanded.

"Soon, Your Majesty," said the whipping boy. "Soon."

Dagnarus frowned. "If you have failed me, Gareth . . ."

"I have not, my lord."

"Ko-kutryx," said K'let, thrusting himself forward. "To prove my loyalty, I have brought you a gift."

"Very well," said Dagnarus, frustrated and impatient. "What is this gift?"

"Him," said K'let.

Raven stood in the shadows of the strange place and tried to make some sense of what was going on. Worn-out by his long and exhausting climb, he was confused by the darkness and the maze of corridors. He had come suddenly out of the darkness into the daunting presence of Dagnarus, Lord of the Void, and Raven was shaken to the depths of his soul.

Raven had heard of Dagnarus from Dur-zor, who had once worshipped him, until Raven had told her of his gods. Even though she said she believed in all that he believed in, Raven still suspected that Dur-zor had not quite given up her worship of her Ko-kutryx. Standing before him, Raven could understand why.

Raven was a military man, and he judged all men in those terms. He knew, at once, that here was a born soldier, a born commander. Dagnarus was not a god, but he was a man whom other men might follow to the Void and back.

To the Void. That old saw held new meaning for Raven. This Dagnarus had given his soul to the Void. He owed his power and his long life to the Void. The handsome, strong, commanding man who faced down

K'let and, with a snap of his fingers, brought the terrifying taan Vrykyl to heel, was Lord of the Void.

Raven shrank back among the shadows, and asked himself, "What am I doing here?"

He had been able to follow the conversation between Dagnarus and K'let. The taan spoke taanic. Dagnarus spoke Elderspeak, his native tongue. Even if Raven had not been able to understand, K'let's fury transcended mere words. Raven admired K'let's temerity, but he didn't think defying this Void lord was very wise. Raven was vastly surprised that Dagnarus did not blast K'let to the ground. The two appeared to mend their differences. Raven was thinking that this was the end of the matter, it would be time to go. And none too soon.

And then K'let said, "I have brought you a gift."

Raven understood the taan word for "gift." He did not understand, at first, that the word applied to him. He found this out when K'let grabbed hold of his forearm and gave it a yank that nearly tore his arm from the socket.

K'let dragged Raven forward, flung him in front of Dagnarus.

The Lord of the Void cast Raven a bored glance. "A fine specimen of a Trevinici, K'let, but at the moment I have all the barbarians I need."

"You do not have all the Vrykyl you need, Ko-kutryx," said K'let. "This R'vn is a valiant warrior, an excellent commander. He has taken a bunch of useless half-taan and transformed them into warriors as skilled and valiant as himself. I know your loathing for Shakur. I know that you think he has outlived—so to speak—his usefulness. Here is a fine replacement. Accept this xkes and make of him a Vrykyl. I will deal with Shakur, if such is your command."

Dagnarus disliked waiting, disliked uncertainty. He was beginning to grow angry at the delay. He wanted what he wanted when he wanted it. The fact that he couldn't have it meant that situation was not entirely under his control. Here was K'let, where he had no business being. The Dominion Lords were *not* here and neither, for that matter, was the Portal of the Gods.

"Any sign of the Dominion Lords, Patch?" Dagnarus demanded.

"My lord, you must be patient—" Gareth began.

"Oh, shut up," Dagnarus snapped. He eyed Raven, who stared at him, stupefied. Dagnarus needed something to do. He needed to show he was master. Reaching beneath his cloak, he removed the Dagger of the Vrykyl.

Shaped like a dragon—with the blade the body, the hilt the head, the crosspiece the wings—the Dagger was an object of revulsion and horror.

"You are right, K'let." Dagnarus grasped the dagger firmly. The hilt had a strange way of conforming to his touch, nestled securely in his grip, almost as if it were alive. "I am sick to death of Shakur's whining, his insubordination. I need a new commander of the Vrykyl. This man is a soldier. Where did you serve, sir?"

Raven stared at the commanding figure, and he stared at the dagger.

"I was a captain in the Dunkar army, my lord," Raven managed to reply.

He had to try twice, to moisten his mouth enough to force out the words. He did not know what was going on, but he sensed danger. He glanced swiftly around, searching for some means of escape. Every Trevinici knows that there is a time to fight and a time to run for your life. This was assuredly the latter.

The Lord of the Void stood in front of him and beyond him was a cul-de-sac, a dead end, nothing but a small, windowless room. The way behind was blocked by K'let, and the walls of the corridor blocked Raven in on either side. He glanced down at the corpse of the murdered man, and his throat constricted.

"You see, Gareth," Dagnarus was saying. "This man is accustomed to obedience. Look at him. He guesses he is about to die, yet you see no panic, no groveling or pleading. He searches for a way out. He sees none. His hand goes to his sword. I fought the Trevinici in my youth, Raven. Your people gave my poor father fits. Doughty warriors, all of your kind, the women as strong and fierce as the men.

"I would very much like to have a go at you, Raven, soldier to soldier," Dagnarus concluded, "but I do not have time. I am expecting guests."

He raised the dagger.

"Do not do this, Your Majesty," Gareth warned. "He is not of the Void!"

"Nonsense, Patch," Dagnarus scoffed. "This human lives among the taan! Isn't that what you said, K'let?"

"True," K'let replied. "He lives among the taan much as you did yourself, Ko-kutryx. R'vn has even killed his own kind in defense of the taan."

"There, you see, Gareth? I'm going to kill you, Captain," Dagnarus told him. "Your death will be quick, painless. I am going to make you like K'let here, a Vrykyl. Only I hope that you will have more sense than K'let and not try to defy me."

Raven understood his fate. He was to become a thing of evil, an abomination to the gods. He would be cursed by every living being, cursed by the honored dead. His soul shriveled within him. Fear seized hold of him, blind panic. Raven gasped and shuddered. He raised his gaze, saw the dragon-headed dagger poised above him.

"Hold him, K'let," Dagnarus ordered. "I must strike to the heart."

K'let reached out his hands. Seizing hold of the Dagger of the Vrykyl, K'let wrenched it from Dagnarus's grasp.

Raven lunged sideways, careened into the wall. Smashing against it, he nearly knocked himself senseless. Dazed, not certain what had happened, he slid to the floor. Beside him lay the corpse of the murdered man. Feeling a strange sort of companionship with him, Raven slumped down next to the shattered skull and the outstretched bony hands and kept as quiet and still as the corpse itself.

"This time, K'let," said Dagnarus, cold with rage, "there will be no forgiveness. I will send your soul to the Void! Give back the Dagger!"

"My prince," said Gareth, coming to stand between Dagnarus and K'let, as he had once stood between Dagnarus and Helmos. "Let it go. You do not need the Dagger. You have the Sovereign Stone."

Dagnarus looked into the dome of heaven and there, standing beneath it, were the four Dominion Lords, armored in silver, armored in light, armored in the blessing of the gods. Around each neck, resting against each heart, was a quarter of the Sovereign Stone, bright against the radiant light, as the evening star dims with the sunrise.

THE DOMINION LORDS STOOD BENEATH THE DOME OF HEAVEN and looked up into the stars and the endless and eternal darkness that bound the stars together, and they knew themselves to be very small and yet very large, for they were made of the stars and of the darkness.

An elderly man stepped out of the darkness and the stars. His face was benign, his eyes wise. The stern lines of arrogance and willful pride that had once creased the mouth had been softened. He was royal as his portraits had portrayed him, yet more frail, more vulnerable. He had cast aside all trappings of his kingship—the crown, the robe, the scepter. He had cast off his human body. He was, as we all are at the end and the beginning, a child of the gods.

The Dominion Lords knew Tamaros, knew him in their souls, and they did him homage, each in his or her own way. He spoke, and they answered, but the words were silent as the emptiness that lies among the stars.

"Captain of Captains," said Tamaros, "Child of Dunner, Lady Damra and Lord of Seeking. I would say that you have fulfilled the oath I once asked of each bearer of the Sovereign Stone, but I know now that the oath I asked and the oath your forebears swore—some falsely, some under constraint, some without true understanding—was not mine to ask. As the Sovereign Stone was not mine to give."

"Then why did the gods give you the Stone?" asked Shadamehr.

"I do not know, Lord of Seeking," said Tamaros. "Sometimes I think

I was meant to keep it secret, keep it safe, use it to work small increments of good where and when I could. Sometimes I think I was meant to know myself well enough to refuse it."

"Yet you must know, Your Majesty. The Church says in death we are given all the answers."

Tamaros smiled. "They are wrong, Lord of Seeking. In death, we are given more questions, as many questions as there are stars. It is our privilege to roam the universe in search of answers, and it is then we come to know what the gods know, that there are as many answers as there are stars and that each answer leads only to more questions. The blessing is that in death, we do not fear either—the questions or the answers.

"When the world was first made, the gods fashioned creatures in the images of themselves to place upon the world and care for it and prosper and thrive. Orks, elves, humans, and dwarves lived together in the world, existing in harmony as the elements themselves exist, Air and Water, Earth and Fire. Content, the people lived from day to day, but they did not thrive, the world did not prosper.

"On that world were two brothers and two sisters, one of each race, much as yourselves. The gods gave to the four a jewel of such radiant, dazzling beauty as none of them had ever seen. They all immediately wanted the brilliant gem for their own. The four, who had once loved each other as siblings, fell to quarreling over it. Their love turned to hatred, so that they could not stand the sight of each other. Each determined, in his or her own heart, to take the jewel and leave his siblings, use the jewel to establish his or her own kingdom. In the night came each brother and each sister and stole away the Sovereign Stone—or thought they did. In reality, each took only a portion of the Stone. Each sibling moved to a different part of the realm. When the jewel was split, the interior was revealed and thus did discord and disharmony, enmity and hatred, sorrow and death enter the world."

The four Dominion Lords could not look at Tamaros, and they could not look at each other. Each knew, with shame, that he or she was a part of the story.

"True, the jewel had a bitter center," said Tamaros, "but each portion of the stone gleamed and sparkled, and rainbows danced within. Only now the siblings could see them, where before they had been blind to the beauty. Death opened their eyes. Realizing that their time was brief, they came to enjoy what time they had and to value it. With sorrow came hope. With death, came life.

"The gods took back the Sovereign Stone. Once more after that, they sent it into the world, but that is another story. Then I asked for it and it was given to me and whether I did right or wrong, only the gods know. And now I ask you, what will you do with your portion of the Stone."

"I know the answer," said Shadamehr. "I give it to my brother."

He held out the portion of the Sovereign Stone in his hand.

"And I," said Damra, holding out hers.

"And I." "And I," said the Captain and Wolfram.

Within the Portal of the Gods, beneath the dome of heaven, each brought the four portions of the Sovereign Stone together. The four parts formed a pyramid of radiant light, beautiful, sparkling, dazzling, gleaming with myriad rainbows. Bright as a sun, the Sovereign Stone shone, and each Dominion Lord withdrew his hand.

The Sovereign Stone fell to the floor of the Portal of the Gods, the floor that was hard and cold and stained with blood. The Stone shattered, broke again into four pieces.

"Why did that happen?" Shadamehr demanded.

"Because you forgot the bitter center," said Dagnarus.

Accoutered in his black armor, which had been forged in his soul to fit his body, the Lord of the Void entered the Portal of the Gods, his steps quick and firm, his hand on his sword hilt. He wore no helm. He looked then much as he had looked two hundred years before, when he had last entered this dome. His auburn hair, thick and carelessly arranged around his face, brushed his shoulders. His handsome face was smiling and certain of his victory.

"Thank you all for coming," he said. "And for bringing the Sovereign Stone. My friend, Gareth—that's his corpse you see, lying on the floor—did his job well. Valura, my dear, I do not like you in that guise. The traitor Silwyth is dead, finally. Let's have no more of him."

The façade of Silwyth rippled, as on still water. The ripples, faded away. The form of a Vrykyl, clad in black armor, emerged from the shadows and came to stand beside Dagnarus.

And then he saw his father.

Dagnarus retained his smile, but his eyes were suddenly watchful, wary.

"If you have come to stop me, Father . . ."

"I would stop you, if I could," Tamaros said. "But not perhaps for the reason you think. I cannot raise my hand to you. I cannot touch you. My mortal body lies at rest. I cannot move you, my son, save only with my prayers."

"And it's late for that, Father," said Dagnarus. "The one prayer you should have prayed, you didn't. The prayer that I had never been born."

Dagnarus reached down to pick up the glittering portions of the Sovereign Stone. A sword blade struck the stone floor near his hand, nearly severing his fingers. Dagnarus snatched back his hand, looked up.

"And who might you be, sir?"

"I am called Shadamehr. And my hand *can* touch you."

Shadamehr had no armor. He wore his usual clothes and his traveling cloak, now much stained with wear, mud-spattered and wet. Dagnarus looked from him to the three Dominion Lords, their armor shining in the lambent light of the flickering stars, and he laughed.

"What's the matter, Baron Shadamehr?" said Dagnarus. "Could the gods find no human Dominion Lords to come to challenge me? Or did they all die of mold and mildew along the way?"

"Strangely enough, I am a Dominion Lord," Shadamehr replied. "I know. Surprised me, too. I didn't want it, mind you. I didn't ask for it. The honor was thrust upon me, so to speak. But," he added, more gravely, "since the gods have chosen me as their champion, I will intervene on their behalf. The Sovereign Stone cannot be yours. It was never meant to be yours or any man's."

"And you are going to stop me from claiming it?" Dagnarus said. He drew his sword. "I should warn you, Baron, that I have more lives than the proverbial cat. You will need to kill me forty times over to stop me."

"Well, then, I guess we had better get started," said Shadamehr, taking his stance.

Dagnarus faced him, but he could not take this contest seriously. His gaze was drawn by the Sovereign Stone that glittered at his father's feet.

Shadamehr watched his opponent's eyes and, taking advantage of his distraction, lunged to strike Dagnarus.

The Lord of the Void, armored in the Void, did not shift his rapt gaze. There was no need. As Shadamehr's sword hit the black armor, the blade splintered, broke apart. Shadamehr dropped the sword's hilt, all he had left of the weapon, and clutched his hand. His palm was covered with blood.

Smiling, Dagnarus reached down to pick up one quarter of the Sovereign Stone.

"He will not be able to touch it," cried Wolfram hoarsely. "The gods will stop him."

"No they won't," said Dagnarus. "They can't."

Grasping the portion of the shining Stone that Shadamehr had carried and Bashae before him and Lord Gustav before him, Dagnarus gazed at the jewel admiringly, turning it this way and that to see it sparkle in the starlight. Then he thrust it into his belt and reached for the next part.

Wolfram stood over the Sovereign Stone, his sword in his hand. His twin, Gilda, stood before him, her shield raised to defend him.

Dagnarus struck the shield with his sword. The blow sliced it in half. Dagnarus ran his sword through her.

Gilda fell, the bright light of her spirit fading. Crying out in grief and rage, Wolfram attacked Dagnarus.

The Lord of the Void plucked the dwarf's sword from his hand and crushed it in his grasp. He dropped the dust onto the dying Gilda.

Reaching down, Dagnarus picked up the second part of the Sovereign Stone.

Damra caught up the elven part of the Stone, held it tightly in her hand.

"My sword was given to me by the Divine and was blessed by the Father and Mother," she said, facing the Void lord without fear. "I may not be able to slay you, but I can unravel the foul magic that holds you together long enough for me to retrieve that which you have stolen."

"I do not steal," said Dagnarus. "I take back what is mine. And you can do your damnedest, Lady, but I will have the Sovereign Stone."

"My lord, she speaks the truth!" Valura cried out. "Her weapon is holy and will do you harm! Do not go near her."

"Be gone, Valura," said Dagnarus impatiently. "I am finished with you. Trouble me no more."

He feinted a lunge, then, shifted his blow, striking at Damra's sword in an attempt to knock it from her hand.

Damra was not fooled by his maneuver. She was ready for his attack and, deftly, she dodged him. The shining blade that had lain for seven years upon the altar of the Father and the Mother slid through the black armor of the Void and pierced to the dust that had once been a beating heart. But the armor was not Dagnarus's armor. The heart was not his heart.

Valura threw herself in front of her lord, took the blow meant for him. The blessed sword filled the Void that was her soul. Valura gave a strangled scream. Her body writhed in agony.

Damra fought to wrench her sword free, but Valura wrapped her hand around the blade and held it fast, though that meant holding the terrible blade within herself. With her other hand, she grasped hold of the Sovereign Stone, tore it from Damra's grasp.

The black armor vanished, revealing the grisly remains of what had been a woman, beautiful and vibrant. Valura shed no blood, for that had been drained from her long ago. Leathery skin stretched taut over her bones. Her hair, ragged and long, flowed over her mummified remains. Moving with pain-filled effort, Valura reached out her ghastly hand, reached for Dagnarus.

He drew back from the horrible touch, stared with loathing at the rotting corpse.

"Dagnarus," said Valura. "I am dying . . ."

"You are already dead," he cried. "And I wish to the gods that I had never brought you back to life. I have long learned to hate the very sight of you!"

"Not me," she whispered, a whisper that was almost all that was left of her. "Yourself."

She crumbled, dwindled, withered to ash, a heap of ash that fell to the floor. Dagnarus reached into the dust of the dead, plucked out the eleven Sovereign Stone. Last to face him was the Captain of Captains.

"Your grandfather sought to try to convince my father to slay me," said Dagnarus. "He saw what none of the others could see. He saw what I would become."

"It would have been better if he had killed you then," said the Captain. She stood with her arms crossed over her chest, the Sovereign Stone in one hand, her blade in the other.

"There are moments, Captain," said Dagnarus, "when I reach the same conclusion. Give me the Stone. For the sake of your wise grandfather, I do not want to harm you."

"For the sake of his wisdom, I give you the Sovereign Stone," said the Captain. Bowing her head, she lowered her sword and held out her hand.

All four parts of the Sovereign Stone were his in the Portal of the Gods, beneath the dome of heaven. Dagnarus stared down at them, the prize he had sought all his life, two of the parts of the jewel sparkling in his left hand, two in his right.

Exulting in their beauty and his triumph, he brought the four pieces together. He remembered, as he did so, the moment that his father had split the sacred Stone. Tamaros saw only the beautiful, radiant rainbows. Dagnarus had looked into its heart and seen the darkness. He did not see the darkness now. He saw only the rainbows. He brought together all four pieces.

One by one, they slipped from his grasp and fell to the bloodstained and dusty floor.

Angrily, Dagnarus bent down to retrieve what he had lost.

"Beg pardon," said Shadamehr politely. "Those belong to us."

He kicked Dagnarus in the teeth.

The black helm of the Void shielded Dagnarus from harm, but the force of the unexpected blow sent him staggering backward.

"The Void take you!" he cried, and tendrils of oily black swirled from his fingers, crawled toward Shadamehr . . .

Toward twenty Shadamehrs. Damra's magic peopled the corridor with Shadamhers. Dagnarus glared furiously from one to another, his own deadly magic coiling about him. He pointed at Damra.

Cracking like a whip, a tendril snaked out, grasped Damra around the ankle and dragged her off her feet. Another curled around her neck, tightening, choking, and her illusions vanished. Damra writhed on the floor, tearing at the tendril to try to free herself, but the tendril was made of the Void. She grasped at nothing, yet nothing was killing her.

Shadamehr made a leap for her.

"Stand clear!" cried the Captain.

She swung her sword, which had been forged in the holy fires of Mt. Sa 'Gra. The blessed weapon severed the Void, freed Damra. With the downward stroke, the Captain sliced off Dagnarus's outstretched hand.

Dagnarus laughed for he assumed the Void would protect him. But Valura's dying warning proved true. The blessed weapon had the power to harm him. He saw his hand lying on the floor, the fingers upturned and curling in on themselves, the red blood pooling around the severed limb.

Then the pain hit, and the fury. He reared up. The Captain plunged the blessed sword into his chest.

The weapon pierced the black breastplate, slid through the Void, but it could not reach his heart. One of the many lives he had stolen, perhaps that of Valura or Shakur, perhaps that of the wretched Jedash or one of the countless others, died for him.

Using his left hand, Dagnarus plucked the sword from his body and, grasping it tightly, he squeezed it in his hand. The metal began to glow red, as if it were once again in the forge fire, and the sword dissolved, flowed into a silvery pool at the feet of the Lord of the Void.

The portions of the Sovereign Stone lay together in a pool of blood. His severed hand crawled toward the pieces of the Sovereign Stone, leaving a gruesome trail behind.

The fingers of the severed hand could touch the portions of the Stone, but only touch. The four parts would not come together.

"One part is still missing," said Gareth.

"What part is that?" Dagnarus demanded, pain making him angry. He clasped his wounded arm to his body, glared down at the bloodstained crystals. "There are four here. My father split it into four."

"He split it into five. The fifth part, I gave you. I gave it out of love, though it cost me my soul."

"Speak plainly, Patch," said Dagnarus. "No more riddles. I had enough of those during those damned Tests I took for a Dominion Lord." He paused, drew in a breath. "That's the answer! You didn't want me to take the Tests. You tried to stop me by bringing me a dagger.

"K'let!" Dagnarus ordered peremptorily. "Give me the Dagger of the Vrykyl."

There was no reply.

Dagnarus turned to look into the darkness that massed at the edges of the dome of heaven. K'let stood in the shadows, the dragon-shaped dagger clasped tightly in his hand.

"K'let," said Dagnarus, "I forgive your treachery. I will make you a king. Bring me the dagger."

Slowly, the taan walked forward. He did not wear the armor of the Vrykyl. He kept the guise of the taan that he had been, his pallid hide roped with scars, the claws on his feet scraping the stone, his face unreadable to those who saw only its bestial snout and fangs and small, alien eyes.

But they were not empty, those eyes. Not empty as the eyes of a Vrykyl should have been empty. The life had not completely drained out of them.

Only one person in the room saw the shadow in the taan's eyes. Raven, huddled against the wall, his soul shrinking as he watched spirits of the dead walking, spirits of the murdered speaking, husks of the dead dying. The darkness was too deep for Raven to see Dagnarus, the light too bright for him to see the Dominion Lords. He could see K'let, however. He had come to know K'let in their long journey together. Raven saw the shadow, like smoke drifting over still, dark water.

K'let came to stand before Dagnarus. K'let held out the Dagger of the Vrykyl, held it in his palms, the blade resting on one hand, the hilt on the other.

"You were different from the others, K'let," said Dagnarus. "You alone gave your life to me willingly. You alone had the will to rebel against me. I have always said that we were brothers."

"So you did," said K'let. "And you killed your brother."

Clenching his hand over the hilt of the dagger, the taan drove it with all his strength into Dagnarus's breast.

The taan gave a hideous cry as the Void shredded him, tore him apart, ground his flesh and bone into nothing. All that remained of him was his skull, bestial, alien. Grinning.

Dagnarus stared down at it and, at first, it seemed he might laugh. But then he felt the pain. Understanding, swift and terrible, came to Dagnarus. K'let had buried the dragon-shaped dagger deep. The accursed blade, sharp as hatred and bitter as jealousy, pierced the black armor. The Dagger cut through all his lives in a single slice to find the last life, Dagnarus's own, buried at the bottom.

Dagnarus slumped to the floor, crouched on his hands and knees above the four shards of the Sovereign Stone.

A spasm of agony made him clench his teeth, but he did not scream or cry out. Grimacing, he clasped the hilt of the Dagger and, with a gasp, wrenched it free.

Blood spewed from the wound, flowed over the four parts of the Sovereign Stone. Dagnarus, his hand shaking, placed the Dagger in the center. He began to gather up the pieces of the Sovereign Stone, one by one.

"My son." Tamaros came to stand beside the shuddering body of his dying child. "The gods are merciful. They are loving of their children, and they understand their weakness."

"Like you, Father?" Dagnarus struck at the spirit, tried to banish it. "Patch!" he gasped, blood trickling from his lips. "Patch, come to me!"

Gareth came to him, stood over him, looked down on him.

"You promised me the god's greatest gift," Dagnarus said accusingly.

"The gods hold it out to you. You have only to ask for it, as I did."

Gareth knelt beside Dagnarus, looked into the eyes of his prince. "The gods' greatest gift is forgiveness."

Dagnarus raised his gaze to the dome of heaven. "No," he said defiantly. "*You* will ask forgiveness of me. For I have . . . the Sovereign Stone."

Grasping the four parts of the Sovereign Stone in one hand, he jabbed the Dagger of the Vrykyl, wet with his life's blood, into the heart of the jewel.

The Sovereign Stone began to glow, its light at first pale and chill, then growing stronger, brighter, more radiant, shining with the aching brilliance that was the mind of the gods. The pure fire illuminated Dagnarus, so that for an instant he was ablaze with argent light. And then the darkness consumed him.

12

NO ONE SPOKE.

The Dominion Lords were too awed to be able to put their feelings into words.

Raven was too shaken.

Shakur was too busy assessing his situation.

The Vrykyl had overheard the conversation between Dagnarus and K'let. Shakur knew Dagnarus meant to banish him to the Void. Shakur might have stopped K'let from slaying Dagnarus, but he chose not to. Expecting to fall into the Void with his master, Shakur was astonished to find himself still here.

He did not know why, except that the Void was always.

Astonishment gave way to pleasure. The Dagger of the Vrykyl was gone. He remained. He had the Blood-knife, made from his own bone. He could continue to use it, continue to steal souls, continue his existence, an existence he hated, but one that might come to be bearable.

"For now I have no master," said Shakur. "No one to order me about, to tell me to go hither or do this. I am free to go where I please, do what I choose. Other Vrykyl are out there. Other Vrykyl who, like me, are now masterless. They will need a leader and who will they look to, now that their lord is gone, but to me."

Shakur had long had plans of his own, plans that he could now put into action. The Vrykyl was not as ambitious as Dagnarus. Shakur had no desire to rule the world. He had other, more modest goals. Shakur slid into the Void, became one with the darkness, and left before the Dominion Lords could find him.

The Dominion Lords looked into the dome of heaven, saw only a ceiling made of wood covered over with plaster, a small room furnished with a bed, a desk, a chair. A single candle, burning with an unwavering flame, stood on the desk. The open door led out into a corridor. The Captain, with a shrug, turned and, ducking her head, walked out the door.

Wolfram started to follow, then he stopped, paused, looking for Gilda. He could not see her and he knew then that he would never see her, not until he joined her to run with the Wolf. But she would always be with him. Sighing, smiling he walked out alone.

Raven retraced his steps down the dark corridor, hoping to avoid talking to anyone. He couldn't move very fast, however, for he had no light, his body was bruised and aching, and he was trembling with the reaction to the overwhelming and mind-numbing sights he had witnessed. He had not gone very far, therefore, when he heard heavy footfalls clumping behind him.

"Wait up, Raven," called out Wolfram.

Raven came to a halt, turned around.

The dwarf had found an oil lamp. He flashed the light in Raven's face, then on his own. "It's me, Raven. Wolfram. Didn't you recognize me?"

"I didn't," Raven lied. "I'm sorry."

"Probably that silver armor I was wearing," said Wolfram, looking embarrassed. The armor was gone, replaced by the dwarf's own comfortable traveling clothes. He looked quizzically into Raven's face. "What are you doing here, anyhow?"

"It's a long story," said Raven. "And one that I don't have time to tell. It is good to see you again. I wish you a safe journey."

Raven started off down the dark corridor.

"Hey, wait!" Wolfram said, doggedly pursuing him. "You're alone. You don't have a light. Do you know the way?"

"No," said Raven. "But I'll manage."

He kept walking, and so did the dwarf.

"Where are you going?" Wolfram asked.

"Back to my people."

"Back to Trevinici lands, huh." Wolfram grunted. "Well, good luck to you."

"Thank you," said Raven. He wasn't going back to Trevinici lands, but the dwarf didn't need to know that. "What about you?"

Wolfram could see that the Trevinici was trying to get rid of him. He slowed down, halted.

"I'm going back to my people," he said, startled to find out that was his destination. He hadn't known it until the words came out. He felt the need of some explanation. "I'm a Dominion Lord. The only one they've got."

Raven didn't understand, but he nodded. "Good luck to you," he said, and went on his way.

Damra waited for Shadamehr, who was aimlessly poking and prodding, looking at the bed, peering into the desk and underneath the chair.

"Lord of Seeking," she said. "Truly a wise choice for you. What do you seek now?"

"I don't know. Some crumb of the Stone, maybe. Left behind by accident."

"I don't think you will find one," she said.

"No. I suppose not." He sighed, stood up. He looked at her, his expression somber. "The Sovereign Stone is gone. That makes me the last of the Dominion Lords."

"Then you must be a good one," said Damra gravely. "And live for a very long time."

"Two of the Vrykyl are gone, but one escaped," said Shadamehr. "I saw it disappear into the shadows, just before the light faded. They are still out there, and who will fight them?"

"The power of the Void has diminished, but it will never be vanquished. Nor should it, as Tamaros said. That is the lesson we have learned."

"I suppose you're right," said Shadamehr. He gave another look around. "I wonder who will be given the Sovereign Stone again."

"Let us hope it is someone wiser than we have been," said Damra.

"Or more foolish," said Shadamehr with a mischievous grin. "Where will you go now, Damra?"

"To find Griffith. We must return to Tromek, take up the battle against the Shield. What about you?"

"I'll find Alise. Or rather," Shadamehr amended cheerfully, "she'll find me. We always seem to, you know. Find each other. It's the knowing what to do with each other that is the hard part."

He looked out the room and into the darkness, an emptiness that was yet filled with possibilities. He thought at last he was beginning to understand, if only just a little.

"The throne in Vinnengael is vacant," suggested Damra, half-teasing, wholly serious. "Perhaps you will be king someday?"

"The gods forfend!" said Shadamehr, alarmed at the thought. "Being a baron is trouble enough. Perhaps Alise and Ulaf and dear old Rigiswald and I will go help the Captain take back her sacred mountain. Or maybe we'll go hunt down these Vrykyl. Or come help you and Griffith fight the Shield."

"Thank you," said Damra firmly. "But I think we can manage."

"Well, if you're sure . . ."

He took one last look about the room, the Portal of the Gods. Then, bending down, he started to blow out the candle.

"No," said Damra, stopping him. "We are meant to take it with us."

Shadamehr lifted up the candle, carried it out the door, and shut the door behind him. Turning around to look, he saw only darkness.

EPILOGUE

IT IS A TEMPTATION FOR THE CHRONICLER TO END THE JOURNEYings of our heroes with this momentous event and pronounce that they lived happily ever after. The truth is that the journey of their lives did not end here, but continued on, albeit in directions that none of them could have anticipated. Their lives were forever changed by the Sovereign Stone, and that is the fate of the hero.

Raven returned to the taan, bearing with him the story of K'let and how he had sacrificed himself to prove that Dagnarus was not a god. The taan were skeptical and more than inclined to think that Raven was lying and were ready to slay him. The shaman, Derl, confirmed the truth of Raven's story, however, as did the taan Vrykyl Nb'arsk, who had witnessed much of what had happened through the Blood-knife. Instead of being tortured and slain, Raven was formally proclaimed a taan and accepted fully into the tribe. From that day forth, no taan ever referred to him as xkes.

Klendist reported to the authorities that a Trevinici had turned traitor and was living with the enemy, with the result that the Karnuans and the Dunkargans both put out bounties on Raven's head. In order to find peace, Raven eventually led his tribe of taan and half-taan back through the Portal to the taan's ancient land, a harsh and brutal and savage realm, where the taan gods were glad to welcome their lost children home.

Having defeated the taan, the Karnuans—being in a martial mood—turned their steely eyes on weakened Vinnengael, floundering about without a king. The officers of the Imperial Cavalry School in Krammes, alerted by Baron Shadamehr, acted quickly to establish order in the city of New Vinnengael. They reinforced the border and took back the Portal at Delak 'Vir. The Karnuans, disappointed, decided instead to pounce upon weakened Dunkarga, which they did.

Wolfram returned to the dwarven lands, where he joined the clan of Kolost, whose fame and glory and great deeds spread across the dwarven nation like lightning-struck fire, which would soon engulf the world.

Damra and Griffith returned to Tromek to do battle against the Shield, a struggle that was long and terrible, for the Shield allied himself with Shakur and several remaining Vrykyl. Before it was finally finished, the battle extended even into the realm of elven dead. One of Damra's first actions, on returning to her land, was to ensure that House Kinnoch was once more restored to a place of honor among the elven Houses.

Bashae was laid to rest in the burial mound that held the body of Lord Gustav. The pecwae joined the ranks of the honored Trevinici dead and, to this day, when the great warriors of history are summoned to aid the living, Bashae takes his place proudly alongside the likes of Ale Guzzler, Skull-Basher, and Bear-Mauler.

Although Jessan had no liking for cities, he found the life of a farmer too dull for his taste, and he was persuaded to travel with a group of his fellow Trevinici to Nimorea, where he served as a mercenary with the army. While there, he renewed his friendship with Arim, the kite-maker, and—so it is rumored—occasionally performed secret missions for the Nimorean Queen.

Ranessa swore Jessan to secrecy regarding the fact that she was a dragon, for it would never do for the Trevinici to know that they had inadvertently reared a dragon child in their midst. (They would have been deeply suspicious of their own children ever after.) Ranessa never returned to the Trevinici. She remained at Dragon Mountain and eventually took over guardianship of the monks upon the death of her mother.

The Grandmother found life intolerable on her return home. The pecwae were so glad to see her and so grief-stricken over Bashae that she could not stand the weeping and wailing. Taking her newly made agate-eyed stick, the Grandmother bid them all good-bye and departed in search of her sleep city. She never returned, and no one ever discovered what became of her.

As for Shadamehr and Alise, the where and how of their eventual marriage was never known, for he would only laugh heartily whenever it was mentioned, at which Alise would fly into a rage and refuse to speak to him for days on end. They apparently loved as heartily as they quarreled, however, for the barony was soon overrun with red-haired children. Though how they found time to either create them or raise them was a mystery to their friends, for they were either off in Tromek assisting the elven cause, or getting themselves nearly killed fighting with the orks to liberate Mount Sa 'Gra, or working with the Council of Dominion Lords to establish new guidelines for their continuation in the absence of the Sovereign Stone, in which the baron, as the new head of the Council, took a very interested and active part.

Last, it is a great temptation for the chronicler of this history to write that the downfall of Dagnarus caused those who had been responsible for his defeat to be honored as heroes throughout Loerem. The truth is that most of Loerem's people were so intent upon living their own lives that they soon forgot the Lord of the Void and those heroes who had sacrificed so much to stop him.

Which, as the Captain, in her wisdom, pointed out, is as it should be, for returning life to the living is the goal of the hero.

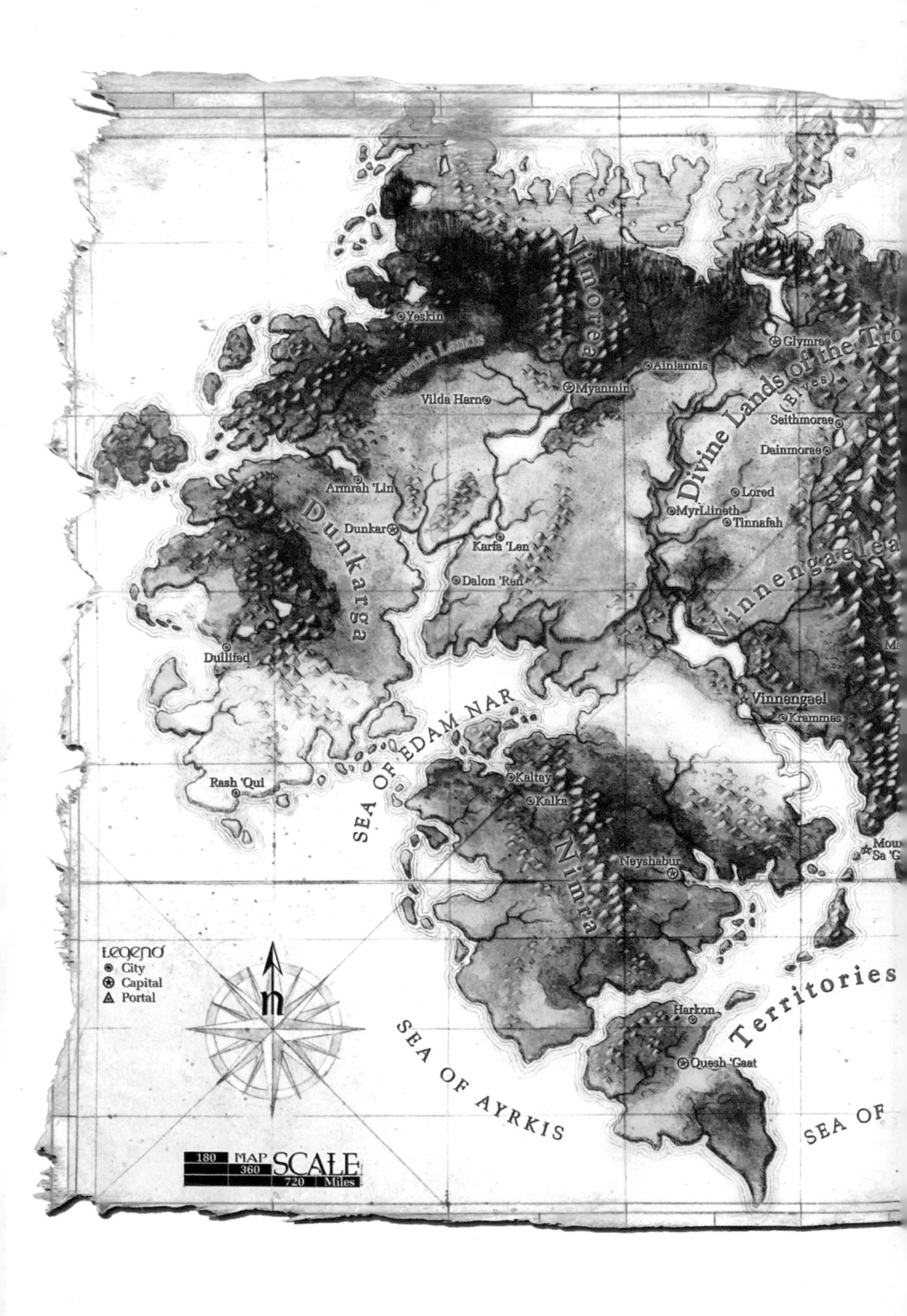
Nimorea
Yeskin
Thevenici Lands
Vilda Harn
Myanmin
Ainlannis
Glymrae
Divine Lands of the Tro
(Elves)
Seithmorae
Dainmorae
Lored
MyrLlineth
Tinnafah
Armrah 'Lin
Dunkarga
Dunkar
Karfa 'Len
Dalon 'Ren
Vinnengaelea
Dullifed
Vinnengael
Krammes
SEA OF EDAM NAR
Kaltay
Kalka
Rash 'Qui
Nimra
Neyshabur
Legend
City
Capital
Portal
n
Harkon
Territories
Quesh 'Gaat
SEA OF AYRKIS
SEA OF
180 MAP 360 SCALE 720 Miles